Echoes from the Past

Book One in the Montana Series

MABEL G. EBNER

PUBLISHED BY FIDELI PUBLISHING, INC.

ISBN: 978-1-60414-976-0

For information, please contact

Fideli Publishing, Inc.:
info@fidelipublishing.com

www.FideliPublishing.com

Dedication

I want to dedicate this book to my beloved brother, Mitchel Jerry Stoumbaugh. His unending patience in helping me complete this tremendous undertaking was extraordinary. Without his invaluable help, I would have abandoned this work long ago. While proofreading the manuscript, Mitchel's constant encouragement made me feel that I could accomplish anything. Unfortunately, Mitchel died of cancer before we were able to make the final corrections.

Foreword

From the time I was a child, my mother read to my brothers and me. As a result, reading is one of my passions. I love books the entire family can enjoy, so I tried to create this novel in like manner. This story first came to me in a dream, then the characters became such a part of me, invading my waking hours, as well as my sleep, that I finally put pen to paper. I have tried to bring the characters to life in such a way as to touch the readers' hearts, thus allowing them to feel empathy for the characters' daily struggles, embrace their joys, and rejoice in their triumphs. If perchance you see your name within the pages of this book, it is purely coincidental.

Although there was a Fort Owen, it was never a military base ... but was used as a trading post. The Fort Owen in my book is not the same as the present day fort, nor is it in the same location. Mine is nestled between the Sapphire Mountains and the snow-capped Bitterroot Range, which is located in a valley between these two mountains. Again, there is a Fort Missoula, but it is not the one I used in the book. The fort's location and description in this work is absolutely fictional.

Because there are so many Indian Tribes living in that area, the tribe in my book is also fictional, therefore there is no tribal affiliation. Although Hellsgate was the original name of Missoula at the time this story would have taken place, I chose to use the name Missoula, not only because I loved the Indian meaning, but also to honor the Salish Indians. The name Missoula means "Near the cold chilling waters." The Missoula River was given many names though the years. Initially the Indians called it Yellow River. Subsequently the name was changed to Clark Fork River, Missoula River, then back to the Clark Fork River, then on to the Bitterroot River.

In life's echoes from the past, perhaps there was a little window of time when the white man and the Indian did live together in harmony. Perhaps in spite of evil, good could and did prevail. So, let go of the known and travel down the trail of the unknown with me now, as I weave a tale of love, honor, courage, justice, and adventure throughout the pages of this book. I hope you enjoy reading this novel as much as I have enjoyed writing it.

Acknowledgment

A special thank you goes to my husband, Maurice Arnold Ebner, who not only encouraged me, but also supported me in every way possible. I wish to thank my daughter, Jennifer L. Nef, for giving me a lot of excellent suggestions as I wrote this novel. A heart-felt thank you goes to Mary Ellison, who did most of the typing for me, assisted by Becky Robinson, who converted the manuscript into Word. I also appreciate Pauline Perkins, as well as Jan and Drew Lyon for proofreading the book. Edna Nasca, with the aid of Leah Buhler, helped with research. I am thankful, too, for all of those who worked behind the scenes to help in any way possible. I am grateful for those who have always believed in me, in spite of myself. Finally, and most importantly, I want to thank my Heavenly Father for giving me the courage, and the talent, to even attempt, let alone accomplish, writing this book.

— Mabel G. Ebner

CHAPTER 1

The Orders

" **C**ompany ... HALT! ... Dismount!"

A troop of cavalry soldiers, from Fort Owen, Montana, dismounted to make camp for the night near the Missoula River. The turbulence of this mighty river was awesome in its beauty, as well as its strength. White water licked at the boulders in its path, creating little eddies in some places, and boiling, swirling rapids in others. The river's roar was deafening, yet there was a calming effect also. It was flanked on both sides by giant pines, rocky snow-capped mountain grandeur shrouded in clouds.

Sergeant Peters issued camp duties, posted sentry duty for the first watch then helped where needed. In no time, tents were set up, wood was chopped, water hauled, as well as the horses' needs taken care of. Soon the hungry, travel-weary men were eating a hearty meal of beans, ham, sourdough biscuits and steaming cups of coffee. The only sounds heard during the meal were the roaring river, the crackling fire, rattling of dishes and the occasional neighing of a horse. Slowly, the sun slipped behind the mountains, leaving behind a magnificent sunset.

Captain Paul Thompson toyed with his food, eating very little. Finally giving up, he left camp to wander aimlessly for a while. With heavy heart he gazed out at the Montana landscape before him. Thompson stood six foot four inches tall in his stocking feet. Although he weighed in at two hundred and fifty pounds, his body was a mass of rippling muscles. He stood by the river, twisting his neatly trimmed mustache. Sandy hair set off his sensitive blue eyes. Thompson's gentle spirit made it difficult for him to hurt others unjustly, yet he was a dynamic force in defense of another's rights.

Thompson took the orders from his shirt pocket and reread them. As he did so, his very soul quaked at the absurdity of its contents:

Exterminate all the Indians at Lost Trail Pass. Take no prisoners.

He bit his lower lip in exasperation. "How can a human being be so cold ... so calculating?" muttered Thompson. The orders went against all of his principles and beliefs. He began walking along the riverbank, trying to figure a way out of this dilemma; yet no matter how hard he tried, he just couldn't find an escape.

Coming to a large boulder overlooking the river, he sat to watch the sun's last glowing rays disappear as it slipped behind the rugged mountains. He gazed in awe as night's shadows spread slowly across the landscape. The moon slowly rose, causing eerie shadows to dance in iridescent splendor. Montana thrilled Thompson more every day. When Thompson was first stationed at Fort Owen in 1845, which would be four years ago in June, he'd wondered if he would ever get used to its many changing moods. It always made him feel as if he were walking on hallowed ground … as if he were glimpsing into a window of time and feeling footsteps echoing from the past.

Some areas of Montana are flat rolling plains, sown into rich-producing fields of wheat, oats, and other grains. Still other areas are comprised of majestic mountain monarchs, reaching heavenward through soft velvet clouds resting against the backdrop of a brilliant indigo sky. It's not uncommon to see rocky mountain goats or big horn sheep playing, feeding, or just standing on the mountains' stony ledges, their fur rippling in the breeze. Waterfalls can be found plummeting or cascading down rugged crags, their mist spewing upward.

Shimmering lakes, rivers, creeks and streams filled with enough fish to fulfill any fisherman's dreams, meander throughout Montana's vast rugged grandeur. Flanked along the rocky shores are many types of multi-colored shrubs. Lush grassy meadows are encircled by giant quaking aspens, gnarly tamaracks, and stately pines, which enhance the state's extraordinary beauty. Wildlife ranges from elk, deer, moose, bear, to mice, rabbits, wolves, coyotes, and many assorted species of birds. Winters can be harsh. Howling winds not only cause blizzards or create huge snowdrifts, but can also plummet temperatures to near forty degrees below zero.

For a while Thompson sat dejectedly upon his boulder, then sighing, he got up to wander farther along the river. Coming upon another large boulder, he knelt down, covered his face with his hands, soon groaning in abject despair. He was still in this position when Sergeant Peters came upon him.

Sergeant Peters was stocky, grizzly in appearance with a thick gray beard. Bushy eyebrows accentuated his mischievous, twinkling blue eyes. A lock of his wavy salt and pepper hair, which was always in constant disarray, fell across his high forehead. He removed his hat, ran his fingers through his hair and then replaced the hat so that it was tipped back on his head. Peters was a bowlegged man, who walked with a proud gait. He paused as he came upon Thompson then hastily turned to retreat.

Thompson looked up when Peters approached. "What is it, Sergeant?"

"Nutten', suh. Ah were jest takin' a stroll when Ah accidentally stumbled onto ya."

"Oh." It was plain by Thompson's countenance that he felt satisfied by this statement.

Peters turned as if to go, then turned back and spit into a bush. Pausing a moment, Peters sifted the wad of chewing tobacco in his mouth. While taking a deep breath, he hitched up his pants. Stepping closer to Thompson, he continued, "Suh, Ah know ya've been given an awful order." When Thompson glared sternly at Peters, he hesitated a fraction of a moment before proceeding. "Ah also know how ya feel, suh, t'wards takin' a innocent life." Thompson remained silent, touched beyond words.

"Know this, suh, thet Ah feels the same way! We know ya'll do what's right in the eyes of the Maker, so ifn' ya decides not ta obey them there orders, suh, the whole troop'll support cha … whatever way ya decide."

Surprised for a moment that Sergeant Peters could know the contents of his orders, Thompson gasped audibly. Peters hitched his pants once more, spit at the same bush, then stood stiffly at attention. Thompson scanned the face before him, all the while struggling to swallow past the lump in his throat. Rising he extended a hand to Peters. "Thanks, Peters. That means a lot to me. It also helps with the decision I must make." Turning toward the river, his hands behind his back, he stood gazing thoughtfully at the turbulent water. Peters watched in silence as Thompson, a giant among men, wrestled with his weighty problem. Turning back to face Peters, Thompson spoke. "You know, I have never disobeyed an order in all of my years as a soldier, yet here I'm facing the most difficult decision in all of my career. I don't want to retire knowing that I have the blood of all those innocent Indians on my hands. On the other hand, if I refuse to kill them, I face court martial … and certain death." He threw up his hands in abject despair. "Some choice, huh!"

"Yes, suh, it shore ez". Peters rubbed his chin thoughtfully then added, "Ah means what Ah said, Suh. We'll do what'er ya decide en let the chips fall where'er they may." He again ran a hand thoughtfully over his beard. "Cap'n, not a man in this here outfit cares much fer Major Thornton, but we do try ta do our best."

"I know. That's why your sticking behind me means so much." He paused to clear his throat. Thanks again, Peters."

Peters waved off the comment. "Don't mention it, suh." Turning, he trudged back toward camp.

Bowing his head, Thompson began praying for help in doing the right thing, and having the strength to stand by his convictions. He expressed his feelings toward Major Thornton's attitude and how he felt about the orders that the major had issued. He knelt for a long time in prayer. Finally, lifting his head erect, he rose with determination, raised a clenched fist skyward, and threw his head back so that he was looking heavenward. With great feeling, he cried aloud: "I won't do it! Let come what may … I just won't do it!" With these words came a peace of mind. There was a spring to his steps as he made his nightly rounds. Turning in for the night, he fell immediately into a deep, restful sleep.

Thompson awoke to the ringing of an axe. Soon the tantalizing aroma of coffee came wafting on the air. Rising, he began to ready himself for the day. After he was presentable, he went again to his private spot to petition the Lord. He needed reassurance that he had indeed made the right decision.

Again receiving confirmation, he cheerfully returned to camp where he ate a hearty breakfast. He had made a decision, now he would faithfully stand by it. Seeing Peters, he motioned for him to join him. The two men walked toward Thompson's tent.

In his tent was a bed, a table with two chairs. A map lay open on the table close to a lantern for light. Thompson motioned for Peters to be seated. Peters sat opposite him, then leaned back in his chair, folded his arms to wait for Thompson to speak. The Captain began, "I noticed that Nataka hasn't returned from his scouting trip yet, so we'll stay here until he returns to report his findings. I want regular guards placed on duty at four-hour intervals. The men can lounge around until Nataka returns."

Sergeant Peters nodded. "Right away, suh!" He stood to go, then as an after-thought, he turned back to Thompson, with a grin spreading across his face. "It shorely ez good ta see ya so chipper, suh."

Thompson smiled. "Thanks, Peters." Peters saluted before exiting. After Peters left, Thompson leaned back in the chair a moment. Rising, he went out to mingle with the men. He grinned as they rose to salute. "As you were, men." Thompson watched the card game for a while, cheering for the winner. Peters challenged him to a game of horseshoes, ribbing his friend unmercifully when he won three out of three games. As he wandered among the men, who were doing nothing but resting, Thompson felt an inner peace flow through him. The day wore slowly and tediously on.

At dusk a soldier rushed up to him. "Rider approaching, sir."

Thompson acknowledged him, "Bring the rider to my tent immediately!"

The soldier saluted, "Yes, sir!" then turned to carry out the order. Thompson entered his tent, lit the lamp then waited.

It wasn't long until a handsome young man, dressed as a scout, entered the tent. Thompson always felt pride when he gazed at this strapping young man. From the time Thompson arrived at the fort, there had been a special spot in his heart for him. Nataka stood six feet tall. He was broad at the shoulders, tapering into narrow hips. His high cheekbones and wide nose lost their hardness when he smiled, making the rich, velvety softness of his brown eyes twinkle. He studied Thompson's face intently as he stood waiting to speak, his hand extended.

Thompson clasped the extended hand before him. "How goes it, Nataka?" With his free hand, he pointed to the vacant chair. "Come, have a seat." After they were seated, Thompson placed his clasped hands upon the table then asked, "Now, what have you found out?"

Nataka placed his hat upon the table, moved his chair into a better position then looked up to meet Thompson's eager gaze. "Well, sir, it looks like you can conquer the tribe easily, as they all seem to be dying off by some disease."

"Do you know what it is?"

Nataka shook his head. "No, sir."

Thompson rose to pace the area inside his tent. Turning to the young man, who hadn't moved, he stepped over to face him, "Nataka …" began Thompson, only to pause in uncertainty. He walked the floor a moment then came to stand across the table from the young man. "Nataka, I know this assignment irritates you. Well … I feel the same way." Nataka blinked in surprise, silently searching Thompson's face. "It's true! I feel that Major Thornton is wrong! After much deliberation, I've decided to disobey his orders." Nataka inhaled deeply as he leaned forward to stare at Thompson as if he'd suddenly gone daft. "I'll not be party to wantonly killing innocent people … no matter what their race!" He paused to let Nataka digest his statement before going on. "What I want to know is this: Will you keep our secret?" When Nataka remained silent, Thompson hastened on. "Another thing to consider is the fact that if we help them … and are caught, it will mean court martial … and certain death for the two of us! Because of the Major's hatred of you, he'll hang you for the sheer pleasure of it." Nataka sat thoughtfully mulling Thompson's words over in his mind, searching for the answer. As he was about to speak, Thompson held up his hand. "Wait just a minute, Son." Stepping to the door, Thompson peeked out in time to see Peters step out of the shadows. "Come in here at once, Sergeant!"

"Yes, suh." Peters turned back toward the tent, entered, saluted then stood rigidly at attention.

"As you were, Sergeant." Peters quickly lowered his arm. "Sit here on the cot," motioned Thompson. Peters sank onto the cot. When all three men were comfortable, Thompson explained the orders he had received. When he was finished, he looked from one man to the other. "Before you give me an answer, I want you both to think it over carefully. If we are all in agreement, we'll help the Indians, then transport them to a safe place."

Jumping to his feet, Peters saluted. "Ah don't hafta thin' it over! Ah ne'er liked it from the beginnin'!" He began to pace excitedly about the tent, stopping near Nataka. ""Sides, Ah only haf two an a haf months left ta go afer Ah kin retire. Shorely they won't find out afer then."

Thompson shook Peters' hand. "Thanks, Peters. I knew that I could count on you."

"I want some time to think things over," said Nataka thoughtfully. "Guess I'd like to understand why you'd go against your orders … just to save these people."

Snorting in disgust, Peters flopped onto the cot. Thompson deliberately ignored him. "That's okay, Nataka," encouraged Thompson. "It's important that you are sure of how you feel, so take all of the time you need. As you do so, take into consideration the fact that the Indians have honored the treaty; therefore, they have done nothing to warrant their extinction.

Nataka nodded appreciatively. "Thank you for understanding, sir. I will take all of this into consideration. I'll give you my answer as soon as I have one."

"That's fair enough, Nataka." Thompson rose, as did the other two. Together they ambled out to join the others for the evening meal.

The air grew colder, with a hint of rain or snow. Being mid-May, the weather was still unpredictable. A slight breeze came up, causing the temperature to dip even lower. Thompson longed to be back at Fort Owen. His thoughts turned to his wife, Kate. How would she feel about the orders if she knew? Somehow he knew that she would go along with his decision, because she was such a kind, gentle hearted woman. He shivered when the wind began to howl in earnest. Soft, misty rain began to fall as he plodded wearily back to his tent. Looking around, Thompson wondered if the rain would turn into ice or snow. Entering his tent, he felt grateful for the tents, which would keep the men dry.

The men, who were not on guard duty, turned in to ensure an early start. He had just taken a seat at the table to pour over the map, when a voice called softly from outside his tent. "Are you busy, Captain Thompson?"

The captain recognized the voice immediately. "No, Nataka," called Thompson. Rising, he walked over to the tent entrance. "Come on in out of the storm." Nataka entered.

Thompson replaced the flap. "Come, take a seat," Thompson invited, motioning to the vacant chair. Nataka moved over to the chair opposite him. When they were seated, Thompson folded his hands before placing them on the table. "Now, what can I do for you, Nataka?"

"Well," said Nataka, brushing at some imaginary speck on the table, "I need to ask you a question, sir."

"Ask away," replied Thompson, watching the young man cautiously.

"I've felt for some time that you know the reason for Major Thornton's hatred toward the Indians. I need to know why." He watched the Captain's face intently. Thompson hesitated, not sure of what to do. "Sir, I know that Mrs. Thornton is my mother." Nataka held up his hand when Thompson would have spoken. "I accidentally overheard my parents talking one night about a month ago, when they thought I was asleep." Sighing, he watched Thompson intently.

"Please! Don't you think I have the right to know now?"

Thompson nodded as he sighed resignedly, "Yes … yes, I do!"

"In order to make a proper decision, I need to know more."

Thompson rose, paced the floor, a habit he had when nervous or uncertain, while Nataka sat patiently. Sighing deeply, Thompson dropped wearily onto his chair. "Colonel Dawson ordered Major Thornton to take a troop of soldiers out for a routine patrol one day … about twenty-one years ago. It was during a period of great fighting between these two groups of people. There were several tribes in the area, many of which were on the warpath, so many troops were either out patrolling or engaged in some terrible skirmish. While the fort was vulnerable, Swift Eagle, chief of those we are now ordered to eliminate, came to the post in Missoula with a large number of Indian braves to raid, rape, and plunder those left behind. Chief Swift Eagle's brother, Storm Cloud, violated Anna Thornton … beat her and left her for dead. Shortly afterward the tribe fled, leaving devastation in its wake. Many people were lost that day. Among the dead were old men, women, and several children." Nataka shivered at the horror of it all.

"When Major Thornton found out about his wife, he went on a rampage that lasted several days. No one could deal with him, least of all Anna. To top everything off, your mother found out a short time later that she was pregnant with you."

Nataka's jaw dropped in consternation. "Are you saying that Storm Cloud is my father?"

"Yes, I am," affirmed Thompson.

"Oh!" Nataka's mind reeled, with the absurdity of it all, making it difficult for his tortured mind to take it all in. How long he sat there, he never knew. To his beleaguered mind, it seemed as if eternity had come and gone.

All at once Thompson's voice drew him back to the present. "Thornton wanted Anna to find a way to get rid of 'the thing', before it was born, by any means she could … but she had refused. When she told Thornton that it wasn't the baby's fault, her words only infuriated him more. Thornton vowed that he would, as he put it, 'kill the brat' when it was born. To protect you, Anna took nineteen-month-old Miles and ran away to Denver, Colorado. Thornton searched for eight long months for her, growing more bitter with every passing day."

Thompson paused to let Nataka digest the facts then went on with the narrative. Nataka remained motionless. "Major Thornton didn't love Anna. I doubt that he ever knew what love was. She was like some type of property … to be used any way he wanted. Her feelings didn't matter in the least. He regularly told her that no one else would want her because she was so ugly.

"Why, your own father couldn't even stand you" was one particular comment he'd fling at her every chance he got. Thompson continued to pace the length of the tent then turned back to face Nataka. "Thornton didn't care who heard him. In fact, if someone did hear him, it pleased him immensely."

Nataka's brown eyes snapped with unspoken anger, but he remained silent. "When Thornton arrived in Missoula, he met Anna's father. Her father, Fred Hawkins, invited Thornton out to his place for dinner. When Thornton met Anna, he became enamored with her, but she disliked him on sight. She made it clear that she wanted absolutely nothing to do with him. Her father pestered her, even going so far as to beat her, all to no avail. Then one night he sold Anna to Thornton … for a measly bottle of whisky!" Nataka flinched as though he'd been struck. "A few nights after the wedding, they found Hawkins in the alley behind the bar … dead. In his hand they found a crumpled note telling Anna that he was terribly sorry for what he had done … although it was now too late … much too late." Neither Nataka nor Thompson spoke, for they were lost in their own thoughts.

Sighing, Thompson continued. "To Thornton, it was a mark against his character for Anna to be pregnant with another man's child … especially an Indian's child! Running away only served to complicate the problem more. You were two months old when he finally found her. Thornton grabbed you to make good his threat when Henry Hansen, who was with Thornton, intervened. He told Thornton that he and his wife, Jane, would raise you. Seeing no other way to spare your life, Anna begged Thornton to let the Hansens have you.

"Seizing the opportunity to strike out at her, Thornton agreed but only if she promised never to have anything to do with you or divulge that she was your mother. He swore that if she ever broke her promise, he'd kill you without hesitation. Everyone present knew he would do so in a heartbeat. Sobbing brokenly, Anna agreed. Thornton watched, smiling fiendishly, as Anna gave you to Henry."

Nataka stared dubiously at Thompson. It was so difficult for him to comprehend an individual so filled with hate that he would take his malicious feelings out on an innocent, defenseless infant. *Is the man crazy?* he wondered. Sighing, he looked over at Thompson. "I don't understand why they named me Nataka. Isn't that an Indian name?"

"Yes, it is."

"Wouldn't that bring Thornton's wrath down on me, as well as my parents?"

A mischievous gleam came into Thompson's eyes then a smile spread slowly across his face. "No one thought of that at the time. It seems that an Indian by the name of Nataka had saved Henry's life, so he wanted to name you Nataka Leroy to honor his father and his savior. Jane wanted to name you Henry Josephus after Henry and her father. To solve the problem, they decided on a compromise and named you Nataka Josephus."

"I see." Nataka rubbed his chin thoughtfully, while digesting this new piece of information. "How did this Nataka save Pa ... I mean Henry?"

Thompson peered at Nataka. I can only tell you the story the way Henry told it to me. True it happened many years ago, but I've heard Henry recount the story to others so often, and a few weeks before we came on this maneuver, that I know it almost by heart. I'm surprised that he hasn't related the story to you."

"If he ever did, I've long since forgotten it."

"Very well, I'll do my best to relate what happened. Shortly after his marriage to Jane, your father, Henry, went hunting where he got stranded in a blizzard. When the visibility got so poor that he couldn't see where he was going, he trusted his horse to get him to safety. All at once his horse heard a cougar scream a short distance away. Snorting in fright, the horse panicked. Throwing all reason to the wind, the horse bolted. Henry was hard-pressed to get him stopped. The horse stumbled, pitched Henry over a rock-filled embankment, rolled a couple of times before plunging to its own death in the ravine below. When Henry caught his breath, he tried to rise, but searing pain pierced through him like a fireball. Looking down at his leg, he was surprised to see that it was turned inward. A strange lump was protruding at the outer side of his pants. The sight terrorized him, because he knew in an instant that his leg was seriously broken. With this thought came the realization that he was so far from civilization that it could be days, weeks, even months before his body was found. When the horse tumbled to its death, it took the rifle, canteen, food supplies, and his bedroll with it. All that Henry had to rely on were the clothes on his back, flint to start a fire, a knife in a sheath at his side, and some jerky in his coat pocket. The loss of the canteen didn't worry him, since he could eat the snow to quench his thirst."

Thompson continued, recalling every word that Henry had told him. "Realizing that he couldn't stay there, because of the exposure to the inclement weather, he looked around for shelter. Seeing none, he gritted his teeth then began to drag his body upward, moaning in agony with every movement. Waves of nausea washed over him, growing in intensity until he began to relieve his stomach. After resting long enough to gain control of the pain, he gathered renewed strength. Again, Henry began pulling himself toward the top. Inching along, beads of perspiration broke out on his face. Many times Henry was forced to pause to rest, until he could summon strength to move on. Finally, trembling with shock, exhaustion, as well as agonizing pain, Henry pulled himself over the top. Lying prone on the ground, Henry closed his eyes as he struggled for control. Shock was setting in, even though he fought hard to remain coherent. Opening his eyes, he looked around for adequate shelter. Seeing a large pine tree nearby, he summoned all his remaining strength and began inching toward it. Crawling under the tree took more effort than he anticipated, causing Henry to lose consciousness."

"Opening his eyes sometime later, he looked around. The snow had stopped, but night was fast approaching. Having to relieve himself, he dragged himself a short distance from the tree, in an effort to preserve the condition of his new shelter. When he got back to the tree, he rested awhile. Feeling hungry, he reached into his pocket to take out a large piece of jerky. Sighing, he took a bite. While he chewed, he pondered his situation. Finding no solution, he finished the jerky in his mouth and put the remainder back in his coat pocket. After finding a comfortable position, he waited for sleep to claim him. No matter how hard he tried, like an elusive shadow, sleep eluded his every effort. Thoughts of home, and visions of his young bride, Jane, both comforted and troubled him. Being five miles from their nearest neighbor left Jane vulnerable. She would worry herself sick when he didn't return that night. Although Henry rubbed himself in an attempt to retain his body heat, the cold continued to slowly seep through his clothes, causing the pain in his leg to intensify. Unable to tolerate the agony, he once more lapsed into the state of unconsciousness. Waking a few minutes later, he was trembling uncontrollably, causing his body to ache with the cold."

Thompson recognized that he was going into great detail about the story, but he had gotten caught up in the drama and emotions, as he watched Nataka's obvious interest. He resumed, "Reality told him that if he didn't get a fire going, he'd freeze to death. Dragging himself over to the trunk of the tree, he removed the knife from the sheath at his side. Peeling away some of the bark, Henry tossed it toward the designated fire spot. He repeated this until there was enough to start the fire. Replacing the knife, he crawled over to some dead wood. Slowly, because of the pain, he dragged it behind him. Resting several times between each trip, he finally had enough to last the night. Clearing away the snow from the chosen spot, Henry arranged the bark and some pitch he'd found to help it ignite the bark. Then taking the flint, he began to coax a fire. At first the fire smoldered, refusing to start. However, through determination on Henry's part, the tinder caught, then began to burn. Satisfied that it was going strong, he placed a good portion of the dead wood on top. Lying back upon the ground, he fell into a deep, restful sleep."

Thompson's voice increased in volume and eagerness, as he continued to relate the most intriguing part of the story. "Awakened by a strange noise, Henry opened his eyes. Cautiously gazing around, he noticed that there were only a few hot coals left of the fire. He made a mental note to replenish it with the remainder of the wood. Raising his arm to brush back a lock of hair from his face, he saw droplets of blood on the coat sleeve. He wasn't bleeding, so how did it get there? Slowly, looking upward into the snow-clad branches, his heart nearly failed him. Crouched, not far above him, ready to pounce, was a large, full-grown male cougar. What an impressive sight it made! Sunlight highlighted the tawny gray body, aggressively flicking its tail back and forth. Shivers of fear ran along Henry's spine. His eyes grew large; his mouth fell slack, causing him to look like a crazed man. The cougar laid its ears back on its short, round head, licked its lips as if in anticipation, then bared his teeth defiantly. Little pinpoints of light flashed from the cat's large brown eyes. Fearing that he provided an easy meal, the helpless, prostrate man lay there, hearing only the deafening beat of his heart. Lying back onto the ground, he waited for death to strike. A deep, full-throated scream rent the air just a moment before the cougar lunged."

Thompson paused at this point. He smiled when he saw that Nataka's interest had been captivated. "No one ever knew for sure if it was the cougar or Henry that screamed." Chuckling softly, he flourished his narrative. "The animal, as if in slow motion, fell from the tree. Henry said his senses were so keen that he could even hear the whoosh of air over the falling animal, and the thud of the body striking the ground. What a shock it must have been to find the animal lying next to him, its head cradled in his lap! Even more shocking was the fur clad Indian, striding toward him with his gun still smoking!" Thompson paused again before abruptly changing the tone of his speech. He smiled in amusement. "Henry told me he did a really brave thing … he passed out."

"I would have done more than pass out. I would have died right there on the spot!"

Thompson smiled knowingly, "Yeah, me too!"

Nataka sat forward in his seat. "But what happened next?"

Thompson took a deep breath to collect his thoughts before continuing the story. "Well, having a broken leg, and being exposed to the inclement weather, Henry was in a bad way. In spite of the fire, his feet and hands were badly frostbitten. Both lips were cracked, making it difficult for him to swallow. The Indian brave built up the fire then searched for straight limbs to make splints. Finding what he was looking for, the Indian returned and set Henry's leg, binding the splints to his leg with strips of rawhide. Through hand signs, Henry made him understand that he needed to relieve himself. The Indian carried him away from the tree. Meanwhile the brave set about finding wood to make a travois. Dumping the wood near the tree, he went to carry Henry back to the tree. While Henry rested, Nataka fashioned the travois. When it was ready, he positioned it for the horse to pull and placed Henry on it. When they were almost ready to depart, the brave slung the trophy cat over the back of his horse. After dousing the fire, he checked to see how Henry was doing. Satisfied that he was as well as could be expected, the brave walked over, untied the horse's reins, then started for the village."

"The chief and others of the band weren't too happy to see Nataka bring a white man into their village, but they relented when they saw how bad off he was. Henry stayed in this man's tepee until he was well enough to go home. A great friendship sprang up between the two men, despite the language barriers."

"Oh, I bet Ma was beside herself with worry."

"If Jane could have, she would have sent out the entire army. However, she hitched the team to the wagon and went to the neighbors for help. After searching for four days, these neighbors told Jane that in all likelihood Henry was dead. Having no recourse but to stay in her home until the end of winter, Jane dealt with her grief pretty much alone. Imagine her surprise when Henry's new friend brought him home."

Nataka sat thoughtfully silent, then looked over at Thompson. "What a great man this Indian must have been! I'm glad they gave me his name." Thompson nodded, moved beyond words. "Why was this Nataka out there in the first place? Why was the animal wounded?"

Laughing, Thompson raised his hands. "Whoa! One question at a time!" Nataka grinned. Thompson drew another big breath before resuming the saga. "It seems the cougar was so old that it could no longer hunt properly. It had been attacking the villagers when they were away from camp. Nataka was out hunting when the cougar cornered him. He got off a shot when the cougar sprang at him. Whipping around, the cat sped away. From the amount of blood on the ground, Nataka knew that he had no choice but to track it so that it didn't come back to the village. He'd tracked it to the tree, unaware that Henry lay there wounded. After the Indian brought Henry home, Henry and Jane thought they'd never see this brave again, but a few weeks later, Nataka and his woman came to see how the invalid was. Moonbeam, his woman, had made the cougar's hide into a lovely vest, decorated it with multicolored beads as well as created a fringe around the bottom. She also fashioned a pair of moccasins from a buffalo hide, decorated them with the same multicolored beads. The patterns on both items were identical. Moonbeam had also made a beautiful tunic with matching moccasins for Jane. Nataka said he felt that Henry should wear the cougar's pelt. Henry started to protest, but the brave waved his argument aside. Remaining adamant, he presented them with the gifts."

"Jane and Moonbeam hit it off well. They shared many of their talents with each other, even taught each other their languages. When the men went hunting with the other braves, Moonbeam came to spend time with Jane. Unfortunately, a neighboring tribe, who raided their village, killed both Nataka and Moonbeam. After their death, Henry joined the army. When he made his current rank, he and Jane moved to Fort Missoula, where they remained for several years. When Fort Owen was opened, he was sent to serve under Major Thornton." Thompson paused to let Nataka think about the story. Looking up at the young man before him, he went on. "I don't think Henry realized when he gave you the name of Nataka that he was openly adding insult to injury. That the name infuriated Thornton was an unknown added bonus."

Nataka grinned impishly as he added sarcastically, "Oh, isn't that just too bad!"

Thompson snorted in surprise. "My sentiments exactly!" Both men burst out laughing, grateful for the reprieve from the mounting tension. It was a while before they were able to regain control.

Finally, Thompson was able to go on. "For a time Anna kept her word to Thornton, though it nearly destroyed her. It was Jane, your ma, who devised the plan for Anna to see you. When Thornton and his handpicked men went on lengthy maneuvers, everyone would meet at some secret rendezvous point. When you grew old enough to talk, the two women concocted a foolproof plan. They would meet in public places as though it were by accident. They never stayed long when they were together, but it gave Anna something to cling to."

Nataka sat thoughtfully rubbing his chin. "I remember when I grew older that, Ma … Jane … said that we couldn't speak to Mrs. Thornton. I guess we finally passed that point when I was about sixteen."

Thompson nodded absently, then rose and paced the floor. Taking a deep breath, he sank onto the chair to resume his story. "Thornton took pleasure in tormenting Anna. He took great delight in teaching Miles to do the same. Your half brother, Miles, was the apple of Thornton's eye; therefore, he could do no wrong. When Anna tried to correct Miles, Thornton would strike her, at the same time calling her a terrible mother. He even threatened to kill her if she didn't leave him alone. Everyone knew that he was dirty enough to do it, too."

When Thompson looked over at Nataka, he wasn't surprised to see anger written all over him. "Why didn't someone do something to stop him?"

"Because he was our superior officer no one dared buck him for fear of bringing his wrath down upon them. You know how difficult he can be sometimes. You have personally tasted his fury."

Nataka nodded thoughtfully before replying, "Yes I have."

Thompson continued, "Then sixteen years ago Anna discovered, to her horror, that she was with child. In an attempt to disguise her condition, she tried hard to gain a lot of weight. Even though the weight gain helped, she knew that she couldn't conceal her condition from Thornton for long. At the time, Jane was very plump, so she could have been in the family way and no one would have been the wiser. Fearing Thornton would learn of the coming baby, she took her problems to the Hansen's. They took her away while Thornton was off on some secret mission. When all returned, the Hansen's ... your Ma and Pa ... had a baby daughter, Sylvia Louise."

Nataka stared at Thompson in stunned disbelief. "Are you saying that Sylvia is really Thornton's daughter?"

"Yes, Nataka," said Thompson softly. "I am!" Nataka shook his head. He could only stare incredulously at Thompson. "I don't know if Thornton ever figured it out, Nataka. If he did, he hasn't let on. Jane and Henry have tried to be good parents to both of you. Anna confessed to my wife, Kate, that she lives in constant fear of Thornton's finding out about Sylvia. He won't hesitate to take her away from your folks so that he can raise her to become like Miles. Anna also told Kate that missing out on the growing up years of both of you has been very difficult for her. So many times she has longed to tell you both that she loved you, also that she is very proud to be your real mother, yet she never dared to speak to you."

Nataka remained silent for so long that Thompson began to worry about him. Finally, Nataka raised his head. Rising, Nataka extended a hand toward Thompson. "Thank you, sir." He hesitated a moment to gain control of his emotions. A mischievous grin lit up his face before adding, "Regarding the orders, sir ... I'm with you all the way ... whatever the outcome. In fact ... I take great delight at the prospect of thwarting old man Thornton. He'll pay for the treatment of my mother ... Anna!"

Thompson rose then clasped the hand heartily. "Good!"

Nataka smiled snidely. "What's the plan in regard to the Indians?"

"Well," said Thompson, reaching for the map. "I thought we could sneak up on them ... take them by surprise." After placing a map on the table, he walked to the tent flap. Throwing it back, he peered out into the inky darkness to speak to the guard, "Private Cooper, wake Peters and tell him to come here on the double."

Cooper resounded, "Yes sir! Right away, sir!"

After the guard hurried off, Thompson re-entered, lowering the flap. "Hopefully, we won't have to harm anyone." Nataka nodded then waited for Thompson to go on. "Then after Doctor McCabe has examined all of them, we'll go from there. My biggest concern is that our men will be affected by whatever is making the tribe ill, also causing our soldiers to die from it."

"I surely hope that's not the case."

"Guess only time will tell." He was prevented from saying more when Peters entered, coming to full attention. Thompson returned the salute. "At ease, Sergeant."

"Thank ya, suh." Lowering his arm, Peters awaited further instructions.

"Sorry about waking you, Peters," said Thompson, "but we need to formulate a plan for when we reach the Indian village." While Thompson spread the map out on the table, the two men walked around to peer over his shoulder. The three men worked far into the night, trying to figure out the best strategy for all concerned. Finally, a few hours before reveille sounded, they got some sleep.

Two days later, sunrise caught the troop nearing Swift Eagle's camp. Nataka was quickly dispatched to check things over. From where he was positioned, Thompson had a commanding view of the camp. What he saw was appalling. Never had he seen such filth in all his life. Knowing how meticulous the tribe usually was, he was able to judge that this disease had been running rampant for some time. Rats brazenly scurried helter-skelter, while dogs fought over what little food there was left to eat.

"No one is stirring, sir," reported Nataka.

Thompson acknowledged him, but remained thoughtful for a moment longer. Finally, turning to his men, he gave the signal for the troops to circle the camp. Soft, misty rain made it seem as if Mother Nature was against them. Wanting to be sure that nothing would go amiss, he watched the Indian village for a few more minutes. Assuring himself that there would be very little resistance, he gave the command: "Charge!" Waving his arm, bugle blaring, the captain saw the men obey as one. The poor Indians were so startled that the tribe was captured without incident or one life lost. Not long afterward, Thompson ordered Doctor McCabe to examine the Indians. This task wasn't easy, as the Indians were so frightened that they hid; thus, the doctor was hard-pressed to get the job done.

Doctor McCabe was a short, wiry man of five foot six inches. His black hair was streaked with gray, especially around the temples. Twinkling, kind brown eyes offset his protruding jaw. He was rather overweight, but that didn't stop him when it came to meeting other people's needs. He was a powerhouse of energy as he struggled to examine each patient. There were many who were too ill to protest, which caused his brows to draw together in concern.

A detail was ordered to set up camp, while another was assigned to begin cleaning up the debris. The stench from the discarded trash made everyone gag. One of the first things on the agenda was to destroy the starving dogs. This was painful, yet it had to be done. Rats were another problem, because they would viciously attack as a group if one of their own squealed in pain or fright, so they, too, had to be destroyed. The soldiers would burn what trash they could, hauling the rest away to bury it. It was also imperative to quickly bury the dead. They would find that all of this would take considerable time to accomplish.

When all of the patients were examined, the four men … Nataka, Peters, Thompson, and Doctor McCabe … met in Thompson's tent. Thompson waited for everyone to be seated then turned to McCabe, "Okay, what is it?"

"Typhus!"

"Typhus!" Thompson repeated. A deadly silence hung in the air, as he stared at McCabe in stunned disbelief. "Are you certain, man?"

"Yes."

Peters expressed what the others were thinking, "What do we do now?"

Doctor McCabe quickly replied, "No one is to drink the water without boiling it first. There are other precautions that must be rigorously followed as well, so I will make out a list of things you'll need to follow. Meanwhile, we need to set up a makeshift hospital."

He turned to Thompson. "Captain, we need the largest tent we have set up in the middle of the village."

Thompson nodded agreeably. "Peters, you see to the rest of the cleanup. I'll assign a few details. One group can set up the makeshift hospital, while another ferrets out those who are affected with the disease. A third detail will be needed to bury the dead."

McCabe turned to Thompson. "I'll need someone from the tribe who is well enough to act as an interpreter."

Thompson nodded to Nataka, "Take care of that, will you?"

"Yes, sir," said Nataka. Further instructions were given, then all the men set about their various tasks.

After the makeshift hospital was set up in the center of the village, Thompson went to check on the other details. He knew they were in for a long siege … that his worst fears were being realized. "Typhus," he groaned aloud. Shuddering, to rid himself of the fear and dread that gripped him, he set about keeping busy … determined not to think about the dilemma before him.

CHAPTER 2

Kate Thompson

Kate Thompson awoke to the sounds of reveille. Groaning, she burrowed deeper under the covers, drifting off to sleep for another five minutes. Slowly, she became aware of the many different sounds outside. Opening her eyes, she noticed sunlight streaming through the window. Flinging the covers back, she sat on the edge of the bed. After yawning a few times, as well as stretching, she struggled to stand up. When she finally achieved a standing position it was very apparent that she was going to have a baby.

Kate, normally a very petite woman, had beautiful auburn hair and green eyes. She had delicately shaped cheekbones and a short well-defined chin that complimented her light complexion, which was generously sprinkled with freckles. Thick sensuous ruby-red lips showed perfectly matched teeth. She had a slight Irish brogue, which became very pronounced when she became excited or angry. Kate was not only fun loving but also generous to a fault. Her greatest delight came from finding ways to serve those in need of help or comfort. Her great sense of humor cheered those around her.

Dressing as quickly as possible under the circumstances, she went to the kitchen. Taking the lid lifter from its place on the wall, she removed the front lid of the range where she added kindling to the smoldering coals. Opening the damper, she replaced the lid. After returning the lid lifter to its place on the wall, she filled the teakettle from the reservoir. The fire was going well, so she added more wood then turned the damper. When the water was hot, she filled the basin so that she could make herself presentable.

Kate had just finished preparing breakfast when someone knocked on the door. Moving the food to the back of the range to keep it warm, she walked over to see who was at the door.

John Whipple, with a covered dish in his hands, smiled at Kate cheerfully. "Morning, Mrs. Thompson. Ma thought you might like a couple of cinnamon muffins with your breakfast."

"Why thank you, John," replied Kate taking the plate. "They smell so delicious!" Nineteen-year-old John beamed at the compliment paid his mother. "Please be sure to thank your mother for me. Hattie has been a good friend."

"That I will!" Stepping inside, John walked over to the counter to pick up two buckets. "I also came to haul water, after which I'll fill the wood box for you." Kate nodded. Smiling, she watched until he had gone outside. Kate set the plate of muffins onto the table then finished preparing breakfast. She had just finished setting the food on the table when John returned with the water. Checking the reservoir, he noticed that it was nearly empty, so he emptied the buckets into it. After several more trips, he returned to place the water buckets down upon the counter. When he went out to chop the wood, Kate ate her breakfast and cleaned up the kitchen before starting her daily baking. When John had filled the wood box, he put a good-sized pile just outside the door for easy access, then left.

As Kate kneaded a batch of bread, she found it difficult because her belly kept getting in the way, and her back felt as if it were breaking. Finally, after what seemed like forever, she had the dough ready to put into a large greased bowl. After placing it in the warming oven to rise, she cleaned up the mess. With that done, she went to the pantry to get some dried apples, placed them into a pan, added a little water, then put them onto the stove to cook.

After adding a stick of wood to the hot coals, she washed her hands so that she could check on the bread. While lifting the bowl from the warming oven, she got too close to the stove. She not only scorched her apron, but also her belly. "Ouch!" she muttered. Finally, she was able to remove the bowl of bread dough, which she placed on the table. She rubbed her tummy then pulled her apron out to scan it critically. "Dad-burn-it! It was my best apron, too!" Lifting the bread cover, she angrily punched the dough down to let it rise again. Replacing the cover, Kate placed the bowl on the counter, so that she would not burn herself again. Sighing wearily, Kate waddled over to the washbasin to wash her hands. As she dried her hands, images of Paul invaded her mind, causing great waves of loneliness to rush over her. *I wonder what he's doing,* she mused. Shaking herself to erase the image from her mind, she went back to work with renewed vigor. "I can't think of him now," she scolded aloud, "or I won't be able to stand it."

Going to the pantry to get the ingredients needed to make the piecrust, she found it difficult to extend her arms high enough to reach the items on the top shelf. Raising her arms put extreme pressure as well as pain on her stretching ligaments and swollen abdomen. After several attempts, she finally succeeded in getting the items needed. Placing the ingredients onto the table, Kate slowly and wearily eased herself onto a kitchen chair. Sighing contentedly, Kate fanned herself with her apron. As she did so, she noticed the huge scorched spot. Rolling her eyes heavenward, she dropped the apron in total disgust. Mumbling under her breath, she set about making the piecrusts. When the dough was ready, she rolled out one crust and placed it into a pie pan. Using the table for leverage, she labored to rise. Once onto her feet, Kate went to the stove to check on the apples. Finding them done, she added cinnamon and sugar and a some flour to the cooked apples, just like her mother had taught her. Getting a teaspoon, she dipped out a small amount of the filling to taste to see if it was sweet enough. Satisfied, she put half of the filling into the pie shell. After rolling out another crust, she placed it on top of the filling. After fluting and trimming the edges, she set it aside to repeat the process with the other pie. She lightly brushed each top with milk, added a sprinkle of cinnamon and sugar then placed them into the oven to bake. Looking at the dishes, with total abhorrence, she willed them to do themselves. However, since that didn't happen, Kate sighed resignedly and began to clean up the mess.

Knowing her work was not yet done, she took the bowl of risen dough from the counter. Molding the dough into four loaves, she placed them into prepared bread pans. Placing a tea towel over the pans, she left the loaves of bread on the table to rise. Oh how she longed to rest, but the loneliness, the longing for Paul grew unbearable. While waiting for the pies to bake and the bread to rise, Kate straightened the house.

This really was no big job because the kitchen and living area was combined into one large room. As one entered the house, the kitchen was to the left, the living area to the right. Left of the door was a large wood box. A Majestic Range was placed next to this. It had a warming oven on top. A large reservoir was attached to the right. On the end wall was a long counter. On the end of the counter near the stove was a washbasin, which was located next to the water buckets. The counter was also used to set the dishpans on when doing dishes. Above the counter was a large window, adorned with white frilly curtains.

Crude cupboards, with green-checkered gingham curtains, began at the right of the window. Another set of connecting cupboards was located on the adjoining wall. A small icebox fit snugly underneath. A doorway on the right led into a small pantry. In the middle of the kitchen area was a wooden drop-leaf table with four homemade chairs.

A small round oak table with claw feet, adorned with a large lace doily and decorative oil lamp, was near the door leading outside. Near the table was an oak wooden rocker. Next to it was a roller-top writing desk with a homemade chair in front. A door at the end of the room led into a spacious bedroom. Left of this door was another oak rocker, similar to the one across the room. Another small oak table, round with claw feet, was adorned with a similar lace doily. There was another decorative lamp on the table, near a large open leather Bible. A basket of needlework was positioned near the rocker. The floors were all made of rough-hewn lumber with a braided throw rug in the middle of the living room floor.

In the bedroom to the right of the door, Kate saw the cradle Paul had fashioned for the baby. A large oak dresser was nearby. Placing her hand on her swollen abdomen, she wondered if the child would be a girl or a boy. Shrugging, she scanned the room. A set of white frilly lace curtains adorned the window near the middle of the room. A large double bed, which was built into the wall, was covered with a wedding ring quilt. A hooked rug lay on the floor at the side of the bed. An oak dresser with a large mirror embossed in gold stood near the bed. To the left of the door was a wide full-length oak wardrobe with decorative double doors.

After quickly making the bed, Kate straightened up the room. She put the living area in order, then went to the stove to check on the pies. They were done, so she took them out of the oven and placed them onto racks in the pantry to cool. After putting the bread into the oven to bake, she added another stick of wood to the stove. When the kitchen was back in order, Kate placed a green-and-white checkered tablecloth onto the table.

While waiting for the bread to bake, Kate went out onto the porch. Not only did she enjoy the fresh air, but as it gently caressed her face, it also brought cool refreshing relief to her tired aching body. Absently brushing back a loose tendril of auburn hair from her face, Kate went to sink slowly, yet awkwardly, onto the porch swing, grateful for the time to relax. For a moment she took advantage of the many sights and sounds of the fort. Gently swinging back and forth, she closed her eyes, all the while willing herself not to think of Paul. No matter how hard Kate tried, visions of Paul invaded her every thought. Finally, shaking herself angrily, she sluggishly rose from the swing. Kate walked back into the house to check on the bread. It was golden brown, so she took it out. After brushing the tops generously with butter, she placed them on racks in the pantry to cool. Kate dipped hot water from the reservoir to pour into the dishpans that she had placed onto the counter. Adding soap, she quickly washed up the pans. When they'd been dried, she put them away. Dumping the water into a bucket, which John would throw out later, she wiped the dishpans. After hanging them up, Kate draped the dishcloth on one pan, then placed the tea towel on the other.

Having nothing more to do, Kate went back outside to sit on the porch swing. Try as hard as she might, she just couldn't block out the overwhelming longing to embrace Paul. To be in his arms at that moment would have been heaven. Thinking back to the day the troops left the fort, she recalled how upset Paul had been, yet he had refused to discuss it. *I wonder what was in those orders that upset him so,* she mused. All at once, Kate felt such a mounting anger for Major Thornton that she felt as though she would burst. She had tried so hard to like Thornton, but had found it virtually impossible. Chuckling softly, she muttered, "It's no secret that he hates me, but then again, Major Thornton hates all women." Gently swinging back and forth, Kate wondered what had made him so bitter against the female gender. Shrugging in disgust, she sighed. While Kate looked out over the fort, thoughts of Thornton continued to plague her. *Major Carl Thornton is so filled with hate and anger that he has even had an adverse effect on his son, Miles,* she mused, nodding her head sadly. *If possible, Miles is more demented than his father!* Sighing, she scolded herself. *What am I thinking of them for?*

Kate thought back to the time when she had first met her husband, Captain Paul Thompson. After the death of her mother three years earlier, she had been living in New York City with Helen Fillmore. Kate's mother, Sarah, had worked for Helen until her sudden death. Paul, who had been stationed in Pennsylvania for the past three years, had come to New York on one of his furloughs to visit his aunt Eileen. They had gone shopping at one of the large department stores, as had Kate and Helen. Neither Paul nor Kate had been watching where they were going, so the inevitable had happened. They had crashed into each other, sending their packages flying helter-skelter. In the confusion, their packages had been mixed up. Kate smiled as she re-lived the scene in her mind.

Eileen began to laugh uproariously. Helen soon joined in. Handing Helen one of her personal cards, Eileen introduced herself. "My name is Eileen Thompson ... and who are you?"

"My name is Helen Fillmore."

Eileen nudged Helen, while at the same time grinning mischievously. Motioning to the two young people struggling to separate their packages, she added, "With the mess these two have made of things, I have a feeling we will be seeing each other in the near future." Kate, who was trying to help the handsome stranger, looked up at the two ladies suspiciously. Helen winked at Eileen. "You may be right, dear." Sighing in exasperation, Kate turned back to her task. After a few moments, she coyly studied the gentleman's manly features.

All at once he looked up, smiling beguilingly. "Well, do I pass?"

Kate blushed a brilliant red from her neck to the roots of her auburn hair, but refrained from commenting. Meanwhile Eileen and Helen had made plans for lunch the following day. It was the beginning of their courtship.

Paul and Kate were only able to spend a month together before his furlough was up, but it was enough time for their love to blossom. Although Paul went back to his Pennsylvania regiment, the couple corresponded. A year later, Paul came to New York on his next furlough. They took time to get better acquainted. Near the end of his furlough, he told Kate that he would have to go to Montana in a few weeks. He had told her that he would be back to visit his aunt to say his goodbyes. On his knee in the park, Paul asked Kate if she would marry him when he returned. For her there was only one answer, and obviously it was "yes". Paul assured her it would only be a short while until they would be able to be together.

It was a difficult time for Kate when Paul went back to his regiment, but Kate kept busy by purchasing her trousseau, as well as making her wedding gown. Helen Fillmore had had a soft spot for Kate and her mother. The three of them had been very close when Kate's mother was alive.

Helen Fillmore was 63 years old, yet didn't appear to be much over 50. She was straight, willowy and carried her five feet six inches with great dignity. Noticing that Helen seemed very pale, Kate also couldn't help thinking that she was much too thin. Her light-blue eyes, as well as her dark-brown hair, which was streaked with gray, made her fair skin even more delicate. Kate had tried to fuss over her, but Helen would have none of it. She was fun-loving, kind, even generous. Helen's greatest desire was to care for others. When they lost Sarah, Helen tried to console Kate the best she could. That was a difficult time for Kate because her mother was the only family she had … that she knew of. When Harold, Helen's husband, died one year later, it was a difficult time for them both. Harold had been like the father that Kate lost in Ireland.

Eileen, Helen, and Kate grew closer as they helped Kate get everything ready for the wedding. Standing five feet tall in her stocking feet, Eileen was plump and robust. She knew how to get things done without quibbling about a little hard work. Work was made easy by her jolly antics and her keen sense of humor. Eileen was sixty-five years old, had snow-white hair, and mischievous blue eyes that gave her away when she was thinking up some kind of mischief. Her face lit up and her eyes became dancing pools of merriment, shrouded in wrinkles each time she laughed. Kate loved being around her and drew great strength from her presence. Though it was a joyous time for Kate, it was also difficult. Many times she wondered how she could leave those dear, precious ladies behind. They had come to mean so much to her, yet she longed for the time when Paul would return and they would be married.

True to his word, Paul returned six weeks later. They were married in a small church close to Eileen's home. The ceremony was beautiful in its simplicity. Helen, Eileen, and a few close friends were all that attended. Kate smiled as she thought of the wedding gown she'd worn. The satin bodice, gathered at the waist, was embroidered with delicate white flowers. White satin sleeves were puffed from the shoulders to the elbow then tapered to the wrist. The satin skirt flowed to the floor, with a long train at the back. A gossamer veil, gathered at the top with a beaded crown, flowed to her waist. Her long thick auburn hair, drawn back from her face, was piled high up on her head. A single ringlet on each side of her face caressed her cheeks. Dainty white shoes completed the desired effect.

After the wedding supper held in Eileen's spacious home, they quickly changed into their traveling clothes. A few minutes later they left for Grand Central Station. It had been previously arranged for their wedding gifts to be shipped after they got settled at Fort Owen, Montana. Eileen's gardener loaded the baggage onto the wagon. He started to the station ahead of the wedding party, while Edwardo, the butler, took the wedding party to the station. It was difficult to say their goodbyes, yet Kate was excited. Little did Kate know that this would be the last time she would see Helen alive, for Helen died three months later from a stroke.

It took them a month of hard travelling to reach Fort Owen. The first face Kate saw when they arrived was Anna's. It didn't take long for the two of them to become fast friends. When Kate met Major Thornton, she disliked him on sight, which surprised her, because she loved people. Major Thornton made no pretense of liking her from the start. In fact, after that first meeting he barely acknowledged her. Kate knew that he even went out of his way to ignore her. This satisfied Kate, who continued to visit Anna amid Thornton's covert glares.

Kate sat fanning herself, trying not to think of the past. Finding it impossible, she gave into the mood. Into her mind came the many times she had taken care of Anna after one of Miles' or Thornton's tirades. Those were the times she felt the strongest repulsions for Thornton as well as for his son, Miles, yet she had managed to remain civil for Anna and Paul's sake.

One morning Kate had taken over a loaf of bread to Anna. She had stayed to visit with her for a few minutes. Thornton came in not long afterward and demanded something from Anna. Kate could no longer remember what the object was that he demanded, but when Anna didn't jump up to do it fast enough to suit Thornton, he bellowed like a mad bull. Picking up a large glass ashtray that was near him, he flung it at Anna, striking her a glancing blow just above the eye. "I said, NOW!" Kate gasped in horror, but Thornton ignored her. Before Anna could move from her chair, Thornton strode over to slug her with such force that she fell backwards, knocking the chair over. Although she was unconscious, he didn't stop there. "Quit faking it, you dirty, filthy wench!" When she didn't move, he kicked her viciously in the ribs two more times. "Get up, you ugly, good for nothing, old hag, or I'll bash your head in!"

Grabbing the butcher knife from the table, Kate rose to position herself between them. With eyes flashing, nostrils flared, the light gleaming from the knife, she looked like one possessed. "Stop it, you rotten fiend, or I'll drive this knife through your dirty, slimy, black heart!"

Thornton started to lunge toward Kate then thought better of it. For a moment he stood staring hatefully down at Kate, wrestling with the idea of grabbing the knife to use it on her. Kate wanted so badly to plunge the knife deep into him for what he'd done to Anna, yet her saner side took over. She gradually grew calmer. Turning sharply, he stomped angrily toward the door. Stopping, he turned to face Kate with pure hatred on his face. "You'll be sorry you stuck your filthy nose in where it wasn't wanted!" His teeth were clenched, his fists were locked tightly against his sides, and the cords in his neck bulged, causing his face to grow red with unspent rage. "You just wait and see, wench!" Turning, he stormed out the door.

When Kate was satisfied that he'd left, she bent over Anna, finding her barely alive. Kate quickly ran to get help. Seeing a soldier passing by, she ordered him to get Doctor Phelps. Doctor McCabe, the army doctor, was with the troops on another maneuver. Phelps was just leaving the fort to check on his patients in the settlement when the soldier reached him. Hurrying over to the Thornton's, he rushed in without knocking. "What did he do this time?" asked Phelps angrily as he knelt over Anna.

"Major Thornton, who was just here, went into a terrible rage because Anna didn't move as fast as he thought she should have," Kate explained, moving aside to let him examine Anna.

"What stopped him from killing her?"

"I did," whispered Kate, so low that Phelps strained to hear her.

Phelps' jaw dropped in consternation as he looked intently at Kate. "You did! How?" Kate shuddered as she thought of how close she had come to stabbing the Major. Sighing, she remained silent. Phelps watched her closely. "Tell me, how did you stop that beast, Mrs. Thompson?"

"I grabbed the butcher knife from the table. I told him …" She couldn't go on for a moment as the memory flooded through her. Taking a deep breath helped her grow a little calmer. "I told him … I'd plunge it into … his dirty black heart!" Burying her face into her hands, she sobbed brokenly. Finally, she looked intently up at Phelps. "So help me, God, I would have done it, too!"

The soldier, who had followed the doctor inside to await further orders, looked at Kate in awe, feeling deep respect. When Phelps turned to him, the soldier saw that Phelps was deeply moved. "Go to the infirmary … get a stretcher, on the double." The soldier, spinning around, hurried out the door. When he was gone, Phelps turned to Kate. "Thornton won't take this lightly, Kate. You damaged his ego when you made him back down."

After dabbing at her eyes, Kate blew her nose before replying, "I know, but I just couldn't let him kill her."

"No, my dear," agreed Phelps, "that you couldn't."

The soldier returned with a stretcher with Henry Hansen close behind. He addressed Phelps, "When I saw Gabe here carrying this stretcher, I figured that Anna was in trouble again, so I decided to see if I could be of some help."

"Thanks, Hansen." Picking up his medical bag, Phelps rose. "We need to get her to the infirmary as quickly as possible." With Phelps barking orders, the men got her onto the stretcher. The men quickly carried Anna over to the infirmary. Gabe left shortly after transporting Anna. Hansen and Kate helped Phelps care for Anna. "He didn't break her ribs, but they'll be pretty sore for a while. What worries me the most is that gash over her eye." Kate could see that it was already swelling and turning black and blue. Phelps probed gently around the wound. When he felt satisfied that there were no broken bones, he stitched up the wound. After putting a dressing on the wound, he went over to the washbasin to wash up. Hansen, with Kate's help, cleaned the work area. "We have to wait until she regains consciousness, to decide how extensive the damage is." Walking over to Kate, he placed a hand gently on her shoulder. "One thing is for sure, Kate … if you hadn't stopped him when you did, he would have killed her!" Kate shuddered as tears ran unheeded down her cheeks. Then he turned to ask, "Hansen, do you think you could stay with Mrs. Thornton until I check on my patients in the settlement?"

"Sure thing, Doc."

Kate looked at Phelps pleadingly, "I can stay with her, too, Doctor."

Phelps smiled gently. "I know you can, but Hansen can handle Thornton if he comes back."

Kate nodded understandingly. "You're right, of course."

"I won't be gone more than three hours," promised Phelps, slipping into his jacket. Going to the medicine cabinet, he took out a bottle of pills. He put one onto a tray. After replacing the lid, Phelps put the bottle back. Picking up the tray, he carried it over to Anna's bedside table. "If Anna regains consciousness before I get back, give her this pill."

"Very well," nodded Hansen. Crossing over to the counter, Phelps picked up his medical bag. Without another word, he left.

Hansen turned to Kate, his face filled with admiration for the Irish lass. "You were really one brave lady, Mrs. Thompson. Not very many people have the courage to go against that rat!"

"I wasn't very brave, Mr. Hansen. I just couldn't let him beat her like that!"

"That may be, ma'am, but lesser men have stood back and done nothing."

"Please, Mr. Hansen, call me 'Kate'. Mrs. Thompson seems too formal somehow."

"On one condition."

Kate watched him warily. "What's that?"

"That you call me 'Henry'."

"Okay," she shrugged. "That's fair enough."

Phelps returned an hour later than he thought he would, but Anna still had not regained consciousness. Paul came into the infirmary shortly after Phelps returned from the settlement, declaring that he had just heard about Anna. Sobbing brokenly, Kate ran into his outstretched arms. Paul wisely let her cry, knowing how special Kate and Anna's friendship was. Finally, Kate stepped back to smile sweetly. "I have surely soaked your uniform, darling."

"You can soak my uniform any time you want to, honey." Thompson kissed her tenderly upon the mouth.

Phelps laughed softly then pretended to become stern. "Wait just a cotton pickin' minute! I'll have you know there'll be none of that mushy stuff in here!"

"Ah, you're just jealous," teased Thompson.

Phelps wiggled his eyebrows tauntingly. "Wouldn't you like to know, Mister? Being as handsome as I am, as well as having such endearingly sweet charms, I have no problems with the ladies." He slowly scanned the room. "Well, not in this room anyway."

Kate giggled softly at Phelps' innate sense of humor. Blushing, Kate tucked her face into Thompson's shoulder. Thompson burst out laughing good-naturedly at Phelps' antics.

Later when they had left the infirmary, they talked about Anna's condition. Kate smiled fondly at how loving, how considerate, how understanding her husband had been, even though he feared for her life when she expressed the desire to see Anna through her dilemma. Kate remembered how anxious he had been for Anna's welfare. He had popped in often to check on her progress.

Kate remembered that Anna didn't regain consciousness until near daylight the next morning. After giving Anna the pain pill, Phelps had redressed her wound. Shortly afterward, she fell into a restful sleep. Only when Phelps told Kate that Anna would sleep for a long time, did she go home. She stayed with her as much as she could, until Doctor Phelps released Anna to go home. Kate walked her home. Getting her settled in bed, she stayed with her until she fell asleep. She walked home, relieved that there was no sign of Thornton. She learned sometime later that Thornton had left on some secret maneuver. For a while things went okay, then one day Thornton went on another rampage, causing Anna to flee for her life. Where she went, no one knew, or no one would tell. She didn't return until he'd cooled off.

Kate's thoughts went back to when she received news of Helen's death. For days she struggled to deal with the loss. One day Helen's lawyer came to the fort to notify her that everything that Helen owned was hers. Paul took her to Missoula, where he put her on the stage to New York so that she could get Helen's affairs in order. Eileen insisted Kate stay with her while she was there. When Kate started to refuse, Eileen held up a hand to ward off the objection. "This old house gets so lonely that it creaks and groans in protest of the silence." Kate chuckled at that, but graciously accepted her offer.

It took a month for Mr. Holbrook to find a buyer for Uncle Harold's business. Helen, who always had a great sense of business, continued to run the business after Uncle Harold's death. She claimed that it kept her from going dotty. Meanwhile, she went through Helen's clothes. With the help of Eileen, Kate was able to find someone who needed them. There were times, especially at night, when the loss was so great that Kate sobbed inconsolably. Eileen would go into Kate's room and slip her arms around the pain-filled woman. She would hold her, rocking her gently until the tears subsided. The two women had worked feverishly to go through the household items. Some of the items they donated to charities; others were packed and shipped back to the fort. Several items were given to Eileen. The furniture, carriages, and other large furnishings were sold at a private auction. After selling the business and huge estate, Kate deposited the proceeds into a New York bank, as she didn't need the money at that time.

When they were done, Kate went to spend a few days with Eileen before starting home. The two grew even closer. Eileen promised to come out west sometime for a visit. It was a tearful parting when Kate boarded the train at Grand Central Station, yet she was comforted by thoughts of soon seeing Paul.

Shaking herself from her nostalgia, Kate got up from the swing to go back into the house. Quickly wrapping up one of the pies, she went to see her friend Lonna Foster. When Jane answered the door, Kate grinned. "Hi, Jane. 'Surprised to see you here."

Jane smiled, motioning for Kate to enter. "Come on in."

Once inside, Kate looked around at the empty room. "It must be time for Lonna's baby to enter this wonderful world!"

Jane Hansen, who was the wife of Henry Hansen, took the pie from Kate. "Yes, Doctor Phelps is with her now." Setting the pie onto the table, Jane turned back to Kate, motioning to the rocker in the corner of the room. "Be seated, dear."

"Thank you, I will." Kate sank wearily into the rocker.

Jane eyed Kate critically. "Can I get you something to drink?"

"No thank you. I'm just fine. Tell me about Lonna."

"Lonna is fully dilated, and the baby is nearly here. I sent John Whipple to get her husband, Lester." Jane looked at the clock. "He should be here soon."

Kate rose clumsily. "Then I won't stay."

"Don't be silly," scolded Jane. "I …" Jane was prevented from saying more when the door burst open. Lonna's husband, Lester, entered.

Placing his hat on a peg behind the door, he turned expectantly toward Jane. "How is she?"

"Lonna's fine," Jane reassured him. "The doctor …" Jane was again interrupted when they heard a loud smacking sound, followed by the lusty cry of a baby in the other room. Lester turned so pale that Kate thought for sure he was going to faint. After quickly washing her hands, Jane went to the bedroom behind the curtain.

Lester was a short man with a medium build. His sandy hair was thinning. Kate knew it wouldn't be too many years before he would be bald. His deep brown complexion came from many hours in the sun. He wore a neatly trimmed handlebar moustache. Anxious blue eyes, usually soft and gentle, peered out from thick bushy eyebrows. She smiled to herself as she watched him pace nervously around the room.

Kate noticed the modest accommodations of the surroundings, which were smaller than her own. One room made up the kitchen and living area. The stove took up space at one end of the room. A few crudely made wooden cupboards and an icebox were on the opposite wall. A large wooden table and two chairs were all the furnishings in the room. Curtains partitioned the room from the sleeping quarters. Kate noticed that the room was tidy yet cramped.

Jane interrupted Kate's thoughts when she brought the baby out to Lester. "Papa, meet your new son." The poor man looked as if he wanted to bolt as Jane walked over to him. Smiling encouragingly, Jane placed the child in his arms. "Don't worry, Papa, he won't break." The baby, bundled up in a soft blue receiving blanket, whimpered pitifully as his tiny rosebud lips made a sucking motion. As Lester gazed down at his newborn son, love and joy, mingled with pride replaced the fear. A few moments later the two of them disappeared behind the curtain, leaving Kate alone.

Kate rose awkwardly to go just as Doctor Phelps emerged from behind the curtain. Although he looked tired and spent, his face lit up at the sight of Kate. "Hey, little mother to be," he greeted. "What are you doing here?" Scowling, he crossed over to stand before her. "I thought I told you to take things easy."

As he chastised her, she grew defensive. "A body has to keep her mind busy in order to stay sane, Doctor."

"Yes, but if I know you, my words went right over your head. I'm nearly done here, so wait for me and I'll walk you home." Kate started to protest, but he held up his hand. "That's not a request … that's an order!"

Kate chuckled resignedly. "Very well, Doctor, you're the boss."

"Don't forget it!" demanded Phelps in mock severity. They both burst out laughing.

Lester, coming out from behind the curtain, spied the pie on the table. He sniffed the air, rubbed his tummy appreciatively then turned to smile at Kate. "I'd recognize who brought that pie in a minute. Only one person other than my wife can make pies like that!"

Kate beamed at the compliment. "Thank you."

Doctor Phelps frowned sternly, shaking his finger at her. "That's my point exactly!" He slipped back behind the curtain, returning a few minutes later. "I'm ready," he announced as he walked over to Kate. "I'll be back later to check on the patients, Lester. Meanwhile, I've left Jane in charge of things."

Lester shook Phelps' hand vigorously. "Thanks, Doctor."

"That's what I'm here for."

Kate studied Phelps covertly as they walked to her cabin. She was amazed at how tall he was. Phelps appeared to be pencil thin. Although Phelps was very homely to gaze at, his personality more than made up for it. Widely spaced brown eyes usually twinkled merrily with life, but when something tender touched him, they would grow velvety soft. His protruding jawbone didn't conform to his small forehead. It made his features seem hard. Those who knew him most knew that he was almost too generous with his time and skills. His once immaculate pinstriped suit was wrinkled. He not only looked disorderly, but he looked haggard from lack of sleep.

Phelps saw her safely inside the cabin, sniffing appreciatively at the lingering aroma. "Yum … It smells like a bakery in here!" Sighing, he turned sternly to Kate. "Didn't I tell you that you were not to get strenuous?" Kate, flinching at his words, remained silent. Seeing her expression, he visibly softened. "I know that it's hard to be alone, but if you want to have a healthy baby, you have got to stop doing too much."

"Very well, Doctor. I won't do any more baking until after the baby is born."

"That won't be too long, now."

Kate nodded affirmatively. "I know." She searched her mind in an attempt to change the subject then brightened. "Have you eaten?"

The doctor paused, thoughtfully scratching his head. Finally he looked over at her. "I've forgotten the last time I've eaten."

"Let me fix something for you."

Kate started toward the pantry, but he stopped her and led her to a chair by the table, where he gently pushed her down into it. "You tell me where everything is …

I'll fix it myself," he insisted. Smiling, Kate gave him the necessary directions. After washing up, Phelps set to work with determination. As he cut the bread, to make sandwiches for them, he began to chat amiably. "During college and my internship, I worked many erratic hours. Dinner was usually over several hours before I got back to the boarding house where I stayed, so I used to have to make myself something to eat. Got pretty good at it, even if I do say so myself!"

A giggle escaped Kate, followed by a teasing light that flashed in her green eyes. "Sure couldn't prove it by looking at you."

Phelps scowled at her, wrinkled his nose, then promptly acted as though she hadn't spoken. Kate was amazed at how quickly he put the sandwiches together. He handed her a fat roast beef sandwich and a large glass of milk. Kate started to protest, but he held up a hand to silence her. "I want you to eat every bite of that without giving me any excuses."

When he was finished, he cut two generous portions of pie, handing one to her. "I expect you to eat every bite. I won't accept any excuses either". Looking at the pie, Kate gulped. Picking up her fork, she obediently proceeded to eat every bite. Phelps poured himself another glass of milk to drink while eating his pie.

After they were finished, Phelps put the food away then quickly did up the dishes.

Turning from the counter, his eyes twinkled mischievously. "I even learned to clean up after myself."

Kate nodded approvingly. "So I see. And all I thought you were good for was dispensing pills or patching someone up!"

"You!" He waved a fist while glaring at her menacingly. Smiling in spite of himself, he walked over to face Kate. "Now, my dear young lady, you go take a long nap." He held up his hand when Kate started to protest. "I don't want to hear that you aren't sleepy! I'm leaving so you had better obey me, or there'll be the hob to pay!" He gently patted her hand. "Thanks for the great lunch." Nodding, Kate watched him leave. All at once Kate realized that she was very tired. Rising clumsily from the chair, she went to the bedroom. Lying down upon the bed, she sighed deeply then promptly fell asleep.

CHAPTER 3

Decisions

T he Indian village became shrouded in darkness when the moon slipped behind a cloud. It was an hour before dawn. All the nocturnal creatures had scurried back to their burrows, nests, or other places of refuge to sleep the day away. Creatures active throughout the daylight hours were still asleep, making the silence complete. The only movements were in the makeshift hospital in the center of the village. Lantern light created silhouettes of those caring men, as well as a few Indian women, who bravely battled the disease.

All at once the tent flap was thrown back, letting a light stream out from within. A figure stood adjusting his eyes to the darkness, while deciding which way to go. As the man closed the flap, the moon came out from behind the cloud. Taking a deep breath Captain Thompson began walking toward his tent. Changing his mind, he turned toward the river. Finding a large boulder, he flopped wearily onto it. Thompson listened to the river's methodical roar, in an attempt to collect his jumbled thoughts. It had been so long since he'd gotten a good rest that he'd lost all track of time.

Not only was Thompson bone-weary, but he was worried as well. Some of the troop had also contracted the disease. Many of them were in a bad way. To top everything off, they were running low on medicine, and they had been at the village far too long. He should have returned to the fort a week ago. Thompson knew that if he were caught, he would not only be court-martialed, but also be executed. Thornton not only delighted in stripping a soldier of his rank, but delighted in making that officer an example, by sentencing him to death. It mattered not that the officer's family was also affected. In fact, it seemed as though this thrilled Thornton more. Thinking of Kate and their unborn child, he couldn't help wondering how all of this would affect them. Taking another deep breath, he chided himself mentally. Let the chips fall where they may!

Thompson pondered the situation from all angles. All at once, he sat bolt upright on the boulder. For a moment he sat in stunned disbelief, surprised at the conclusion he had reached. Shaking his head back and forth, he began mumbling to himself. "The answer is so simple. Why didn't I think of it before?" Getting up, he walked briskly to his tent. After lighting the lantern, he got out some writing material. Taking a seat near the table, Thompson began writing quickly. He wrote for a while then paused to read it. Finally, collecting his thoughts, Thompson continued to draft the letter. When he was satisfied that he'd written it the way he wanted, he blew on it to dry the ink. Folding the letter, he put it into an envelope. Sealing the envelope, he addressed it. Rising from the chair, he walked over to Doctor McCabe's tent.

The Doctor was just getting ready for bed when Thompson called softly out to him. "Come in, Captain," responded McCabe. Entering, Thompson waited for him to light the lantern. The tent contained a bed, a table, and a chair. McCabe usually placed his medical bag on the table. He motioned toward the chair. "Be seated, sir." Thompson sank gratefully onto the chair, while McCabe plopped onto the cot. Sighing wearily, McCabe leaned forward, rested his head in his hands, then placed his elbows on his knees. He sat this way for a few minutes before looking over at Thompson.

"Now, what can I do for you?"

"I've come to a decision, but I need your help." McCabe nodded in acknowledgment, yet remained silent. "First of all, we are running awfully low on medicine and food and other staples needed to care for everyone. It's imperative that we replenish these items soon. Second, we need to cover our tracks with the Major, because we have been gone way too long. Make up a list of what medical supplies we need, making sure that it isn't so large that it draws attention. Get it to me as soon as possible. I will send a man back to the fort to get the supplies."

Rising, McCabe began to rummage through his things. "I'll get on it right away, sir. The list will be ready for you in about an hour."

"I'll leave you to it then." Rising, Thompson walked wearily to the tent entrance. Pausing, he turned back to address McCabe. "Bring it to my tent when you are ready, Doc." McCabe nodded absently as he began to prepare the list.

Leaving McCabe's, Thompson crossed over to the tent of Corporal Wilson. "Corporal Wilson, he called out softly." When no one answered, he lifted the tent flap enough to peek in. Wilson was snoring softly. Thompson walked in to roughly shake the man. "Come alive, Wilson!"

Groaning, Wilson opened his eyes. Struggling to rise, he asked, "Who is it?" Seeing who it was, he jumped to his feet. Coming to full attention, he saluted.

Thompson grinned in sympathy. "At ease, Corporal." Wilson relaxed. "We need to be sure there is enough food to sustain us until we reach the fort. I want you to get dressed, go to the mess tent, and take an inventory. When you're done, prepare a list of what's needed for two weeks. Bring it to me in an hour."

"Yes, sir! It's as good as done, sir."

"Very well. See you in a few moments." Turning, Thompson walked out, leaving Wilson to dress.

While he waited, Thompson wandered along the riverbank, feeling comforted by its mighty roar. Arriving at the first boulder, he sank gratefully onto its cool surface. As he listened to the river, his mind began to reflect back to the past two weeks. It had been surprisingly easy to take control of the Indian village. The biggest challenge was trying to get the Indian people as well as his men through this awful epidemic. Dr. McCabe and several able-bodied persons fought a good fight, but there were many casualties.

He remembered the day a young woman and her infant son were brought to the infirmary. The woman, Thompson remembered, was very beautiful, with dark-copper skin, highlighted by her long raven-colored hair. Willow, the female interpreter, called her Morning Dove. She told Thompson that a few days before the soldiers came, the woman's husband had died. Morning Dove had been found too late. She died shortly after being brought into the infirmary. Thompson, who had been awake for 26 hours, took over full care of the infant. In spite of all they did, the baby continued to worsen. Doctor McCabe tried to spell Thompson off for a few hours, so that he could get some much-needed sleep, but he had refused. While caring for the baby, Thompson couldn't help thinking of Kate and his unborn child back at the fort. For the rest of that day and far into the night, Thompson wrestled with the angel of death. He had so desperately wanted the infant to live, yet no matter how hard he struggled, nothing helped. In the hour before dawn, the angel of death won. The infant's spirit joined his parents.

The Indian woman who prepared the dead for burial reached out for the infant. "No, I'll prepare him for burial myself," snapped Thompson. The woman jumped back in surprise. As he sat there gently stroking the baby's lifeless fingers, feeling angrily helpless, he wondered, *Why couldn't I save him?*

Becoming aware of someone touching his shoulder, Thompson looked up to see McCabe watching him with a mixture of concern and compassion. "He must be put to rest as soon as possible, Captain."

Acknowledging the comment, he turned his attention back to the infant. Rising, he went to get the things needed to prepare the body for burial. He lovingly washed the tiny body. When he'd finished the task before him, Thompson gently cradled the infant in his arms. He tenderly bent to kiss the now still cheek, unaware of the tears streaming from his eyes. Thompson, gripped in the throes of agonizing grief, sat rocking and caressing the lifeless form. Everyone there was deeply moved by the tender scene. Tears flowed down the cheeks of the strongest, the bravest men and women there.

A soldier entered the makeshift hospital. Finding the doctor, he walked over to whisper something in his ear. McCabe walked over to place a hand gently on Thompson's shoulder. "It's time to lay the child to rest, Captain."

Nodding, Thompson rose to follow the others out to the gravesite where the infant's mother had been laid to rest. The soldier took the infant from Thompson. After tenderly wrapping the blanket snuggly around the still form, he placed the tiny body into the grave at his mother's feet. Not wanting to see him buried, Thompson hurried back to the infirmary.

Chief Swift Eagle, who had also been quite ill with the disease, was still recuperating. He was released from the infirmary shortly after the infant's death. So much had happened since the soldiers had taken over his village. He walked to his lodge very perplexed indeed. It was apparent that he had much to sort out in his mind. One question constantly plagued him: "What does it all mean?"

Thompson, lost in his own thoughts, was oblivious to his surroundings. All at once, he became aware of someone standing behind him. Stiffening, he turned slowly around to see who was there. Chief Swift Eagle stood silhouetted in the moonlight, which caressed his rough, copper skin. He was wearing a tan buckskin shirt with matching pants. The sleeves and legs of the outfit were fringed. The front of the shirt was decorated with assorted shades of blue beads. Matching moccasins completed the desired effect.

Thompson wasn't able to see the chief's eyes clearly, but he could feel them penetrating him. Uncertain what to do, he remained silent. Chief Swift Eagle gazed expressionlessly into Paul's face a long time before he spoke. "I watch your men take us captive. I know we too sick to stop you." Swift Eagle paused a moment, then went on. "I fear we all die. I not know what to do! Then I see you … with your men … try to care for my people. For a time I not understand why you no kill us. I say nothing … I wait … see." As he talked, he gestured gracefully with his hands. "Then I begin to see something different in here." He tapped his heart emphatically. "I see a big man who cares a lot for my people. The night you try to save boy child, I know you not like Chief at fort. So now I want to know why you no kill my people." He made a sweeping gesture of the village. Thompson thought he made a striking figure, standing with his arms folded across his broad chest. He proudly held his head high.

As Thompson listened to the chief, he knew that it took a lot for him to say what he did. A huge respect for this great man welled up inside of him. For a few moments he stood there, looking directly at Swift Eagle, searching for adequate words to answer the chief. Finally, realizing there was no other alternative but to tell the truth, Thompson plunged in. "I was given orders from the chief at the fort that I could not in all good conscience obey." Swift Eagle watched Thompson warily. "The orders were to find your village … kill your people … sparing no one." Swift Eagle's face became hard as he waited for Thompson to explain. "That's not all, I was told to burn the village completely to the ground." He paused when he saw Swift Eagle's countenance become angrier. Taking a deep breath, he hurried on. "I have a much higher chief to answer to than the one at the fort, Swift Eagle. I knew that He didn't want me to kill your people. Not only that, but I could never kill someone because they were different from me." Swift Eagle looked at Thompson strangely. "Because I have gone against my chief's orders, I will face certain death. I do not fear dying, because in going against these orders, I know that I have pleased my higher Chief. You know this higher chief as the Great Spirit. Thompson was relieved to see the chief softening a little. "Swift Eagle, it is extremely important that we get your people strong enough to move them to a safer place … someplace where the chief of the fort can't find them."

Swift Eagle stood staring at Thompson incredulously, as if he'd lost what senses he possessed. "Why? Why, does chief at fort want us dead? We have done nothing to break white man's treaty, yet white man kill buffalo, run game away, break treaty of chief in Washington, now he wants us all dead. Why?"

"The chief, Major Thornton, is a hateful, bitter old man, who has lost all sense of right or wrong." Thompson paused to collect his thoughts. "When your people attacked the fort sometime prior to signing the treaty, Major Thornton became very angry when your brother, Storm Cloud, raped his wife. Since the time she gave birth to Storm Cloud's son, Major Thornton has grown more bitter with every passing year."

Swift Eagle seemed to be trying to digest this information. Finally, he looked questioningly at Thompson. "Storm Cloud had a son?"

"Yes. The young man who has been helping Doctor McCabe to find the sick and dying is Storm Cloud's son."

Swift Eagle shrugged matter-of-factly. "Storm Cloud went to happy hunting ground a few days before your men come."

"I'm truly sorry about that," replied Thompson compassionately. Neither of the men spoke for a time. Finally, Thompson broke the silence. "The people at the fort have also felt this man's wrath. If we dare go against him, he punishes us the worst way possible … sometimes even killing us." Thompson paused to let Swift Eagle contemplate the information.

Swift Eagle was so stunned that he was unable to speak. Thompson continued, "Will you please take your people to another place, where you can all be safe … at least until Major Thornton has cooled off, or has been replaced?" When Swift Eagle still didn't speak, Thompson began to plead. "Swift Eagle, if you don't go, Major Thornton will send men who will not stop with just killing your men, but will take fiendish delight in desecrating your women … especially your fair maidens. When they have finished with them, they will kill them as well. I must ask you once more, Swift Eagle, to take your people away from here!"

Swift Eagle bowed his head; his shoulders drooped in abject misery. Thompson watched Swift Eagle grow very sullen. It seemed to Thompson that he was taking an inordinate amount of time to weigh each alternative. Finally, the chief nodded submissively. "We go! I see that you come as friend … not as enemy. I glad in here!" He thumped his great chest passionately. "I not go any other time, but see this must be so. I go for sake of the women … the children. They must be made safe."

"Thank you," replied Thompson, greatly relieved. "I know that this is hard for you, Swift Eagle. Oh, how I truly wish this didn't have to be."

"I want you know, that I not always willing to give into white man at fort!" Thompson nodded. Swift Eagle hastened on, "For now, must see to needs of my people."

"I understand, Swift Eagle. Perhaps I would feel the same way if our places were reversed." Thompson sighed wearily. "We hope you know that we don't want to fight your people."

"I do!" Swift Eagle answered without hesitation.

Thompson seemed relieved. "We have come to have a great respect for your people." The two leaders clasped each other's arms, looking intently into each other's eyes, searching the other's soul. It was evident that there was a deep respect, one for the other.

Thompson grew thoughtful a moment, and then faced the Chief. "In a little while I am going to dispatch two men. One is to go to the fort for more food and medicine, while the other will carry a letter to Colonel Williams at Fort Missoula. This man's authority is greater than Major Thornton's. The letter will tell of the orders I have been given and my reasons for disobeying them. Meanwhile, we will do our best to help the sick and dying." Swift Eagle nodded once more before walking briskly away.

Pausing a moment, Thompson walked over to Peters' tent, calling out softly, "Peters." There was no answer, so he called a touch louder. "Peters!" A groan was the only answer he got. Poking his head inside, Thompson wasn't surprised to see Peters lying prone upon his cot. He smiled to himself when he heard Peters snoring loudly. Entering, he walked over to roughly shake him while calling into his ear, "Come alive, man!" Peters struggled to pull himself into a sitting position. That accomplished, he tried to rise in order to salute. Thompson chuckled in sympathy. "At ease, Sergeant." Sinking gratefully back upon the bed, Peters waited for Thompson to speak. "Find Corporal Jefferson and Private Cooper. Tell them to report to my tent in fifteen minutes. I expect to see you there, too."

"Right away, suh." Grabbing his clothes, he started getting into them as Thompson retreated.

Exhaustion began to overtake the captain as he walked slowly back to his tent. He paced the tent in an attempt to clear his head. A few moments later, Thompson walked over to light the lantern on the table. When it was going well, he got out the letter he'd written earlier. Setting it onto the table, he sank gratefully into the chair to wait. It wasn't long until he heard muffled voices drawing near the tent. Rising, he went to open the tent flap, stepping aside to let the men enter. "Come in, men." They saluted, entered, coming to full attention. "As you were, men." Walking over to the table, he sank wearily into a chair.

Before he could speak, McCabe quietly called to him. "Captain? Are you there, sir?"

"Come on in, McCabe."

After entering, McCabe paused to let his eyes adjust to the light in the tent. Finally, he looked around at the expectant faces before him, acknowledging each individually with a nod. Walking over to Thompson, he saluted. Reaching into his pocket, he extracted a slip of paper, which he handed to Thompson. "Here's the list you asked me to make, sir."

Taking the paper, Thompson leaned closer to the light in order to scan it quickly. "Thank you, Doctor. This is great! I'll take care of the rest from here." McCabe nodded, then departed. Sighing, Thompson slumped wearily back into his chair before addressing the men. He looked from one to the other then began, "Peters, I want you to fix provisions for these men, get the best saddle horses we have, as well as pack-horses. Have them ready to ride within the hour."

Peters, snapping to attention, saluted. "Yes, suh! Right away, suh!" Turning, he walked out.

When Peters was gone, Thompson turned his attention back to the two men. He gazed intently at Jefferson, who stood at his left. Corporal Harold Jefferson, a tall, thin, young man of perhaps 21, was always polite, even respectful to Thompson. His uniform was always neat. His straight coal-black hair was always neatly combed. Wrinkles around his sparkling brown eyes gave him the appearance of a tease, yet Thompson knew that he took life seriously. Thick lips softened his high cheekbones and protruding jaw. He loved being around people and laughed freely, always championing the underdog. Thompson couldn't remember ever hearing a complaint from Corporal Jefferson regarding a job given him, even when it was distasteful or strenuous. Captain Thompson admired the man's tenacity and stick-to-itiveness. Large, work-worn hands twisted his hat nervously as he waited to receive his orders.

Thompson turned to gaze at the other man in the room. Private Michael Cooper was short, with a medium build. He was nearly twenty-nine years old. He had bushy red eyebrows. His thick curly auburn hair was usually unkempt because it was difficult to manage. Laughter lines and soft delicate cheekbones accentuated his mischievous green eyes. Thompson, who remembered the many times this joker had played tricks on the other men, chuckled inwardly. *He has surely made life fun at the fort, but I like him,* he thought.

As he watched Private Cooper, a smile began to tug at the corners of his mouth. *Perhaps it's because he reminds me so much of how Kate pulls her antics,* he nodded. Although Cooper had a strong dislike for Thornton, he was always willing to do what was asked of him. Thompson, who knew how fussy Cooper was with his dress uniform, was surprised to see him dressed so haphazardly. Looking down at himself, he smiled to see that he, too, was dressed just as sloppily.

Thompson sharply brought himself back to the present. "Corporal, I want you to take this letter to Colonel Williams at Fort Missoula." Jefferson stepped forward to take the letter then waited for further instructions. "Remember, Corporal, you cannot enter the fort because of the epidemic. Remain a safe distance outside the fort while you talk to the guard on duty. Inform him that you have been exposed to typhus, but that you have an important message for Colonel Williams, which you need to deliver personally. Select a spot within sight of the fort where you can meet privately. It is imperative that you keep a safe distance from him at all times.

"Yes, sir!" Jefferson placed the letter inside his shirt pocket.

"If he isn't there, wait for him. Do not discuss your mission with anyone. When you have delivered the message, wait for his reply then hurry back." Thompson intently studied the face before him. "I'll await your return before going back to the fort. Are there any questions?"

"No, sir."

"Good! Go get your gear corporal and report to Sergeant Peters for your horses and supplies."

"Yes, sir." Saluting, Jefferson hurried out.

Turning to Private Cooper, Thompson studied him a moment. "Private Cooper, you have perhaps the most difficult job of them all."

Cooper swallowed nervously. "Yes, sir."

Wilson called from outside the tent, "Captain Thompson, are you in there, sir?"

"Yes, Corporal, come on in."

Lifting the tent flap, Wilson entered. It took a moment for his eyes to adjust to the light. Thompson waited patiently. "Sir, here is the list you asked me to make. I'm sorry, but it took longer than expected."

"That's alright. It's better late than never."

Stepping forward, Wilson handed him a large sheet of paper. "Thank you, sir. Here's the list."

Taking the list, Thompson quickly scanned it. "This is great. That will be all. You're dismissed."

After Wilson was gone, Thompson picked up another slip of paper from the table. He handed both lists to Private Cooper. "These are lists for food, medicine, as well as other supplies needed from the fort." Taking the papers, Cooper put them inside his shirt pocket. "Cooper, what I'm about to tell you, you are not to divulge to another living soul as long as you live."

"Yes, sir."

Rising, Thompson began to pace the circumference of the tent. After a few moments, he turned back to face the young man. "I was given orders to exterminate all of the Indians in this tribe, including men, women, and children. After much deliberation, I came to the conclusion that this would not only cause many repercussions, but it would be morally wrong as well."

Cooper blinked in stunned disbelief. "But, sir, that means you will be court marshaled. Knowing Major Thornton the way we do, he'll take fiendish delight in making an example of you."

"I know, but what could I do? There was no way I wanted their blood on my hands! I would rather face death many times over than kill innocent people!"

"I have to agree, sir … I would, too!"

"It's critically important that you follow my orders to the letter. Do not go into the fort, but tell the sentry that you need to speak to Doctor Phelps and Major Thornton just outside the gate." When they appear, tell them that the orders have been carried out. Report that the troops have contracted typhus."

He stared at Thompson incredulously, and then began to speak. "Begging your pardon, sir. Are you telling me to tell the Major the Indians are dead?"

"Yes, Private, that's exactly what I want you to do!" Cooper nodded then waited for further instructions. "We need to buy some time for the Indians, as well as ourselves. Telling Thornton that we have typhus will keep him from coming out to check on us. We desperately need those supplies." Again Cooper nodded. "Tell Major Thornton that we will return to the fort as soon as we have the disease under control. After reading both lists off to them, instruct them to put the items onto packhorses. Instruct them to tie the animals a safe distance from the fort. When they have complied, wait five minutes before getting the horses. Once you have them, hurry back here. Meanwhile, stay a safe distance from the fort." Cooper nodded absently as he listened to Thompson's instructions. "Are there any questions, Private?"

"No, sir."

"Very well then, get your gear, report to Peters for your horses and supplies. Be on your way as soon as possible." Saluting, Cooper turned to leave, but Thompson called to him. "Private," called Thompson as Cooper reached the tent entrance, "I can't say enough about how important it is for you to follow my instructions to the letter. Otherwise, Private, it will spell trouble for many people. Thornton has no qualms about killing these Indians. It's up to us to see that the treaty is not broken."

"I understand, sir. I will make sure that your orders are carried out to the letter." The tone of Cooper's voice reflected firm conviction and commitment.

"Thanks, Cooper. You're dismissed." Saluting, Cooper turned and walked out. Thompson felt drained. He turned off the light, quickly undressed, and slipped gratefully under the covers. Sighing, he turned onto his right side and was soon fast asleep.

✧ ✧

Cooper and Jefferson began their missions simultaneously. A couple of hours later they parted. *It's such a beautiful day for a ride,* thought Cooper. He pushed his horses as fast as he thought safe, while his mind raced with the orders Thompson had issued. Cooper, not a praying man, now wished that he knew how. Many miles slipped away, as the hours rushed by. At noon, he stopped at a shady spot along the river to fix himself something to eat. Leading the horses to water, he let them drink. After they were finished, he took them back to a nearby tree, where he tied them securely. Removing the pack from one of the horses, he searched through it until he found the nosebags, which he hung around the horses' necks. Working quickly, he soon had a fire going. Cooper again rummaged through the supplies, taking out what he needed to prepare the meal. When it was ready, he dished up a good-sized portion. Sitting on a log near his campsite, he hungrily wolfed the food down. Sighing contentedly, he set about cleaning up his mess. After repacking the supplies, he put the pack back onto the packhorse. Cooper doused the fire until he was satisfied that it was out. He went to the river to fill his canteen. Placing it on the saddle horn, he removed the feedbags, which he placed with the pack. Untying the horse, he tied the lead rope securely to the saddle horn. Gathering the reins of the saddle horse, he mounted and looked the campsite over to ensure himself that all was as it should be. Cooper rode hard and fast toward the fort.

Cooper kept this grueling pace up all day, stopping only long enough to let the horses rest. That evening he rested a couple of hours before pushing on. When the moon had risen, it was so bright that he had no problem seeing where they were going. Squeaking leather, hoot owls, and the sounds of other night creatures kept him company.

As he rode along, Cooper slowly, yet meticulously, scrutinized the orders he'd been given. He hated Thornton with the rest of them; still it went against his grain to openly lie. "What should I do?" he asked aloud. The hours passed as he continued to examine each aspect of the orders. All at once, he began to catch a glimmer of the full spectrum. "Perhaps it is better to tell one lie than to be the cause of so many innocent people's death," he muttered aloud. A smile began to play around his lips as he rode along. "Yes, sir, I see why this must be so. I will give it my best shot!" He patted the horse's neck affectionately then began to hum an old Irish tune.

Cooper got to the fort quite late the next afternoon. He stopped at a safe distance from the fort calling out to the sentry. "Yow, the gate!"

A guard appeared at the top of the wall, scrutinizing Cooper suspiciously. "Who goes there?'

"Private Michael Cooper. I'm here with a message for Major Thornton and Doctor Phelps from Captain Thompson. Bring them to the gate on the double, sir!" When the sentry hesitated, Cooper shouted again. "It's imperative that they obey this strange request."

Even though the sentry wasn't convinced, he turned to obey. "Very well. Wait there until I return!"

"Okay, but hurry." The guard hurried off, leaving Cooper alone with his thoughts. Waiting became torturous for him. He began pacing nervously back and forth, in an attempt to shake off impending doom.

It wasn't long until Cooper saw the big doors of the gate slowly swinging open and two figures emerging. Major Thornton looked surly while Doctor Phelps remained calm. Thornton began to bellow angrily, "What's the meaning of dragging us out here in such a disgusting manner?"

When Thornton started toward him, Cooper raised his hands. "Stop where you are, sir!"

Thornton stopped in surprise then scowled at the insubordinate upstart with undisguised contempt. "How dare you order me around like this!"

Cooper flinched, but quickly recovered. He began to speak, "Begging your pardon, sir, but it is vitally important that you remain where you are. First of all, Captain Thompson wanted me to tell you that the orders have been carried out." Thornton grinned, but remained silent. "We are not able to return to the fort, because the men have contracted typhus!" He paused when he heard Phelps gasp in horror. Thornton seemed to be slowly digesting the information. "There aren't enough medical supplies, food, and other miscellaneous items to take care of them all, so I have been dispatched to procure these items. I have two lists that I am to read to you. One is for medical supplies and miscellaneous items needed. The other is for food items."

Thornton remained sullen, but visibly softened. "Very well, let's hear the lists."

Phelps took a pad and pencil out of his shirt pocket then looked at Cooper expectantly. "Please read each list slowly, Private."

"Yes, sir." Cooper began with the medical list, reading it off as slowly as possible. When he was finished, he began reading the list for food items. He tucked the lists back into his shirt pocket when he was finished.

When Cooper fell silent, Thornton, who had been pacing, turned to glower at him. "Is that all, Private?"

"Yes, sir, that sums up both lists, sir. Captain Thompson gave specific instructions on how you are to proceed. You are to pack the items onto packhorses, leave them a short distance from the gate, then go back inside. When I have gotten the horses, I'll leave." The men nodded understandingly. "Captain Thompson said to tell you that he'll return to the fort just as soon as the men are well enough to travel."

"Very well, Private, wait there!" Thornton turned impatiently toward Phelps. "Come on, Phelps! Shake a leg, man … we've got a lot to do!" After entering the fort, the gates closed. Cooper was alone once more.

While he waited, Cooper impatiently walked around. Finally, he went to his horse to get down his canteen. Going to the nearest boulder, Cooper gratefully sat down to wait. Reaching into his pocket, he took out a large piece of jerky. After eating the jerky, he uncapped the canteen to drink greedily from it. When he was finished, Cooper recapped the canteen. Getting up, he went to put the canteen back on the saddle horn. He gave the two horses well-deserved attention, then went back to the boulder to wait. Several hours later, the sun slipped behind the hills. Cooper gloried in the magnificent sunset left behind. While night's shadows began to spread across the land, the birds stopped singing.

All at once, the gate swung open. Cooper watched in fascination as light streamed out. A man, leading three packhorses laden down with supplies, emerged. Leading the horses a good distance from the fort, he tied them to a tree. Glancing around as though someone might spring at him with deadly intent, the man hurried back inside. Once the gate was closed, Cooper waited five minutes before retrieving the packhorses. He led them back to his horses where he fastened the lead rope. He secured each horse to the rope then tied the ropes to the saddle horn. Mounting, he rode off.

As darkness enveloped him, crickets began to chirp loudly while an owl hooted some distance away. Not long after that the moon rose high, illuminating his way. Cooper rode several hours before stopping to make camp. Quickly unpacking the horses, he led them to the river to drink, then took them to a grassy area, where he hobbled them. Leaving them to eat, he walked back to camp. Cooper slipped gratefully into his bedroll, too tired to eat.

The sun had climbed high into the sky by the time he awoke the next morning. Cooper quickly prepared breakfast and ate heartily. He cleaned up camp, doused the fire, and packed his gear. Going to the horses, he slipped their bridles on, removed the hobbles, led them back to camp, and tied them to a tree. He loaded the packhorses, and then saddled his horse. Removing the canteen from the saddle horn, he went to the river, where he filled it. Capping it, he walked back to hang it on the saddle horn. Mounting, he took one last look around before riding out of camp.

Cooper decided to make up as much time as he could, so he pushed the horses relentlessly most of the morning. At noon, he stopped long enough to let the horses drink. While the horses ate their noon meal, Cooper rested. Taking a cold biscuit and some jerky from his pack, he stuffed them into his coat pocket. Removing the nosebags, he put them away. Mounting, Cooper pressed on. The food tasted good, reviving his spirits. Reaching for the canteen, he lifted it from the saddle horn. Uncapping it, he drank heartily. Feeling refreshed, Cooper recapped it. After placing it back onto the saddle horn, Cooper clucked softly to his horse, pleased when it picked up speed. They didn't stop again until he made camp late in the afternoon.

Dismounting near a small stream, Cooper tied the horses to a tree. Removing the packs, as well as the saddle, he rummaged through one of the packs until he found the hobbles. Laying them aside, he searched for the halters. Slinging them over his shoulder, he untied the horses. Leading them over to the stream to drink, Cooper waited until they were finished before taking them to a grassy meadow. After tying them to a tree, he removed the bridles, quickly putting on the halters. When Cooper had their hobbles on, he turned them loose. He watched as they started to munch on the tender blades of grass, then he went back to camp.

Cooper gathered rocks to make a circle, making sure that the area around it wouldn't ignite. He started a fire inside the circle. When the kindling had started going well, Cooper added larger pieces of wood. When he had a hot fire going, he gathered a large quantity of wood. Picking up the bucket, he went to the stream to fill it. Cooper placed it onto the bank while he washed up. Rising, he picked up the bucket, went back to camp, and set it down near a stump. Rummaging through the pack, he took out the items he would need to prepare his meal.

He mixed up a batch of biscuits, placed them into a Dutch oven then put the lid on them. Slicing a couple pieces of ham, he placed them into the hot frying pan to cook. The fire had died down, providing a good bed of coals, so he buried the Dutch oven into the hot coals. The ham was done, so he set it onto a tin plate, near an old stump. Placing two eggs into the pan, he seasoned them. When they were done, he put them onto the plate of ham.

Brushing the coals from the Dutch oven, he lifted it from the hot coals, setting it down near the fire. Lifting the lid, Cooper saw that the biscuits were golden brown.

He promptly placed two biscuits on the plate of ham and eggs. Savoring the tantalizing aroma, his mouth salivated in anticipation of what was to come. Filling his cup with icy cold water, he sat near the fire to eat. Taking a bite, he realized just how hungry he was. By the time he was through with camp duty, it was growing dark.

He quickly cut some pine boughs, which he placed a short distance from the fire. Satisfied that it was the way he wanted it, Cooper spread his bedroll on top of the boughs. Adding more wood to the fire, he went to check on the horses before turning in. They nickered when he came into sight then went back to eating. Satisfied that all was well, he went back to camp. Removing his boots, Cooper got into his bedroll. While listening to the crackling fire, the horses munching, and a myriad of other night sounds, he drifted off to sleep.

All at once, Cooper woke with a start. For a few minutes, he struggled to figure out where he was. Some sixth sense told him something had awakened him. Turning, he noticed that the fire had died down to a few hot coals. He started drifting back to sleep when he heard the scream of a cougar. He quickly tossed a handful of dead grass onto the hot coals to get the fire started, then added a large amount of smaller fuel to get a bright blazing fire. When he was satisfied that it was blazing brightly enough, he grabbed his boots and hurriedly slipped them on. Jumping up, he grabbed his rifle and some rope then headed for the horses. Again the cougar screamed, sounding like it was near the horses. Slowly, yet cautiously, he approached the frightened horses. When he got close to his horse, it snorted, while the packhorses squealed in fright. Cooper reached out to slip the rope through the horse's halter, making sure that it was securely tied. He tied the other end of the rope to a nearby tree.

Again the cougar screamed closer to them, causing the packhorses to squeal in terror. Several times Cooper attempted to control the frightened horses, while attempting to put ropes in their halters. Finally, after several unsuccessful attempts, he was able to secure the ropes to the halters. Tying them to the tree where he had tied his horse, he removed the hobbles. Untying the horses, he led them back to camp, being hard-pressed to keep them from bolting.

When he got to camp, he retied the horses. Quickly gathering his gear together, Cooper loaded it onto the packhorses. When he had finished saddling his horse, he took his canteen from the saddle horn. Picking up his rifle, Cooper hurried to the stream. He kept a watchful eye on the horses as he filled his canteen. Capping the canteen, he walked back to his horse. He had just placed the canteen onto the saddle horse when all at once the cougar screamed closer to camp. The startled horses snorted in fright. They reared back, straining against their bridles. Their eyes grew large with fright. Their ears were laid back on their heads, their nostrils flared, while their mouths gaped open as they screamed in mortal terror. Cooper struggled in vain to get them under control. Finally, he stepped back from the horses, injected a bullet into the chamber of the rifle. Raising the rifle, he squeezed the trigger. The sound was deafening as it echoed through the crisp night air. Relief washed over Cooper, when he heard something bolt off to the right. The horses gradually grew calmer, as he talked soothingly to them.

Cooper doused the fire until he was sure it was out. Untying the packhorses, he tied the lead rope to the saddle horn. Untying his horse, he mounted. Turning the horse in the direction of the Indian village, he rode off. Cooper put the horses to a brisk pace for the first few miles until satisfied that they were far enough away from the cougar, then he slowed them down.

Several hours later, Cooper watched the new day dawn, thrilling at the spectacular scene unfolding in the sky. Knowing that he was near the village, he pushed the horses harder. Cooper got to the village just after lunch. He rode directly over to Thompson's tent. Dismounting, he called out, but no one was there. Seeing Peters coming out of the makeshift hospital, he led the horses toward him. Before he got to him, Peters ducked inside, returning with Thompson. Doctor McCabe joined them. The four men unpacked the supplies at McCabe's tent. Once the items were unpacked, the men began to sort through them. The medical supplies, as well as the miscellaneous items, were stored there, while the foodstuff was transported to the mess tent.

When they were done, Thompson ordered Cooper to report to his tent as soon as he had taken care of the horses. Nodding, he complied with Thompson's wishes. A few minutes later he reported to Thompson, who was there ahead of him.

Opening the tent flap, Thompson moved aside for Cooper to enter. "Come on in, Son." Private Cooper saluted, removed his hat then entered. Thompson walked over to sink onto a chair, motioning to Cooper. "Be seated, Private."

Cooper softly chuckled. "Begging your pardon, sir, but I prefer to stand. I've been doing too much sitting lately!"

The captain laughed as he nodded understandingly. "Very well!" Leaning back in the chair, he watched Cooper intently while the man collected his thoughts. "Now," he sighed, "let's have it all!"

Cooper gave him a full account of what took place at the fort. "Thornton seemed pleased when he heard that the Indians were dead, sir." He shuddered at the memory.

Thompson sighed disgustedly. "I thought as much!"

Private Cooper bowed his head thoughtfully a moment, then looked intently over at Thompson. "He appeared to be displeased because we had contracted typhus … that we were detained from getting back to the fort."

Thompson sat forward, scowling angrily. "Well, isn't that just too, dad-blamed bad!" Cooper smiled in spite of himself. "Is that all, Private?"

"Yes, sir!"

"Very well. You're dismissed!" Saluting, Cooper turned to walk away, but Thompson detained him a moment longer. "And by the way Cooper, good job!"

"Thanks, sir." Cooper walked out.

Thompson sat thoughtfully reviewing the report. We've bought some time, he told himself. His attention was diverted when someone stopped outside of his tent.

He stood up to see who was there. Swift Eagle stepped back in uncertainty when Thompson appeared at the tent's entrance. Smiling in greeting, he moved aside for the chief to enter. "Come in, Chief." Swift Eagle entered, but stood to one side of the tent entrance. "Please be seated," invited Thompson, pointing to a chair.

Ignoring Thompson's invitation, Swift Eagle began to speak. "I think much after we talk. I think you find yourself in heap big trouble for helping us!"

"You could be right, Chief."

"I come up with plan." Thompson looked surprised, but remained silent. "If you get into trouble, come to village … we help."

Thompson beamed his approval. "Thank you, sir. If you are in any danger, we'll send Nataka to alert you."

"That good!" The men clasped arms emphatically. "I go now!" Before Thompson could add anything, Swift Eagle was gone. Thompson sank into the chair, placed his head into his hands in an attempt to clear his mind. A few moments later, he rose to return to the makeshift hospital.

Thompson was in his tent, when Jefferson rode into camp three days later. The soldier stepped out as he dismounted. Thompson moved aside, motioning to him to enter. "Come in, Corporal."

When they were both inside, Jefferson saluted then took a letter out of his shirt pocket. Jefferson hesitated for a moment then handed it to him. Taking the letter, Thompson ripped open the envelope, extracting the letter. As he read it silently, his face was void of expression. When he had finished reading the letter, he placed it back into the envelope. Looking at Jefferson expectantly, he asked, "Was there anything else?"

"No, sir!"

"Hum!" Thompson thoughtfully tapped the envelope against his leg. Finally, he looked up at Jefferson. "That will be all, Corporal. You're dismissed!" Saluting, Jefferson left. Thompson took out the letter to read it again. A perplexed expression crossed his face. Slowly, he placed the letter back into the envelope then placed it inside his jacket pocket.

Putting out his light, he undressed for bed. Once in bed, Thompson clasped his hands behind his head while looking up at the tent ceiling. Although he was bone-weary, his mind refused to let him go to sleep. Sighing audibly, he gave into his thoughts. Picturing Thornton's attitude about being delayed from returning to the fort, Thompson grew delighted at his discomfort. Turning onto his right side, he pulled the covers up around his neck and sighed contentedly. A few minutes later, he was asleep.

CHAPTER 4

Letting Go

Kate woke later than usual, feeling more exhausted than when she went to bed. Struggling out of bed, she began to slowly dress. She was nearly finished when someone knocked at the door. Rising, she slowly walked over to open the door. John Whipple stood grinning back at her. Smiling, Kate motioned to him to enter. "Why, good morning, John."

Removing his hat, he stepped inside. "Morning, Mrs. Thompson. I won't take very long to do the chores this morning." While talking, he went to the counter to get the water buckets, then hurried outside. Closing the door, Kate went to start the fire in the stove. While she waited for it to catch, she filled the washbasin with water from the reservoir. After setting the basin on the counter, she turned the damper on the stove. John entered with fresh water, which he poured into the reservoir. When he went back for more, Kate quickly performed her daily procedures. When he returned, he set the buckets on the counter for easy access. That job finished, he went out to chop some wood. A few minutes later the wood box was full. True to his word, it didn't take John long to complete the chores.

"Thank you, John."

"You're welcome, ma'am." Hesitating at the door, he turned back to face Kate. "I asked Gabe Wilson to do my chores for a few days, while I go to Missoula on some business." He watched Kate intently. "Will that be all right with you?"

Kate nodded. "Of course, John. I appreciate your doing the hard jobs for me." She smiled when John sighed in relief. "Go have a good time, but be careful. You mean a lot to me."

"I will," he grinned. "Right now, I'd better hurry."

Kate chuckled softly, waving her hand toward him. "Okay, be off with you!"

"See you when I get back." With those parting words, he was gone.

Kate watched him hurry off, then went to prepare breakfast for herself. Kate didn't feel much like eating, but she knew that she had to for the baby's sake. After she was finished, she cleaned the house. Wrapping a loaf of bread in a clean towel, she left the house. The sun felt warm on her person as she lumbered along. Many people stopped to chat with her, or they called to her cheerfully. A slight breeze blew playfully about her.

Anna was sitting on the porch swing, knitting, gently rocking back and forth on the porch swing when Kate arrived. "Oh, what a pleasant surprise!" Excitedly laying the knitting in the basket, Anna rose to hug Kate. Linking her arm through Kate's, she gently pulled her toward the door. "Come on in and sit a spell." Chuckling, Kate allowed herself to be drawn forward. When they were inside, Kate offered Anna the bread. "Let's have some of this, shall we?" Smiling appreciatively, Anna took the bread. "Thank you." She hugged Kate's arm affectionately before carrying the loaf to the table. "Please, be seated while I cut this bread."

Kate sat on a chair at the end of the table. Sighing wearily, she watched Anna bustling about the room. Anna went to a drawer near the counter to get out a large butcher knife, which she placed near the loaf of bread. After taking down two plates, two glasses, and the honey from the cupboard, she went to the icebox to get out the butter and a large pitcher of milk. Picking up the butcher knife, she cut two thick slices of bread onto each plate. After setting the items onto the table, she poured the milk into two tall glasses.

Standing five feet tall, Anna was very thin. Her dull, prematurely gray hair was neatly combed, braided then coiled around her head. Her sunken cheeks and her pointed chin gave her ashen features a hawk-like appearance. A full-length white apron covered her ankle-length pale-blue dress, which had long straight sleeves attached to a simple bodice. The color matched her light-blue eyes. Kate smiled as Anna stopped to survey the table.

Anna cheerfully returned the smile. "I guess we're ready."

Anna's whole face lights up when she smiles, thought Kate.

They chatted amiably as they ate. Kate told Anna of Lonna and Lester's new baby boy. "He is a big healthy guy. Boy, has he ever got a good set of lungs!" They chuckled heartily, then Kate sat for a moment lost in thought. Sighing, she looked down at her swollen abdomen. "I wonder what this baby will be like."

"Big, strong, handsome, just like his father, or witty, charming, beautiful like his mother," teased Anna.

"Ah, you've been kissing the blarney stone again!"

Anna mimicked Kate's Irish brogue, "Not at all! Fer one thing, it's a might too far away to be kissin', en fer another, I'd be hanged afer they'd lower me out a drafty old window … upside down to boot!"

Kate laughed so hard she had to hold onto her sides as tears ran down her cheeks. "Oh what I wouldn't give to see them try."

Anna thought about it a moment, then began laughing, too. Dabbing at her eyes, she looked up at Kate. "Well, what did they name this big, healthy boy?"

"Rodney James. They'll probably call him Rod."

Anna nodded approvingly. "I like that. It sounds so strong!"

Changing the subject, they talked of many other things. As Kate scrutinized Anna closely, a smile began tugging at the corners of her lips. "You seem a lot more chipper this morning, my dear friend."

"Last night I heard Carl telling Miles that they would be leaving on another one of those secret maneuvers." She grew sullen. Kate watched her expression of anger spread across her face. "I abhor that man so much that sometimes I wish he were dead!" Anna unconsciously brushed a strand of hair back from her face. "It seems as if I'll never be free of him." Kate, who understood her hatred, shuddered in spite of herself. Remaining silent, she watched her friend anxiously. "Sometimes, I hope he'll be killed on one of his maneuvers, but like a bad penny, he keeps coming back." Sighing deeply, she tossed her head determinedly. "There's no use of our talking about it … it doesn't solve a thing!"

Kate reached out to gently lay her hand on Anna's. "It's all right for you to state your feelings to me, dear, because I know that it has been very difficult for you to endure his horrible tirades." She gently squeezed Anna's hand. "Be patient a little while longer, Anna. Remember that God will see you through any trial … large or small. I'm certain that he has something wonderful in reserve for you."

Anna pondered Kate's words a moment before speaking. "I certainly hope so!"

A twinkle came into Kate's eyes as a mischievous grin played around her lips. "Aren't I always right?"

Anna grinned mischievously. "Well …"

"Don't answer that," said Kate, quickly cutting her off. Both chuckled, relieving the tension in the room. Drinking the last of her milk, Kate rose and took her dishes to the counter. Turning back to face Anna, she asked, "When does the Major leave?"

"Sometime today," Anna replied thoughtfully. "At least that's what I heard him tell Miles last night, when they didn't think I was around." Rising, she took her dishes to the counter. "It's not soon enough for me." Kate helped her straighten up the kitchen. Neither one spoke as they worked, for each was lost in thought. Kate hung up the dishtowel, while Anna dumped the water.

"How long will he be gone this time?"

Anna hung up the dishpans and wiped the table and counter before answering. "Carl told Miles they would only be gone for the afternoon."

"Too bad it isn't longer … we could have had dinner together." Kate shrugged resignedly then commented, "Maybe the next time he leaves, we can get together. It would be nice to just forget about Carl for a while. How does that sound?"

Anna turned excitedly toward Kate. "Wonderful! You're on!" She grew thoughtful then added, "I don't know if I can forget him, but I'll try!"

"That a girl!" Kate reached out to squeeze Anna's hand. "We'll talk about it the next time he leaves."

"Okay," she conceded. Stepping closer to Kate, she placed a hand on Kate's shoulder as she looked at her intently. "Thank you, Kate, for being such a great friend."

Kate smiled, pleased at the compliment. "That's easy. You're special to have as a friend." She grew thoughtful a moment before proceeding. "Too bad Carl is so blind that he can't see the rare, beautiful jewel he has before him." Anna gasped in surprise, staring incredulously at Kate. "I must go now, but I'll keep in touch," smiled Kate.

"Goodbye, dear." Anna dabbed at her eyes, struggling for control. "I truly don't know what I ever did to warrant getting such a great friend as you are to me. Never have I known a sister's love, but you're as close to me as if you were my blood sister." Her voice cracked, preventing her from speaking for a moment. Finally, she smiled at Kate. "I love you so much."

"Thank you, Anna." Kate was touched more deeply that she could express. "Like you, I never had a sister, yet I have had a special friend that showed me what it was like. I missed that until I got to know you better, as well as the other women here at the fort." A tear fell unheeded down her cheek. "I love you too, Anna!" Kate reached out to hug Anna. "I'll see you later." Anna could only nod. Kate went home, feeling warm and happy inside.

Time passed slowly for Kate that day, yet somehow she was able to keep busy. That night after the supper dishes were done, Kate went out to sit in the porch swing to relax. The house was so warm that she enjoyed the light breeze playing around her face. Kate watched in fascination as daylight gave way to night's lengthening shadows. Looking up, Kate wasn't surprised to see a vast canopy of stars twinkling in the sky. Slowly, the full moon rose higher in the sky, illuminating the objects in the fort. Closing her eyes, Kate gave in to the moment, grateful for the peace that enveloped her. A dog barked off in the distance, a wolf howled for its mate, yet she remained as she was. Some sound nearby snapped her back to the present. Looking anxiously around, she saw John on his way home. She noticed that he seemed a little flighty, even preoccupied. *I wonder why John has returned so early,* Kate mused. Her attention was diverted when she heard a baby crying. As she leaned back in the swing, Kate began to think about the baby she was carrying. *What will he be like? Will he be fussy or calm? Will I be a good mother?*

These thoughts, plus others whirled around in her mind. The child, as if knowing what she was thinking, began to kick her. Some of the blows struck her in the rib cage. "Whoa!" she moaned aloud, wincing with each blow. "I know you are in there, little one, but you don't have to kick your poor mother to death to get her attention!" Still, the baby continued to kick her. When Kate despaired of getting any relief, the baby settled down. "Momma loves you!" she whispered, resting her hand on her abdomen. The baby kicked a few more times, then ceased.

Struggling out of the swing, Kate went into the house. She got ready for bed then sat in one of the rockers to read her Bible. Reading the Bible always brought her a feeling of peace. All at once, exhaustion overtook her so she laid the Bible on the table. Turning off the lamp, Kate went to bed. Kate was asleep soon after her head touched the pillow.

John didn't say much when he came to do the chores the next morning. He wasn't rude, yet he wasn't his friendly self. "I thought you were going to be gone for a few days," stated Kate nonchalantly.

"Something came up, so I decided to come back," he replied evasively. Grabbing the buckets, he hurriedly left. Kate stood looking at the closed door, trying to figure out what had made him so jittery, so defensive. Shrugging, she went back to work. John never spoke another word, but went straight to his chores, leaving shortly after finishing them. This really puzzled Kate, because John was always so considerate. "Why, he didn't even say good-bye," she mumbled aloud.

It wasn't until the next day that Kate found the opportunity to speak with John further. When he came at his usual time to do the chores, Kate noticed that he was even moodier than the preceding day. Grabbing the buckets from the counter with intention of making a hasty exit, John was prevented from doing so when Kate barred the way. Watching him intently, she hastened to ask, "John, are you all right? You seem … so different."

As he stood there like a trapped animal, a strange expression crossed his face. Sighing, he looked quickly away. When he turned back, he was his old self. "I'm fine, Mrs. Thompson," he assured her. "I just have a lot on my mind. That's all."

When Kate stepped closer to place her hand gently on his arm, John flinched slightly. Searching his face, she knew that he had just lied. "John, if you're in trouble, you know that I'll do all that I can to help you."

For a moment, John seemed about to speak, but he changed his mind. Taking a deep breath, he tried to smile. "Thank you, but I really am fine." As he started to bolt out the door, Kate clung tenaciously to his arm. With a look of desperation, he started to pull away. "I've got to go now."

"Please wait, John. I know that something is very wrong for you to act this way." Kate anxiously searched his face, noting that he again looked like a trapped animal searching for a way to bolt. "You can explain your problem to me." Still John hesitated. "Nothing can be so bad that we can't somehow solve the problem together. I know that I can help you!"

He hesitated a moment, then sighed resignedly while setting the buckets down. "Okay, ma'am, but my telling you may put you in danger, too. That I don't want to do! Besides, I'd have Captain Thompson to answer to."

Kate smiled reassuringly. "That's no problem. I'll take care of the Captain myself. Now, please tell me your problem."

Relief crossed John's face. "Thank you, ma'am. I really do need someone to talk to." Removing his hat, he stood thoughtfully twisting it, while struggling to come to a decision. Finally, taking a deep breath, he began, "I promised your husband that I would watch out for you. If I tell you my problem, I may be putting both of our lives in danger." Seeing Kate's look of determination, he sighed. "But I guess that can't be helped."

"Come, be seated," Kate invited, suggesting a seat at the table. "We might as well be comfortable."

John shook his head politely, but remained where he was. "No, thank you ma'am, I would rather stand."

"Very well." She plopped gratefully into a chair at the kitchen table then waited for him to begin.

John was not one of the soldiers at the fort, but was the son of Corporal Jonathan and Hattie Whipple. Hattie was one of Kate's special friends. At nineteen, John was very responsible and mature. Although he stood five feet eleven inches tall, John was thin yet wiry. His straight jet-black hair, parted at the side, was always neatly combed. A lock of hair fell across his forehead, making his handsome features even more boyish. He had a soft jaw line and a high forehead. His deep blue eyes were always alert and attentive. As he paced the floor, twisting his hat nervously in his hands, Kate noticed that he was dressed in a dark-blue plaid shirt, which was tucked into the waist of old faded blue jeans. Black boots, polished to perfection, completed his attire.

As he turned toward Kate, a pained expression crossed his face. Taking a deep breath, he began, "The other night while heading to Missoula, I saw something that chilled me to my very soul. I was going to stop in to see Melissa Martin, as well as her parents for a few minutes. Nearing their homestead, I heard several horsemen approaching. Knowing there had been Indian raids lately, I took the precaution of hiding behind some large bushes amidst some trees. It wasn't long until a small band of Indians came into sight. I shivered, grateful that I was well hidden."

"I watched in horror as they stormed into the Martin's house, their guns blazing. My blood ran cold as I listened to them whooping … hollering with evil glee." John shuddered at the memory it evoked. "Hearing Melissa's screams, I realized that she was being raped. When I heard the loud booming voice of Corporal Reno echoing through the crisp night air, my heart lurched in surprise. I realized it wasn't Indians; the white men were committing the dastardly deeds. I heard him say, 'Now that I'm done with her, kill her! Might just as well burn the house to the ground while you're at it!' I died a little when I heard three shots ring out. I wanted to help them, yet I knew that I could do nothing, because I would have been murdered, too. Why? Why couldn't I have saved them? Instead, like a butterfly wrapped in its cocoon, I lay huddled in my hiding spot, like some dirty rotten coward! Now, all I have left are those awful screams … gun shots … this extreme guilt."

Great soul-racking sobs wrenched him, making it impossible to continue. Kate sat frozen in horror as she listened to the grizzly details, then compassion filled her heart. Leaping to her feet, she reached out to hold him while tears streamed down their faces. After gaining a semblance of composure, John stepped back. "I never wanted so badly to kill anyone as I did at that moment! Yet, all I could do was watch in horror!"

"That's awful!" Kate blurted out passionately. "I know how close you were to the Martins, especially to Melissa." She tried to console him, but he was beyond noticing. "Please go on, John."

Running his hands nervously through his hair, John stared strangely off into space. "A few moments later he was able to continue. "Soon the house was fully engulfed in flames. With the flames greedily licking the structure then slowly reaching heavenward, the men mounted and rode away. They rode off toward Missoula, laughing fiendishly. Knowing this, I dared not go on to the fort." A strange expression crossed John's face. "As they rode away, I noticed the strange markings on one of their horses. I'll know it when I see it again." When a look of pure hatred filled his eyes, it sent chills down Kate's spine. "That night I promised to get even with those miserable, slimy snakes … if it's the last thing I ever do!"

A deadly silence filled the room, with the only sound coming from the crackling fire in the kitchen stove. Kate sat silently watching John as he paced the room like a caged tiger, wondering what to say. She silently uttered a prayer for guidance. While pondering the situation, Kate flinched as an idea came to her … a memory that she hoped to never remember let alone talk about. Sighing, she looked at John, who was still nervously twisting the hat in his hands. "John," she called softly, waiting until he looked up. "I've got a story to tell you." He looked at her intently. "I've kept this secret from everyone, except my mother's friend Helen, and, of course, Paul."

John came to the table where he sank expectantly into a chair. "Would it be too hard to tell me about it?" he questioned, not wanting to trouble her.

"Yes, but I think I need to share it with you, if only to show what happens when we allow hate to dominate out lives." He nodded. "I was a child of nine, living with my parents in Ireland on a share cropper's farm. Papa did the best he could to get the farm to yield a large crop, but the landlord was a nasty man, who took fiendish delight in tormenting my Papa." Kate sighed deeply at the painful memory it evoked.

"One night I heard my parents talking late into the night. Papa told Momma that he was worried because the farm wasn't producing as it should. He suggested that she prepare for the worst. I fell asleep shortly after that."

"I'll never forget the last time I saw my Papa alive. That morning he kissed us both tenderly before going out to the field. A few minutes before noon, Momma sent me to the field to tell Papa that lunch was ready. I often went out to the field to be with Papa. I felt it was a privilege when Momma asked me to take something for him, or tell him to come eat. I never dreamed that that day would be so different." Kate shuddered at the painful memory. "Momma spent most of the morning baking, so the house smelled heavenly. It's strange that I should think of the following events every time I smell fresh bread baking, but I do."

"Papa's screams reached me long before I got to him. My heart beat fast as I ran toward him. Fear gripped me so hard that I could hardly breathe." Kate took a deep breath, then began again, "The landlord was whipping Papa with a blacksnake."

John looked at Kate strangely then asked, "What is a blacksnake?"

"It can be a long tapering braided rawhide whip or a leather whip with a snapper on the end. It is so called because of the way that it wraps around a person or object. When the blacksnake was used on an animal or a human being, it would curl around a body like a snake. When the person using the whip pulled back, it tore the flesh, causing the person to scream in agony. If a person were beaten long enough, it would kill him because he would literally bleed to death. These blacksnakes were lethal weapons!"

"I'm surprised that Major Thornton hasn't used one on the men of the fort as well as the animals."

"Either he doesn't know about a blacksnake, or he knows that would be going too far ... even for him."

"What type of blacksnake did the landlord use?"

"The braided type. The landlord never carried a gun. Instead his weapon of choice was that blacksnake. I learned later that he had beaten many men with it. No one had survived to tell about it." Kate paused again in an attempt to gain control. Retelling the story was more difficult than she realized. It took a while for her to go on, yet John waited patiently. Taking another deep breath, she was able to continue. "I screamed for him to stop. He laughed shrilly even as he continued to beat Papa. Running to the landlord, I tried to push him away. Mr. O'Hara, the landlord, slapped me so hard that I fell to the ground. Jumping up, I put myself between them, wrapping my arms around his waist. Mr. O'Hara tried to pull me off, but I held on for dear life. Grabbing my hair, he yanked my head backwards. I almost turned loose, but somehow I knew that if I did, he would kill my Papa. When I felt the whip bite into my back, I screamed in agony." Kate began to sob brokenly. John winced, not sure what to do. Finally, he reached out to gently touch her hand, but Kate remained unaware that he was touching her hand. "As my arms flew out, Mr. O'Hara pulled me off. He shook me like some dirty old discarded rag doll, then threw me onto the ground to the side of him."

"I lit right next to Papa's pitchfork. Instinctively, I grabbed the handle of the fork. Standing up, I waited for my opportunity. As Mr. O'Hara pulled the whip back to strike Papa again, he staggered. With all the strength that my young body could muster, I rammed the fork forward then upward, striking him squarely beneath his rib cage. As one of the tongs drove through the middle of his heart, his eyes met mine. As a look of shock registered on his drunken face, I watched the color drain from his face ... life drain from his face ... His body quivered then crumpled into a heap on the ground ... dead. My eyes were riveted on his lifeless form. I could not move. Then all at once, like a frightened deer, I bolted over to my Papa. By now he was unconscious. I knelt to cradle his head in my lap, stroking his hair, his face, all the while sobbing uncontrollably. I kept yelling for him to wake up."

"Hearing a voice calling my name, I looked up as Grandpa approached me. I laid Papa gently on the ground before getting up. I stared at Grandpa in horror. *What will he think of me? What will he think of what I've done? Will he hate me? Will he disown me as his granddaughter?* These and other thoughts ran rampantly through my tortured mind. He knelt before me while reaching out for me. I hesitated a moment, unsure of what to do, then I ran gratefully into those loving outstretched arms. I felt safe as he wrapped his huge arms around me. Then with one hand, the other one still holding me close, he softly caressed my hair. Ever so often he would kiss my cheek tenderly, all the while talking soothing words of comfort to me. Snuggling closer, I buried my face in his neck, sobbing uncontrollably. "I killed him, Grandpa! I killed Mr. O'Hara!"

"Hush, Katie girl … it's alright," he whispered as he rocked me gently. "Ye did the only thing ye could, child! I'm mighty grateful to ya fer trying ta save yer pa!" This surprised me, because I was afraid he'd be mad at me for what I'd done. Leaning back, I gazed anxiously into his eyes, but there was no anger or hate there, only sweet love and compassion."

"My grandpa was a large burly man, who stood six feet two inches tall in his stocking feet. His once red hair was peppered gray, as were his thick beard and eyebrows. Wrinkles covered his face, revealing the ravages of time, while merry green eyes twinkled with life. Broad at the shoulders with narrow hips, he made quite the picture. He always wore baggy gray plaid britches, held up with a pair of black suspenders. The bottoms were rolled up a couple of times. A blue flannel shirt, although clean, was patched at the elbows. He always rolled the shirtsleeves up to the elbows, disclosing faded longjohns. Brown boots, laced up the front, stuck out from under his pants. A gray derby sitting precariously upon his head completed his outfit. His large, thick, massive hands were very gentle. A smile played softly around Kate's lips. "I can still remember how much I loved touching Grandpa's large gentle hands as I sat upon his knees."

Kate paused with her head bowed thoughtfully then raised her head, gazed at John, and continued with the story. "Grandpa hugged me tightly once more, moved me from him so that he could check on Papa. I stood back as he quickly examined him. It was plain to see that Papa was still unconscious. Turning, my grandpa told me to run to the house for Momma. He told me to have her bring the wagon which he'd left at our house, out to the field. Without another thought, I bolted toward the house. When Momma came out of the house and saw me covered in blood, she nearly fainted. It took me a while to tell her what had happened because I couldn't stop crying. She was finally able to piece the facts together. She quickly hugged me close to her before leading me to Grandpa's wagon. Momma drove that team out to the field like a mad woman! Wrapping the reins around the brake handle, she leaped from the wagon to rush over to Papa's unconscious form."

"By the time I got to Papa, Momma was shaking him in an attempt to revive him. Moaning in extreme agony, he begged her to stop. "Please, just let me be," he snapped. He tried to smile in an attempt to soothe his sharpness, but he was just too weak. "It's too late to help me, dear." Gazing tenderly into Momma's eyes, he struggled to reach for her hand. Pulling her hand close, he kissed it then told her that he loved her very much. With tears flowing down her face, she pressed his hand affectionately to her cheek. After kissing the back of it softly, Momma lovingly leaned over to kiss his lips."

"Finally, he motioned for me to come closer. Kneeling beside Momma, I nervously took his hand but remained silent, too frightened to speak." Tears coursed down Kate's face as the memory flooded back. "I'll never forget the last words my Papa said to me. 'Oh, me precious girl! Proud I am to call ye daughter. Thank ye for tryin' to save me life, honey. I hope someday ye'll find it in yer heart to be forgivin' him for this awful thing that he has done. Mr. O'Hara was a very sick man.'" Kate looked intently at John. "I nodded, but in my heart I secretly vowed never to forgive him. Papa told me that he loved me very much then asked me to take care of Momma. I was told to do all that she asked of me. I told him that I would, that I loved him, too. I bent to kiss his cheek."

"After that, Papa was so still that I was afraid he was dead. Sighing, he opened his eyes to look at Grandpa, who asked, "Why did Mr. O'Hara beat you this time?" Papa told Grandpa that he must have made Mr. O'Hara angry when he told him the crop was blighted. He said he tried to explain how the soft rot in the potatoes was due to the heavy amount of rain received that season. Snorting, Grandpa said that everybody was suffering from soft rot. He asked Papa to start from the beginning … if he could."

"Slowly, painfully, Papa unfolded the awful story. In the early spring, Papa patiently tried to explain to Mr. O'Hara about crop rotation. He told Mr. O'Hara that the soil needed a rest every seventh year in order to yield the best crops. Mr. O'Hara had grown furious with Papa, telling him to mind his own business. As he so aptly put it, he didn't need 'some lowly commoner' telling him what to do. Papa went on to tell us that he did as he was told, knowing what the results would be. That it rained incessantly all that spring and summer didn't help, either."

"Papa had been examining the potatoes that fateful day, when he heard Mr. O'Hara's buggy tearing into the field. He drove that thing like a man possessed, whipping the horses into a terrible frenzy. It careened precariously around the corner, nearly tipped over, before righting itself. Jumping out, Mr. O'Hara staggered over to Papa in a drunken stupor. Mr. O'Hara stood tapping the whip against his leg. Papa said that he didn't see anything strange about him tapping the whip against his leg, because he was always doing that. Throwing the potatoes to the ground, Papa looked at them in disgust. He realized he had made a terrible mistake when he looked up just in time to see Mr. O'Hara's fist strike him in the face. When he fell to the ground, Mr. O'Hara began whipping him with the blacksnake."

"Grandpa angrily muttered something under his breath, but I didn't hear what he said. Momma was crying softly while resignedly caressing Papa's hand. Looking lovingly at each of us, Papa told us once more that he loved us, then sighed. I knew by the way he lay so still that he was dead!"

"As bad as Grandpa was hurting, he could see my grief. Tucking his grief deep inside, Grandpa tried to console me. Feeling those strong, loving arms wrap around me again, for a moment I felt safe from the world. Setting me on his lap, Grandpa gently kissed me on the cheek, then told me that he loved me." Great soul-racking sobs shook Kate's body.

John rose to kneel beside her, slipped his arms around her shoulders. He held her close until she was able to gain control. Finally, Kate drew back. Brushing the tears from her eyes, she took the handkerchief from her pocket to blow her nose. John watched her anxiously. "Can you go on?"

Sighing, Kate nodded affirmatively then resumed the narrative. "Kissing my cheek, Grandpa tenderly lifted me from his lap, then rose. Gently helping Momma to her feet, he hugged her tight for a moment. Looking from one to the other of us, he said he would go for the constable. Before leaving, he explained how important it was not to touch anything at the scene. Momma nodded understandingly. Walking over to take my hand, Momma led me to the wagon. She told me to go with Grandpa. She told me that he would take me to stay with Grandma until she came for me. As we drove away, I saw Momma walk over to kneel beside Papa. Something inside of me died in the field that day." After that, Kate fell silent, lost in the bittersweet pain the memory evoked.

John asked, "If I'm not prying too much into your affairs … why did your grandfather come out to the field?"

Sighing, Kate looked at him. "That morning, Grandpa received a letter, telling him that his father had died, leaving him a modest sum of money." John gasped in surprise.

"He came to tell Papa that he would help us leave that farm. We could start over again somewhere else."

Neither spoke for a few moments, as each was lost in their private thoughts. Finally, Kate began to speak. "When we got to Grandpa's, he helped me from the wagon. After hugging me once more, he told me to go find Hector, his dog. I ran toward the barn, leaving him to talk with Grandma. When I found Hector, I fell to my knees, wrapped my arms around him, and buried my face in his neck, where I sobbed brokenly. Usually Hector would have nothing to do with me, but somehow he sensed my need, so he allowed me to fondle him. When I cried myself out, he whimpered, licked my face, and lay down so that I could lay my head on his side. Winding my hand deep into the fur around his neck, I began to tell him all my troubles. You know, after all the years, I can still remember what he looked like."

"What did this dog Hector look like?"

"Hector was a terrier, with a soft curly coat the color of ripe wheat. The long hair of his head fell forward over his eyes. He also had V-shaped folded ears, a black velvet nose, and a strong jaw with a square muzzle. He had a deep chest as well as a muscular neck, which was moderately long. His docked tail was pointed up. I had always thought Hector was ugly, but that day he really looked beautiful to me!"

Brushing at an imaginary speck on the table, Kate continued her story. "I had just finished telling Hector all of my troubles, also how beautiful a dog he was, when Grandma found me. Gently calling my name, she helped me up. As she led me to the house, Hector followed, checking to see that I was all right." Kate chuckled softly at some private joke. She looked at John, "Dear old Hector refused to stay outside when we went in. Patiently Grandma helped me wash up, then changed my dress, all the while telling me what an angel I was. When we were finished, Grandma kissed me soundly upon the cheek. Leading me to the divan in the living room, she gently pulled me down next to her, holding me tight as fresh tears started from my eyes. Hector jumped upon the divan with us … something that was unheard of in Grandma's house. It seemed as if she was always fussing about one thing or another." Kate smiled at the memory. "That she let him into the house was strange, let alone allowed him up onto the divan! Crooning softly, Grandma held me until I fell into an exhausted sleep."

"I woke up when Momma and Grandpa came in. I heard Grandma ask them what would happen next. Grandpa said that from the way Papa had been beaten, along with the puncture wounds in Mr. O'Hara's side, the constable felt there was no need to press charges. The first thing I noticed was that Momma had changed her clothes. Sitting close to me on the divan, she hugged and kissed me, as she told me how proud she was of me. She even petted Hector, who was lying on the floor next to the divan. When Grandma told them how Hector refused to leave me, Grandpa just shook his head in bewilderment. Glancing down at the dog, he called softly for the dog to follow him. For the first time ever, Hector refused to go to Grandpa. Shrugging, he went out to take care of the horses."

"Looking up at Grandma, standing near Momma, I thought she was so very beautiful. Standing four feet eleven inches tall, she was not only thin, but spunky as well. Wrinkles around her mouth and her close-set blue eyes, gave one the impression of being hard or unfeeling, but she was the gentlest, most caring woman one could ever have had the privilege of knowing. Her hair, pulled back at the nape of the neck, was cotton white. She wore a green gingham dress with a wide crocheted lace collar and straight sleeves. The skirt, gathered at the waist, flowed to her ankles. A white full-length apron completed the ensemble. Oh, how I loved this tiny wisp of a woman with all my heart!"

"Momma, on the other hand, was five feet three inches tall. She was also slightly plump. Her dark chestnut hair was parted in the middle then tightly pulled into a bun on the top of her head. Her deep green eyes sparkled with life. Momma had dimples in her cheeks, so when she smiled, which was often, they were prominent. She was wearing a brown dress which was simply made. It was trimmed with a small crocheted collar and long straight sleeves. The full skirt, gathered at the waist, flowed to her ankles. Black high-top shoes added to the drab appearance of the dress. A white full-length apron completed her attire. I always thought Momma was an angel ... yet when Momma hugged and kissed me that afternoon, I knew she was an angel."

"Momma kissed me once more before rising to go out to the kitchen to help Grandma prepare lunch. When I followed them, with Hector close behind, Grandma never said a word. As I think back on it, I know Grandma must have been frustrated when she stumbled over him so many times, yet she wouldn't allow anyone to take him from me. Scooping me up, Grandma set me closer to the table, then asked me what I would like to eat. I told her that it didn't matter, that I liked anything she made. Beaming at the compliment, she set about fixing a meal fit for a king. Eating was very difficult for me, but no one seemed to notice."

"I listened as the grownups chatted amiably about nonsensical things," Kate said. "Momma said that she thought she would like to move somewhere away from the farm, as it was just too painful for her to live there after what had happened. Turning, Grandpa looked strangely at Grandma, who nodded then looked back at her plate. Perplexed, Momma watched each one intently, as her eyebrows knit together. Calmly Grandpa ate a few more bites, then laid his fork on his plate and wiped his mouth, slowly placing the napkin on the table. Leaning back in his chair, he laid his hand on his stomach, belched loudly, followed by a contented sigh. I laughed when Grandma punched him on the arm as she told him to mind his manners. At first Grandpa looked hurt when I chuckled, then smiling he winked at me. When I looked over at Grandma, she was smiling a little."

"Growing serious, Grandpa told Momma about a ship sailing to America. He informed her that he and Grandma wanted to go on it. Momma gasped, then stared at Grandpa as if he'd gone daft. Grandpa told Momma that he had wanted to go for a long time, but there just wasn't any way they could afford it. Now with the money from his father's estate, they could also take us with them. When Momma continued to stare strangely at Grandpa, he went on to tell her that he thought it would be a good place for me to grow up, a place where I could forget about what had happened at the farm. For a while, Momma sat absently toying with the food on her plate, digesting Grandpa's words. I watched Momma, wondering what she thought, but she continued to toy with her food. Finally, laying the fork on the side of her plate, she looked up to smile at Grandpa. She told Grandpa that she felt that it was best to get as far away as possible ... that going to America seemed like the best way to accomplish this. We grew excited as we listened to Grandpa give us all the details. When Grandpa talked about the Bertain, the big ship that was going to take us to America, I felt awed by it all. It was decided that Grandpa would speak to the captain of the Bertain about booking passages for us."

Rising, Grandpa took his hat from the peg near the door, then went out to hitch up the team. When I heard him drive away, I reached for Hector to assure myself that he was still there. Finding that he was, I absently stroked him as I watched Momma and Grandma put the kitchen to rights.

Kate was quiet again as she thought about her grandparents' home in Ireland. Glancing at John, she decided she ought to think out loud. "The kitchen was huge! A wood cook stove took up one end of the kitchen, with a large wood box beside it. The stove had a warming oven at the top, but did not have a reservoir like the one I have now. There was a window over the door leading outside with another large window in the middle of the wall to the left. Cupboards and counters filled the walls on the right, while at the end of the room leading into the living area was a large buffet. I can still remember how on the holidays, that buffet as well as all of the extra counters were laden with food. A large oak table with huge claw feet surrounded by six matching chairs sat in the middle of the room."

"When the kitchen was in order, Grandma and Momma went into the living room to sit on the divan to relax while they visited. For a while I sat in Grandpa's chair, listening to them talk about the things Papa had done in his life. All at once I missed Papa so much that I couldn't sit there any longer. In an attempt to escape the pain, I began wandering aimlessly about the house. With Hector following close behind, I looked longingly at the different bric-a-brac. When that didn't interest me any longer, I examined the other household furnishings. Although I was never allowed to touch anything, I could gaze lovingly at them from a respectful distance. As I looked at every little thing, the thought of never seeing this beloved home again, filled me with an overwhelming sadness. I just had to explore each nook and cranny one more time."

"What was the rest of the house like, if you don't mind my asking?"

Pausing a moment, Kate leaned back in the chair and folded her hands, resting them on her tummy. A faraway look came into her eyes as she recalled the appearance of each room in her grandparent's home. "Well ... The living room, slightly smaller than the kitchen, was beautifully decorated. There was a large window on the right of the door as one entered the house. There was a large window on the adjoining wall farther to the right. To the left before the entrance to the kitchen was a large bedroom. A staircase straight ahead and to the right led to two more bedrooms above. The multicolored divan sat near the window that was beside the door leading outside, with an oak end table located on each side. Matching doilies with decorative lamps adorned each table. Two matching straight-backed chairs were placed nearby. Placed between the kitchen and staircase was a roller-top desk. A large hutch, stuffed with different bric-a-brac, stood to the left. Other shelves, placed along the walls, also held bric-a-brac. The pictures on the walls and a braided hooked rug covering the hardwood floors gave one a cozy feeling of home."

"The bedroom to the left was simply decorated. Two small hooked rugs covered the wooden floor near the bed. Stands, one on each side of the bed, contained large white crocheted doilies with matching decorative oil lamps on top of each. A closed book lay on the stand to the right, while an open Bible lay on the stand to the left. I just remember how beautiful my grandparents' home was. I still miss it. I think if Grandma knew what I did, she would have had my hide for sure."

"Gosh, you must have done something pretty awful for her to have your hide."

"As far as Grandma was concerned, it would have been horrible."

"Now you've really got my curiosity piqued!"

A mischievous gleam came into Kate's eyes. "Walking over to the stand, I lovingly caressed the doily then the pages of the open Bible."

John blinked in surprise. "What's so terrible about that?"

"Grandma was the only one allowed to handle that Bible. I can't tell you how many times she told me that she'd tan my hide if I so much as touched a corner of it." Kate leaned forward to eagerly gaze into John's face. "Can you imagine how shocked she would have been, if she'd seen me caressing that sacred book?" John could only shrug his shoulders and shake his head. "If that wasn't enough to get me into hot water, I lay down on the bed, which was covered with a white laced spread over the coverlet … with my shoes on. That was really taboo! However, to make matters even worse, I patted my hand on the bed, inviting Hector to join me! He did so without hesitation. But the truth of the matter was I needed to feel the comfort that bed afforded me. As I lay there, scratching Hector's ears, I looked around the room. Noticing the window with the white lace curtains fluttering in the breeze, I thought how it brightened the room. Pictures of different types of landscapes gave me the sense of being outdoors. Lying there on the bed, I felt comforted by a sense of peace for the first time that day."

After a while we got up to explore the rest of the house. We wandered from room to room, where I fondled all those things I had been forbidden to touch. Hector and I had to lie on every bed covered with homemade quilts just to see what it felt like." A mischievous gleam again came into her eyes while a smile played around the corners of her lips. "You know, John, I never even straightened those beds."

John laughed heartily. He seemed relieved that the conversation had been lightened up. "It's a good thing she never found out, or I have a feeling we wouldn't be having this conversation."

Kate readily agreed then added, "Instead, I'd probably still have an awful sore sit down!"

"Well, we couldn't have that happen now, could we?"

Ignoring him, she went on with the narrative. "When Hector and I came downstairs, Momma and Grandma were still talking. Not wanting to listen, we wandered out to flop on the porch swing. I'll always remember that beautiful enclosed porch with the heady, tantalizing aroma of Grandma's potted plants. To this day I can still hear her humming as she worked. From the swing I had a commanding view of the large red barn and chicken coop, as well as the many fields nestled against a backdrop of hazy blue mountains that reached heavenward. My Grandpa wasn't rich by the standards of the world, but he wasn't poor either. The farm and most of the equipment was inherited from both sides of the family. It grew so hot on the porch that Hector jumped down but stayed nearby. I grew so tired that I lay full length on the swing, still absently scratching behind Hector's ears. I finally gave in to the sights and sounds around me. I was startled when Grandpa returned, slamming the porch door. He reached out to lovingly ruffle Hector's ears, tweaked me playfully on the nose then went into the house. Not wanting to be left out of anything, we followed closely behind."

"While I went to sit between Momma and Grandma on the divan with Hector lying at my feet, Grandpa sat in one of the straight-backed chairs. When we were all settled, Grandpa began by telling us that the Bertain was sailing in two weeks. After hesitating a few moments, he told us that he had booked passage for us all. Momma and Grandma groaned when Grandpa told them that it would take a month for the ship to reach America. He said that Captain Masterson had assigned them two cabins close together. Grandma and Momma began to bombard him with questions, growing so excited that they didn't give him time to answer. Finally, holding up his hands, Grandpa hollered 'whoa.'" Kate smiled as she lifted her hands like he had.

"Grandpa told us that he'd stopped to talk with Mr. Kilpatrick, who'd been pestering him a long time about purchasing the farm. Grandpa said that Mr. Kilpatrick had agreed to purchase the farm. They were to take care of the business end of it the next day. Leaning forward, Grandma gasped in surprise. "Ye sold it already?" Smiling, he nodded. Not giving them a chance to bombard him with questions, he went on to talk of other things. I listened as he told them they would have a public sale to dispose of the items we couldn't take. Grandma and Momma began to quibble about there not being enough time to get ready, but Grandpa said that if we started right away, we could do it. Seeing that there was nothing left to do but get started, they fell silent, each trying to wrap their minds around the information just given to them."

Kate paused a moment then continued her story. "Grandpa listened patiently while they discussed plans for Papa's wake, readily agreeing with the decisions they'd decided upon. A short time later, we gathered our things so that Grandpa could take us home. When I was lifted into the wagon, Hector jumped into the back with me. Although he adored Grandpa, he sensed my need for companionship, so went home with me. From that time on, he was my constant companion, never straying far from me."

"The next two weeks were only a blur to me, yet somehow I got through Papa's wake. When I looked into his bier to say my last goodbyes, he looked like he was asleep." Tears filled Kate's eyes, and her voice became a little shaky. "I walked beside Momma as we wound our way to the cemetery, but I don't remember anything else. It was very difficult for me to leave Papa there, knowing I would never see him again."

She turned away just long enough to regain composure then went on. "After the wake, Momma was busy day and night getting our things in order for the sale. Even though Grandpa was busy with his own place, he came over often to help where he could. There was just so much to be done that it seemed as though we would never be ready in time for the sale. In spite of the many challenges, we were ready for the sale in a week and a half. I still remember when Grandpa took the last of the furnishings over to his place, for that was where the sale was to be held. I was surprised at how empty the old house seemed now that all the furniture was gone. The things we were taking with us were sitting on the porch waiting for Grandpa's return."

"Running out of the house with Hector close at my heels, I left Momma to sweep the floors. Standing at the end of the long lane, I gazed longingly back at our house, which was nestled between a thick grove of trees. The chimney peaked up from the thatched roof, which overlapped the whitewashed stucco walls. The field where Papa died was off to the right, where the dew glistened in the early morning sunlight. To the left was a large red barn with stalls for our team and our Guernsey milk cow. There was a small tack room to the right of the door. The loft was filled with sweet-smelling hay. A chicken coup and a pigpen were both located between the barn and house."

"A couple of days earlier a man had come to purchase our milk cow. Other men had come to buy our pigs, chickens, and our team of horses with the wagon. Still, others had come to take back the farm equipment belonging to the landlord. As I stood gazing into the barn, I felt almost as empty as it was. Feeling lost and lonesome, I wandered back to the house. Although I wondered if the future would be better than this, I felt ready to tackle whatever it held for me."

"Together we walked to the little cemetery a good distance away. Removing the old flowers, Momma put fresh ones on the grave. While watching her, I thought of Papa. The realization of not seeing him again in this life was so overwhelming that my throat constricted, causing me to nearly choke on the pain in my heart. "I couldn't think of him lying cold in that ground without tears smarting behind my eyes." Kate's speech became broken. "Momma looked up in time to see the tears begin to spill down my cheeks. Rising, she brushed the dirt from her hands. Reaching out, she pulled me to her, holding me until I had cried myself out. Kissing the top of my head, she stepped back to gently brush the tears from my eyes. Taking my hand, we walked back toward the house, with dear Hector not far behind."

Kate paused, "Papa was a robust jolly man, built like Grandpa only a little shorter. Twinkling mischievous green eyes peeked out from under thick bushy red eyebrows. His clean-shaven prominent jaw jutted determinedly out. Red suspenders always held up his pants, which he always had rolled up a couple of turns. He always had his shirt open at the neck, revealing thick curly red chest hair."

"The things I remembered most about Papa were the many times he played his fiddle. One of his thick massive hands reverently yet gently clasped the bow, while he tucked the instrument lovingly under his chin. When that bow touched the strings, heavenly music echoed throughout the room. I think I could have listened for hours as he played ballad after ballad. We had tucked his silent fiddle into one of the trunks that would go with us to America."

"We arrived just as Grandpa drove down the lane. Pulling my hand free of Momma's, I ran to hug him. While Grandpa loaded our belongings into the wagon, we looked around the house one more time. When Momma began to sob brokenly, I walked over to slip my hand into hers. We hugged each other, then silently left the house. As Momma closed the door softly behind us, we knew it was the last time we would ever see those wonderful walls again. Helping us into the wagon, Grandpa climbed up beside us. Gathering the reins, he tapped the reins lightly on the horses' backs, yelling giddy up. Creaking in protest, the wagon started forward. Turning to take one last look, I was surprised to see how quickly the house slipped from our view." Kate instinctively placed her hand over her heart, falling silent for a few moments.

"The next few days melted into each other, as we held the public sale and prepared to leave. Mr. Kilpatrick drove us to the docks on the day of our departure. Once there, he helped Grandpa take our things to our cabins. As I stood on deck, I stifled my fears by watching the people coming or going along the dock. Finally Momma came back to get me. Taking a deep breath, we went aboard. As the big engines began to hum and we pulled out of port, I ran along the rail, waving excitedly to the people still on shore. That night as we went to bed, it felt strange sleeping in a bed that kept swaying."

John chuckled at the thought. "Not having ever been on a ship, I can't even begin to imagine what it would be like."

Kate sighed absently, "Little did I know at the time that there would be some really rough times to endure ... days and nights when during some awful storms the ship tossed to and fro, while giant waves struck the ship. One time I thought we were goners when a storm raged furiously above. Giant waves washed over the ship as we pitched back and forth as effortlessly as though we were rag dolls. During that storm, I lost Hector when one of our trunks broke free. It pinned him to the side of the ship, crushing him to death. When the storm abated, Captain Masterson allowed me to wrap Hector in an old rag. After praying for him, Grandpa lowered him over the side of the ship. Oh how I cried as I bid farewell to my best friend!"

Kate paused to wipe at her tears, "The storms finally abated, allowing the ship to sail peacefully on. I loved to stand at the side of the ship because I loved to watch the ocean's many changing moods. The moon on the ocean made it appear as a sea of glass, while the gleaming sunsets were something to behold! During this time we met Mr. and Mrs. Harold Fillmore, a wonderful couple who became our lifelong friends. Aunt Helen, as I learned to call her, didn't have any children of her own, so she took me under her wing. She had been a schoolteacher in Ireland, but they decided to move to America because of her husband's health. I went to her cabin during the day to do my lessons or look at her huge collection of books. Not once did I grow tired of examining or reading those wonderful books."

"We were all visiting in the Fillmore's cabin one night after dinner. The grownups were visiting while I was looking at some pictures in one of Aunt Helen's books. While slowly turning the pages in the book, I ran across a picture of a pitchfork!" Kate's voice halted momentarily, then became rapid and animated. "Memories of Papa's death flashed before me. I began to scream and sob hysterically. Though Momma tried to console me, I was beyond hearing. I ranted and thrashed about. The pain, the anger just couldn't be held inside any longer. Hate welled up inside as I began to scream,

'I hate you! I hate you!' at the top of my lungs! Finally, exhausted, I fell limply in Momma's arms, still sobbing softly. As Momma held me close, rocking me gently, Grandpa told the Fillmore's why we had left Ireland. Aunt Helen cried openly as she listened to all that I'd been through."

"I woke up the next morning in our cabin, never knowing how I got there. As for the book … I never saw it again. After that, Aunt Helen went out of her way to do special things for me. I learned to love her very much. Uncle Harold intently listened to my childish chatter, always seeming to enjoy my company. When Grandpa was busy, I could always go to Uncle Harold to find comfort. He also became an anchor in the storms of my life. I learned to love and treasure him as well."

"When we lost Grandpa, two days before docking in New York, I thought I would die as I watched them lower his blanket-wrapped body overboard. I could no longer eat. I slept fitfully, waking often with terrible nightmares. As you can imagine, I was very bitter by the time we docked in New York."

"After our arrival in New York, we found a small house to rent. Because of our few possessions, it didn't take long to move in. While Momma went to work for the Fillmore's, Grandma took care of our home. For some time things fell into a routine, as I went to school during the day then studied hard at night. But once again, tragedy was just around the corner. Poor Grandma grieved so much for Grandpa, as well as my father, that she died of a broken heart six months after our arrival in New York. Momma and I moved in with the Fillmore's, where Momma worked. We stayed there together until Momma's death five years ago. Uncle Harold died four years ago from pneumonia. I lost Aunt Helen three months after Paul and I were married."

"Prior to Momma's and Uncle Harold's deaths, the four of us had become insepa-rable. Aunt Helen had taken over the duties of my education, while Uncle Harold had spent his time spoiling me. I learned much from Uncle Harold's quiet example, his sweet disposition. I had come to regard him like the father I had lost. Now that I think of it, I don't remember him ever becoming angry with me."

"Momma and Aunt Helen's great examples enabled me to learn to love as well as trust other people. They taught me that I have a greater friend, on whom I can always rely. Through their unerring patience and loving tutelage, I found joy, peace and a quiet inner strength when I prayed or read the scriptures. They were my greatest tower of strength, as my Savior came to be. I never doubted their love for me. John, it was the Savior who taught me to forgive Mr. O'Hara."

John stared at her in amazement, not sure what the Savior had to do with any of it. "You have gone through so much in your short life. You have suffered so many losses, that I don't know if I would have come through it as well as you have." He paused while thoughtfully considering her story, then shook his head. "What I can't understand is how you could ever forgive that rotten landlord!" He stared at Kate as though she were daft. "That really flabbergasts me!"

"Yes I forgave him, but it wasn't an easy thing for me to do." Kate sighed thoughtfully. "In fact, it was a slow often painful growing process."

John gazed at her with renewed respect and said, "I never believed in God." His eyebrows knit together in anger. "I always wondered if there really was a God, how could He let people hurt one another!"

Kate sat thoughtfully pondering the best way to answer him. "I think it's because He gave us our free agency. Although we can choose the path we'll lead, I believe that those who hurt others will suffer, too. There is an old law that states, 'What goes around comes around.'"

"It can't happen soon enough to suit me!"

"It is my opinion that when those who do evil have ripened in iniquity, He removes them." John shrugged, plainly not convinced. Ignoring John, Kate went on, "It doesn't matter what happens to them. What does matter is that we must forgive all of our enemies."

John glared defiantly at Kate. "I don't see why!"

Sighing, Kate patiently began to explain. "You see, John, hating only puts us in the same league as the one who hurts us. Perhaps when we learn to overcome obstacles in our way, we become the victor. Aunt Helen used to say that going through the refiner's fire ... trials ... strengthens our characters. The important thing for us to know is that when we forgive, we become free. When we are filled with hate, it consumes us until we are so possessed with getting even that we are bitter, spiteful, unpleasant to be around. We are so bound down by these feelings that we become slaves to it! I learned that when I forgave Mr. O'Hara, the pain as well as the anger grew dimmer, until I didn't think of it anymore." Kate watched John closely. "So, please, my friend let it go! If you don't, it will destroy you."

John flinched, then sat thoughtfully staring at the hat in his hands. Finally, he looked up at her. "I don't know how!" He said it so low that Kate had to strain to hear him. "In fact," he added passionately, "I don't know if I want to."

"I know that it's hard, but we must pray for our enemies more fervently than we do for our friends and loved ones."

"You've got to be joshing me!"

"No," said Kate patiently, "Only the Lord has the power to soften their hearts. If they choose to continue hating, then it will be upon their heads, not ours. I found peace and comfort through prayer as I struggled to forgive Mr. O'Hara ... You can, too." John didn't seem convinced but held his own counsel. Kate got up, walked around to John's chair to gently place a hand on his shoulder. "John, you have got to take this information to Missoula."

John jumped as though he'd been slapped. "I know, but I don't want to!"

Kate gazed at him tenderly. "I know you don't, but it has got to be done." He sat nervously twisting his hat. "Melissa and her parents' deaths have got to be reported, because these fiends just can't be allowed to get away with what they have done. They must be brought to justice as soon as possible.

"I know you're right, but I don't know if I can go through the retelling of it all again."

"It will be difficult, however, you just can't keep something like this a secret. Bottling it up inside can destroy you." John nodded slightly. "Check with Gabe Wilson to see if he'll do your chores for a few days. If he can, go right away."

Rising, John began nervously pacing the room, then walked determinedly over to Kate. "I'll do it right away." Before she could say anything else, he bolted out the door.

Kate walked back to the table to sink heavily onto the chair. She found that although it had been painful telling John of her past, it was a healing time for her as well. Rising, she prepared a quick breakfast. When she had finished, Kate struggled to her feet to straighten up the room. While she wiped the table, someone knocked at the door, so she walked over to answer it. Seeing that it was John, she smiled. Moving aside, she motioned to him to enter. "Come on in, John." When he was inside, she closed the door before turning to face him.

"I came to tell you that Gabe will take over my chores starting tomorrow morning."

"Good!"

"I'll do the chores today, then get ready to leave as soon as possible."

"What about your parents?"

"I talked to them just before coming back here. I told them that I was going to go fishing for a while."

"I see."

John defended his position. "I haven't told them anything, as I feel that it's safer for them."

"I agree."

"Well, I'd best get these chores done so that I can be on my way."

Kate watched him take the buckets and walk out the door. He was still restrained, yet his steps seemed lighter. It didn't take him long to complete the chores. Within the hour, he popped in to tell her goodbye.

"Let me know what happens as soon as you get back, John. I'll be anxious to know all about it." He nodded, smiled briefly, then was gone. Going about her work, Kate struggled to put everything out of her mind.

CHAPTER 5

John Whipple

That day, John left the fort later than he planned. After completing Kate's chores, he went home to pack his gear. He walked over to the stove where his mother, Hattie, was frying doughnuts, to kiss her on the cheek. Hattie turned to smile at him. "Are you still planning to be gone for a couple of weeks?"

"Yes. "

"When are you leaving?"

"As soon as I can get my gear together." He paused a moment before making his next statement. "I may be gone even longer, as I have some business to do in Missoula." Hattie intently studied his face. "Where will you go, son?"

`"I thought I'd go fishing someplace around Missoula. You know, I haven't been fishing for so long that I doubt whether or not I can even remember how to bait a hook."

"Fat chance of that happening!" declared Hattie, lifting a doughnut from the hot grease. After placing it with the rest on a plate in the warming oven, she silently placed several more doughnuts into the hot grease. When she was finished, she turned to smile softly. "I guess it has been a long time since you've been away from the fort." A mother's intuition warned her that something wasn't right with her offspring. She walked over. Placing a hand on his shoulder, Hattie looked at him intently. "Son, is there something else that you're not telling me?"

John nearly flinched but caught himself in time. *She knows me all too well,* he thought. He turned to her with a smile on his face. "What makes you think there's something else, Ma?"

Shrugging, Hattie moved around to turn the doughnuts before speaking. "You just seem different somehow." When the doughnuts were done, she lifted them and placed them onto the plate in the warming oven. "You'll at least wait until I finish the baking so that you can take some of it with you, won't you?"

Eyeing the doughnuts appreciatively, John nodded affirmatively, "I guess I can wait that long." John walked over to the cupboard, got down a small plate then walked over to the warming oven. After placing two doughnuts on the plate, he set the plate on the table. Going back to the cupboard, John got down a glass, then went to the pantry to fill it with milk. Returning to the table, John sank gratefully onto a chair to devour the doughnuts. He sighed with delight as he bit into the first doughnut, "Yum, these are delicious!"

Hattie beamed with pleasure. "Thank you, Son." All at once John became aware of another aroma wafting through the air. It was bread baking in the oven. He watched silently as Hattie checked to see if the bread was done. Satisfied, she took the bread pans from the oven and dumped the loaves onto metal racks to cool. After buttering the tops of the loaves, she covered them with a dishtowel.

John began to study his mother's features. Hattie Whipple, who stood four feet eleven inches tall, was pleasingly plump. Her light brown hair streaked with gray was parted in the middle, which she pulled into a knot at the back of her head. The faded light-blue dress, which gathered at the waist, flowed to her ankles. John noticed that it had three-quarter length sleeves. A white starched frilly apron covered the front of the dress. Merry blue eyes crinkled at the corners when she smiled or laughed. Her thin red lips always had a smile about them. Her face was wreathed in wrinkles, which made her appear older. John particularly loved her short pudgy hands. He remembered well the many times she had lovingly brushed away a tear or administered to him when he was ill. *To some people, she may not be much to look at,* he thought, *but to me, she'll always be beautiful!* A great wave of love for this grand woman swept over him as he sat watching her go about her work.

Sighing, John looked around their humble abode. It was very much like Thompson's cabin, with the kitchen and living room combined, yet there were two bedrooms with a large back yard. The stove where his mother was working was also a Majestic, complete with a reservoir and warming oven. It was positioned a little way from the wall to the right of the door leading outside. A huge wood box filled to overflowing sat at the left of the stove. Crude cupboards ran the full length of the wall at the right with a door leading into the pantry. Counters ran under the cupboards close to the stove. The crudely built kitchen table with six matching chairs were positioned in the middle of the room. When the table was not in use, it was covered with a green checkered tablecloth. The pantry was small yet was capable of holding a great quantity of supplies.

Their living area was simply decorated with a wing back chair at each corner and a small round table near each chair with a doily on top of each. A decorative lamp sat on each table. A pipe stand with a canister of tobacco sat on the table to the right, while a Bible with reading glasses on top sat on the table to the left. There was a divan near the window on the left with a large white lace doily thrown across the back. A large multicolored rug covered the roughly hewn wooden floor.

Rising, John stood and took his dishes to the counter. "This isn't getting me ready to go, so I guess I'd best get a move on!" He kissed his mother again and hurried to his room to get a few articles of clothing, which he stuffed into a canvas bag. Taking several necessary items from the shelves, he placed them into another canvas bag to be added to his grip. John always enjoyed his room, so it's no wonder that wonderful memories flooded over him as he gazed around. The bed, which had been built into the wall at the right, was neatly made. He remembered watching his mother make the handmade comforter that covered his bed. With his father's help, they had built some shelves so that he could store his few possessions.

John left the room, closing the door behind him. Hurriedly gathering the rest of the items needed, he piled them near the door. Quickly packing some food for him to take, Hattie placed the bag near his gear. "I'll be back as soon as I requisition a packhorse, as well as saddle Blacky." Not waiting for an answer, he darted out the door.

Blacky, a five-year-old gelding, had been given to John three years earlier by his father. Jonathan Whipple, John's father, had rescued the horse from an irate farmer, Keith Langford, who lived in the settlement. Langford hated the horse because it tried to bite him every chance it got. It would also buck at the drop of a hat. Blacky's favorite trick was stepping sideways whenever anyone tried to mount. This had so infuriated Langford that he vowed to kill the horse. John's father persuaded the distraught man to sell him the horse. Langford, thinking he was getting the better part of the bargain, conceded. John and Jonathan worked patiently with the horse to rid him of all his bad habits. Because the horse responded more to John than he did to Jonathan, Blacky was presented to John that Christmas. Blacky stood fifteen hands high and was black, except for the white blaze that ran down his face. He had a mighty sweet tooth which John readily gave in to. Through love, John taught Blacky to come when he whistled.

John had just finished saddling Blacky when his father entered the stable and walked over to him. "I heard you were getting ready to leave, Son. Did you get a pack animal requisitioned?"

"Yes, sir." John gave the saddle cinch one last hard tug before tying it off. Lifting the stirrup from the horn, he patted the horse affectionately.

Grinning, he turned to face his father. "They gave me old Baldy."

Jonathan groaned. "Not him! That knock-kneed old pile of bones ain't worth the powder to blow him to hell and back!"

John nodded affirmatively. "I know!" John's eyes were twinkling as he turned to his father. "Oh well, I guess a horse is a horse. At least I don't have to ride him."

Whipple snorted in disgust. "I should hope not!" Turning, his father slowly made his way toward the end of the stalls, shaking his head disgustedly while muttering to himself. Smiling, John followed his father. Jonathan stopped at a stall at the far end of the stables and gazed critically at its occupant. "That has got to be the ugliest horse God ever created!"

Old Baldy was a black gelding with white stocking feet. That was his only beauty, for he was sway-backed and knobby-kneed. A long bald streak and several nasty scars, ran down his left side. He had received these marks when attacked by a bear three years earlier. The poor old fellow had gone quickly downhill health-wise after that — so much so that he lost weight until his ribs showed grossly, giving him the added appearance of a skeleton. He walked with a strange little shuffle-wiggle that caused one to laugh.

Stepping into the stall, John gently patted the horse's neck. "Ah, Pa," he chided in mock severity, "Ya shouldn't say such things in front of the poor creature." Whipple again snorted in disgust. "It ain't his fault that he's so dad-blamed ugly, Pa." They burst out laughing. It was awhile before they were able to gain control. John brushed away the tears in his eyes. "I guess the only thing I can do is be nice to him. Maybe … just maybe … I'll get something out of him."

Whipple threw up his hands in exasperation. "I give up!" He went to get a bridle, as well as a pack frame. Between them, they got Old Baldy ready to go. Jonathan led Old Baldy, stopping to get a good-sized piece of rope, while John followed leading his horse Blacky. Together, they led the horses back to the house where they quickly packed the gear onto Old Baldy.

John, who suddenly remembered his fishing pole and tackle, hurried off to get them. It wouldn't do to forget that, he chided himself. After all, that's the excuse I gave Ma for leaving the fort in the first place. He quickly hurried outside and packed everything on to Old Baldy. When they were finished, the men went back into the house.

Whipple kissed his wife, Hattie, gently upon the lips. She blushed with pleasure then scolded him for interrupting her. Laughing playfully, he tweaked her ear. "Why, you dirty old....!" She turned to swat him, but Jonathan ducked. Again, Jonathan tweaked her ear as he moved away. Shaking her finger at him, Hattie threatened to get him when she got the chance. Laughing, Jonathan wrinkled his nose impishly, and blew a quick kiss at her, before grabbing a doughnut. Chuckling good naturedly, Hattie shook her head before going back to her work.

John smiled as he watched his parents banter back and forth. As he looked closely at his senior parent, John's heart swelled with pride. Jonathan Whipple was a strapping five feet eleven inches tall. He was solidly built. Laughter lines grew more prominent around the corners of his eyes as well as his mouth whenever he smiled. Dark blue eyes twinkled often from beneath dark eyebrows. Large ears stuck out from his head, giving him the appearance that he was about to fly. His short dark hair was neatly combed back from his face, revealing a high forehead, highlighted by high cheekbones. Whipple had a wide jutting jaw. His uniform, that of a corporal, was always neat and orderly. His boots were polished to perfection. Corporal Whipple wasn't a handsome man, but because he was always honest, gentle, and kind to all he met, no one noticed.

After filling his canteen, John kissed his mother. Walking out the door, his father followed him. Placing the canteen on the saddle horn, John tied one end of the rope to Old Baldy's bridle, then tied the other end to the saddle horn. He was about to mount when his father placed a hand on his shoulder. "Son, ya ain't foolin' me none with this fishing trip business." John could only stare dumbly back at his parent. "I know something happened the other night that's spooked ya." John started to protest, but

Whipple raised a hand to stop him. "It's all right, son. Whatever made ya come back early from Missoula must have been pretty bad." Silently, John watched his father, wondering what to say. "Just make sure ya watch yer back, ya hear?" John nodded affirmatively as Whipple looked lovingly into his son's face. "I want you to know that you can tell me anything, son. When you're ready to talk, I'll be here."

John coughed to clear the lump in his throat before tenderly answering. "I know, Pa!" Reaching out he quickly hugged his father tightly to him. "Thanks for all your help." Turning, he mounted Blacky. Turning to smile at his father reassuringly, John added, "I'll be all right, Pa." Jonathan nodded when John waved, then watched as John turned his horses toward the gate. Whipple watched in concern until he was out of sight. Sighing, he turned and went into the house.

As John absently rode along, he ignored the passing scenery, for he was busy trying to sort through the jumbled thoughts in his mind. Many times he struggled to find a way to tell Colonel Williams about witnessing the fate of Jared Martin's family, but no matter how hard he tried, there just wasn't an easy way to talk about it.

When he wasn't dwelling on this, he wondered if he would ever see the horse with the strange markings again. No matter how hard he tried, he just couldn't fully remember what was so different about the horse, yet in his mind he knew he would recognize it when the time came. *At least,* he told himself, *I hope so!*

There were other times when a battle raged within causing him to wonder if he really wanted to forgive those evil men who had murdered the Martins. Great bouts of anger shook him as he relived the events over again. At these times, John plotted sweet revenge. Then while in the deepest throes of heated passion, he heard Kate Thompson's gentle voice admonishing him to release the pent-up emotions. Angrily he tried to push these thoughts back into the deepest recesses of his mind, but it was no use. Kate's remarks continued to invade his thoughts. Slowly as the passions within grew dimmer, the image of Thornton's hate-filled countenance penetrated his brain. No matter how hard he tried not to face the facts, the realities were still the same. If he didn't let go of the feelings of revenge, he could very well find himself in the same league with Thornton. As he pondered the situation, he was forced to ask himself if this was what he wanted. His soul quaked within, as he raised his fist and shouted, "No! A thousand times, no!" He struggled to rid himself of the feelings that he found not only difficult, but almost impossible to let go. Again, Kate's words came to his rescue. He remembered how she described the difficult, painful struggles she had gone through in order to forgive the man who killed her father. "What was it she'd said?" he asked aloud. Slowly the words came flooding back, so he decided to try them. Time passed as he struggled to find a way to forgive the fiends while finding peace in his troubled heart.

All at once, John realized that he was nearing Jared Martin's farm. As he drew closer, he noticed men digging in the rubble for bodies, while others were digging graves. All at once he began to shake uncontrollably, followed by gripping panic.

He didn't want to talk to anyone … let alone watch as the dead were buried. Jerking Blacky's head to the right, John kicked him hard in the ribs. The startled horse snorted, laid his ears back and flared his nostrils as he complied with John's wishes. A soft cool wind, ripping through John's hair and clothes, began to soothe his jangled nerves.

Finally, after they'd traveled a good distance from the farm, John slowed the horses to a steady walk, then stopped. Dismounting, John saw that Blacky was blowing hard. When John went to console Blacky, he noticed that his eyes were large with fright. Blacky tossed his head reproachfully as he warily watched John approach. As John reached out to touch Blacky, the horse stiffened. Letting the reins dangle, John walked around to the horse's head, talking softly and soothingly to him. Reaching into his pocket, he took out a piece of candy, which he held out to the trembling horse. Blacky watched John anxiously a moment before taking the proffered candy, then nickered softly. While stroking the horse's neck affectionately, John apologized for being such a rotten person. Slowly, Blacky began to settle down under John's loving touch. When John was satisfied that Blacky was calmed down, he went to check on Old Baldy. The poor old fellow was trembling with the exertion of the ride. Lather covered his body, while he wheezed as he struggled to catch his breath. John's heart nearly failed him when he saw the horse's plight. After hurriedly removing the pack, he rubbed him vigorously with dried grass to remove the foam from his ugly body. As he worked, he talked soothingly to him. Old Baldy began to breathe normally. A few minutes later he stopped trembling. John hated to put the pack back onto him, yet as there was no other choice, he quickly replaced the pack. Mounting, he rode off.

They traveled for several hours before stopping to make camp for the night. Finding a good hiding place near the river, he dismounted. John tied the horses to a nearby tree. After removing the pack from Old Baldy as well as the saddle from Blacky, he led them to the river to drink. When they were finished, he led them to a grassy area where he hobbled them, leaving their halters on. He made a hot fire, gathered plenty of wood, and then went fishing. After half an hour of fishing he caught two fish, which he cleaned. When he was finished, he went back to camp to cook them over the hot fire.

After he finished eating he started to clean up camp. Suddenly his father's parting words came to him. Just make sure ya watch yer back. All at once, he felt very vulnerable. Quickly reorganizing his gear, John went to get the horses. Bringing them back to camp, he packed Old Baldy. The urge to flee grew stronger as he saddled Blacky. When he was sure that the fire was stone cold, he left camp. John found a secluded spot about a quarter of a mile away from the first camp. He didn't remove the pack or saddle from the horses after tying them to a tree in case he needed to get away fast. When he was satisfied that everything was fine, he went back to the first camp.

Finding a safe spot between the river and campsite, he hid in some bushes where he had a commanding view from all angles of camp. John knew that he wouldn't be easily detected. Should the need arise he could get away quickly. The sun had barely gone down when he heard the rumbling hoof beats of approaching horses. From the sounds the hoof beats made striking the ground, John knew there were at least four riders … probably more. Listening, John waited for the riders to come fully into view. John was glad he had remembered his father's caution about watching his back. Otherwise he would have been an easy target. But now, secluded as he was in the bushes, he felt safe. As six riders came into view, they continued coming directly toward him. John's stomach began to knot with dread. He no longer felt so safe. The approaching riders had a certain roughness about them that caused John's senses to become even more alert. When he recognized the horse with the strange markings, his heart beat faster. For a moment he found it difficult to take a deep breath. His mind flashed back to the last time he had seen that horse. In his mind's eye he could see the horse illuminated by the light of a burning cabin. It was a horrible image that he would never forget. Had he inadvertently camped near the outlaws' hideout? All of a sudden he wished he were somewhere else.

The horse with the strange markings was a thoroughbred gelding, standing at least seventeen hands high. Every muscle in the horse's body rippled in perfect symmetry as he strutted forward. His sleek chestnut coat glistened in the fading daylight. His two front legs were white from the knee down. There was a long white blaze across his right flank, while a jagged white blaze ran along the left shoulder. A white star appeared from under a lock of his straw-colored mane, spreading to his eyes. His straw-colored tail, held high, fluttered in the slight breeze which had begun to blow. Snorting, the gelding proudly tossed his head up and down, then back and forth. John nearly gasped aloud at the beauty the horse displayed in the fading light.

John's attention was drawn to the rider, who was a large burly sort of man that stood at least six feet tall. He wore a navy-blue shirt that fit his upper torso to perfection. Black pants conformed to his hips. The hat tied under his chin had silver spangles around the wide hat brim. Black boots decorated with bright silver spurs jangled when he walked. Cold, calculating, close-set brown beady eyes gazed unseeingly at the scenes around him. His thick black eyebrows were drawn together in an evil frown. A slightly hooked nose and pursed lips made his chiseled features appear even harder. When the man's clean shaven jaw jutted out defiantly, John shivered in fear, for he sensed that this man was a cold-blooded killer. John realized when he heard the man bark orders to the rest of the men that he was looking at the outlaw leader responsible for the death of Jared Martin's family.

As a man came strutting boldly toward the leader, John felt an overwhelming wave of anger consume him. Looking into the face of Corporal Reno, John knew that this man had raped and murdered Melissa Martin. It took every ounce of strength John had to remain calm, yet somehow he managed to do it.

Reno stood five feet ten inches tall. He wore a red, long-sleeved shirt with tan pants, rolled up a couple of turns at the legs. Straight stringy brown hair jutted out from under the hat's light-brown floppy brim. His brown widely-spaced eyes were cold and calculating, like those of the leader, yet there was a sneer about the thin-lipped mouth. High cheekbones accentuated his prominent Roman nose, making Reno's features ugly, grizzly, and hard to gaze upon. John waited with bated breath as Reno drew near the outlaw leader. What he heard caused him to writhe in disgust.

"Listen, Reno," began the stranger, looking around to see if anyone was listening to them, "I want to strike Hans Pedersen's place around midnight tonight." Nodding, Reno leaned closer and listened eagerly as his leader continued. "I heard from a reliable source that they purchased more horses and another herd of cattle. I hope I can get more horses like Champ."

Reno looked covetously at the horse, then back to the stranger. "That sure would be fine by me, Maines."

Maines, ignoring Reno's comment said, "When we've finished eating, bring out the stash of booze. Let the men lounge around to gamble for a while. They deserve it for the great job they did during the raid on Jared Martin's place." Maines chuckled fiendishly, causing John to grow enraged at their audacity.

Sneering, Reno sat on his haunches as he scratched absently in the dirt. "I would like to have a go at that oldest gal of Pedersen's. Boy, she is really some looker!"

Maines' satanic chuckle sent shivers of terror throughout John. Terror turned to anger when he heard Maine's next comment. A snide, roguish smirk spread across the leader's face as he said, "Ya, I'd like to have a go at her, too! Why, I would like to have a go at the next one down!" They continued to talk crudely, while John secretly vowed to spoil their vile plans. The only problem he had with that thought was how to do it. The two men went back to the campfire to eat. When dinner was over, Reno announced that they could lounge around or gamble. This pleased the men, who wasted no time in complying with the lieutenant's news. Reno rummaged through one of the packs shoved up against a tree, bringing out several bottles of booze. Uncorking one of the bottles, he poured a generous portion of the amber liquid into each man's tin cup. John saw a glimmer of hope when he saw Reno fill the cups to the brim. While the men drank or played cards, John noticed that there was a guard near the horses, as well as a guard at the other end of camp. Maines and Reno joined the men at the card game. Soon, both became engrossed in the game in front of them. John watched in disgust as money passed hands while they greedily guzzled their cups of liquor.

His attention was drawn to the man at the end of the camp. John wasn't surprised to see him sneaking a drink from a bottle every chance he got. As soon as the sentry finished the bottle, he pulled out another from inside his coat. The sentry proceeded to make short work of this bottle, too. John couldn't help but smile as he saw the window of opportunity growing wider. Turning to the guard by the horses, he saw that he was also ingesting secretly. The man guzzled a large bottle of whisky like it was water. John was amazed at how well he held his liquor. When the second guard had finished the bottle, he went back to one of the horses, reached inside the saddlebag extracting another. He looked around to see if he had been noticed, then went back to his secluded spot, where he uncorked the bottle. The man had walked with such a stagger that John doubted that he'd finish the new bottle. John was surprised when no one removed the saddles from the horses, then thought perhaps it was because of easy access for the intended raid.

Again his attention was drawn back to the card game when the leader, Maines, jumped up spewing curses at a lean, red-faced man. Bellowing like a mad bull, he pointed a finger at the doomed man. "You cheated!" Jerking his gun from its holster, he shot the man point blank. The others sat in stunned disbelief as the man fell into a crumpled heap before them. "Get rid of him," ordered Maines, turning back to the game. Mumbling something under his breath, he scowled menacingly, "I hate a cheat!" No one spoke, but sat looking intently at their cards. Two men came forward. Picking up the body, they carried it out of camp. Another man, picking up several shovels and a pick, grimly followed them.

Maines, grabbing a lighted lantern, stormed out of camp. Pausing, he gazed suspiciously around to see if he were being followed. Satisfied that he was alone, he slunk deeper into the night's shadows, coming dangerously close to John's hiding spot. John held his breath, trembling for fear that this demon-filled monster would discover him. Again Maines hesitated, to nervously look around. Sighing audibly, he went to a dead tree nearby, reached into its hollow trunk to extract something from its depths. Even with the lantern light from Maines' lantern, it was so dark and far away, John couldn't discern what Maines had withdrawn from the tree. John was reminded of an animal being stalked by some large predator, when Maines again paused, cautiously peering into the darkness, listening intently for any little noise. Feeling reassured, Maines took the lantern, moving even further from the camp. He was no longer in John's view. John couldn't see clearly enough to discern what Maines was doing, but he made a mental note to remember the location of the tree. Half an hour later, Maines returned to the tree. He stuffed whatever had been taken out earlier, back into the hollow cavity of the dead tree. Glancing around to satisfy himself that all was well, he returned to camp from a different direction.

John noticed that the booze began to flow more freely after the shooting, causing the men to grow more lewd in their language and more temperamental as time passed. John was disgusted at the amount of liquor the men consumed. The bottle was continually passed from one to another. Looking up at the full moon, he figured that it was nearly 9:30. As John slowly moved into a more comfortable position to wait, a wolf howled in the distance, answered immediately by another wolf a short distance away. The card game broke up an hour later, and the men nursed their drinks, passed out, or got into their bedrolls near the fire.

Maines, entering the camp immediately assessed the situation. Again standing dangerously close to John's hiding spot, Maines called to Reno. From the firelight, John could see angry flecks of light flashing in Maines' eyes. Reno, oblivious to the anger in the outlaw leader's eyes, strolled jauntily over to his boss. "Where'd you go, boss?"

"Never mind where I've been," snarled Maines. All at once he started bellowing loudly, "I told you to let them have a drink or two, not inhale it." Reno, who knew he'd brought down Maines' wrath upon him, waited for the tirade to dissipate. His head was bowed, so he didn't see Maines fingering the gun in his holster. Maines started to lift the gun out of the holster, then thinking better of it, let it fall back into place. John didn't think he could witness another killing, yet wondered what could he do to prevent it from happening? "You're lucky I don't kill you on the spot for spoiling my plans."

"Sorry, boss ... I won't let it happen again."

"See that you don't ... or I swear there'll be a parting of the ways!"

Reno slunk away like a whipped puppy to lick his frayed nerves. Getting a couple bottles of whisky, Maines went to sit by the fire. Drinking straight from the bottle, he stared moodily into the fire. Like a parched man in the desert, Maines downed the bottle. Grabbing the other bottle, he continued to gulp it down. Half way through the second bottle, he corked it, slouching down near the fire. A few minutes later, Maines began to snore heavily. John was relieved to see that he'd passed out.

When he saw the guard at the end of camp slouched over in a strange position, he realized that he had passed out. Turning to the guard by the horses, he was surprised to see him still drinking heavily. Most of the men were asleep when John saw the guard finally rise, then fall over in a drunken stupor. John waited patiently until he was sure they were all in a heavy sleep before moving from his spot.

Slowly, yet cautiously, he crawled along, stopping every so often to listen. When he was satisfied that it was safe, he continued to inch forward. It seemed like forever until he got to the outlaws' horses. John noticed that the horses were securely tethered to a rope stretched between two trees. John quietly untied one end of the rope, then proceeded toward the opposite tree. He looped the first end of the rope around the reins, tying it so that the horses couldn't break free. He then untied the other end of the rope. He took one more look at the outlaws. Satisfied that they were still out, John slowly led the horses away.

At one point the horses nickered. The guard moved a little. John crouched quickly, waiting breathlessly until the guard was settled before continuing away from camp. He continued to lead the horses to where he'd left his own. He tied the rope of the lead horse to Old Baldy's pack board. Satisfied that it was secure, John tied the old horse to Blacky. After gazing around to see if he had missed anything, John took a deep calming breath. Gathering the reins, he mounted. Glancing back at Old Baldy, John wished that he had time to put the pack on another horse. Knowing he couldn't do anything about it at that time, he nudged Blacky forward. John rode slowly for a distance, before he dared take them faster. When he was satisfied that they wouldn't be heard, John rode quickly toward Missoula. Two of the horses started to get temperamental, causing the others to become skittish. John struggled with the horses for several miles, wishing he could get rid of them. His head ached from the stress of the past few days, and the fact that he hadn't gotten much sleep. Knowing he had to get a safe distance from the outlaws, he forged on. He pressed on for another hour or two. Satisfied that the outlaws couldn't catch up with him, John slowed the horses to a gentle walk to cool them. Coming to a good campsite he stopped to make camp.

After watering the horses, he led them back to camp, where he tied them to a large tree. Removing the saddles from the horses, he piled them together a short distance from the intended fire site. When John went to remove the pack from Old Baldy, he became alarmed at finding him wheezing. His body was trembling so hard that John feared he'd expire where he stood. Taking one of the blankets, John began to rub him vigorously. John made the decision not to put the pack back onto him, as he just wasn't fit enough to handle it. It was some time before the wheezing and trembling stopped. Feeling guilty, he continued to stroke Old Baldy gently, talking in soft undertones until he was satisfied that he'd calmed down. Going back to the area where he planned to camp, John began to get organized.

After gathering a good-sized pile of wood, John prepared a blazing fire. When he was satisfied that it was going strong, he cut some pine boughs and laid them a short distance from the fire. When he had enough, he laid out his bedroll. Rummaging through his gear for something to eat, he came across a cloth bag. Opening it, he found a large quantity of doughnuts and several sandwiches at the bottom. *How did I miss this?* he wondered. A grin spread across his face. *Leave it to Ma to think of everything.* John went back to rummaging through the pack. He found the coffeepot and some ground coffee, took the coffeepot to the river to fill it, then brought it back to place it on the fire. Scooping up some of the ground coffee, he placed it into the coffeepot then closed the lid. An owl hooted close by, then John heard the whirling of wings as it flew off. When the coffee was ready, he rummaged for a cup. Finding one, he filled it with the boiling coffee. He hurriedly ate two sandwiches and dank two cups of coffee.

When camp was put to rights, he placed more fuel onto the fire. While he sat on the bedroll, he stared moodily into the flickering firelight. Taking out his watch he leaned toward the fire to study it intently. "01:30," he mumbled aloud. Putting the watch back into his pocket, he removed his boots. Slipping gratefully inside the bedroll, John turned onto his back. The full moon bathed the landscape in purple-shrouded hues. A canopy of diamond-studded stars twinkled amidst a curtained backdrop of marbled ebony. Sighing, he turned onto his side, closed his eyes in hopes that sleep would claim him. No matter how hard he tried, sleep eluded him.

John tossed and turned in an attempt to find a more comfortable spot. When he did close his eyes, horrible images rushed into his mind. Giving up, he lay watching the flickering firelight dance, like ghostly shadows on the outer reaches of camp. Sometime during those sleepless hours, John realized that he had won a sweet victory over the outlaws, when he'd prevented them from raiding, even killing Hans Pedersen's family. Still, he knew that he must come to terms with the bitterness and hatred he held inside. So it was that slowly, yet painfully, he struggled to free himself from the awful chains of hate that held him captive.

Kate's words on how to find this peace entered his mind. Raising himself to a sitting position, he began to pray for the first time in his life. As tears streamed down his face, the bitterness as well as the anger he had so wanted to hang onto began to slip away. He knew there was still a long, bumpy road for him to traverse, but for now, it was a good start.

When a faint rosy light appeared in the east, John got up. After slipping into his boots he stirred the fire. After tossing more wood onto the hot coals, he placed the coffeepot near the fire to reheat. John went to lead the horses to the river to drink. When they were finished, he led them to camp, where he re-tied them. When the coffee was hot, he wolfed down several of his mother's doughnuts. John also drank his fill of coffee. Leaving out the bag of doughnuts, he poured out the last of the coffee, rinsed out the pot then placed it with his pack, which he quickly organized. Rolling up his bedroll, he placed it near the gear then doused the fire. When he was satisfied that it was completely out, he picked up his canteen. Going back to the river, he refilled it.

He began to saddle the horses, which was no small task. John, deciding not to place anything on Old Baldy, because the old fellow was still showing signs of fatigue, placed his gear onto a beautiful sorrel mare. He didn't try to keep the two troublemakers, but turned them loose to forage alone. He slipped the canteen over the saddle horn, along with the bag of doughnuts. After tying the horses together with one rope, he tied the other end to the pack frame. Mounting, he rode slowly out of camp. The sun was beginning to crest over the hill as he headed toward Missoula.

After pushing the horses relentlessly for several hours, John stopped to eat the last of his doughnuts while giving the horses a chance to rest. Old Baldy was again showing great signs of stress, even without a pack or saddle. John felt anger toward Thornton well up inside of him, both for the way he treated people and animals. When he finished the doughnuts and was satisfied that Old Baldy could continue, he mounted. Looking around once more, he rode on.

Arriving at the fort late that afternoon, John was surprised when a guard at the gate pointed a rifle at him. "Who goes there?"

"John Whipple from Fort Owen to see Colonel Williams." He waited anxiously for the gate to open.

Slowly, creakily, the gate opened up to let him enter. Several soldiers swarmed excitedly around him as he rode through the gate leading the string of horses. Dismounting, John tied the horses to a hitching post. As he walked towards Williams, a tough-looking sergeant came toward him.

"Who are you, and what's your purpose here?"

"I'm John Whipple from Fort Owen. I'm here to see Colonel Williams."

The sergeant studied him intently then turned. "Very well, follow me." Taking the saddlebags from the horse, he followed closely behind the sergeant. As they entered a building at the end of the fort, a soldier sat at a desk busily doing paper work. "A man to see Colonel Williams," announced the sergeant.

"One moment, Sergeant Aimes. I'll see if the Colonel has time for him." Rising, the orderly walked toward the door to the right. He hesitated a moment before knocking.

John had time to look around him as he waited. The room was small yet clean and neat. There was a flag of the United States to the left as he entered the door. A large wooden desk with a chair was also to the left. A long table, with benches positioned on each side and two wooden chairs at the ends, was located at the back of the room. On the wall near the table was a picture of James Polk, President of the United States. It was the only decoration in the room.

The sergeant interrupted John. "Why do you have all those horses, boy?" Not giving John time to answer, he interrogated him further. "In particular, what are you doing with Corporal Maines' mount?"

John was spared from answering when the orderly came out of the room and spoke to John. "Colonel Williams will see you now." He moved aside for John to enter.

"Thank you." John grew suddenly very nervous. Sighing, he wearily moved toward the open door. Just before he entered the room he turned politely toward the orderly. "Would you please see to the horses?" With a grunt, the orderly bobbed his head once affirmatively that he would take care of the horses. "Thank you." Completely ignoring the sergeant, John entered the room. He stood just inside the room as the door closed quietly behind him. Colonel Williams continued working as though John weren't there.

While waiting for the colonel to acknowledge him, he looked around, nervously twisting the hat in his hands. A large gray desk with three chairs was all the furniture in the room. The large American flag stood just to John's left. There was a window behind the colonel, and a large potbelly stove stood to the right of the room.

John turned to study the colonel. He guessed that he was in his late fifties. His once light-brown hair was streaked with gray, as were his mustache and bushy eyebrows. William's had high cheekbones and a prominent chin that accentuated his wide Roman nose. His light-blue eyes were alert, yet watchful. The colonel's skin appeared to be rough, even leathery, which John guessed was due to inclement weather. John looked at the colonel's wide thick hands as he worked at the desk. He couldn't help feeling that even though they were tough, they could also be authoritative when necessary. Something inside him caused John to feel that they could also be kind or gentle. The colonel's neat orderly uniform looked as fresh as if he'd just put it on.

He was to the point of fleeing when Williams looked up. "Be seated, young man." When John was seated, the colonel folded his hands then placed them on the desk in front of him. "Now, what can I do for you?"

Still twisting his hat nervously, John wondered how to begin. Finally, looking at Colonel Williams he said, "My name is John Whipple. I am from Fort Owen. I have some disturbing news to tell you, sir." Sighing, he paused to gain control of his emotions before going on.

"Go on," prompted Williams kindly.

"A few nights ago I came upon a horrible scene." Again John was unable to go on. Seeing his distress, the colonel waited patiently for him to continue. "I guess I should start at the beginning." Slowly, painfully, John wove the gruesome tale of how the Martins were not only robbed but were murdered. When he was finished, he stepped back.

Colonel Williams listened intently until he had finished then asked, "Is there more?"

"Yes, sir. Last night on my way here I felt uneasy camping in the open, so I decided to move my camp out of sight to a secluded spot. It wasn't long until a group of men rode up near my first camp, where they dismounted. It was then that I recognized the horse ... the one with the strange markings that I'd seen on the night of the murders." By now, John, was having a difficult time trying to control his emotions. "The leader of the gang, I heard a man call him Maines, had ridden him into camp."

Williams blinked in surprise. "Did you say Maines?"

"Yes, sir, I did."

"Describe this man to me!" Shuddering, John complied with his wishes. As he spoke, Williams' countenance changed. He grew livid, while his eyes seemed to smolder with pent-up rage. "I see." Williams spoke so low that John had to strain to hear him. "Please, go on," he coaxed.

"The men bragged about what they had done at the Martins. Growing lewd in their talk, they discussed their next plan ... that of robbing Hans Pedersen, raping his daughters, then murdering all of them around midnight." John shuddered involuntarily. "After they were finished with the meal, Corporal Reno brought out several bottles of alcohol for the men to drink while they gambled." John paused thoughtfully for a moment to gain control. "Even the two guards were drinking while on watch. When one of the men cheated at the game, Maines shot him point blank. While the man was being buried, the card game continued on as if nothing had happened. This man called Maines went off by himself."

"Did you see where he went?"

"Yes, sir." John proceeded to tell of Maines coming near his hiding spot, as he went to remove something from the hollow of a tree. He meticulously described how to find the tree. As he spoke, Colonel Williams hastily wrote it all down.

When John paused, Williams looked up questioningly, "What happened next?"

After Maines had disappeared from the camp, the alcohol began to flow more freely until the men either passed out or fell into a deep sleep. Coming back to camp, this outlaw leader assessed the situation. Growing furious, he began to bellow at this lieutenant about his plans being ruined. His henchman is none other than Corporal Reno, from Fort Owen. My dad said that he had been missing for quite a while. Anyway, for a moment it looked like there would be another killing, but Maines calmed down, only threatening him if it ever happened again. Then Maines drank a bottle and half of whisky. He finally passed out beside the fire. When I was sure they were all asleep, or in a drunken stupor, I snuck over to their horses. Leading them out of camp, I took them to my waiting horses. Mounting, I rode far enough away that I knew they couldn't follow me. Then I stopped for the night. This morning when I was getting the horses ready to travel, I left two troublemakers at camp. The two of them were so ornery that they stirred up the rest of the horses, making it impossible for me to handle them. I thought it was better to leave them than fight trying to bring them here." John described the horses, going slowly enough so that Williams could write down the details. "That's everything, sir."

Williams laid the pen back in its holder before looking up at John with awe. "To steal their horses was pretty smart thinking," praised Williams. It was plain to see that he was greatly impressed. "Because of your quick thinking, they'll be easily captured." Rising, he swiftly opened the door to look into the other room. "Hawkins," he bellowed, "Come in here at once!"

Entering, Hawkins came to full attention, saluted then stood rigid as he replied, "Yes, sir."

"Get Major Brown in here on the double!"

"Yes, sir." Saluting, Hawkins left the room.

"I know this must have been difficult for you, son, but I am eternally grateful that you came forward." He sat back in the chair, folded his hands, placing them onto the desk. "We have been hard-pressed to find out who was behind these raids." He paused thoughtfully before continuing. "I never did believe it was Indians, but evil men who would benefit by starting another Indian uprising. That way we would be so busy suspecting the Indians that they could continue to carry off these heinous crimes without detection. Because of the brave thing you did, we can finally put an end to these raids."

"I must admit that I wasn't brave at all, sir." John looked at his hat, which he was twisting nervously in his hands. "A really special friend helped me see that it was important that I come forward with what I knew."

"I'm glad this friend had the wisdom to help you see how truly important it was that you come forward." He was interrupted by a slight knock at the door. "Come in!" A handsome, young man entered. "Come on in, Major Brown," greeted Williams, watching as the young man stepped inside. The orderly closed the door behind him.

Major Brown removed his hat, tucked it under his left arm, as he snapped to attention. Standing five feet ten inches tall, Major Brown was broad at the shoulders, with lean well-shaped hips. An immaculate uniform fit his frame perfectly. The legs of his pants were tucked into his well-polished high-topped boots. Major Brown's dark complexion was flawless and his features were pleasant to gaze upon. As he stood rigidly at attention, his manner was carefree ... easy going. His deep blue eyes were warm and inviting as lashes peeked out from under well-shaped dark eyebrows. His black curly hair, neatly combed with one curly lock falling across his forehead, gave him a boyish appearance.

Colonel Williams began to speak. "At ease, soldier."

"Thank you, sir." As Brown lowered his hand, he visibly relaxed. For the first time he noticed John sitting in the chair. He glanced inquisitively in his direction, then turned expectantly back to the colonel.

"Major Brown, I want you to meet John Whipple. Mr. Whipple is from Fort Owen."

Brown politely nodded. He greeted John brightly, while extending his hand. "Pleased to meet you, young man."

John was amazed at the way Major Brown's whole face appeared to become one big smile. *Even his eyes smile*, he thought. Taking the proffered hand, he winced in pain as the major gripped it heartily. "The pleasure is all mine, sir."

Major Brown nodded affirmatively, then turned back as Colonel Williams began to issue orders. "I want you to get a detail of twenty men together and leave immediately, Major." Brown again nodded and remained silent. Williams continued, "There are some men a full day south of here who may be responsible for the raids we have been having lately." Williams took a deep breath then went on. "I want them brought back to the fort for questioning." Brown's eyes brightened with interest. "I have reason to believe, Brown, that the leader is none other than Corporal Horace Maines, whom you reported absent without leave several weeks ago."

Brown stared at Williams in stunned disbelief. "Begging your pardon, sir, but did I hear you say that Corporal Maines is the leader of those raids?"

"You heard me correctly, Major. Bring them to my office immediately upon your return." He peered at Major Brown intently. "Is that understood?"

"Yes, sir! Right away, sir!" He started to exit, but Williams called him back.

"One more thing, Major."

Brown turned back expectantly. "Yes, sir."

Colonel Williams gave him the descriptions of the horses, as well as the tree that Maines had stashed something into. "See if you can find the two horses, then send one of the men back to the fort with them while the rest of you proceed to the outlaw's hideout. There were six of them, until Corporal Maines killed one of them for supposedly cheating at a game of poker. The five of them should be easily captured, because of being left afoot. Even so, they are armed and dangerous, so proceed with caution." Williams paused to take a deep breath, "Do you understand your orders, Major?"

Major Brown had remained impassive as he listened intently to Williams' instructions. Nodding once he came to full attention as he replied, "Yes, sir! I understand your instructions implicitly, sir."

Williams rose, stepped up to gaze intently into his eyes, "I want this whole thing to remain top secret! You are to tell no one why you are bringing these men in. Is that clear?"

"Yes, sir, I will follow your orders explicitly, sir."

"Very well, that will be all!"

"Very well, sir." Brown saluted, pivoting on his left toe. He marched calmly out of the room, closing the door behind him.

When the door was closed, Williams turned to John. "This order goes for you as well, son." John nodded. Williams continued, "I have some things that have to be attended to, so it will be awhile before I will be off to Fort Owen. I would appreciate it if you didn't tell anyone that I am coming." John looked at Colonel Williams in surprise, but held his own thoughts at bay.

"It is very imperative that you tell no one … not even your friend … that I am coming."

"I understand, sir. I won't tell anyone."

"Thank you, son," said Colonel Williams, placing a hand on John's shoulder. "In spite of what you say about not being brave, it took a lot of courage to come here … even greater courage to steal those horses!" A smile crossed Williams' lips while his eyes sparkled merrily. "I'd be proud to have you on my side any time!"

John felt a great pleasure as Williams squeezed his shoulder affectionately. "Thank you, sir." John rose to leave.

"Wait a minute." Stopping at the door, John turned back in surprise. Watching him intently, Williams voice was filled with compassion. "How long has it been since you've had a good night's sleep?"

"I don't know for sure, sir," mumbled John, wearily taking a deep breath. "It seems like forever!"

"I thought as much when I observed you just now. I think it would be best if you stayed here for a few days to get some rest." John was startled. "And I also think you should be here to identify the men when they arrive." John started to protest, but Colonel Williams raised his hand for silence. "It's for the best, son. We want to stop those murdering beasts in their tracks, so that no one else will be hurt."

John thought this over for a moment then knew that the colonel was right. Sighing, he raised his head. "I can see that you're right, sir! I definitely want all of this to stop. I will see it through!"

"Good! Be seated a minute!" When John was back in his seat, Williams walked over to open the door to the outer office. John jumped when he yelled, "Hawkins, come here at once!" Hastening back to his desk he began writing on a small piece of paper.

Hawkins entered, snapped to attention then saluted. "Yes, sir." He glanced in John's direction then promptly looked back at Williams.

"I want you to take this note to Mrs. Williams for me." Williams continued to write, ignoring the two men.

Hawkins, who appeared to be carved out of stone, stood rigidly erect. The uniform was flawless, as were his boots. From his boyish look, one would think that Hawkins was in his late twenties. Long blonde lashes with thinly shaped eyebrows accentuated the private's steel-gray eyes. Small cheekbones, a short shapely nose, and thick well-defined lips highlighted his perfectly shaped face. Thick light-brown hair framed his flawless complexion. In spite of his snobbish disposition, he was very handsome.

Colonel Williams folded the note, placed it into an envelope, sealed it, then handed it to Hawkins. "Take this note to Mrs. Williams on the double!" With a wave of his hand he added, "Be quick about it."

Saluting, the orderly left, not once looking in John's direction. John realized that Hawkins was intentionally snubbing him. Puzzled, he wondered to himself, *Why did he ignore me? I've done nothing to him.* Shrugging, he let it pass.

John turned when Williams began to speak. "I'm taking you to my home so that I can keep an eye on you."

John looked nervous. "I don't want to be a bother, sir."

"Nonsense, we've plenty of room." He smiled softly at some private joke. "My wife would skin me alive if I didn't bring you home with me. JaNae loves to think she is a mother for every soldier here." A look of love, even pride filled his countenance. "And if the truth be known … she is!" He chuckled, causing John to smile in spite of himself. "I have to see that the detail is dispatched and do a few things here before I can get away. Tell you what you do … have a look around the fort. I'll meet you back here when I'm done."

"I'd love to have a look around, sir. I've often wondered what it looked like."

"Good! I'll try to get back here in say … half an hour?"

"I'll be here," promised John. "Goodbye, sir. Thank you for your hospitality." Williams nodded. John quietly ambled out of the room.

A look of admiration crossed Williams' face as he watched Whipple wearily walk out of the room. *Now there's quite a man!* He was very impressed with John's quick-thinking ingenuity. He began to laugh gleefully at the thought of the outlaws' plight. *Oh, how I'd love to have been a field mouse, when those men woke to find their horses missing! Stealing those horses was just plain genius!* It was a few moments before Williams could gain control. *Yes, sir, he's quite a man!*"

Sighing, he rose to pick up his hat. He mumbled aloud, "I'd best get back to the business at hand." With that said, Williams left.

CHAPTER 6

Little Princess

L eaving the Indian Village proved to be an overwhelming experience for the troops. When they first arrived at the village, they brought with them a lot of preconceived ideas, as well as tumultuous, pent-up emotions. Time brought healing for some, learning for others. There blossomed an eternal love for all. Through sleepless nights and arduous labor came the realization that there are others — not of their skin coloring — with feelings like theirs. Although they'd wrestled with the angel of death many times, the victories were bittersweet. Parting from those whom they'd come to love, was even more grievous than ever imagined. Anguish gripped their hearts as they bid farewell to their newfound friends, knowing their separation might be forever.

Early that spring morning, a quiet somber group of men left for the fort. All grieved for those who had perished from the disease. Creaking saddles, snorting horses, and their plodding footsteps echoed in the crisp, tangy air. When they camped for their noon meal, orders were carried out with precision but without much conversation. Most of them toyed with their food, unable to shake the thoughts running rampantly through their heads. When camp was set to rights, they continued on toward the fort. Silence reigned throughout the day, continuing when they made camp for the night.

Sergeant Peters finally stopped eating, as the lump in his throat felt as though it were breaking. He wandered away from camp. For this large burly man, parting had perhaps been the most difficult thing he'd ever had to do in his life. It was not often that Peters allowed anyone into his heart, but as far as Little Princess was concerned, it was not a matter of choice. She had quietly yet unobtrusively shattered the barriers, then took up permanent residence in his heart forever. It was the Little Princess who invaded Peters' thoughts as he walked along the riverbank. He couldn't forget her angelic face, nor did he want to. Peters' first love had always been the army; therefore, he had never wanted a family before. Never had he so keenly felt the loss as he did now.

It had been a very rough day when Little Princess softly entered his life clutching tightly at his heartstrings. Since there had been a lot of admissions to the little makeshift hospital, all able-bodied people were hard-pressed to keep up with the demands of it all. Several of the troops were barely clinging to life. Peters had just finished washing his hands, when a trooper brought her into the makeshift hospital. Peters rushed over to look tenderly at the tiny waif of a girl and waited for Doctor McCabe to examine her and then give instructions for her care. Her long jet-black hair, fanning her copper-colored face, spilled haphazardly about her pillow. *The little tyke can't be more'n two-years-old, ifn' she's thet,* thought Peters. He listened intently to Doctor McCabe's instructions for the little girl's care. When the doctor was finished, Peters sat on the chair beside the bed so that he could begin to care for her. From the way she was thrashing and groaning on the cot, he knew that she was in a bad way. Little whimpers escaped her, each one tearing at Peters' heart. Something about the little girl's struggles pierced Peters' soul. As she fought for her life, Little Princess stole quietly into his heart.

For the remainder of that day until late into the night, Peters fought a tough battle with the angel of death. There was one point, just after midnight, when it looked as if he were going to lose the battle. After lifting the limp form onto his lap, Peters wrapped a blanket around her. As he held her close to him, he gently bathed her fevered brow. While Peters worked, he began to plead with her. "Please hang in thar, honey. Ever' thin's gonna be awright … ya hear?" A trooper tried to spell him off, but he refused. "Naw, Ah'll be jest fine." He didn't even look up to see if the trooper left, but continued working on the little girl. As he took care of her, he continued to speak tender words of encouragement. Many times throughout the long torturous night, he loving called her 'Lil' Princess'.

The sun had been up several hours when the child settled down enough to sleep peacefully. Peters helped change her soiled garments and made her comfortable, then settled in for the long wait. Many times while watching over her, Peters nodded off. How long he sat there he never knew. The stirring of the child woke him. When he bent over, he saw her watching him. Peters smiled encouragingly. This caused her gorgeous brown eyes to grow large with fright. All at once her tiny bottom lip began to quiver. Like a frightened fawn, she lay there, watching every move Peters made. Lovingly, Peters tucked the blankets around her, talking softly as he worked. Feeling for fever, Peters was relieved to find her brow cool. He tenderly brushed his rough, calloused hand on her cheek. Still she didn't move, but watched Peters closely to see what else he would do. Squeezing out a cool cloth, he gently bathed her face. Sighing contentedly, she closed her eyes, falling into another deep, restful sleep.

He had just laid the child back onto the cot, when Doctor McCabe came over to the bed to examine her. "The fever has finally broken."

"So … she'll be awright?"

"Yes, Peters, she will."

Peters sighed with relief. "Saints be praised!"

"Why don't you get some sleep, man? You look totally wiped out."

Sighing, Peters stood up to stretch. "Thin' Ah'll git some vittles first. It seems like ferever sence Ah hed some decent belly timber."

McCabe smiled while nodding in agreement. "Good idea."

"See ya later."

"I'll wake you if there is any change; otherwise, sleep as long as you can. You deserve it!" It was easy for the doctor to see that Peters cared deeply for the little child.

Nodding, Peters crossed to the tent entrance, where he pushed the flap open enough to step out into the warm sunshine. It was so bright after being in a semi-dark tent that he had to wait until his eyes became adjusted. Stretching, he breathed deeply of the cool, rich mountain air. Walking away from the makeshift hospital, he wandered to the outskirts of the village. All at once, he was so bone-weary that he had to find a place to sit. Finding a large flat boulder near the river, he sank gratefully onto it.

Suddenly he heard someone approaching, followed by the sounds of hushed voices. Not wanting to talk to anyone, he looked around for a way to escape. There was no other way back to the village, so he settled back on the rock to wait. At first the voices were too far away to discern. He knew that the voices weren't from Indians, but for the life of him, he couldn't recognize them. The men stopped a few rods away to talk in earnest. It was then that Peters recognized them as Samuel Zook, Ralph North, and Theodore White.

Zook seemed to be monopolizing the conversation. "I'm disgusted with this whole business. I didn't come here to be a nursemaid to a bunch of dirty stinking Indians! Seems to me that there must have been another reason for our coming to this rotten place, other than this ..."

"You'd complain about taking care of your own mother, Sam."

"I don't see you liking it, Ted."

"Well, I don't! The truth is ... it has to be done, so why complain about it?"

"Ted is right, Sam. I don't relish putting them on the chamber pots or bathing them, either ... but the way I see it, someone has to ... so why gripe about it? Pa used to tell me that griping was only a terrible waste of energy. When a job needs doing, get it done and over with. When it's done, you never have to do that chore again. Just get in, do it, soon you'll be done with it — that's my motto."

"Okay, you're both right," Sam admitted. "But I still don't understand why we're here! There is no way Thornton would ever issue this kind of order. He hates Injuns 'most as much as I do, so I'm tellin' ya that I smell a rat in the woodpile."

"Who cares why we're here, Sam? Ralph and I have come to care what happens to these people. We know that you've always had a problem with Indians, but for the life of us, we don't understand why."

Zook looked spitefully at his friends. "I'll tell you why!"

Hearing the anger in Zook's voice surprised Peters. Zook complained about a lot of things, but he had never displayed this type of anger before. Peters leaned eagerly forward to hear Zook's answer.

"You and Ralph came from New York just a few months ago, so you don't know about the Injun trouble. My folks, my kid brother, as well as myself moved to Missoula about sixteen years ago. At first the Injuns were friendly. Oh, they stole things once in a while, but for the most part they were friendly. Then for no reason we could see, they started looting, plundering ... even murdering the whites. For a while we were spared because Pa went out of his way to help them. Then one night, a group of bloody, murdering savages came to our cabin, where they killed my folks. They took my baby brother prisoner. Earlier, Pa had sent me to get the cows. When I had gone to put them into the corral, one old cow broke loose. I watched in frustration as she ran into the woods. Those Injuns came riding in just after I hurried after Old Bessie. Chasing her saved my life! Being ten, I was so scared I hid in some bushes behind the barn until they left. They took the horses, cows, and the chickens before burning the house and barn. I wandered aimlessly for several days before Thornton, who was still stationed in Fort Missoula, found me. He took me to the fort where a couple from Missoula took me in and raised me as their own. I joined the army when I turned nineteen. When Fort Owen opened eight years ago, Major Thornton was given the commission of running it. I was one of the soldiers stationed under him. The rest is history."

"That's too bad, Sam! Guess Ralph and I have been pretty sheltered."

North nodded. "Yes, we have. My parents and sister are still living in New York. Even though I haven't seen them for some time, I don't think I'd feel any different if something that horrible happened to them."

Zook turning on them blurted out, "Then don't nag me about taking care of these mangy savages!"

Both men readily agreed, then all were silent. Ralph North was the first to speak. "We have the next shift, so we'd best get back."

Zook groaned and shortly after that Peters heard their receding footsteps. He waited awhile, then stood up. Wearily, he ambled over to the mess tent, where he ate a hearty breakfast. There were a few others in the tent, but they were too weary to speak. When Peters was finished eating, he rose, took his dishes to the cook, then stepped out into the bright sunlight. Hitching his pants, he lumbered over to his tent. Once inside, he sank wearily onto the cot, removed his clothing then slipped gratefully into his bedroll. Peters fell immediately into a deep sleep.

Several hours later, Peters slowly opened his eyes and looked around the tent. He lay there feeling as though he hadn't been asleep in weeks. Stretching, he pulled himself up onto the edge of his cot and dressed as quickly as possible. The night was bitterly cold. It seemed to seep into the marrow of his bones. After making himself presentable, Peters put his tent in order. Satisfied that all was as it should be, he got his hat and headed to the mess tent for something to eat. When Peters was finished, he returned to the makeshift hospital.

Entering the hospital tent, Peters looked around the room. There were approximately sixteen beds, with walking room only down the middle of the room. All of the beds were full. A table, some wooden crates filled with medical supplies, clean bedding, and other necessary items took up the remaining area. Peters marveled to see both cultures struggling together to help the sick or dying. His heart grew heavy at the casualties they'd had. Twelve of the thirty-five troops as well as twenty Indians had died from the disease. Shaking himself sternly, in an attempt to rid himself of glooms-day feelings, he went to speak to Doctor McCabe. Upon learning that Little Princess was doing much better, he worked cheerfully at various tasks while the little girl slept. Several times he went over to the cot to check on the child, satisfying himself that she was indeed all right.

It was at one of those times that Peters found her awake. He smiled encouragingly, tucked the blankets more comfortably around her, then sat on the chair beside her. She lay watching him curiously, following his every movement with her large velvety-soft brown eyes. "Well, Lil' Princess, ya finally woke up. Ah were 'bout to give up on yer wakin' up this year!" Chuckling at his own comment, he absently stroked the baby-soft fingers of her left hand. "Ya feelin' some better now, honey?" There was no answer. Peters smiled encouragingly. "Well then, 'er ya hungry fer some vittles?" The tiny, bottom lip began to quiver, tears glistened in her eyes, and she mumbled something Peters couldn't understand. Turning, he motioned for Willow to come forward. Watching her waddle toward him, he was reminded of the day she became their interpreter. Nataka had had a tough time finding someone, because he couldn't speak the Indian's native language. When he approached her, she made it plain by her actions that she didn't like the soldiers. Acting as their interpreter didn't please her at all. In English, Chief Swift Eagle speaking from his sickbed had asked her to help. The Indian woman had been interpreting for them ever since. Willow stopped by the cot to listen as Peters spoke. "Tell me what she wants."

Willow spoke to the child in her native tongue, listened to the reply, then turned brusquely toward Peters. "She want mother."

Peters slowly scanned the room then looked back to Willow. "Where's her ma?"

Willow pointed to a woman on another cot across the room. "There!"

It was apparent that the woman was too ill to help her daughter. "Where's her pa?"

Again Willow pointed across the room. "There!"

Peters, seeing a very ill man lying on a cot knew that he wasn't able to help his daughter, either. "Tell her they can't come to her."

Willow turned to the child again speaking in their native tongue. The child's eyes filled with tears. They began to flow down her cheeks. Without hesitation, Peters scooped the tiny bundle into his arms. Rocking her gently, he softly crooned little words of love as well as encouragement. Finally, exhausted, the child fell asleep. Holding her as effortlessly as though she were a china doll about to break, Peters continued to croon a soft off-tune lullaby.

He was still holding her a couple of hours later when she awoke. This time she didn't try to move out of his arms, but gazed at him timidly. Surprisingly, she reached out to touch his beard, and then quickly pulled back as a quizzical expression crossed her face. Again, she slowly reached out to touch his beard. All at once she gave it a slight tug. After raising his eyebrows and wiggling his chin, Peters chuckled at the expression on the child's face. A tiny smile crossed her lips as she ran her tiny fingers through the beard. Sighing, she snuggled closer to this rough old fossil. The heart of Peters belonged forever to Little Princess. A special bond began to develop between them from that moment on. It was at those tender moments, that Little Princess learned to know what "love," "sweetness", and "honey lamb" meant.

It was several more days before Little Princess was well, but no one hurried her out of the makeshift hospital. Peters cared for her as often as time allowed. Little Princess followed him around the room with her soft velvety doe-like eyes. When Peters approached her, her eyes would light up with eager anticipation, as she reached eagerly out to him. Scooping her into his arms, she would wind her arms around his neck for a special hug. Little Princess would lean back to run her tiny fingers through his beard, while gazing intently into his eyes. One day as he entered, she ran eagerly to him with arms raised for him to lift her. Wrapping her arms around his neck, she clung to him with all the energy of her tiny body. "Woves! She whispered into his ear. "Me woves!"

Peters, gasping for joy, buried his face into her hair. "Aw, Lil' Princess," he murmured brokenly, "Ah love ya, too!" They stood this way for a while, then Peters carried her back to the chair beside her cot. He combed the long black tresses, washed her face and hands, then played with her for a few minutes. Scooping her to him, Peters tickled her neck with his beard. He laughed heartily at her squeals of delight. "Thar's sum'n ta see ya!" Although she didn't understand his words, she trustfully wound her arms around his neck, allowing him to carry her to the other side of the room. Nearing a cot, the woman called her by name as she hungrily reached for her. With a glad little cry of joy, the child sprang eagerly into those loving, open arms. Peters moved away so mother and daughter could be alone. He walked over to Thompson, who was struggling to save an old man. "'Kin Ah hep ya, sir?"

"No thanks. I can manage." He laid a cool cloth to the man's brow then looked up to smile at Peters amiably. "Thank you anyway, Peters." Nodding, Peters walked away.

Trying to find something to do, Peters saw a young brave watching him with interest. Knowing that he was the little girl's father, he hurried over to reassure him that his wife and daughter were going to be fine. The brave, not understanding his words, looked at him suspiciously. Sighing, Peters turned and motioned for Willow.

As she sauntered over to them, Peters was amazed at her agility, because she was not only stooped but was quite large. However, this didn't affect her ability to move quickly whenever necessary. She was four feet eleven inches tall, and he thought she had to be almost as wide as she was tall. Her copper skin was wrinkled and leathery from many years of inclement weather. Braided coarse gray hair hung almost to her waist. High cheekbones accentuated her dark-brown eyes, which gave one the feeling of gazing into the eyes of a hawk. Peters judged her to be in her late seventies. In all the time they had been there, Peters couldn't remember seeing Willow smile once. Because Willow seemed suspicious of the soldiers, she warily approached Peters, glaring at him with such disgust that it made him uncomfortable.

Smiling, Peters motioned toward the young brave. "Tell this here brave thet his family's gonna be jest fine," pleaded Peters. He had time to study the young man's features as Willow spoke to the young man in low guttural tones. The handsome face, wane upon the pillow, watched Peters suspiciously. Peters wasn't able to discern how tall the young man was because of the way he lay on the cot. High cheekbones and soft inquisitive brown eyes accentuated his coppery skin. Long straight black hair framed his handsome face as it spilled loosely upon the pillow.

Peters' attention was diverted when Willow turned to speak to him in crisp broken English. "Him not believe white man! Him wants see girl child and his woman." Grinning snidely, Willow waited for Peters to make the next move.

"Tell'm thet his woman is too sick ta come, but I'll git the girl." Peters waited until the woman spoke and the man answered.

Willow turned back to Peters. "Brave Eagle say that be good!"

Peters hurried over to the mother, with Willow close behind. "Tell Meadow Lark thet her man's better so he wants ta see the girl." Begrudgingly, Willow turned to comply. Smiling, Peters remembered how Willow resented giving him the name of Little Princess' parents. It was plain to see that she didn't want to tell him but did so only when she felt compelled to do so. Peters watched as Meadow Lark looked first at the child, over to Peters, and back to the child.

Slowly she looked over to where her husband lay watching them. Kissing her daughter, Meadow Lark handed her to Peters. Gently taking the little girl, he carried her over to Brave Eagle. Little Princess squealed with delight at the sight of her father. She reached out eagerly for him as Peters drew near the cot. Chuckling lightly, he then set the child into her father's arms. Embracing his daughter, Brave Eagle spoke tender words to his beloved child. Peters, so moved with the scene before him, quickly left them alone. When he returned sometime later to take the child to her mother, Willow helped him tell Brave Eagle that he was glad their little family was going to be fine. Brave Eagle showed genuine gratitude, as well as relief.

The time spent with the Little Princess was not always a joyous time for Peters. The knowledge that they would soon have to part ... perhaps forever ... was always nagging at him from the back of his mind. He was happy for them, yet at the same time it was a difficult thing to face. He couldn't help asking himself, his heart heavy with the pending departure, how he would live without having Lil' Princess in his life. Even as he pondered the question, he knew that he would have to find a way to deal with it.

The day finally arrived for the Indians to travel to their new home, while the troops returned to the fort. Nataka and Swift Eagle, along with a small group of elders, had recently returned from seeking a new site. Thompson and Nataka were the only ones to know where the site was. It seemed safer that way.

That morning Peters sat upon a rock, watching in silence as preparations were nearing completion. The troops were almost ready to go. It wouldn't be long until the tribe was ready, too. As he watched the preparations, thoughts of the troop caused him to remember Zook and his friends. After the conversation, Zook seemed to become moodier, more difficult to handle. Peters had felt forced to talk to Thompson about Zook's attitude. They decided to give him assignments outside the village. He, along with several others, hauled water, cut wood, or hunted. This seemed to please him, because he didn't have to deal directly with the Indians.

A few days later, his friends contracted the dreaded disease. When they became ill, Zook begged to care for them. Reluctantly, Thompson had given in. Zook had worked relentlessly to save them, allowing no one to spare him from his efforts. When White died, he showed no emotion whatsoever, but turned his full attention to North. The night North died, as Doctor McCabe covered the man's face, Zook rushed out into the night. When he was gone for several hours, Thompson asked Peters to search for him.

In his search, Peters took the same path he'd taken the morning he'd overheard the three friends talking. He remembered the rock he had been sitting on that day, so when he came within sight of the rock, he wasn't surprised to see Zook sitting exactly where he had been. Peters had hesitated a moment to collect his thoughts before going towards Zook. When Zook saw Peters, it looked for a moment as if he would bolt. Zook must have thought better of it, because he had waited. Peters remembered their conversation as though it were yesterday.

"I haven't deserted, Sergeant."

"Didn't thin' ya had, Zook. When ya didn't return, we all got worried 'bout ya, especially Captain Thompson."

"I just had to get out of there so I could get my head straightened out … that's all."

"Kin Ah hep ya eny?"

"No. I have to sort some things out on my own. If I come back now, I think I'll explode!"

"Ver' well. Take all the time ya need. We'll be waitin' fer ya."

"Thanks, Peters. I appreciate that very much."

"Ifn' ya need ta talk, Ah'm a good listener. Maybe we kin sort it all out together."

"I might take you up on that."

"See ya back at camp, Zook."

Nodding, Zook turned back to stare at the scenery. Peters watched a moment, then went to speak to Thompson.

He remembered finding the captain about to enter his tent, so he had hurried over to him. "Cap'n, might Ah haf a word wit' ya?"

"Sure, Sergeant. Come on in." When they were inside, Thompson folded his hands and placed them on the table in front of him. "Now, what can I do for you?"

"Ah found Zook jest outside the village. He told me thet he didn' desert or eny-thin' like that. Said he jest needed time ta sort through sum things. He feels like ifn' he returned now, he'd blow up. After seein' him, Ah were 'clined ta 'gree with him, so Ah gave 'im the time he needed."

Thompson nodded thoughtfully. "It has been difficult on all of us here, but especially for him. He has done his best, even though he did a lot of complaining and has a great dislike for these people. White and North were all the true friends he had, so ..."

"Plus losin' his family 'cause ah Injuns ... it all adds up ta truble."

"My thoughts exactly."

"Then ya agree wit me fer givin' 'im permission ta return when he were ready?"

"Yes, Sergeant, I do."

Peters sighed, relaxing visibly in his chair. "Thanks, Cap'n."

"Sergeant, I trust your judgment implicitly in such matters. Sometimes a person has to have time to sort things out in order to come to the right decision. Private Zook is no different. Perhaps he'll be able to come to terms with his hatred as well as his anger for all Indians."

"Ah certainly hope so!"

Sighing wearily, Thompson leaned back in his chair. "Let's get on with our work, shall we? We won't worry about him for now."

"Yer right, suh." Rising, Peters saluted, then left.

Zook returned later that night, tired, hungry, as well as mentally spent. Peters saw him coming, so waited for him. "Sergeant ... May I have a word with you, when you have time?'

"Ah've got time now, ifn' ya'd like."

Relieved, Zook sighed wearily. "Thanks that would be great."

They walked out of the village, along the river until they came to a mound of boulders, where they could sit and talk without interruption. When they were comfortable, as much as they could be under the circumstances, Peters turned to face Zook. "Whut's on yer mind, Private?"

"For a lot of years, I've hated Injuns. No matter how hard I've tried, I just couldn't wipe out what they'd done ta my family."

Wanting to convey to Zook that he understood his struggles, he decided to confess that he knew the man's story. "Ah were sittin' on the boulder ... ya know ... the one Ah found ya sittin' on today? Ya were a talkin' ta North and White 'bout what'd happened ta yer family."

Zook stared dumbfounded at Peters. "You were?"

"Yes, Private, Ah were. Jest' like ya, Ah were needin' time out from thin's en Ah didn' wana be disturbed. When ya three comed t'wards me, Ah decided ta remain hidden. Ah'm sorry, but Ah couldn't hep heerin' yer story. An' Ah were real' sorry ta learn a yer great loss."

Zook assumed that Peters was referring to the loss of his family, though he was still keenly feeling the loss of his friends, too. "Well, it's all water under the bridge now."

"Beggin' yer pardon, Private, but Ah don' thin' it ez. By holdin' yer strong feelings inside, it's still ver' much a part a ya'. Ya kin hide it, but ya kin't run frum it."

Sighing Zook nodded affirmatively, "You're right, sir. That's why I've come to you. I don't want to have these feelings any longer, but I just don't know how to get past 'em."

Peters thought about his dilemma a moment, then looked at Zook. "Ah've awlez found thet thar's a lota angles ta a problem. When ya peer at it from all sides, one kin usually find a good reason fer what sum'n did. Jest like the Injuns attackin' yer family. Somethin' purty torrible musta happened ta make them attack, 'pecially after all yer father did fer'm. Did ya ever ask yersef why?"

Still clinging to his strong feelings, Zook snapped back, "No … I was just too angry to think about it!"

"When Ah comed ta Fort Missoula four years ago, Ah heerd 'bout the Injun trouble. Major Mathews told me 'bout it. It seems a group a rebellious Injun boys hed been 'sponsible for lootin', plunderin', en murderin' the settlers fer some time. Colonel Watson, hed been ordered ta find en stop 'em. It didn't hep when a group a hotheaded settlers 'cided to git back at the Injuns. Them hotheads went inta a village when they knowed the men were off huntin'. Old men, women, en children were all thet were left in the village. Them monsters struck without warnin' en done kilt most nigh onta all in that thar village. Those thet got away were maimed en dyin'. Ah thin' there were only five Injuns thet made it out alive.

"I had no idea that's what happened."

"By listening ta those thet were left, our own Major Thornton were involved."

Zook's jaw fell slack as he stared at Peters in shock, "No!"

"But it ner could be proved. The way he hated Injuns, Ah wuldn't been atall surprised ifn' he hed been involved. Since it couldn't be proved, there twern't enythin' left ta do, but drop it. When the hunters returned en saw the state a thar village, they plotted and then delivered their revenge. 'Twern't nary a white man thet twere safe 'round Missoula fer a while. Colonel Watson were hard-pressed ta git them Injuns ta stick ta the treaty. Sumtime after thet, the rebels were caught en punished by thair chiefs. As fer the settlers, they was severely punished, too."

Zook pondered the comments a moment before looking up at Peters incredulously. "You know, Sergeant, I never thought of 'em as humans. Why, I never even thought of 'em as feeling the same kind of pain or loss as us. Having lost my family, I think I understand what they went through.

Peters was pleased with the insight Zook had gained. "Twon't be easy ta let go, but if'n ya keeps busy takin' care a thair needs, time'll hep ya take care of the rest."

Zook responded with determination, "I will."

"C'mon then, Ah want ta intra'duce ya ta the sweetest lil' angel chil', God e'er created."

Walking back to the makeshift hospital, they entered. Little Princess, squealing with delight, ran eagerly to Peters. Grinning from ear to ear, he scooped the little girl into his arms hugging her tightly to him. She tugged at his beard then wrapped her little arms around his neck. Pulling back, she looked lovingly into his eyes. "Me woves," she whispered. "Me woves!"

Peters forgot Private Zook momentarily as he and Little Princess greeted each other. Zook was moved more than he thought possible. When the little girl put her head trustingly on Peters' shoulder, he turned to Zook. "This here's the sweetest lil' angel Ah e'er knowed." Zook was surprised to see this rough, tough old sergeant become such an old softie, but it was plain to see that he was putty in this little girl's hands. "Lil Princess, Ah'd like ya ta meet muh friend, Sam."

Little Princess watched Zook intently, then did a strange thing ... she reached out for him. Surprised, Zook took her from Peters. As he felt those arms wrap around his neck, he relished the wet sweet baby kisses raining on his cheeks. From that time on, she played a huge part in healing his sad, aching heart. When her parents were released from the hospital, Little Princess went with them. The hospital seemed so empty without her, but Peters rejoiced about the wellbeing of the little family. Whenever she saw Peters or Zook, Little Princess would run eagerly to them to hug them to her. Slowly, Zook came to realize that these people were the same as him only their skin and traditions were different.

The time came when Zook met Peters on his way to the mess tent. "Sarge, may I have a moment of your time?"

"Shore, Sam. Whut's on yer mind?"

"Thanks for setting me straight, also for sharing Lil' Princess. Through her sweet example and following your tonic for dealing with my feelings of hate, I've come to have a new slant on things."

The sergeant beamed at Zook, as a smile flashed across his face. "Thet's great!"

"I'll never look at Major Thornton without feeling pity."

"Tis a pity thet he's allowed hate ta destroy 'im."

Looking intently into Peters' eyes, Zook told him, "When I think of my attitude, it scares me to think that I could have ended up the same as Thornton. Thanks, Sergeant." The men talked a few more minutes, then parted.

Peters remembered shaking himself sternly when his thoughts returned to the present. Looking past the noisy preparations to the beauty surrounding the village, he sighed resignedly. As he listened to the river's thunderous roar, he felt somewhat comforted. A soft gentle breeze ruffled his hair while also lightly caressing his face. Closing his eyes, he gave in to the mood. Feeling someone beside him, Peters opened his eyes. He was surprised to see Willow intently watching him. Rising, he removed his hat, smiled at her respectfully. Greeting her pleasantly, he added, "Mornin', Willow. What kin Ah do fer ya?"

Peters noticed that there was something different about Willow. Golden shafts of sunlight highlighted the copper features, which had been scrubbed clean. Her coarse, gray hair had been washed, combed, rebraided into one long braid, which hung down her back. The fresh, buckskin dress, which she filled sufficiently, was decorated with multicolored beads that also matched the moccasins and wide headdress. She is really beautiful, thought Peters.

When Willow stood motionless, her brown eyes searching his soul, Sergeant Peters was again reminded of a hawk about to pounce on its prey. He waited patiently, wondering what was on her mind. Sighing, she began to speak. "When soldiers come to village, I not trust! Then I watch with new eyes, see much kindness. This strange … because in moons past … soldiers come … kill … do real bad things to my people." She paused to collect her thoughts before continuing. "I learn from great man who teach much love." Grinning, she emphatically tapped Peters breast as she gazed intently into his eyes.

As Peters searched her face, he knew that it took a lot for her to tell him this. "Ah knowed thet it were hard fer ya en yer people ta put up wit us, Willow, but please believe ma whin Ah say thet we haf nothin' but the deepest respect en admiration fer ya all!"

Nodding, Willow did a strange thing. Stepping forward, she clasped Peters' right hand with both of hers giving it a hearty squeeze. "I 'specially proud to know you! You showed much love … cared for all. You big man with big heart!" Again she tapped his chest emphatically. "Thank you, for all you do!" Releasing his hand, she stepped back to again watch him intently.

Her words touched Peters deeply. "The pleasure's all mine, Willow. Ah feel Ah'm a better man fer it en Ah'm mighty grateful thet I hed the chance ta be a service ta ya en yer people." He paused, struggling to master his feelings. Finally, he was able to go on. "It's such a shame thet so many had ta suffer en die." Placing a hand on her shoulder, he squeezed it gently. "Yer one really grand lady, Willow!" Gasping in surprise, Willow quickly turned away.

Hearing a slight movement to the side of him, Peters turned toward the sound. It was Little Princess along with her parents. Brave Eagle, Little Princess' father, was dressed in a suit of buckskin. The front of the shirt was beaded in many different colored patterns. There was fringe on the sleeves and the sides of his legs. Matching beaded moccasins adorned his feet. A thick wide headband held his long straight black hair back from his face. Two feathers from a bald eagle were inserted in the back of the headband. His coloring was back to normal, which made him even more handsome than when Peters first met him. He watched in fascination as Brave Eagle reached out to place a hand on his shoulder. Brave Eagle spoke softly, but Peters didn't understand a word of it.

Willow stepped forward to interpret. "Him wish to thank man with big heart for giving family back to him."

"Tell him thet it twere a great honor ta serve him en his family. Also tell em thet Ah will ne'er forgit'm." He listened while Willow delivered his message. Brave Eagle nodded once before turning to his wife.

Peters thought Meadow Lark, Little Princess' mother, was very beautiful. She was dressed in a buckskin dress, which was decorated with multicolored beads. It fit her tall slender frame perfectly. Her graceful movements were like a breath of fresh air as she walked up to him. Straight jet-black tresses, flowing to her waist, were adorned with a beaded headband. She wore beaded moccasins on her dainty feet. High cheekbones enhanced the doe-like softness of her velvety brown eyes and copper features. Sensuous red lips parted to reveal perfect white teeth. Peters couldn't help but wonder if Lil' Princess would look like her mother when she was fully-grown.

Meadow Lark stepped forward. Standing on tiptoes, she tenderly kissed him on the cheek. This sweet gesture was almost Peters' undoing. He swallowed hard and blinked several times to keep the tears back. Smiling Meadow, Lark stepped back. Peters gasped and fell back against the rock.

A familiar presence made her way to him. It was Little Princess, her body clad in buckskin with beaded moccasins on her baby feet. Long straight jet-black tresses, streaming down her back, were tossed helter-skelter about her cherubic features. Her soft copper skin glistened in the early morning sunlight. Peters' heart seemed to be breaking, as he saw her soft velvety brown eyes gazing intently up into his tear-filled eyes. Neither of them moved but seemed to be drinking in the other's features, filing the images away into the deepest recesses of their minds for future references. It was Little Princess who broke the spell as she drew closer to place both of her tiny hands on his knees. Peters reached out to scoop her to him. Wrapping his arms lovingly around her, he gently hugged her to him. He felt as though his heart would burst as those precious arms tightened around his neck. Broken sobs shook his frame as those sweet baby fingers roamed through his beard. "Me woves!" came the tiny whisper. After a moment she leaned back in his arms to gaze lovingly into his eyes. Her fingers continued to roam through his beard. Before he could discern her intent, she grabbed him by his ears, planting a good-sized kiss on his lips. "Me woves," she repeated softly. Squeezing his ears, she planted one more kiss directly on his mouth, climbed down from his lap, studied his face one more time, then went to her mother.

As they walked away, tears fell unheeded down Peters' face. "Oh, be safe ma lil' angel princess, fer Ah love ya, too!"

All at once Peters became aware of another presence. Looking around, he saw Chief Swift Eagle standing to his left. As a sign of respect, he brushed quickly at his tears, rose to wait for Swift Eagle to speak. Swift Eagle looked proudly at the little girl, then back to Peters. "Little one be safe. I see to that!" Chief Swift Eagle paused a moment for Peters to digest the information. "She is Bright Star, my son's daughter!"

"Please, see thet she ne'er wants fer enythin'." He paused thoughtfully. "Ah wish ... Ah wish Ah could see her grow up!" He sighed resignedly. "Please, see thet she gits someone ta love en honor her when she takes a mate. Hep ... hep her children know what'a sweet mother they twere blessed ta haf."

Swift Eagle nodded briskly. "I do!" Tapping Peters' chest, he hastened to add. "I teach them of brave man with big heart ... who save her family." Again Swift Eagle tapped Peters on the chest. "I hope someday our people live in peace."

"Ah'd like nothin' better," Peters agreed. Then without reservation, Peters added, "But with men like Thornton, it's doubtful."

"Then we must live in hopes that someday there be peace." Again he thumped Peters' chest. "But I glad in here ... there be men like you ... Captain Thompson ... your people were there when we need help. We learn not all white men bad. Must search hearts ... they not lie!"

"Thank ya, Chief." They clasped each other's arms, then the chief joined his people. The troops watched the Indians leave camp, then turned to the business at hand. Though necessary, burning the village was difficult, as it took a part of them with it. After the village had been completely burned and the fire extinguished, the troops started back to the fort.

Something caught his attention, bringing him fully back from his deep contemplations. It was a doe with her fawn, coming down to drink. Peters watched as the two drank their fill, then disappeared from view. Sighing, he rose to saunter back to camp. Getting gratefully into his bedroll, Peters thought of Little Princess. Little did he know that a little child was thinking of her bearded friend as she snuggled into bed.

The minds of the troops were crowded with many disturbing thoughts as they turned in that night. Crackling fires, chirping crickets, howling coyotes, horses munching grass, and noises from other nocturnal creatures were the only sounds in camp. With a heavy, aching heart for his sweet little angel child, Peters turned onto his left side, and fell into a troubled sleep.

CHAPTER 7

Surprises

Kate awoke feeling as though she had not slept in weeks. Struggling to rise, she slowly sat up on the edge of the bed. After stretching, she dressed as quickly as her condition would allow. Going to the kitchen, she started a fire in the stove. When it was going strong, she banked it, then began to perform her daily ablutions. Someone knocked on the door as she was putting the last hairpin in her hair. Quickly pouring her wash water into the slop bucket, she put everything away, and walked over to open the door. Gabe Wilson was impatiently rocking back and forth on his toes then his heels.

Gabe wore bib overalls that were too short for his legs, a dirty wrinkled red flannel shirt, and dusty loosely-tied boots. Brown locks of uncombed hair peeked out from under a dirty army hat, which was smeared with sweat around the band and streaked with dirt on the brim. Pimples made his fair complexion unsightly, although it was apparent that he had washed his face. A wide thick nose, bushy eyebrows and a short stubby chin made him appear homely. Stepping to the side, she greeted him.

"Good morning, Gabe."

"Mornin', ma'am. I come to do John's chores."

"I know. Won't you come on in?"

"Thanks."

Hurrying into the room Wilson went over to the counter. Grabbing the water buckets, he headed outside, banging them hard against a chair. Kate groaned inwardly as she saw a dent appear in one of the buckets. Gabe returned a few minutes later, slopping the water on the floor as he went to fill the reservoir. He was in such a hurry to fill the reservoir that he slopped more water onto the floor. Turning to grab the empty bucket, he struck the side of the stove with the bucket he'd just emptied. Each time he returned with the buckets filled with water, he would slop some of it onto the floor.

As Kate watched Wilson go about his work, she was reminded of John. She wondered how he had managed the visit with Colonel Williams. It had been two weeks since the day he'd shared the gruesome tale concerning Jared Martin's family. Gabe was always punctual but did his work carelessly. John, on the other hand, was careful. When Gabe returned with two more buckets of water, he set them onto the counter.

Kate was relieved. While he went out to cut wood, she went to the pantry for the mop. She soon had the floor wiped up.

She had just returned from putting the mop away, when Gabe came in with a huge armload of wood. As he threw it haphazardly into the wood box, wood dust and shavings fell onto the floor. Walking through the mess, on his way out to get the kindling, he made tracks across the floor. Returning with his arms laden with kindling, Kate wasn't surprised to see him toss it, helter-skelter, near the wood box. Kate, growing impatient with Gabe's sloppy manner, was relieved when he was done.

Gabe turned from the wood box, straightened his hat, hooked his thumbs through the front of his overalls then rocked back and forth. A grin, which Kate thought was more like a sneer, spread across his face. "I'm done, ma'am."

"Thank you very much, Gabe. That will be all for today." Nodding, Gabe hurried out the door. Sighing, Kate got the broom and dustpan to sweep the floor. Seeing the wood sticking haphazardly from the wood box, she knew that she had to reorganize it. As she removed the wood from the box, Kate became more disgusted with Gabe's sloppy job. When the wood was stacked neatly back into the box, she wasn't surprised to see that it was only half full. *It's a good thing I'm not baking today,* she thought. The kindling was soon placed neatly on top of the bigger wood, then she swept the floor. When she had finished cleaning Gabe's mess, she leaned wearily against the broom thinking of Paul. An overwhelming longing to see him engulfed her. "Oh, Paul," she moaned aloud. "I wish that you were here!" Sighing, she put everything away. After washing up, Kate prepared a bowl of bread and milk. Carrying it to the table, she sank wearily onto a chair to begin to eat. When she was finished, she did the few dishes and finished her daily chores. While she was making the bed, her back began to feel as though it were about to break in two.

To get her mind off of the pain in her back, Kate decided to go see Lonna Foster's new baby. Donning her shawl and bonnet, Kate went out the door. A gentle breeze ruffled her hair as well as her clothes, while the warm sunshine bathed her back and face. A special rendition from robins mingled with meadowlarks filled the air with their sweet joyful melee, filling her soul with peace.

Knocking gently on the Foster's door, she entered at Lonna's bidding. Lonna invited Kate to come to the bedroom. Lonna was still tired from giving birth and taking care of the new baby, but she greeted her friend cheerfully. Kate admired her flawless, china-doll complexion, framed by long curly black tresses, which spilled from her shoulders onto her pillow. Thinly-shaped eyebrows with long lashes accentuated her light-blue eyes. A dainty nose softened her delicate cheekbones. Full ruby-red lips parted, revealing sparkling even white teeth. Her white cotton nightgown was ruffled at the neck with lace across the bodice. Noticing Lonna's long thin tapering fingers folded gently on the coverlet, Kate smiled. "You are a vision of loveliness, my friend!"

Lonna blushed prettily. "Thank you so much, Kate. I don't feel very lovely today." She gazed proudly over at the baby lying asleep in his cradle. "It's wonderful having my beautiful son, but I still feel so bone-tired, besides it's a lot of work to take care of a new one."

"That's to be expected, dear. It will take some time before you get your sass back." Smiling, she patted Lonna's hand. "You've got to be patient." Looking at her swollen abdomen, she giggled softly. "I don't think I have much room to talk, though. I'm already so impatient that I'll probably be a bear cat when it's my turn."

"Bah! I've never known you to become irritable when things don't go your way."

Kate grew thoughtful for a moment. "I must admit that I'm ready to have this baby!" Rising, Kate walked over to pick up the sleeping infant. He opened his eyes, stretched lazily, pursed his lips as though nursing, sighed deeply, then went back to sleep. Grinning, Kate kissed him gently upon the cheek. Tenderly cradling the baby in her arms, she sat on a chair by the bed.

For a moment Lonna was forgotten as Kate gazed at the sleeping child. Removing the blanket, she lovingly caressed the long thin feet. Twitching, he pursed his lips. Kate grinned at Lonna. "He's ticklish!" Smiling, Lonna nodded. Lifting one of the feet, she gently kissed it. Again the baby twitched. "Oh, you beautiful doll," she crooned. Wrapping the blanket around him, taking one of his tiny hands, she lightly straightened the fingers. Softly kissing them, she was amazed at how long and tapering they were. A button nose, thin eyebrows, rosebud lips accentuated his chubby cheeks. His dainty slightly curled chin quivered in his sleep. The hair on his head was so light that he appeared bald. "He's so gorgeous, Lonna!"

Lonna smiled proudly. "I know!"

A great longing welled up inside of Kate as she watched the sleeping infant. Lonna looked proudly on, touched by the tender scene. Noticing that Lonna looked tired, Kate laid the baby back into the cradle. She turned in time to see Lonna trying to stifle a yawn but failing. "I'll leave so that you can get some rest."

"Thank you for coming, Kate. Please come again soon!"

She squeezed Lonna's hand gently. "I will. Take care and enjoy this precious angel."

Lonna nodded, as a smile spread across her face. "I will!"

Kate took one last peek at the sleeping baby, then left. Not wanting to face the house alone, she decided to see how Anna was making out since Major Thornton's departure. She had watched the four men leave on her way to Lonna's, feeling relieved that he was no longer at the fort. Remembering that he'd returned the day after John left for Fort Missoula, she couldn't help but hope he would stay away for a longer period of time.

As Anna stepped out of the Mercantile, her arms laden with packages, she saw Kate approaching. Her face lit up with joy at the sight of her friend. "Good morning, Kate."

"Here," cried Kate, with outstretched arms. "Let me take some of those packages for you."

Anna gratefully handed a few of the smaller packages to Kate. "Thank you. I guess I got a little carried away with my shopping."

Kate was pleased to see her friend so happy, so carefree. She guessed that it was the knowledge that she was free of Carl for a while. "It's wonderful to see you in such a good mood, dear." A teasing note crept into her voice, while her eyes twinkled mischievously. "I'd be willing to bet it's due to the fact that Carl left the fort for another secret rendezvous."

Anna laughed good-naturedly. "I'm caught red-handed with my hand in the cookie jar! I feel so free with him gone, that I guess it shows."

Hugging her friend's arm, Kate smiled cheerfully. "It does, but who cares? It's wonderful to see you so chipper." Stepping up onto the porch, Kate felt relieved to have reached their destination. Opening the door, Anna moved aside for Kate to precede her. When she was inside, Kate placed the packages onto the table before addressing Anna. "How long will Carl be gone this time?"

Anna thoughtfully laid her packages onto the table before replying. "I don't know for sure. Said he'd be back in a day or two."

"Then you don't know how long he'll be gone?"

"No. That's all he would tell me." Sighing, she began to sort through the items on the table and put them away. "He was his usual evasive self."

"Then at least we can have that dinner I promised you last time. How about five o'clock tonight?"

Anna watched Kate in concern. "Do you feel like cooking? You don't look like you are feeling very well."

"I'll be fine! Besides, it will be fun to visit for a while without fear of Carl coming in to spoil everything." Anna remained unconvinced, but Kate plodded on. "We both need the change."

"Tell you what we'll do. I would really enjoy getting away from here, but not at the expense of your health. How would you feel if I prepared the meal and brought it over? That way we can still have dinner together, but you won't have to cook."

Seeing the logic, Kate gracefully relented. "Thank you. You're right of course."

"Of course! Haven't you figured that out yet?"

Kate playfully slapped at her. "Oh you!"

Both laughed heartily, then Anna grew serious. "Would it be all right if I brought dinner over at eighteen hundred hours?"

"That would be just fine."

"Good, then it's settled! I'll see you then, Kate."

"See you then." Kate walked out of the cabin into the heat of the morning. She paused a moment on the porch to gaze around her. Being so advanced in her pregnancy wasn't easy, but to feel the heat so early in the morning was even more difficult. Needing some items from the Mercantile, she headed in that direction. The Mercantile, located to the right as you entered the gate, was a huge building. It was adorned with a covered full-length wooden porch.

Lumbering along, she thought of the kind gentleman who ran it. Garth Adamson came to the fort a year ago and purchased the Mercantile soon afterward. His teasing lackadaisical manner earned him many friends. He was an older gentleman, who always joked about his hair deserting him. A fringe of hair around the sides and back was all that was left of his once curly dark-brown hair. He always wore a white shirt, with the sleeves rolled to his elbows, disclosing thick dark hair on his massive arms. Piercing blue eyes seemed to see into one's soul. When he smiled, they seemed to disappear into an endless multitude of wrinkles around his face. High cheekbones, a large prominent jawbone, hidden by a thick double chin, reminded her of a jolly roly-poly clown. Black suspenders held up his baggy corduroy pants, and brown heavy boots completed the outfit.

It was so dark when she entered the store after being out in the bright sunlight, that she had to pause to let her eyes adjust to the room. A long counter at the back of the room was fraught with several glass jars filled with pretty colored candies. On the end of the counter was a large scale. Several men were leaning against the counter, haggling with Adamson over their furs. Along the walls were several shelves laden with many types of merchandise. On one long flat table were large bolts of different types of material along with other sewing notions. Another was laden with decorative lamps, lanterns, clocks and other paraphernalia. A long aisle separated the two. At the end of the table, closest to the counter, were several barrels of salt pork, crackers, and beans and a large crock of dill pickles. In a corner to the right of the room stood a large pot-bellied stove. To the side was a small table, upon which sat a game of checkers. A door at the back of the room led into a spacious storeroom. Another door to the right led into a room that had been converted into a saloon. Here the men could drink and relax after a tough grueling day. Kate could see several round tables around the room. To the left was a long bar which Garth's oldest son, Thad, was manning. A few men were seated around the tables, drinking coffee, laughing loudly, or talking amiably.

As the men turned to leave, Adamson carried the furs to the storeroom. Coming back into the room, he saw Kate. Greeting her cheerfully he said, "Why, good morning, Mrs. Thompson. How are you doing today?"

"Hello, Mr. Adamson. I'm doing just fine. Thank you."

"Great! Glad to hear that! How can I help you today?"

"I came to purchase a few items."

After she handed him a list, he scanned it and then set about filling it. When she had paid for it, he turned to call to a young man from the back room. "Seth, get out here on the double!"

Kate jumped in surprise, then grinned at the young man as he entered. "Hello, Seth. It's great to see you. How are you doing?"

"Jest fine, ma'am! Jest fine!"

"I want you to carry these packages home for Mrs. Thompson."

"Be glad to, Pa."

"That won't be necessary. I'll be just fine."

"I won't hear of it! It's much too hot for you to be carrying packages. Besides, Seth needs something to do anyway."

"Pa's right, ma'am. All ma chores er done. To tell the truth, I'm bored clean outa ma gourd."

Kate smiled in spite of herself. "Thank you, Seth. I appreciate that."

Picking up the box of supplies, Seth waited for Kate to precede him out the door. As they walked along, Kate covertly studied the young man. His thick dark brown curly hair was in disarray, along with several locks that fell recklessly across his forehead. Sparkling blue eyes twinkled from beneath lush long lashes. His prominent jawbone and high cheeks appeared to be sculpted from potter's clay. His full lips and flawless complexion all enhanced his manly features. She wouldn't have been surprised to learn that he was a terrible tease. Being seventeen, he was not only tall, but also willowy. He seemed to be all legs, and she found herself struggling to keep up with his long strides. Finally, noticing her dilemma, he slowed down.

"Beggin' yer pardon, ma'am, but I fergets about ma long legs. Ma usually hauls off an whops me a good un to let me know ah better slow down."

A teasing light came into Kate's eyes. "Your mother had a good idea, but somehow I don't think I'd get away with that." They continued on, happy to be out in the fresh air.

By now they had reached Kate's home, so Seth carried the packages inside, setting them on her table. After Kate thanked him, Seth darted out. As soon as she took care of her purchases, she prepared and ate a quick lunch. By the time she'd cleaned up her lunch dishes, she was feeling so tired as well as achy that she decided to take a nap. Kate fell into an exhausted sleep as soon as her head hit the pillow.

Opening her eyes, Kate looked around the room, then at the clock on the dresser, gasping in surprise. Realizing that she had slept too long, she struggled to rise from the bed, then groaned. The pain in her back was more intense. She was also experiencing more discomfort in her abdomen. Ignoring the pain as much as possible, she rose. After going to the kitchen, she started a fire in the stove. When it was going well, she banked it. Preparing a pot of coffee, she placed it in the front. As she washed her hands, the thought of food became abhorrent to her. Removing the tablecloth, she quickly set the table.

Kate was sitting in the rocker trying to read the Bible when Anna knocked. Struggling out of the rocker, she went to answer the door. Moving to the side, she motioned for Anna to enter. "Come on in. The table's ready." Anna, carrying a large basket, looked at Kate anxiously. "Are you sure that you're up to this?"

Kate nodded, not daring to look at her. "I'm fine … just tired and achy."

"We can do this another night, you know!"

"No, I'll be all right. Please, come in."

"If you're sure."

"I am."

Stepping inside, Anna waited for Kate to close the door. "Just tell me where things are and we'll soon be ready to eat." While they worked to put the meal on the table, they began to visit. "I'm glad that we have this time together, Kate"

"I agree. It's been a long time since we've had a really good talk. Personally, I've missed it."

"Me, too."

"Were you able to get much accomplished this afternoon?" Kate asked.

"Yes." A smile tugged at the corners of Anna's mouth. "I love being alone with my own thoughts … a bad habit, I suppose."

"It's good to be alone once in a while." Kate stated. She continued to help Anna put food on the table. They were soon ready to eat.

Soon after the prayer, the pain grew even stronger. She struggled to keep the conversation flowing so that Anna wouldn't worry about her. Thinking they were pre-labor pains, which she had been experiencing lately, she decided to ignore them. They'll pass, she told herself. The pains did not pass as Kate thought they would, but increased in intensity. Biting her lower lip as a pain stronger than any of the others gripped her, she moaned in extreme agony.

Looking up from her plate, Anna peered at her anxiously. "You can't tell me there's nothing wrong!" Rising she went to Kate's side. "You're having contractions, aren't you?" Kate could only nod affirmatively as the pain continued to linger.

"Come on, honey, let's get you into bed, then I'll get Doctor Phelps." Helping Kate to her feet, she led her toward the bedroom. Kate had only taken a couple of steps, when her water broke. Anna patted her hand reassuringly while continuing to fuss over her like an old mother hen. "It's all right, honey. We'll have you taken care of in no time!"

They nearly had Kate ready for bed, when Kate groaned, grabbing her abdomen. Anna supported her as best she could, until the contraction was over. "Oh," moaned Kate in agony, "that was a real beaut!" Sighing, she struggled to rise so that she could get into bed, but found it an almost impossible feat to accomplish.

"It's all right. Just take your time, dear." Kate leaned trustingly against Anna as she tried to catch her breath. Finally, with Anna's help, she was in bed. Again, Anna patted Kate's hand reassuringly. "I'll be right back. I'm going to get Doctor Phelps."

Kate was prevented from answering, for she writhed as another contraction washed over her. "Ah!" Anna waited until the contraction was over, and then rushed from the cabin in search of Doctor Phelps.

Throwing open the door to the infirmary, she rushed over to the orderly. "I need Doctor Phelps immediately!"

The orderly looked at Anna as if she were daft. "Doctor Phelps is not here."

"Then where can I find him?"

"Doctor Phelps rode out four hours ago to deliver Jessie Morgan's baby. I don't know when he'll be back." He went back to fussing with something on the counter, completely ignoring Anna.

Realizing she would get no help from the orderly, she wrung her hands in frustration. "Thank you," she offered in disgust. Turning, she rushed from the room, leaving the door wide open. When she was no longer in sight of the infirmary, she paused in an effort to try to collect her tangled thoughts. She was so angry with the orderly, frustrated with the situation, so scared for Kate that she had a hard time thinking clearly. All at once, she knew what to do. "I'll go to Jane. She'll know what to do." Without another thought, she hurried over to the Hansen's cabin. After knocking, Anna quickly burst into the room. Panting from the exertion, she struggled to get a deep breath. Not only that, but she had to wait until her eyes became adjusted to the bright light. Meanwhile, startled out of his wits, Henry threw his pipe into the ashtray, jumped hurriedly to his feet and started towards her.

Jane, gasping in shock, almost dropped the dishes that she was slipping into the dishpan. Wiping her hands anxiously on her apron, she, too, hurried toward Anna. "What's wrong? Why are you so upset?"

"It's ... it's ... Kate! She has gone into labor and Doctor Phelps is gone. The orderly told me he went to deliver Jessie Morgan's baby four hours ago. I need your help, Jane."

"You bet!" Jane removed her apron, throwing it across the back of a chair. "Just give me a moment to collect my things."

Anna nodded and watched her leave before turning toward Henry. "How are you tonight, Henry?"

He laughed lightly, then sighed in relief. "Now that the shock is over, I'm fine. In fact I'm as fine as frog's hair."

Anna smiled, feeling a little embarrassed. "Sorry about the scare, Henry."

As he smiled, she felt relieved. "No problem, Anna. Everybody needs woke up by a good scare ... once in a while. Keeps the old ticker in shape that way."

Anna stood looking at this "Rock of Gibraltar," who was always there for her when she needed help. He was tall, had broad shoulders and was solidly built. Long thick sideburns and bushy eyebrows now streaked with gray, enhanced what was left of his once thick golden curly hair. Wrinkles nearly obscured his merry deep-set hazel eyes when he smiled. A wide Roman nose accentuated kind, gentle features. Anna noticed that he was no longer dressed in his corporal's uniform, but he was wearing a blue-checked flannel shirt, rolled part way up the arm. Black suspenders held up his dark-blue trousers. She smiled to herself when she saw him standing there in his stocking feet.

Anna glanced quickly around the familiar room and asked, "Where is Sylvia?"

"Maude Tiddle asked her to care for their children while they went to see some people in the settlement."

"Oh." Anna started to say something else, but was prevented from doing so when Jane returned.

"I'm glad to see that you are bundled up well," declared Henry. "Don't want you catching your death of foolishness!"

Chuckling, Jane kissed Henry affectionately on the cheek. "I'll take good care of myself. I don't know when I'll be home, dear."

Slipping an arm around her, he patted her arm affectionately. "You just do what you have to do. Don't worry about us. We'll be just fine!"

"Thank you so much, Henry. I don't know what I'd do without Jane's stabilizing influence."

Henry held the door open for them as they walked out into the crisp night air. Shivering, Jane drew her shawl tighter around her. As the cold gripped her, Anna realized that she'd forgotten her shawl in her haste to get Doctor Phelps. Hugging her arms tightly to her, she began rubbing them vigorously in an attempt to keep warm. While they walked briskly toward Kate's cabin, Anna was grateful to be near her dear friend.

Jane Hansen, standing five feet tall, was a thin wisp of a lady. Her once golden hair, now streaked with gray, was pulled tightly back into one long braid down her back. A stubby hooked nose accentuated light-blue eyes. High gaunt cheekbones emphasized her protruding jaw connected to a pointed chin. These combinations made her taut features appear hard. Jane had on a solid-gray cotton dress set off by a wide crocheted collar. The simple bodice was gathered at the waist, with the slightly flared skirt flowing to her ankles. Long tapered sleeves were rolled up to the elbow. A frilly white crisply-starched apron covered the front of the dress.

All at once, Jane began to question her. "How long has Kate been in labor?"

"I really don't know. She seemed tired and pale when I saw her this morning, but I thought nothing of it. Then when I arrived for our prearranged dinner, she seemed to be in pain. That's when I really became worried about her. I told her that we could do this some other time, but she wouldn't hear of it." She paused thoughtfully for a moment, then went on. "All at once I noticed that she was not only as white as a sheet, but was biting her lower lip in an attempt to deal with the pain."

"Hum!" murmured Jane thoughtfully. "If I know Kate, and I do, she's probably been in labor for a while."

"I wouldn't be surprised! She always thinks of others instead of herself." Jane nodded "When I went to get Doctor Phelps, Jim Brolen, the orderly on duty, said he had no idea when he'd be back."

"I see." Jane fell thoughtfully silent.

They walked the rest of the short distance in silence, each lost in her own thoughts. Reaching the cabin, they entered without knocking. Removing her shawl, Jane laid it over a chair. Going to the counter, she got down the wash pan where she filled it with hot water from the reservoir. Turning and placing the pan onto the counter, she washed her hands thoroughly. Going into the bedroom to check on Kate, Anna found her moaning as well as writhing upon the bed as the pain gripped her.

Jane entered and quickly examined her. She looked up with a deep frown on her face. "She's more than ready, so things should be happening by now."

"Well, maybe you just didn't examine her right. Maybe you should check her again."

"Perhaps you're right." After re-examining her, Jane grew more perplexed. "The baby is not in the right position. I can't tell for sure, but I think it's breech." Anna looked anxiously from Kate to Jane. "Something just isn't right, but I'm not experienced enough to figure out what it is!" Anna turned visibly pale but didn't speak. All at once, Kate began to bear down as a new contraction came on. "Take it easy, honey. I know you feel like pushing, but you can't because the baby may be breech."

Kate obeyed at once, but struggled to endure the pain. Hours passed, and still there was no baby or relief from the pain. Jane tried unsuccessfully to turn the baby. Tears of frustration glistened in her eyes while beads of perspiration ran down her face. Finally in exasperation she stood up and left the room. As she washed and dried her hands, Jane tried to sort out her tangled thoughts. Seeing the mess on the floor, she quickly cleaned it up. After again washing her hands, she put away the food on the table but left the dishes. This small distraction helped calm her frayed nerves, so she washed her hands once more before going back into the bedroom. Anna turned thoughtfully to gaze at Jane as she entered the room but again remained silent.

"It's all right, dear. I just needed to get my mind focused again. Nodding, Anna turned to wring out a damp cloth.

Kate began to weave in and out of reality. There were times when she felt as though she were floating on an invisible river. She could feel its enormous power drawing her downward into its great dark murky depths. At other times she felt as though she were on fire as hot fingers of pain coursed through her pain ridden body, leaving her limp and drained. Again hot waves of searing pain surged through her tortured body. "Oh," she cried aloud, "it hurts so much!"

"I know, honey, but you have to hang in there." Anna gently bathed her face with a cool damp cloth, while speaking soothing words of comfort.

A great longing to see Paul filled Kate until she felt she couldn't endure it. In her delirium she began to writhe, moan, or cry out, "Where is Paul? Will he be here in time? He said he would be." Great gulfs of despair washed over her as ever-present waves of pain surged through her. "Paul! Where are you, Paul?" She pleaded with such longing, such anguish that it tore at the hearts of her friends. As time passed, Kate grew more anxious. "Paul! Paul, where are you?" Sobbing brokenly, the tears rolled unheeded down her ashen cheeks. Kate began thrashing around. Anna tried to reassure her, but Kate was past listening. Each contraction became more unbearable.

Floating in and out of consciousness, Kate was no longer aware of what was real or what wasn't. Distorted images began to weave in and out of her troubled mind. She heard someone telling her to hang in there, but she couldn't figure out to whom the voice belonged, nor did she understand why she wanted her to hang in there.

Oblivious to the pain, Kate found herself walking effortlessly through a lush green meadow filled with a vast assortment of exquisite wild flowers. Kneeling upon the ground, she picked a bouquet and pressed the flowers to her nose to drink of their robust, titillating aroma. Raising her head, she gazed in awe at the opulent rainbow of colors before her. Glancing at the bouquet in her hands, she began to examine the flowers closely. Such illustrious vibrant colors, whose beauty defied all description, affected her as never before. As she gazed hungrily around, a peace beyond anything she had previously experienced filled her being. A gentle breeze played with her long auburn hair, causing strands of it to tickle her face. Rising, she continued to investigate her surroundings, marveling at how easily she moved. I'm as free as a bird in flight, she thought. How can this be? Scrutinizing the perfection of her hands, Kate was surprised because the scars or flaws were no longer there. She struggled to learn what it meant.

Realizing that someone was calling her name, Kate turned slowly to the left, then to the right, but no one was there. Hearing her name called once more, she turned to look behind her giving a jubilant cry of joy. Kate called back, "Momma!" With outstretched arms, she ran eagerly toward her mother.

The woman quickly raised her hands. "Stop where you are!"

Bemused, she stopped. Lowering her arms, Kate waited expectantly. Like a panorama, the events of Kate's past began to unfold before her, revealing both the good as well as the bad she had ever done. Everything was there for her to scrutinize in great detail. Kate sighed in relief as the scenes finally came to a close, for she knew that she had nothing of which to be ashamed. Going expectantly toward her mother, who was gazing at her lovingly, Kate waited for a sign that it was all right for her to approach. An illuminating smile spread across Sarah's face as she reached out hungrily for her. With a glad little cry, Kate rushed eagerly into those loving, outstretched arms. Oh, how sweet was Kate's joy, as those loving arms enveloped her. Finally, stepping back from the embrace, she studied the blessed face before her. How long she stood there, Kate never knew nor really cared. Clasping Kate's hand, Sara gently pulled her forward.

Meanwhile, Jane grew more desperate as the situation continued to worsen. Looking at the clock on the dresser, she was amazed to see that it was four o'clock in the morning. "If something isn't done soon, we are going to lose Kate." All at once, the door burst open. Doctor Phelps entered. Taking off his coat, he lifted the lid on the stove to build a fire. Checking to see that there was plenty of water in the reservoir, he turned the damper. Taking the washbowl from the counter, he filled it with hot water. After washing his hands thoroughly, he placed his instruments into a pot of water, which he put on the stove. Satisfied there was nothing else he could do, he went into the bedroom to examine Kate.

A sigh of relief crossed Jane's face when he entered the room. "The baby is breech. If that isn't enough, something else is terribly wrong." Phelps grunted then concentrated on the task before him. "I tried to turn the baby, but it was impossible."

Phelps began to bark orders that kept both women hopping for a long time. Finally, when they'd despaired of saving the baby, it emerged into the world. The baby, a boy, was in great stress as the cord was wrapped around his neck twice. Doctor Phelps worked quickly over the baby, while Jane gathered the items needed to care for him. Meanwhile, Anna continued to bathe Kate's face. Finally, tipping the baby over, he gave him a good swat on the behind. Nothing happened, so he checked the baby over, again. Tipping him, he swatted his behind once more. A lusty cry rent the air … a wonderful sound to all present. Doctor Phelps handed the baby to Jane to care for, then continued to work over Kate.

A strange expression spread across his face, and then a wide grin softened the weary, haggard lines. "I thought as much, but now, I know for sure!"

Placing the baby in the crib, Jane walked over to join him. "What's wrong?" She peered over his shoulder, straining to see. All at once, she gasped in stunned disbelief. "Doctor, it's …"

Anna grew alarmed as she looked from Phelps to Jane. "I don't understand what's happening."

Phelps chuckled softly and nodded. "You will in a little bit, Anna. Just keep talking to her." Ignoring the women, he tended to Kate's needs.

Kate, unaware of the conversation going on around her, wondered why her mother was leading her away from the meadow. All at once, she heard a baby crying from somewhere close by. Pulling away from her mother, she started to follow the sound. A force mightier than she knew was drawing her nearer the sound. Sarah called to her softly, and Kate turned and began to walk with her once more.

Again, Kate heard a baby crying; only this time it seemed even closer. Turning toward the sound, Kate couldn't find anything. When the baby continued to cry, she grew concerned. *Something is terribly wrong,* she thought. *Why don't they take care of it?* Kate turned to gaze questioningly at her mother, but she only stood there, waiting patiently for Kate to decide what she should do.

Turning once more to the crying child, Kate saw a woman holding a newborn infant in her arms. As the vision became clearer, she saw herself lying on the bed. Jane was holding her child. All at once Kate became unsure of what to do. Gazing at her mother, she felt she was being given the choice of going with her mother, or returning to help Paul raise their child. The scene changed, revealing Paul sitting on a chair, his elbows resting on his knees with his head in his hands. There was such agony and such longing on his face that love as well as compassion swelled within her. She could not go with her mother but must return.

Turning to express her decision, she was surprised to see her mother smiling. She knows! Kate was gazing lovingly at her mother, as if to take the memory back with her, when something distracted her. When she turned back to her mother, she was gone.

From some deep recess in her mind, Kate became aware of voices. Someone was persistently calling her name. Kate struggled to follow the voice, but it took too much effort. She grew impatient, thinking why don't they just leave me alone? Why don't they just let me sleep? Again, someone called her name. Struggling desperately to identify the voice, it became clearer.

"Oh, please come back to us, Kate. You have so much to live for."

All at once Kate recognized Anna's voice, pleading with her to return. Kate struggled to let Anna know that she heard her, but she felt weighted down, unable to speak. Following Anna's voice, she slowly began the long climb upward through the deepest depths of darkness with murky shadows until she could feel warmth upon her face. The pain was no longer intolerable, yet Kate found it difficult to open her eyes. Slowly, she opened them to gaze into the worried faces of her dear friends. Although she heard a baby crying from somewhere nearby, the reality of it all didn't sink in.

Anna excitedly hugged Kate to her in a warm embrace. "Oh, my dear, dear girl! You're going to be just fine!" Kate smiled at Anna weakly, then closed her eyes. She longed to slip back into the other place, but Anna wouldn't let her. Kate listened to Anna's soothing gentle words of comfort, until blessed sleep claimed her.

When Kate opened her eyes some time later, she felt much stronger. Anna was still sitting by her bedside and sunlight streamed in from the crack in the curtains. Anna grinned. "Well, sleepy head, welcome back!" Kate could only smile weakly at Anna. "You have someone here, who's waiting to meet you."

Kate blinked in surprise. "I do?"

"You surely do!" Both women chuckled as Jane laid first one, then another baby into Kate's arms. Doctor Phelps, a pleased look on his face, was leaning against the doorway of the bedroom.

Kate looked first at one, then the other in surprise. "I have twins?" She was so surprised that she didn't know what else to say. Realizing it was true, a smile slowly spread across her face. "Well ... how about that? I ... Kate Thompson ... the mother of twins!" Lovingly, she tenderly kissed their tiny cheeks.

"A boy and a girl," said Jane proudly. "A right handsome pair!" Puffing out her chest, she began imitating the Irish Brogue. "E'en if I do say so meself!" Everyone burst out laughing at her strange antics.

Moving from the doorway, Phelps walked over to Kate. "Well ... we all agree that you pulled a real surprise on us!" Kate smiled as he squeezed her hand gently. He moved back to stand by the two women. "Let's give this mother some peace while she gets to know these wee tykes, as she'll no doubt be callin' them." He winked at the two women before following them from the room.

An impish gleam came into Kate's eyes. "Wait, Doctor Phelps."

He stepped anxiously back into the room. "Yes."

"I'll be havin ye know thet I'll be callin' them me wee bairns."

Phelps grinned, shook his head as he started out of the room. Grumbling under his breath he said, "Just like a woman ... always has to have the last word in everything!"

Jane smiled impishly. "Always!"

"Women! There's no living with them!"

Gazing lovingly at her babies, Kate couldn't get over the surprise. Love along with pride flowed through her as she watched them sleep. *Wait until Paul returns,* she thought. *Won't he be surprised?* She smiled at the image of Paul's reaction. The smile faded, as she wondered why he wasn't there. Jane returned to put the infants back into their beds. Tears glistened in Kate's eyes, as she watched Jane work.

Seeing the unshed tears, Jane anxiously peered into her face. "What's wrong, honey?"

"I was just thinking of Paul. I was wondering why he isn't here."

"Don't go worrying your pretty head about the Captain, honey ... He'll be back before you know it."

"But, something must have happened, or he would have been here."

"Sometimes they're gone a long time when they're out on maneuvers, so please don't worry, or you'll make yourself sick."

"Perhaps you're right." Kate wasn't convinced, but she let Jane make her comfortable.

"Aren't I always?"

An impish gleam came into Kate's eyes. "Well ..."

"Don't you answer that," quipped Jane.

Giggling, Kate nestled deeper under the covers. Sighing, she was asleep before Jane left the room.

When the baby girl was born, there was no bed for her, so Jane had quickly pulled out a dresser drawer. Emptying the contents onto the top of the dresser after putting a pillow in the bottom, she prepared it as though it were a regular cradle. Tucking the covers around Kate, Jane vowed to find another cradle with more baby clothes as soon as it was possible. Satisfied that all was well, she went to join the others.

Doctor Phelps was drinking a cup of coffee. Anna was standing at the stove cooking some bacon and eggs. Jane sniffed the air appreciatively. "That smells heavenly, dear."

Anna beamed. "Thank you. When I learned that Doctor Phelps hadn't eaten since lunch time yesterday, I decided he deserved a decent meal."

Jane turned to look critically at Doctor Phelps. He raised a hand of protest when she started to speak. "I know that I should take better care of myself, but I didn't have time to eat before going out to deliver Jesse's baby. When I got back to the fort, I learned that Kate was in labor. I hurried over here as soon as I could."

Jane softened visibly. "Oh, all right. I guess you do have a good excuse for not eating."

Phelps exaggeratedly wiped his brow. "Phew! For a moment there, I thought you were about to give me one of your famous Irish blessings!"

"I was. However, since you saved Kate's life, I'll forgive you." She ruffled his hair, as she walked past him.

"Ah," he cried in mock pain, "Ya just messed up my beauty." He patted his head as if to put his hair back into place.

Jane burst out laughing at his antics. Unable to resist the chance to tease, she hastily added: "What beauty?"

He leaned forward to pout, "Now ya done it! I don't think I'll wait for that delicious smelling breakfast if I have to put up with the likes of you!"

"Ah," cried Jane with a toss of her head, "you're just feeling sorry for yourself again. You get a good breakfast into ya, and there'll be no livin' with ya!"

That was too much for Phelps, who burst out laughing good-naturedly. "I never could put one over on you, Jane Hansen!"

"I'm always surprised that you even try." They all guffawed. Soon thereafter Anna announced that breakfast was ready. When they were seated at the table, Anna blessed the food. They soon made short work of the meal.

When he was done, Phelps leaned back in his chair to pat his stomach. "I think I'll live now." He sighed in satisfaction. "For a while, I do believe my stomach thought my throat had been cut!"

Jane shook her head, "Sometimes I wonder about you."

"Good! That means I always have at least one ace up my sleeve."

Anna shook her head hopelessly. "I don't know about the two of you. From the way you two act, you'd think you were bitter enemies or something."

"Not us! Why, this here is one of my favorite girls."

Jane beamed, then grew serious. "I don't want to be a wet blanket to all of this fun, but we do have a problem." Phelps and Anna turned expectantly. "We need another cradle as well as some more baby clothes."

Phelps nodded thoughtfully while rubbing his chin. "I'll check around today. There may be someone in the settlement that has a crib. I think I know of someone, but I need to make sure before I say anything." Both women nodded understandingly. "I'll get back to you as soon as possible." Sighing, he rose to go. Turning to Anna, he rubbed his stomach appreciatively. "That was one of the best meals I've ever eaten! Thank you, for the belly timber, Anna. I greatly appreciate what you've done for me."

Anna smiled, pleased at the praise Phelps paid her, "You're more than welcome, Doctor."

Nodding, he strode to the door and picked up his medical bag. Opening the door, he replied, "See you both later."

"Hey, mister, you can't leave yet!"

Phelps turned back to stare at Jane in surprise. "I can't? Why ever not?"

"In all of the hubbub, you forgot to tell us what the Morgan's had ... a boy or a girl!"

An amused smile tugged at the corners of his lips. "They had a healthy baby girl. Both mother and daughter are doing fine." Turning, he walked out, closing the door behind him.

When the women had tidied up the house, they cooked a meal for Kate to have later on. By the time they were finished with everything, it was four o'clock in the afternoon. It had been a long, frightening night for them both. No friend could have been more loved than Kate was by these two great women.

Jane sighed wearily. "I've got to go home for a little while to take care of my family." She removed her wrap from the hook near the door. "I'll send Sylvia over to stay with you until I can get things under control." Anna nodded, watching Jane leave.

A few minutes later, Sylvia knocked softly, then entered. Gazing at her daughter with pride, Anna couldn't help but stare. Long straight chestnut hair framed her oval face. A spattering of freckles ran across her delicately-shaped cheekbones and tiny button nose. Soft hazel eyes, thinly-shaped red lips, and a protruding chin all flattered her pale porcelain features. Sylvia, who stood four feet eleven inches tall, was very petite. She was dressed in a light green dress, which was adorned with a white crocheted lace collar. The straight-fitting bodice had long sleeves which tapered to the wrist. The full ankle-length skirt gathered at the waist. Black button-topped shoes stuck out from under the skirt.

Anna smiled sweetly at the young woman, "Good afternoon, Sylvia. Thank you for coming to stay with me."

"That's no problem. I'm really happy to do it." She looked toward the bedroom. "Ma said that Mrs. Thompson had twins. Do you think I could see them?"

"I don't see why not."

She had just tiptoed into the bedroom, when there was another knock at the door. When Anna answered it, she was surprised to see Doctor Phelps standing there. Stepping to the side, she motioned to him to enter. "Hi, Doctor. Won't you please come in?"

"I'll be right back." Turning, he headed toward his spring wagon. Sylvia emerged from the bedroom as he returned, carrying a cradle, which he placed in the living room. "Would you mind helping me, Sylvia?"

She smiled amiably. "I'd be happy to help you, Doctor Phelps." They made several trips to the wagon, each time laden down with baby things.

Anna stood staring at them aghast as they entered with the last load. "My goodness ... what did you do, Doctor ... rob a store?"

Throwing his head back, Phelps roared. "No. I went to see George Fredrickson today." He paused long enough to empty his arms. "Do you remember about a month ago when his wife, Rachel and their baby died during child birth?"

"Yes."

"Well, I took the chance that George might still have everything. George said that he'd been wondering what to do with these things. It seems that he was getting rid of a lot of unnecessary items because he was selling out. He and his brother, Joseph, are going to leave as soon as they get their affairs in order."

"Do they know where they are going?"

"They said they were going somewhere back East. George said they would decide that as they travel along."

"I see." Sighing deeply, Anna began sorting through the items on the table. Phelps helped them scrub the cradle. When they were finished, Anna placed a crib sheet in it. Anna lifted the baby out of the drawer so that Phelps could empty it. After placing the drawer back into the dresser, he put the cradle in its place. He watched, as Anna laid the sleeping baby in the cradle then tenderly covered her up. Kate stirred, but didn't wake up as they quietly left the room.

Jane returned as they emerged from the bedroom. After she sent Sylvia home, Jane wanted to know where everything came from, so Phelps filled her in. She shook her head as she listened to Phelps's account of George Fredrickson. "Saints be praised! God surely moves in mysterious ways, doesn't he?"

Phelps shrugged his shoulders nonchalantly. "Can't prove that by me!"

They all turned in surprise as the door burst open. Major Thornton angrily entered. Jane glared at Thornton in disgust as he surveyed the room's occupants. "Haven't you ever learned to knock before entering a room, Major?"

Thornton was a large burly man who stood six feet tall. He had closely-set, beady, light-gray eyes that were cold and calculating, and stared hawk-like under his bushy gray eyebrows. What was left of his hair was lightly peppered with gray. A day's growth of black stubble caused his face to appear dirty. It made his nasty disposition more repulsive. The once immaculate uniform was streaked with dirt. He didn't even have enough respect to remove his dirty hat. The cords along his thick neck bulged, while his face grew red with unspent rage as he attempted to remain cool. Failing miserably, he turned to look at Jane contemptuously. Phelps saw something akin to hatred cross his face.

"What a cozy little party we have here." He gazed around the room in disgust. "Where's your nosey friend, now? Leaving you in the lurch like all brain dead scallywags?" Laughing fiendishly at his own private joke, he stomped haughtily over, bellowing to Anna, "What are you doing here at this time of day?" Before Anna could reply, Thornton grabbed her roughly by the arm, pulling her towards the door. "You're coming home now!" Seeing Jane's expression of hate, as she stood with her hands on her hips, he laughed sadistically, then curling his upper lip said, "Don't you know better than to hang around where you're not wanted, wench? But then maybe you've lost your way home." Condescendingly, tossing his head sideways in disgust, he hastened to add, "You women are all alike! The only good woman is a dead woman!"

Doctor Phelps rose to confront Thornton, but Jane beat him to the draw. Rising to her full height, she took a deep breath to gain control of her emotions, as she calmly faced him. Glaring at him with something akin to loathing, she began to give him a piece of her mind. "You're not worth the powder and dynamite it would take to blow you to hell and back, Carl Thornton! Nor are you sane enough to call the kettle black! Not that it's any of your business, but we've been here all night, and all day, helping Doctor Phelps deliver twins." At his blank stare, she smiled as though placating a naughty child. "Why don't you go where you're wanted, Mr.? But, then again … sir … I doubt that you could ever begin to find out where that is!"

For a moment, Thornton struggled with the thought of striking her. "Why you lowdown, good-for-nothing, filthy wench!" He was prevented from saying more when the door flew open.

Turning to see who it was, Jane failed to see the look of pure hatred that crossed Thornton's face. A glad little cry escaped her as she saw Captain Thompson standing in the doorway. "Oh, won't Kate be surprised!" Grabbing his arm, she pulled him inside before Thornton could protest. "Come, I'll take you to Kate." Thompson looked inquisitively at each one as they left the room.

As Paul gazed down at the sleeping infants, his mouth gaped open in shock. "I'll be a monkey's uncle," he whispered. Grabbing the startled Jane in a hearty embrace, he kissed her hard upon the cheek. "I've got twins!" He kissed Jane's scarlet face again before releasing her. Growing serious, he went to Kate's side, leaned over to kiss her tenderly upon the forehead.

Slowly, Kate opened her eyes, blinked a couple of times in an attempt to get fully awake. She gazed intently into Paul's eyes. As recognition crossed her face, she raised her arms hungrily to embrace him. "Oh, Paul, you're finally here!" Jane left the room as Paul gently took Kate into his arms.

She was in time to see Thornton roughly pull Anna from the house. "Come on, you hag, let's leave this dump!" Jane started forward, but Phelps signaled for her to remain where she was. Sighing, Jane complied, though it took all her strength to do so. Anna cried out in pain as Thornton half dragged her from the house.

Jane stared angrily after them. "That fiend!"

Phelps gently patted Jane's shoulder. "I know."

She studied his face intently. "Why did you stop me?"

"If you had interfered, he might have hurt her more … but then perhaps he will anyway." Sighing, Jane allowed him to lead her out onto the porch to give Paul and Kate some privacy. Tender were the moments that followed for the little family.

CHAPTER 8

Making New Friends

Walking outside after the conference with Colonel Williams, John blinked several times in an attempt to adjust his eyes to the sunlight. All at once he felt someone standing beside him, so he took a deep breath of the fresh air before slowly turning to see who was there. John felt nervous as he looked into Sergeant Aimes' suspicious-looking eyes, then decided that the best thing he could do was to stand his ground. "Can I help you, sir?"

Aimes glared angrily at John. "What are you doing with all of those horses? Most especially, why do you have Corporal Maines' horse?"

John watched Aimes closely to see what he intended. Aimes' uniform was immaculate. His boots were shined to perfection. His coal-black hair was not only straight, but also unruly. John watched him impatiently remove his hat, push a lock of hair back from his face, then replace the hat. His dark-brown eyes were set wide apart, obscured by thick eyebrows, knit tightly together. A thick slightly hooked nose with a protruding jaw, set and defiant, caused John to shiver in spite of the late afternoon heat. Sergeant Mitchel Aimes was not ugly by any stretch of the imagination, yet his nasty disposition caused him to appear so. As Aimes stood impatiently tapping a riding crop against his leg, he glared at John with every muscle taut. John, who thought him cold ... even calculating, didn't trust him.

"I don't see that it is any of your business, sir."

Aimes' face reddened with anger. He clenched then unclenched his fist as he struggled to control his temper. Somehow after several moments, he managed to remain calm. "I don't like sassy brats who are still wet behind the ears!" Fiery darts of light leaped from his cold, calculating eyes. Suddenly he began to taunt John, "It's apparent that you have no respect for your elders, sonny." He stepped toward John, who stood his ground by leering back at him. "Perhaps you need to be taught a lesson or two!" He jerked John's arm in an attempt to drag him away.

John visibly jumped when he heard a deep booming voice close by. "That will be quite enough of that, Sergeant!" Aimes released John as though he were a hot potato then flipped around to see who was behind him. When Major Brown stepped forward, Aimes looked like a whipped puppy.

Aimes jumped to attention, "Beggin' yer pardon, sir, but we were just talking."

"I heard your conversation, Sergeant, so spare me!"

"Yes, sir."

Gone was the easy mannered gentleman John had met inside the colonel's office. In its place was a confident, authoritative figure that wasn't afraid to speak out. John liked him more at that moment than when he'd first met him. "Get your gear and be back here ready to ride in twenty-five minutes, Sergeant."

Aimes saluted. "Yes, sir!" Pivoting on his right foot, he fled.

Major Brown turned to John, smiling politely, "You must guard your back at all times, friend." John, swallowing past the lump in his throat, could only nod. "Sergeant Aimes is not a patient man at the best of times."

"Thank you, Major Brown. I appreciate your advice." He paused a moment before adding, "I'll remember to do just that!"

Brown tapped John hard on the shoulder. "I hope we meet under better circumstances, John. I like your spunk!"

John smiled in spite of himself. "Thank you, sir."

Brown nodded. "Goodbye for now!" Turning he sauntered off.

John watched until he was out of sight and then went to check on his horses. John was so bone-tired that it was all he could do to function. *Oh, what I wouldn't give for one good night's rest,* he thought. Sighing, he headed toward the stables. A stable boy saw him as he entered the stables, but was so busy that he only nodded. John didn't mind, as he was interested in the proceedings.

Glancing around, John noticed that many horses were saddled, waiting to be led out. A couple of privates entered the stable to help the stable hands lead the horses out to the waiting men. For a while, everything seemed so chaotic that John didn't have a chance to look for his horses. However, he did notice that the horses he'd brought to the fort were placed into stalls. They also had been rubbed down. Being concerned about Old Baldy, John began to walk down the row of stalls.

The stable was huge, housing a great quantity of horses. With only a few hands working in the stable, John was amazed at how quickly the work got done. There was an enormous tack room off to the right, which not only fascinated him, but also made him yearn to explore it. Deciding that he'd better tend to his own business, he didn't go inside. Finding Old Baldy resting comfortably in a stall, John stroked his neck affectionately before walking over to the young stable boy.

The short thin lad, who was near John's own age, had brown curly hair that stuck out from under his dirty hat. Streaks of dirt ran down his suntanned face. Captivating dark-blue eyes twinkled merrily. John noticed that the boy's bib overalls, streaked with sweat mingled with dirt, were too big for him. He also noticed that the legs of the overalls had been rolled up a few turns. His dirty plaid gray shirt was faded, patched and worn. Both also had the sleeves rolled part way up the arm.

John smiled as the boy sauntered confidently over to him. "Hello, I'm John Whipple."

He shook John's hand vigorously. "Howdy. Name's Joshua Taylor."

"Pleased to make your acquaintance."

"Hey, that was some string of horses you brought in! I especially like that gelding in the stall over there. He's a real beaut!"

"Yeah, he is." John intently looked the boy over. "Say Joshua …"

"Just call me Josh," interrupted the lad. "Everyone else does!"

"Very well, Josh. Have you seen my saddle horse or the horse I used as a pack animal?"

Josh scratched his head thoughtfully, replaced his hat then looked at John. "I saw the sergeant move them just after you got here. I think he moved them to the corral at the back of the stable. Said he thought you ought to look for them a spell." John's eyebrows knit together in concern. Josh thoughtfully started moving to the back of the stables. "I thought I'd get them when he was gone, but then our boss came into the stable in a great huff and told us to get eighteen horses saddled for some kind of maneuver." He paused a moment, then sighed apologetically. "Sorry, but I got so busy that I clean forgot about them."

"It isn't your fault, Josh. I'm just trying to figure the sergeant out. For the life of me, I don't know why he should be so nasty. Why, I don't even know him."

"No one knows why Sergeant Aimes acts the way he does!" Josh shook his head in disgust. "Then again, he is a creep all the time." A look of pure disgust flashed across his face. He stopped at the door at the back of the stables to face John. "I have always tried to stay out of his way as much as possible." He started to push the door open then paused again to face John. "I once saw him lay into a feller just because he didn't like the way he did something. Boy, did he ever lose it! Aimes called the feller an imbecile, a lop-eared, empty-headed, mangy jackass. He went on to call him some words I wouldn't want my own dear grandmother to hear."

"Sounds like a real peach of a guy to me!"

"Ya, right!" It was plain that neither meant their statements to be complimentary. "If his nasty disposition weren't enough, there's the company he keeps."

"What do you mean?"

"Well, for one thing, he's always following Corporal Maines around like some lovesick puppy dog." John jerked as though he'd been slapped at the mere mention of the name. He was relieved when Josh didn't notice. "I think I dislike the Corporal most of all!" Josh spit emphatically on the ground at his side. "That man is not only mean, but rotten clean through. I don't think very many of the men like him, other than Sergeant Aimes." *You can add my name to the list of those who don't like him,* thought John. "But this isn't finding your horses, is it?"

"No, it isn't."

Josh pushed the doors open, "Come on, let's see where your horses are."

John followed close behind, his thoughts running rampant as he tried to sort out all that Josh had told him. John blinked as they walked out into the sunlight. Both of the young men had to wait for their eyes to adjust to the bright light. When their eyes had adjusted to the light, they went in search of the horses.

Anger welled up inside of John when he saw the horses tied to a stake near a large dung heap. They were tangled up in the lead rope so tightly that their heads were bowed. To make matters worse, Blacky was still wearing the saddle. The other still had a pack on. As the two men rushed to untie the horses, John noticed that a great swarm of flies were driving them crazy.

"Poor things!"

Blacky nickered softly, as did the sorrel mare, when they drew closer. The two men worked as fast as they could to untie the horses, then led them to the stable to care for them. John took the saddle off Blacky, while Josh removed the pack from the mare. They then began to rub them down vigorously. Blacky quivered in appreciation as John worked over him. He talked soothingly to Blacky while raging anger battled inside at the cruel treatment given.

As Josh rubbed down the packhorse, he studied the animal intently. All at once he stepped back from the horse. "I've got it!"

John turned from working on Blacky. "What have you got?"

"I kept thinking that I've seen this horse before," Scratching his chin, he continued to study the horse. "I couldn't believe it was the same horse I've taken care of many times."

John grew frustrated. "Well man ... Are you going to leave me in suspense?"

Josh laughed and turned to face John. "This horse belongs to a wealthy rancher, named Jason Walters. He lives on a huge ranch on the other side of Missoula. I've never been there, but I heard that it is a great distance from here." He paused a moment, then staring intently at John said, "Why do you have this horse, John?"

"It's a long story, Josh, but right now I don't have time to go into it." Josh wisely refrained from speaking. "When I can, I'll fill you in on everything." Josh nodded absently, as he continued to work on the mare. For a time, neither spoke. Both became preoccupied with their own thoughts. Finally, curiosity got the better of John, "Is Walter's ranch located near Fort Owen?"

"No. I think it's found somewhere around three miles from Superior."

"I see." John thoughtfully continued to work on Blacky.

Josh was silent a long time. All at once, he began to speak. "I've heard some of the men talk about how Mr. Walters has been pressuring some of the ranchers over towards Fort Owen to sell him their lands." John turned toward Josh, growing fascinated by what he had to say. "I don't know if any have sold out to him, though." John began to see the picture clearly now, but kept his comments to himself. Shrugging, Josh patted the mare absently. "There's probably nothing to the story though."

John watched as Josh finished rubbing the horse. The horse, a beautiful sorrel mare, was solidly built. As Josh led her toward an empty stall, she lifted her head proudly, then slightly nudged him in the back. Josh nearly tripped over his own feet when the mare nickered softly. She nudged him again. Josh took out a carrot from the pocket of his overalls, placed it in his hand then held it out to her. John chuckled when she greedily accepted the carrot and quickly ate it.

Josh chided her, while gently rubbing her neck. "You old beggar! I'd be mighty proud to own a horse like you." After leading the horse to a stall, he motioned to the stall nearby. "Put your horse in this here stall." Looking from Blacky to the mare, he smiled. "After his trying ordeal, he deserves to be next to this beauty!"

John smiled when he realized that Blacky would also be near Old Baldy. "Thank you, Josh. That'll put him between the beauty and the beast!"

Josh scratched his head, clearly puzzled. "Between the beauty and the beast? What are you talking about, man?"

"Look in the other stall."

Josh whistled when he caught sight of Old Baldy. "I say there, old man, what is this creature?"

John laughed good-naturedly. "I think it's a horse, although he is so old, scarred, sway backed that no one knows for sure."

"You sure could have fooled me!" Slowly, walking around the horse, he shook his head in disgust. "This old beast should have been put out of his misery long before this. How did you come to get this beast anyhow?"

Thoughts of Major Thornton's treatment of animals made him angry. "The major at Fort Owen is a mean spiteful man, who thinks nothing at all of using Old Baldy. His pitiful condition didn't matter in the least."

Josh snorted disgustedly. "Reminds me of Corporal Maines, it does!"

"When I went to get a packhorse, this is what I was given." Josh just nodded sadly. "Thanks for helping me rub the mare down, Josh."

Josh stepped back from Old Baldy's stall. "Not a problem."

Looking at his watch, John realized that it was nearly time to meet Colonel Williams. "Thanks again, Josh. With a wave of his hand, he called out, "See you soon." Turning, he sprinted out of the stables.

Colonel Williams emerged as John drew near. "You're just in time, Whipple. It's this way to my home." Smiling, he took John's arm to turn him in the direction he wanted.

They walked in silence for a while, then John began to speak. "Sir, are you sure it won't be an imposition having me there?"

"Not at all, son." A smile tugged at the corner of the Colonel's mouth. "Just wait until you meet the missus. She'll put your mind to rest."

John sighed, grateful for the Colonel's generosity. "Thank you, sir."

It wasn't long until they entered the Colonel's home. JaNae met them at the door. When she saw John, she clapped her hands excitedly. "Why, bless my soul, Jedidiah. What a pleasure to have company!" She bustled around John like a protective old mother hen.

JaNae Williams was a thin wisp of a woman, who bubbled with life. Her thick black hair was tightly pulled back into a bun at the nape of her neck. Her beautiful dark brown eyes flashed from under thinly-shaped eyebrows as well as through long silky lashes. Her deep dusky-brown complexion was flawless. A small well-shaped nose and a soft jaw line added to her beauty, as did her full lips, which parted to reveal perfect white teeth. Her rich full-throated laugh tinkled like silver bells. JaNae had on a light-green dress, which gathered at the waist and flowed to her ankles. Ruffles at the bottom of the full skirt added to the beauty and charm of the dress. The bodice had a white ruffled V front, with sleeves that puffed at the shoulders tapering to the wrist. Dainty light-green slippers peered out from beneath the dress. John thought she was very beautiful.

"Now, Ma," chided Williams. "Don't fuss so!" It was evident to John that Colonel Williams adored his beautiful wife, as she did him. It touched him deeply to see them fussing over each other.

Chuckling, JaNae stood upon her tiptoes to kiss her husband gently upon the lips. Williams beamed, then pretended to be embarrassed, but John saw right through the ploy. He found himself smiling, immediately feeling at ease around them. "Show our guest to his room, Jedidiah, while I get supper onto the table." Without waiting for a reply, she hurried off toward the kitchen.

Smiling good-naturedly, the colonel turned back to John. "Come on, Whipple, I'll show you where you'll bunk."

John was taken to a beautiful room off to the right. He noticed that the room was small, yet well decorated. The bed situated to the left was simply decorated with a blue comforter. A small round wooden table, upon which sat a decorative oil lamp atop a white crocheted doily, stood next to the bed. There was a handcrafted wooden chair positioned close by. One long window, adorned with frilly lace curtains, was found above the table. The tall wide mahogany-colored, crudely designed bureau, decorated with another white crocheted doily, was found to the right of the door.

"What a lovely room, sir! Thank you for allowing me to stay here."

"You're more than welcome, son." Williams noticed that John was empty handed. "What did you do with your gear?"

"I left it in the tack room of the stables.'

"Perhaps you'd better get it. I think it would be better to keep it in your room." John nodded, making a mental note to get it after dinner. "I think you have time before dinner to fetch it, but you better snap to it."

"Right away, sir."

Rushing from the house, he ran to the stables. John was leaning against a stall, still struggling to get a decent breath, when Josh came out of one of the other stalls.

"You forget something?"

"No. I just came to get my gear."

Josh nodded, leading the way to the tack room. "I'll help you carry it back to the colonel's." Opening the door to the tack room he entered, with John following close behind.

John noticed that the tack room was neat, not only orderly, but with everything in its place. It had also been labeled for easy access. Anything and everything needed to run the stables efficiently was stored there. He was amazed at how much more orderly this tack room was, compared to the one at Fort Owen.

Between the two of them, they were able to carry everything back to John's room at the Colonel's home. JaNae asked Josh to stay for dinner, but he declined saying that he had to finish his jobs that he had back at the stables.

"Sit down and eat before everything gets cold," called JaNae as John emerged from the bedroom.

The dining area just off from the kitchen was simply decorated. In the middle of the room was a round oak table with claw feet, and six matching chairs. A white crocheted tablecloth set off the blue design in the china pattern. Gazing down at the table's place setting, he thought the design on the china was the most exquisite he had ever seen. He was reminded of the simple, yet serviceable dishes back home. His attention was drawn to a long oak sideboard at the right of the room, laden down with covered dishes that John guessed were part of dinner. On a green glass cake plate sat a cake decorated with white frosting.

Above the sideboard was a large landscape painting, which added to the room's beauty. To the left was a large oak buffet, decorated with another crocheted doily with a few knickknacks. An oak china cabinet, filled with china, was found near the buffet. A rug braided from multi-colored material covered the floor.

An unlit, decorative lantern hung from a beam in the ceiling. As they gathered around the table, John marveled at the meal before him. Taking a bite, he sighed appreciatively, thinking he'd never tasted food such as this before. "This is delicious, ma'am! Could you tell me how this is made, so that I can get Ma to fix it sometime?" JaNae beamed with pleasure. "I've never eaten anything so delicious, and Ma's a great cook, too!"

It was plain to see that she was deeply touched by John's compliment, "Why, thank you, Mr. Whipple. What a sweet compliment!"

Before either could discuss the different dishes, Colonel Williams gazing proudly at his wife started to speak, "JaNae is from France, John. The food you are eating is French cuisine." John's eyes widened with surprise. "Let's see … the soup is French onion, and the bread and the main course are from an old French recipe. The dessert is also a wonderful French delicacy." It was plain to see that Colonel Williams was proud of his wife's culinary skills. JaNae eyed her husband appreciatively as he sang her praises.

John leaned back in his chair, a teasing light in his eyes. "You know, Colonel, I just figured out why you're so jovial!"

Williams stared at John suspiciously. "Oh, you do, do you!"

John nodded then leaned forward. "Yes, sir! Not only do you have a beautiful gracious wife, but she is a great cook. She's an interior decorator as well!"

JaNae beamed at the high praise bestowed her, which caused the colonel to chuckle good-naturedly. "I've been had!" He winked at John, then looked over at JaNae with a mischievous gleam in his eyes. "Don't compliment her too much, Whipple, or there'll be no living with her."

"Well, I never!" JaNae looked indignant, until Williams burst out laughing, then joined in. A tiny smile began to tug at the corner of John's lips, as he watched their jovial bantering. When the meal was over, the men retired to the living room, while JaNae did up the dinner dishes.

John noticed that the living room was just as elaborately decorated as the dining room had been. A piano stood along the wall between the two bedroom doors. It, too, was adorned with a white crocheted dresser scarf, which ran the full length of the piano. In the center was a large candelabra surrounded on both sides with family pictures. One large window, covered with a white set of frilly lace curtains, was found to the left of the door leading outside. At the end wall was a large stone fireplace, with huge scented candles on the mantle. As the room was already warm, there was no fire in the fireplace. There was a small divan under the window, decorated with a white, wide, crocheted doily on the back. Several small stuffed pillows sat on each end. A small round oak table with claw feet was placed at the end of the divan. It was covered with a white crocheted tablecloth and a decorative oil lamp. Next to the table was a comfortable stuffed French chair. It sat a little way out into the room so that when the door was open the door rested against the back of the chair. Throw rugs were scattered strategically around the wooden floor, giving it a comfortable, homey feeling.

When JaNae was finished in the kitchen, she joined them in the living room. Williams persuaded her to play something on the piano. As the sweet lilting refrains of music filled the room, John began to feel at peace, soon growing exhausted. Williams noticed and motioned for JaNae to stop playing. "You don't need to feel obligated to stay up until we retire, son. Feel free to go to bed when you feel the desire."

John rose and stretched lazily. "Thank you. The music is so beautiful, but I don't think I can stay awake much longer." Yawning, he turned and headed toward his room.

Williams smiled as he watched John walk away. "Good night, son. I hope you sleep well!"

"Good night, sir and thanks again for your kind generosity."

"You're welcome." JaNae nodded and started playing something softly on the piano.

As John undressed for bed, he thought of the Colonel and Mrs. Williams. *What a sweet couple.* A sweet peace began to steal over him, causing him to feel bone-weary. Sighing, he slipped gratefully under the covers and was soon fast asleep.

ஒ௳ ௳ஒ

John woke up the next morning still tired, but feeling a lot more rested. Dressing quickly, he went out to the dining room. Hearing him, JaNae came out of the kitchen. After telling him where to wash up, she went back to the kitchen to prepare his breakfast. John went out to the porch, just off from the kitchen, where he found a washbasin near a bucket of water. Near the basin was a bar of soap. A white towel hung on a peg above. After hurriedly washing up, John went back to the dining room to sit on a chair near the table. JaNae came from the kitchen with a plate filled with a large stack of pancakes, a huge sausage patty, along with two eggs. "Here you go," replied JaNae, "Eat hearty." In front of the plate was a tall, frothy glass of milk. John's eyes bulged at the sight before him; nevertheless, he did full justice to the meal. JaNae didn't stay in the room but bustled about like an old mother hen.

He had just finished when someone knocked at the door. JaNae came from the kitchen, drying her hands on a dishtowel as she walked over to open the door. Seeing Josh standing hesitantly on the threshold, she smiled and moved aside for him to enter. "Come on in, Josh. What brings you here at this time of the day?"

Taking off his hat, Josh timidly stepped into the house and took a deep breath. "I came to get John."

John stood up and walked anxiously over to Josh. "What is it, Josh?"

"It's that strange, old horse you brought to the fort yesterday. He collapsed in his stall this morning and we can't get him to move."

John started toward the bedroom. "Let me get my hat and I'll be right there!" He didn't wait for Josh to say anything else, but hurried from the room. Josh was gone when he came back into the living room.

"Thank you for a wonderful breakfast, Mrs. Williams."

"You're welcome, John."

He hurried out the door, taking time to close it behind him. Hurrying toward the stables, he noticed that the sun was not yet up.

The doctor was working over Old Baldy when John entered the stall. John's heart lurched when he saw the poor old fellow lying on his left side, barely breathing. Going over to Old Baldy, he knelt upon the straw, lifted his head and placed it onto his lap. Absently stroking the horse's neck, he began crooning words of encouragement. Looking at John with a mixture of disgust and anger, the doctor was appalled at the horse's condition. "Where did you ever get such a miserable bag of bones?"

John glared angrily at the doctor. "Major Thornton doesn't believe animals should be well treated or protected by their owners. He cares about this poor old guy about as much as he does any other human being and this isn't much. When I left the fort, I was only allowed to use this horse for a pack animal."

Snorting, the doctor grew angrier. "Well, the major should be shot for allowing this poor old cuss to live like he has!"

Tears of anger glistened in John's eyes. "My sentiments exactly! I tried to spare him on the trip here, but he suffered sorely." John watched as the Doctor worked patiently over the horse, growing anxious when Old Baldy didn't respond to the treatments given him. "Will he be all right, sir?"

Shaking his head angrily, he looked up into John's anxious face. Softening visibly, he replied, "No! I'm surprised he lasted through the night."

Turning his attention back to Old Baldy, he continued to stroke his neck. "I'm so sorry that you've had to suffer like this, Baldy!" Something about the horse touched John deeply as Old Baldy tried to respond to John's gentle, soothing words. Old Baldy nickered softly then with a little shudder, he slipped quietly away. John didn't realize how much the horse had come to mean to him, until he saw him expire. Tears spilled unheeded down his cheeks, yet he was grateful that Old Baldy was finally at peace. He was free to roam the big pasture in the sky. Stroking the horse one last time, he gently placed the head back onto the straw, then rose to face the doctor, "Thanks Doctor, for trying to help him." John didn't wait for the doctor to speak, but turned, blindly staggering out of the stall, then ran out through the back of the stables.

Anger for Thornton welled up inside of him when he thought of the treatment given Old Baldy. Then he grew angrier with himself for allowing himself to be duped into using the horse. He knew what condition he was in, so why didn't he insist on another horse? Stooping to pick up some stones, he tossed them angrily toward the dung heap. Slowly, the anger began to subside until he was able to gain a little control of his emotions. It was at this time that he decided to go fishing. Perhaps, I can find some peace of mind, he mused. Rushing back into the stables, he found Josh cleaning out Old Baldy's stable. "Josh, could you please saddle a horse for me? I need to let Blacky rest up a little before I ride him again."

Josh nodded affirmatively. "Sure thing! I have the perfect horse for you."

"I need to speak to the Colonel before I leave, so I'll be right back."

"No problem. I'm right on it." Turning he went to get a horse.

John, going in search of Colonel Williams, found him in his office. While the orderly went to tell the colonel that he was there, John paced like a caged tiger. Hawkins returned to say that the colonel would see him in his office.

As John entered, Colonel Williams stood up to greet him cheerfully, "Good morning, Whipple. I trust you slept well."

"Yes, sir. Thanks to your kind generosity, I am more rested today."

"Good! Good! You looked awful tuckered out yesterday."

"That I was." John watched the colonel intently for a moment then began to present his request, "Sir, I was wondering if I might have time to go fishing before the men return."

Williams slapped John lightly on the back. "That's a capital idea, son. It would give you time to sort through all that you've been through as well as time to relax before you have to deal with what's coming."

For a moment it seemed as though he were going to break down, but he quickly squelched those feelings enough to reply, "Thank you, sir. I won't be gone long."

"Take all the time you need. It will be awhile before the men get here. Then we have to wait for Sheriff Hill to get here from Missoula."

"Good." Turning, he walked out into the outer office. Taking a deep breath, he walked toward Hawkins, who looked up from his work as John approached. It was then that John decided to take the bull by the horns and confront him. Stepping closer to the desk, John extended his right hand while looking the orderly straight in the eye. "I think we got off to a bad start yesterday, sir, and I would like for us to start over. For starters, my name is John Whipple."

Blinking in surprise, the young man stood up, uncertain how to respond to John's overtures. Taking the proffered hand, he slowly smiled. "My name is Private Sid Hawkins. I, too, would like very much for us to start over." They shook hands heartily, then Hawkins looked at John a moment before proceeding. "I apologize for my attitude yesterday, but Sergeant Aimes glared at me every time I started to speak to you."

John's jaw went slack as he stared at Hawkins in confusion. "I don't understand! Why would he not want you to speak to me?" Hawkins shrugged, but did not answer. "I've never done anything to him. Why, I've never even met the man before yesterday!"

"No one knows what makes Sergeant Aimes tick. We just try to get along with him when we have to. The rest of the time we ignore him."

"I see." Shaking off the doldrums, John went on. "Well, I hope we can get to know one another better."

Hawkins grinned. "I'd like that, too!"

"Good! I'll see you later."

Hawkins smiled and nodded affirmatively. "You bet!" He watched John leave, then sat back in his seat.

John hurried back to the colonel's house, where he knocked softly on the door. JaNae opened the door, smiled cheerfully, and said, "Come on in, John." When he was inside, she placed her hands on her hips and scowled at him. Seeing her expression, John flinched, then took a step backward. "Young man ... as long as you're here at the fort and staying in this home, you don't need to knock before you enter."

John stared at her in stunned disbelief. "Yes, ma'am."

"And another thing, please call me JaNae." John blinked, remaining speechless. Grinning at John's expression, she went on, "Calling me Mrs. Williams makes me feel old ... haggard."

John chuckled in relief. "Okay, JaNae it is." His eyes twinkled as he watched her, "I wouldn't want you to feel old and haggard!"

JaNae laughed heartily then punched him lightly on the arm in mock severity. "Okay, smart aleck, that will be just about enough from you!" John laughed, readily seeing through her ruse. "Now, what brought you back here at this time of the day? I thought you and Josh would be off gallivanting around some place."

"Josh is busy working hard in the stables, so I decided to go fishing. I also want to have a look around the area."

"I see."

"I'll get my fishing gear and be out of your hair soon." JaNae nodded, watching until he entered his room. Turning, JaNae then went back to the kitchen. Quickly gathering his fishing gear, John left the room.

JaNae called to him from the kitchen as he was about to go out the door, "Please wait a moment, John." Surprised, he set the gear down, turned back toward the dining room to wait. He didn't have long to wait until JaNae emerged from the kitchen with a sack in her hands.

She handed it to him as she explained what was inside, "I thought you might get hungry before you got back, so I've packed you something to tide you over until dinner. There are a couple of sandwiches and a large slice of the cake."

Smiling appreciatively, he took the sack. As John went to pick up his fishing gear, he uttered, "Why, thank you, ma'am." Looking up he saw JaNae scowl as she opened her mouth to speak. "Oops, I mean, JaNae!"

Smiling, JaNae nodded in acknowledgment, "You're welcome." John smiled in relief. As he turned and started toward the door, JaNae called out, "Good luck with your fishing."

"Thanks." JaNae turned back to the kitchen, when the door closed behind John.

Josh had the thoroughbred gelding saddled when John got to the stables. "I can't—"

Josh held up his hand. "Well, he needs to be worked out so that he doesn't get lazy."

John sighed resignedly. "Thank you, Josh. I'll try to take good care of him." Josh nodded before going back to his work. Leading the gelding from the stable, John mounted and rode out of the fort. He rode slowly along the river until he found a good spot to fish. He tied the gelding to a good shade tree with plenty of good grass to eat. Removing the gear from the horse, John went to fish. He quickly caught three large fish before they stopped biting. He didn't mind, as it gave him more time to think.

At noon he ate his lunch, thoughtfully walked along the river for a while, then returned to fish some more. John hadn't been fishing long, when he heard a wagon approaching. Feeling vulnerable, he quickly hid and waited to see what would happen.

As the wagon drove past John's hiding place, he noticed that the rider was a surly heavyset man with rugged features. Pulling hard on the reins, he bellowed loudly to the team. "Whoa, ya dad-blamed mangy old nags!" Anger welled up inside as John saw the driver pull harder on the reins, which strained their necks. The horses stopped, snorted, and their eyes grew large with fright. Tossing their heads up and down, their ears twitched nervously. Loudly issuing forth more foul oaths, he turned the team so the back of the wagon was next to the river. John waited anxiously. Struggling to the ground, the man walked behind the wagon.

As the man unhooked the tailgate, John was able to see him more clearly. Black beady eyes glared out from under thick grey eyebrows, which were knit tightly together. Thick lips emerged from his long dirty beard. His wide hooked nose made his rugged features appear even harder. A dirty wide-brimmed hat covered his head, yet a few curly strands of dirty hair fell across his long forehead. His red flannel shirt, the sleeves rolled up to the middle of his arm, was dirty with a few patches here or there. Bib-overalls, the legs rolled up a few turns, were also dirty. They too were patched in several places. He was wearing big heavy boots. John wondered what kind of life the man led, then decided he didn't want to know.

John's attention was diverted when he heard pups yipping in the back of the wagon. A mother dog whimpered softly. The man struck her with the back of his hand so hard that she rolled over. Yelping once, she sat up with her head bowed dejectedly. After stooping to pick up a rock, which he stuffed into a burlap sack, he hurriedly tossed the pups along with the female inside. Grabbing a heavy piece of rope, he tied it shut.

All at once John, realizing his intent, angrily stood up. Scurrying quickly over to the man, he yelled, "Hey, Mister! If you're just going to drown those dogs, I'll take them off of your hands!"

The man jumped guiltily. Slowly he faced John. Watching John approach, he grew sullen, "Who are you?"

Remaining calm, John stared into the man's angry eyes. "It doesn't matter who I am, sir. I just want to have the dogs you're planning to drown."

Scowling, the man watched John intently for a moment, then turned back to the dogs in disgust. "If you want them so all fired badly, you kin have them!" Grabbing the sack, he tossed it roughly to John, "Here ... and good riddance!" John caught the sack before it could hit the ground, but not before he heard one of the pups yelp in pain. Turning, the man shuffled to the front of the wagon, climbing up onto the seat. Grabbing the reins, he bellowed loudly to the horses. Another string of foul language spewed from his lips as he struck the team with a whip. Squealing with fright, the horses bolted, causing the wagon to careen to the left, then to the right until it finally disappeared.

John placed the bag gently onto the ground. Working at the string, he finally got it open. As John opened the bag, the female growled deeply, drawing back further into the bag. John began to talk softly to her, something she wasn't used to. Finally, she slowly poked her head out of the sack. When John didn't strike her but continued to talk to her softly, she crawled timidly out of the sack. With her ears laid back, her tail tucked between her legs, she skulked over to John. Tenderly examining her, he was relieved to find her in good condition. Chuckling softly, he ruffled her ears. "Why, you're no bigger than a minute, my lady."

John couldn't tell what breed of dog she was—only that she was small, with short thin hair. Her smooth, sleek coat was mostly tan with a few black markings around her eyes, ears, and muzzle. The underside of her lifted tail, which was white, flared out into a flag. This caused John to envision a white-tailed deer in flight. Her soft velvety dark-brown eyes watched John intently. Her distinctly pug black nose sniffed at him warily as he reached for the sack. Setting the bag near her, he reached inside pulling out a pup.

As a white squirming mass of furry fluff emerged from the sack, John noticed that its long curly hair made it appear larger than it was. John laughed softly as he tried to examine it closely, because it kept squirming in an attempt to get to its mother. After making sure that it wasn't hurt, the mother licked its face to comfort it. He couldn't help grinning as the little male waddled over to his mother to suckle.

Reaching into the sack, John pulled out a roly-poly female, who whimpered as he tried to examine her. Again, the female sniffed him over thoroughly to insure herself that John wasn't hurting her. Satisfied that the pup was all right, she licked its face lovingly, then looked up at John as if to say thank you. As it wasn't hurt, he placed it near the mother dog to nurse. John smiled when he noticed that the pup was a small miniature of the mother dog. Unlike the male pup's curly coat, hers was smooth and sleek.

As he reached into the sack, his heart nearly failed him. He couldn't feel any movement from the pup. Ever so gently, John lifted the still pup from the sack. Like her brother, her body was a white ball of curly fluff. However, there were more tan hues to her coat, with brown on her ears and muzzle. Red stains near the left ear worried John, but he continued to examine her, aware that momma was also conducting her own examination. She whimpered softly, as if that would wake it, but it remained still. As John's fingers gently explored the wound, he was relieved to see that it wasn't deep. When it still didn't move, he grew more worried. Placing his hands on her side, he felt a slight heartbeat, which made him feel better. Again, he ran his fingers over the tiny body, but couldn't find anything else wrong. Finally, when he despaired of her coming around, she took a deep breath and slowly opened her eyes.

The female licked its face ever so gently. She nudged it in an attempt to make her rise. John placed the stunned pup near its brother and sister in hopes that it would start to suckle. It lay there listlessly, trying to gather its strength, while momma licked her all over. Finally, the pup reached out for a teat. While they nursed, John removed the rock from the sack, tossing it into the river. Gathering his fish, John put them next to his fishing gear. He went to get the gelding. When he had everything ready, he placed it on the horse. Coming back to the dogs, he found the pups fast asleep while momma dog watched his every move. Picking up the sack, he placed the pups, one by one, inside. Placing the sack over the saddle horn, he made sure it was open so they could breathe easily. The female whimpered as he put the sack on the saddle horn, not sure of his intent. Stooping, John gently lifted the mother dog stuffing her inside of his shirt. Holding onto her, he untied the gelding. Mounting, John rode back to the fort as quickly as possible.

CHAPTER 9

Cornered

When John rode to the fort, he went directly to the stables, where Josh came out to meet him. "Thanks for the loan of the horse, Josh."

"Don't mention it," grinned Josh, taking the reins. At sight of the dog in John's shirt, he grew inquisitive. "What cha got there?"

Removing the mother dog from his shirt, he stroked her absently. Finally, he handed her to Josh, who dropped the horse's reins. The horse stood as if securely tied ... a sign of good training. "I ran across a man today at the river who was planning to send this female along with her pups to a watery grave."

"Humph! A man who abuses dumb animals should be taken out and shot."

"I agree!" Dismounting, John turned to lift the sack of pups from the saddle horn, setting it onto the ground.

One by one, he took them out of the sack.

"Oh, what corkers they are!" Kneeling on the ground, Josh began to examine each one. "A male and two females." Lifting one of the pups, he examined her, then turned anxiously to John. "Say, this lassie is hurt! What happened to her?"

"The man had put them into this burlap sack, along with a huge rock. He was about to toss the sack into the river, when I told him that I wanted them all. Angrily grabbing the sack, he tossed it at me. When I caught the sack, the impact hurt her."

Stroking the soft fur, Josh brightened. "Mrs. Williams will know what to do with her." Josh gently put her back upon the ground. The male pup staggered inquisitively over to chew on Josh's shoes. Chuckling, he gently scolded the culprit. "Hey, those are my shoes!" The male pup ignoring him continued to chew on Josh's shoelaces.

John laughed heartily at the expression on Josh's face. "I think he likes you."

All at once, Josh grew excited. "Do you think I could have this little tyke?"

"Won't your parents have a fit if you bring him home?"

"My parents died when I was ten, so I live with Albert and Janice Jefferson. They love animals almost as much as I do." Picking up the pup, he grinned when it started chewing on his ear. "They told me once that I could have a dog, but I never saw one I liked until now." Laughing, he gently disengaged the pup from his ear.

"Then he's yours!"

"Thanks, John," replied Josh feelingly. He studied the pup a moment, then looked over at John. "This pup is just plumb lucky you come along to save him and his family, so I think I'll call him Lucky!"

One of the other stable hands, Mort Bridgford, came out to see what all the excitement was about. "'Body could'a heerd the two a ya all the way t'other side a Missoula! Whut's gwan on out here, enyhow?"

While John retold the story, the healthy female started tugging at a horse blanket that had slipped from a stall gate. Mort grabbed at the blanket in an attempt to extract it from the pup. "Leave that alone, you little varmint!" Placing the blanket back onto the stall gate, he turned back to chat with the young men. The little female jumped, grabbing the blanket with her teeth. She started dragging it away. They laughed out loud when tripping over the blanket, she tipped forward. "You can't have that, you little rascal!" Growling, the pup refused to relinquish her hold on the blanket. When Mort persisted, the pup began pulling backwards. Mort chuckled heartily at the pup's antics. "You're a bandit for sure! I'd take you home to the kids in a heartbeat!"

"She's all yours, sir."

"Thanks, son! The kids'll surely get a kick out of her!" Stooping to scoop up the pup, he held her close to him constantly scratching her behind her ears. After wiggling and squirming her way to his shoulder, she started chewing on the collar of his shirt. Holding the pup out at arms-length, he surveyed her closely. "I'm a gonna call ya Bandit, cause ya just plumb stole my heart!" Still scratching behind the pup's ear, he walked home to show his family.

"Can I leave Pugger here, Josh, while I take the hurt female to Mrs. Williams?"

Josh looked at the mother dog strangely, then back to John. "Pugger?"

John smiled. "I called the mother dog that because her nose is so pug."

"So, does that mean you're going to keep her?"

"Yes. I feel that we belong together … especially after saving her little family."

"I'm glad! Just leave her with me. It will give her time to be with my pup."

"Thank you, Josh."

"Don't mention it. I'll take care of the gelding while you take the pup over to Mrs. Williams." Tucking his pup more firmly under his arm, he gathered the gelding's reins and whistled softly while leading him toward the stables. "Come on girl, let's go."

John watched until they had entered the stables, then hurried over to the Colonel's home. Knocking once, he entered. Coming from the kitchen, JaNae blinked in surprise as she saw a pup tucked under his left arm while a string of fish dangled from his right hand.

"What have you here?"

John grinned at her strange expression. "While I was fishing, a man drove to the river … he was going to drown a mother dog as well as her three pups. This pup was hurt when he angrily threw the bag at me. You see … he'd placed a large rock inside to weigh them down."

"Where are the mother dog and her other pups, now?"

"Josh took the male. Mr. Bridgford took the other female. Josh said that you'd know what to do for this one, so I brought her over to see if you could help her. I left the mother with Josh."

"I see."

"Can you help her?"

"Let's have a look, shall we?" Taking the hurt pup, JaNae began to examine her carefully. Looking up from the pup, she smiled encouragingly at John. "The wound isn't serious, but she does need some attention." Scooping the pup up into her arms, she began to croon to it tenderly.

"Thank you for helping her, ma'am." JaNae started to scowl. "Oops! I mean JaNae."

She smiled. "You're welcome. Leave her with me, and I'll see what I can do."

Smiling gratefully, he was relieved to see the pup's needs met. When John started to leave, JaNae called to him, "John …"

John turned anxiously back, "Yes …"

"I'm so glad you rescued the dogs."

"Me, too!" Turning, he walked outside while she turned her attention to the pup.

Closing the door, John leaned thoughtfully against it as he struggled to gain control of his emotions. He suddenly realized just how close the dogs had come to drowning. He never thought of having a dog of his own or how his parents would feel about it but somehow he didn't think they would mind. Finally, moving away, he inhaled a deep breath of crisp clean fresh air. As he started toward the stables, he heard the sentry at the gate yell out, "Riders coming." His heart skipped a beat as he turned toward the Colonel's office.

Colonel Williams was emerging from the office with the sheriff, as John approached. Seeing John, he smiled encouragingly. "Hello, John. Have you met Sheriff Zachariah Hill?"

"Yes, sir." They politely shook hands. "Hello, Sheriff Hill."

"Hello, Whipple."

"Well … it's obvious that you two know each other well."

"You bet! John and I go way back!"

"I see. Anyway, he is our main witness." Sheriff Hill nodded understandingly. Turning to John, Williams went on. "It won't be long now until it's over, son." John could only nod nervously. Their attention was diverted when the gates swung wide open, allowing Major Brown's detail along with their captives to enter.

Williams turned sternly toward John. "Are those the men you took the horses from?"

Again, John nodded affirmatively. "Yes, sir. They are."

"Very well. That will be all until I send for you."

"Yes, sir." Turning, he started briskly toward the stables.

As Colonel Williams walked over to the detail, he began to bark orders. Finally, he turned to address Major Brown, who saluted, then stood rigidly erect.

"At ease, Major."

"Thank you, sir."

"Bring these men to my office immediately, Major."

"Yes, sir!" Turning, he began to address several officers. "Welch, Drisco, Smith, Hayes, escort the men to the Colonel's office on the double." John paused to look at the miserable surly men sitting in the back of a wagon. When the soldiers moved forward to comply, John saw Major Brown reach inside his saddlebags and remove a bag. Turning back to the Colonel, Brown handed it to him. "I found this in the tree you indicated. Mr. Whipple described the location so well that it wasn't difficult at all to find."

"Very good, Brown, that will be all for now. I'll see you at the office in a few minutes."

"Yes, sir." Brown saluted, leaving Hill and Williams staring at the contents in the Colonel's hands.

Williams went back to the office with Hill close behind. Hill took a seat near the wall, while Williams sat behind his desk. Opening the bag Major Brown had handed him, Williams reached inside. He took out a bottle of ink, a quill pen, then lastly a book. Upon opening the book, a key fell out onto the desk. Knowing that the prisoners would be there soon, Williams quickly scanned the book's contents. As he read the words, he turned visibly pale. Hill went to stand behind him so that he could see, too. All at once Hill gagged. He looked at Williams with disgust, "How could anyone do those awful things, let alone brazenly keep a journal of it all?"

"I don't know," replied Williams, still reeling from the horror of it all. He reached into his pocket to take out a key. Unlocking a desk drawer, he buried the book in the bottom. Relocking the drawer, he put the key back into his pocket.

Williams took his seat near the wall just as they heard footsteps in the outer office, followed by a knock on the door. "Enter," ordered Williams.

Major Brown entered, followed by five men bound with strong cords. "The men are all present and accounted for, sir." Brown saluted, then stood rigid.

"Very well, Major Brown. That will be all." After saluting, Brown started to leave. "Stay in the next room until I call for you."

"Yes, sir." Again saluting, Brown exited the room.

"Colonel Williams looked at each man in the room, noting that some of the men present weren't part of the military. Feeling disgusted with the whole lot, he folded his hands and placed them on top of the desk. He again looked intently at each man. As his eyes rested on Maines, he felt such a strong feeling of revulsion that it was difficult not to show his emotions. Inhaling, he began the business at hand. "I am placing all of you under arrest." He was surprised when they sat stoically staring forward. "Because of the heinous crimes committed ..."

Maines, growing surly, jumped to his feet with his fists raised to show the cords binding his hands. "I understand why Reno and I were arrested, but I fail to see what these men have done to deserve being dragged in here like this"

Williams was amazed at how calm Maines was in the face of it all. Either he didn't get the full impact of what it all meant, or he just didn't care. "You will in time, Corporal," stated Williams flatly. "You will in time." Removing the key from his pocket he unlocked the drawer and removed a knife. Rising, he leisurely approached the first man. "Stand up and turn around." The man hesitated a moment, then complied. Williams cut the cords loose from his hands, continuing down the row until they were all released from their restraints. "Sit," he ordered irritably. When they were all seated, he went back to his desk, placed the knife back into the drawer, which he locked. Tossing the key up and down in the palm of his hand a couple of times, he looked defiantly at the men, then slipped the key back into his pocket. Slowly, yet deliberately, he went to open the door. "Major Brown, come in here at once!"

"Yes, sir." He quickly entered, saluted, then stood rigidly at attention while awaiting orders. Williams took his watch out of the watch fob to study it intently for a moment. "It's now fourteen hundred hours, so we'll hold court at zero nine hundred hours two days from today." He looked over at Sheriff Hill for confirmation, plainly relieved to see him nod his head. Turning back to Major Brown, he continued. "I want you to assign three details. One is to arrange the Community Hall for court proceedings. The second detail is to be dispatched to Missoula, where they are to appoint ten men to act as jurors for these civilians. The third detail is to inform the defendant's families of their arrests. They are to give them the time as well as the place for these proceedings." For the first time, Williams saw the men flinch nervously. Some even went pale at the mention of their families. "For those without means of travel, see that they are brought to Missoula and put them up in the hotel, then see that the bill is brought to me. The day of the trial you are to bring them here."

"Yes, sir."

"That will be all, Major. You're dismissed!"

"Yes, sir." Saluting, Brown went out, making sure to close the door securely behind him. Because of the strained silence in the room, Williams could hear his footsteps in the other room.

Williams turned back to the accused. "I have appointed Lieutenant Jared Gillespie to act as your counsel. Doctor Richard Stanley will act as the prosecuting attorney." He looked over to Sheriff Hill, who again nodded. Sheriff Hill and I will act as judges over the proceedings. Rising, he stepped over to open the door. "Hawkins, get in here on the double!" Hawkins timidly entered, saluted, then waited for further instructions. "Bring Lieutenant Gillespie to my office at once."

"Right away, sir." Saluting, he hurried out the door, slamming it shut behind him.

Williams was debating what his next move was when there was a knock at the door. Hawkins entered. "Lieutenant Gillespie's here, sir!"

Williams rose. "Very well then. ... Don't just stand there. ... Show him in."

"Yes, sir." Moving to the door, he motioned to someone in the outer office. "The Colonel will see you now, sir." Moving to the side, he let Gillespie enter, then went back to his desk.

Saluting, Gillespie waited further instructions. "At ease, Lieutenant."

"Thank you, sir." Lowering his hand, he visibly relaxed.

"These are the men I spoke to you about last evening. I've already told them that you will be representing them."

"Very well, sir."

"The trial has been set for two days from today at zero nine hundred hours. Can you be ready by then?"

"Yes, sir."

"I'll leave these men to your discretion." Williams motioned to Hill to follow. Together they left the room.

⋮

Closing the door, Gillespie walked over to sit behind the desk, placed his hat on the desk, spread out some papers, and then situated an inkbottle for ready use. Nervously brushing at a speck of dust on his immaculate uniform, he took a deep breath before facing the men. "As you know, Colonel Williams has assigned me the task of being your counselor in the forthcoming proceedings which will convene in two days." He waited a moment to let this sink in, then proceeded, "I would suggest that you level with me, so that I can present the best defense possible." When no one spoke, he grew exasperated. "Were you told why you are being prosecuted?"

Maines leaned forward to leer at Gillespie condescendingly. "No, we weren't! We were brought in here against our will. We were told that we were being arrested. Reno and I know that we were absent without leave, but we don't understand why these men were brought in here like common criminals."

"Surely you know the reason why you've been arrested?"

"I'm telling you that we don't!"

"Then let me enlighten all of you. You have all been arrested for a multitude of crimes — namely: theft, rape, murder, horse stealing, and cattle rustling. You and Corporal Reno will also be tried for desertion from the Army. How do you plead?"

Gillespie, who was able to see all of their faces, noticed that those closest to Maines turned to get his reaction. As far as he could discern, Maines was the ringleader. When he remained detached, and calmly leaned back in his seat, the men followed suit. All at once Maines rose and peered arrogantly down at him. "We plead ... not guilty!"

Gillespie wanted to leave them all to sink or swim, but as that wasn't an option, he leaned back in his chair and folded his hands across his chest. He felt repulsed against them. Putting his feelings aside, he addressed them. "Well, I hate to be the one to throw cold water in your faces, but I know, for a fact, that they can prove that you are guilty on all counts. The only choice that you have is for you to come clean."

Maines grew extremely angry. "No way! As far as their having proof of our guilt, I don't believe you! You're trying to trick us into confessing to a crime we didn't commit." Turning, he sank back onto his chair to sulk.

Ignoring Maines, Gillespie concentrated on the men. "So, do all of you feel this way?"

"Yes!" they cried as one.

Gillespie sighed resignedly. "Very well. I'll do what I can to get you off. But let me make one thing abundantly clear. There really is proof of your guilt." Rising, he walked over to open the door. "Sheriff Hill, would you please come in here?"

Sheriff Hill emerged. "The prisoners are ready to be taken to the stockade until their trial." Without another word, he picked up his hat, then strode out of the room without so much as another word.

Hill turned to the outer office. "Will you please come in here, Major Brown?" Turning back to face the room, he noticed that Maines was eyeing the door, seeking the opportunity for escape. Calmly removing his gun from his holster, he aimed it at the men and pulled the hammer back. Maines slumped back in the chair, appearing not to notice. Brown entered, standing near the door. "You can escort these prisoners to the stockade. See that they are made presentable then give them something to eat. When that has been accomplished, inform Colonel Williams."

"Yes, sir." Turning, Brown barked orders to the waiting soldiers, who quickly complied.

When the room was cleared, Hill turned to Hawkins, smiling half-heartedly. Without saying a word, he went out. Sighing sadly, Hill went in search of Williams.

✦ ✦

The day of the trial, Hill found Whipple behind the stable tossing rocks at the dung heap. Because of the recent traumatic events, John jumped and whirled around when he heard Hill's footsteps behind him. Seeing how terrified the young man looked, Hill's heart went out to him. Tossing the remaining rocks on the ground, John rubbed his hands against the side of his pants then waited for Hill to join him. Colonel Williams sent me to tell you that the trial will begin in a little over an hour. When John glanced around in panic, Hill placed a comforting hand on his shoulder. "You've been very brave up to now, son. Just hang in there a little longer and it will all be over before you know it."

Sighing dejectedly, John lowered his head. "I wish it were all over with now, so that I can start putting this ugliness behind me."

"I know, but these things take time." Turning John so that he could look him in the eyes, he smiled encouragingly. "Thanks to the evidence you brought to Colonel Williams, the trial shouldn't last very long."

John's shoulders drooped wearily. "Even so, it's hard to go in there knowing that what you have to say will sentence five men to an awful fate." When Hill started to speak, John hastened on. "I know that they've brought it onto themselves, but still it's hard to think about their families learning about their awful crimes. You know, Sheriff Hill, when all of this terrible stuff happened, I wanted revenge. Coming here … waiting for the trial to be over with … I've had a lot of time to think about it. I don't care about revenge anymore … I just want to have this awful trial over with so that I can go on with my life." Sighing audibly, John bowed his head. "Right now, I don't know what to do until time to go inside."

Hill's eyes twinkled merrily. "You can always throw more rocks at the dung heap."

John smiled sheepishly. "I seem to be doing that a lot lately."

They stood thoughtfully silent until all at once Hill began to laugh heartily. "When Williams told me that you stole the crook's horses, I was mighty impressed." He enthusiastically patted John upon the back. "Darn smart thinking, son!" John looked inquisitively at Hill, but remained silent. "You sure do have spunk!"

"Thank you, sir. Truth is … I didn't feel very smart. I was not only angry, but scared out of my mind."

"Being angry is no sin, as long as it's controlled. Fear is a feeling that I've tasted many times throughout my life—especially as the sheriff of Missoula"

"Thanks for understanding."

"No problem at all." He squeezed the young man's shoulder one more time before lowering his arm. "Don't let this get you down. Find a way to be happy. I'll come get you when it's time."

"Thank you, sir. I'll try." He watched Hill walk away, then stooped to pick up a handful of rocks, absently tossing them at the dung heap.

⁕⁕⁕

An hour later, John saw the big gates swing open. People came in on horseback, in spring wagons, surreys, and several other means of conveyance. His heart skipped a beat at the sight of the families. For a moment, he felt that he was going to be ill. Taking several deep breaths, he was able to gain control of his emotions.

Hearing steps behind him, he cautiously turned around. He sighed in relief when he saw Hill approaching. Smiling at John encouragingly, he beckoned for him to follow. "Come on, son. We better get over there, so that they can get started." Nodding, John fell into step with him as they walked to the Community Hall. Standing on the threshold, John felt as if he were going to suffocate. As panic gripped him, he had an uncontrollable urge to run. Sensing his feelings, Hill placed a calming hand on his shoulder. "Take a deep breath, son." John tried to obey, but it was so difficult. Trying once more, he succeeded in growing calmer. Walking nervously to the front, John took a seat in the second row to the right, behind the prosecutor's chair while Hill joined Williams at the head table.

Not having ever seen a trial, John was curious to know what would happen. Noticing a small platform, he was surprised to see a medium size table, with two chairs facing the people. When he saw another chair positioned at the side of the table, also facing the people, his curiosity almost got the better of him. No matter how hard he tried, he couldn't figure out why a chair would be placed like that. Shrugging, he continued to scan the room. He saw two tables, one on each side of the room, each with a chair facing the platform. Gillespie was sitting at the table to the left of the room. Doctor Stanley was sitting at the table to the right. Seeing twelve chairs along the wall to the left, he wondered who would be sitting there. *Whoever they are, they would have a commanding view of everything.* Chairs were placed in rows all the way to the door, with an aisle down the middle. John supposed they were for the families or spectators to use. The first two rows to the left were filled with the men who were on trial.

John sat quietly, absorbed in his thoughts. Sighing, he looked around the room, now packed with family members along with some spectators. As he looked into the anxious faces of the families, he felt an overwhelming feeling of pity for them. Knowing they would be the ones hurt most from these proceedings, it really bothered him; yet, in his heart he knew that because other families had been hurt, these men had to pay for their crimes. He couldn't help wondering what the families would do when they learned how low their loved ones had fallen. Sighing, he turned his attention to the front of the room and waited for court to begin.

John was glad to see Sheriff Hill, although he wished it could have been under better circumstances. As the Sheriff removed his hat, John smiled to see how much balder Hill had become. His pate, which was as shiny as brass, glistened with beads of perspiration. There was a snow-white fringe around the sides and back of his head. His steel-gray eyes and bushy eyebrows made him look hard as flint. Under a black vest he wore a cream-colored shirt, sleeves rolled to the middle of the arms. John noticed that the badge, pinned to his vest, sparkled when the light hit it. The well-polished colt .45, ready for easy use hung in the holster close to his right hip. The brown hat held loosely in his hands had a wide brim with a high crown. Enormous wide thick hands, scarred around the knuckles, absently stroked the brim. A wide gold wedding ring adorned the third finger of his left hand. John marveled at how calm he was as he leaned back in his chair to place his leg across his knee.

A movement to the left caught his attention. Gillespie was absently running his fingers through his thick dark-brown curly hair, which had receded slightly back from his forehead. His eyebrows were knit together in consternation as he turned to gaze at the prisoners. John saw disgust run momentarily through Gillespie's light-blue eyes before he quickly veiled them. John felt a thrill course through him. A long jagged scar ran down his right cheek, where a muscle twitched slightly.

John couldn't help wondering what had happened to give him such a scar. *Was it from fighting Indians?* he wondered. *Or, was it from some wild animal?* He made a mental note to ask Josh then promptly dismissed it from his mind as he continued to study his features. The rough leathery skin, stretched tautly over his face, was browned from the sun and inclement weather. Gillespie had a wide thick Roman nose, also a protruding jaw, which made him appear rough … unfeeling. Yet as John studied him more closely, he felt that this wasn't really so.

Turning to his papers, Gillespie began to chew on his thin bottom lip. Folding his hands together, he placed his elbows on the table and pressed his clasped hands against his forehead. At that moment, he was filled with extreme empathy and compassion for Gillespie.

John's attention was drawn back to the front, when Colonel Williams banged hard on the table to silence the crowd in an attempt to bring a semblance of order to the proceedings. "Silence in the court room! Silence in the court room!" John was surprised at how quickly the room fell silent. "Sheriff Zachariah Hill and I, Colonel Jedidiah Williams, will be presiding over these proceedings. The prisoners will all rise." Slowly they rose, as did Gillespie, waiting for the axe to fall. "Corporal Alvin Reno, Corporal Horace Maines, you have been absent without leave for some time. How do you plead to these charges?"

"Guilty, sir."

"Due to the following charges, we will dispense with the sentence for now. As to the other charges … horse stealing, cattle rustling, theft, rape, and murder … how do you all plead to the charges placed before you?"

"Not guilty!" echoed the men.

"Very well then, let the proceedings begin. You may take your seats." When the men were seated, Williams turned to Doctor Stanley. "Doctor Stanley, call your first witness."

Picking up a piece of paper, Dr. Stanley walked around the table. "I call Adam Sanderson to the stand." As the man rose, he skulked arrogantly toward the chair at the side of the table. John recognized the guard he had seen protecting the horses. He was a short dumpy man with a red face, which John guessed was due to his excessive drinking. Cold, calculating hazel eyes peered around the room when he reached the chair. Long mangy black hair and the dense dark beard covering his protruding jaw gave his ugly features a grizzly effect.

Hawkins stepped forward with a Bible in hand, extended it toward Sanderson. "Place your left hand on the Bible and raise your right hand, sir." Sanderson hesitated a moment, then complied. "Do you solemnly swear to tell the truth, the whole truth, and nothing but the whole truth, so help you God?"

"Yes, sir."

"You may be seated." Lowering the Bible, Hawkins went to sit behind the doctor. Stanley walked over to face the prisoner. "State your full name."

"Adam Michael Sanderson," came the brusque reply.

"Where were you on the night of April fifteenth of this year?"

"That was five days ago, so how am I supposed to remember where I was?"

"Think back and perhaps you'll remember," Stanley mumbled sarcastically.

Stanley waited a moment for the man to think. Clearing his throat, he continued. "All right, where were you on the night of April fifteenth of this year?"

"I don't remember."

"Do you know Corporal Maines?"

"Yes, sir."

"How do you know him?"

"We met at the Bluebird Saloon in Missoula."

"When?"

"Let me see. I think it was a year ago."

"Were you with him on the night of April fifteen?"

"I told you … I don't remember where I was on that night, so how am I supposed to know who I was with?"

Stanley turned toward Gillespie. "Your witness."

Gillespie, writing on a piece of paper, didn't even glance up. "I have no questions at this time."

Williams leaned forward to scowl at Sanderson. "You may step down."

Rising, the man smiled snidely as he walked back to his seat. When the man was seated, Stanley looked down at a sheet of paper on the table. "I call Corporal Alvin Reno to the stand." Rising, Reno sullenly headed toward the chair. Once there, Hawkins swore him in. When he was seated, Stanley turned to study the man before him. "Please state your full name and military rank."

"Alvin Montrose Reno. My rank is that of a Corporal."

"Where are you from, sir?"

"Fort Owen."

"Do you know Corporal Horace Maines?"

"Yes, sir."

"Where were you on the night of April fifteenth of this year?"

"I don't remember."

Stanley studied the man a moment. "Are you telling me that you can't remember five days back?"

"Yes, sir. I am."

"Very well, your witness."

Gillespie looked up to smile politely at Stanley. "I have no questions."

Sighing resignedly, Williams turned to Stanley. "Call your next witness, Doctor."

Nodding, Stanley turned toward Maines, watching him intently for a moment. Maines sat as though carved from stone, reminding him of a dead fish. Turning, Stanley looked over at John. "I call John Whipple to the stand."

Everyone turned as John rose to walk to the front. He was shaking so hard that he barely heard Hawkins' instructions. Placing his left hand on the Bible, he raised his right hand. "Do you solemnly swear to tell the truth, the whole truth, and nothing but the truth, so help you God?"

He looked at the prisoners then to Stanley, who smiled encouragingly. Taking a deep breath to settle his nerves, he pulled himself to his full height then replied, "Yes, sir."

"Be seated." Hawkins returned to his seat, while John took the witness stand.

When he was seated, Stanley walked over to stand by the chair. "Please state your name and where you are from."

As John took a deep breath, his eyes met those of Corporal Reno. A little feeling of satisfaction washed over him when he saw the man squirm. "My name is John Leroy Whipple. I am from Fort Owen."

"Tell us what happened on April fifteenth, which was approximately five days ago."

John sighed deeply, looked around the room then back to Doctor Stanley. He didn't want to tell the story again, but as there was no other alternative, he took another deep breath then began. "It was late at night. I was on my way to Missoula to do some business. I had just reached Mr. Martin's ranch when I heard riders approaching." He paused to gain control before continuing, "With the Indian threat, I decided to hide behind some trees with thick bushes in front to see who it was before I ventured out."

As the memory flashed before him his heart began to pound, his ears rang, causing him to feel as though he would go mad with the grief. The desire to bolt became so overwhelming that it took all the effort he could muster just to remain seated. "It wasn't Indians I saw ride up, but a group of white men, dressed as Indians!" Everyone in the room groaned in surprise at John's words, then a hush fell over the room. From his chair, he saw the men turn to Maines, but Maines remained impassive. Seeing this lent strength to John.

"Are you sure that it was white men and not Indians that you saw?

"Yes, sir … I am."

"Very well, please go on."

John nodded and took a deep breath. "Imagine my surprise, when I learned that it wasn't Indians who rode up to the farm house, but white men dressed like them. Dismounting, they drew their guns as they rushed into the house. All at once, two more shots rang out. I heard Melissa scream in terror. I heard some of the men running through the house while others drove the horses out of the corrals, while still others chased the cattle from the field. Again I heard Melissa screaming in terror, but I couldn't do anything to help her." John started shaking so hard that he couldn't go on.

"Take your time, son. We can wait."

It took a few minutes for John to gain enough control to go on. Swallowing past the lump in his throat, John proceeded. "Sometime later, I saw Corporal Reno come out of the house, straightening his clothes. My heart nearly failed me when I heard him say that he was done with her. He ordered someone to kill her, burn the house and buildings to the ground. I saw a man who went inside. Shortly after that, I heard three shots. When he came back out, covered in blood, I knew that they'd also killed Melissa and the other people." Looking at the accused, John wasn't surprised to see that they were unmoved by his statement.

"Please go on," encouraged Stanley.

"The scoundrels whooped and hollered in fiendish delight as they set all the buildings on fire." He looked down at Reno with contempt. "When the villains rode past me, I saw a horse with strange markings. I knew I would recognize it if I ever saw it again."

"Did you ever see the horse again?"

"Yes, sir!"

"Please tell us about it."

"I went home for the next two days. I tried to sort through my grief. I was afraid to speak to anyone about it.

"What caused you to come to Fort Missoula to report it?"

"I finally talked to a special friend, who convinced me that I couldn't let it go … that it was important for me to alert Colonel Williams about what I'd seen. That night, after I'd made camp and finished eating, I remembered my father telling me to watch my back. All at once I had a really eerie feeling come over me to get the heck out of there. It was so strong that for a minute I felt weak all over. Like a man possessed, I began slamming things around. Before I knew it, camp was torn down, my horses packed, then I made sure the area was swept clean. After dousing the fire until I was satisfied it was out, I mounted, riding hard as if the very devil himself was after me.

"I object to this line of questioning," declared Gillespie. "The witness is being too melodramatic. He is suffering from an acute case of an overactive imagination."

"Sustained. Just stick to the facts, son and leave out all the flowery stuff," cautioned Williams.

"Yes, sir."

"What happened next?" prompted Stanley.

"Finding a secluded spot, I dismounted. I tied the horses securely to a tree for an easy getaway. Sitting on a boulder by the river a couple of hours later, I had an overwhelming need to know why I felt so strongly that I must leave. I was cautiously making my way back to the first camp, when I heard horses approaching. I had just gotten well hidden near my old camp, where I had a commanding view of the entire camp. I waited to see what would happen. Not long after that I saw a group of six men riding into my old camp. Seeing the horse with the strange markings, I quickly dropped to my stomach, finding myself in a den of rattlesnakes."

Gillespie raised his head to glare at John defiantly, "I object! You cannot refer to the defendants as a bunch of rattlesnakes."

"Sustained. The men are innocent until proven guilty. Therefore, they are not to be referred to in that vernacular … by that name," corrected Williams.

John took a deep breath in an attempt to gain control of his emotions. I was so scared I couldn't move. I felt like I was going to vomit, when Corporal Maines, whom

I didn't know at the time, came riding up on the horse with the strange markings. My heart nearly failed me when they dismounted. Both Maines and Reno advanced toward my hiding place. While the rest of the men set up camp, these scoundrels began bragging about what they had done to Jared Martin's family. A deep smoldering hate surged through my entire being, consuming my very soul, when I heard Maines and Reno planning the job they were going to do next. They were planning to raid Hans Pedersen's family later that night. Oh, how I wanted to stop their evil deeds before they could accomplish them, but I just didn't know how. So I just lay there listening to their grizzly plans."

"What happened then?"

"After they ate, liquor was passed around. They began guzzling it as if there were no tomorrow. Two guards had been posted ... one over the horses and one at the other end of camp. Even they were freely gulping that swill like one would water. At first, I wondered why they left their horses saddled, but after hearing Maines and Reno discussing their grizzly plans, I knew it was because of their planned raid. They gambled for a while, when all at once Maines' countenance grew ugly. Bellowing like a mad bull, he accused a man of cheating. Before I could discern his intent, he pulled out his pistol, shooting the man point blank. He ordered some of his men to get rid of the body."

Several in the room began mumbling among themselves. All at once, pandemonium broke loose. Williams and Hill banged the table hard in an attempt to get the crowd's attention. "Order! Order in this court, or I'll clear it!" Slowly the noise died down until silence again filled the room. "Please go on, Whipple."

"Taking a lantern, Mr. Maines disappeared from the men for a long time. I watched him slink toward some trees, looking around often to see if he were being followed." John looked at Colonel Williams to see if he should proceed. When Williams nodded affirmatively, facing front, John continued, "Mr. Maines stopped in front of a dead tree where he removed something from it." He again looked at the accused being rewarded by the sight of Maines slouching in his seat.

"Were you able to see what it was he took out of the tree?"

"No, sir. It was too dark ... too far away, even with the aid of the lantern's light."

"From that time on the men began to drink more heavily. One by one, they passed out. When Mr. Maines came back to camp and saw the men, he called Mr. Reno over to him. He began yelling at him for ruining his plans. I thought he was going to shoot his friend, because he would lift and lower the gun in his holster. Finally calming down, he only threatened him. When Reno went to the fire, he continued to drink heavily. Mr. Maines did the same. That was when I had my first glimmer of hope at stopping them.

"Explain yourself, please."

"When I saw the guard at the end of camp slouch over in a strange position, I knew he'd passed out. Everyone else was in such a drunken stupor, that they were sprawled out all around the campfire. Only the guard by the horses was still awake, but he was showing signs of doing the same. Seizing the opportunity given me, I crept closer to the horses. I waited until this guard had also passed out. Untying the horses, I led them a safe distance from their camp where I tied them to a tree. I hurried to get my horse and pack animal. Then I returned to the secured horses and tied the lead rope to the pack animal. Mounting, I rode off."

"Did you ride straight to the fort after that?"

"No, sir,"

"What did you do then?"

"After riding hard for several hours to make certain they wouldn't catch me, I stopped to set up a new camp. I took care of the horses, ate a little, then tried to go to sleep."

"How long did you stay there?"

"Just until daylight. Then I rode here to the fort where I met with Colonel Williams.

Stanley intently watched Maines to see how he would react to John's testimony. Maines was not only squirming, but was fidgeting in his seat. The other prisoners kept glancing suspiciously at their outlaw leader. Although he was aware of them, he refused to look in their direction. "Is there more?"

"No, sir. Only that Colonel Williams told me that I was needed as a witness."

"Thank you, Mr. Whipple." Stanley turned to face Gillespie. "I have no further questions of this witness. You may cross examine." With that, he took his seat.

Gillespie rose, dusting at an imaginary speck on his suit as he sauntered anxiously over to face John. "That was some tall tale you told, young man."

"It wasn't a tall tale, sir. It really happened!"

The prisoners heaved a sigh of relief. Finally, there was a little glimmer of hope. Gillespie acknowledged John's comment with a grunt. "You said that you saw a horse with strange markings on the night of the murders."

"Yes, sir."

"If it was late at night when the alleged incident took place, how could you see what the horse looked like?"

"Because, the rider rode past the burning buildings, and the leaping flames revealed it."

Gillespie began to taunt him. "Maybe you were the one who killed Martin and his family." Stepping closer to John, he leered at him accusingly, while sweeping his arm toward the defendants. "I think you killed them then blamed it onto these men!" John gasped as his jaw dropped in shock, looking first at the accused, which were smugly watching their defender, then back to stare at Gillespie.

Emotions began to run rampant among the families and spectators. For a moment, it appeared as if some were going to attack Gillespie, while others were going to attack the defendants. Loud murmurs began to fill the room. Some of the men pulled their pistols. Brown and several of the soldiers quickly thwarted any attempts at trouble. Gillespie had stopped to swallow past the lump in his throat when he realized how closely they had come to having a riot.

Something snapped inside of John causing him to shake uncontrollably. Tears glistened in his pain-filled eyes. He began to speak reverently. "I have known Melissa since we were children. She was like a sister to me. Mr. Martin and I used to go fishing and hunting together. I always thought Mrs. Martin was an angel." Spreading out his hands pleadingly, as deep, soul-searing pain along with anguish engulfed him. A few moments later, he went on. "Why would I kill them or do all those dastardly things to them? I loved them … so much!"

Gillespie seemed unmoved by John's feelings. Pushing his face close to John's, he began to bellow. "That's a good question! So why did you do it?"

John began to sob brokenly. "I didn't do anything to them."

"A likely story!"

Williams slammed his fist so hard on the table that the noise reverberated throughout the room. "Enough, already!"

Gillespie jumped as though he had been dealt a severe blow. "Yes, sir! Begging your pardon, sir." He smiled sheepishly before bowing his head. "Guess I did get a little carried away."

"That's a gross understatement, Lieutenant!"

"I was so determined to serve the defendants, that I lost all perspective for a moment. It won't happen again, sir." Looking sorrowfully at John, he sighed wearily. "I have no further questions." Turning, he quickly took his seat.

Williams smiled kindly. "You may step down, son."

"Thank you, sir." Rising, John tread wearily back to his seat.

Stanley rose to look at the accused men. "I call Corporal Horace Maines to the stand." Corporal Maines slowly uncrossed his legs, rose to his feet and then sauntered lazily over to the chair. After Hawkins swore him in, Maines dropped into the chair looking at Stanley defiantly. "Please state your name and rank!"

Maines smiled snidely. "You know who I am … sir!"

"I order you to state your name and rank!"

"Corporal Horace Eugene Maines, sir!"

"Where were you five nights ago?"

"I'm not going to answer that!"

Stanley turned to Williams then Hill pleadingly. "Would you please instruct him to answer all of the questions placed before him?"

Williams turned to address Maines. "You will answer any and all questions placed before you. Is that clear?"

Maines slouched further into the chair then scowled at Williams. "Yes, sir!"

Stanley walked closer to the chair. "Where were you five nights ago?"

"Who knows? That was five nights ago."

Sighing in exasperation, Stanley walked over to the table, picked up a sheet of paper, and walked back to hand it to Maines. "Is this your handwriting, Corporal?"

Taking the paper, Maines looked at it critically. Handing it back to Stanley, he snapped, "You know that it is!"

"Thank you, Corporal." Taking the sheet of paper from Maines, he walked over to hand it to Hill, who read it before handing it to Williams. Glancing at the paper, Williams laid it aside.

Gillespie rose, walked over to examine the paper then handed it back to Williams. Turning brusquely, he took his seat.

Picking up the book on his table, Stanley patiently moved closer to the witness chair. He held up the book that Williams and Hills had examined on the day the accused were captured. "If that was your handwriting on the sheet of paper, then do you recognize this book?"

Maines' demeanor changed drastically. "It looks like a book, sir."

"Do you recognize this book?"

Gone was his sassy manner. "No, sir!"

Stanley looked at the book thoughtfully. "Hum! Now that's interesting." He opened the book to a marked passage, which he read aloud. "Now, do you recognize this book?"

"No, sir."

John realized that Doctor Stanley was toying with the corporal, like a cat with a mouse. He again handed him the book. "Is this your handwriting?" Maines looked at the book, but refrained from commenting. Stanley, now losing his patience, bellowed loudly. "Is this your handwriting, Corporal?"

Maines looked at the men then around the room. It was apparent that he was feeling cornered, and he looked at Stanley. "Yes, sir," he said in a low tone. He spoke so low that no one could clearly hear his answer.

"Would you speak up, sir? We didn't hear you." Turning, Stanley watched the men in the front row.

"Yes, sir."

The accused squirmed restlessly, feeling their necks slowly slipping into the noose. Hearing women quietly sobbing in the back forced the outlaws to face the realization of just how incredibly low they had fallen. For the first time, the weight of their evil deeds pressed in on them. Although they felt their families' pain, they refrained from looking at them. Feeling betrayed, they glared at Maines menacingly.

"Would you read the entry I marked?" Maines sat staring at the book as if it were a red-hot poker. Stanley leaned over to point to the place he wanted read. "Right here, Corporal." Maines squirmed visibly, then looked into the anxious faces of his men. "We're waiting, Corporal!" He read the entry, which caused those in the room to moan in horror, then handed the book back to Stanley. Turning to another page, he handed the book back to Maines. "Now, read this passage." Like a trapped animal,

Maines looked down at the designated page then back to the Doctor, who nodded encouragingly. "Go ahead, read the passage!" Taking a deep breath, he did as he was told. Turning to one last passage, he again instructed him to read aloud. Once more, Maines complied. The passage gave the names of those men who had taken part in the heinous crimes mentioned in the preceding passages. Stanley moved in for the kill. "Are these men present in the courtroom?"

Maines paused to look at the accused, then at those in the room. Finally, sighing audibly, he looked at the Doctor. "Yes, sir."

"Would you point them out to us?"

Maines grew paler by the minute, as he tried to weigh his options. Finding that there really weren't any, he pointed to the accused. "They are all sitting in the row behind Lieutenant Gillespie."

Stanley watched Maines closely. "Let me get this straight. Are you admitting that the details in this book are true?" Maines didn't answer but stared at a spot on the floor. "And are you also admitting that the rest of the accused helped you carry out these dastardly deeds?" He peered intently at Maines, who could only nod affirmatively. "I want to hear it coming from your own lips, Corporal."

Head bowed low, he sat there like a whipped puppy waiting for the club to fall. "Yes, sir."

Doctor Stanley turned to Sheriff Hill and Colonel Williams. "In light of this man's confession, I suggest that we dispense with the jury and pass sentence."

Gillespie rose to face the accused with a look of disgust. He turned to Colonel Williams and Sheriff Hill, "I have no objections." He sank onto his chair completely ignoring the men behind him.

The two men looked at the accused shuddering in spite of the heat in the room. "Sound advice!" Williams turned to face the twelve men sitting next to the wall. "The jury is dismissed." None of the men on the jury moved, but they all sighed in relief. Turning his attention back to Corporal Maines, Williams scowled menacingly. "Take your seat, Corporal." Slowly rising, Maines slunk back to sit with his men.

While he took his seat, Williams and Hill conferred before pronouncing a verdict. Finally, Hill turned to the defendants. "The Defendants will now rise." The men slowly got to their feet to face the judges. "Never, in all my years as a lawman, have I heard or seen anything that equals the heinous crimes you have committed. We hereby sentence each of you to die before the firing squad at dawn tomorrow morning ..."

A woman screamed hysterically, rising as quickly as her eighth-month pregnancy would allow. "No! Anything, but that!" Clutching at her chest, she stretched out a hand to stop the judge, then as the strain became more than she could bear, she fainted. One of the accused started to go to her, but Major Brown grabbed him, thus preventing him from getting to her.

Ignoring the woman, Hill continued to pass sentence on the men. "Your bodies will then be buried with headstones, which will state your name, date of birth, death date also the word "MURDERER" in bold letters beneath it. May God have mercy on your souls." Some women among the spectators were weeping softly, while several women were hovering over the distraught wife. "Colonel Williams and I will see that the sentence is carried out."

Leaning back in his chair, he looked at the condemned men. "The men are to be held in the guard house until their executions. Court's adjourned."

Colonel Williams turned to Major Brown. "Major Brown, see that these men are restrained then escorted to the stockade where you are to lock them up. Place two guards around them at all times."

"Yes, sir." Brown saluted respectfully. He saw that these men were restrained by tying them together to prevent escaping. He turned to face a group of soldiers to the right of the room. "Corporal Harris, Private Hanks, Private Townsend, and Private Smith, take these men to the stockade, undo their restraints, then lock them up." The soldiers named rose to come forward. "Corporal Harris … Private Townsend … you take the first watch." Saluting, the soldiers went to carry out their orders. The men were taken through a side door while those in the room filed out.

A short, small-boned woman stepped out from the rest of the crowd. She walked up to Sheriff Hill and Colonel Williams. "Pardon me, but I wonder if I might have a moment of your time?" asked the woman of Colonel Williams.

Both men paused to give her audience, "How can we help you, ma'am?"

Unconsciously raising her head proudly, she began to speak with great dignity. "My name is Maude Walters." Williams bowed slightly then waited for her to continue. "My husband was one of those on trial. He is the one responsible for getting those animals to do those awful things to those poor families." John could tell that it wasn't easy for her to confess this. He felt a great respect for her welling up inside of him. As she stood collecting her thoughts, he had a chance to study her closer. She was dressed in a light blue dress trimmed with a medium-blue collar around the top. A cameo, set amid a backdrop of gold, was pinned at her throat. Puffed sleeves at the shoulders tapered to her wrists, trimmed with the dark-blue. The ankle-length skirt hung straight in the front, with a bustle in the back. A slight train touched the ground. Well-shaped eyebrows, and long lashes enhanced her hazel eyes. A light-blue bonnet, trimmed with white roses amidst long feathered plumes, sat askew on her head. It accentuated her dark-brown tresses, which were done up on her head. A well-defined nose and ruby-red lips favorably accentuated her small cheekbones and her well-shaped jaw. White pointed button-up shoes appeared from under the hem of her dress.

He was brought back to the conversation when he heard her say, "I am going to sell our ranch. I will give the entire proceeds to the relatives of those poor victims."

In astonishment, Williams replied, "We don't require that you do something as drastic as that!"

"I won't live on the place any longer than it takes to sell everything. I definitely don't want any of that tainted money!" Williams nodded understandingly, but remained silent. "As soon as the property is sold, I will take some of the money to get my family a ticket back east, where we can make a new start." She paused thoughtfully for a moment then proceeded. "When I married my husband, I had ten thousand dollars for a dowry. I'll deduct that much from the sale of the ranch."

Williams kindly stepped closer to her to lay a hand lightly on her arm. "That's more than fair, ma'am. Please ... make sure that you don't cheat yourself."

"Thank you, sir." Turning, she quickly walked away.

Colonel Williams turned to look at John. "Well, son, it's over with. You did a good job!"

"Thank you, sir. I'll get my gear together so I can be gone within the hour. Could I have the loan of a packhorse, sir? Old Baldy, the horse I brought with me from Fort Owen, died the morning after I arrived.

Williams stood rubbing his chin thoughtfully. "I would really like it if you stayed until I was ready to go to Fort Owen. It will only be for a few days. I know JaNae enjoys your company as much as I do."

John fumbled for an answer. "I ... I ... I don't want to be in anyone's way, sir."

"Josh Taylor doesn't have many fellows his age to hang around with, so if you were to stay around for a while, there will be lots of opportunities for you two to go fishing."

John thought that over for a moment, then with a smile looked over at Williams. "You drive a hard bargain, sir. Before leaving, I told Ma I was going fishing, so now I won't have told a lie."

Williams chuckled heartily at that statement, then slapped John upon the back. "Good! Then I take it, you will stay?"

John nodded affirmatively. "Thank you, sir. I'll stay."

Williams became elated. "Good! Let's go find out what's for dinner, shall we?" John nodded. Together they walked to the colonel's house. The sight that met their eyes when they walked in was comical.

JaNae was on the floor wrestling with the little female pup. She was on her hands and knees, playing tug a war with an old tea towel. Seeing the two men staring at her, she quickly jumped to her feet and tucked up a stray lock of hair that had fallen down her cheek. John couldn't help but notice how radiantly beautiful she was, standing there in disarray. "Oh, my goodness! I must look a real fright!"

Williams' eyes twinkled merrily while a teasing smile played around his mouth. "I thought I was seeing things when I saw you playing with this little ball of fluff." As he bent down to pick up the pup, the little dog growled at the inconvenience. Williams chuckled. "She surely is a spunky little thing, isn't she?"

JaNae smiled when the colonel looked at the pup curiously. "You would never believe she was even hurt."

John told him how he saved the little family of dogs. "When Josh told me your wife was good with animals, I brought her here."

Sighing, the colonel looked sternly at JaNae. "I knew it! Now I suppose you're going to ask me if we can keep her, aren't you?"

JaNae began to plead softly. "Well ... I would really like to have her company."

He hedged, rubbing his chin while intently studying the pup. It was apparent even to John that he was stalling. "I don't know!" All at once Williams handed the pup to JaNae. "Since you are so set on having her ... helped to make her better ... you can have her."

JaNae, forgetting John, threw her arms around her husband's neck. "Oh, thank you, darling!" That was more than the colonel could bear. He hugged her to him, kissing her gently upon the lips. John turned to look at the fireplace to give them some privacy. JaNae laughed impishly. "Oh look, Jedidiah, we've embarrassed John!" They both chuckled heartily as John's face turned slightly red.

John decided to change the subject. "What are you going to name the pup?"

JaNae looked at the pup intently. "I think she should be called Spunky because she has so much spunk."

"A good name for her," said Williams. They chatted about the dog for a while, grateful to have the day's events behind them. As John watched their interaction with the pup, he was surprised at how much he admired this couple.

CHAPTER 10

Getting Acquainted

Hunger, mingled with passion filled Captain Paul Thompson as he gazed lovingly into his beloved's eyes. Dropping to his knees by the bed, he drew her close to him, rained kisses over her eyes, her cheeks and her neck. A soft moan escaped Kate as his lips touched hers, and she returned kiss for kiss until, too spent physically, she went limp in his arms. Paul peered anxiously into Kate's flushed-face, watching her intently, until she slowly opened her eyes to look lovingly up at him. "I do believe I died and went to heaven, sir! You have never kissed me like that!" She sighed contentedly, as a teasing smile played about her lips when she saw Paul's look of concern. "I'd gladly go there, if it meant I'd get kissed like that again!"

Paul threw back his head laughing heartily. "You little imp!" Scooping her into his arms, he again drank hungrily of her sensuous lips, tenderly kissed her eyes, then kissed her soft lips passionately once more. Laying her gently back onto the bed, he asked, "Now, what do you think of that, you little Vixen?"

"Now I know for sure I died and went to heaven!"

It was difficult to know who was happiest at that moment ... Kate or Paul. Kate was relieved to know that Paul was well and alive. She sensed something wasn't quite right with her husband, but held her own council, deciding to wait until another time to question him. Sinking gratefully back into the pillow, she sighed contentedly. Kate reached up to caress her beloved's face. Taking her hand, Paul pressed it to his cheek, closed his eyes in order to tuck her image into the deepest recesses of his mind. Tears glistened in Kate's eyes when he tenderly kissed the palm of her hand. The moment was so poignant that neither spoke for fear of breaking the spell.

As Paul gazed into Kate's love-filled green eyes, his heart skipped a beat. Her auburn hair lay helter-skelter about the pillow. A few moist strands clung to her ashen face, making her even more beautiful. *I love this woman with every fiber of my being,* he thought. A sob escaped him as he slumped to the floor burying his face on the bed beside her.

While great heart-wrenching emotions ran rampant through his body, Kate gently stroked his hair. "Oh my darling, Kate," he whispered feelingly, as he drew her to him, "I love you so much!" For a moment, the only sound in the room was the ticking of the clock as he held her to him. "I don't ever want to lose you, darling, for my life would be worthless without you!"

Kate smoothing back a lock of hair tried to comfort him. "It's all right, love. I'm going to be just fine!" She tapped him playfully on the arm in an attempt to change the subject. "Besides, ye haven't been properly introduced to yer wee bairns." She chuckled at the strange expression on his face. "Well, ye haven't!"

Paul rose to peer at the sleeping babies. Paul gently reached into the crib closest to the bed. Lifting his son, he tenderly kissed the soft cheek. "And who might you be, sir?" The baby pursed his rosebud lips then continued to sleep.

"I would like you to meet your son, Prince Aaron Joseph Thompson!" Kate declared proudly. She hesitated a moment. "I named him after my father Aaron, your father Joseph, and you." She anxiously watched Paul for any adverse reactions. When he bowed to his son, she sighed in relief.

"A wonderful name for my son." He hesitated as he realized that he truly had a son. "MY SON!" Smiling broadly, he bowed in mock humility. "Well hello there, Prince Aaron! I'm right proud to make your acquaintance, your most royal highness!" A smile began to play about his lips as he lovingly watched the sleeping child. "Well, son, I can see right now that I'll have to beat the girls away from you!" A tiny quiver of the infant's bottom lip was the only notice his son paid him. Paul gently kissed his cheek, then laid him back into his crib.

Kate laughed softly, and then feigned seriousness. "This I've got to see!"

"You hush, woman. Time will tell!"

"Uh huh! As I said before, this I've got to see!" They both chuckled.

Kate smiled, as Paul gently picked up his infant daughter. "Now, Mr. Thompson, please meet yer wee daughter, Princess Sarah Anna-Heleen." She paused to take a deep breath before continuing. "I chose such a big name because I didn't want to miss anyone important."

"I know that you miss your mother, dear, so I think naming her Sarah for your mother was a fantastic idea." Looking tenderly at the sleeping infant in his arms, he smiled proudly. "I can't begin to imagine Anna's reaction to the news."

Kate sighed. "I hope she'll be pleased."

"There's no doubt of that. I think it was ingenious how you rhythmically combined Helen and Eileen into one name. Won't Aunt Eileen be proud as a peacock when she gets the news?"

"Thank you, darling." Feeling pleased that he had liked her choice of names, she sighed contentedly watching the tender scene before her.

"Maybe, it will be the thing that finally drags her out to see us." He tucked the blanket around his daughter then absently stroked her tiny fingers. "Heaven knows, we've pleaded and enticed hard enough." Paul looked lovingly at his sleeping daughter. Kissing her cheek, he bowed to her. "Right pleased to make your acquaintance, Princess Sarah Anna-Heleen!" Her eyebrows knit together, as if she were about to cry. Her bottom lip quivered slightly in her sleep. "Sarah, you surely are a mighty pretty little thing. Almost as beautiful as your wonderful mother!"

Kate laughed outright. "Be off with ye now, ye flatterin' rogue!"

"You can laugh all you want to, but what I say is true!" Gently laying the infant back into the crib, he sat back on the edge of the bed. Taking her hands he said, "I'm tickled pink at the names you gave the children. They fit them somehow."

"Thank you. I didn't know what to do when you didn't come back."

"I'm back now."

She nodded. They began to talk about the hopes and dreams they had for little Aaron Joseph and Sarah Anna-Heleen. Like all parents, they had many great aspirations for them. So they wove their magical dreams until the twins interrupted them. It was apparent by their cries that they wanted attention now ... they wouldn't wait for anyone or anything. Paul guffawed. "Now, I know why you call them the Prince and Princess." Rising, he lifted Aaron from his crib. He placed him into Kate's arms, where he began to suckle. "It's plain to see that they're going to be the rulers of this roost!"

Kate smiled happily, as she gently stroked her son's fingers. Jane came in from outside, as if on a cue, to help with the twins. Jane took care of Sarah's needs then handed her to Paul, who rocked and crooned to her. Sarah wasn't satisfied at all with this attention; she was hungry. There was nothing doing until she got what she wanted. Jane shook her head thoughtfully. "That tyke has a good set of lungs!"

Paul laughingly nodded. "No one would ever guess how hard a time she had coming into this wicked old world!"

The women readily agreed. When Aaron was finished, Jane took him so she could change him. Paul laid Sarah in Kate's arms. The infant, settling down immediately, began to drink greedily. Meanwhile, Jane finished with Aaron, so handed him to his father. Eagerly taking the infant, Paul kissed his tiny cheek. He proceeded to croon a short ditty while gently rocking him back to sleep. Aaron didn't seem to mind that the tune was off-key, but snuggled closer. It wasn't long until he was soon fast asleep. Taking him from Paul, Jane placed him back into his crib and gently tucked a blanket around him. She paused to stroke his tiny cheek.

When Sarah had finished drinking her fill, Paul scooped her up into his arms so he could kiss her tenderly. He tried to croon the same tune, which was just as off-key, but she wouldn't stop fussing. Kate tried to smother a smile, but Jane snickered. Paul looked pained. "Isn't that just like a female? Just plain persnickety!" Both women tried to look sorry for him, but it was plain that they could barely contain their mirth. "Well, my pretty one," Paul said to Sarah, "you'll get nothing better from me, so ya just better learn to like it!" Unable to contain themselves any longer, Jane and Kate burst out laughing. Paul drew Sarah closer to him and whispered just low enough for Kate and Jane to hear. "Between you, me, and the old bed post, sweetheart, I can't say that I blame you." Whimpering softly, Sarah snuggled closer.

This caused the women to laugh even harder. "I'd cry, too, if I had to listen to the likes of that," teased Jane.

Paul joined in on the merriment. Kissing the tiny cheek, he whispered, "Sweet dreams, honey. Papa loves you!" He handed the infant to Jane, watching as she laid her in her crib, then gently tucked a blanket around her. Yes Sir, you are the spittin' image of your sainted mother. Paul admitted to himself that these newcomers had quickly wound their way into his heart. This knowledge touched him deeply.

Jane turned to gaze at the proud parents. "Well, what did you name these little angels?" When Kate told their names, Jane's eyes glistened with unshed tears. "Oh, that will please Anna so much! She so adores you." Then her eyebrows knit together in consternation. "It's such a shame that she has that old coot for a husband!"

Paul nodded. "I agree."

Kate couldn't speak for a moment as she searched for a way to make Jane understand that she hadn't deliberately left her out. "I couldn't figure out a way to add your name, too, Jane. The fact is … I admire you just as much as I do Anna."

Jane waved her hand toward Kate, "What's a name got to do with it anyway? Knowing how you feel about me is the most important thing to me … not a name!" She started to leave the room then turned back with a smile. "Besides, I like the names you gave these angels just fine. It fits them somehow." Kate and Paul smiled proudly as she left the room.

Paul bent to kiss Kate. "Well darling, you have had far too much excitement for one day, so I'm going to leave so that you can rest." He held up his hand when Kate started to protest. "There'll be no arguments from the boss' quarters!" Smiling, Kate shook her head affirmatively, suddenly realizing that she was very tired. Paul saw her close her eyes before quietly leaving.

Jane was busy at the stove when he emerged from the bedroom. He wearily walked over to the table where he sank onto a chair. Jane turned and placed a cup of hot coffee before him, then placed her hands on her hips. "I bet yer a mite hungry, too."

He eyed the steaming kettle on the back of the stove. "I could eat a bite, if it were available."

Jane turned to bustle about the tiny kitchen. "I thought as much. I have never known a time when a man wasn't hungry." She soon placed a bowl of stew in front of him, along with bread, butter, and a jar of preserves she had brought from home. Paul quickly did justice to the meal. He was just starting on his second cup of coffee when Jane put a big slice of apple pie in front of him.

His eyes lit up as he sighed appreciatively. "Oh! This looks wonderful … smells divine!" Taking a large bite, he groaned in delight. "Um, this is heavenly! Where did this come from? Heaven?"

It was apparent that he had thrilled as well as embarrassed her. Blushing, she waved a hand at him. "Ah, cut that out! It really isn't that good! Why, I whipped it up yesterday morning, so taint nothing special to go on about!"

"You may have whipped it up yesterday, but it really is something worth going on about!"

She waved her hand impatiently then went back to sorting the baby clothes. "Thank you for the compliment, sir."

Paul nodded then continued to eat his pie. When he had finished, he rose to take his dishes to the sink. Seeing that there was hot water, he started washing his dishes. Jane started to protest, but he smilingly waved her aside continuing to finish them. "I'm a big boy, dear friend. I can help a little!" Grabbing the dishtowel, he dried the dishes and put them away. After hanging up the towel, he affectionately walked over to Jane, slipping an arm around her shoulder. Before she could protest, he leaned over to kiss her cheek. "Thank you so much for being there for my beloved Kate. I'm mighty beholden to you … as well as Anna … for all you did for her."

Dabbing at her eyes, she began to scold. "Off with you, you old scallywag! 'Twern't nothin. Besides, anybody would have done it."

"Maybe so, but it doesn't change the fact that the two of you were here to make things better for Kate."

Jane was so moved that she couldn't speak, so lowering her head, she continued to sort the clothes. "These clothes have been stored so long, that I'll have to wash them before the little angels can wear them."

Smiling, Paul walked over to his desk. "I guess I'd better get to my report before the major comes looking for me."

Jane snorted. "Huh! He's probably taking his frustrations out on poor Anna!"

Pondering the truth of her statement, he could only shake his head in agreement. Paul sat watching her a moment, then opened his desk. Taking out some paper and a bottle of ink, he prepared to write his report. Nothing came to mind so he sat for a long time just staring at the blank pages. His attention was broken when he heard Jane sigh. Turning, he saw her staring at a pile of clothes strangely. "Is there something wrong?"

"No. I was just wondering if I should check on my family, or at least let Henry know that I'm going to stay over tonight to make sure that Kate will be all right. That is, if you think I should."

"Staying over tonight would be a good idea. I would appreciate the help. "I'm such a new parent that I don't know the first thing to do when it comes to helping my little family. Perhaps you can show me what has to be done. Jane nodded agreeably. He looked into the room at his sleeping family. "Now is a good time for you to tend to your family's needs, Jane. Don't worry about us. I'm sure they will all sleep for a while. Besides, you need a good break!" He waved a hand at her and scowled as though he were angry. "So be off with you." Seeing her look, he smiled so that she knew that he wasn't serious.

"Very well then. I'll hurry so that I can be back as soon as possible."

"There's no need to hurry. Take all of the time you need." Rising, he walked to the door with Jane, where she took her outdoor items from the hook before walking out. Paul stood watching her retreating figure for a moment, grateful for all that she had done. Closing the door, he went to check on his little family. Satisfied that all was well, he went back to his desk to prepare his report. Reaching into his inner pocket to remove the letter from Colonel Williams, he unfolded it and began to scan its contents.

He hadn't gotten far, when there was a knock at the door. Rising, he went to open it. Surprised to see Doctor Phelps, he smiled cheerfully. "Hello, Doctor. Won't you please come on in?"

Phelps entered and removed his hat. "Thanks, Paul."

"What can I do for you?"

"I have to go back to the settlement in a few minutes, so I thought I'd check in on Kate and the twins before I leave. She had such a rough delivery that I have been concerned about her."

"Well, she is sleeping right now."

"Then I'll check on her tomorrow after I get back to the fort."

"You can do it now, if you'd like."

"No, it's not that important. Sleep is what she needs more than anything else right now. If there are any problems, you can send someone out to Hank Thurman's place to get me."

"Thank you. I'll do that, should the need arise." Thompson paused a moment, then continued. "Doctor Phelps, I want to thank you for helping Kate during her hour of travail."

"That's what I'm here for. I have come to respect Kate's spunk ... her tenacity in the face of any challenge. In fact, I had a sister like her once."

"What happened to her? That is, if you don't mind my asking."

"I don't mind. When I was sixteen, cholera struck our little community near London, England. It took my entire family." It took him a moment to collect his thoughts before he could go on. "I had gone to my Uncle Peter's villa in France, so my life was spared. With the loss of my family, I decided to pursue a medical career."

"I'm so sorry for your loss, but very grateful that it led you to become a doctor," murmured Thompson sympathetically.

Phelps shrugged his shoulder nonchalantly. "Well, I have come to accept the loss. Helping others has eased the pain. Hannah, that's my sister, had red hair with green eyes. Smiling, he added, "She was just as big a tease as Kate! I guess that's why I value Kate's friendship so much."

Thompson was greatly moved. "I'm glad the two of you are such great friends."

Phelps moved toward the door. "I better get going. Hank was bucked off of one of his broncos a while ago, and they think he has broken his leg."

"That's too bad about Hank. Don't worry about us, Doctor. We'll be just fine!"

"Good! Then I'm off. See you tomorrow!"

"You bet."

Paul saw him to the door, watching as he saw him saunter toward the infirmary. Quietly closing the door, he went back to his desk. Sinking wearily onto the chair, he picked up the envelope, thoughtfully turning it over and over in his hands. He felt as if he were sitting on a keg of dynamite, with the fuse in place ready to be ignited. *Where is Colonel Williams? Will he be here before Thornton discovers my terrible secret? If he does, what will happen to Kate and the children? Thornton's hatred for her is so strong. Will he make her life miserable, too?* These thoughts along with many others ran rampantly through his mind. Like a rat in a trap, all he could do was wait. Paul picked up the letter scanning its contents again, as he had so many times before. He was puzzled by its context. What could be more pressing than the treaty between the Settlers and the Indians? Sighing, he softly read it aloud.

"Attention: Captain Thompson: Have received the message regarding your situation. Continue as planned. I am unable to assist you at this time, as there are more pressing problems here which must be resolved. Return to the fort when able … await orders. Keep own council. It's imperative that you do not discuss the present outcome with Major Thornton. I will take care of the matter personally, when possible. Prepare a necessary report as follows: Orders completed.

"Sincerely, Colonel Jedidiah Williams."

Paul placed the letter into the envelope. Picking up a pen, he began to work quickly. It wasn't long until the report was ready to deliver to the Major. Kate stirred in the bedroom, so Paul went to her.

"What time is it?"

"Nearly 7:30 P. M."

"Oh, my goodness! I didn't realize that I'd been asleep for so long"

"You needed the rest."

Sighing, she stretched lazily. "The bad part is … I don't feel like I've even been asleep."

Paul smiled. "I can imagine. Your body took a real beating when the twins were born." Tucking her in, he leaned down to kiss her. "Just sleep all you want, honey. Jane and I'll be here to take care of whatever needs to be done."

Kate yawned. "Okay, I will." It wasn't long until she was fast asleep.

Paul looked at the twins, gently touching each cheek. *What a tired trio*, he thought. He tiptoed quietly from the room. Someone knocked at the door, so he quietly walked over to open it. Seeing that it was Jane, he invited her in. "I need to get this report to Major Thornton as soon as possible. Do you mind staying with the family while I take care of this?"

Jane removed her shawl, hanging it on the peg by the door before answering. "Of course not. I'd be happy to stay." She hesitated a moment, then began to speak. "Henry told me that he has heard a lot of yelling by Thornton. He also said there's an awful ruckus going on at the Major's. I'm very worried about Anna."

Paul's brows drew together as anger washed over him. "I was afraid of that! I'll let you know what's up when I get back." He started out the door then turned back. "I'll get a cot for you along with some bedding when I've finished with the Major." Jane thanked Paul as he walked out.

CHAPTER 11

Anna

Pulling his coat tightly around him, Captain Paul Thompson stepped off of the porch heading toward Thornton's office. He hadn't gone far when Peters caught up to him. "Hello, Peters. How goes it?"

Peters saluted. "Fine, suh. Jest fine!"

"At ease, Sergeant."

As Thompson continued toward Thornton's office, Peters fell in with him. They walked awhile in silence until the silence had grown uncomfortable. Peters turned to face Thompson. "Ah heard from Henry Hansen thet yer missus hed twins."

Paul smiled proudly, while unconsciously puffing out his chest, "That's right, Dan."

"How's the missus en the babies doin', suh?"

"Great! Jane is staying with them while I deliver this report to Thornton. When I left, they were all sleeping like babies." He laughed heartily at his own pun.

Peters stopped walking to frown at Thompson. Referring to the Captain's play on words, he said, "Oh, thet's torrible!" The two men laughed as they continued strolling toward Thornton's office. "Bet ya were a mite surprised ta find she hed twins."

"To say the least! I'm still a little dazed over it all."

Smiling, Peters shook his head thoughtfully. "Two blessings in one can be quite a bit ta handle, 'specially in the times we is livin' in."

"That's true, but I wouldn't change these blessings for all the tea dumped in the Boston Harbor."

As they neared the Major's quarters, they heard Thornton bellowing like a mad bull. They immediately knew Anna was in grave danger. As they looked worriedly at each other, they heard a loud thud coming from inside the house. Both gasped. They paused outside the door to contemplate the best course of action. "What shud we do, sir?"

Thompson remained silent as he pondered the situation. Finally, he turned to whisper to his companion. "Peters, I want you to wait out here until I return." Peters nodded. "Move into the shadows … act as though nothing is happening, but remain close in case I need you."

"Yes, suh!"

"I'm going to try to distract the Major. If what I suspect is happening, Mrs. Thornton is going to need immediate medical attention."

"Ah understand, suh." Looking around to see that no one else was in the vicinity, Peters moved back into the shadows. Thompson stepped onto the porch, hesitated a moment, then stepped inside.

The door to the Thornton's living quarters was open, furnishing Thompson with a full view of all that was happening. Anger welled up inside of him as he watched Thornton's treatment of Anna. Ranting and raving like a mad bull, the major was shaking Anna as though she were an old rag doll. Seeing a chair lying on the floor to the left, Thompson realized it had been the cause of the loud noise they'd heard earlier. Before Thompson could do anything, Thornton struck Anna hard in the right eye with his fist, causing her to lose her balance and fall backwards over the chair.

When she didn't move, he grew angrier ... bellowing even louder. "Why, you filthy good for nothing rotten ugly witch! Get up or I'll kick your guts out!" When Anna didn't move, Thompson realized that she was unconscious and mercifully beyond hearing. Paul nearly lost control of his emotions when he saw Thornton kick Anna repeatedly in the ribs. He was about to deliver another blow when Thompson coughed. Thornton whirled toward the sound, his face filled with unspent passion and blind rage. "What do you want?"

Thompson smothered the anger inside and meekly saluted. "Excuse me, sir. I didn't know you were busy. I came in to deliver my report." Swallowing, he took a step backward. "I can come back later."

"No! I'll finish this little matter later." He entered the office, closing the door to the living quarters. Crossing to the desk, Thornton dropped heavily into the chair. Looking impatiently over at Thompson, he demanded. "Okay, let's have it!"

Thompson was amazed at how callously Thornton could ignore the still form of his wife, lying helplessly on the floor in the other room. With all the will power that he could muster, Thompson again smothered his anger before speaking. "The orders have been completed; however, while destroying the village, the men contracted Typhus. Because it was so contagious, we couldn't return to the fort until they were all well. As you'll read in the report, it took some time for the men to overcome the effects of the disease. There were some that didn't make it." Reaching into his pocket, he took out a large piece of paper. Unfolding it, he handed it to Thornton. "I took the liberty of preparing a list with the individual names of those soldiers who perished from the disease."

Thornton, after quickly glancing at the list, handed it back to Thompson with a look of disgust. "Contact the families of these men and give them my condolences."

"Yes, sir." For a moment, he became so enraged that he had to look at his hands a moment to gain control. Finally, he looked at Thornton, who was waiting for him to speak.

When he remained silent, Thornton asked, "Did you conduct a thorough search of the area to see if there were any stinking savages in hiding?"

"Yes we did, sir, but there weren't any."

Thornton grew very excited as he shook Thompson's hand vigorously. "Great! Very well done, Captain!" He slumped back into his chair, struggling to appear calm and failing miserably. Leaning forward, he glared at Thompson. "That will be all. You're dismissed." Saluting, Thompson left the office. Everything inside of him wanted to punch the major until he was as helpless as his wife, but as Thornton was his superior officer, he knew he dared not touch him. Closing the door, he was surprised at how calmly he had acted to the situation. Peters moved cautiously out of the shadows when Thompson motioned to him to follow. Thompson filled Peters in on what transpired with Thornton as they walked a short distance from the office. There they waited in the deepest shadows for the opportunity to help Anna.

Thornton emerged from his office smoking a cigarette. After taking a few drags of the cigarette, he threw it onto the porch, crushing it with his foot. Looking intently around to satisfy himself that all was well, he stepped down from the porch. He started roughly heading to the officers' quarters. Within minutes, Thornton along with three of his friends emerged crossing over to the saloon. Hearing the men laugh gleefully as they neared the Mercantile, Thompson felt an overwhelming urge to silence them. They waited a few more minutes, even though they knew that the men would be celebrating the major's victory far into the night. Satisfied they weren't coming back, he turned to face Peters. "Go get Doctor Phelps now!"

"Yes, suh!"

"Wait!"

Peters stopped to stare at Thompson wonderingly. "Yes, suh?"

"Phelps went out to Hank Thurman's place to set his broken leg. Send Corporal Stevens out right away. Tell him that it's imperative that he speaks to no one. Go to the infirmary. Tell the orderly to bring a stretcher and a small medical kit on the double."

"Right away, suh." Turning, Peters ran toward the officers' quarters.

Turning, Paul entered Thornton's living quarters. Seeing Anna lying prostrate on the floor, he hurried over to kneel beside her. Compassion combined with anger vied for dominance as he felt for her pulse. Fear gripped him as he realized the extent of her injuries. "You poor thing! You're barely alive!" Paul quietly murmured.

Anna's upper lip was bleeding profusely. Both cheeks were also cut, one worse than the other. Even though they were bleeding, they were already beginning to swell, bleeding slightly and beginning to bruise. From the angle of her arm and the bulge at its side, he feared her arm was broken. When Thompson moved the overturned chair lying near Anna's head, he saw a small pool of blood. He knew that she'd struck her head on the chair when she fell. As he gently turned her face toward him, he noticed blood flowing freely from a large cut on the side of her left temple. There was so much blood coming from the wound that he couldn't tell how bad the injury was. Glancing quickly around the room, he saw a clean neatly folded dishtowel lying on the counter. Rising quickly, Thompson crossed the room, snatched up the towel, and plunged it into a nearby water bucket. After wringing it out, he again knelt beside the still form. Thompson applied the towel to the wound in an attempt to stem the flow of blood.

Anna moaned softly then lay still. Thompson didn't know what else to do, so he began to talk softly to her. "I never got a chance to tell you how grateful I was for what you did for my Kate. Carl took you away before I came back into the living room." Anna didn't stir. Paul wondered if she were even able to hear him. As there wasn't anything else to do, he decided to keep talking to her. "Wasn't that a real surprise … our Kate having twins? Just wait until you hear what Kate named them. In all the hubbub going on here at the fort, we didn't have much time to decide on a name for the baby, so Kate made the final choice." Groaning, Anna tried to rise, but didn't have enough strength. Moaning once more, she fell silent.

Thompson went over to the bucket to rinse out the towel. He reapplied it to the wound. *Too bad McCabe went to Missoula for supplies,* he thought. "You just hang in there, Anna. We need your sweet presence around to keep things sane. I promise that Carl won't ever get the chance to do this to you again."

He was prevented from saying more when Peters threw open the door. He entered, followed by the orderly. Leaning the stretcher against the table, he looked down at Anna. "Corporal Stevens rode out ta git Doctor Phelps. He shud be back here in no time."

"Good!"

Jason Bernhardt, the orderly in charge, moved over to kneel beside Anna. Slowly and meticulously he felt for broken bones. "How long has she been this way?"

"At least ten minutes." Bernhardt mumbled something under his breath, which Thompson couldn't discern. "I've been trying to stem the flow of blood coming from the wound she sustained to her head, but it's still flowing heavily. She has weaved in and out of consciousness a few times, but not for long."

"I see. She's in a very bad way, sir. We need to get her to the infirmary so that we can better attend to her needs." That was a lot coming from Bernhardt, considering he never did much speaking at any one time.

"Very well then, let's get her onto the stretcher as carefully as possible."

They had barely gotten her onto the stretcher, when the door flew open. Doctor Phelps entered. While carefully examining her, he cursed Thornton vehemently. He glanced toward the men. "That man has got to be stopped somehow, or he'll kill this dear lady! I know he'll get his just desserts someday, and just between us, gentlemen, I'm looking forward to that day! So help me, Hannah, I am!"

Peters scowled, "Ah feels the same!" Bernhardt nodded, but refrained from speaking.

Thompson grew sullen as he looked at each of them. "I promise all of you that he'll never get another chance to hurt her like this again!"

Straightening, Phelps turned to the waiting men. "We must get her moved to the infirmary as soon as we can! It's not safe to remain here. Thornton may return at any moment to prevent us from attending to her wounds. If that were to happen, she might die. I don't want to take that chance. Thompson, get a blanket from one of the beds. I don't want her to go into shock while we transport her to the infirmary."

Thompson did as he was told, soon returning with a blanket. As Phelps gently wrapped it around her, Thompson noticed that the right eye, now badly bruised, had swollen shut. The lacerations on her cheeks, still oozing blood, were also dark and swollen. Tears glistened in his eyes as he instinctively reached for one of her hands. "All because you helped my Katie girl," he said remorsefully.

Anna lay still … silent as she was carried to the infirmary as fast as they dared. Thompson and Peters waited outside while the doctor attended to Anna's injuries. Turning to a nearby tray, Phelps picked up a pair of scissors. After cutting the hair away from her head injuries, he gently felt around the area. "I don't like this bump on her head," said Phelps. "This is a very bad cut, too." Phelps, with Bernhardt's assistance, proceeded to clean the area. After suturing the wounds, he put on a dressing. When he was finished, Phelps began to examine the other cuts around her face. The cut under her left eye required three stitches, as did the cut on her lip. The gash on the right cheek required 30 stitches. After stitching the wound, a dressing was applied.

Bernhardt anxiously peered over Phelps' shoulder, watching him run his fingers lightly over her ribs. "How many of the ribs are broken, Doctor? When I examined her at her home, I thought there were at least two."

"I could tell there are at least three. By the sight of the bruising, I wouldn't be surprised if there aren't more." Phelps turned to get the items needed to wrap her ribs. "Thank goodness none of them punctured the lungs." After Anna's ribs were wrapped to Phelps' satisfaction, he turned his attention to her left arm.

Bernhardt gasped at the sight of the arm. "In order to have the arm look like that, he had to have twisted it in an unnatural way."

"I agree."

When Phelps straightened to start toward a cabinet, the orderly took another look at Anna's arm. The sight made him wince in disgust. "This looks really bad!"

For a moment, Phelps scanned the young man's face then sighed, "It is. The wrist is broken, the forearm has sustained a fracture. If that isn't enough, the arm has been pulled from the socket."

Bernhardt's eyes glistened with unshed tears, which surprised Phelps. In all the time he'd worked with the man, Bernhardt had never once shown any emotion. Blinking twice, the young orderly was back in control. "Tell me what you need, Doc. I'll help any way possible."

Phelps began barking orders, which the orderly started to do. For a while, things grew hectic. When they had done all they could, Phelps stepped back and sighed wearily. "Now all we can do is wait for her to regain consciousness." Phelps looked over at Bernhardt with a smile. Thanks for your help, Jason."

"Glad I could be of help, sir." He took a deep breath. "You know, sir, I've come to have a great respect for Mrs. Thornton. She never lets things keep her down." He paused a moment then continued, "if only something could be done to stop the Major from hurting her again."

Phelps pondered the orderly's words then sighed resignedly. "Let's put her into the bed near the window." With Bernhardt's assistance, the two of them moved Anna to the bed, making her as comfortable as possible. Phelps went to the door. "It's all right for you to come in now." He moved aside to let Thompson and Peters enter, and they anxiously took seats close to Anna.

A few minutes later, Anna began groaning, thrashing about to find relief from the pain. "Oh, I hurt so bad … my head."

Phelps gently tried to calm her. "I know Anna … but you must lie still, or you'll hurt yourself even more." Anna tried to comply, but the pain was more than she could bear at the moment. Phelps quickly stepped over to a medicine cabinet, took down a bottle of Laudanum and quickly prepared a dose. Putting the bottle back where it belonged, he closed the door, moved back to her bed where he administered it to her. Patiently stroking her hand, Thompson talked soothingly to her. Tears streamed down Anna's cheeks as she valiantly tried to tolerate the pain. When the medication began to take effect, she grew calmer. Finally, she fell into a fitful, troubled sleep.

Phelps flopped into the nearest chair, anxiety showing on his face. Thompson sat next to Anna, absently stroking her fingers, while he struggled to control the rage that threatened to consume him. Peters walked over placing a hand on his shoulder. "When ya interrupted the major tonight, ya saved Mrs. Thornton's life, Cap'n." Thompson shuddered then looked at Peters curiously.

Turning toward Thompson, Phelps noticed how haggard he looked. "Peters is right, Paul. Thornton wouldn't have stopped until he'd killed her."

Thompson shuddered again at the thought before turning toward Phelps. "I have no doubt that you're right, sir." He looked beseechingly from one to the other. "I also know that she is in this condition because of helping my wife, Kate."

"Yore right, suh. Thet's why Ah thin' it's best thet we don't tell Kate 'bout Anna's condition 'til she's much stronger."

"Peters is right, Captain. It will only worry her, as well as make her feel bad." Thompson readily agreed. "Her friendship with Anna is special, but right now we need to let her gain her strength without worrying about Mrs. Thornton."

"I agree with both of you! Kate would fret something awful." Paul sat thoughtfully for a moment. An amused expression crossed his face. "If I know my wife, and I do, she'd find a way to go tell Thornton off."

Smiling, Phelps nodded slightly, "That's just what we want to prevent her from doing. First of all it would set her recovery back a long way. Second, it would probably be enough to send Thornton over the edge. Thompson nodded in agreement. "Now, you'd both best get out of here and go home. It would never do for Thornton to catch you here."

Sighing, Thompson gently patted Anna's hand in concern. Looking at her, Thompson nodded affirmatively. "You're right, of course."

"Thornton is vile and evil, but also smart enough to know that it was you that got help for Mrs. Thornton. With his hatred of Kate, it wouldn't be good for either Anna or Kate. So let him cool off awhile before you have to confront him."

Nodding, Thompson rose to leave. "I'll be back tomorrow to check on her progress. Phelps nodded. "Good night now." Peters and Thompson reluctantly departed. Thompson's mind was in a state of chaos as he trudged wearily home. He leaned against the porch post a moment, fighting to gain control of his emotions before entering the house. He went directly to his little family. Jane was just finishing with the twins when Paul entered the bedroom. "Hi, sleepy head," he said to Kate.

"Why did it take so long to present your report, dear?"

"I got to talking to Peters and Doctor Phelps. Somehow I lost track of time. How are you doing since I've been gone?" He could feel Jane's penetrating eyes on him but didn't acknowledge them.

"I feel much better, except that I feel like I've been asleep forever." A smile began to play around her lips. "Sort of like that fellow who slept for one hundred years … what's his name?"

Jane grinned. "Do you mean Rip Van Winkle?"

"That's it! Like him, I feel like I've been asleep for at least one hundred years." Everyone laughed.

"Good. You need to go back to sleep for the rest of the night, at least!" said Paul.

Wrinkling her nose, Kate saluted him smartly. "Yes sir, boss! Right away, boss!"

Paul playfully tweaked her chin. "That's my girl!" Kate smiled then snuggled further under the covers. Paul leaned over to kiss her gently upon the lips. "Good night, honey."

"Good night, Paul." She was soon fast asleep.

Jane and Paul tiptoed from the room. When they were safely out of the room, Jane spun around to face him. "Okay, spill it!" When she saw that he wasn't going to say anything, she grew impatient with him. "Listen, Paul Thompson, I could tell by your face, when you walked into this house, that something wasn't right!" Placing her hands on her hips, she stared at him. "So spill it!"

"I saw him shake her like a burlap sack. Making a fist, he hit her hard in the eye. She fell backward over the chair and lay unconscious upon the floor. When she didn't move, he cursed her then began kicking her viciously in the ribs. I coughed loudly to distract him."

Thompson had to stop to gain control of his anger. "For a moment I wanted to kill him. I wanted to ignore the fact that he was my superior officer. I wanted to thrash him until he was as helpless as Anna ... maybe even break a few of his bones! But some inner voice snapped me back to reality. At that moment, I knew I dared not give into my feelings. To do so would not only destroy my family, but would put me in the same league as him."

He looked intently into Jane's angry face. "Do you know that he was so anxious to know what was in the report, that he left Anna lying there on the floor?" Jane blinked then started at Thompson in disbelief. "It's true! When he got the news he expected, he went off to get good and roaring drunk with his cronies!"

Jane, who had turned visibly pale, continued to intently study his face. "What about Anna? Is she going to be alright?"

"Yes, but it's going to take a while, because she was pretty badly beaten."

Jane could no longer control her emotions. "I've seen Carl Thornton stoop pretty low during the time I've known him, but even I didn't think he would sink this low!" She fought valiantly to gain control. Taking a deep breath, she was able to go on. "You know, Paul, sometimes I wish someone would kill him!" Thompson could only stare at her incredulously. "It's true! If I were anything but a lady and a Christian, I'd laugh over his grave when he was gone!"

"I understand your feelings, Jane. All of my life I've tried to treat my fellow man with respect. I can even respect a man who has forsaken God, but I can never respect a man who abuses his wife!"

Jane nodded, growing thoughtful, "Paul, how long will God allow Carl to go on hurting or taking advantage of others?"

Thompson sat thoughtfully pondering the question. Finally, he looked at her sympathetically. "I don't know, Jane. I know that God allows all men the right to make their own choices, good or bad, but only God can determine when they should be stopped." They fell silent, each one lost in private thoughts, then Paul exhaled. "To answer your question, Jane, I just don't know how long He will allow Thornton to go on hurting others! Only God can answer that question, I guess. One thing I do know for sure is that Kate can't know about Anna's condition until she is stronger. It would be too hard for her to bear because of her feelings toward Anna."

"I understand, Paul. Please don't fret about me because I can keep quiet."

"I know you will, Jane. I have no fear of that!"

"Why don't I pour you a cup of coffee. Could I also fix you a bite to eat?"

"I'd love a cup of coffee, but nothing more to eat. Well, maybe another piece of that delicious pie I had for lunch."

After getting the pie and coffee, she sat down to talk to Paul while he ate. "Tomorrow when Kate and the children have been taken care of, I would like to go over to the infirmary to check on Anna."

"I think that's a great idea. She needs the support of her friends right now."

They talked for a while about other things, then said good night and retired to their separate beds.

Thornton came out of the Mercantile around midnight, feeling testy, looking for a fight. Staggering, he ran into a hitching post and nearly got kicked by a horse that hadn't been put in the stables. Righting himself, he staggered on toward home. He began to sing loudly, as he reeled along. At one point, he tripped over his own feet, which sent him sprawling onto his face in the middle of the road. Cursing, he struggled to his feet. He squinted his eyes in an attempt to clear them from their drunken haze. When he reached home, he tripped on the step and fell face forward onto the porch. Grumbling under his breath, he again scrambled to his feet, then staggered into the house.

Bellowing like a mad man, he yelled for Anna to get out to the kitchen. When there was no answer, he staggered to the bedroom and threw open the door. Yelling out her name as he swaggered to the bed, he struck her side of the bed with an awful blow. Finding the bed empty, he began ranting and raving, throwing things around the room, like a man possessed. Staggering back out to the kitchen, he lit a match to see the room. The chair had not only been righted, but had been pushed back into place at the table.

"Thompson!" He bellowed at the top of his lungs, blowing out the striker. Hate so strong, so all consuming, filled him. Striking another match, he gazed at the spot of blood on the floor. "Thompson was here!" Whirling around, he started for the door. Still walking unsteadily, he made his way into the crisp night air. After looking groggily around, Thornton raised his arms heavenward with his hands clenched tightly into fists. "Thompson, you'll be sorry you ever meddled in my affairs!"

A soldier came running anxiously over to him. "Are you all right, sir?"

"No, you dunderhead! I'm not all right!"

The private, Gordon Jamison, watched Thornton nervously. "How can I help you, sir?"

"Tell me where she is."

Jamison looked at Thornton, "Where she is? I don't know who you are you talking about, sir?" Jamison had hoped not to be the one to deliver the news to Major Thornton.

Thornton grew angrier. "The hag I had the misfortune of marrying. Who else do you think I'm talking about, you fool?"

"I just heard that your wife was taken to the infirmary, sir." Yelling, Thornton waved his clenched fist in the air as he spit out murderous threats against Thompson. Frightened, Jamison took a step backward, then fled.

Thornton was so angry that he didn't even notice that the soldier was gone. Cursing with every step, he staggered crazily toward the infirmary, intent upon finishing what he'd begun. It didn't matter that he'd awakened most of the people in the fort.

He just wanted to wreak havoc on Anna. When he finally reached the infirmary, he threw open the door and staggered inside.

Phelps rose from his seat beside Anna. Slowly coming toward Thornton, he tried to calm the turmoil that churned within him. "What do you want at this time of the night, Major Thornton?"

"You know darn well what I want, Phelps, so let's not beat around the bush, shall we?"

Gazing intently at Thornton, Phelps was reminded of a rattler about to strike. "Oh I do, do I?" It was obvious that he was not going to volunteer any information. "And just what might that be?"

Thornton began moving toward Anna. "You have my wife in that bed over there, and I came to take her home!"

"I think not!" replied Phelps, defiantly stepping in Thornton's way.

Thornton looked dumbly at Phelps, growing so angry that the veins in his neck bulged and his face turned red with unspent passion. "What did you say?"

Phelps remained calm as he stared back at the Major. "I said … I think not!"

Thornton moved to step around him. "We'll just see about that!"

Phelps quickly stepped back in front of him. "You have no jurisdiction in this infirmary, Major Thornton, so if I say you aren't going to take her home, then you aren't going to take her home."

Leering at Phelps, Thornton started to threaten him. "I can dismiss you without a qualm, so you'd better think twice before you cross me!"

"I have no fear of you, Thornton. McCabe told me that he was free to retire as soon as he returned from Missoula. That makes me the only doctor here for miles around." Thornton glared at Phelps, who remained impassive. "You can try to get rid of me, but you'll find that it will bring down the wrath of Fort Missoula, and that you don't want."

"Why, you're nothing but a low down mangy good-for-nothing rotten cur! You'll rue the day you ever dared to cross me!" Turning, he stormed out of the infirmary staggering toward home.

∞◈ ◈∞

Morning came all too soon for Thompson, as he woke to the sounds of the reveille. Looking over at his sleeping wife, he couldn't help thinking how beautiful she was. Sighing, he rose, dressed quickly, then went quietly to start a fire in the stove. Jane, who lay with her back to him, didn't stir as he bustled about. When he was satisfied that the fire was going well, he turned the damper. Taking the washbasin, he went to the reservoir, filled the pan then went back to the counter to prepare for the day. When he was finished, he cleaned up his mess and quietly left the house.

The morning air was crisp but clear as Thompson walked toward the troops, who were assembled for parade. They came to full attention as he approached. Peters saluted Thompson before turning back to the men. Thompson took his time inspecting them, greatly impressed at how good they looked. "Very good, men! At ease!" As one, the men relaxed to listen as Peters gave them their orders for the day. Thompson and Peters were about to go about their various duties after dismissing the soldiers, when Thornton emerged from his office. Although he was immaculately dressed, he appeared to swagger slightly. "Wait up, Thompson! I want to see you for a moment!"

"Yes, sir!" Saluting, Thompson stood rigidly at attention, while struggling inwardly to steel against the onslaught of anger he knew was coming from his superior officer.

Thornton's only notice of Thompson's salute was a grunt. "As you were, Captain." Lowering his arm, Thompson waited for the axe to fall. Thornton turned to glare at Peters, who wisely walked a little distance away. Thornton turned his attention back to Thompson. "I came home to find Anna missing, so I went in search of her. I found her at the infirmary." He paused, glaring hatefully at Thompson. "Do you know what Phelps told me, when I told him I was taking her home?"

"No, sir."

"Well, he had the unmitigated gall to inform me that she was going to remain there under his watchful care!" Thompson remained silent as Thornton rambled on. "That old hag is just faking it to get attention!"

Thompson lost all control at Thornton's last comment. "Excuse me, sir, but Mrs. Thornton is not faking it. In fact, if we hadn't gotten her help when we did, she would have died. You would have been charged with murder!"

Thornton stared at Thompson in amazement then stiffened. Every cord and vein bulged in his neck, causing his face to turn red as rage engulfed him. "It's bad enough that your wife tries to meddle into my affairs, but I will not tolerate you sticking your rotten nose into them as well! If you ever try to intervene for her again, you'll be sorry! Do I make myself clear?"

Unknown to Thornton, Peters stood behind him making warning gestures. Thompson watched Peters a moment then turned his attention back to Thornton. "Yes, sir! I understand you implicitly, sir!"

"You'd better!" Turning, he walked briskly back to his office, slamming the door so hard that the windows rattled.

"Ah'd say thet he were jest a tad bit angry, suh," said Peters.

Thompson nodded, looking toward the office. "Thanks for making those gestures, Peters. They helped me keep from losing complete control."

Shrugging, Peters grinned impishly. "Aw, Ah were doin' thet so's not ta hit him over the head with somethin'! Ah'm glad ifn' it heped ya."

"I didn't remain too calm, though!"

Peters chuckled. "Well, ya could'a fooled me!"

Thompson shrugged. The two men walked toward the infirmary.

CHAPTER 12

A Time for Healing

The following days proved a challenge for Thompson. Being an only child, he had never been around other children or infants in his growing up years. Paul didn't know the first thing to do with his children. Jane patiently undertook the task of teaching him how to properly care for them. Many times she had to turn her back so that Paul didn't see the smile that tugged around her lips. It was decided the next morning that Paul would bathe Aaron Joseph. While he dressed the child, Jane would then care for Sarah.

Bathing his son proved very difficult. Jane patiently instructed him on how to undress the infant. He did just fine until he got to the diaper. There was a strange smell emanating from that region of his son's person. Wrinkling his nose distastefully, he turned toward Jane in the hopes that she would bail him out.

A teasing gleam came into Jane's eyes. "Now's as good a time as any for you to learn how to change a diaper."

Again he wrinkled his nose, staring at the diaper as if it would change itself. When it didn't, he sighed in frustration. "Aw, shucks! I've never done this before, Jane."

"As I said, this is as good a time as any to start."

"Do you mean to say that you won't help me?"

"That's what I'm a saying." He was so absorbed in the task ahead of him that he didn't see the smile tugging at the corners of her mouth. "You're a father now, Captain, so you've got to learn to help in these matters."

"Yes, ma'am!" He was plainly not convinced.

"First of all, let me show you how to fold a diaper." She slowly folded a diaper, explaining each step to him as if he were an errant child. When she was done, she shook it out before handing it to him. "You have to do it yourself."

"Very well." Taking the diaper from Jane, he began to fold it. When he was finished, he looked at Jane with a proud smile. "There!"

"It appears that you're ready to begin."

"Removing the pins, he gagged a few times when he removed the flap. Lifting the child, he started for the bucket on the counter. Jane, guessing his intentions, moved quickly toward him. "No! You can't put him in that icy water!"

Paul stopped to stare at her dumbfounded. "Why ever not?"

"You'll shock his little system, that's why not."

"Oh!"

"Bring him back here and I'll show you what to do."

Slowly, he sheepishly walked back to Jane. "Guess I didn't think about it hurting him."

Jane snickered. "That was evident!" Seeing Paul's confusion, she instructed him on how to clean him up. "Now, it's time to give him his bath."

For a moment Paul appeared as if he were ready to bolt. Only the love for his child kept him there. "Will that be as hard as the diaper?"

"It shouldn't be. Just do as I tell you, and you'll be done in no time."

"Lead on!"

Jane taught him how to test the water and how to hold Aaron while he bathed him. "See, that's not so bad."

"That's easy for you to say! This is all old hat for you!"

"Really, Captain, you're doing great."

"Thank you."

"The more you do this, the easier it will become."

"That remains to be seen."

Finally the job was done. It was now time to dress Aaron. Smiling, Jane decided to warn him. "It's always better to diaper him first."

"Very well." Paul struggled valiantly to get the diaper snug enough to ensure its staying on, then pinned it. Triumphant of his job, he proudly lifted the child for inspection. "There! That's done!" His mouth gaped open in stunned disbelief as the diaper he'd so patiently worked to get right, hung sloppily on the infant's hips. It was slowly sliding off. Jane snorted, grabbed her sides laughing uncontrollably. "Laugh, will you!" Seeing the humor in it all, he willingly joined her.

When Jane was able to gain control, she again showed Paul how to properly fold the diaper. "For one thing ... you've made the diaper too big."

After painstakingly folding the diaper, he started to put it back onto his son, but it was too late. A stream of liquid hit Paul in the chest, completely soaking his once immaculate uniform. "Ah!" he exclaimed.

Again, Jane laughed uproariously at Paul's shocked expression. "That's why ... I told ... you ... to put ... the diaper on first!" Jane could hardly get the words out.

"Now, I know why it's women's work. Only they have enough patience to deal with surprises like this!" He grinned in spite of himself as he removed his coat jacket. Sighing, Paul started over. With Jane's patient tutelage, Paul finally mastered the diaper, then got Aaron dressed. After donning a new jacket, Paul proudly picked up his infant son to gently kiss the tiny cheek. Aaron's bottom lip began to quiver, while his eyebrows puckered threateningly. "That was a difficult ordeal to undergo, wasn't it old man?" Again, the tiny lip quivered.

Smiling, Jane cleared away the mess then prepared the water for Sarah's bath. She went to the bedroom to get the sleeping child. Paul gently rocked Aaron while he watched the procedure with Sarah. When Sarah was dressed, Jane placed her in Paul's other arm. Stepping back, she watched the beautiful interaction of father, daughter, and son. "Now, that's a picture, if ever there was one!"

Paul smiled lovingly at his infant daughter. "How's my little beauty this morning?" Paul couldn't help smiling as Sarah yawned sleepily. Sighing, she closed her eyes. Rising, he walked into the bedroom, where Kate waited anxiously. "Good morning, Momma!"

"Good morning yourself, Papa." When Kate reached out for a baby, Paul placed Sarah into her arms, then sat on the edge of the bed. He gently rocked Aaron while Sarah drank her fill. By the time she was finished, Jane had straightened up the kitchen. Joining them in the bedroom, Jane took Sarah, laying her over her shoulder to burp. Paul placed Aaron in Kate's arms watching as he began to suckle. There was a sudden knock at the door. Paul rose to answer it.

"Why, Ilse, what a pleasant surprise!" Ilse stood in the doorway holding a container with a dishtowel wrapped around it. Moving aside, he motioned to her to enter. "Won't you please come in?"

She held the container out to him. "Danke! I don't vant to disturb Katie if she's resting. As I was baking, I thought ya might like some fresh rolls."

Paul took the container. "We'd love some. They feel hot!"

"Ya, I took zem out a few minutes ago."

"Please, come in, Ilse. Kate will be delighted to see you. You won't be disturbing her at all, as she is feeding the twins."

Ilse hesitated, unsure what to do. "If yer sure tis no botter."

"No bother at all!"

Ilse stepped inside. "Vell den, I'd like to see her, too."

Paul placed the container of rolls onto the table then turned back to Ilse. "This way." He led the way to the bedroom.

Kate smiled excitedly. "Hello, Ilse! This is such a wonderful surprise!"

Ilse beamed, greeting the women cheerfully. "Danke. Gutten morgan, Katie." Turning to Jane, she smiled as she nodded slightly. "Mornin', Mrs. Hansen,"

"Please, just call me Jane. Calling me Mrs. Hansen makes me feel old … worn out."

Paul snorted. "Huh! You old and worn out! That'll be the day!"

"Don't pay any attention to him, Ilse," chided Jane good-naturedly. "It's so good to see you. How have you been doing?"

"Yost fine … danke."

"Good!"

Kate patted the bed invitingly. "Come sit on the bed beside me, dear."

Ilse walked over to the cribs. "Let me peek at zee kinders first." She excitedly clapped her hands together. "Oh, vat little engels!" After gently touching each cheek, she walked over to sit on the edge of the bed.

"Now, my dear, tell me how your family is doing."

Ilse started chattering in her broken English. "Vell, my Hans is plowin' and plantin' like a crazy vool!" She sighed resignedly, and then continued. "Here tis Yune and already he haf our garden in and two fields of veat and two fields of hay planted. Our cows broke down zee fence yesterday, so today, my Hans and zee tree older boys are oust mending fences." She paused thoughtfully before continuing. "Seems like farm vork never ends. Alvays somesink ta do!" Ilse sighed wearily, folded her hands in her lap smiling. "Oh vell ... It keeps vun humble as vell as out a trouble, I guess."

Kate patted Ilse's hand sympathetically. "I'm glad that you took time out of your busy day to come see me. We haven't seen you for quite a while, and frankly, I've missed you."

Ilse smiled broadly. "Danke."

Ilse, a tall, buxom woman of German descent, was seven months pregnant and walked with difficulty. Thick golden braids wrapped around her head like a crown and her high cheekbones accentuated her piercing, light-blue eyes that sparkled with life from her pale complexion. Her light-blue, checked dress was covered by a white apron that was crisply starched. Her sleeves, were full to the wrist, were gathered with a wide cuff. A white collar, trimmed with tatted lace and a small cameo broach pinned at her throat were contradictions to the heavy men's boots that stuck out from under the hem of her dress and her rough, work-caloused hands. Even though she'd had 17 children and worked beside her husband on their 20-acre farm near the fort to eke out a small living, Ilse was still quite beautiful.

Thompson thought of the time he had talked to Hans about his huge family. He remembered asking him how he ever managed to care for so many children. Hans had laughed at some private joke before telling what their life was like. It all came flooding back into his mind, causing him to forget about those in the room.

With such a large family, even the older children were forced to work. The older girls were not only responsible for the younger children but were required to work beside their mother. There were pies, cakes, cookies, along with huge batches of bread that needed to be made fresh every day. Daily, several large loads of clothes needed to be washed on a scrub board then hung out to dry. After they were dried they were taken from the line. Sad irons were placed on the back of the stove to heat.

One sad iron was always left on the stove to remain hot. When the sad iron being used became too cool, it was placed back onto the stove. The girls then used the hot one. This procedure was repeated until all the clothes were ironed. There were floors to be scrubbed, butter to be churned and huge mountains of dishes to be done before day's end. In the midst of all this activity, if that wasn't enough to do, three square meals had to be prepared.

The boys didn't have it any easier, either. Long before daylight, they rose to milk the cows, slop the pigs, feed the chickens and care for the other livestock. Horses had to be harnessed so that they could be hooked up to some kind of conveyance. In the spring there were fields to plow, harrow, then plant. Gardens had to be plowed, planted, and cared for as well. Calves and other farm animals were born. Then came the hot breathless days of summer, when the fields of pungent, sweet-smelling hay were mown down with scythes.

After the hay had matured a few days, it was hauled to the barn to be hoisted to the loft. In the autumn, there was the garden to harvest, fruit to pick and can, and wood to haul for the long winter evenings. This was also when they usually butchered their pigs. Ham and bacon were placed into a smokehouse to cure. On and on went the list of the things they had to do. It was a time of "early to bed, early to rise," yet in spite of all of this, there were fun times, too. Families bonded through sharing the heavy loads.

They chatted about the news around the fort or settlement, yet no one spoke of Anna or Thornton. Each was content to be in the other's company. Finally, an hour later, Ilse rose to leave. "Vell, I'd better git back and git dinner started before mine vamily comes lookink fer me."

"Please, come again soon, dear friend!"

"Danke. I vill try!"

Paul walked her to the buggy helping her up. "Thank you for the wonderful rolls, Ilse. They are greatly appreciated!"

"Ya betcha! I'm glad to do zat!" Clucking to the horses, she drove off. Paul watched until she left the fort, then went back inside.

✨ ✨

The days merged, one into another, bringing joy to the Thompson's. Kate asked after Anna often, but each time after a brief answer the subject was changed. This not only bothered her, but made her feel uneasy. *Why won't anyone talk about Anna,* Kate wondered. Sighing, she made up her mind to know the truth once and for all. She decided the next time Jane came over she would ask Jane point-blank why she refused to talk about Anna. The opportunity came sooner than she thought.

Kate grew stronger every day, gradually doing more things by herself. It was decided that Jane would come every other day to do the baking, washing, or other difficult tasks around the house. The twins were asleep, while Paul worked at his desk. Kate was finishing the dishes when Jane arrived to do the washing. Kate answered Jane's knock at the door inviting her in.

After looking sternly from one to the other, Kate placed her hands on her hips and plunged in. "I want to know why neither of you will answer me when I ask about Anna." She watched them suspiciously. Jane, knowing the questions would keep coming, remained impassive as she turned to look at Paul.

"It's no use, Jane," said Paul. "She'll hound us to death until we tell her the truth. Besides it's really time she knew." Paul rose to place his hands on Kate's shoulders, while gazing intently into her eyes. "Before I say anything, honey, you have got to promise to behave." Kate's eyes grew large with fright as she looked at one, then back to the other. "I mean it, or it's no deal!"

"I promise. Please tell me. I know something isn't right by the way both of you keep hedging every time I ask about her."

"The day the twins were born, Thornton found Anna here." Kate gasped, knowing what was coming. She immediately felt anger well up inside her. "Well, Thornton grew furious, grabbed her arm and dragged her out the door."

"The monster!"

"You promised to behave, honey." Kate nodded trying to stem the mounting anger. Paul gently patted her arm. "That's a good girl. Why don't you sit in the rocker while I tell you the rest of the story?" Nodding, Kate sank into the rocker by the desk, as Paul began to tell what happened. Kate winced as she heard the tale, and tears began to flow unchecked down her flushed cheeks. "I watched most of it, Kate," Paul concluded. "It was terrible."

"You were there?" Kate cried out.

"I had gone to deliver my report to Thornton that night. I heard noises of fighting inside the house. I went in to see what was happening. Thornton didn't even know I had come in."

"What did you do?"

"I coughed to divert his attention."

"Did it work?"

"Yes."

"What happened then?"

"He was so intent on hearing the report that he left Anna lying there on the floor. Shutting the door to the living quarters, he went and sat at his desk. He acted like nothing was going on. He never mentioned anything about it until he heard my full report."

"Oh, that man is nothing but a rotten monster!" Kate did not realize that she was squeezing Paul's hand hard, until he winced in pain. Releasing her grip, she gently rubbed his hand. "I'm sorry, honey. Please go on."

Paul continued to reveal the events as they happened, ending with Thornton giving him a great tongue-lashing for meddling into his affairs. When Paul was finished, he sat on the floor beside her absently rubbing her hands to give her time to adjust to the horror of it all.

"Oh, Paul," she sobbed brokenly, "It's so hard not to wish him dead! Yet I know that it isn't right to harbor such ugly thoughts." Sighing, Kate sat thoughtfully pondering it all. Finally, she looked anxiously at Paul. "How is she now?"

"She is improving daily, although she is still in the infirmary. She will be for a while longer. It's all right, honey. Right now, it's the safest place for her to be." Kate thought that over for a moment before nodding. "Doctor Phelps is trying to figure out a way to prevent her from going back to Thornton, but he still hasn't found one. He just needs time to work it all out."

"I'm glad that he is keeping her away from that barbarian!" She grew quiet a moment then again looked intently at Paul. "When do you think I will be able to see her?"

"I'll talk to Doctor Phelps as soon as I can. Let's let him decide when you can go. For now, you have to do what he told you to do. Most of all, you are not to worry about Anna."

Kate sighed resignedly. "Very well."

"That's my girl. Besides, it wouldn't do to have Thornton see you going into the infirmary to visit her." He paused a moment to let Kate digest this statement before adding, "In fact, it wouldn't help her at all."

"You're right, but it's hard to wait!"

"I know, but you will do this, won't you?" She nodded affirmatively. "Good!" He tenderly kissed her on the lips. "Since you kept your promise to behave yourself, I'll ask Doctor Phelps today when you can visit Anna."

"That would be nice. I really am anxious to see her."

"I'll let you know what Doctor Phelps' decision is tonight." Rising he went back to his desk to work. While Jane started the wash, Kate rose to go check on the twins.

Jane waited until Kate was out of the room then turned to Paul. "I must admit that I was very worried when you decided to tell her about Anna. Now I'm glad that it's out in the open."

Paul sighed. "Me, too!" Returning, Kate sat at the table to visit with Jane as she began to sort the wash.

As Paul headed out to inspect the troops one morning, he reflected upon the time since his return to the fort three weeks earlier. In spite of his duties or what had happened to Anna, it had been wonderful having time with his little family. Thornton had been very distant since he'd told Paul off, but that didn't upset Paul at all.

Walking along, his thoughts became so jumbled that he had a hard time sorting them out. He was brought back to the present when he saw horses tied to the hitching post in front of Thornton's office. Four of them had saddles, and two were laden with camping equipment. *Now what is he up to?* he wondered. Thornton emerged from his office, looking surly, just itching for a fight. Hesitating long enough to collect his thoughts as well as control his emotions, Paul stepped forward. Saluting, he smiled while greeting Thornton. "Good morning, sir."

Thornton grunted, but neglected to return the salute. Stepping around Thompson, he looked at the three men waiting by their horses. Looking toward them, Thompson wasn't surprised to see Miles, along with his two cronies. Corporal Hank Jennings, Private Tom Jones, also Miles went everywhere with Thornton. Ignoring Thompson, Thornton addressed the three men. "Mount up."

Not willing to let it go, Paul stepped before the mounted men. "Is there anything that I should know before you go?"

"No! I'll let you know of our mission when I get back. Meantime, you're in charge!"

"Yes, sir." Even as Paul started to speak, he knew he was probably invoking Thornton's wrath. "Can you at least give me an approximate time of your return, sir?"

Thornton peered snidely at Thompson. "When you see us! In other words, Captain … when I get dad-gum good and ready to return … you'll know it!" Thornton watched Paul's face for a moment, then whirling his mount around hard, he rode toward the gate, laughing fiendishly. As the three men turned to follow their leader, Thompson felt disgusted with the whole lot of them.

Paul watched the retreating men leave the fort before heading over to the troops. The feelings of disgust were replaced with peace. After inspecting the troops, he dismissed them. Turning to Peters, he said, "Sergeant, I want you to find Nataka. Have him report to Thornton's office immediately."

Peters saluted. "Right away, suh." Turning, he hurried off toward Hansen's.

Thompson started toward Thornton's office when he heard his name called. "Captain Thompson." Turning in the direction of the voice, he saw Samuel Zook approaching.

"What is it, Zook?"

"Captain Thompson, may I have a moment of your time, sir?"

Seeing the concern on the young man's face, it softened Thompson. "Come into the Major's office." They walked to the office in silence. When they were inside, Thompson surveyed the room, remembering the last time he'd been there. Shaking himself to rid himself of the memories, he walked over to the desk, flopping onto a chair. Zook stood twisting his hat, nervously watching Thompson. "Be seated," ordered Thompson.

Zook seemed about to flee. Thinking better of it, he took the seat behind the desk. "Now how can I help you, Private?"

"I may be the cause of the Major's attitude, sir."

Paul's eyebrows knit together in concern. "How so?"

"Last night, when I was in the saloon off of the Mercantile, he came to sit at my table. At first I didn't think anything about it until he started asking all kinds of questions."

"What kind of questions?"

"He wanted to know if you'd obeyed your orders. Did you indeed kill all of the Indians?"

Thompson struggled to remain calm, impassive. "What did you tell him?"

"I told him that I didn't know what he was talking about."

"I see. Go on."

"Well, he asked if all of the Indians were dead. Something about his manner bothered me. I know about his feelings toward these people, so I suspected that you'd gone against the orders he'd given you. So … not sure what to do, I hedged a bit. Again he asked me if you'd killed the Indians."

"What did you answer?"

"After hemming and hawing a while, I said I thought he'd better discuss that with you. There was no way I would talk behind someone's back, no matter what the topic."

"I see."

"Then the Major ordered me out of the saloon. I didn't have to be told twice. When I was out of the room, I slipped behind the stove in the store to listen."

When Zook hesitated, Paul leaned forward. "Please go on."

"Well, Corporal Jennings said something was fishy about my attitude. Miles and Jones agreed with him. Thornton sat there as still as a mouse, but I could see his face from my spot behind the stove. He was growing angrier by the minute. As he swirled his drink around in his glass, the cords in his neck began to bulge … his face grew red. I knew it wasn't good. Then I heard him slam the glass onto the table. When he spoke, the words sounded like a hissing snake. In spite of the heat in the room, I shivered and slunk deeper into the shadows."

"Is that all?"

"No, sir. They decided to go out to the Indian village to check for themselves. Major Thornton said that if he wasn't satisfied, they would hunt for the village until they found it. When they did, they would come back for troops who would obey his orders." He hesitated a moment, not sure if he should go on.

"It's all right, Zook. Don't worry about my feelings, as I can take it."

Zook sighed, plainly relieved. "He said he was going to take care of you real good, after he was done doing what you should have done. He said that he would hang you to the highest tree as an example to the men. From the way he said it, I knew he'd do just that. All the respect I'd ever had for him went out the door. I worry most about you, sir."

"Thank you for coming forward with this information, Private. It will help me with the decisions I must make."

"I was afraid that you'd think I was nothing but a snitch. That was something I couldn't handle."

"Not at all. It was most important for you to apprise me of the situation."

"Thank you, sir."

"Keep our conversation under your hat. Too many people would be hurt by the knowledge of Thornton's intentions. Peters told me that Major Thornton was a friend of yours."

"Yes, sir, he was, but he has grown more bitter with every passing year until he is no longer the person I once knew. You don't have to worry about my feelings, sir. There was a time when I would have defended his honor to my death. Now, I detest all that he stands for. Sergeant Peters and a precious little Indian child taught me the real meaning of love. When I saw the rage on Major Thornton's face, I realized that I never really did know him."

"It's hard to see someone we hold in high esteem brought low. For a long time I wasn't sure of you, Private. Now, after serving with you in our last campaign, I have come to have a great respect for you. In spite of your tremendous loss, you have risen above it all. You have become a giant of a man."

Zook gulped in surprised, then began to beam. "Why, thank you, sir. That means a lot to me. During the time with the Indians, I saw your great concern for some people not of your color. When you didn't discipline me when I ran away from camp, I gained a greater respect for you. If I can be of further use to you, please let me know."

Thompson rose to proudly shake the young man's hand. "I will!"

"I'd better get to work before Sergeant Peters sends out a search party for me."

Thompson grinned. "We don't want that. Thanks again for coming forward."

Zook nodded., "You're welcome, sir." Saluting, he hurried out the door.

Not long after Zook left, Peters along with Nataka knocked on the door and entered. Saluting, Peters turned to leave. "Wait, Dan. You need to hear this, too."

"Yes, suh."

"Pull up a chair and get comfortable." The two men obeyed, placing the chairs across from the desk. When they were ready, Thompson took a deep breath and began, "Private Zook was just here to inform me that Thornton's group are on their way to the Indian village. Our secret has been found out." Both men inhaled deeply amd looked at each other and then back to Thompson.

He continued, "When we were in the Indian Village, I sent a message to Colonel Williams describing our dilemma. He sent back word that we had to wait because he had more pressing matters to attend to. I have a plan I'm going to share with you. If it works, I think it will buy us some time for the Colonel to get here. Perhaps it will prevent any senseless bloodshed.

A determined look crossed Thompson's face. "Nataka, I want you to take another route than that of Thornton's. Ride hard. It's important that you apprise Chief Swift Eagle of the situation, which will allow him time to prepare for Thornton's arrival. It's really important that you make them understand that there must not be any bloodshed. If that were to happen, it would break the peace treaty."

Nataka nodded understandingly. He patiently listened carefully to the rest of Captain Thompson's instructions. Peter's eyes began to twinkle merrily as he tried to conceal the excitement, thrilling to the thought of the impending justice that would surely come. All at once unable to control himself, Peters doubled over with a fit of laughter. Thompson took notice of Peters' reaction. Smiling, he finished detailing the orders. Nataka watched Peters until he couldn't contain himself any longer. He, too, doubled over with uncontrolled laugher. "I ... I ... I'm sorry, sir ... but ... but the justice of it all ... along with the picture it conjures up in my mind ... is more than I can take." Nataka doubled over laughing until tears ran down his cheeks.

Thompson thought that over a moment, and then as the picture became clearer in his mind, he began to laugh as well. His laugh was so contagious that the other men again lost control. Every time they would gain control, someone would start chuckling, causing the laughter to ring out again. Finally, Nataka pulled himself together, rose and saluted Thompson. "I'd best get started if I want to beat them to the village." Turning, he walked over to open the door and stepped out into the bright sunlight.

Peters dabbed at his eyes with a handkerchief. "Is there enythin' else, suh?"

"Don't let a soul know what went on in here today!" Peters nodded, rising to salute. "That will be all, Sergeant. You're dismissed."

"Yes, suh." Saluting again, Peters hurried out the door.

Thompson sat behind the desk struggling for control. A few minutes later he was able to walk out with a straight face. A few men walking across the compound kept looking at him strangely. That they were curious about the laughter going on inside was very evident in their faces. However, he was not about to enlighten them. He walked on without so much as an acknowledgment.

✒ ✒

Two days later, Sylvia came to stay with the twins so that Paul and Jane could take Kate to see Anna. Paul tried to prepare her for the worst, but still Kate winced when she saw Anna's bruised, lacerated face. Kate had barely pulled herself together when Anna turned to face them.

"Oh, Kate," was all Anna could say, as tears glistened in her eyes. Anna reached out to accept Kate's embrace. Anna patted a place on the bed for Kate to sit. "I'm so happy that you are well enough to be up and around."

Kate sat on the bed taking Anna's hand. "I'm so sorry you had to go through this, dear."

"I'm going to be all right, Kate." She smiled sweetly. "In fact, since I found out that Carl left the fort, I've felt much better." They all chuckled heartily at Anna's great sense of humor. Looking at Kate, then at Paul, she grew anxious. "By the way, what did you name the twins? I forgot to ask Paul or Jane when they came to see me. I haven't been able to do much visiting until now."

"We thought Kate should be the one to tell you their names. After all it was her idea in the first place. We didn't want to burst her bubble."

Anna turned to search Kate's face. Kate toyed with her for a moment before replying, "I named our son, Aaron Joseph." Kate intentionally paused, enjoying Anna's look of anticipation.

"And the girl," prompted Anna, growing impatient.

"We named her Sarah Anna-Heleen." Anna stared at Kate incredulously. "That's right. We named her Anna, after you."

"Really!"

Kate gently squeezed Anna's hand. "Yes, really!"

Anna's eyes grew misty. "I've never had anything as special as this done for me before. Thank you so much. I really appreciate this sweet gesture."

"That's the least I can do, after learning how hard you worked to save my life. I just wish I could have named her after Jane as well."

Jane responded, "I'm happy that you named her after Anna! I know how you feel toward me, without giving my name to your child."

"There will be more children, I'm sure. If there's another girl, she'll be named for you!" She held up her hand when Jane began to protest. "That's the end of that!"

Everyone laughed heartily. "Well, it looks like you've lost the battle, Jane."

"Perhaps. Only time will tell."

For a time they rattled on about nothing in particular, just happy to be together. Paul sat contentedly listening to the women chattering like magpies. All at once he sat forward on his chair as an idea, too rich and wonderful to let slip away, began to take shape in his mind. Paul began to notice that the two women were growing tired, so suggested they leave. They could come back another time. The women hugged, promising to see each other soon. As they started home, Paul took Kate's arm to steady her.

On the way home, Kate tried to appear calm, yet as she thought of what Thornton had done to Anna, anger mounted inside, threatening to engulf her. Paul, noticing how quiet Kate was, guessed at the turmoil going on inside. He wisely let her work her way through it.

Reaching home, Jane sent Sylvia home then helped Kate into bed. Kate started to protest, but Jane held up her hand for silence. "There'll be no argument from you, young lady. You've had too much exercise for one day. A good nap will do you a world of good." Kate, smiling at the way Jane mothered her, secretly vowed to find a way to show her appreciation. Jane turned back the covers, stepping away to wait for Kate to lie down. "I'll wake you when I've prepared a bite to eat. Besides, the twins will sleep for a while yet, so don't argue with me ... cause you won't win!"

Kate gratefully snuggled under the covers. "Yes, ma'am!" She was asleep almost before Jane was out of the room.

When Jane went to the kitchen to prepare dinner, Paul was standing near the door with his hat in his hands. "I've got to run out for a while, but I will be back in time to eat." Jane nodded. She began to prepare lunch as Paul walked out the door.

From the time the idea had first come to him at the infirmary, Paul had a difficult time containing the mounting excitement. Seeing Peters talking to a guard at the gate, he hurried over to him. As Thompson approached, Peters turned and saluted, before greeting him cheerfully. "Afternoon, Cap'n."

Thompson returned the salute. "As you were, Sergeant." Peters lowered his arm. Thompson began to speak, "Come walk with me." Turning he started walking toward Thornton's office. Even though Peters quickly caught up with him, they walked the remaining distance in silence. When they were inside, Thompson closed the door. Indicating a seat near the desk, Thompson added, "Be seated, Peters."

"Thank ya, suh." Curious, Peters took the preferred seat across from him.

When he was settled, Thompson smiled at him encouragingly. "I got an idea when Kate, Jane, and I visited Anna in the infirmary a few minutes ago. It really has me so excited that I wanted to talk it over with you … get your opinion on it." Peters leaned expectantly forward in his chair watching Thompson intently. "In four days, it will be the fourth of July." Peters nodded, continuing to watch Thompson expectantly. "I thought since Thornton won't be here to object, we should celebrate it." Peters' eyes lit up, as he sat on the edge of his seat. "It would have a great healing effect on the fort and the community. What do you think about the idea, Sergeant?"

Peters jumped excitedly to his feet. "Thin' 'bout? It's a great idea, suh!" He began rubbing his hands together gleefully, bubbling with the excitement of it all. "This ole fort has needed lots a laughter en merriment fer a long spell, en celebratin' the Fourth'd provide thet very thin'!"

His excitement was so contagious that Paul found himself growing even more elated. "Good! Come over to the house later. We'll discuss it with Jane, Henry, and Kate. They'll know what to do to get the people at the fort and the settlement excited enough to participate. Besides, they would skin us alive for springing this onto them without letting them have a say in it."

"Humph! Ya kin say thet agin! Jest tell me when ya want me ta come, en I'll be thar."

"Come around Nineteen hundred hours."

Peters rose to go. "See ya thar."

Seeing his friend so excited made Paul grin. "Bring some ideas with you. Let's keep everything amongst the five of us until tomorrow afternoon. We'll announce it then." Peters readily agreed. Thompson rose to place a hand on Peters' shoulder. "Thanks for agreeing with me, old friend! Somehow, I knew you would." The two men left the office, each already thinking about their plans for the forthcoming event.

CHAPTER 13

A Tender Heart

As reveille echoed over the crisp morning air, it penetrated deep into the inner reaches of John Whipple's mind. Slowly he clawed his way back to wakefulness. Groaning, he turned onto his left side, burrowing deeper under the covers. Opening one eye, he glanced around the room. Noting that it was already daylight, he quickly closed his eyes in an attempt to ignore the wake-up call. It worked until sweet, tantalizing aromas of ham frying and fresh boiled coffee came wafting into his room, playing havoc with his already growling stomach.

Flinging back the covers, John rose to sit on the edge of the bed. After stretching like the proverbial cat, he sat enthralled, watching the rising sun stream into the room. The wind coming through the open window caused the crystals around the lamp to vacillate, causing a soft tinkling sound as they bumped against the base. Miniature rainbows of prismatic light shimmered as they bounced rhythmically around or across the walls of the room. As the sun rose higher, the rainbows began to slowly recede, until they had completely disappeared.

His attention was diverted when he heard Colonel Williams walk past his door. Dressing quickly, John turned to straighten his room. After making the bed, he put the pillow neatly on top. A smile formed around his lips. *Here I am making my bed as a regular habit, while Ma used to have to nag me to death just to get it done. What a waste of time and energy for nothing.* Taking one last look around the room, John walked out, making sure the door was securely closed.

Colonel Williams greeted John cheerfully when he joined him at the washstand located just outside the kitchen door. "Good morning, Whipple."

"Good morning, sir." Waiting for his turn to wash up, he looked around, marveling at what he saw and heard. A pair of blue jays sat in a nearby tree, chattering at some real or imaginary enemy, while the robins, bluebirds and other songsters vied for equal time to rend their particular melodies. Squirrels scurried back and forth, squawking angrily at some interloper trying to steal their juicy tidbits.

A soft breeze playfully ruffled John's hair as it rustled the leaves in the nearby trees. Golden shafts of sunlight bounced along the rooftops, the boardwalks, even across the dusty streets. Horses nickered, cattle bawled and dogs barked, each adding to the melee going on in the fort. All at once, he felt a deep inner peace, thrilled by the beauty of the day.

"You going to stand there all day?" asked Williams.

Flinching in surprise, John turned to Williams with a blank look. "What?" Realizing that he'd been daydreaming, he smiled sheepishly. "Oh, excuse me, sir. I guess I was lost in the beauty around me."

Williams smiled teasingly. "I know. You were so wrapped up in what was going on around you that you looked as though you'd been carved out of stone." Both laughed good-naturedly. "Hurry up or JaNae will have our hides, saying we spoiled breakfast."

John nodded. He hurriedly made himself presentable. After making sure that everything was as neat as it should be, he went in to breakfast. John was in time to see JaNae remove a large platter filled with ham and eggs from the warming oven above the stove. "Here, let me carry that for you."

"Why thank you, John." JaNae gratefully handed him the platter, then reached into the warming oven to remove another platter filled with pancakes. Closing the door, she reached out to pick up the coffee, then proceeded toward the table. Taking the platter, John placed it onto the table, while JaNae began to pour the coffee. She placed the coffeepot onto a hot pad lying on the sideboard. When everyone was seated around the table, a short prayer was given.

When the edge was taken off of their hunger, they began to chat amiably about various subjects. JaNae took a swallow of coffee and then looked up at Williams. "I was wondering, Jedidiah, if I could borrow John for a while."

Williams looked up in surprise. Looking over at John before facing JaNae, he said, "He's free to do as he pleases, my dear. You'll have to ask him if you can borrow him." He smiled, looking pleased with himself, as he went back to consuming his breakfast.

"What can I do for you, Mrs. Williams?"

"I wondered if you and Josh Taylor could drive me over to Maude Walters' ranch today." John flinched slightly, not sure what to say to this request. Colonel Williams looked up in surprise but remained silent as his wife went on. "When I met Maude the day of the trial I promised that I'd be out to visit her first chance I got."

Williams smiled, nodded thoughtfully. "I see."

John, growing anxious, began to express his concerns. "I'm not sure Mrs. Walters would be pleased to see me. After all, I was the one who turned in the evidence that convicted her husband. What with him dead only a few days, it might be too painful to have me around."

JaNae laid a hand compassionately on John's. "It may be painful at first, but as you render service she'll come around." John looked unconvinced, so she hastened on. "Besides, how do we know how she feels if we don't go? Letting our feelings dictate our actions may be misconstrued as our blaming her."

John's eyes grew large with surprise. "I never thought of it that way!"

"Right now she is hurting deeply. No matter what, we must show our support by helping her in spite of herself. It's important that we let her know that no one holds her responsible for her husband's actions."

Williams laid his fork on the plate so that he could take a couple swallows of coffee. Placing the cup back onto the saucer, he dabbed at his mouth with his napkin before saying anything. "I think that your idea is a good one. What do you propose to do?"

"I thought I'd go out to her ranch, look the situation over, then decide from there. If I need to stay longer, I'll procure rooms at the hotel close to the ranch for the three of us. We'll go back and forth each day, until we're no longer needed. I don't know how long all this will take … several days … maybe a week or more.

"My biggest concern is how Alvin Hoffsteader will try to take advantage of her situation. That man is notorious for bilking widows or older women. He has no conscience when he does it, either. I think he enjoys watching them squirm and wants to see just how much he can get away with. It's really too bad he heard her comments to you, darling."

"That has greatly troubled me as well. I tried to discourage him afterward, but he only smiled. Doffing his hat, he strode away. Too bad someone doesn't bring him down a peg or two from his high horse."

JaNae smiled sweetly. "Maybe someone will." Williams eyed her suspiciously but remained silent. "I'll have Mrs. Forbes come in to cook for you each day I'm away."

"That won't be necessary, my dear. I'm a big boy who is more than capable of taking care of myself." He held up a hand when she started to protest. "Now don't start frettin' before you've gone," he teased. "Besides, it will do me good to be on my own. It will make me appreciate you more!"

"Oh, you!" JaNae tried to appear stern but failed miserably. Pouring herself another cup of coffee, she turned to John. "Would you mind driving me out to Mrs. Walters', John?"

"Not at all! That is, if it's all right with you, sir."

"Who am I to stand in the way of compassionate service? Before it's laid in concrete, though, you should check to see if Taylor can go or not."

JaNae looked anxiously up at her husband. "Do you think that Josh wouldn't want to go with us?"

John rose to go. "I'll check right away and let you know."

Seeing John's partially eaten breakfast, Williams reached out to place a hand on his arm. "It can wait until you've had your breakfast. If I know my wife … and believe me I do … she'll work you to death."

Laughing, JaNae shrugged her shoulders. "I do have that tendency."

"Very well," conceded John, sitting down to eat. "This food is so delicious that I would have hated having to leave it." This caused the Williams' to laugh. John readily joined them. The three finished breakfast while making plans for the trip.

Williams laid his napkin beside his plate. Pushing his chair back, he rose. "Guess I'd better get over to the office before someone sends out a search party."

JaNae started scolding John when he started to clear the table. "I'll do that! You go talk to Josh, then when you get the answer hurry back to let me know if he can go."

John set the dishes back onto the table. "Okay, I'm as good as gone."

The two men left the house together, leaving JaNae to clear the table. When they were a short distance from the house, Williams stopped John. "Tell Bridgford that I gave Taylor permission to go with the two of you."

John beamed. "Yes, sir!"

"Let me know what the three of you decide."

As Williams turned to go, John called out, "Colonel, sir?"

Williams turned back in surprise. "Yes, son. What is it?"

"Sir, I really admire the love that you have for JaNae." The colonel seemed pleased at the praise. "Also I want to thank you for all the hospitality you have shown to me while I've been here at the fort. I promise that I will do all in my power to see that Mrs. Williams is well taken care of."

Tears glistened in Williams' eyes. His respect for John raised a notch higher. "Thank you, son. Never once would I have doubted that you wouldn't bring her back safely. JaNae will be the first to tell you that I never hand out compliments easily … so believe me when I tell you that we regard our newfound friendship with you as one of our greatest treasures."

John blinked in surprise. "Thank you, sir. That really means a lot to me."

He clasped John's shoulder fondly. "See you later." John nodded, watching Williams stride away. John looked around a moment at the busy fort, marveling at how orderly everything was. Shaking himself, he hurried off to find Josh. He found him in the stable, currying a pinto mare. Josh turned when he heard steps behind him, brightening at the sight of John's smile. "Good morning, Josh."

"Howdy, yourself. What's up?"

"Where can I find Mr. Bridgford?"

Josh continued to rub down the horse as he answered John. "He's out back talking to Sergeant Aimes. He should be back any second now."

"Good!" He watched Josh work for a while, fascinated at how gently the lad worked. He began to think of the fishing trip they had taken a few days earlier. The day had been ideal for fishing. Bridgford had given them permission to take two horses and JaNae had prepared them a picnic lunch. They took the lunch, their fishing gear, the worms they dug up the night before, and a rifle for possible danger. Mounting, they rode toward the river. When they were a good distance from the fort, they decided to race. Making a goal line, they were off.

Josh, beating John by a head's margin, commenced to heckle him. "He who snoozes … loses."

Bantering back and forth, they rode on to a very good fishing hole that Josh knew of. They quickly dismounted, placed their lunch in the shade, took care of the horses, then baited their hooks. They threw their lines into the water.

Nothing happened for a few minutes, then John caught the first fish. It was a real beauty. Proudly holding up the fish, he began to taunt Josh. "Well, you may have won the race, but I got the first fish!"

Josh scowled disdainfully, watching as he put the fish on a stringer, which he slipped back into the water. "I wouldn't brag about that puny thing, if I were you. It's so small they'd need a magnifying glass to see it."

"Ah, you're just jealous cause you didn't get the first one. Oh well … it doesn't matter; the first one you'd get would be even smaller, so why complain?"

All at once, a fish took Josh's bait doubling his pole over. It took a while, but he finally reeled it in. It was, indeed, much bigger than John's. Of course, he couldn't resist the opportunity to torment John. He stuck out his chest while sticking out his tongue. "Told ja I'd get the biggest fish!"

"Ya, ya, ya … brag all ya want. But let me tell ya, it ain't over til it's over … so we'll just see who ends up with the biggest fish."

And so it went for at least half an hour that first one and then the other caught a fish. It didn't matter the size of the fish. They just heckled one another for the sport of it. Finally the run was over. As fast as it started, it stopped. Although they sat in silence patiently casting their lines back and forth, it was no use; the fish just weren't biting anymore.

After a few minutes, Josh sighed. Turning hesitantly toward his friend he asked, "John, I don't mean to pry, but why did you come to the fort?" John jumped as the horrible memories flashed into his mind. "I know it had something to do with the trial."

John didn't want to discuss the past, but he knew that Josh deserved an answer. The memory was very painful so it took a moment for John to speak. Finally, taking a deep breath, he began. "I had a friend named Melissa Martin, who lived on a ranch near Fort Owen. Because we grew up together, she was like a sister to me. I taught her to fish, so she taught me how to dance." He smiled at the memory. "Teaching me to dance turned out to be the toughest job of the two."

" Two days before I came to the fort, I saw something terrible happen to the family. I was almost to their house, when some men came riding up …" The painful memory tore at John, making it impossible to go on. Josh turned to look at him, then wisely waited. John was forced to take several deep breaths before he could continue. "Thinking they were Indians, I hid. I watched in horror as they broke into the Martin's house, with guns blazing."

"They immediately killed her parents …" again, he was forced to pause. Finally able to continue, he said, "A man assaulted Melissa. When he was done, he gave the order to kill her. I was helpless to stop them, Josh! I … I …" He broke down sobbing brokenly. Josh sat motionless, wishing he could help, but he didn't know how.

John reached into his pocket and pulled out his handkerchief. He wiped the tears away and blew his nose. Replacing the handkerchief, he took a deep breath. "When they were riding away, I saw a horse with strange markings and knew that I would recognize it when I saw it again."

John then told Josh about the night he saw the same murderous group camped out. How, after recognizing the horse with the markings, he had stolen the murderers' horses, then had come to the fort.

"That was so smart to steal their horses when they were drunk. I doubt that I would have ever thought of it!" Hearing a twig snap, they turned as one gasping in shock. Sergeant Aimes, with a fishing pole in his hand, stood staring at them strangely. John started to rise, then thinking better of it, he remained seated.

Sergeant Aimes pointed to some trees to the right. "I didn't mean to eavesdrop on your conversation just now, but as I was over there, I couldn't help but hear." He shifted nervously from first one foot, then to the other. Finally he continued, "When you first came to the fort, John Whipple, I didn't like you!"

"I know!" John spoke so low that Aimes had to strain to hear him.

"Well, I've watched you when you didn't know it. I have found that you're all right." John blinked. He stared at Aimes as if he had heard incorrectly. "I never had many friends in my life, so when Maines treated me square, I was pleased. Sometimes I was suspicious, but who am I to judge? I see now that I was wrong to think that he was so hot. The worst part is knowing that he would have sold me down the river at the drop of a hat!" John could tell that this knowledge hurt Aimes. "I'm even sorrier for what happened to you and your friends. Just thought you should know."

John's respect for Aimes rose dramatically. "Thank you, sir!" Aimes nodded before turning to leave. Something about Aimes' demeanor touched John. He gazed inquisitively at Josh, who nodded with a smile, then turned to see Aimes retreating. "Sergeant Aimes."

Aimes slowly but suspiciously turned around. "Yes."

John hesitated, uncertain of Aimes' feelings. Seeing no animosity in his countenance, he sighed in relief. "You have two new friends … that is … if you want them."

Aimes' mouth dropped in surprise. "I don't understand. After my treatment of you … you'd want to be my friend?"

"That's right! We aren't here to judge others, because we make too many mistakes of our own." Sergeant Aimes just stood there staring at John as if he'd gone daft. "You can drop your line in here with ours. There's plenty of room! We haven't caught anything lately, but maybe you'll change our luck"

Still Aimes hesitated. "I don't know!"

"Aw, come on. Mrs. Williams made us a huge lunch. We'd like to share it with you … that is, if you'd like."

Smiling, Aimes walked toward them. "Thanks, Whipple. I'd like that a lot!" They found a real friend in Aimes that day. They knew that he enjoyed their company, too. John came back to the present when he heard his name called. "John."

Josh was looking at him strangely. "Where did you go just then? I had to call your name twice. For a moment, when you didn't answer, I thought you'd been turned into a Roman statue."

John grinned apologetically. "I'm sorry, Josh. I was just thinking about our fishing trip with Mitchel Aimes."

"That sure was fun, wasn't it?" He grew thoughtful a moment then remembered what he was going to say. "I tried to get your attention to tell you that Mr. Bridgford has just come in."

"Oh, thanks!" John stepped over to Bridgford. "Excuse me, sir. I was wondering if I could take a moment of your time."

Bridgford turned to smile at John, "Sure thing. What can I do for you?"

"Mrs. Williams was wondering if Josh along with myself could take her out to see Mrs. Walters. The colonel wanted me to tell you that he said it was okay to let Josh go."

Bridgford grinned. "I figured when you said Mrs. Williams wanted to have the two of you take her out to see Mrs. Walters, that he had already given his okay. What Mrs. Williams wants, Mrs. Williams gets. It's fine with me, son."

They walked over to join Josh, who was standing in front of a stall, suspiciously looking from one to the other. "What're you two hatching up now?"

"Mrs. Williams wants us to drive her out to see Mrs. Walters."

Josh looked over at Bridgford in concern. "Really?"

Bridgford grinned. "I told him you could go. Besides, who am I to go against what the colonel tells me to do?" Josh just stood dumbfounded. Chuckling, Bridgford reached out to take the currycomb from his hand while shooing him away with the other hand. "Go on, son. I'll get the two James brothers to fill in while you're gone."

"Thank you, sir."

John's eyebrows drew together as he bowed his head thoughtfully. "I don't know how long we'll be gone."

"I've already figured that out. It's all right. Mrs. Williams never asks for much, so when she does, everyone tries to accommodate her." John looked relieved. "Go on before I change my mind. I'll have the surrey brought over to the colonel's quarters in 20 minutes, along with a horse for one of you to ride."

"Thank you for letting me go, sir."

"You bet!" He watched the two young men leave, before going to search for the James brothers.

When they were outside, John placed his hand on Josh's shoulder to stop him. "Go get a few things packed. When you're done, meet me at the colonel's in fifteen minutes."

"I'll be there." Josh started running toward his home, while John hurried back to the colonel's as fast as he could.

JaNae opened the door to John's knock and promptly began to scowl. "Let's get something settled right here and now, John Whipple! You don't have to knock when you come here. After all you're staying here."

John smiled apologetically, "Okay." He stepped inside. "Josh has gone home to pack a few things. He will meet us here in 15 minutes. Mr. Bridgford will bring the surrey, along with a horse for one of us to ride, in 20 minutes."

JaNae rubbed her hands together excitedly. "Good! I'll be ready by then. I've already packed a few things, just in case it worked out. I was just preparing a little basket of goodies to take along to eat."

"Can I help?"

"No, no," she cried, waving him aside, "I'm almost finished."

"Then I'll go throw a few things together."

JaNae nodded before heading back to the kitchen. "That's a good idea."

It didn't take him long to pack a few things into his cloth bag. Walking into the living room, he stared in surprise when he saw the "little" basket of food JaNae said she was packing. It turned out to be three or four large containers. He couldn't resist the opportunity to rib her. "Were you preparing to feed another army, Mrs. Williams?"

"It does look like that, doesn't it," she responded. "Not knowing what the conditions will be like when we get there, I've decided to take some extra things along just in case they're needed. It's better to be overly prepared, then to be found lacking."

John nodded, then set his bag down near the food. "You're right, of course. I just couldn't resist the chance to tease you a little."

She was prevented from commenting when someone knocked at the door. When she went to answer it, John looked at the clock on the piano. He was amazed to find that it had only taken them ten minutes to get ready. He silently made a mental note of self-praise. Way to go, Whipple! Hearing the door open, he turned to see who it was.

Josh stood at the door, a cloth bag in his hand, smiling nervously. "Come on in, Josh. You can put your things here with the rest of the items." All at once, she remembered something she'd forgotten in the kitchen. "Oh dear, I forgot something. Excuse me a moment while I get it." Turning, she bustled toward the kitchen.

John reached down to pick up Spunky and ruffled her ears. As he stroked her fur, he was pleased to see that Spunky had fully recovered from the wounds she'd received when the farmer tried to drown her little family. She had become quite a feisty little ball of fluff. He remembered JaNae telling how she had nearly worn everyone in the household to a frazzle. He set her down when he heard the buggy pull up outside. Opening the door, they stepped outside.

Bridgford stepped down from the conveyance just as John reached him. Tied to the back was a large white gelding. John guessed it to be at least sixteen hands high. After tying the team to the hitching post, he turned to Bridgford. "Thank you for everything, Mr. Bridgford."

Bridgford scowled. "Please, just call me Harold."

John smiled. "Okay, Harold it is."

Bridgford sauntered back to the stables calling, "See the two of you when you get back! Have a good time." All at once, he stopped to face the young men. "I'll tell the colonel that you're leaving as soon as you get loaded."

"Thanks, sir. I'd appreciate that." John playfully tapped Josh lightly on the arm. "We'd better get loaded before the Colonel or Mrs. Williams tan our hides."

Josh snickered. "As if they would!"

Laughing they went into the house. They had nearly finished loading when the colonel came toward them. He smiled when he saw the loaded surrey. "It appears as if she's leaving for good, doesn't it?" The young men nodded.

JaNae came out with a small container in her hands. She beamed when she saw the colonel. A naughty gleam came into her eye, and there was a teasing tone to her voice. "Why, Jedidiah, you've come to see me off!"

"You knew I would, you little scamp."

John offered, "Let me take that container for you, ma'am."

Taking the container, the two young men moved away to give the couple time together. Colonel Williams kissed his wife affectionately then began fussing over her like an old mother hen. "Did you get a warm wrap to take with you, dear?"

"Yes, dear. I had the boys load it so that I could get to it if I need it."

"Good. I can't have my favorite girl coming home ill."

JaNae beamed as she kissed him warmly. "I left something for your supper. All you have to do is heat it." She stepped back to study her husband critically. "You will take care of yourself, won't you, Jedidiah?"

"I promise to be really good, my dear. I wouldn't want to get my favorite girl angry with me."

JaNae tried to appear stern. "You better remember that, sir." She reached up to tweak his ear affectionately.

Snapping to attention, he saluted while his eyes twinkled mischievously. "Yes, ma'am!"

JaNae punched him lightly on the arm. "Oh you!"

Colonel Williams kissed her again. He lovingly slipped his arm into hers as he slowly guided her to the surrey. As he helped her inside, Josh mounted the gelding, leaving John to climb in beside JaNae. Williams turned to John with what appeared to be a stern look. "You take good care of my girl."

John looked from Williams to JaNae then back to Williams. "Yes, sir. We will!"

"Good." Turning to JaNae, he patted her hand lightly. "Have a good time … don't worry about me … hear?" JaNae nodded as Williams stepped back. John clucked to the horses, and they were off. JaNae turned to wave and the colonel returned the gesture.

As they approached the gate, the guard saluted respectfully then leaned to open it. "Have a good day, Mrs. Williams."

JaNae smiled sweetly. "Thank you, Mr. Forbes. With two such gallant escorts, I'm sure that I will."

When they were a good distance from the gate, Josh rode up beside the wagon. "It's a beautiful day for a trip, isn't it, Mrs. Williams?"

JaNae gazed appreciatively at the passing scenery a moment before answering. "Yes, Josh, it is."

They rode for a time in silence, no one wanting to break the spell that Mother Nature wove into the scenic tapestry spread before them.

JaNae flinched as a grouse was flushed from its resting place near the road, thrilling as it took flight. She gasped in surprise as she watched an eagle swoop down, catch an unwary rabbit in its massive golden talons, then fly effortlessly away. The trio rode companionably along, each lost in their own world, yet content to be together.

The day grew warmer as the sun's rays touched down upon them. JaNae opened the top button of her brown tweed traveling suit. Taking a handkerchief, she wiped her face. Removing the matching hat, she laid it in the seat between them. "It is growing unbearably warm already. That means we are in for another scorcher."

"I was thinking the same thing," said John.

"It's so unusual for this time of year. Hope we get a good soaking rain soon, or we could be in for trouble."

"Don't remember it ever being so warm before."

"I wouldn't know that. We arrived here two years ago, so I've only hearsay to go on."

John continued, "We've had a few hot summers, but none as bad as the year before we moved to Fort Owen. It was so bad that crops failed, and everyone battled forest fires all over the place."

"Sure hope it doesn't get that bad again."

"Me, too." Seeing her distress, he hastened to console her. "It won't be long now until we get to town. We'll get something refreshing to drink there."

JaNae sighed wearily. "That sound's wonderful! I think I'll survive until then."

Not long after that, like a beacon to a fog-shrouded ship lost in the night, the town of Missoula hovered along the horizon. John tugged the horses with the reins as he hollered, "Getty-up." Snorting, the horses picked up a little more speed. As they rode into town, JaNae placed her hat back onto her head. Missoula's streets were long and dusty, with crude buildings lined up along the way.

John pulled up near a small eating establishment. Jumping from the surrey, he tied the horses to the hitching post. He came back to the buggy and helped JaNae down. Josh alighted from his horse and tied him to the hitching post. He joined them on the boardwalk. Taking JaNae's arm, John led her inside. A waitress escorted them to a table near the window. After taking their orders of tea, milk and pie, she returned with their orders.

JaNae, taking a sip of the cool sweet tea, sighed contentedly. "Oh, this is heavenly!" Both men nodded in agreement. They sat there long after their drinks were finished, grateful not to be moving. Finally, JaNae leaned anxiously toward John. "Would you mind asking the waitress how to get out to Maude Walters' ranch?"

"Not at all." Rising, he walked toward the waitress. JaNae watched the interaction between them. She saw the waitress walk over to the counter and pick up a sheet of paper, which she handed to John. They exchanged a few more words then John came back to the table. After handing the sheet of paper to JaNae, he took his chair. "When I spoke with the waitress, she gave me the directions. She also handed me this sheet of paper."

JaNae scanned the paper, then looked up at her escorts. "According to this, Mrs. Walters is having a public sale out at her place on Friday." She paused a moment, then continued. "That's just a week away!"

"The waitress told me that we go west about three miles. We will take the first road, which leads to the Walters' ranch.

"Very well. Josh can help me outside while you pay our bill." Extending the money to John, JaNae rose to leave.

Josh extended his arm, while John gave the waitress the money for their refreshments. He joined them in time to see Josh help JaNae into the surrey. Untying the team, he got in beside JaNae. Picking up the reins, he waited for Josh to get mounted. When Josh was mounted, John turned to smile at JaNae. "Guess we're ready to go."

"Then we'd best be on our way."

He whacked the reins lightly against the horses' rumps, as he spoke softly, "Come on, boys, let's get a move on." The horses snorted, tossed their heads up and down then strained into their harnesses.

They made good time after leaving Missoula. There wasn't another living soul on the road, which stretched out flat before them. They traveled for two more hours, coming to a spot near the river. John could tell that the heat was getting to JaNae, so he watched for a good spot to pull off. Finding a shady spot with plenty of grass near the riverbank, he turned the horses into it. "Whoa." JaNae looked at him in surprise. "I thought this would be a good place to rest the horses while we have lunch. Would that be all right with you?"

JaNae nodded her approval. "That's a capital idea!"

John got out to tie the team to a tree. While Josh dismounted, John helped JaNae down. After leading her to a shady spot near a rock, he went to the back of the rig to find a tin cup. Going to the river, he dipped it into the water's icy depths. Bringing the water back to JaNae, he extended the cup encouragingly. "Perhaps this will help to cool you off a little."

JaNae gratefully took the cup from his hand, taking a few swallows of the icy liquid, "Oh, you angel! This feels so good going down." John smiled as she quickly drained it. Sighing, she handed him the empty cup. "Thank you."

John watched her in concern. "Would you like another cup full?"

"No thank you. I can wait until lunch is laid out to have another. Thank you so much for your thoughtfulness, John."

"You're more than welcome, Mrs. Williams."

JaNae stood up, then with John following her, they went to the back of the surrey. Meanwhile, Josh had unhitched the team, with intentions of leading all three horses to the river to drink. John joined him just as he had untied the gelding.

"I'll take the horses to water, if you'll help JaNae."

Josh replied, "I'll be happy to do that very thing."

As John led the horses toward the river, Josh carried the lunch basket to a shady spot. After washing up, he helped JaNae spread the basket's contents onto a blanket. A few minutes later, John led the horses back to the surrey, where he began tying them to trees with lots of good grass. He finished just as JaNae called, "Lunch is ready, John."

"Okay, be there as soon as I wash up."

Josh called out, "Better hurry up, old man. Everything smells so good that I'll have it eaten before you get back."

John snorted in derision, "Humph! Fat chance of that happening! I'm too speedy when it comes to Mrs. Williams' cooking!"

JaNae beamed fondly at the two of them as they bantered good-naturedly. "If you both don't stop jabbering and get over here, I'll just pack it away. Neither one of you will get it! What do you think of that?"

"I think I'll behave myself," meekly lamented Josh. "I'm so hungry my stomach thinks my throat got cut!"

"Mine too, ma'am. I'll hurry!" Thus saying, he hurried to the river. It wasn't long until he was back eyeing the food appreciatively. As they ate, JaNae entertained them with stories of her girlhood.

"I lived in France until I was nearly fourteen years old. Then my parents decided to come to America. I still remember how frightened I was of that big boat. Momma and Papa got motion sickness soon after we left port, so I was elected to take care of them. Three days out I got ill from motion sickness, too. A kind lady who'd traveled several times by boat took care of the three of us. We finally got better a few days before time to dock at Ellis Island. That's near New York City. I was never so glad to plant my feet on solid ground as I was that day."

"We stayed in New York City for the winter, then moved to Louisville, Kentucky, where I lived until I married Jedidiah. I was well acquainted with his sisters, Margaret and Belinda. The three of us were like three peas in a pod. We went everywhere together, did everything together ... even got into trouble together."

John grinned as he winked at Josh, "I can't picture you getting into trouble, ma'am."

"Oh, but I did!"

Josh rubbed his hands together gleefully. "Oh, how I would like to have been a little mouse in the corner when that happened."

John nodded, knitting his eyebrows together thoughtfully. "Me, too."

"I just bet you would," grinned JaNae.

Josh grew thoughtful as well. "I try hard to stay out of trouble, but somehow it always seems to find me. I'll be glad when I get older so that quits happening to me."

JaNae smiled reassuringly. "I don't want to disillusion you, Josh, but the truth is, trouble has a way of finding you when you're old, too."

Both young men groaned. John spoke for both of them. "Does that mean we'll have to battle trouble all of our life?"

"I'm afraid so! The secret to life is, when you're dealt a dirty blow, endure that hardship the best you can. Always honor your mothers and fathers. Never do anything to bring shame to your name. The primrose path to sin is strewn with very appealing temptations, however there are lots of briars and thorns hidden along the way. There are some people, because of selfishness, greed, or clouded judgments, who make grievous mistakes. They don't realize, or perhaps don't care at the time, that they are dishonoring and even deeply wounding those whom they profess to love the most. The loved ones must face the brunt of their actions. As you encounter life's trials and temptations, always remain as loving and conscientious as you are now, because it is an honor … indeed a joy to be in your presence."

Josh sighed resignedly. "I'll try to remember that the next time I'm tempted to do something I shouldn't. As to this enduring thing, I've had to learn that early."

JaNae and John turned anxiously toward him. Reaching out, she gently took his hand looking him in the eye, "Please share with us how you learned this."

Plucking at a blade of grass, Josh struggled to formulate his thoughts. Finally he looked up at his friends. "I was ten when a band of Indians killed my parents. In my dreams, I'm haunted by that awful … AWFUL day. The memory always reminds me of a circling eagle about to dive upon its unsuspecting prey. To my dying day, I'll hear their screaming war cries as they rode into our yard. My baby sister and I were quickly placed into the root cellar under the kitchen floor to protect us. My parents shot off a few rounds, but they were so outnumbered that it was over real quick. When we smelled smoke, we knew the house was on fire. The Indians stole what they wanted; then rode away, leaving us alone … close to death from all the smoke."

JaNae shuddered. "That's horrible!"

Josh paused, shivering as if cold. "We thought we were goners, but our neighbors rode up to the house. They knew of the cellar, so headed there after finding my parents. They barely got us out of there before the entire house was consumed with flames. Mr. Jefferson, the neighbor who adopted us, was severely burned while getting us out of the house."

"I wanted to ask you about the scars on his hands and face, but didn't know how to bring it up," said John.

"Jedidiah told me about him being hurt in a fire, but never elaborated on it further," added JaNae.

"My sister Becky was also burned, but not as severely. Ma Jefferson said she healed so well because she was so young. She was six when we lost our parents."

"I'm so sorry," chorused the others.

"We had a lot of wounds inside that had to be healed, too. Becky adjusted to the new home easier than I did. It took me nearly six months to come to grips with our folks' death. The only way I made it was through the wonderful love and patience of the Jefferson's. Their patience finally helped me see that I wasn't alone. We were and are very much loved."

Puzzled, John looked at Josh. "I don't remember meeting Becky since I came to the fort, Josh."

Pain momentarily filled Josh's eyes. "Becky died three years ago, when her appendix burst. Doctor Stanley tried to save her, but it was just too late. She never let on that she was even sick until Ma found her moaning and groaning on her bed that morning. She died during the surgery."

John looked sympathetically at his friend, "That's really awful! I'm so sorry for your loss."

"As I said, love got me through." Deciding to change the subject, he turned to JaNae. "I don't want to talk anymore about me. How did you meet Colonel Williams?"

Understanding, JaNae changed the subject. "He came home on leave the summer I turned sixteen, to see his parents. What a dashing figure he cut at twenty-two in his captain's uniform. One afternoon his sisters and I were coming home from a shopping spree, my arms laden with packages. I was laughing at some antic Belinda had pulled, not watching where I was going.

"Hearing our girlish laughter, he came out of the house to see what the ruckus was about. I ran smack dab into him, knocking him onto his back, then fell on top of him. I was so flustered, and tangled in packages and my skirts, that I couldn't get up." Both of them were whooping boisterously at the picture it painted in their minds. "It was pretty funny! Maggie and Belinda weren't any help at all because they were doubled over in a fit of laughter. Jedidiah's father came out to help disentangle us.

"To say I was humiliated would have been a gross understatement! Jedidiah must have enjoyed our accidental 'entanglement,'" JaNae added with emphasis, "because he came to call on me a few days later. I was so embarrassed about what happened that I refused to see him. He left without our meeting again.

"When Papa learned that Jedidiah had come calling … and that I had refused to see him, he told me that I was going to be a lady and see him, or he'd turn me over his knee. I politely but firmly told him that I was much too old for that rot."

John dabbed at his eyes. "That must have made him happy … I guess not!"

"Papa stood to his full height of six foot two. Towering over me, he told me that I was still under his roof … that I'd darn well better act like it. Knowing my father as well as I did, I knew that he would turn me over his knee. Two nights later, Jedidiah, as arranged by my father, came over to meet with me. When I walked into the parlor, there he stood in his Corporal's uniform. I gawked at him like a lovesick calf, almost embarrassing myself all over again.

"Right there on the spot I fell head-over-heels in love with Jedidiah Williams. Oh, I fell for him hard! Ours was a whirlwind courtship, ending with our marriage three weeks later." JaNae paused a moment then continued, "That night I fell in love with Jedidiah's good looks ... also his uniform, but during our short engagement I got to know him from the inside, too.

"How long have you been married, Mrs. Williams?" asked Josh in between bites of his sandwich.

"Please, call me JaNae," she scolded.

"Yes, ma'am."

"You too, John."

He sighed. "I keep forgetting."

"Well then, don't forget!" JaNae, smiled to take the edge off of her words. "To answer your question, Josh, we've been married nearly thirty-five years. Or we will be in two months."

Josh was plainly impressed. "Gosh! That's wonderful!"

"I agree!" cried John in awe. "My folks have been married for twenty years now. I thought that was a good record!"

"It hasn't always been easy," said JaNae thoughtfully. "Three boys and two girls were born through our union. We lost our oldest son along with our oldest daughter to smallpox. Jack had just turned three ... Julia was fourteen months. Then eleven years later cholera took our last two sons and our remaining daughter. It seemed as though my life had ended with theirs. I sank into utter despair.

"Jedidiah tried to console me, but I was past feeling. I avoided him, because I thought it was his fault that we were out there in this Godforsaken country." She unconsciously clutched at the front of her dress as poignant memories beset her.

"I didn't even realize the pain he was feeling. One day when I went to the wood-shed to get some wood, I heard him crying." Tears glistened in her eyes as she talked. "When I went to him, I found him crouched into a ball, sobbing brokenly. Seeing that tenderhearted man in the throes of such deep mortal agony, it softened my heart. It not only filled me with love but a deep compassion.

"At that moment I realized just how much he'd lost, too. Not only had he lost his children, but also I had shut him out through my deep despair or moody indifference to him. I rushed over, knelt beside him to throw my arms around him. We told each other how very sorry we both were. We wrapped our arms around each other and cried for a long time."

John and Josh struggled to swallow past the lumps in their throats. They couldn't speak. "I decided right there that I would devote the rest of my life to my husband, also to those in need of assistance. Ever since then, we just can't bear being apart for a long period of time. Things have been better in our marriage. We have bonded in many ways because of our need for each other."

Josh dabbed at his eyes, "Colonel Williams isn't the only one with a tender heart!"

John was unable to speak. He had come to love this couple dearly in the short time he'd stayed with them. Hearing of their sad story filled him with a greater appreciation and a deeper respect for them than he had before.

When they had finished eating, JaNae cleared away the lunch things while she re-packed the basket. The boys put it back into its place in the rig. After taking care of the horses' needs, they hitched them to the surrey. Helping JaNae inside, John climbed aboard. Picking up the reins, he turned to see if Josh was ready to go. Seeing that he was, John called to the horses. They were on their way.

Finding the road to the right a couple of hours later, John turned into it. Traveling became difficult, as the road was full of wagon ruts. The further they went, the more twisted the road became. No one paid attention to the passing scenery as they wound around each curve.

It took all they had to concentrate on the task ahead. JaNae clung tenaciously to the side of the seat, as she was pitched to and fro. John slowed the team, but it didn't help. After what seemed like an eternity, they saw a house not far ahead, nestled among some trees.

They weren't able to estimate exactly how large the house was from their view, but it appeared massive in size. Smoke was coming from the dual chimney, dissipating into the blue crispness of the azure sky. To the left of the house were pigpens, a chicken coop, and a huge barn. Several feet away to the left stood a long stable, surrounded by several corrals or holding pens.

Rolling plains stretched out along the horizon. Several large herds of horses along with huge herds of cattle dotted the landscape as far as the eye could see. A string of bunkhouses, set further back from the house, was located to the right of the main house. As the three of them gazed around, each was in total agreement that the surrounding view was indeed ... spectacular.

CHAPTER 14

Nataka

After Nataka left Thornton's office, he headed directly to the stables. There he procured two horses ... one to ride, the other to carry his gear. Nataka chose Chester, a large dapple-gray gelding that stood seventeen hands high. Nataka often took Chester with him because of his gentle, easy-going spirit. The horse nickered as Nataka approached. "Good morning, old boy. Are you ready to go on a little trip?" The horse nickered, pressing his nose into Nataka's shoulder. Nataka chuckled as he affectionately scratched behind the gelding's ear. "Okay!" Going to work, he soon had the horse ready.

When Chester was ready, Nataka went to stand in front of another stall. The occupant inside snorted impatiently as Nataka started to open the door. "Good morning, Hurricane!" Hurricane was a strawberry-roan quarter horse gelding that stood seventeen hands high, weighing about fifteen hundred pounds.

As Nataka approached, the horse nickered softly, nudging him gently. No one at the fort liked riding Hurricane because of his unpredictability. He loved to wait until his rider became relaxed and carefree, then he'd pitch a fit that always ended by unseating the rider. It had been no different with Nataka; only when he pitched a fit, he wasn't able to unseat Nataka. Gradually a special bond grew between the two.

Nataka stood thoughtfully stroking the horse, remembering how Hurricane got his name. When Peters arrived at the fort three years ago, he was a tough crotchety very hard to live with man. He laughed in disgust when the men told him how nasty and mean-tempered the strawberry roan was.

On his first maneuver, Peters made it known that he was going to ride the gelding. He turned a deaf ear to the repeated warnings the men gave him, bragging to everyone who would listen, "No hoss hes e'er throwed me! En what's more, Ah doubt one e'er will!" Shrugging, the men continued to lead their mounts from the stable. As Peters led the docile horse out of the stable, he smirked. He proceeded to taunt the men. "Unpredictable, ma eye! Why, he's ez gentle ez a lamb!"

The roan stood meekly while Peters mounted. When he was settled, Peters nudged him gently. The horse snorted excitedly, tossed his head up and down then patiently followed the other horses out of the fort. Peters couldn't resist rubbing their noses into the fact that the horse was so obedient. "Where's yer wild hoss? Ya'll must be nothin' but a bunch a sissies ta let a lil' ole hoss like this rattle yer cages." The men remained silent, knowing what was coming. They had gone approximately six miles from the fort when Hurricane showed his true colors. "Ya'll jest wanted ta pull ma leg. This here's the best b'haved hoss in the whole outfit."

All of a sudden, Hurricane lowered his head. Before Peters could decide on his intent, the horse began bucking. Each time the horse touched old Mother Earth, Peters was jarred so hard that it seemed like every bone in his body was breaking. Finding that he couldn't unseat his rider, the roan tried another tactic … the trick that had always worked.

Bucking high into the air, the roan flipped his massive, fifteen hundred pound body in a manner for which no rider could ever be prepared. Sure enough, as he performed his famous trick, Peters went sailing through the air, landing hard upon the ground. Peters lay there, struggling to get the air back into his oxygen-starved lungs. When he got a good breath, he tried to rise, but fell back upon the ground, groaning. "Ah'm a dyin'!" he cried.

Thompson laughed with the rest of the men then tried to console Peters. "Nah! You're just a little beaten up, but you'll live!"

By the time Peters was back on his feet, two soldiers led the horse back to him. He hobbled over to the horse eyeing him critically. From the twinkle in the horse's eyes, Peters knew the horse was pleased with himself. He stared at the horse in stunned disbelief. "Ah'll be horned swaggled! Ah've finally met the hoss thet kin throw me!"

The soldiers struggled hard not to laugh, but it was no use. One by one, they began to laugh uproariously. "Laugh, ya fiends!" Peters grew stern. "Jest laugh en see ifn' ah care!" A grin began to form around the corners of his mouth until he, too, joined in on the merriment. From the way the horse moved his mouth and tossed his head, Peters was sure he was laughing at him.

Thoughtfully rubbing his chin, he critically looked the horse over. "Ah ain't never seed a hurricane, but Ah heared onct where they destroy all thet's in their path. Ridin' ya is like bein' in one a them there wild storms … peaceful one minute, then wild en woolly the next! Ah don't know what they called ya afore, ya old reprobate, but ya'll always be Hurricane ta me!"

Nataka snapped back to the present when Hurricane nickered impatiently then nudged him to get more attention. After Nataka had the roan saddled, he led the horses to his home. He hitched them to the hitching post before going inside. Relieved to find no one home, he quickly gathered the items needed and put them in a tarp. When he was finished, he went to load Chester.

Satisfied that the pack was securely on, he took his canteen inside to fill it. Setting the canteen on the table, he wrote a note to his parents, stating that he had something important to do, that he would be back when he could. Placing it where it would readily be seen, Nataka picked up his canteen, gathered his rain gear along with his bedroll, then went out to the waiting horses.

Hooking the canteen over the saddle horn, he tied his raincoat and bedroll on behind the saddle. Untying Chester, he tied his lead rope to the saddle horn. That completed, he untied Hurricane and mounted.

Once outside the gate, Nataka reached down to pat Hurricane's neck affectionately. "We have a good piece to travel before nightfall, ol' boy, so don't let me down." Hurricane quivered slightly then strained anxiously at the bit. Nataka turned the horse in the opposite direction from Thornton's group. He rode the horses hard for a while. He let Hurricane have his way. After a few miles, he slowed him to an easier gait.

Nataka spent a good portion of the ride surveying the landscape around him. Coming to a grove of trees, he pulled the horses down to a walk before he entered. His attention was taken up with picking an easy path for them to travel. At one point, he dismounted, tied the horses to a tree so he could scout the terrain. Finding a deer trail, he decided to follow it for a while.

He went back to untie the horses. Mounting, he worked around until he got to the deer trail. Nataka followed it for a ways then turned back into the brush. Trees concealed the sun, casting eerie shadows around or in front of him. He rode on, watching intently for possible dangers to the horses. Finally, when he saw sunlight straight ahead, Nataka heaved a sigh of relief. Riding out of the grove of trees, he clucked to Hurricane and the horse picked up a little more speed.

Cattle dotted the landscape as he rode along. He noticed that the grass was higher here than when he entered the grove of trees. Hurricane was tempted to eat the grass, but Nataka kept a tight rein on him. Knowing how much Hurricane wanted to stop and eat, Nataka kept a wary vigil on the horse.

As the sun rose higher in the sky, Nataka grew so warm that beads of perspiration rolled down his neck and face. He reached into his back pocket to get a handkerchief, which he used to wipe away the perspiration. He stopped once to take a good drink from his canteen, letting Hurricane nibble at the sweet lush green grass. A gentle breeze began to tug at Nataka's shirt and ruffle his hair. Feeling refreshed, Nataka capped the canteen, hooking it over the saddle horn. He gathered the reins tighter as he clucked softly to Hurricane. For a moment the horse seemed about to pitch a fit, but as he couldn't lower his head, he thought better of it as he began to canter. Nataka smiled, knowing that he'd won that battle.

They traveled steadily for the next three hours. Nataka figured that Thornton would head first toward the old Indian village, located at the base of the Bitterroot Mountains. Finding it empty, it would take him some time to figure out what had happened. Nataka didn't have any doubt that Thornton would figure it out, because Thornton was like a bloodhound when he was determined. He figured he had about a forty-eight-hour lead before Thornton would reach the new village. As everything depended on that lead, he nudged Hurricane gently. The horse responded by going faster.

Nataka heard the river long before it loomed into sight. He knew from the height of the sun that it was nearly noon. He stopped at a shady spot close to some trees. Dismounting, he took the weary horses down to the river to drink. Returning with them, he led them to a nearby tree. Getting the feedbags from the pack on Chester, he placed one feedbag onto Chester. He rubbed his neck affectionately while the horse ate. His dapple-gray color glistened in the sunlight. "You're quite the horse, old boy," declared Nataka affectionately. The horse blinked, quivering under Nataka's gentle touch. It was obvious that Old Chester enjoyed the unusual attention given him.

Nataka patted the horse's neck one more time. "Enjoy your oats. You earned them!" He took the other nosebag over to Hurricane, who nickered softly as he reached out greedily for it. "Okay, hold yer taters!" chuckled Nataka, "I'll get it on as fast as I can!" When the bag was securely in place, Nataka gently patted the horse's neck. Quivering appreciatively, Hurricane blinked, continuing to munch on his oats.

Removing the pack from Chester, Nataka put the gear in the shade a safe distance from the animals. Sunlight, as it filtering through the trees, cast golden beads of light onto the pine needles below. The pungent pine scent caused Nataka to close his eyes while inhaling deeply. Thrilling to the pine scent, he drank in several more deep breaths before going in search of firewood.

When he had gathered a good-sized pile, he went in search of some large river rocks, which he placed in a wide circle. He cleaned the area around the circle of rocks to ensure that no sparks could ignite anything. Satisfied, he started a fire in the center of the rock circle.

When it was going well, Nataka picked up a bucket and went down to the river. Setting the bucket down on the bank, he washed up. Cupping his hands, he again thrust them into the river's artic moistness, filled his hands, then leaned down to drink from them. He repeated this process several times before he was satisfied. Picking up the bucket, he plunged it into the water's frigid depths, bringing it up full. Rising, he returned to camp and set the bucket near a tree. While he waited for the fire to burn down to coals, he removed the nosebags from the horses and placed them near the pack.

Rifling through the pack, he got out the things needed to prepare a meal. Washing his hands, he quickly set about preparing lunch. Lifting the steaming pans from the fire, he set them onto a huge stump. After pouring himself a cup of coffee, he set the pot back from the fire. He placed the cup beside the coffee pot, while he generously filled a tin plate. When he was ready, he picked up his cup of coffee. Sitting near a tree, he set his coffee beside him. Leaning back against the tree, he ate heartily. Nataka paused every so often to reflect upon the beauty around him.

When he was finished, he set the plate down beside him. While watching the horses greedily munch on the grass, his attention was drawn to a chipmunk to the right of the horses. The little animal was scolding the horses for being in the way of his spoils, though they paid no attention to him. Cautiously, he approached to grab a tidbit, promptly stuffing it into his cheeks. He'd look first at the horses, then at Nataka.

Satisfied, he stuffed another tidbit into his cheeks. He repeated this operation until his cheeks were full, then scurried up a nearby tree to deposit his goodies into a hole somewhere at the top. He reappeared to repeat the process again several more times as Nataka watched in fascination.

For a time Nataka watched his brother, the chipmunk, gather his winter supply. Feeling comfort against his back, he felt a kinship with the trees. The roar of the mighty river was like a balm of Gilead to his soul. The crackling fire, the munching horses, and the screaming of an eagle in flight all seemed to lend wings to his spirit. For as long as he could remember, he had had questions that could not be answered; now they were crystal clear.

After Thompson told him of his birthright, he found himself dwelling on it. Now here he sat dwelling upon it once more. He felt an overwhelming need to express his feelings aloud. "I knew I was different, but I never knew why. I've wondered why I love nature so much; why my skin was so different from that of my mother, my father and my sister; why my eyes were so brown where theirs are so blue; why I tanned so easily in the summer while they burned." Slowly a smile spread across his face, as realization dawned on him that he was a half-breed Indian, with all the characteristics of one. Oh how good this knowledge made him feel.

Reluctantly Nataka gathered up his dishes, placing them in a dishpan. He turned to the fire where he had hot water heating and took down the containers. Filling the dishpans, he proceeded to clean up his lunch mess. Working quickly, he soon had camp chores done. Taking the bucket, he poured the water into the fire pit, spread the wood out, then went back to the river for another bucket of water. Nataka poured half the water onto the fire to douse it, stirred it to make sure it was out, then dumped the remainder of the water into the pit. Satisfied that it was out, he packed the gear, then loaded it onto Chester's back. When he was satisfied that the pack was secure, he tied the lead rope to the saddle horn and mounted Hurricane.

When they neared the river, Hurricane hesitated. Bending over, Nataka patted the horse's neck encouragingly. "Come on, boy, you can do it." Hurricane snorted his disgust then gingerly stepped into the water. Nataka kept a tight rein on him while nudging him gently. Hurricane decided there was no other way out, so continued. Unconcerned, Chester followed behind Hurricane. Near the middle of the river, the swirling eddies taxed the horses' strength, so Nataka wisely let them choose the course they thought best. The current pulled them downstream a ways, before they were able to make it to the opposite shore. As they rode up the bank, Nataka felt relieved that they'd gotten across without incident. He gently pulled on the horses' reins, "Whoa!" He stepped down from the saddle to let the water-soaked horses take a breather.

He checked the pack on Chester, satisfied that it was still secure. Nataka kindly patted the gray's neck. "That's a good boy!" Chester nickered, nudging Nataka in an attempt to get attention. Turning to Hurricane, he grinned at this gallant horse who was chomping at the bit and stamping his feet impatiently. His black eyes sparkled with life along with vitality as he turned to look at Nataka. He nickered softly, as if telling him to get on with it. Nataka let the horses drink their fill before leading them away from the river. Mounting, he rode toward the Sapphire Mountains. The surroundings became more breathtakingly beautiful as he rode along. Thick lush green grass came up to the horses' knees. Hurricane wanted to stop to partake of the bounty before him, but Nataka wouldn't let him. Hurricane stiffened a moment, but Nataka kept a tight rein on him. For a moment the air was charged as Hurricane weighed his options. Then the horse relaxed, deciding that he'd better obey his master. He tossed his head up and down in defiance but continued on.

Nataka pushed the horses relentlessly on until they stopped to make camp near the base of the mountain just before sundown. Tying the horses to a tree, he unloaded the pack from Chester. He carried the pack to a rock formation, where he set it down. Following the sound of running water, Nataka found a small stream tumbling over and around some boulders. Tall stately pine trees lined the bank on one side, with a lush green meadow on the opposite bank. "This is where I'll camp," mumbled Nataka aloud. Turning, he walked back to where he had left his pack. Picking it up, he carried it back to the stream, placing it near a tree. Hurrying back to where he'd left the horses, he led them to the stream to drink.

When they were finished, he led them across the stream to the meadow where he hobbled them. They began to munch on the tall, thick, tender shoots of grass, as Nataka hurried back to set up camp. The first item on his agenda was to gather enough wood for cooking and to last through the night. When that was accomplished, he gathered some large rocks to place in a circle. Checking to see that nothing could be ignited from flying sparks, he started a fire. Taking up the bucket, he went to the stream for water, which he set near the pack. Cutting some pine boughs, he laid them between two trees. Satisfied that he had enough, he rolled his bedroll out onto them.

Going to his pack, he took out what he needed to fix supper. He washed his hands and prepared a quick meal. When he was finished, he filled his plate and poured himself a cup of coffee and went to sit near a tree to eat.

It didn't take him long to polish off the meal and do his camp chores. Refilling his coffee cup, he went back to lean against the tree to sip his coffee leisurely. He watched in awe as old Mother Earth took prolific colors from nature's palette and splashed them in a blaze of glory across the sky. Too soon the colors faded and night's shadows slowly spread across the terrain.

Nataka turned when a twig snapped close by, and saw a large bull elk a short distance away. From his stance, it was apparent that he was just as surprised as Nataka. With eyes bulging and nostrils flaring, he watched him suspiciously. A huge rack of horns covered in velvet adorned the elk's regal head and his body was sleek and plump from spring's bounty.

He lowered his head and displayed his antlers threateningly, while Nataka remained motionless. Eventually, the elk snorted and then plunged into the nearby thickets. Shaking himself, Nataka went to check on the horses. Finding all well, he returned to camp, put another pile of wood on the fire and got into his bedroll.

For a long time Nataka lay listening to the night sounds. The sighing wind, rustling of the leaves in the trees, the horses munching grass, the frog croaking, a cricket chorus, the water bubbling around the rocks in the stream, and the scream of a distant cougar all lent an air of peace to Nataka's soul. Looking up at the canopy of stars overhead, he felt grateful to be alive. Finally, after turning onto his side, he closed his eyes and was soon in a deep, peaceful slumber.

Having skipped breakfast, daylight found Nataka a good distance from his camp. Suddenly, he surprised a mother grouse, with her fledglings, scratching in the dirt. Nataka looked to his right in time to see a rabbit disappear down a hole. A few minutes later, he watched a male moose lumber into a nearby stream to feed. Nataka reveled in the peace of it all, feeling right with the world.

The sun grew warm upon his back, while a gentle breeze playfully ruffled his hair and shirt. It felt cooler than the day before, yet there wasn't a cloud in the azure sky. Nataka relentlessly pressed on, anxious to make the Indian village before nightfall. At noon he stopped to rest the horses, but he didn't start a fire. He ate some of the biscuits from his saddlebag, washing them down with water. When he was done, he traveled on.

An Indian brave met him late that afternoon. Nataka knew him so greeted him cheerfully. "Hello, Whispering Wind."

"Ugh," came the surly reply.

"It is very important that I see Chief Swift Eagle immediately."

The brave nodded, "Come, I show the way!" Turning, he began to trot effortlessly ahead of the horses.

It wasn't long until they entered the Indian village. Children ran behind or beside them, while women and braves watched. The brave who had led Nataka to the village stopped before a large teepee. As Nataka dismounted, Swift Eagle emerged raising his hand in salutation. "How!"

Nataka thrilled as he gazed at his uncle. "Hello, Swift Eagle. Captain Thompson sent me to speak to you concerning a grave matter."

"Come," ordered the chief, motioning to Nataka to enter his teepee. Nataka entered, followed by Swift Eagle, who motioned to a place near the fire. "Sit!" As Nataka sat down, the chief sat across from him. Swift Eagle looked over at Nataka. "How Thompson?"

"He's worried! Major Thornton, the chief of the fort, left early yesterday. Thompson suspects Thornton knows what happened when we were at your old village." Swift Eagle remained motionless. "Thompson believes Thornton went to check out your old village. When he figures everything out, he will search until he finds where you went. He will come here to finish off the job himself." Swift Eagle flinched then remained motionless. "Captain Thompson wants you to watch for Thornton's group. Surround them, but do not harm them in any way. To do so would break the treaty. This would cause a lot of problems for both Indians and white men. Once they are captured, I will finish carrying out the orders Captain Thompson gave me. When the orders have been carried out, we need two of your most trusted braves to follow them. These braves are needed to ensure Thornton and his men get safely back to the fort, and help them in case of any unforeseen dangers."

"I see that be done."

As Nataka mapped out the rest of the plan for Thornton's group, he saw the chief's eyes begin to twinkle. Swift Eagle shook his head emphatically, "It be done!" Nataka gazed at the chief anxiously. All at once, the chief grabbed his sides as he burst out laughing. When he gained control, he looked at Nataka. "Thompson one wily old fox!" Nataka nodded, joining in on the hilarity of it all.

Finally when they had gained control, Swift Eagle turned, and the two of them walked outside. Once outside, Swift Eagle motioned to Whispering Wind to come to him. When the young brave stood before him, he began to address him in his native tongue. "Tell all of the braves in the village to meet at the council lodge immediately. Tell Willow we need her to act as interpreter. Now go! Hurry!" Whispering Wind dashed away. Swift Eagle turned to another brave still speaking in their native tongue. "Take care of Nataka's horses. Afterwards put his things into an empty teepee." When the brave led the horses away, they walked over to the lodge together.

The braves were already assembled when they arrived at the lodge, which amazed Nataka. As they entered, the braves watched Nataka intently. Some nodded politely, while others sat motionless. Swift Eagle motioned to Nataka to sit on his right. When Nataka was seated, Swift Eagle again addressed the braves in their native tongue, while Willow interpreted for Nataka. He told them what Thompson suspected and what he proposed to do.

The only sign of their feelings was the twinkle that appeared in their eyes. Swift Eagle gave orders for guards to be placed further down the trail, while others were to be stationed closer to camp. "When Thornton's men are spotted, send the chosen runner to relay the information to the guard near camp, who will then relay it to me."

Swift Eagle paused to look at each man assembled. "Take your weapons, but do not use them unless absolutely necessary. You are not to hurt any of Thornton's men! We will not be the ones who break the white man's treaty. Let them come close to camp, following them without their knowing it. Surround them completely then wait for me. Remain hidden until I give the signal. This is important to ensure the element of surprise." Swift Eagle turned to two young braves. "Whispering Wind, Yellow Dog, stay where you are." He motioned to the others to leave. "Go now!" The braves left as one to do as they'd been commanded.

Seeing the two young men who were awaiting further instructions, Nataka was impressed with their calm demeanor. "You will have the toughest job of them all. After the orders have been carried out and they are headed back to the fort, you are to follow them. Your role is to make sure they are safe from harm. Do not let them see you, but stay close in case of trouble. They have much hatred in their hearts for us. Their greatest desire is to see us dead. Even so, this does not give us the right to harm them. Again, I want you to understand how important it is not to break the white man's treaty." The two young braves nodded solemnly. "We understand," said Yellow Dog.

"Good! Go make ready!" The young braves quickly darted away.

Swift Eagle led Nataka to a vacant teepee near his own and informed him that he would have his wife, Little Flower, bring him something to eat. "Thank you, Swift Eagle," said Nataka. The chief nodded in acknowledgment. Turning, he nonchalantly moseyed back to his teepee. Nataka thought him quite an imposing figure, dressed in buckskins with a decorative headdress.

As he watched the chief disappear into the teepee, he not only felt a deep pride in the fact that this wonderful man was his uncle, but that he was indeed blessed with a vast heritage. He tucked this knowledge deep within his heart as he entered the teepee. There on the ground in the corner to the right were his camp gear, bedroll, saddle and his canteen. He spread his bedroll on the straw mat, found to the right of the teepee. He had just finished when there was a rustling noise close by. Raising his head, he was just in time to see Little Flower step inside.

Nataka smiled to himself when he saw Little Flower, for Little Flower wasn't little at all. She was as wide as she was tall. Her graying hair, parted in the middle, was slicked back with braids hanging down her back. When she smiled, he noticed some of her teeth were missing, while some were broken or decaying. Multiple wrinkles etched their way along her face, adding to the leathery texture of her skin. Her brown eyes twinkled merrily as she watched every move he made. In her hands was a beautifully decorated pottery bowl, filled with steaming stew. The tantalizing aroma caused his mouth to salivate with unknown pleasures. Inside the bowl was a hand-carved wooden spoon.

"I bring food."

"Thank you, Little Flower. I didn't realize how hungry I was until I smelled this."

"I like to see man eat." Before Nataka could utter another word, she quickly departed.

Two days later, while Nataka was walking around camp, he saw a runner approach Swift Eagle's teepee and enter. From the expression on the brave's face, he knew something was up, so he decided to investigate. As Nataka reached the chief's teepee, two braves emerged. The runner went back the way he came, as Swift Eagle joined Nataka. "Thornton's men spotted coming. Not wait much time now." Nataka nodded falling into step with Swift Eagle.

They reached the guard near camp where they waited. They hadn't settled in completely, when Thornton's men came into view. Nataka's heart lurched when he saw

Thornton riding in front, sitting stiffly in the saddle. He turned to gaze at Swift Eagle to watch his reaction.

Swift Eagle crouched behind the huge boulder and was so still that to Nataka, the two seemed as one. Turning to the waiting braves, Nataka was not surprised to see them waiting patiently. He was reminded of a cat waiting to pounce on an unsuspecting mouse. The air became charged with electricity as they waited.

Finally, when Thornton rode past their hiding place, Swift Eagle gave the signal to attack. As one, fifty braves sprang up, surrounding the startled group. Thornton knew at once that it was no use fighting, so he stopped. Moving his hand away from his weapon, he waited. The others in the startled group followed the actions of the major. Five braves came forward to disarm them.

Thornton's face grew red with rage, while the cords and veins in his neck bulged, yet he wisely remained silent. Thornton along with his men were pulled unceremoniously from their saddles then forced to move a short distance away from their horses. The same five braves forced them to the ground. Stepping back, they waited further instructions. Swift Eagle and Nataka stepped out to confront Thornton.

When Thornton saw Nataka, he grew even angrier, if that were possible. He started to speak then thought better of it. Swift Eagle turned to Nataka. Nataka, stepping forward to face Thornton, ordered, "Get up! Undress down to your longjohns … also, remove your boots and socks."

Thornton growing indignant began to bellow like an angry bull. "We will do no such thing!" Several braves stepped forward, with rifles poised. Thornton looked at them angrily, but seeing their immoveable expressions, decided to do as he was told. Thornton glowered at Nataka, while pulling off his clothes.

Nataka was grateful at that moment that looks couldn't kill, or he would be lying dead upon the ground. Thornton hesitated for a moment, but seeing that it was no use to protest, he grunted in disgust. When he was undressed, he tossed everything on top of the growing pile of military clothing. "You'll be sorry for this, Nataka Hansen," he snarled, glaring at Nataka hatefully. "You mark my words! You'll be sorry for this!"

Nataka showed no emotions whatever. "Remove your hats, too!" The men groaned, but did as they were told. He took a canteen from one of the horses. Noticing that it was nearly empty, he handed it to Whispering Wind. "Would you please fill this at the stream?" Nodding, Whispering Wind took the canteen, then hurried off to do Nataka's bidding. Thornton puckered his eyebrows in concern, but watched in silence. The other three men looked on, feeling miserable and disgusted.

Whispering Wind returned with the full canteen. Handing it to Nataka, he stepped back. "Thank you, Whispering Wind." Swift Eagle came forward with a large leather bag filled with food, which he handed to Nataka, who smiled respectfully. "Thank you, sir." Nataka shoved the canteen along with the bag of food at Thornton. "This canteen and the bag of food are all that you'll have to take with you on your walk back to the fort. If you use the food sparingly, you'll do fine. Inside the bag you'll find a flintlock to help you start a fire."

Thornton mechanically snatched the items from Nataka, staring at him in stunned disbelief. All at once, the impact of Nataka's statement hit him. "Walk back to the fort?" Nataka smiled as he calmly nodded. Thornton flew into a fit of rage, calling Nataka everything but a human being.

Nataka calmly waited until his tirade was over, then peered angrily into his face. "You can yell at me all you want to, sir. You can call me anything you want to, sir, but you are … going to walk back to the fort!"

Screaming with unspent rage, Thornton plunged toward Nataka. It was evident in his hate-filled eyes that he wanted Nataka dead. "Why, you …" Two braves grabbing Thornton threw him backwards. He fell like a lump of lead to the ground. He lay there snarling like a snake, hissing vehemently through clenched teeth. "I should have killed you when I had the chance!"

Nataka stood looking at him dispassionately, while inside he quaked with the audacity of the man. "Well … you didn't when you had the opportunity … so you'd better find a way to make the best of your situation now."

Thornton jumped up to glower at Nataka spitefully. As blind rage engulfed him even more, his nostrils flared, and the veins in his neck bulged. Thornton's face grew red with unspent passion. Pressing his arms tight against his sides, he clenched and opened his ugly massive fists several times. Nataka shuddered unconsciously, watching in grim fascination as Thornton lost all rhyme or reason, becoming totally insane. Like a caged animal, he paced back and forth, bellowing like a man possessed but moving ever closer to Nataka. Before his intentions were recognized,

Thornton lunged at Nataka, getting a death grip on his throat. The braves were hard-pressed to restrain him, but finally they pried him loose. After several minutes, Thornton grew quieter. Shaking the men off, he turned to look at Nataka. "If it's the last thing I ever do … I'll kill you!"

For a moment only, fear gripped Nataka, then a feeling of impending doom coursed through him, leaving him drained. As he watched, Thornton traipsed determinedly back the way they'd come, with murderous threats flowing from his vile mouth. Nataka couldn't help feeling saddened by the man's wasted life. Thornton had harmed so many people.

Jones and Jennings stared in shock, unable to comprehend it all. Miles stared after his father, then turned to look dubiously at Nataka. As reality sank in, he looked down at his nearly naked person. "Surely you jest about walking back to the fort … like this!"

Nataka nodded his head, as if placating a naughty child. "No, Miles. I'm dead serious!"

Miles' mouth dropped in consternation. All at once, he began to yell like a mad man. "You're nothing but a rotten mangy cur! If Pa doesn't kill you … then I will!"

Turning he went to join his father. Jones and Jennings looked at Nataka in disgust then turned to join the other men. Nataka watched until they had disappeared out of sight, before he turned to Swift Eagle.

Swift Eagle tried to console him. "Not fear! My braves see them safely to fort."

"Thank you, Swift Eagle."

Swift Eagle nodded, then motioned for the two braves to follow the men. "Remember make sure they don't see you, but keep your eyes on them at all times." The braves nodded, and picking up their gear, they moved noiselessly away.

Stooping to gather up some of the items left by the men, Nataka headed back to the village. Several other braves helped, while some led the horses. There he bundled everything up. A brave brought him a horse belonging to one of Thornton's men to use as a pack animal and also brought some skins to pack the clothing in.

When he had the bundles tied together, he placed them with his pack. He placed the skins onto the packhorse, making sure they were secured in place. He loaded Chester with his things, then saddled Hurricane. When he was ready to go, he tied all five horses together with a lead rope, which he hooked to the saddle on Hurricane.

Nataka dreaded the long ride back to the fort leading five horses. As he made hurried preparations to leave, Nataka recalled Thompson telling him that Colonel Williams was coming from Fort Missoula to deal with the situation concerning Thornton. I hope he gets here before it's too late, he mused.

He started to mount Hurricane but stopped in mid-air as Swift Eagle came toward him. Placing a hand on Nataka's shoulder, Swift Eagle looked fondly into Nataka's eyes. He spoke gravely, "Two times you and Thompson save my people. I not forget!"

"Thank you, Swift Eagle."

"Watch back all times," warned Swift Eagle. "Thornton crazy here!" he exclaimed, pointing at his head.

"Thanks. I will!" The two men clasped arms, each feeling a deep respect for the other. Mounting, Nataka slowly rode out of the village, not once looking back.

Nataka was so full of mixed feelings that he knew he would never be able to sleep, so he didn't stop to make camp at sundown. Using the bright light of the moon he continued to ride toward the fort. Stopping once, Nataka led the horses to water to let them drink, also to allow them to rest. For Nataka, the night wore tediously on, as Thornton's threats echoed repeatedly throughout his mind.

Fear such as he'd never known before plunged Nataka deep into utter despair. *Will my mother also reap the whirlwind of Thornton's rage?* he wondered. "Oh, yes!" he cried aloud. The knowledge pierced to the very center of his soul, plunging him into throes of terror … not for himself but for his mother, Anna.

Deep anger soon replaced the fear. For the first time in his young life, Nataka tasted hate's bittersweet passion. All that Jane taught him as a young boy, concerning forgiveness or turning the other cheek, was momentarily forgotten. So engulfed was

Nataka in these new emotions that visions of revenge entertained his tortured mind. "You'll be sorry for what you've done to Mother!" he vowed passionately.

All at once Thornton's raging image flashed before Nataka, unveiling a man so bitterly consumed with the hatred which had trapped him, that he was like the proverbial fly caught in a web. No longer was Thornton able to discern the feeling of love and compassion. Thornton would live out his miserable existence in this prison of his own making. Nataka realized that he had a choice. He would become entrapped in the same web, unless he forgave Thornton and left his fate to a higher power.

Nataka wrestled with his feelings long into the night. Daylight brought little relief, yet he was now past seeking revenge. The sun began to climb high, though many times dark menacing rain clouds obscured the sun. By midmorning, a stiff breeze came up, howling eerily through the trees. The grass rippled like giant waves on the river.

Nataka knew by his surroundings that the river wasn't far away. When they reached the river, Nataka stopped. Dismounting, he tied the horses to a tree. Looking up at the menacing sky he knew that rain wasn't far off. He walked over to survey the river, growing alarmed at how choppy it was. He walked back to the horses to check to see that the lead rope was secure.

Satisfied that it was, he went to check on the packs. Chester nickered wearily when Nataka approached. He began scratching behind the horse's ear. "I know, old boy," he whispered affectionately. "It's been a rough trip, let alone a long night." Finding both packs were secure, he led the weary horses down to the river to drink.

When they were finished, Nataka mounted and nudged Hurricane in an attempt to get him to cross the river. Hurricane didn't hesitate but stepped confidently into the water. The other animals followed without protest.

As the water grew more treacherous, Nataka let Hurricane choose the best course to follow. As with the previous crossing, the current began to carry them downstream, but at a much faster more dangerous pace. The powerful horses, their eyes wide with fear, struggled against the current. Nataka felt sorry for Hurricane as he fought valiantly to get across.

About midway across, the river appeared to rage erratically. Nataka began to doubt the wisdom of making the river crossing in such conditions. All the while, the packs were being splashed with water. Just before he despaired of making it to the other bank, Hurricane found firm footing. Struggling up the bank, Hurricane's great sides heaved from the effort. The other horses accompanied them up the bank.

Nataka rode along the riverbank until he came to his old campsite. Both he and the horses were so weary that he decided to make camp. Dismounting, he hobbled the horses in a grassy spot and spread out the contents of the wet packs to dry before doing anything else. When he was finished with this task, Nataka gathered wood, started a fire, then prepared a meal.

When the meal was over and the camp chores were done, Nataka went back to check on the horses. Satisfied that all was well, he returned to camp. Replenishing the fire, Nataka slipped into his bedroll, quickly falling into a deep sleep.

Two hours later, Nataka awoke to the sounds of distant thunder. He rose, rolled up his bedroll, then quickly carried it over to place it near a stump. He quickly packed the now dry contents into the packs.

When he was finished, he placed the gear near his bedroll. After dousing the fire several times to ensure that it was out, he went to get the horses. Tying the lead rope to their bridles, he tied them to a tree, then went back to get Hurricane. Slipping the bridle on Hurricane, he started toward the tied horses.

Hurricane protested, pulling against the bridle. "Come on, boy," coaxed Nataka. "We haven't got all day!" Finally, Nataka succeeded in leading him to the other horses. Working quickly, he soon had the horses ready to go. Looking around to see that all was in order, Nataka untied Hurricane. Mounting, he began to push the horses relentlessly to a grove of trees.

As they neared the grove, Nataka slowed the still tired horses. He entered as thunder continued to rumble even closer. As they emerged from the trees, the sun was slipping behind the mountains. Lightning flashed, followed by the echoing thunder. He nudged Hurricane gently but hurriedly on toward the fort. Nataka hoped to arrive home before the rain. Two hours later, Nataka rode wearily through the gates.

Dismounting in front of Thornton's office, he tied the horses to the hitching post. Removing the packs containing the clothes, he went inside. Thompson and Peters were in Thornton's office when he entered. Nataka laid the pack onto the desk before saluting.

Thompson gently motioned to a nearby seat. "Be seated, Nataka." After Nataka was seated, Thompson began to speak. "Tell me everything that happened. Spare me nothing!"

Nataka quickly obeyed, going into great detail. Thompson congratulated him on an assignment well done. After thanking him, he was dismissed. Nataka saluted, then lumbered wearily out the door. Untying the horses, he led them back to the stable where he turned them over to the stable hands. Picking up his gear, he started home, feeling bone-weary. There was no one home when he arrived, so he took care of his gear. When he was finished, Nataka went to his room, where he fell across his bed, immediately falling into a deep sleep.

CHAPTER 15

Restitution

As JaNae, John and Josh drove into the yard, they saw an empty buckboard nearby with horses still hitched. John got down and went up to knock on the door. A little girl answered the door. Josh and JaNae heard her tell John that her mother was out showing some men around. John asked if they could wait for her, and the little girl agreed. He was just about to return to the surrey, when he heard a man's deep booming voice a short distance away.

John turned around as three men and Mrs. Walters came into view. He didn't recognize two of the men, but the third one made him shiver. It was the man that was going to drown his dog along with her three pups. He recognized John as well, but other than scowling, he paid no further attention to him. He was wearing the same dirty, patched bib-overalls, the legs of which were rolled up a few turns. The shirt was blue-checked, with the sleeves rolled to the elbows. The same dirty wide-brimmed hat covered his head with a few black curly strands of dirty hair falling across his long forehead. John thought he looked just as menacing as he had the first time he'd met him.

John heard the older portly gentleman refer to the younger man as his nephew Donald. As he was a couple of inches taller than his uncle, John thought the man had to be at least six feet three inches tall. Donald was not only straight as an arrow but dressed like a gentleman. The man was not handsome by any stretch of the imagination. There was an arrogant uppity manner about him. Prominent cheekbones, hooked nose, with an upturned chin reminded John of a wizard. He was dressed in an immaculately clean gray pinstriped suit, with a white cravat around his throat. A black top hat sat askew on his head.

His attention was drawn back to the conversation between the woman and one of the other men. It was plain to see that Mrs. Walters was very upset. "Your offer is way too low, sir."

The older heavyset gentleman's arrogant voice boomed across the yard as he peered at her condescendingly. "Personally, madam, I think the offer is more than fair!"

"Five thousand dollars isn't enough for a 2000-acre ranch! I can do far better than that."

212

"If you'll forgive my blatant honesty, I don't think so. Everyone is aware of what kind of husband you had, so they won't want to give you much of anything for this place."

"Selling this place has nothing to do with what my husband did or didn't do." Angry flecks of light flashed in her eyes. For a moment, John thought she was going to order the men off of the property.

JaNae motioned to Josh to help her down. She brushed her hand over her clothes to straighten them, then quickly joined the group. Politely turning to the largest of the men, she smiled sweetly. "Good afternoon, Mr. Hoffsteader! What a pleasant surprise to see you."

Hoffsteader jumped as though he'd been slapped. Turning pale, he became very flustered. He was a tall heavy-set man who enjoyed manipulating people. Deep-set dark-brown eyes glared at JaNae from beneath bushy eyebrows. His thick nose dominated his face that sported huge jowls framed by porkchop sideburns. The fringe of hair around the back and sides of his head was straight and peppered gray. Beads of perspiration glistened on his shiny, balding pate, and there were dirt streaks on his face where he'd used his dirty red bandana to mop the sweat. The sleeves of his shirt were rolled to the elbows, and grungy longjohns stuck out from beneath the sleeves. Black suspenders held up his baggy pants and heavy black boots caked with dirt stuck out from his pants legs.

Again he mopped his face with the bandana, then stuffed it back into his hip pocket. "Mrs. Williams! Why, fancy meeting you way out here!"

"Yes, isn't it!" She gazed all around her, then turned to Hoffsteader. "Frankly, sir, I was surprised to hear what you offered this sweet lady. I wonder what Jedidiah would say about it, since I know that he told you that we were going to make a bid for the property."

Hoffsteader began to fidget from first one foot, then the other. JaNae appeared not to notice, but turned her attention to Maude Walters. "My husband and I have been talking about purchasing a place nearby when he retires. This ranch would be ideal." Hoffsteader gawked at JaNae a moment, growing furious.

The gentleman with Hoffsteader glared at JaNae furiously, but she ignored both of them. Again, she looked slowly around. "Would you sell it to us for … say … ten dollars an acre? That would come to twenty thousand dollars." A deep breath escaped Hoffsteader as he stared at JaNae with a mixture of shock and anger.

"Humph!" snorted the gentleman standing near him. "That's pretty gutsy of you to make such an offer, when you knew that we were here first!"

"Excuse me, sir. I don't believe I know you, let alone what you have to do with this matter!"

"My name is Donald Hoffsteader the Third. I came here from Boston two weeks ago to live with my Uncle Alvin." He paused to nod toward the portly gentleman that JaNae called Hoffsteader, and then indicated the other man to his left. "Uncle

Alvin and Mr. Jinks have graciously brought me out here so that I could purchase this property."

"I see." Placing her hands on her hips, JaNae glowered at the man as if he were an errant child. "Well sir … out here it is customary for the highest bidder to get the deal."

The younger man turned to his uncle, who begrudgingly acknowledged the fact with a slight nod. Alvin Hoffsteader looked at JaNae questioningly, "How can you afford this on your husband's military pay?"

"When I lost my father, he left me with a great deal of money … not that it's any of your business," she added. Hoffsteader fell silent.

The younger Hoffsteader, ignoring JaNae, calmly turned to face Maude. "Very well then, I will raise my offer to forty thousand dollars."

JaNae, felt that the offer for the ranch should be higher, due to the fact that there was a large herd of cattle along with several hundred head of horses. There was also the farm equipment to consider in the deal. Glancing first at the young Mr. Hoffsteader, whose arrogant attitude made it clear that he thought that he'd pulled off the biggest deal of all time, JaNae felt repulsed by his demeanor. For a fleeting moment, JaNae had an irresistible urge to tweak him on the nose.

Restraining herself, she turned to Alvin Hoffsteader. Seeing the haughty look on the older Hoffsteader's face, she realized that he didn't believe that she really had enough money to purchase the ranch. From the way he puffed out his chest, she knew that greed and arrogance were playing a major part in the balance of things.

Even though she knew that she was taking a great chance, JaNae decided to bring them down from their high horses. *Yes si-ree bub,* she thought, *it is indeed time to bring these men to their knees.* Turning to face Maude Walters, she said, "I'll make it 100,000 dollars."

The younger Hoffsteader looked at his uncle in shock. Gone was his arrogant attitude. JaNae smiled inwardly when both men grew sullen. Knowing that the older Hoffsteader was greedy, she surmised that the nephew was a chip off of the old block. Showing no emotion whatsoever, she watched the younger Hoffsteader mulling things over in his mind. Finally, he turned to Maude. "I'll pay you one hundred and fifteen thousand dollars. That's my final offer."

Once more JaNae looked around the ranch, taking her time. Through peripheral vision, she was pleased to see the men squirm. Maude looked at the young man, then back to JaNae, not sure what to do. To those around her, it appeared that JaNae was thoughtfully weighing the options. Finally, sighing sadly, JaNae turned back to the gentlemen. "I guess you get the deal, sir, as it is two thousand dollars more than we are willing to pay." Turning to Maude, Donald humbly asked, "Is this price suitable to you, madam?"

Maude, astonished by both the new offer and the speed of the whole transaction, stood mutely trying to take it all in. Finally, she looked up at young Hoffsteader, nodding in agreement. "Yes, that will be acceptable."

"Very well then. Let's draw up the agreement together, shall we? After we're satisfied that everything is to our satisfaction, we can both sign it."

"That will be fine with me."

"Good. I didn't bring out enough cash, so I'll bring out a bank draft for the remainder tomorrow. Would that be alright with you?"

Gasping in stunned disbelief, Maude's knees threatened to buckle. Quickly gaining her composure, Maude searched the young man's face for signs of deception, but she didn't see anything but a very humble man. "Yes, sir, that would be fine."

"Thank you, ma'am. In the meantime, you keep the bill of sale until I come back tomorrow. I'll bring the sheriff with me as another witness to the transactions."

"Okay, that seems fair enough."

Donald Hoffsteader, sighing in relief, replied, "Good! Let's get to it then, shall we?"

Maude turned to start walking toward the house. "Please come inside." Stopping to look at JaNae, she smiled politely. "Please, won't you come in, too?"

JaNae smiled sweetly. "Thank you. Don't mind if I do." When all were inside, they watched as the agreement was written out. Hoffsteader signed the document, then Maude signed it.

Maude turned to JaNae, "Would you please sign as a witness?"

"I'd love to." Taking the pen, she signed below the first two signatures.

Maude then turned to Jinks, "Would you mind signing as the second witness, sir?" Jinks hesitated a moment then took the pen, dipped it into the ink, then signed his name below JaNae's signature.

Hoffsteader shook Maude's hand to seal the deal. "By the way, the buckboard and the team will go with the house, but I won't relinquish them until I've gone to Missoula for the last time. I'll leave everything at the stable, where you can pick them up at your convenience."

That will be just fine." Bowing slightly, he started toward the door.

JaNae's little group waited while Maude showed the three men out. JaNae looked around her, surprised at what she saw. The room they were standing in was a large parlor. Exquisite paintings, elaborate furniture and ornate furnishings filled the huge room. Adjacent to the room was a large dining room that would easily seat twenty to thirty guests.

A crystal chandelier hung over the long oaken table, which was adorned with a white crocheted lace tablecloth. In the center of the table was a bouquet of multicolored roses. Located along the north wall was a long sideboard, flanked on both sides by china hutches filled with matching china and crystal goblets.

Another door led to the kitchen on the south wall. A winding staircase led to the upper floors. JaNae guessed from the size of the lower floor, that there were several bedrooms on the upper level.

It wasn't long until they heard the buckboard rattle off. A tiny smile played around JaNae's lips.

Maude walked back to look at JaNae suspiciously. "Excuse me, ma'am, but were you really serious about purchasing this place?"

JaNae laughed until her sides ached and tears ran down her face. Gaining control, she dabbed her eyes with her lace hanky. "No. I've known Alvin Hoffsteader for about a year now. That man is notorious for bilking all people, especially widows or older ladies. I also knew that he wouldn't let me outbid him. From the nephew's attitude, I gambled that he was the same."

This invoked laughter from them all. Still giggling, Maude struggled for control. "Well, you surely did have me fooled. You know … you really took an awful chance."

JaNae just shrugged. "Perhaps!"

John looked at JaNae in awe. "That was the best acting job I've ever seen!"

Josh nodded. "I'm surprised that he didn't challenge you about your authority to purchase the land without your husband being with you."

"I was, too," confessed JaNae, "but I think they were just so determined to get the land that it probably never even occurred to them!"

Everyone nodded affirmatively. "I'm so grateful that you showed up here when you did, Mrs. Williams. No one else has even been out to make me an offer … so I was getting desperate."

"I've been thinking about you ever since I met you after the trial. I was concerned that you might have a few problems getting your affairs settled, so I decided to pay you a visit to see if there was something I could do to help."

Maude sighed wearily. "I'm at my wit's end! There are so many things to do that I just can't seem to decide what to do first. There are the animals to take care of, the farm equipment to sell; then there are the items in the house to decide upon. I can't seem to get anything in order and I only have a week until the public sale!"

JaNae slipped an arm around her. "There, there, don't fret about it. There are three more able-bodied people here who can help. You tell us what you need help with, and we'll help you any way we can."

Maude sighed. "Thank you. That would be great!"

"I brought a few things from home that I thought you might need," said JaNae, turning to the young men. "Could you help me with them, boys?"

John headed for the door. "Sure thing!"

JaNae turned anxiously back to face Maude. "Before I forget, is there a hotel in Superior or is the nearest one in Missoula?"

"Hotel! After the miracle you performed a few minutes ago, I'll not hear of you staying anywhere else but here!"

"I don't want to put you out."

"You won't be putting me out, JaNae. There are several empty bedrooms in this old house, just aching to be used. Come, let me show you your rooms, then these handsome young men can bring in your things."

"Thank you," replied JaNae. "That is … if you're sure!"

"I'm more than sure!" Turning, she led the way while JaNae, John and Josh followed. JaNae noted that she guessed right. There were six rooms on the upper level. Maude showed them to their rooms. Shortly afterward, the young men brought in the items from the buggy. When that was done, they went to take care of the horses, while JaNae helped with dinner. The women hit it off immediately. They were soon chatting like old friends. The children, four-year-old Stephen and eight-year-old Janie, took to JaNae right away.

When dinner was ready, Janie went to tell Josh and John to come in to eat. They quickly washed up before coming inside. John hesitantly drew back, afraid that Maude wouldn't want him there. He was about to go back outside when she approached him, placed her hands gently on his shoulders. Looking him in the eyes, "I don't blame you for testifying against my husband, son. What my husband did was inexcusable. He deserved the punishment he got." John sighed audibly. "We'll never speak of it again. Okay?" John nodded. "Good. Now let's eat."

After dinner, JaNae helped Maude with the cleanup, while the young men entertained the children. They were a great hit, as they told them story after story. "Tell us another one," begged Stephen.

"Okay, children, it's time to go to bed," announced Maude, coming into the living room.

Janie looked pleadingly up at her mother. "Oh, Mommie, can't we stay up for a while longer?"

Maude gently smiled at her daughter. "No, sweetheart. You need to get your beauty sleep!" Grudgingly they stood up and walked over to kiss their mother good night. Maude hugged Janie close for a moment then gently kissed her cheek. "Good night, honey."

"Good night, Mommie," replied Janie.

Stephen stepped closer to his mother, sighing contentedly as she enfolded him in her arms, where she drew him closer. Cuddling closer he exclaimed, "I wuv you, Mommie."

"Good night, pumpkin!" she crooned into his ear, kissing him tenderly upon the cheek.

"Night, Mommie," answered Stephen, snuggling closer for a moment. Turning, he ran over to quickly kiss JaNae on the cheek. "Night, night, pretty lady!"

JaNae gasped in pleasure. "Night, honey!" Stephen ran toward the stairs.

"I love you both!" Maude called after them.

"Love you, Mommie!" They chorused.

"I'll be up shortly, to tuck you in and listen to your prayers."

"Okay!" They chorused.

After the children were in bed, the four adults sat around the dining room table to make a list of the things that needed to be done. JaNae asked for some writing material, which Maude quickly placed in front of her. Looking over at Maude, she smiled encouragingly, the pen poised to write. "You tell us what has to be done and I'll write it down. When we've done that, we'll make assignments. Would that be all right with you?"

"That's a marvelous idea."

"Very well, let's begin."

As Maude specified what needed to be done in time for the sale on Friday, JaNae quickly wrote it down. John was amazed to see how long the list grew. When the list was completed, they began to break it down into specific jobs.

When the job list was re-written, John reached for the list JaNae handed him, surveyed it a moment then offered, "Josh and I can organize the items in the barn and the property. We'll gather up all the stray cattle along with the horses and put them into the corrals. Then we'll attack the barn and the other buildings. Before we go out to round up the stock, we'll slop the hogs, take care of the chickens … we'll even milk all of the cows. That will leave you both free to do what has to be done inside the house."

Maude studied him thoughtfully. "I … I don't know. That seems like a great undertaking for just the two of you. After all there are at least ten thousand head of cattle and approximately five hundred horses."

"Where is the rest of the crew?"

"I was wondering the same," said Josh.

Maude sighed. "They along with the household staff left the day after the trial. I think they all thought they wouldn't get paid anymore. I've been trying to do it all by myself."

John leaned eagerly forward. "Would it be alright if we asked one of your neighbors to help us for a few days?"

"I don't mind if you ask, but don't be surprised if you're turned down flat."

Josh grew surly as he leaned forward in his chair. "If they don't help, then we'll manage to do it ourselves. It may take a lot more time than we expected, but we'll get it done."

Maude smiled at their spunk. "I do believe you will."

JaNae interrupted the conversation. "Didn't the stock go with the sale of the property?"

"No. I thought I'd be able to get more selling them separately. I'd just told Mr. Hoffsteader when you drove up. That's when they started to turn ugly, only offering me a pittance for the land."

"I see." A mischievous gleam came into her eyes. "No wonder Mr. Hoffsteader was so irate when I started bidding the land up." She clapped her hands together, laughing gleefully, "I just realized how good I got it over on Alvin Hoffsteader. Wait until I tell Jedidiah!" The others watched in surprise as this dignified lady laughed so uncontrollably. Realizing the impact of what had happened between JaNae, Alvin and Donald Hoffsteader, they quickly joined in the fun.

"I didn't know that they should go with the property," said Maude. "I just thought the property should be sold by itself."

"One thing you can bank on for sure … is the fact that they'll both be here Friday, greedy as ever."

"I hope so," retorted John. "I know horseflesh. Part of my father's job at Fort Owen is buying cattle and horses. I've gone with him so many times, that I know I can get you a good price on every one of these. The pigs and chickens may be a little different, but we'll do our very best."

Tears glistened in Maude's eyes. "What a blessing it was that you came when you did." She began to shake uncontrollably. "Sometimes, I think I'll go mad from anger … or fear … I've been experiencing since Jason's trial."

JaNae reached out to cover Maude's hand with hers. "This would be a difficult thing for anyone to face! Please, don't be so hard on yourself. What you're feeling is very normal."

"Thank you for understanding." Maude dabbed at her eyes with a lace handkerchief. "I was so excited that morning … that is until the soldiers came to tell me about the trial … because I'd just found out that I was going to have another child."

Leaning forward, JaNae excitedly squeezed her hand. "Oh Maude!"

Sighing, Maude bowed her head in dejection. "When the trial was over, I didn't know what to do. I not only felt betrayed, but I'm angry at Jason's greed … his selfishness. Sometimes I hate him … other times I miss him so badly that I can hardly bear it. Now here I am … alone … pregnant … forced to start all over again. The thought of starting over is so very overwhelming that I feel panicky! I'm so afraid of how people will treat the children. Will we be ostracized? I couldn't bear to see the children treated that way. The thought of starting over is so very overwhelming. I sent a telegram to my parents but haven't heard from them. Where will we go if they reject us? All of these things have been running rampant through my mind until I can't think, let alone function!"

John felt as if he were suffocating. *JaNae was right when she said our loved ones would suffer the most from our evil acts,* thought John. *Although it's true that Mr. Walters deserved the punishment he got, Maude and the children were the ones left to pay the price. They still had to live in a world filled with hate and prejudice. They are the ones who had to pick up the pieces after his death. Jason Walters' family would be the ones to suffer from people's attitudes.*

People frown at women who are single. Children cruelly taunt other children who don't have a father in the home. Somehow, I've got to make it up to them, by doing all I can while I'm here, he mused. "We'll do anything we can to help you, ma'am," said John aloud. "Just tell us what you need. It's as good as done."

Josh nodded. "What I don't know how to do, I'll learn by following John's lead. I've never milked cows before, but I have fed and watered the chickens ... even slopped the hogs. I can do almost anything with horses, so I know my way around the stable... so that will help." He smiled ruefully. "As to herding cattle or horses, well that will be a new experience for me."

Smiling, John thumped him on the back. "We'll learn together!"

Josh looked at John strangely. "Do you mean to say that you haven't milked before either, John?"

"No, I can milk a cow, but I've never herded stock before. This will be very interesting indeed. I suggest that we ride over to the neighbors in the morning and see if we can enlist some help. If we can, great! If we can't, then we'll do the best we can, hoping it's enough."

Josh nodded. "I'm with you all the way!"

"Ma'am ..."

Maude grimaced. "Oh, please call me 'Maude'. That 'ma'am' business makes me feel so out of place."

John smiled. "Maude it is. Maude, we have a slight problem with getting the stock in from off the range."

"What's that?"

"We only have one horse, and it's not a cow pony."

"That's not a problem! Take all the horses you need. In fact, use whatever you need from the barn or other buildings to get the job done."

"Thank you, Maude. That will help us a lot."

JaNae thoughtfully surveyed the list. "Well, we surely have our jobs cut out for us, that's for sure!"

"You can say that again," responded Josh.

Laying the list on the table, she smiled at them confidently. "We'll just take it one task at a time. Before we know it, we'll have everything ready." Not long afterward, everyone retired for the night.

The next few days were very hectic, as everyone worked on his or her particular list. True to his word, the next afternoon, Donald Hoffsteader brought out a bank draft for the remainder of what he owed on the property. When the transactions were taken care of, he turned to Maude to ask, "Will you be selling any furniture at the auction?"

"Yes, all of the heavy furniture will have to be sold."

"Would it be an imposition for me to purchase some of the furniture ahead of the public sale?"

"I don't see that that would be a problem."

"Good. I'll be back in a few days before the sale to decide what I'll like to purchase. I'll pay you for them at that time."

"Very well, see you then."

"By the way, when can I expect that you'll have vacated the premises?"

"I'll be out by Saturday night. You can take over the property any time after that."

"Wonderful!" He bowed slightly then turned to leave, calling over his shoulder, "See you soon."

Earlier that morning, the boys went to the neighbors west of Walters' to ask for help. Fred Johansson and three of his sons agreed to help them drive the stock into the corrals. He was a congenial man, who was always ready and willing to help. John liked him the moment they met.

As he gave instructions to his sons, John took note of Johansson's appearance. He was five feet seven inches tall with black hair that was streaked with gray. He had honest brown eyes, a wide nose and high forehead, and was wiry-thin with a quick look about him.

The evening of the first day found them so exhausted that they turned in not long after the dinner dishes were done. Each day became more grueling, yet somehow they managed to shorten the list. Poor Josh and John became so saddle sore that it was all they could do to keep from crying out.

Two days later, Josh turned his horse to block the path of a cow, when a stitch in his side nearly doubled him over. Yelling out in pain, he nearly fell out of the saddle.

Grabbing the saddle horn was all that saved him. He stopped the horse, struggling to get a deep breath while waiting for the pain to subside. Doggedly, he kept up with the grueling pace. That night as they rode into the yard, Josh was so saddle sore that he couldn't dismount. John, with the aid of Mr. Johansson, helped him down. Between the two of them, they got him inside and into bed. He was asleep before they left the room.

The next morning, both of them were so stiff that it was comical to see them staggering into the dining room. Heading for the coffee on the sidebar, Josh eased into a chair, moaning and groaning with every effort. "Oh … I think I've been run over by a huge herd of buffalo!"

John, too, had eased into a chair by now. "My sentiments exactly! Only thing is, I don't think they were satisfied with running over me once, they had to do it at least two or three more times!"

The women struggled not to laugh outright at the pitiful sight they presented. Maude walked over to place a hand on John's shoulder. "Believe it or not, this too shall pass. By the end of tonight you will both be seasoned riders."

John moaned, "Oh great laws a massy, I hope so! These old bones feel like they're about to fall apart!"

Maude laughed. "I have a feeling … those old bones, as you call them, will see many more days like this."

"Oh … I was afraid of that!" lamented Josh.

JaNae joined in on the fun, as she walked around the table refilling their cups. "Ah, boys, what 'cha need is a good breakfast under your belts, and you'll be as good as new."

Josh moaned again, before he took several large gulps of coffee. Setting his cup down, he sighed. "Ah, that's better! Maybe you're right, JaNae. It seems like three days since I've eaten anything. My poor stomach thinks my throat got cut sometime during the night. Bring it on, I'm ready for it!" At that moment, breakfast was served.

It took them four days to round up the stock. Maude had been right; they were seasoned riders by the end of the day. In spite of the fact that the work was easier, John was relieved when it was over.

As he sat astride his horse surveying the stock, he was amazed to see how large the herds were. He wouldn't have been surprised to learn that there were well over ten thousand head of cattle and seven hundred head of horses. The count would have been higher, if Mr. Johansson hadn't purchased all of the new spring calves along with half of the new colts. He had also purchased all of the chickens.

The next few days were spent in cataloging the tack room, also the farm equipment. Fred Johansson lent a helping hand where needed. One evening, Maude went out to the barn to let them know dinner was ready. Hearing them talking seriously, she hesitated, uncertain if she should interrupt them. Peering inside, she saw John standing by a stall, watching Josh use the currycomb on a sorrel mare. She didn't want to eavesdrop on their conversation, but intuitively, she felt the need to listen. "You know, Josh, you act like that horse is your best friend."

"Well, it's like this. When Mr. Walters came to the fort to visit Corporal Maines, he always rode this beauty to the stables. He always requested that I take care of her. I have done so off and on for about a year now." John opened the stall to step out of the way so that Josh could lead the horse out. Nickering softly the mare nudged him in the back, nearly causing Josh to fall over his own feet. "Aw, girl, I know you want a carrot, but I don't have one." He lovingly stroked her neck. "I'm sure going to miss you!"

"Well, it's plain to see that you love this horse," said John.

Josh sighed sadly. "I surely do." He continued to stroke the sorrel's neck for a moment longer. "I surely hope she gets a good master ... one that will love her as much as I do."

Maude, touched by the love between the horse and boy, knew what she had to do. Stepping into the barn, she quickly hurried toward Josh. "It's as plain as the nose on my face that the two of you belong together."

Josh's jaw dropped, as he stared at her in confusion. "I ... I don't understand, ma'am."

Putting a hand on his shoulder, Maude gently turned him to face her so that he could look intently into his eyes. "You and this horse love each other so much, that I know my husband would want you to have her. He always called her his 'Molly Girl.' He rode her everywhere."

Tears glistened in Josh's eyes. For a moment, he couldn't believe that he'd heard correctly. "Are you saying … are you saying I can have this horse?"

"Yes, Josh. That's exactly what I'm saying." By now, tears were glistening in her eyes as well. She smiled sweetly, feeling good about what she was doing. "After all that you've done for me, Josh, it's the very least I can do for you."

Losing all control of his emotions, he buried his face in Molly Girl's neck, sobbing brokenly. "Oh, Molly Girl … I never thought this could happen to me." John stood back, moved beyond words. Before Maude could discern Josh's intent, he turned to hug Maude tightly to him, kissing her on the cheek. "Oh may God bless you forever, ma'am! No one has ever done anything like this for me before. I'll be eternally grateful!"

Maude turned a beautiful rose color, then stepped back, lifting her apron to dab at the tears in her eyes. "That'll be enough of this mushy stuff," she teased. "I came out here to tell you that dinner was ready, so let's get a move on."

John smiled, reading through her harshness. "We'll be in as soon as we put Molly Girl away and get washed up."

"Good enough. See you inside." With that, she rushed away.

Two days before the public sale, several men came out separately or in groups to purchase farm equipment or livestock. Calvin Jinks, Alvin Hoffsteader along with his nephew Donald were the first to arrive. Mr. Johansson was helping them sort through the things in the barn. Calvin Jinks snubbed John. Alvin Hoffsteader's blustery attitude grated on everybody's nerves. They condescendingly scoffed at the farm implements.

While Jinks and Donald Hoffsteader went to look at the stock in the corrals, Alvin Hoffsteader strutted arrogantly around like a proud peacock with its feathers in a full fan. He mopped the glistening beads of perspiration from his balding pate with the same dirty, smelly bandana. Walking over to the stall that housed Molly Girl, Hoffsteader hung his arms on the gate greedily eyeing the sorrel. "How much you want for this sorrel?"

"That horse is not for sale, sir," politely muttered John, not bothering to look up as he polished a saddle.

"Aren't you being a might persnickety, boy?"

"No, sir. I'm just telling you that the horse is not for sale."

Hoffsteader grew testy, as greed possessed his soul. "Who said it's not?"

"It was a present. Mrs. Walters gave the horse to my friend Josh."

Hoffsteader, growing sullen, spun around to face John. "How do we know when her husband committed those horrible crimes that she wasn't also part of that gang? After all, birds of a feather do flock together. She should be grateful that my nephew Donald bought this ranch." Anger flashed from John's eyes as he struggled to control his temper. Hoffsteader either didn't see, or didn't care. "Besides, with an estate such as this, everything should have been sold together … not separately! It appears that she learned to bilk poor unsuspecting men like us out of our hard earned money!"

Fred Johansson, who came into the barn shortly after Hoffsteader started his spiel, became so enraged that his body began to shake uncontrollably. He stalked angrily over to Hoffsteader, until they were eye-to-eye and nose-to-nose. "I happen to know that Mrs. Walters is the most caring, honest woman I have ever met. I suggest that you shut your mouth … kindly tend to the business at hand … or get off the property … now!"

"Oh, I see that she has you hoodwinked, too! Or why else would you be so ready to defend a woman like her?"

John saw Fred Johansson's body stiffen, his right arm swung out, his fist connecting perfectly with Hoffsteader's wide Roman nose. Hoffsteader grabbed the tender member as blood spurted from it, trickling down through his fingers. "Ah! Ya broke my nose, man!"

"If you think that's all yer gonna get, Mister, ya got another think comin'." Bouncing from side to side, fists poised for action, his short wiry body darted in before Hoffsteader could sidestep him, slugging him hard in the stomach. As air escaped the portly man, he doubled over in pain. Johansson finished him off with a hard right uppercut under his jaw. Jinks and the younger Hoffsteader rushed in to see what was going on. They arrived just in time to see Alvin Hoffsteader stumble backwards then crumple into the corner of the barn, like a limp burlap sack.

"What's the meaning of all this?" yelled Donald Hoffsteader.

Johansson turned calmly to the irate gentlemen, smiling coyly. "We're just teaching your uncle proper manners, sir. My mother always taught me to hold women in highest esteem. I will not tolerate a woman being slandered by anyone. Mrs. Walters is not only genteel, but the most honest, fair-minded woman I've ever met. Now, will you kindly remove this baggage from the barn?"

Donald Hoffsteader turned to Jinks. "Come help me get my uncle out to the buckboard." Between the two of them, Hoffsteader was removed from the barn.

Josh dashed from the barn toward the house, running like a man possessed. "JaNae, Maude, come quick! There's been a fight in the barn!"

The women came tearing out of the house, with their skirts gathered in their hands so they could run without being hampered. As they hurried toward the barn, they were in time to see Jinks and Hoffsteader's nephew carry Hoffsteader to the buckboard. They paused in shock. Fear flashed from their eyes as they saw the overpowered man positioned between his two companions. Blood was flowing freely from Hoffsteader's broken, disfigured nose. There was a huge bruise on his chin, which was quickly swelling.

The women glanced at each other, then rushed on to the barn, concerned and bewildered. As they stepped inside, John and Johansson were talking. John looked at Johansson in awe. It was obvious that he was pleased with what the old man had done.

"You surely gave that man what for! I never thought I'd be so tickled to see a man get a licken as much as I was with Mr. Hoffsteader. Thank you for championing Maude."

Johansson was holding his bruised fist, feeling ashamed of losing his temper, yet feeling very good. "When Hoffsteader insulted Mrs. Walters, I saw the perfect chance to knock him off his high horse. The truth of the matter is, I don't like him, or his arrogant attitude. Seems like the old coot always sticks his nose where it doesn't belong. I just taught him how to mind his own business."

Maude rushed over to Johansson, took his hand in hers to observe it closely. "What's been going on in here?"

"Just teaching a few lessons on manners, ma'am."

JaNae chuckled mischievously. "Well, at least the right man is still standing. Knowing Hoffsteader the way I do, he has had this lesson coming for a long time!"

"I never liked him much, but when he insulted Mrs. Walters, something inside me wanted to whop him up aside the head to make him shut his fat mouth ... so I did!"

Releasing his hand, Maude stood on tiptoe to quickly kiss his cheek. Stepping back, she looked him in the eye. "Thank you, Mr. Johansson, for defending my honor. I'll always remember that."

Johansson's eyes grew misty as he struggled to gain control of his emotions. Swiping at his eyes with the back of his hand, he sniffled, turning shyly away. "Dad-blamed animals are kicking up so much dust that it makes a body's eyes water." He quickly got busy doing something else. Smiling, the women went back to the house.

When they got Alvin Hoffsteader's bleeding under control, he stayed in the buckboard while the two went to look over the livestock. They had just finished cutting out the stock they wanted, handing John the money, when others arrived. Donald made other purchases which John or Josh marked "sold." They placed the items where they were safe. Without so much as a "thank you", the two men went to join Alvin and shortly rode away.

At the end of the day, most of the stock and the farm equipment were sold. It was an impressive sight to see huge groups of cattle or horses being driven away. It reminded John of several small cattle drives. That night at dinner, when they handed Maude the proceeds from the sales, she was impressed with the outstanding sum they had gotten for everything.

Every day, while the men had been busy doing their tasks, the women had been tackling the interior of the house. The house, being the women's territory, presented a great challenge to them. They sorted through the household items, deciding what to pack, which things to ship, and what to sell. As they sorted, they thoroughly cleaned each room. The items Maude wanted to keep were placed in one room, while the items to be sold were placed in another.

When they finished going through each room, they washed down the walls and the windows and cleaned the floors. For days, the women worked like Trojans, sorting, cleaning and preparing meals. Every day became a blur as they worked side by side. A friendship, greater than either could imagine, blossomed into something beautiful.

All of the rooms had been gone through except the back bedroom, which had been Jason's office. Maude had put this room off until last, because it was too painful to go into. Entering, they began to tackle the room's contents. The room's two windows, adorned with simple curtains had a commanding view of the farm. A large desk occupied the middle of the room, with a large plush stuffed chair behind it.

Two matching chairs were positioned against the opposite wall with round end tables. Beautifully decorated matching lamps sat in the center of the tables. An ornate liquor cabinet was located near the far left of the room. Several pictures decorated the walls. An oriental rug covered the hardwood floor. These simple furnishings proclaimed it a man's room.

JaNae began taking the pictures from the walls, while Maude went through the desk. There was a ledger in the top right hand drawer, which Maude placed on top of the desk. The other drawers held paper with lots of writing paraphernalia. The other drawers yielded nothing. Wiping her brow with the back of her hand, Maude wearily rubbed her aching back. Sitting in the chair, she went through the ledger. There was nothing earth shattering in it, only business transactions concerning the running of the estate.

When JaNae removed the final picture, which was behind the desk, she cried out in surprise, "Oh."

Maude swung around in her chair to see what had startled JaNae. Stunned, she rose to peer critically into the gaping hole in the wall. "Oh, my goodness! Look at this hole!" Her eyes grew large with shock, causing her to shake uncontrollably as she reached into the cavity. She pulled out a bankbook. Reaching in again she pulled out an inordinate amount of cash. Reaching in one last time she pulled out their marriage certificate. As Maude examined the document, tears sprang into her eyes. Feeling such utter despair, she grabbed the bankbook and marriage certificate and rushed to her room. The bankbook she placed in her handbag to take to the bank. Maude quickly buried the marriage certificate in between clothes in her trunk.

Finding a satchel, Maude went back to the office. JaNae was removing the last bottle of liquor from the cabinet when Maude entered. Seeing Maude's ashen face, JaNae went to hold the satchel open while Maude filled it. Neither spoke as they worked, but it was apparent that Maude was nearing the breaking point. When the hole in the wall was empty, Maude hung one of the pictures over the hole before fastening the clasp on the satchel. When she was finished, she wiped her hands on her apron.

While Maude went through the pictures and the other items in the room, in an attempt to decide what she wanted to keep, JaNae got a bucket of hot water and cleaning supplies, then began washing down the walls. Maude took the items she intended to keep to the room with the items waiting to be packed, crated or shipped.

Everything else was placed with the other sales items. The large furniture would be brought down later, unless Donald Hoffsteader purchased them. When the room was finished, they went out.

When everything was sorted, they packed the larger items into crates. The smaller items were packed into the steamer trunks, while the items needed for their trip home were packed in satchels to be taken with them. Finally, they were ready to set up the table for the sales items.

Early one morning, Johansson and Josh took the crates and several steamer trunks to Missoula to ship them. They returned late that night tired and hungry. Josh let Johansson off at his ranch then rode on to Maude's. Once inside he handed her a receipt. "They told me at the shipping office that it would take about six weeks to two months to deliver everything."

"Thank you, Josh," said Maude. "I'm glad that job is over with."

"You're welcome, ma'am. Glad I could be of service." After eating, he went to bed, immediately falling asleep.

By Thursday night, they were ready for those who were coming out for the sale. JaNae made Maude sit down while she prepared dinner. When it was ready, everyone made short work of it. During dinner, Maude informed everyone there that her little family would be traveling with them to Missoula. There Maude would procure rooms at the local hotel until they left the following Thursday.

JaNae told Maude they, too, would get a room at the hotel for the night. They would go back to the fort after helping Maude finalize some business the next morning. Being bone-weary, they all decided to retire early so that they would be ready for the crowd.

Long before daylight, each member of the group was busily working at some task. JaNae looked out the window while cooking breakfast, watching a rosy glow appear in the east. There was not a cloud in the sky. The birds were chirping merrily in the treetops, ensuring good weather for the sale.

The group had just finished clearing away the breakfast things, when a wagon pulled into the yard. It was Donald Hoffsteader. JaNae called to Maude before going to the door. Hoffsteader greeted her amiably as he removed his hat. "Good morning, ma'am. Could I please see Mrs. Walters?"

JaNae moved to the side, motioning to him to enter, "Of course. Please come in."

Maude joined them as JaNae closed the door. "Good morning, Mr. Hoffsteader."

"Is it too early to make purchases?"

"No, please look around, then we'll talk."

"Thank you, ma'am." JaNae and Maude were surprised to see him acting so gentlemanly toward them. A short time later he returned to the parlor where they were putting last minute touches on the sale items. "I'm ready to make my deal."

As he named off the items, JaNae wrote sold on a piece of paper, listed them on a separate sheet in case the paper flew off, then put the "sold" tags on the items sold. JaNae was surprised when he paid her handsomely for everything.

Shortly after his departure, they were soon so bombarded with the onslaught of people that at times they were hard-pressed to keep up. By late afternoon, it was all over. Even all of the farm equipment was sold. The team and buckboard, which Donald Hoffsteader had loaned them to haul their luggage, were all that was left. As she looked around the empty house, Maude felt just like it looked.

JaNae put her arms around the children then motioned for John and Josh to follow her. She looked at the children, "Come on children, let's all go so that Maude can have a little time alone."

Maude smiled through her tears as everyone began to leave. "Thank you, JaNae." Slowly Maude walked from room to room, reliving the bittersweet memories. She remembered the day her husband brought her to this home. Unbeknownst to her, he had purchased the land and then had the house built.

When it was ready, he told her he wanted to go riding. As they drove the wagon into the yard, Maude remembered gasping at the beauty before her. Jason had helped her out of the wagon. Taking her hand in his, he excitedly led her to the house. Flinging open the door, he scooped her up into his arms to carry her over the threshold. Just inside the door, he kissed her passionately before setting her down.

"Welcome home, my love. Welcome to your new home." She couldn't believe he had pulled it off so easily without her knowing anything, but he had. Now here she stood in the middle of the empty parlor, feeling betrayed, forsaken, angry, scared; but most of all, she felt so incredibly lonely.

She crumpled to the floor, as tears coursed down her cheeks, struggling to find a way to deal with the indescribable pain. "Oh, Jason, how could you fall so low?" After a few minutes, she rose. Walking to the kitchen sink, Maude splashed water on her face to make herself presentable, while at the same time composing herself.

Taking a deep breath, Maude calmly joined the others waiting near the wagon. Maude was so very thankful for those few precious minutes in the empty house alone, for now she felt as if she could cope more easily.

John helped her onto the seat, then went around the wagon to climb up. He would drive the buckboard with Maude and the children, while Josh and JaNae followed in the surrey. Molly Girl and the white gelding were securely tied to the back of the wagon as John clucked to the horses. As the horses strained into their harness, the creaking wagon slowly moved out of the yard. They were on their way.

"What were you doing all by yourself, Mommie?" asked little Stephen.

"Oh, just saying goodbye to the house," she calmly replied.

"Did it tell you goodbye, Mommie?"

"In its own special way, son. In its own special way." Stephen scratched his head, but said no more.

All at once Janie looked up at her mother. "Mommie, when is Papa coming home?"

Maude's heart skipped a beat. She had known this question would come up sooner or later, but had secretly been hoping that it would be much later. Now that she was facing the question, she didn't know what to do. Taking a deep breath, she turned to smile at her daughter. "Papa isn't coming home, honey."

Janie watched her mother, confused and hurt. "Why not?"

"Papa did a really bad thing which he had to pay for. He went to a place where we can't go."

"Where's that?"

"Papa died, honey."

"Oh … does that mean he went to Heaven?"

Maude paused for a long time, wondering how to answer her daughter, so that she could understand. Knowing there was no other answer, save it were the truth that would suffice, she plunged in. "Do you remember when your Papa and I told you about consequences?"

"Yes, a little."

"Remember, I told you that when we do a wrong, we have to be punished?" Janie nodded. "Well, when we do a little wrong, we are punished a little, but when we do a big wrong, we are punished a lot. Papa did a really big wrong that will take a long time to be worked out. To answer your question … is he in heaven … I don't know."

Janie sat back in the wagon trying to digest the information her mother had just given her. Maude was so grateful that Stephen was too young to be interested in the conversation. He sat watching the horses at the end of the wagon. For a long time they rode in silence, then John turned to Maude and spoke in a hushed voice. "You really handled that situation well, Maude."

"I don't know about that. It was so difficult, and it's not over."

"No, but you made a good start."

Several hours later, they rode into Missoula, stopping at the livery stable. Alighting from the wagon, John went inside the stables to speak to the proprietor. He left instructions for the buckboard and the team to be picked up by Hoffsteader. Untying the horses from the back of the wagon, he took them inside.

After procuring the rooms, they went to Aunt Em's Cafe across the street to eat. The same waitress they met going to Maude's led them to the same table. JaNae smiled at the waitress sweetly. "What special are you serving tonight?"

"We have the ham special, which consists of ham, mashed potatoes and gravy, and biscuits. Or we have a steak with the same trimmings."

"Please, give me the ham special."

"I want the steak," said Josh.

John nodded, "Me, too."

"The children and I will have the ham special."

"What would you like to drink?"

"The children and I will have milk."

"I'd like coffee," chorused the others.

It wasn't long until the waitress returned with their meals. They ate in silence, grateful to have the day nearly over. The chatter and clatter of other diners failed to dim their peace. When the meal was over, they went back to the hotel lobby. After saying good night to each other, they retired to their rooms.

Meeting in the hotel lobby early the next morning, they went to eat their last meal together. By the time they were finished, all of the businesses were open. Maude turned anxiously toward JaNae. "I wonder if the sheriff is in his office by now?"

"Let's go find out," said JaNae, linking her arm through Maude's. Entering the Sheriff's office a few minutes later, they saw Sheriff Hill sitting at his desk.

Hill rose, hurrying over to the women. He took JaNae's hand in his. "Good morning, Mrs. Williams! What can I do for you this bright sunshiny day?"

JaNae nodded toward Maude. "I don't know if you remember Mrs. Walters, Sheriff."

The sheriff turned to peer intently at Maude. "Yes, I remember you!" Releasing JaNae's hand, he reached out to take Maude's. "That was a rough blow dealt you, my dear." The compassion in his voice completely unnerved Maude. It took a moment for her to gain control. "How can I help you, Mrs. Walters?"

Taking a deep breath, Maude let it out slowly in an attempt to collect her thoughts. "At the trial, I stated that I was going to sell my ranch after which I would return the proceeds to the victims' families." Hill nodded. "Well, I'm here today to do just that." Before he could discern her intent, she set a satchel on his desk.

Blinking, he looked at her as if she'd gone daft. "Wait a minute! Let me see if I've got this straight!" He scratched the stubble on his chin thoughtfully. "You want to give everything you got from the sale of the ranch to the victims' families?"

"Yes, sir! Everything but ten thousand dollars, the full amount of my dowry." She paused to gain control before continuing. "I will need that to get started again."

Opening the bag, Hill gasped at the contents inside. "You got this much from the sale?"

"Yes, sir." Taking the bank draft from her handbag, she handed it to him.

Casually looking down at the amount, Hill's jaw went slack. Looking at her with a blank expression on his face, he asked, "What am I supposed to do with this?"

"I need you to go to the bank with me so that you can deposit everything into your account. You know who the families are, so it is best to leave it in your capable hands. Your reputation for being honest earns you the right to do this job, sir. My children and I are leaving Thursday for Boston, so I will not have time to do anything more with this matter."

Hill looked down at the floor for a moment in an attempt to collect his thoughts. "There is no easy way to say this, ma'am, but I feel that you must be told the truth.

Upon investigation, preparatory to your helping the families, we made a terrible discovery. When your husband's gang did their dastardly deeds, they made sure no one was left alive."

The fact that she was pregnant and the horrific shock of his words, made Maude begin to swoon. Hill caught her before she hit the floor while JaNae knelt to gently rub her hands. A short time later Maude opened her eyes looking blankly up at Hill. "Oh, what happened?"

"The shock was too much, my dear. You fainted," said Hill. He helped her to her feet directing her to a chair. When she was seated, he knelt at her feet. "Now we need to have a talk."

"Yes, sir. I'm listening."

"I know this was a terrible shock, but you're a strong, courageous woman. I admire you so much for trying to put things right, but it just can't be."

"But can't this money help someone? You see, sir, I don't want this tainted money."

"I know, my dear, but you have the children to think of now. The money from the sale of the ranch will help to educate them. Don't think of it as tainted money, but as a blessing to see you through the rough times ahead."

Maude thought that over then nodded. "Very well, but only for the children's sake."

"Good!" As he gently patted her hand, tears glistened in his eyes. "You're quite a lady, Mrs. Walters. Quite a lady!" Closing the satchel, he gently handed it and the bank draft to her, while he smiled encouragingly.

"Thank you, Sheriff." Rising, she put the bank draft back into her handbag. Picking up the satchel, the women left.

JaNae linked her arm through hers. "Let me steady you for just a little ways."

"Thank you. I would really appreciate that."

Together, they walked over to the bank.

The bank president escorted them into his office. Closing the door, he motioned to two chairs in front of his desk. "Won't you both please be seated?" When they were all seated, he asked, "Now, how can I be of service to you?"

Maude gently set the satchel onto the desk. Reaching into her handbag, she extracted the bank draft and bankbook and handed them to the bank president. Maude spoke, "Sir, I've never done any banking before. My husband took care of those matters so I don't know what I'm supposed to do. Would you mind adding all of this up and giving me the total owed on my account?"

"I'd be more than happy to do that, madam." He placed the bank draft and bankbook on the desk. He pulled the satchel over, opened it and peered inside. What he saw inside made his face go chalky white, his mouth gaped open, his eyes bulged, and he started to shake. For a moment he appeared about to faint. "My dear, madam! Have you been carrying this around town?"

"Yes, sir. Is there a problem?"

"I should say so! I'm surprised you haven't been hit over the head by now." He removed the contents, arranging them into piles on the desk. Working quickly, he calculated the sum, and then entered it in the bankbook. Finally, he looked at Maude, "Were you aware of what was already in your husband's account, ma'am?"

"Not totally, sir. My husband never discussed business with me."

"Well, you are one very wealthy lady."

She sat there stupefied. Finally, curiosity overcame her. "I am? Just how wealthy am I?"

"There is now slightly over one million dollars in your account."

Maude sat there, too shocked to speak. Finally gaining control, she blurted out, "Surely you are mistaken."

"No, ma'am, I'm not."

She leaned forward to rest her elbow on the desk, and slapped her forehead. "Oh my gosh, JaNae! Did you hear that?" She began to shake her as if she'd been asleep. "Did you hear that? What do I do? Tell me, what do I do?"

JaNae calmly rested her hand on her friend's shoulder. "It's all right, honey. Just let Mr. Peabody decide what's best. He knows what to do."

She nodded in agreement. "You're right, JaNae."

Trying to appear calm, she turned back to the bank president and took a deep breath. She paused to formulate her thoughts, then smiled and said, "I am leaving for Boston on Thursday. I need thirteen hundred dollars to pay a bill, buy our tickets and take care of any other unforeseen incidentals while we travel."

"We'll write you out several bank drafts. You can take them to any bank along the way and cash them. We'll also give you thirteen hundred dollars in cash. Do you think that will be sufficient?"

"Yes. Thank you, sir. Would you mind giving me some paper, ink and an envelope?"

"Not at all." He quickly placed the items in front of her. Preparing to leave the room, he said, "I'll be just a moment, ma'am." Rising he left the room. JaNae sat patiently while Maude quickly dipped the pen in the ink before writing. When she was finished, she blew on the paper to dry the ink. Folding the note Maude placed it on top of the envelope. When that was done, they talked quietly while they waited for Mr. Peabody to complete the transactions. Not long afterward, he returned, patiently counting out the thirteen hundred dollars.

Maude took a small cloth pouch from her handbag. After stuffing the money inside, she put it back into her handbag. Mr. Peabody handed her the bank drafts, which had been tied together. These Maude added to her handbag. Rising, she sighed wearily. "Thank you, sir. You have been very helpful"

JaNae stood up as they shook hands. The bank president escorted them from the office. He watched until they were out of sight. Shaking his head in disbelief, Peabody went back to work.

JaNae accompanied Maude to the stage office, where she procured their tickets. Taking the letter she had written in the bank president's office, she stuffed some money between the folds of the letter. Then she put everything into the envelope, making sure that the envelope was sealed. That done, they went back to meet John, Josh, and the children, waiting for them in the hotel lobby. A clerk came toward them with something in his hand. A telegram has arrived for you, Mrs. Walters."

"Thank you, Ben." Taking the telegram, her hands began to shake so badly that she handed it to JaNae. "Would you please read this? If it's bad news, I don't want to be the first to know."

JaNae took the telegram from her trembling hands. Opening it, she scanned the contents. A huge smile broke out on her face. "It's good news. Do you want to read it ... or should I?"

"You read it, please."

JaNae looked at her in concern. "No, I surely think that you should read it first."

Maude took the telegram from JaNae and began to read. As she read the telegram, a smile spread across her face. Maude read it aloud: "Dearest Maude. -STOP- Anxiously awaiting your arrival. -STOP- Nothing to forgive. -STOP- Love's unconditional. -STOP- Hurry home. -STOP- Love, mother and father. -STOP-

"Oh! Praise be! Oh, JaNae, read this!" Looking at the children she said firmly, "It's from your grandpa and grandma. We're going home. We're really going home! Everything's going to be fine now."

Maude was already disconnecting herself from the empty house she had just left. Since the moment she had learned the hideous truth about her husband, she began to feel a need to distance herself from the house they had lived in. Then, an excitement she hadn't experienced since that awful trial permeated her soul. She grabbed the children and hugged them.

She turned to a teary eyed JaNae and hugged her tightly too. "Thank you for everything, JaNae. I shall never forget your generosity and kindness. I could never have done it without the three of you." She unconsciously straightened her back and her shoulders and added confidently, "We'll be fine from now on."

JaNae dabbed at the tears in her eyes. "You will never be forgotten, dear. I want to wish you all the luck in the world. When you are settled, write to let me know how the three of you are doing. I'll be especially curious to know about the new baby."

"I'll write as soon as I get settled," promised Maude. "I'm still wondering how I'll handle having a new baby in my life." She giggled shyly. "I thought Stephen was my last!"

JaNae patted her hand. "You'll do just fine! Goodbye for now, dear."

Maude hugged Josh, "Thank you for all your help."

As Josh stepped back, he replied, "You're welcome."

Maude hugged John, "Thank you for everything." Stepping back, she stuffed an envelope into his shirt pocket. "I want you to promise me that you won't open this envelope until you are alone in your room."

"I promise, Maude. I'll always be grateful for the privilege of getting to know you. You're one spunky lady."

Tears glistened in Maude's eyes, as she looked at the young man before her. "Thank you, John."

As John and Josh walked on each side of JaNae, they felt the awful pain of parting from a newfound friend. They stopped and turned for one last look. "Goodbye," they chorused.

"Goodbye!" answered Maude.

The three stopped to have lunch before continuing their journey. On the return trip, after securing Molly Girl to the back of the surrey, John mounted the gelding, leaving Josh to be with JaNae. They made good time back to the fort. After unloading the surrey, they took it along with the horses to the stable.

CHAPTER 16

Encounter

T hings weren't going well with Thornton, or his men. In fact, nothing had been right from the time they left the Indian encampment. None of the men were used to walking in their bare feet, so each step they took caused them great pain. Walking caused huge blisters to break, as the rocks, sticks and pine needles all cut into their tender feet.

Thornton's disposition became nastier, if that were possible. Not only did Thornton breathe out murderous threats against Nataka, but he also bellyached about everything. The men grew so tired of Thornton's foul attitude that it grew ever more difficult for them to remain silent.

Miles, standing five feet nine inches tall, was lean and wiry. Thick golden curly hair was his only real beauty. Thin lips, usually drawn into a smirk or sneer, short cheekbones and a flat chin made Miles ugly. Bushy eyebrows, usually scowling, accentuated cold, calculating, dark-blue eyes. Although there had been a softer side to Miles, his father taught him well.

Thornton's injurious attitude instilled in Miles the love of hurting others. Under his father's demented tutelage, he learned to watch eagerly for the opportunity to strike out at someone. Usually the victim was some unsuspecting female. While there were times when Miles could have cared less whether his father loved or hated him, the little boy inside yearned for love and his father's acceptance.

Corporal Hank Jennings was a mystery. His thick black hair, which he combed back from his face, was never out of place ... until now. His spotless uniform was always neatly pressed. High cheekbones, a delicately shaped chin and a long shapely neck combined to complement his six-foot frame perfectly. Thin eyebrows and a neatly trimmed moustache over thick, sensuous lips accentuated his beautiful light-blue eyes.

One would never guess from first contact that underneath that handsome physique beat a cold, ruthless, evil heart. He took fiendish delight in hurting others just for the pure pleasure of it. However, when any derisive plan was foiled, he became testy or sullen, silently skulking away to wait for the next opportunity to wreak havoc on the one who dared to cross him.

Private Thomas Jones, "Tom" to his friends or acquaintances, was a follower, not a leader. Although he was now mean, crotchety, even nasty-tempered most of the time, he wasn't so far gone that there was no longer the possibility of change. However, because of the company he chose to keep, that possibility lay concealed in the deepest recesses of his brain. His five-foot-four-inch height never stopped him when it came to taking on someone bigger or stronger than he was. He would dive in or around the person, striking accurately in vulnerable spots. One lock of his short, straight, brown hair, always in constant disarray, fell across his high forehead. Thin eyebrows highlighted his cold, deceitful gray eyes. Combined with thick cheekbones, a pointed chin, thin sneering lips and a wide beefsteak nose made him downright ugly.

Such were the temperaments of Thornton's men ... a group of vile, spoiled, hard-hearted, hate-filled men bent on revenge. So poisonous were the prisons of their own making that these men could die without ever having tasted the fruits of pure love and the sweet joy of serving others.

They had gone about two miles when the sun slipped behind the mountains. A stiff breeze began to blow, penetrating their longjohns. Growing chilled, they decided to make camp early. Jones and Jennings went in search of wood, while Miles gathered stones for a fire pit, placing the stones in a circle. Thornton sat upon a rock bellyaching incessantly. Miles looked over at him in disgust then continued to lay the stones into a circle. Jones and Jennings brought several large armloads of wood, which they dumped into a pile in easy reach of the fire.

When Miles had the circle completed, making sure the area around it was completely clean, he prepared a roaring fire. He used the flint provided by the Indians. Thornton moved closer to enjoy the fire's warmth. He continued to bellyache about their situation, constantly picking at everything the men tried to do. The three men remained silent ... disgruntled by Thornton's attitude.

Thornton turned sullenly towards Miles. "Where's that food bag?" Miles hobbled over to get the bag, which he handed to Thornton. Impatiently rummaging inside, he pulled out some jerky and some Indian fry bread. Looking at the items with contempt, he shoved them back into the bag. He flung the bag back to Miles. "This isn't fit for man or beast!"

Miles reached into the bag, pulling out some jerky, which he hungrily munched on. After a few chomps, he shuddered in disgust. "This tastes like a block of salt!" Shrugging, he continued to chew. "Oh well, I guess it's better than nothing." With disdain, he handed the bag to Jones, who took out a generous portion of fry bread before passing it on to Jennings.

Reaching into the bag, Jennings took out a large portion of fry bread and a piece of jerky. Biting into the fry bread, he moaned in delight. "Yum! This is delicious!" Thornton wrinkled his nose in scorn, then turned away. Jennings shrugged at Thornton's indifference as he continued to eat the food. When they were finished, they sat staring into the fire, willing their aching bones to get warm. Growing sleepy, one by one they lay down near the fire, soon falling asleep.

Morning found them struggling painfully toward the fort. The morning air was not only crisp but was also breezy, causing the men a lot of discomfort. They were so disgruntled that they failed to see the beauty around them, or to hear the songsters' different renditions. Because of the abuse to their feet, they had to rest often. As the sun climbed high into the sky, they were hard-pressed to endure the hot sun on their heads. To make matters worse, when they sat down to rest their tired aching feet, the buzzing flies tormented them.

The two braves sent to escort the four men back to the fort lay hidden from Thornton's men, but they were thoroughly enjoying the men's discomfort. The braves were not vindictive, but knowing what these men had intended for their people, they only felt that justice was being meted out. They watched in fascination as Thornton's group struggled along. They couldn't help wondering if they would make it to the fort.

Near noon Thornton looked up at the sky. He grew anxious when he saw dark storm clouds gathering in the distance. He turned to look at the men, who were also studying the sky. Rising from the rock where he had been resting, Thornton started walking. He was so lame that it was almost impossible for him to walk a step. Only his hatred of Nataka and his desire for revenge let him continue walking toward the fort.

As the day grew hotter, it became sultry. Still the men struggled on. They were determined to accomplish a goodly distance before the storm struck. The air stood still, making the heat unbearably stifling. Static electricity danced along the hairs on their arms, stretching their already frayed nerves to the breaking point. They constantly bickered back and forth like naughty children, accustomed to getting their own way. Thornton cursed the impending storm while the men cursed each other. Although it was difficult to endure the strain each step demanded, they doggedly hobbled on. The surveying braves looked at each other. They could only shake their heads in disgust.

Finally late that afternoon a slight breeze blew. A break in the heat was a relief, even though it was only a prelude to what lay ahead. Not long after the wind increased, menacing storm clouds billowed angrily across the sky. Soon the clouds obscured the sun. Lightning flashed in the distance, soon to be followed by rumbling thunder. This concerned the men, who knew that they were at the mercy of the elements. With heavy hearts, they trudged on. In spite of their great determination, the men were required to take several breaks in order to endure the heat or extreme pain in their feet. Meanwhile, the storm grew ever closer.

It was getting late in the day when they decided to make camp. It was decided that they would prepare a shelter to protect themselves from the ever-approaching storm. The breeze continued to grow in velocity until it was a real squall. At first the spring air was cool, even refreshing, providing much needed relief from the heat. As the wind continued to grow in intensity, it penetrated their underwear. Since the long-johns provided little protection, the men began to shiver. Trees bent under the wind's mighty force, causing some of the limbs to snap. The men jumped when they heard a dead tree fall to the right of them.

Miles searched for rocks to make a pit. Jones gathered the wood and the other men attempted to prepare a lean-to. They acted like two old tomcats vying for the same territory, as they argued over how the shelter should be constructed. Thornton wanted to do it one way, while Jennings wanted to do it another. Somehow through all the bickering, just as darkness arrived, the lean-to was finally up. Jones got a good fire going so the men huddled around it. Feeling the heat of the fire helped to soothe their distraught nerves.

The rain began as a soft, gentle, misting shower then burst into a heavy deluge. Disheveled, the men sat huddled in the lean-to, feeling miserable from the cold. The deluge had put the fire out, leaving them sitting in total darkness, except for the constant, illuminating lightning strikes. They didn't keep track of how long they sat under the leaking lean-to. Evil filled their cold calculating hearts, as they plotted "sweet" revenge against Nataka.

They were snapped back to the present when a tree close by was struck by lightning. The sound was deafening, as the thunder echoed along the canyon walls. The tree, like a giant warrior, quivered then crashed noisily to the ground. The pungent sulfuric smell of charred wood caused their eyes to water and their noses to run. Unconsciously, they moved closer together, concerned about what might lie ahead.

Relentlessly the storm raged on. Wind howling mournfully through the trees caused unseen branches above the crude shelter to scratch eerily against it. The constant scratching motion grew nerve-racking. Neon swords of lightning pierced the shield of inky blackness in the dark ebony-shrouded night, followed by clapping thunder that reverberated through the heavy damp air. Embers of fire burned across the sky, like glowing wood chips in a campfire.

"That horrible smell reminds me of rotten eggs," grumbled Jones.

Thornton mumbled something indiscernible while the others remained sullenly silent. Sleep was out of the question for the four nerve-racked men. Silence reined inside the lean-to while icy fingers of fear clutched tenaciously at each man's heart. Slowly and tediously, the stormy night wore on.

Toward morning, rain completely penetrated the crudely constructed lean-to, soaking the already miserable men. Tempers again began to flare, as each blamed the other for the situation they were in. Miles and Jones got into a fistfight that destroyed the sagging lean-to. This brought damnation upon their heads from Thornton. Jennings grew more sullen, yet wisely held his peace.

A cold, gray, misty morning finally dawned, bringing temporary relief to the sad lot. They opted to forgo breakfast from the food bag in order to get an early start. By so doing, they hoped to find mental relief through the vigorous exercise. Groaning, the men attempted to rise. Accomplishing this feat, they struggled to put one foot in front of the other. After several unsuccessful attempts, they were finally under way. Morose and testy, they silently plodded along, slapping their arms to keep the circulation going so that they could bring their cold aching bodies warmth. Mud oozing through their toes cushioned their sore, aching, blistered feet even as it stripped them of their heat.

Thornton's little band hadn't gone far when the rain began to pour in earnest, soaking the already drenched men. With tempers flaring, a verbal war was waged against Nataka. As there was no relief in sight, the cold, weary group pressed on.

The braves followed safely behind, keeping Thornton's group in sight at all times. Their lean-to had also provided the braves little safety from the angry storm, but watching Thornton's group suffer had made the braves' discomfort worth it. The braves marveled in the beauty created by old Mother Earth, grateful for the rain's moisture. Though they eventually got soaking-wet, they ignored their discomfort as they kept a vigil on the group ahead. Listening to the disgruntled men bickering among themselves, they knew they were a long way from being repentant.

The day finally drew to a close and found the men still exposed to the elements. They were so bone-tired and sore, that it became impossible for them to construct a lean-to. They gathered wood, but it was so wet that it wouldn't ignite. Finally, giving it up as hopeless, they huddled together for warmth. When it wasn't raining, they were tortured from the dripping trees. Sometimes the men grew so desperate that they had to hobble around the camp in an attempt to get some warmth into their tortured bodies.

Around midnight the wind began to blow in earnest, while the rain came down in sheets. It seemed to the distraught men as if the lashing raindrops were tiny needles driving into their flesh. No longer did they have enough strength to curse the elements, let alone bicker among themselves. Like whipped puppies, they sat down near a tree, wrapped their arms around their legs, and laid their heads upon their knees. It was a sad, dejected lot that struggled to endure the long, tedious stormy night.

"Perhaps the Gods are involved after all," said Yellow Dog.

"Maybe so, Yellow Dog … maybe so." The braves settled in for the long night, storing memories to tell around the campfires.

Morning found the four men hobbling painfully along, so lame and bone-weary that it was a tremendous effort for them to put one foot in front of the other. The rain, a light misting drizzle, no longer penetrated the minds of the weary men. When the rain stopped at noon, the tired hungry men stopped to rest.

The food bag was still dry, as it was made of skin, but only yielded a large quantity of jerky. Like ravenous wolves at a fresh kill, the men devoured the jerky. Leaning back against a tree the men tried to sleep, but the dripping branches teased their strained nerves. Giving up, they trudged doggedly on.

Whispering Wind and Yellow Dog shook their heads in dismay, to see the men's dogged determination. "They're like a dog with a bone," observed Yellow Dog. Whispering Wind nodded. They cautiously followed Thornton's group.

Stopping early in the evening, Thornton's group was able to construct a lean-to that protected them from the dripping tree branches. By tearing open dead logs, they found enough dry wood to start a fire, which helped to calm their jangled nerves. As they looked up, they were relieved to see the storm clouds scurrying away. Bright blue indigo skies appeared overhead. As the sun slipped behind the mountain, they crawled under the lean-to, falling immediately into an exhausted sleep.

Daylight found the men still asleep in the lean-to. The two Indian braves followed the sound of running water. They came upon a thundering falls, plunging down a rocky mountain wall coming to rest near their feet. Nestled away from the trail, the falls weren't easily seen by the human eye. The Indians took a long drink from its icy sweetness, then returned to camp. Thornton's group was beginning to stir but remained close to camp.

Thornton, bellowing like a mad bull, caused tempers to flare. Whispering Wind shook his head in disgust. "Well … white man back to old selves!" Walking to their lean-to, he entered, emerging a few minutes later with something to eat. He handed some of the food to Yellow Dog. "Might as well eat … be comfortable. No telling how long we must wait for them to leave."

Yellow Dog took the proffered food. "Good idea!" The two young men sat down where they were well hidden but had a commanding view of Thornton's group. As they began to eat, they were well entertained by the white men's antics.

Miles got up to hobble from camp to some nearby trees. He had become impatient with the whole group because of their disgruntled attitudes and the fact that no one paid any attention to him. He was too self-centered to realize that everyone had his own set of problems to deal with.

Before he realized it, Miles had walked a good distance from camp. His only desire was to find a solution to the rotten mess they were in. He found several massive boulders deeply embedded in the ground, which were placed between two huge pine trees. As he examined the surrounding area, Miles realized that it would be nigh unto impossible to move the rocks, which were nestled against a sheer cliff. The long drooping branches provided a protective covering against detection. "Hmm!" he muttered aloud. "This would make a good place to hide."

When Miles looked to his left, he realized that he was close to a one-hundred-foot drop-off. There were a few trees to the right and to the left, with several in front of him, surrounded by a large lush green meadow. Some of the trees' massive branches were gnarled or twisted from the ravages of time. The seasons' harsh elements also played a large part in shaping them. Majestic snow-capped peaks loomed high above the tree line while sunlight filtered through the trees, glistening on the pine needles. As Miles took in the surrounding scenes, it failed to move him.

His attention was drawn to a movement to the right. Two roly-poly grizzly bear cubs emerged from the edge of the trees. Growling the cubs playfully rolled or tumbled. Miles jumped unsure of what to do. He started to climb behind the boulder he'd been sitting on, but the cubs antics intrigued him, so he sat back down to watch the cubs intently. His movement attracted the cubs' attention.

Being curious like all cubs are, they decided to check out the strange creature near the boulder. One of the cubs hung back, while the bolder cub waddled up to smell the leg of Miles' longjohns. The cub jumped, backing up a little to take in what it all meant. Shaking his head to and fro, the cub sneezed. When the cub came back to sniff again, Miles couldn't resist the urge to touch the cub.

The more timid cub, becoming frightened, cried out. The bolder cub along with his sibling ran up a nearby tree. Upon hearing a ruckus to the right, Miles knew that trouble wasn't far off. He had only gotten into his hiding place behind the huge boulders, when his attention was drawn to the trees. He saw a large tree swaying wildly. Miles watched the tree intently. *There's no wind,* he thought. *What is causing that tree to sway like that?* When his answer appeared in front of him, his eyes grew large with fright and every hair rose on the back of his neck.

A large, cinnamon-colored male grizzly, weighing at least fifteen hundred pounds, ambled forward. It was obvious that he was unaware of impending danger. His black eyes sparkled when the light hit them. Miles watched in fascination as the grizzly waddled sluggishly along, sniffing at the ground.

He turned over several rocks, eating what he found beneath. He looked up with an expression of pure delight on his face, while thick saliva drooled from his mouth. Golden sunlight danced along his thick fur coat, like mischievous imps at play. *What a magnificent specimen,* thought Miles.

His attention was quickly drawn back to the right, as a sleek female grizzly came crashing out of the trees. Miles noticed her cinnamon color as he marveled at her fury. Growling a deep, full-throated challenge, she rose to her full height and raked the air with her right paw. She held her head held high as her eyes blazed with rage. The female smacked her lips in an attempt to warn the male that he was too close to her young.

The male, hungry from the long winter's hibernation, looked up but refused to leave his grubstake. She slowly advanced a few steps on her hind legs, still smacking her lips. All at once, she dropped to all fours and rushed him.

Their bodies, locked in mortal combat, were writhing, growling blurs. At times, it was difficult for Miles to see what was happening; the dirt they kicked up was making a dust cloud. Though he couldn't see, he could hear the rending of flesh and the breaking of bones. Although the female was smaller than the male, she more than made up for it with her raging mother's fury.

The battle grew more heated. At one point, they came close to Miles' hiding place. They hit the rock and tree closest to him, throwing dirt in his face. Miles feared detection, but they were too into the battle to notice him. On and on they fought, two raging dynamos, struggling to be the victor.

At one point, the male got a good hold on the female's neck. Miles watched in horror as the male began shaking her violently. Somehow she broke his hold and dove for the male's middle. He sidestepped her, only to have her flip around to make another attempt. Again, she dove into the male's middle, rending flesh. The sound chilled Miles to the bone.

All at once, the male dropped to the ground. Snorting, he tried to rise. After quivering a few moments in the throes of death, he exhaled one final time and was still. The female slapped the male a time or two. She circled him, only to slap him again. When he still didn't move, she raked him with her paw. Satisfied that he could never hurt her cibs, she left him.

As she passed the tree where the frightened cubs sat huddled, she called to them. Hurrying down the tree, they followed her into the woods. She paused one last time to look back at the male and give one last deep-throated growl. She tested the air, then waddled off into the trees, limping from an injury to her right hind leg.

Noticing the dark, bloody gashes on her neck and side, Miles knew she would not be following her foe in death. *Well,* he thought as he watched her waddle slowly through the trees, *perhaps the old adage is true after all. The bigger they are, the harder they fall!*

He listened a long time after they were gone. He watched the male grizzly, afraid that he really wasn't dead and would come after him, but the bear never moved. Satisfied that he was dead and the grizzly family was long gone, Miles slowly made his way out of his hiding place.

Pausing in front of the dead grizzly, he stared in awe. Miles wiped his brow. *Whew! Am I ever lucky! That could have been me!* All at once, he began to tremble and grow weak in the knees. *This must be my lucky day!* He laughed to himself as he took a few unsteady steps forward.

Cautiously, he started back to camp, every so often looking back over his shoulder to assure himself that he was truly out of harm's way. There were times when his overwrought imagination caused him to feel as if the male were breathing down his neck. Shivering involuntarily, he would stop to look around, but there was only a calm scene behind him.

Whispering Wind, who had opted to follow him from camp, looked over at the bear before he hurried back to report to Yellow Dog. The young braves shook their heads at the way Miles got out of that predicament.

Thornton and his men watched Miles as he came slowly toward camp. His hair was disheveled, his eyes bulged with fear, and his dirty face was void of color. Breathing heavily, he staggered as though drunk. Miles was almost back to camp when his right leg struck something, knocking it to the ground. He looked down in time to see a black swarm of hornets stream out of the broken nest. Immediately, his body became covered with a mass of angry insects, and he cried out in pain and terror.

Like a crazy man, he began running helter-skelter toward the men, flaying his arms in an attempt to ward off the hornets. The angry insects continued to surround him, stinging him unmercifully.

Seeing him running toward them, the men tried to get him to stop, but Miles was beyond hearing. Yelling, they tried to get away from him and the cloud of insects following him, but it was no use. Hornets swarmed everywhere, stinging everyone they possibly could.

The men's bare heads, their hands and their feet were all perfect targets. They swatted and screamed, but all to no avail. The angry hornets clung tenaciously to them like hot glue. Finally, in desperation, the four men ran for the nearby river and dove in. After they dunked themselves several times, some of the hornets stopped stinging. The men had to duck under the water several more times before they were finally left alone.

When the hornets began to swarm the four men, the two braves began to laugh uproariously, almost revealing their hiding place. They moved to a safe distance, holding their hands over their mouths. Then they laughed until their sides hurt. "Those hornets ... are better ... than a switch ... to teach them a lesson!" whispered Yellow Dog. Whispering Wind grabbed his sides as another spasm of laughter struck him. Finally, gaining control, the braves snuck closer to see what would happen next.

As Miles continued to tread water, he frowned in bewilderment. "Humph! So much for the lucky day theory!"

Jennings turned to Miles with disgust. "What are you blabbering about?" It was plain that he couldn't have cared less.

"Son," began Thornton, "what in the world was all that ruckus about back there in the woods?"

Miles grew pale at the mention of the woods. "I guess you deserve an explanation after the episode with the hornets." Swimming to shore, he slowly emerged from the river, filled with pain.

It was a sad, wary lot that followed Miles out of the water. Not only had they been sunburned, windblown, rained upon, had blisters upon blisters on their tender feet, and were miserable in general; now they also had huge, red welts that were swelling more with every passing moment. No one wanted to have anything to do with Miles, yet curiosity got the better of them.

Miles waited while they sat down before telling the men of seeing the two grizzly bear cubs, then what had transpired. Several times, he had to stop to gain control of his emotions. When he was finally through, the men stared at Miles incredulously.

Jones stared at Miles in astonishment. "What possessed ya to touch that cub, man?"

"They were such cute little roly-poly balls of fur that they fascinated me. Besides I was curious."

Jennings snorted in disgust. "Dumb is more like it."

"Lucky!" cried Jones, in awe.

"Ah, you're an idiot!" Jennings waved his hands in an attempt to ward him off. "Just stay away from me!" Rising, he hobbled a short distance away.

Thornton just sat staring at Miles as if he'd gone daft. "What a crazy, fool thing to do, son! A real fool thing to do!" He lowered his head thoughtfully.

Jennings sneezed several times. "I feel rotten!" He struggled to stand, then hobbled around camp. He was so lame that it took every ounce of effort he had just to get going. Miles, Thornton and Jones ignored him, wallowing in their own self-pity.

The sound of distant thunder brought them back to the present. Thornton looked up at the menacing sky groaning in abject misery. "We'd better get under way, before we're hit again."

Groaning, the men began to follow Thornton out of camp, with Whispering Wind and Yellow Dog following closely behind. While Thornton's men were miserable, the two young braves couldn't have been happier. They would have many tales to share around the campfires for generations to come.

One hour later the rains began in earnest, again chilling as it soaked them thoroughly. Thornton began to complain. "We've been out in this miserable weather for three days and three nights. I doubt that we're any closer to the fort than we were before." The dejected men nodded, but continued to walk in silence.

Jennings began to sneeze fitfully then hold his head. "Blast this weather!" Again, he sneezed, holding his aching head to ease the pain. "Oh, how I'll love torturing Nataka when I get the opportunity!" Groaning, he sneezed as he continued to struggle on.

"You'll have to get in line!" snapped Thornton.

Miles grunted, and then remained silent. *I'll be hanged if I'll stand in line to get even with Nataka,* he mused. His mind became filled with possible ways of getting revenge. Jones was so miserable that he decided to plot his own type of revenge.

The rain continued through the afternoon, letting up by nightfall. Jones and Jennings were hard-pressed to keep up with Thornton and Miles because of the fevers that racked their tortured bodies. The men, realizing that camping was a waste of time, because they wouldn't sleep anyway, decided to plod on. They stopped to rest a few times, but anger, hunger, cold and fever drove them relentlessly on. Dawn found them two miles from the fort, so they trudged wearily on. When they were in sight of the fort, the braves left to return to their people. As Thornton's group drew closer, they were surprised to see so many Conestoga wagons sitting outside the fort.

"I wonder what's up," questioned Thornton aloud.

Jennings sneezed, growing even testier. "Who cares? I just want something to eat, a warm bath, and a place to lay my head. And I want them in that order, too." Miles and Jones walked on in silence.

As it was full daylight, the group decided to wait until it was dark to enter the gates. When they were again presentable, they would wreak sweet revenge on Thompson and Nataka. "Let's see how they feel about the treatments we give them," mumbled Thornton fiendishly. The only comments from the rest of the group were grunts.

CHAPTER 17

Making Plans

J ohn Whipple felt his pulses quicken as he heard Colonel Williams telling his wife about his plans to lead a company of troops to Fort Owen the next day. The three of them were having dinner together when Williams broke the news to them. "I have some necessary business that I have been putting off for some time, which needs my full attention."

John watched JaNae, whom he'd come to respect a great deal, as she sat thoughtfully sipping her coffee. Finally raising her head, she looked directly at her husband. "When do you plan to leave?"

"At dawn," he nonchalantly replied. "We should get there two days before the fourth."

JaNae nodded, "I see." She lowered her head to take another sip of her coffee. "I see." She spoke so low that John wasn't quite sure that he had heard her.

John turned to look at Williams, who smiled and winked, suddenly becoming noncommittal. John's eyebrows knit together in wonderment. "I thought perhaps you'd like to go along for the ride," he continued without changing expressions. JaNae's head snapped up, revealing surprise. John tried not to smile, but it was impossible. "That means that we will miss the fun festivities here at the fort. Oh well, perhaps there will be some there as well."

"Not if Major Thornton has anything to say about it!" John retorted.

Williams blinked before asking, "Don't you celebrate the Fourth of July?"

"We haven't celebrated any of the holidays for years. Major Thornton thinks it's a waste of good time, so he gives us heavy workloads on those days."

"I see," said Williams. He sat for a moment, thoughtfully stirring his soup. Turning to address JaNae he continued, "Well, no matter! The offer still stands, my dear."

"I really would like to talk with Kate and the other women at the fort," she confessed. She grew thoughtful a moment. "My going along won't hamper anything will it, dear?" She intently watched her husband's face for signs of disapproval, but there weren't any.

He smiled to reassure her. "I'd love to have you along, my dear."

"Then I'll go!"

Williams snickered heartily. "I thought you would." Nothing more was said as they continued to eat their dinner. John, anxious to know how things were at the fort, found it difficult to finish his meal. Finally, giving it up as hopeless, he asked to be excused. He rose to leave the room, then paused to look down at the colonel. "Sir, I know this is highly unpardonable of me to ask after all that you've done, but would it be all right if Josh came along with us?"

Williams gazed up at John smiling excitedly. "That's a capital idea, John. I wonder why I didn't think of that before." Then he grew stern. "After all this time, I thought you would feel free to ask me for anything you needed!"

"Yes, sir, but I don't want to impose on your kind generosity."

"That'll be the day," Williams responded. He stood up to face John, placing his hands on his shoulders. "Son, it has been a real pleasure having you in our home. You have touched our lives deeply. We'll never forget you."

John's eyes grew moist, making it hard to speak for a moment. Finally, he gazed at this giant of a man, "Thank you, sir!" Williams nodded then sat down on his chair. John turned to JaNae, who was beaming at her husband. "Thank you for a wonderful supper, ma'am!"

JaNae smiled as she nodded affirmatively. She watched as John walked over to enter his room. Her eyes misted as she turned back to her husband. "I will miss him when he goes back. I have come to think of him as one of our sons." There was a catch in her throat, making her unable to go on. Williams dared only to nod in agreement.

John emerged from his room. Stopping before Williams, he asked, "Do you mind if I give Josh the good news, sir?"

"Not at all, son," approved Williams. "Take all the time you need."

"Thank you, sir. I won't be gone long." "Yes sir, that is one very special young man," declared Williams, after the door had closed behind John. As John strode along, he felt at peace for the first time since the horrible events that had brought him here to Fort Missoula.

John had always been thrilled by the beauty of a sunset. Tonight was no different. A rosy glow touched all the buildings and trees, silently spreading along the dusty road. A cool breeze ruffled his hair as he paused to take in the sights. The only activities about the fort at this time of day were the guards walking back and forth along the boardwalk above. Delicious aromas wafting through the air taunted him, even though he was much too excited to eat. His sensitive ears caught the sounds of a neighing horse followed by the lowing of cattle. *Somehow,* he thought, *this makes things feel homey!*

All at once, he had the distinct feeling that he wasn't alone. Swinging around, he saw a man standing in the shadows of a nearby building. Realizing that he'd been seen, the man stepped out of the shadows to walk toward John. "Hello, Sergeant," greeted John cheerfully. "You startled me a little bit."

"I didn't mean to intrude, John," said Aimes. "I saw you coming. I was about to speak when I noticed how intently you were studying the surroundings. I didn't want to intrude into your thoughts, so I just waited. I'm sorry if I startled you."

"It's all right. Besides, I was going to look for you after speaking to Josh anyway. I'm glad you're here, sir."

Aimes looked at him in surprise. "Oh?"

"Colonel Williams just told us at dinner that he was going to take a troop of soldiers to Fort Owen in the morning." He paused to let Aimes absorb the information, then continued, "That means that I will be leaving with them."

"I see." He fell thoughtfully silent, as he pondered the news. After a few minutes, he looked sadly over at John. "I will miss the great fishing trips the three of us had together." Stepping closer to John he put a hand on his shoulder. "Most of all I will miss you, friend. You have taught me so much about people." He squeezed John's shoulder, before removing his hand.

"I'll never forget those fishing trips, either. I will always regard our friendship as one of my most treasured possessions, because you, too, have taught me so much, Sergeant." John took a step closer in order to look Aimes squarely in the face. "Thank you for being my friend, sir!" Aimes was startled, taken aback by John's statement. Shaking hands, John said, "Goodbye, sir."

"Goodbye, John … good luck to you!" Before John could say anything else, Aimes hurried off. John watched until he was out of sight, then dashed over to Josh's house.

Stepping up to the door, he knocked. Josh opening the door smiled broadly at seeing John. "Hey, John! What brings you here?"

"I came to talk to you, Josh. Do you think we could go for a walk?"

"Sure thing. Let me get my coat and tell Ma where I'm going."

"Thanks. I'll wait out here." Josh nodded. Going back inside, he closed the door. John walked to the edge of the porch to wait. When Josh came out of the house, they stepped off of the porch, heading toward the stables. Neither spoke, content to be in each other's company.

After a while, John broke the silence. "Josh," he began, "tomorrow Colonel Williams is taking a troop to Fort Owen, so I will be going with them." Josh stopped anxiously turning to face John. "It's true, Josh." John watched his friend struggle to deal with the news. Finally he smiled. "I asked the Colonel if you could go with us, which he readily agreed."

Josh swung around in surprise. "He did?"

"Yep. He did!"

"Then I won't have to say goodbye so soon!"

"Does that mean that you're going with us?"

"You bet yer sweet Aunt Petunia, it does!"

John laughed at Josh's strange answer. "Good! That's settled then. Let's go tell Jeffries we need help getting my dog home!"

"Okay," agreed Josh. I'll beatcha there!"

"We'll see about that!" Off they raced, happy for the diversion from sad thoughts. Josh won the race by only a scant margin, but needled John unmercifully about being out of shape. John punched him hard on the arm before entering the stables.

ᔆᕒᑯ ᔆᕒᑯ

When supper was over Paul did the dishes so that Kate could care for the children. After finishing the dishes, he wiped off the table. As he turned to rinse out the dishcloth, a knock sounded at the door. Wiping his hands on the dishtowel, he walked over to open it. Sergeant Peters stood with his hat in his hand, smiling excitedly. "Howdy, Cap'n."

"Come in, Peters," greeted Thompson stepping away to let him enter. When Peters was inside, Thompson closed the door. "Please, have a seat while I finish these dishes." Thompson walked back to the counter to rinse out the dishcloth. Washing off the table once more, he dumped the dishwater. Wiping out the pans, he hung them on their designated hooks, draping the dishcloth over one, the dishtowel over the other. Peters sat near the table, crossed his legs and set his hat on the table. "Looks like ya got KP duty tonight, suh."

"I seem to be getting that even more lately," Thompson lamented. "Those two little scallywags of ours sure do demand a lot of Kate's time." Peters could tell by the pride in Thompson's eyes that he didn't mind the new chores at all. Thompson was spared from saying more when someone knocked at the door. He walked over to answer it. Seeing that it was Jane and Henry, he smiled motioning to them to enter. "Come on in, you two. Yum!" Paul grinned, appreciatively eyeing the covered dish in her hands. "What do we have here?" He asked reaching out to lift the cover.

Jane laughed, playfully slapping at his hand. "No fair peeking. You'll see when the time is right, Mr. Impatience!"

Drawing back his hand, Paul feigned hurt pride. "Ah, is that anyway to treat a friend?" Jane only smiled as she promptly pushed past him. Peters stood to greet her cheerfully. "Ev'nin, Mrs. Hansen"

Jane set the dish onto the table while greeting Peters. "Hello, Sergeant Peters!"

Henry, joining her, reached out to shake Peters' hand. "How goes it, Serge?"

"Jest fine ez hen's teeth, suh!"

"Good!" Hansen was prevented from saying more when Kate emerged from the bedroom to join them. "What a perfect picture of loveliness," praised Hansen. Peters nodded in agreement.

"Ah, such sweet music to a bonnie lass' ears!" she replied. "Truth a the matter bein' that ya been kissen' the blarney stone agin, kind sir."

"Whatever that is," mumbled Hansen in mock surprise.

"You don't want to get her off on that subject, Henry," cautioned Paul. "I will say this though ... that it all started in the palace of the Queen of Ireland. It seems a court jester was constantly teasing the Queen. In exasperation, she accused him of kissing the blarney stone." At their strange expressions, he continued, "There is some castle where a large stone dangles below one of the garret windows. In order to kiss the stone, someone lowers you out of the window, backwards of course, while holding your feet. To get to the stone you have to stretch for it. It is believed that when you kiss the stone, you'll be blessed with the gift of blarney, or the ability to speak in a flattering manner."

Hansen slapped his hat against his leg hooting good-naturedly. Peters slapped Hansen lightly on the back as he roared with laughter. "Oh, thet's rich," Peters cried, "jest rich!"

Kate kissed Hansen on the cheek. "Never mind these jokers," she soothed. "I loved the compliment immensely!"

Peters began to pout, acting as if he were being sorely neglected. "How come he gits sich royal treatment?" he huffed in mock disgust. "What 'bout us lowly commoners? Peers ta me we deserve sumpin' too!"

"Why, Daniel," gasped Kate. "I had no idea you felt so left out!" Before Peters realized her intent, she moved over to him to plant a kiss on his rough old cheek.

Jumping, Peters grumbled, "Ah were only funnin' with ya," he exclaimed. The others ribbed him unmercifully as Peters nervously ran his fingers through his hair.

Kate stepped back with an impish grin on her lips. Her eyes twinkled merrily at the trick played on this great giant of a man. "Why, sir," she replied in mock surprise, "how was a lady like me to know the intent of your heart?" The twinkle remained in her eyes as she coyly tilted her head to watch him squirm.

Grinning, Paul came to his friend's rescue. "Why don't we all sit down at the table?" As everyone went to sit around the table, Paul went to his desk, where he picked up some writing materials. He sat at the head of the table.

Kate reached out to lift the covered dish on the table. "Yum! This smells as good as it looks heavenly, Jane!"

"Thank you, dear! I thought we'd be famished after we got through discussing whatever we're here for." Looking over at Thompson, Jane wrinkled her nose at him. He smiled.

Kate added, "You're probably right, knowing my husband!" Thompson looked hurt but remained silent. Kate stood up to place the dish on the counter. "We'll make them wait to see what you have here. That will make them more appreciative of it that way." Jane nodded in agreement.

Thompson said, "Let's get started, shall we?" Everyone nodded. "That way we'll be able to find out what smells so heavenly under that cover." Jane beamed, but remained silent. "Four days from today it will be the Fourth of July." As he looked around the table, Thompson noticed that everyone's interest was immediately piqued. "Since Major Thornton's away, I thought it would be good if the fort celebrated the holiday. We'll include those at the settlement." When he paused to look at those assembled, he was pleased to see them growing excited. "When I talked to Peters about it this afternoon, he readily agreed." Peters smiled, but refrained from speaking. Turning toward Kate, Thompson continued. "We knew how hurt you and Jane would be if you weren't included in the planning, so I called this meeting to discuss what we want to do."

Jane rubbed her hands together gleefully as she turned to her husband, "It's a marvelous idea … you're absolutely right about our being hurt if you hadn't included us!"

Thompson smiled. "Well, this meeting is now open to suggestions."

"It jest wouldn't be fitten' not ta have a foot race," said Peters. "Then, too, havin' a hoss race would be interestin' ta the fellers."

"That's a grand idea, Peters," agreed Hansen. "I also think it would be good to have a wood chopping contest along with a log splitting contest for the farmers." Paul wrote every suggestion down as it came to him.

Jane spoke up quickly. "We should have all types of booths—booths for displaying homemade items, such as quilts, embroidering, tatting, knitting, and sewing. There should also be a booth for children to bob for apples."

The men sat back, letting the women chat uninterruptedly. "Oh, yes, and there should be judges assigned to decide which handmade item is the best in each category," said Kate.

"There should also be judges for breads, cakes, pies, and other homemade food."

"Jane, what do you think about making ribbons for the different prizes? We could make blue ones, red ones … even some white ones. We need to involve the women in the settlement, as well as those in the fort."

"I think it's a great idea! We can send out information about it with the men."

"I don't want to be a wet blanket here, but what about the food?" questioned Paul.

"Why don't we have a huge potluck dinner?" replied Jane, thoughtfully.

"A good idea," everyone chorused.

Peters volunteered to assign riders to alert the settlement of their plans. The people would be asked to join in on the celebration. It was decided that Thompson along with Hansen would supervise the preparation of the booths, racecourses, or other necessary jobs. The women agreed to oversee the potluck luncheon and organizing the booths. Peters also agreed to choose judges for the booths, races, along with the other events.

When the events were finally hashed over with everything decided upon, Peters cleared his throat to speak. His eyes sparkled like diamonds in the early morning sun, "Thar's one thin' needed most in them thar booths, en thet's a dunkin' device."

"Do you plan to be the person dunked, Sergeant?" bantered Thompson.

Peters looked at the others in the room as an impish grin played around his lips, "Oh no, suh, but Ah does have someone in mind who'd work out jest right."

Thompson looked at him suspiciously. "And who, may I ask, is the poor devil you have in mind?"

"You, suh!"

Thompson could only stare at Peters in disbelief. Both women burst out laughing gleefully. "Not on your life!"

Peters began to plead in earnest. "Thin' 'bout it, suh. The men respect ya en t'would be a boost ta their spirits ta git the chance ta dunk ya." Thompson didn't seem too convinced, but listened thoughtfully as Peters continued. "'Sides, the proceeds 'id be far greater than ifn' someone else were ta did it."

"I have to agree, Paul," exclaimed Kate between fits of laughter. "It would be a great way to release their tensions, and raise money for the needy."

Looking around it wasn't surprising to see his comrades' attempts at being serious. He smiled in spite of himself, "I guess I can be a good sport for a good cause," he mumbled sternly. Then as everyone burst out laughing, he joined in on the merriment. All at once, he grew gravely serious. "Okay Sergeant, your turn is coming … even if it takes the rest of my life to arrange for it!"

"Ah'll personally see to it thet the dunkin' machine ez made jest right," volunteered Peters, not scared in the least by Thompson's threats. "After all … we wouldn' want somethin' ta make it go down afore time."

"I just bet you don't!" responded Thompson. Again, there was a good amount of hilarity. It was awhile before they grew serious.

When all of the assignments were made out, the women rose to serve the contents under the covered dish. Kate moved the coffee forward onto the stove, while Jane placed the dish's contents onto little plates. Kate served the coffee, while Jane placed the plates onto the table. The men's eyes widened with pleasure as they saw the long awaited treat.

"Aw," sighed Peters, "Ifn' Ah'da knowed ya were a hiden enythin' ez delicious ez this, Ah'da ne'er been able ta thuk a enythin' else." On each plate sat a slice from a three-layered, yellow cake covered with a white, creamy frosting.

"Why, you old, scallywag!" Jane said, plainly pleased with the compliment.

Taking a generous bite, Thompson closed his eyes in delight. "Oh, yummy! This is wonderful!" Jane beamed at the compliment paid her, then continued to serve the cake. They lingered at the table long after they were finished with their snack, content just to be together.

Peters finally stood up to go. "Ah'd better git some shut eye, er Ah won't be fit fer enythin' tamarra." Picking up his hat, he started for the door.

Kate and Paul rose to see him out, "Thanks for helping with the plans, Sergeant."

"Muh pleasure, suh," replied Peters. Turning, he shook hands with Kate. "Yer a real peach of a lady, Mrs. Thompson, en it'sa pleasure ta comed ta yer home!"

"Thank you, Daniel. Please feel free to come again." Peters nodded before stepping out into the night.

Jane and Henry walked over to them. "We'd best be going, too," declared Henry. "Daylight will be here before we know it, then there's work to be done."

"Thanks for everything," said Thompson. "I think we should have a great time."

The Hansen's walked out the door. "Good night," they called.

"Good night!" answered Paul and Kate. After the others were gone, Paul slipped an arm around Kate's waist to pull her closer. They stood on the porch looking up at the big golden moon. All at once a cloud obscured it from sight. "Looks like we might have a little rain to contend with," he whispered.

"I hope not!"

"Time will tell, but right now it's time for us to go to bed." Kate nodded. Together they went inside.

CHAPTER 18

The Journey

John, who had tossed and turned for most of the night, rose to sit on the edge of the bed. He was experiencing so many emotions that he was having difficulty sorting them out. It was just barely light outside, so he reached over to pick up his pocket watch so that he could see what time it was. He was surprised to see that it was only o-three forty-five. I still have an hour to do what I want to do, before everyone gets up for the day, he mused. Laying the watch back onto the nightstand, he stood up to light the lamp. He dressed as quickly yet as quietly as possible, so that he wouldn't wake up the colonel and his wife.

A dog barked some distance away, which made him smile. *So, something else is up at this unearthly hour,* he thought. When he was dressed, he started packing his few possessions, still trying to sort out his feelings. He dreaded leaving his newfound friends, but at the same time, he was looking forward to returning home to all that was familiar.

Shaking himself sternly, he continued to prepare for the trip. As he removed his trousers from the bureau, he noticed a fat envelope. All at once, he remembered Maude stuffing it into his shirt pocket while making him promise to wait until he was alone to read it. By the time they got to the fort and took care of things, he had been too tired to open it. Promising himself he would read it in the morning, he had put the envelope inside the drawer then promptly forgot it.

Curious, he went to sit on the bed, yet was still unsure if he should open it. Sighing, he quickly tore it open before he could change his mind. As he removed the contents from the envelope, he noticed something green inside the letter. All at once, everything spilled out. John gasped at what he saw. Money! Lots of money lay strewn in his lap. Shaking like a leaf in the wind, he gathered it into a pile. He could only stare dumbly at it. Finally laying it aside, he picked up the letter, unfolded it, and quickly scanned the neatly written lines. As he began to read, an excitement like no other encompassed him.

"Dear John,

When I first saw you standing beside JaNae, I had a strong feeling of anger wash over me. I wanted you off of the property. Then, when JaNae rescued me the way she did, I held my own counsel. You were so considerate of my feelings that I was deeply touched. It was then that I realized that you weren't at fault ... it was my husband's fault. An overwhelming feeling of peace enveloped me, and I knew that it would be all right.

Oh, dear friend ... I hope you'll let me call you that. How can one ever repay what you've done for me? You and Josh, together with Mr. Johansson, accomplished a feat that most people would have deemed impossible. They would never even have attempted it. Your unwavering service to the children and me will never be forgotten. In the short time we were all together, I learned to rely upon you for many things. Never once did you let me down.

You taught me to laugh again ... to hope in the face of despair. You showed unfailing courage. My children will sorely miss the stories you shared with them. I promise to speak of you and the others often. The greatest example you showed me was that of forgiveness. Every day I watched your spunk ... your tenacity in the face of difficult obstacles, and I marveled. You must have the greatest parents in the world, for you are growing to be a giant among men ... a hero that my children can emulate ... grow from. For this, I am eternally grateful, because I cannot honor their father. After much deliberation and talking with JaNae, I finally arrived at a way to say 'thank you.' Please accept this money as a token of my gratitude ... my friendship.

Your friends forever,

Maude Walters and children"

Not believing what he read, he started at the beginning and read it through again. It touched him so deeply, that for a few moments he could only stare at the letter. After placing the letter back in the envelope, he picked up the money. As he slowly counted the money, his jaw dropped in surprise. *Wow! There are one thousand dollars here!*

Tucking the money back into the envelope, he buried it deep in his cloth bag. John finished his packing then straightened up the room. Satisfied that all was in readiness, he sat by the nightstand. The emotional turmoil returned, so he stood up to quietly stroll across the room. A few minutes later, when he still couldn't gain control of his emotions, he walked over to blow out the light. Going back to bed, he closed his eyes, willing himself to go back to sleep.

Try as hard as he might, it just didn't work. Sighing in exasperation he rose, remaking his bed. Tiptoeing from the room, John went to the kitchen for a drink of water. Noticing the nearly empty bucket and the partially empty wood box, an idea struck him. Smiling to himself, he picked up the bucket. As he went out the back door, he saw another empty bucket near the washstand. Picking it up he went to the well.

John stopped to look up at the cloudless sky with its canopy of stars, marveling at Mother Nature's beauty. Gazing upward, the stars began to fade, replaced by a rosy glow which began to appear in the east. John knew that he didn't have long to complete his plan. As he hurried toward the well, a slight breeze ruffled his hair and his clothing. The fresh, pure exhilarating air not only thrilled him, but also made him feel grateful to be alive.

After setting his buckets down on the ground, into the well he lowered the well bucket, which was tied to the rope on a pulley. When it hit the water below, he pulled it back up. He emptied the bucket into one of those sitting on the ground. Again, he lowered the bucket bringing it up full. He poured it into the other empty bucket, leaving the well bucket on the ledge of the well.

Stooping to pick up the buckets, he carried them to the house. After tiptoeing into the house, he emptied the buckets into the reservoir. John made several more trips until the reservoir was full, then filled the teakettle with the remaining bucket of water. John went back to the well one more time. After refilling the buckets, John went back to the house, where he set one of the buckets near the washstand. He took the other inside putting it on the counter.

That job finished, he went to the kitchen to start a fire in the stove. Taking down the lid lifter, he raised the lids on the range, being as quiet as possible. After building a fire in the cook stove, he replaced the lids, making sure the lid lifter was put back into its place. When the fire was going well, John banked it.

Preparing the coffee, he set the pot near the back of the stove to boil. John went out to the woodpile, where he quickly gathered an armload of wood. Carrying it back into the house, he arranged it neatly into the wood box. This process was repeated until the wood box was overflowing. Then he brought in a load of kindling, which he laid in easy reach near the wood box.

By the time he was finished bringing in the wood, the coffee was beginning to boil. Seeing that he had made a mess while hauling in the wood, he went to get the broom to sweep it up. John was returning from putting the broom away when the Williams emerged from their bedroom.

They sniffed the air appreciatively. "Is that coffee I smell?" questioned JaNae.

"By gum," exclaimed Williams, "it sure enough is!" Noticing the full wood box along with a full bucket of water on the counter, he turned to stare at John. "I know that you went to bed last night," he teased, "but did you sleep any?"

"I tried, but I just couldn't sleep long, so I decided that working was better than tossing and turning."

"Well, one thing's for sure. I don't have to worry about doing my chores this morning!" Walking over to John, Williams placed a hand affectionately on the lad's shoulder. "That's about the nicest thing anybody has ever done for me. I won't soon be forgetting it." John nodded, beaming at the praise paid him by this man, whom he'd come to admire so much.

JaNae surprised John, when she stood up on tiptoe to kiss his cheek. "You're about the dearest boy I know," she whispered tenderly. "Jedidiah and I won't ever forget the joy and pleasure you have brought into our empty lives." John could only stare at this grand lady. Williams smiled at his confusion, enjoying the tender moments immensely.

"I know that I will never forget either of you, nor the hospitality that you have extended to me. I only wish I could have done more."

"I had better get breakfast or we'll be starved long before lunch time," laughed JaNae. She started for the pantry to get the things needed to prepare the meal. You men busy yourselves for a few minutes while I get things ready." She bustled busily around the room, precise yet graceful in her movements. John turned to see Colonel Williams watching his beloved JaNae as she worked to prepare the meal.

Shaking himself, he turned to smile at John. "We'd better find something else to do, or we'll find ourselves in hot water." JaNae pretended to be angry with her spouse, but Williams only laughed heartily.

"Could I at least set the table for you, JaNae? That way the meal will be ready sooner." JaNae started to protest, but John hastened on. "Ma used to tell me that I had to learn women's work along with that of a man, so I was taught at an early age to help in the kitchen."

JaNae beamed. "Thank you. I would really appreciate that."

Williams sat at the table, where he could watch the two of them. *Yes,* he thought, *like JaNae, I will miss this young man, too.* He had to admit to himself that it had been a lonely time without the children. Somehow, John had temporarily filled that empty void.

Soon the meal was on the table. After grace was said, they began to do justice to the meal. When it was over, JaNae hustled to the kitchen to clean up their breakfast dishes, then get things ready to be loaded in the carriage, while the men went to finish what they had to do.

Williams went to the parade grounds to inspect the troops, which consisted of three hundred and fifty men, and to assign a detail for the trip to Fort Owen. Meanwhile, John carried his gear to the stables to procure a packhorse and have Blacky saddled. After inspecting the troops, Williams turned to Major Brown. "Get a detail together for a trip to Fort Owen. Inform them that they are to be ready in thirty minutes."

"Yes, sir." Major Brown saluted before hurrying off to carry out the orders.

Williams headed for his office. Entering the outer office, he cheerfully greeted his clerk. "Morning, Hawkins."

Private Hawkins stood to salute, "Morning, sir." He then waited until Williams had entered his office before he went back to his duties. Private Hawkins had been working for the colonel for two years, yet he always grew nervous when he entered the room. This time proved to be no different.

Williams placed his hat on a hook near the door, walked over to his desk to plop into his chair. Reaching into his right-hand pocket, he took out a small, silver key. Unlocking the bottom drawer of his desk, he pulled it out so that he could begin to search through its contents.

Finding what he wanted, a large thick packet, he removed it from the drawer. Setting it on the desk, opening the packet, he browsed through it a moment until he was satisfied that it was the packet he wanted. He meticulously searched through the papers, taking out what he needed to take with him.

When he was finished, he closed the packet, placing it back into the bottom drawer. Closing the drawer, he locked it. After placing the key back into his pocket, he scooped the papers into a neat pile. Picking up a brown leather bag, he began to stuff the papers inside.

Fastening the clasp, he rose, taking time to push his chair snug against the desk. Tucking the leather bag under his left arm, Williams reached for his hat, which he placed upon his head. After looking around to make sure that everything was in order, Williams walked out of the office.

Hawkins stood to salute. Watching Williams closely, he asked, "Is there anything I can do for you, sir?"

"I'm going to Fort Owen on business. We shouldn't be gone too long, but I've left Major Brown in charge while I'm gone, so if any problems arise, check with him."

"Yes, sir!"

"You'll answer to him until I return."

"Very well, sir!"

"That will be all, private." Hawkins saluted. Williams was leaving later than he had planned, but that was all right with him, as he would make up for lost time when they got under way. Seeing Aimes standing near a small group of men, he called out to him. "Sergeant Aimes!" Aimes spun around coming to full attention as he saluted. "Have you done what we talked about last night?"

Aimes smiled slightly. "Yes, sir."

"Good! Let's get on with it, shall we?"

"Yes, sir!" Aimes saluted once more then fell into step with Williams.

John was having problems with Bridgford when they entered. "I don't understand, sir," he exclaimed. "Why isn't Blacky saddled and ready to go?"

"He's not saddled, but he is ready to pack anytime you are." Bridgford showed no expression whatever, which greatly surprised John. Pugger, the dog John rescued with her pups, wiggled up to him, but he didn't notice. Williams and Aimes entered the stable, which spared Bridgford from answering John.

"Aren't you ready, Whipple?" Williams bellowed.

John blinked in surprise at the tone of voice the colonel used. "No, sir! Mr. Bridgford told me that Blacky, whom I always ride, is ready to be packed. Then, when I asked for permission to use a packhorse, I was denied ... I just don't understand." It was plain to all present that John was very frustrated.

Williams almost lost his sternness at John's confused expression. It was plain to everyone but John that something was in the air. Williams turned to Bridgford in feigned agitation. "Didn't you get him another horse?"

"Well…" Bridgford turned to Josh who gave the prearranged signal.

When Josh turned to hurry off, John turned to look first at Colonel Williams then Aimes, but they remained expressionless. When he turned to look back at Bridgford, his eyes caught sight of Josh leading the thoroughbred gelding that Maines had ridden. John's jaw went slack. He stared in bewilderment, as Josh led the horse up to him, handing him the reins. "I don't understand!" cried John. Turning, he was surprised to see Williams smiling broadly at him. The only emotion on Aimes' face was a twinkle in his eyes and a tiny smile that played around his lips.

Williams took pity on the young man's confusion and walked up to place a hand on his shoulder. "We searched for the true owner of this horse son but learned that he was killed along with his family, so it was decided that you should have the horse."

"Me, sir?" John just couldn't believe his luck. He turned to look at Aimes in concern. Aimes smiled while shaking his head affirmatively.

Williams saw the look that passed between the two men. "It was Aimes who suggested that you have the horse, John." Gasping in surprise, John turned to stare at Aimes. "Yes, son, he thought that it took a lot of courage for you to turn those men in," affirmed Williams. "It won't bring your special friends back, but maybe … just maybe, it will help you remember the new friends that you made here at the fort."

"Oh, sir!" That was the only statement John was able to make before burying his face in the horse's neck. It took a few minutes for him to gain control of his emotions. Finally, he lifted his head wiping his eyes. Turning, he looked at each person there before him. "Thank you all so much! I'll never forget what happened here today, nor will I ever forget any of you." Choking up again, he turned to stroke the horse lovingly. "From now on you'll be called Beauty."

Williams tried to appear stern but failed miserably. "Well … let's not dillydally any longer, or we'll never get out of here before midnight." Saluting, the men got busy. Williams turned to look sternly at John, "You'd better shake a leg, John, or we'll leave without you!"

"Yes, sir."

As John darted off to get ready, Williams smiled inwardly. Yes, sir, that lad will be sorely missed around here, he muttered to himself as he leisurely strolled out to the waiting troops.

John quickly placed the gear on Blacky, then placed Pugger into the crate Bridgford had prepared for the trip home. Strapping it on top of the pack, he led the two horses out to join the rest of the troops.

Josh, who was holding Beauty's reins, as well as those of his own saddle horse, smiled as John walked up. John tied Blacky's lead rope to the horn of the saddle that was on Beauty, then took the reins from Josh. Mounting Beauty, the horse snorted, pranced in place a little, while tossing his head, plainly declaring that he was ready for something to happen. John reached down to pat the horse's neck. "Easy, boy!" he crooned. "We'll be on the way soon!" John couldn't believe his luck, as he gazed at the magnificent horse beneath him.

JaNae, sitting in the carriage with Private Jackson as the appointed driver, looked over to grin at John. Filled with curiosity,and unable to stand the suspense any longer, John rode over to look at JaNae. "Were you also in on this surprise, JaNae?"

"Yes, I was. When Jedidiah told me what Aimes wanted to do, I was more than pleased."

"Thank you, JaNae. I'll treasure that knowledge forever."

He rode back to Josh to wait for the order to leave while observing what was going on around him. On a Conestoga wagon, which John guessed was the famous chuck wagon, sat a burley, heavily bearded man. He, too, was waiting for the signal to get under way. There were several packhorses heavily weighted down and tied to the back of the wagon.

Williams went to the head of the column. Gathering the reins to his stead, he mounted. Turning in his saddle so that he could look down the column a moment, Williams bellowed, "Mount up." When the men were mounted, Williams raised his arm then waved it forward. "Move out!" The column of troops slowly rode out of the fort. The surrey carrying JaNae was positioned in the middle of the column, followed by the Conestoga wagon. Once out of the fort, the horses picked up speed. They traveled this way for several miles.

Williams called a halt at lunchtime, where there was plenty of grass for the horses and plenty of shade where the men could rest. JaNae spread a blanket on the ground under a large shade tree, then sat on it to rest while lunch was being prepared. It wasn't long until the cook called them all to eat. No one had to be told twice, as they fell to it with hearty appetites.

Thirty minutes later, the group mounted and continued, with Williams pushing them relentlessly on for the rest of the afternoon. They hadn't been back on the trail long when a stiff breeze began to blow. John, looking up at the sky, wasn't surprised to see storm clouds gathering off to the left of them. He hoped the impending storm would hold off until they got to the fort, yet as he watched the gathering clouds, he knew that it wouldn't be long before the storm came.

John, feeling different about the return trip, surveyed the surrounding beauty. He was so intent that he didn't see the colonel ride up beside him. It wasn't until he heard the horse snort that he realized that he had been daydreaming again. Jumping in surprise he turned his head, seeing Williams smiling at him. "Oh," gasped John, "I didn't realize you were there."

"I'm not surprised, son. It was plain to see that you were daydreaming … again."

John, embarrassed at being caught off guard, quickly changed the subject. "How's JaNae, sir?"

"Fine!" Williams' eyes twinkled with merriment, but he wisely remained silent. They rode companionably along, content to be in each other's company. Williams was the first to break the silence. "I was wondering, John, if you'd mind riding with JaNae for a spell." John started to speak but Williams continued. "She enjoys your company so much. The truth is Private Jackson is so shy, she can't get more than three words out of him at any one time."

John responded good-naturedly. "I'd be happy to ride with her, sir."

"Good! I'll call a halt for a moment so that you can trade off with Jackson."

"I'll head back there right now, sir." Williams nodded before heading back toward the head of the column.

Turning Beauty towards the rear, John rode back to the carriage. JaNae smiled gratefully up at him. "Hello, John. Did you get tired of riding up ahead or did you long for a little taste of dust?"

John, realizing she was teasing him, was glad she felt free enough to do so. "Colonel Williams asked me to relieve Jackson." JaNae sighed in relief. John couldn't resist the opportunity to tease a little. "Truthfully, I was so desperate to talk to somebody that I was hoping for a break. I was grateful he asked me to ride with you, that is if I wouldn't bore you."

JaNae saw right through him and smiled. "Well … I guess I could put up with you for a little while."

"Good!" John could tell from Jackson's expression that he was more than grateful for the break. John had to smile to himself at the man's timidity. Just then, Williams gave the signal for a halt. Riding back to check on JaNae, Williams was in time to see John smile at JaNae. John dismounted, handing the reins to Jackson. "You're in for a real treat. Beauty rides like a dream!"

Jackson looked at John in surprise. "Thank you for giving me the privilege of riding him. I promise to be easy with him, sir."

John smiled encouragingly. "I know you will, Jackson. Of all the soldiers at the fort, I've seen how gentle you are to the animals. I admire that."

Jackson beamed at the praise given him. "Thank you, sir! That means a lot coming from you." John watched Jackson mount, then climbed into the surrey. Gathering up the reins he said, "I'm set, sir."

"Good! Let's get under way then!" He rode back to the head of the column, where he gave the order to move out.

When they had gone a little way in silence, JaNae turned to smile at John. "Oh, am I ever glad that you agreed to ride with me. I was amazed to see how little conversation you got out of that dear man." John smiled, but remained silent. "That's more conversation than I got out of him since we left the fort."

"He isn't much of a talker, is he?"

JaNae nodded emphatically. "Indeed, no!" They laughed a moment then started to talk of other things. The wind picked up and the impending storm drew ever closer. Lightning flashed in the distance, followed by the rumbling of thunder. As the day wore on, the storm threatened to break any moment. Dark menacing storm clouds obscured the sun. John feared that they would be caught out in the storm, but still the column moved on.

Two hours before dark they reached the place where John had first camped. By now the storm was almost upon them. Colonel Williams barked orders, which the travel-weary soldiers carried out. John, after seeing that JaNae was comfortable, set up the colonel's tent. After chopping a good amount of wood, he built a fire for the camp cook. When those chores were done, John hauled water and helped Josh and Private Smith place a large canopy over the fire, and position the wood under the canopy to protect it from the inclement weather.

John went over to talk to JaNae, "Your tent is ready, ma'am. Is there anything you need?"

"Yes, John. Could you please ask someone to bring some hot water to my tent so that I can freshen up?

"You bet. I'll tend to it myself." John went down to the river for a bucket of water, which he poured into a large container to heat. When it was ready, he took it to the colonel's tent, setting it near the tent's door. "Here is the hot water, JaNae. I'll get a bucket of cold water so that you can make the water temperature to your satisfaction. Taking an empty bucket to the river, he filled it. Setting the bucket near the tent door he called out, "I have the cold water for you."

"Good, please bring it inside."

When JaNae no longer needed him, John went to see about his horses. They'd been cared for by Jackson, who had hobbled them before turning them loose with the rest of the horses to forage. John marveled at how Beauty's mane and tail flowed in the breeze. He walked over to stroke the horse a moment before going over to give Blacky ample attention. He looked around for his gear and saddle, but they were nowhere in sight. John went in search of Jackson, who was emerging from one of the tents. "Have you seen my things, sir?"

"Sure," replied Jackson pointing to the tent he'd emerged from, "I put them in there."

"Thank you."

"No problem!" Jackson walked away. John watched him a moment, then went inside.

Josh was already there, preparing his bedroll. He looked up as John entered the tent. Pointing to an area near him, Josh said, "Jackson stowed your gear over here by me, John. Come get comfortable." John let Pugger out of her crate to have a good run before unrolling his bedroll. They had just finished, when Pugger came back inside the tent and snuggled next to him for some attention.

He laughingly complied, scratching her behind the ears. "You're quite the dog. I'll let you out again before we go to bed, but for your protection, I'm going to put you back into the crate." Pugger didn't like that even a little bit, but allowed him to put her back. When the clasp was securely fastened, they emerged from the tent to hurry near the fire.

The camp cook began banging on a tin pan. "Come and get it, before I feed it to the wolves."

Colonel Williams and JaNae were the first to get their meal, then the soldiers. John, finally getting his plate filled, went to sink down upon a stump, grateful for the rest. As he began to inhale the contents of his plate, he realized that he was famished. He made a mental note to save something to feed his dog.

The smell of rain was intoxicating, as it made the air fresh and pure. Lightning followed by thunder began to crash in around them like a magnificent symphony. The troops went to their tents for their rain gear. John and Josh had just finished KP duty when the storm broke with a vengeance, pelting the earth with huge raindrops. John, who loved a good storm, watched from under the canopy as the rain soaked the thirsty ground. A horse nickered in protest of the storm, then only the sounds of the falling rain prevailed.

Williams, who had retired to his tent a few minutes earlier, emerged dressed in his rain gear. While walking determinedly over to the fire, soldiers resting under a canvas tarp rose as one. They came to full attention before saluting. "At ease, men." John watched in fascination as the colonel began barking orders. "Privates Howell, Fulmar, Jefferson … you take the first four-hour watch. Corporal Holmes, Private Watson, Corporal Davis … you take the next four-hour watch. Private Smith, you and Private Hendricks tend to the horses. You can decide who will take the first watch or who will take the second. Private Walton, Private Shaw, Private Scott, you take the watch before dawn."

"Yes, sir," chorused the men as one man. Saluting they hurried off to do as ordered, each taking up a position around camp.

"Meanwhile, those not on duty now better get to sleep, as tomorrow will probably be a difficult day." Everyone saluted once more before hurrying to their tents, while Private Hendricks headed toward the horses. "John, I want you and Josh to haul more wood for the fire. Stack it under the canopy, to ensure that it won't be too soaked to use."

"Yes, sir!" echoed John and Josh.

"Make sure you wear your rain gear," cautioned Williams. "Don't want you to catch your death of foolishness." The two men grinned then headed toward the tent, while Williams walked back to his. John gave Pugger the remains of his supper, before slipping into his rain gear.

John and Josh worked hard to get a good quantity of wood stored under the canopy. When the job was done, they added some of the wood to the fire before going to their tent. John released Pugger from her crate to have another run while he got undressed. She soon came back to snuggle up next to him. She was wet, so he rubbed her down with his shirt. He didn't mind letting her slip into his bedroll. After hanging his shirt up to dry, he slipped in beside her, grateful for the reprieve. From Josh's light snoring, John could tell he was fast asleep. As he listened to the rain gently striking the top of the tent, he, too, was soon fast asleep.

⌘ ⌘

John moaned, burrowing deeper under his covers when the bugler sounded reveille. Josh stirred but didn't rise. "Get up, sleepy head!" John slowly rose into a sitting position. "Sounds like it's still raining," added Josh. Pugger stretched, then waited while the men quickly dressed.

Slipping into their rain gear and grabbing their hats, the two men went out to the fire. Pugger went off for a little jaunt, soon returning to snuggle closer to the fire and John. He reached down to pat her on the head. "Well, old girl, let's see if the cook has something for you to eat, then it's back into the crate for you." The dog didn't understand a word he said, but wagged her tail happily. John asked the cook, "Do you think I might have a few scraps for my dog, sir?"

"I ain't hired to feed no dad-blamed dog!"

Colonel Williams came up to them in time to hear the cook's remarks. "There's more than enough to spare a small dog something to eat, Snodgrass," thundered Williams.

"Yes, sir!" Snodgrass went over to the griddle to pick up a hot cake. Placing it onto a tin plate, he handed it to John.

John politely took the plate. "Thank you, sir." He called to Pugger as he headed toward the tent. Putting the dish inside the crate, he called the dog over. Pugger sniffed the air appreciatively, slipping quietly inside the crate. John patted her gently as she started to eat. When she was finished, he removed the plate, closing the door and making sure the latch was securely clasped. "You be good while I'm gone, old girl." Pugger whimpered, then curled up and watched as he pushed back the flap and disappeared behind it.

After breakfast, Josh and John cleaned up while the cook prepared to pack the wagon. When they were finished, they helped the cook get the wagon ready, then went to help with the other chores. The rain continued to plague the men as they worked, but it didn't stop them from getting camp dismantled.

John went out to help with his horses. Jackson had packed Blacky and was saddling Beauty when he got there. Seeing John's look of surprise, he hastened to explain, "Josh brought out your gear while you were helping the cook, as well as the crate with your dog in it."

John nodded, then stooped down to lift Pugger's crate. Placing it onto Blacky's pack, he made sure it was secure. John scratched behind Pugger's ear while talking to her. Finally, he went over to Beauty to give him the same attention. He went back to get Blacky's lead rope, which he tied to Beauty's saddle horn. When he was ready, he went to check on JaNae.

Seeing John coming towards them, Colonel Williams called to him, "Just a minute, John." John turned to face the colonel as he walked up to him. "Would you mind riding with JaNae again today?"

"Of course not, sir."

"Good! She said the trip was easier when she had someone who'd talk to her." Both men chuckled.

John looked around then turned back to the colonel. "Where is she now, sir?"

"I walked her over to the surrey."

"Very well then. I'll head on over that way."

"Fine!" Williams turned to leave then paused to turn back. "Do you mind if Jackson rides Beauty again today?" It was plain that he was concerned about John's feelings.

"No, sir! He is really good to the horse. Besides I trust him."

"Very good. I'll inform Jackson of the plan."

John nodded. After watching the colonel walk toward the horses, he went toward the surrey. JaNae smiled as he approached her side. "Good morning, JaNae."

"Good morning, yourself, John. What brings you over here?"

"Looks like you'll have to put up with me for the rest of this trip."

JaNae clapped her hands together excitedly. "Wonderful! I was afraid Mr. Jackson would be my companion for the day."

John smiled then teasingly added, "You might wish for Jackson after I've talked your leg off."

"That'll be the day!"

John was spared from speaking when Williams gave the order to mount up. John got inside the surrey. Gathering the reins he slapped the horses' rumps with them as he called, "Get up." When they were in formation, he stopped to wait for the command to move out.

"Company, ho!" called Williams. They slowly moved out of camp as the rain continued to beat relentlessly down upon them. John watched the steam rising from the horses, as they pulled the surrey through the muddy road. He looked to see that JaNae was comfortable and staying dry. Seeing that she was, he then turned his attention back to the horses. There wasn't much time for small talk, as the muddy road demanded all of his attention. Because of the mud and rain the group could only inch along. It seemed to John as if several hours had passed, while in reality it had only been an hour since they left camp.

They had traveled for two hours when trouble began to visit them. It all started when the Conestoga became bogged down in a mud hole. The horses tried valiantly to pull it out, all to no avail. They unhitched the team from the surrey so that they could hook them to the front of the wagon. The men got handholds on the sides or back of the wagon. Even though they pushed hard, the wagon wouldn't budge an inch. In fact, it became even more bogged down.

"Privates Smith, Walton, get an axe," barked Williams. "Then go chop down a couple of thick long poles!"

"Yes, sir!" The men hurried off to obey the colonel's orders.

It wasn't long until the two men returned, dragging two long thick poles. "Put them under the wheels!" The men complied. Soon the logs were in place. Several troops put their weight onto the poles, while others found good handholds on them to push. "Go!" yelled Williams. The men along with the horses gave it all they had. At first nothing happened, then slowly the wagon shook. There was a loud sucking sound as the wagon began to rise out of the hole. The team tugged a little harder, as did the men, until the wagon moved forward. Slowly the wagon inched forward until it was finally freed of the mud hole.

"Whoa!" called Williams. The trembling horses stopped pulling. They stood there struggling to get sufficient air into their overtaxed lungs. Unhitching the lead horses, John led them back to hitch them to the surrey. When all of the men were mounted, Williams gave the command to move out. To ensure that there were no more surprises lurking around the corner, Williams sent two men ahead to scout for mud holes.

Still, the rain poured incessantly upon the weary travelers. John grew concerned for JaNae's welfare, but she assured him that she was doing fine. Hoping to set his mind at ease, she changed the subject. "Tell me about your mother, John."

John sighed at mention of his mother. "Ma's a real peach of a woman! I remember how lovingly she taught me to read." He paused, smiling at the memory. "That wasn't an easy task for her because I was always more interested in what was happening outside than I was in reading." JaNae laughed at the picture he presented. "But somehow she got through to me when she began reading adventure stories. My love of reading grew until I could read the stories by myself." He paused to see what was happening ahead of them. Seeing that all was well, he continued. "My most treasured moments with Ma were those times that she read to me."

"She sounds really special!" replied JaNae, remembering her own mother.

"She is! Ma has always tried to help others out when they were in need. She also loves being around nature and watching the wild animals."

"I hope you'll introduce her to me when we get to the fort."

"I'd be proud to do that very thing."

"Good!" JaNae, looked thoughtfully out at the passing scenery. She was prevented from saying more when the scouts returned a few minutes later. They reported a huge bog hole a mile further down the road. Williams scowled at the news but continued to push the group on.

When they were near the bog hole, Williams called a halt. He went to examine the hole. Seeing that it was not possible for the wagon to go through, he studied the area around the hole. Feeling confident that it was possible for the wagon to pass around it, he sent a soldier back to get Snodgrass.

He soon approached the colonel, looking very concerned, "How bad is the hole, sir?"

"Too deep to go through it, but I think it's passable if you go to the left of the hole." Snodgrass nodded looking to the left. "You'll have to go really slow in case of unforeseen problems." Again Snodgrass nodded but remained silent. "We'll let you go first so that, if necessary, we'll be there to help you out."

"Very good, sir!" Snodgrass returned to the wagon.

Williams turned and noticed a soldier standing nearby. "Corporal Howell, go tell the men to dismount and get up here on the double."

"Yes, sir!" Corporal Howell saluted before hurrying off toward the men.

The Conestoga pulled up next to Williams, where it stopped. By then the men had joined them. Williams waved his hand forward as he shouted to be heard above the storm. "Move it out!" Snodgrass hollered at the horses. The wagon slowly moved to the left of the bog hole, creaking in protest as the horses strained to pull it. Anxiously the men watched as it continued to move along, unconsciously willing it not to mire down.

Half way around the huge bog hole, the wagon moved more to the left then back to the right. Still the men watched in fascination, wondering if the driver would make it. Finally, the wagon moved out onto the road, then stopped. Everyone shouted for joy as Snodgrass got down from the wagon. Sauntering back to the waiting men, he was visibly relaxed.

While the men slapped him on the back, Williams praised him highly. "Good work, Snodgrass. I couldn't have done it better myself!"

Snodgrass smiled at the compliment paid him. "Thank you, sir!"

"Let's get the surrey through the same way," commanded Williams. John, who had remained with JaNae, called to the horses and slowly, yet steadily, steered the team to the left of the mud hole. Again the men waited with baited breath. Slowly John inched around the hole. At one point it seemed as though they would sink, but they doggedly continued. To John it seemed as though they would never get around the bog, but the horses strained into their harnesses, and the surrey continued to inch forward.

Again the men waited with baited breath. Just as they drew near the Conestoga, the surrey slid toward the edge of the road, nearly slipping into the wet grass, but John guided the horses to the right until they inched back into the wagon tracks. When they finally came out onto the road behind the Conestoga, the men cheered. Williams grinned, then grew serious, "Get mounted, men!" Turning, the men went back and mounted their horses. "Move them out!"

Because they had lost so much time, Williams decided not to halt for noon break, but continued to press forward. The day wore tediously on as they rode toward the fort. Grateful for no more delays, Williams sighed when the fort loomed into sight just before dark. He was surprised to see so many Conestoga wagons positioned outside of the fort. As they came abreast of the wagons, he made a mental note to check them out.

The great doors of the fort swung slowly open as they drew nearer. As they entered the inner confines of the fort, Williams was surprised to see so much activity going on. "Company ... HALT!" He waited for the group to come to a full stop before lowering his arm. "Dis-mount!" After stepping out of the saddle, he removed the leather pouch from his saddlebag, tucking it under his left arm.

As the weary men dismounted, soldiers came running to take their horses and the conveyance to the stable. While Snodgrass stepped down from the Conestoga, John helped JaNae down, supporting her until she was able to stand on her own. Colonel Williams came toward them to take his wife's arm. "Thanks for watching out for my beautiful JaNae," exclaimed Williams.

John grinned, "My pleasure, sir! You see, I got the best of the deal!"

JaNae beamed at the compliments given her. "Why, thank you, kind sirs!"

Hattie Whipple ran up to throw her arms around her son. "Welcome home, son!"

"Hi, Mom," greeted John, returning the hug. "Mom, I'd like you to meet Colonel Williams and his wife, JaNae. I stayed with them while in Fort Missoula."

Hattie pumped the colonel's hand vigorously. "I'm so glad to make your acquaintance, sir." Turning, Hattie took JaNae's hand excitedly into her own. "Thank you for taking such good care of my boy, ma'am!"

"It is I, madam, who should thank you." She touched Hattie's cheek with her free hand. "You have raised a fine son, dear. He has brought so much happiness into our home. We shall sorely miss him." JaNae was unable to go on because of the great emotional turmoil in her heart.

"Please, allow me to take you to our home to freshen up and rest."

JaNae sighed wearily. "Oh I would appreciate that so much!" Hattie linked her arm through JaNae's as she led her away.

Colonel Williams was touched by Hattie's kind gesture. John looked at him in concern. "Can I do anything for you, sir?"

"Yes, John. Could you lead me to Major Thornton's office?"

"You bet!" While John escorted him to Thornton's office, the troops were shown to the barracks.

Thompson joined Colonel Williams, who was about to enter Thornton's office. Saluting, he stood at attention, then waited for Williams to speak. "At ease, Captain! I would like to speak with you and Major Thornton at once."

"Major Thornton isn't here, sir," calmly replied Thompson. "Please come into the office where I'll try to explain everything.

"Very well, Captain, lead the way!"

"Yes, sir." Turning, Thompson led the way into the office.

CHAPTER 19

Conestogas

Late the next afternoon, Paul Thompson stepped out of Major Thornton's office onto the porch, pausing to look up at the sky. All afternoon the storm clouds had been gathering until the sun was now obscured. A stiff breeze was blowing, while lightning flashed, followed by thunder rumbling in the distance.

Paul's attention was drawn to the activities going on in the fort. Earlier that morning, Peters had sent several soldiers out into the settlement to inform the people there about the upcoming events. They had ridden back an hour before to report that everyone at the settlement was excited about the celebrations. Several men volunteered to help make the booths, as did some of the settlers closer to the fort. Smiling to himself, he placed his wide-brimmed captain's hat on his head, then stepped off the porch.

Seeing that Hansen was approaching, Thompson waited. As Hansen reached Thompson he stopped. Coming to attention and raising his hand, he saluted Thompson. Thompson acknowledged the salutation as they walked on toward the working men. "The booths are coming along faster than we expected, sir. The men are relaxed … even enjoying themselves."

"Great! I was hoping the thought of celebrating the fourth would make them more jovial."

"I've never seen Jane so excited about anything before. When I left her a little bit ago, she was baking up a storm!"

"So is Kate!" the captain responded.

"Say, I've been looking up at the sky and not liking what I see."

"Me, too."

"Well, what if it does rain on us? It will spoil everything in the booths."

"I've been deliberating on that very thing,"

"What if we set the booths up in the community hall?" Hansen inquired. When Thompson stood thoughtfully considering the possibility, Hansen continued on, "The room is big enough to accommodate the booths, yet still have room to set up tables for the food."

"That's a great idea, Henry," Thompson became elated. "Do it!"

"Right away, sir!" Saluting, Henry started away.

Thompson called him back. "Just a minute, Henry!" Hansen turned curiously back to Thompson. "When we are together talking about the celebration for the Fourth of July, you don't have to be so formal with me."

"Yes, sir! It's just habit, I guess, that makes me do it, sir."

"Well in this capacity, we're friends. We don't have to stand on ceremony to be friends doing a fun thing together." He smiled to take the edge off of his words. "Besides, I was on my way to see what has been done on the construction of the booths. We might as well walk along together."

"Thank you, Paul, I'd like that a lot." The two men hadn't gone far when a guard came running excitedly up to them. "Captain ... a rider's coming!"

"Very well, that will be all. Carry on men." Without a backward glance Thompson strode briskly toward the stairs leading to the upper tier of the fort, taking them two at a time. The guard whirled around immediately standing at attention. Thompson returned the gesture, then struggled to get a good view. "Can you make out who it is?"

"Looks like Nataka, sir."

"Wonderful! Send him to Thornton's office when he arrives."

"Yes, sir."

Thompson acknowledged the guard's salutation, "As you were, soldier!"

Captain Thompson quickly descended the stairs. Peters came up to Thompson pausing to salute. "I was on my way to find you, sergeant."

"Whut's all the confounded ruckus 'bout, suh?"

"Nataka is returning to the fort and should be here any minute."

Peters blinked in surprise. "Thet were a fast trip!"

"Yes it was. Come with me to the office!" Nodding, Peter's fell into step with him. They had just entered the office when Nataka entered. He looked strained, even haggard from lack of sleep. Thompson motioned to a nearby seat, "Please be seated!"

Nataka grinned pleadingly. "Please, sir, if it's all the same to you, I'd prefer standing. I have been in the saddle so long that I feel stiff."

"As you wish. Tell me everything that happened ... sparing me nothing!" It was obvious that Thompson was very apprehensive, as he gazed intently into the young man's face. Nataka took a deep breath, twisting the hat in his hands, while thoughtfully cataloging the events as they happened.

When he was ready, he gave them the complete details, leaving nothing out. The two men listened intently to Nataka's report. It was plain to see that Peters was having a hard time keeping a straight face. Thompson had to smile, in spite of himself, at the sergeant's attempts to remain calm.

When Nataka was finished speaking, Thompson asked him a few pertinent questions, which Nataka answered. When he was finished, Thompson sat reflectively pondering the details. "Is there anything else I should be aware of?"

"No, sir!"

"Very well then, that will be all. Thank you for your excellent report, Nataka." The young man nodded, saluted, then turned to leave. Stopping, he turned slowly back to unflinchingly face Thompson.

All at once, his eyes twinkled merrily, while his lips twitched slightly. "The chief called you 'one Wiley old fox'." Before Thompson could reply, Nataka walked out the door, slamming it behind him.

For some minutes Thompson sat mulling over Nataka's report and its implications. After a few minutes, he turned thoughtfully toward Peters. "What do you make of the report, Peters?"

Peters began to laugh heartily while slapping his leg. "Ah wish so dad-blamed badly thet ah could'a been a little mouse in them thar rocks soz ah cuda watch Thornton's reactions, suh … thet Ah kin hardly stands it!"

Thompson thought a moment about the dilemma Thornton's little band of troublemakers had been put through. Looking at Peters, Thompson replied, "You know … what we did to Thorton will get us in terrible trouble. He is, after all, our superior officer. Once he returns we will not only be court-marshaled and stripped of our ranks, but we will face a terrible death."

This reminder immediately sobered Peters. "Yer right, suh!"

Thompson continued as if he hadn't heard Peters comment. "Even with all of this I must confess … I would also like to have seen Thorton's reaction." With that said, Thompson and Peters began to laugh. Finally, they rose to leave. "Keep what happened in this office under your hat, Peters! It's nobody's business what we did!"

Peters nodded. "Mum's the word, suh!" He saluted before going toward the barracks. Thompson stepped off of the porch while starting back to the community hall.

A private hurried toward Thompson forgetting to salute. "Captain, wagons are coming!"

Thompson stopped to look at the soldier in surprise. Together they rushed up the stairs to join the guard. The wagons looked like tiny white specks against their scenic backdrop. Lifting the spyglass, he studied the train more closely. "It's a train of Conestoga wagons. From the looks of things, the train is quite long, Harris. Better get Peters to assign some men to help them set up just outside of the fort."

"Yes, sir." Harris ran down the stairs.

Again looking through the spyglass, his brows knit together in consternation. Lowering the glass, he turned to the guard. "They seem to be pushing forward at a harried pace. Perhaps they are trying to beat the impending storm." Thompson continued to study the approaching train. All at once he could clearly see the lead wagon and the teamster upon the wagon seat.

As he watched, a woman poked her head out of the tent flap. She spoke quickly to the driver and then retreated behind the canvas. The driver, growing sterner, slapped the reins. The horses, already giving their best, tried to obey. Lowering the spyglass, Thompson walked over to the rail. "Corporal Adams, come here on the double!"

"Yes, sir!"

Thompson didn't wait to see him salute, but went back to watch the caravan. He had just raised the glass when the corporal joined him. He turned to see the soldier salute while standing stiffly at attention. Thompson acknowledged the greeting. "At ease, soldier!" Adams lowered his arm visibly relaxing. "I want you to go get Doctor Phelps immediately. If he isn't in the fort, find out where he went, then go get him. Bring him here at once!"

"Yes, sir!" Saluting, Adams hurried off to comply with Thompson's wishes.

Thompson lifted the spyglass and watched as the train inched closer. "Something is driving that man," he retorted aloud. Lowering the glass, he was surprised to see Adams arriving with the doctor. Both were out of breath as they quickly climbed the stairs. "That will be all, Adams. The corporal saluted before retreating.

Phelps, not seeing an emergency, looked quizzically at Thompson. "What's so all fired important that you had me run around like a man possessed?"

"We have a Conestoga wagon train approaching at breakneck speed. I think from the expression of the man in the lead wagon that something is terribly wrong. I want you to get down there and be ready for them in case there is trouble!"

"I'm as good as gone." Phelps hurried down the stairs then over to his office.

Thompson turned back, no longer needing the spyglass to pick out the wagons.

They weren't far from the fort, when several soldiers emerged from the gate. Thompson wasn't surprised to see that Phelps was among them. A few minutes later the wagon train pulled up outside of the fort. Thompson hurried down the stairs, rushing out the gate to meet them.

The driver of the lead wagon, a tall, thin, agile man, was stepping down from the wagon when Thompson arrived. He was dressed in bib-overalls, the pant legs tucked into heavy black leather boots. A red-checked shirt, its sleeves rolled almost to the elbow, revealed dingy white long-johns. Steel-gray eyes snapped with life from beneath thick, unruly eyebrows. Strands of gray hair, falling out from under a black beret, enhanced his weather-beaten face. A full graying beard covered sunken cheeks and a jutting chin.

Thompson stepped up to the driver with an extended hand, "I'm Captain Thompson."

The driver clasped the proffered hand in his own massive hand, shaking it heartily. "The name's James Payne." He looked anxiously around as if searching for something. "Is there a doctor here at the fort?"

Phelps, with his medical bag in his hand, stepped forward. "I'm Doctor Phelps. What can I do for you?"

"The wagon master took sick yesterdey, en we grew a might worried when he took a turn fer the worst a few hours ago."

"Where is he?" asked Phelps.

Payne pointed toward the lead wagon. "Here in this wagon. His missus is with him now."

"Very well, let's take a look, shall we?" Phelps walked to the back of the wagon, where he climbed inside, while everyone waited anxiously outside. He was only gone a few minutes, when he stuck his head out. "Thompson, I need a stretcher immediately." Two men disappeared inside the fort and returned shortly with a stretcher, which they took to Phelps. Thompson walked over to see what was needed. Phelps barked orders to the two men, who hastened to carry them out. The man was soon lifted out of the wagon, then carried back inside the fort with Phelps following closely.

Thompson turned when a tiny wisp of a woman emerged from the back of the wagon, assisted by one of the men from the wagon train. She was short and thin, and her shoulders were bent by the ravages of time. Large brown eyes, enhanced by thin white eyebrows, were filled with fear.

Although her once-beautiful face was wreathed in wrinkles, her smile more than made up for these imperfections. Her snow-white hair was fashioned in a style that reminded Thompson of a rabbit. She wore a plain brown dress, covered by a full-length flowered apron, and heavy brown boots encased her tiny feet. As he watched, she pulled the brown shawl, draped around her shoulders, tighter around her.

Thompson quickly stepped up to speak to her. "Good afternoon, ma'am." She blinked in surprise. "My name is Captain Paul Thompson."

"Hello, Captain. My name is Sadie Atkinson, and my husband's name is George."

Thompson bowed slightly and politely tipped his hat. "I'm pleased to make your acquaintance, ma'am. I just wish it was under better circumstances." When she nodded, Thompson remained silent. Gently touching her elbow, he offered, "Let me take you to your husband, while the soldiers help Mr. Payne get the wagons situated."

Sadie sighed in relief. "Thank you, sir. I would appreciate that very much."

As Thompson led her into the fort, he began to ask questions in an attempt to distract her. "Where is your wagon train coming from?"

"Not this spring but last spring, we started out from Missouri headed to Wyoming." She paused reflectively. "George was hired as the wagon master because he'd been there before. He tried to tell those thick-headed Missourians that they wouldn't be happy there, but they would have none of it." Thompson chuckled lightly at her choice of words. "One winter in that God-forsaken country was enough for George and me. When George got sick during the winter, we nearly lost him a few times.

"One day when the weather was better, some neighbors came to visit us. George was up ... doing some better by then. The men told us that they had had more than enough of that country. They wanted to move on toward Oregon or maybe up toward Canada. I was appalled when they asked if he would lead them there."

Again, she sighed wearily. "I was afraid for his health, but at the same time I knew that if we stayed another winter, it would kill him. I wasn't surprised when he readily agreed." They were nearing the infirmary, so she hurried her story. "Several times I feared that George wouldn't be up to the trip, but he assured me that he was. There aren't many things that I can be certain of in this life, but of one thing I can be sure. Once my George makes up his mind to do something, no one can change it."

"I see." Thompson paused thoughtfully to give her a chance to gain control. "Please go on."

She nodded and sighed audibly. "Then yesterday … yesterday he clutched at his chest. Moaning he crumpled over." She looked up at Thompson in concern then went on. "We stopped early to give him time to rest up, thinking that would help, but by morning he was no better. Mr. Payne said that we were close enough to the fort, that perhaps there would be a doctor there. Thinking it over, we decided to make a run for it." She was unable to go on for a moment.

"If anyone can help him," soothed Thompson, "it's Doctor Phelps." She sighed and remained silent. "We're finally here." He helped her inside.

Phelps looked up from the patient as they entered, then went back to work. Thompson led her to a chair in the corner where they could wait. Phelps lifted the sheet, gently placing it over the man's face.

Phelps turned to face Sadie, who had turned visibly pale. Her brown eyes grew large with shock while a little cry escaped her as she watched Phelps walk toward her. "Are you this man's wife?" She could only nod affirmatively. Phelps reached out to get a chair, which he placed in front of her. When he was seated, he folded his arms, resting his foot on his other leg before speaking. "He didn't have much of a chance to make it. His heart was just plain worn out!"

Sadie looked at him in surprise. "His heart?"

"I would guess that he has been ill for a very long time, hasn't he?"

"Yes."

"When I examined him, I was surprised that he was still breathing. From the sound of the heartbeats, or lack of, he should have died sooner. Your husband was just plain worn out, ma'am!"

"I knew that he'd been sick, but I didn't think it was his heart. He never told me what bothered him … no matter what I asked or tried to learn. He would keep telling me that it was nothing to worry about, that it was just the cold climate in Wyoming." Tears sprang to her eyes, slowly sliding down her old wrinkled cheeks. Thompson slipped an arm around her while wisely letting her cry. When she had gained control, he helped her to her feet.

"Paul," called Anna from her sick bed. "Take her to my house, please. See that she wants for nothing."

"Thank you, Anna." Paul replied gratefully. Thompson started to lead her from the infirmary, but she stopped to touch her husband's arm. "I'll see that a grave is prepared for him, but what you need right now is a place to rest and get something to eat." She allowed him to lead her from the infirmary. When they reached Thornton's house, he took her over to a chair. Thompson waited to speak until she was seated. "I'll have some dinner brought over to you. Jane Hansen can stay with you tonight."

Sadie gasped and blinked in surprise. "That won't be necessary."

"Now, there is no use of your arguing with me … because you won't win."

"Very well, Captain," she answered resignedly. He smiled, relieved that she had accepted his help. As he started for the door, Sadie closed her eyes. All at once she opened them calling out his name. "Captain Thompson!" He turned back into the room. "Thank you so much for your thoughtfulness. I truly appreciate it."

"No thanks necessary, ma'am. I'll return when I've seen to all of the arrangements."

"Very well." She closed her eyes, as Thompson softly closed the door behind him.

A few moments after that, lightning flashed and thunder rumbled through the air. Thompson looked up at the angry sky. Perceiving that the storm wasn't far off, he hurried back to his home for his rain gear. He quickly kissed Kate then filled her in on the news. "When I prepare dinner, I'll prepare a little extra for you to take to them," said Kate.

Paul hugged her up close, "I knew I could count on you, honey." He kissed her once more. Grabbing his rain gear, he left. After slipping into his rain gear, he went to find Peters, who was helping Hansen with the booths. They turned as one when Thompson approached them.

Saluting, they came to attention. "As you were, men." Dropping their hands, the men relaxed. "The wagon master, George Atkinson, just died."

They shook their heads sadly, as Peters spoke what was on their minds. "Thet's too bad, suh. He seem like an awful nice feller, at least ez fer ez Ah gots ta know him, en thet t'weren't much."

"His widow seems like a wonderful person, Peters," commented Thompson. "I feel really bad for her. I want you to assign a detail to get a grave dug as soon as possible. The storm is coming in fast, so we need to get the man in the ground before it does."

Saluting, Peters started to move away. "Yes, suh!"

Thompson watched him leave before addressing Hansen. "Henry, I have an awfully tall order for you to do in such a short space of time."

Hansen laid down his hammer to watch Thompson expectantly. "Yes, sir!"

"I need you to find Carl Jensen. See if he has already prepared a casket. If he hasn't, help him construct something."

"Right away, sir!" Saluting, Hansen hurried off.

Thompson walked out to the wagon train in search of James Payne. He found him rummaging through his wagon. "Ho the wagon."

Payne stuck his head out of the back then stepped down from the wagon. He greeted Thompson cheerfully. "Why hello, Captain. I was just about to come looking for you. I wanted to find out about George."

Thompson sighed sadly. "That's why I'm here. Mr. Atkinson passed away a few minutes ago. We took his wife to the home of our major to rest and collect herself."

Payne's mouth went slack with shocked disbelief. "George is gone?" He dropped down upon the ground with his head lowered. Thompson waited until Payne could gain control of his emotions. Finally, Payne lifted his head to stare at Thompson. "I knew he was sick, but I honestly didn't think he was that sick. What was it that took him?"

Doctor Phelps said that his heart was so tired … so worn out that it just stopped working."

"George never let on that he was that bad. He'd been under the weather last winter but always assured me that it was nothing." He tried to swallow past the lump in his throat but found it difficult to do. "I truly never knew that he was so bad."

"As you can see," said Thompson, indicating the sky, "a storm is about to come in upon us. It is imperative that we get Mr. Atkinson buried right away." Payne looked up at the sky and nodded. "I was wondering if you had someone in your group who would like to sing a hymn for him, as well as someone who would like to give a eulogy?"

"Mr. Rathbone has a beautiful tenor voice. He often sings for special occasions." Rising Payne looked reflectively back at the wagons. "I'll speak to him, then let you know."

"Thank you."

He paused to scratch his head thoughtfully. All at once, he looked over at Thompson. "I've known him the longest … so I'll gladly give his eulogy!"

"Great! Tell everyone who wants to be at the service to meet at the cemetery in two hours. They'll find it located just outside of the fort to the north."

"I'll get right to it." When he was gone, Thompson trudged back into the fort. Seeing Corporal Adams, he called to him. "Corporal Adams, I need you to spread around the fort that we have lost the wagon master from the wagon train that pulled in an hour ago. The services will be at the cemetery in two hours, if anyone wants to come."

"Yes, sir." Adams hurried off, while Thompson absently watched him go. Corporal Adams was a young man in his late twenties with curly raven-colored hair that stuck out from under his hat. Deep blue eyes augmented his dark complexion. Traces of a dark beard were showing along his well-shaped jaw, highlighting full thick sensuous lips. His uniform, always clean and neat, revealed a well-shaped muscular body. Adams stood five feet eleven inches tall in his stocking feet. Thompson smiled as he remembered all the stares Adams got from the young ladies.

Thompson went to inform Atkinson's widow of the plans. He knocked softly upon the door then went inside. She was sitting in the same chair that he had left her in. It was plain to see that she had been crying. She took out a hanky, dabbing at her eyes before looking at him. "I'm sorry to intrude upon you, Mrs. Atkinson, but I thought you'd want to know what is happening with the arrangements."

"You're not intruding, Captain. I would greatly appreciate any news you may have for me." As quickly as possible, Thompson told her what he had accomplished, relieved when Sadie nodded approvingly and reached out and took his hand. "I want to thank you for everything, my dear sir. When it first happened I wasn't thinking too clearly."

"I'm more than willing to help you in any way that I can, ma'am." Sadie dabbed at her eyes again. "I'll be back for you as soon as everything is ready. For now ... just get some rest." He patted her hand reassuringly then left the house.

Peters came up to him. Saluting quickly he spoke, "The grave's ready ta receive the wagon master, suh!"

"Very good, Peters! See if Jensen and Hansen are ready with the casket."

"Right away, suh!"

Thompson looked up at the sky once more, as lightning was flashing all around the fort, followed by crashing thunder. Counting the time between the flash and the thunder, he knew that the storm was only twenty miles away. "Hopefully," he told himself, "the storm will hold off until the funeral is over."

Peters soon returned to report. "Well Sergeant ..." Thompson looked at him a little impatiently.

"Mr. Jensen hed a casket finished, which he hed planned ta sell in Missoula. They was taking it over ta the infirmary, while Ah come ta tell ya the news."

"Thank you, Peters. Take a wagon from the livery stable over to the infirmary. When the body is in the casket, place it into the back of the wagon. Take it out to the Thornton's. Those in the fort will follow the wagon out to the cemetery."

"Yes, suh."

Thompson rushed over to knock on the Hansen's door. Jane opened the door greeting him warmly. "Come on in, Captain." Thompson removed his hat before he stepped inside. "What can I do for you?"

"A wagon train pulled in almost two hours ago. The wagon master was very ill, so Doctor Phelps had him taken to the infirmary, where he died of heart failure."

"Oh, that's too bad!"

"His widow is over at Anna's until the funeral. Would you mind staying with her tonight, so that she doesn't have to be alone?"

"I'd be happy to stay with her! Just give me a minute to finish my chores, then I'll be ready to go."

Thompson was relieved to see Sylvia come out of her room just as Jane turned back to the counter. Sylvia walked towards him with concern. "I'm sorry to hear about the wagon master."

"Thank you, Sylvia. Do you mind staying with the twins while we conduct his funeral?"

"Sure! I'll go over now so that Kate can get ready."

"Thank you so much."

"You're welcome, Captain." Thompson smiled inwardly as Sylvia kissed Jane on the cheek before leaving. It pleased him to see her so considerate of her mother. "See ya later, Ma." She rushed out the door only to stick her head back in, "Don't worry about supper, Ma, 'cause I'll be back in plenty of time to fix it." Not waiting for an answer, she closed the door. Listening intently to the ditty she was humming, Thompson realized it was an Irish tune. It was obvious that Sylvia not only felt happy but was content with her world as well.

"I'm ready to go." Spinning around in surprise, he saw Jane striding toward him. Thompson stepped back to allow her to precede him then followed. Jane kept him busy answering questions about the planned activities for the fourth of July.

They were interrupted when the wagon carrying the casket passed them on its way to the Thornton's. "You won't need to worry about supper for the two of you," said Thompson, "because Kate offered to send something over."

"Good. That will give us the chance to get acquainted. Tell ya what we'll do. I'll introduce myself, after which I'll let her in on what's to take place, while you go get Kate. Let's meet back here so we can go to the funeral together."

Thompson had to accede to her practicality … even cherished it. "Leave it to you to come up with an easy solution." Jane eyed him oddly, unsure of his meaning. "But then again, you always did have that special gift."

Jane stopped to curtsy. Throwing her head she arrogantly replied, "Thank you, sir. It's my sad lot in life to mingle with those beneath me!"

Thompson began to howl gleefully at her ridiculous antics. All at once, he was seized with an uncontrollable urge to flick her on the nose. "Be off with you, madam, before I forget my gentlemanly manners and flick you on your haughty little nose. Nothing would give me greater pleasure than to knock you down from your high horse."

"Well … I never!" Indignantly raising her nose higher in the air, she huffed off toward Anna's. She had only gone a few steps, when she wheeled around to face Thompson. Scowling, she placed her left hand on her hip while shaking her finger at him, "You'd best be careful of who you knock from their high horse, Captain. Otherwise, you might find yourself with a black eye or bloody nose!" Without another word, she continued her course to Anna's. "See you soon," she called over her shoulder. From her posture and jaunty air, Thompson knew that she was pleased with herself for getting in the last lick.

Still shaking his head at Jane's funny capers, he went to get Kate. She met him at the door, still issuing last minute instructions to Sylvia, "We shouldn't be gone long."

"Don't worry, ma'am," assured Sylvia, "they'll be fine."

"We better hurry, dear," encouraged Thompson.

"I'm ready."

He held the door for her then waved at Sylvia, "Be back soon."

When they got to Thornton's, Jane's introductions were given. Coming out to the waiting wagon, they were soon on their way to the cemetery. Both women plied Sadie with questions to take her mind off the task ahead.

Thompson was amazed to see so many people standing there. Lightning struck all around them as the service commenced, followed by loud rumbling thunder. Thompson knew that it wouldn't be long before the storm hit. Slipping an arm around Kate, he pulled her closer to him. A reverent hush fell over the people when the casket was lowered into the ground.

The service was short, yet sweet. Payne delivered the eulogy, while a few close friends shared their feelings. Then Mr. Rathbone sang Rock of Ages, his rich, clear tenor voice singing crisply across the open air. When he was finished, no one moved, not wanting to break the peaceful spell that lingered. Finally, Mrs. Atkinson bent down to pick up a handful of dirt, which she tossed onto the grave. Then one by one, each person threw in a handful of dirt. Many offered condolences to the widow before leaving the cemetery to continue with their individual business.

When everyone had gone, the burial detail completed its task of burying the wagon master. They had just finished when the heavens opened. The rain descended while lightning flashed. The thunder reverberated through the air. Static electricity seemed everywhere. Grabbing their shovels, the men hurried back of the wagon. Even though the driver pushed the horses to go faster, by the time the crew had reached their barracks, they were all soaked.

CHAPTER 20

The Newcomer

Paul Thompson wasn't surprised to find that it was still raining when he awoke the next morning. Rising, he quickly dressed. Going to the kitchen, he started a fire in the cook stove. When it was going well, he banked it. After filling the wood box, he filled the reservoir with water. Getting two more buckets of water, Thompson placed them on the counter.

He had just finished making himself presentable when Kate came out of the bedroom. He stood gazing at the vision of loveliness she presented. Her long auburn hair was in disarray. She was dressed in a light pink dressing gown. A sloppy pair of slippers appeared from under the hem of her gown. Kate stretched lazily then inhaled deeply. "Good morning, sleeping beauty."

"Is it really morning … or am I up in my sleep?" Kate asked, coming over to kiss Paul squarely upon the lips.

"The way it's raining I'm not sure, but since I heard reveille an hour ago, I'm forced to assume that it is."

Kate groaned. "I was afraid of that!"

Thompson couldn't resist the temptation to tease. "Perhaps the bugler is up in his sleep, too!"

"Huh! Fat chance of that happening!" Kate shuffled over to the counter to perform her daily toiletries. "I don't even feel like I've been asleep!"

"I don't wonder, what with the twins fussing for most of the night." He went to slip his arms around Kate's waist, pulling her to him. "Why don't you just go back to bed while I get myself some breakfast?"

"Um," sighed Kate, "I think I will." Thompson nibbled on her ear a moment. "You'll never get breakfast if you keep that up," Kate teased, turning to slip her arms around his neck. "Thanks for taking such good care of me," she mumbled into his neck. "I love you so much, Paul Thompson!"

Thompson responded by kissing her passionately upon her sensuous lips. "You better get, while the getting is good," he snickered, slapping her playfully upon the rump.

Giggling she moved out of his arms. "Who says I want to get away?"

Thompson grabbed for her, but she eluded him as she headed for the bedroom. He called out, "You little imp!" She tittered softly as she disappeared into the bedroom. "You just wait, Miss Tease!" Paul heard her giggle happily.

Thompson prepared a light breakfast. Taking a seat at the table, he began to eat. When he was finished, he not only did up his dishes but he also straightened up the room. Satisfied that it was the way it should be, he got into his rain gear, removed his hat from the hook at the door, then slipped quietly out the door.

He leaned against the porch a moment to survey the sky. From the dark menacing clouds, it didn't appear that it would stop raining very soon. Stepping off the porch, he went to give the troops their orders.

The day dragged slowly by as they continued to prepare for the upcoming celebration. The men from the settlement showed up shortly after breakfast to help where needed. Thompson went to the wagon train to visit with Payne. He found him rummaging through his Conestoga for something. He hesitated a moment, then called, "Can I see you a moment, Payne?"

The racket inside the Conestoga stopped, then Payne poked his head out. "Good morning, Captain." He quickly climbed out of the wagon to join Thompson. "What can I do for you this nasty rainy morning?"

"Are you aware that there will be a commemoration for the Fourth of July day after tomorrow here at the fort?" Payne nodded as he waited. "Would you spread the word that everyone from your train is invited to join us?"

Payne grew excited. "Sure thing, Captain! How can we help?"

"There are still a lot of preparations to be completed before we're ready. Can you ask every able-bodied man to help?"

"You got it! I'll have all of the men there in a jiffy!"

"Wonderful! I'll send Peters over to guide you to the community hall. By the way, tell the women that there will be booths for them to display their needlework, their baked goods or both."

"Very well! I'll do that very thing!"

"Fine! I'll see you there." Payne nodded. Thompson went back inside the fort, leaving Payne to speak to those in the wagon train.

Thompson went to inform Hansen that the men from the wagon train were coming to help. Hansen sighed in relief. "Good! There is still a lot to do!"

"Then I'll leave you to it." Thompson went back to the office to work on some paper work. No matter how hard he tried, he just couldn't concentrate on it. He took the letter he'd received from Colonel Williams from the pocket of his jacket. He slipped the paper out of the envelope then began to reread the contents. *How long will it be before he gets back to us?* Thompson wondered. *Can't think about this now,* he chided.

He slipped the letter back into the envelope placing it back into his pocket. Thompson had kept the letter with him so that it wouldn't be found accidentally. The last thing he needed was to have the letter pose problems he couldn't deal with. He tried again to sign the papers that Corporal Hadley, Thornton's clerk, had prepared for him.

Settling down, he worked until noon, when his mind began to wander once more. Wiping the pen, Thompson laid it by the inkbottle, which he had recapped. Closing the folder, he rose and walked over to the door, slipped into his rain gear and removed his hat from the hook. Stepping onto to the porch, he inhaled deeply of the pungent rain-filled air before heading home for lunch.

Kate had dinner on the table when he entered. Thompson removed his outerwear then hung the coat and hat on the hook near the door. He sniffed the air appreciatively, sighing in delight. "Um, that food smells delicious!" Kate smiled as she continued to dish up the food. "I'm as hungry as a male grizzly bear after awakening from his long winter's nap."

"Ah, you poor dear," she crooned, kissing him tenderly, "it's ready when you are."

Thompson quickly washed up, then walked over to the table where he plopped wearily into a chair. After Kate took a seat, they said a short prayer. They ate in silence until the edge of their hunger was appeased. "How have the little ones been today?" Thompson asked companionably.

"They have been little darlings. When they'd been given their baths had drunk their fill, they went to sleep like little lambs. They've been so quiet that I keep going in to check on them."

"That's a switch. Usually they're yelling their heads off for something."

"I know. I've been able to get caught up on my work. Several times I would check to see if they were all right, because they never made a fuss."

They continued to talk about the commotion at the fort, those at the wagon train, including Sadie Atkinson. All too soon lunch was over. It was time for Thompson to get back to the office. He rose to kiss Kate tenderly. "Thanks for a wonderful meal, darling. It was delicious!"

Kate grinned. "Thank you, kind sir."

Thompson started for the door. "Best get back to work. See you tonight, honey." He kissed Kate once more then left.

Thompson started to the office, but then decided to go over to Anna's cabin to check on Sadie Atkinson. Stepping up on the porch, he knocked and stepped back to wait. Jane opened the door, smiling as she greeted him pleasantly. "Come in, Captain."

Removing his hat, Thompson stepped inside, glancing around for Sadie. Seeing her washing dishes, he went over to greet her cheerfully. "I came to see how you are doing today."

She hastened to reassure him. "I'm doing great, considering everything. We were just tidying up before I go back to the wagon train."

"You don't have to hurry off so fast."

"I have things that have to be done, and I best get at them." As she began to wash up the table, Sadie paused. "Thank you so much for your concern, Captain." When the table was washed, she turned to do the same to the counter. Thompson watched her work, feeling concerned for her welfare.

Jane sensing his concern hastened to put him at ease. "I'll look out for her, Paul."

"Thank you, Jane."

Sadie, wiping out the empty dishpan, hung it back on the wall, then draped the tea towel over it. "Jane has been telling me about the upcoming celebration. Sounds like a lot of fun!"

"Yes, it does. I was just out to the wagon train, where I told Payne to pass the word along that everyone was invited. I also told him to tell the women that there were going to be booths where they could display their needlework, baked goods or both."

Sadie grew very excited. "That will be wonderful! I didn't have much to do during the winter months except needlework, so I'll have something to display. Not only that, but it will help keep my mind from thinking about what has just happened."

"Not only will there be booths for needlework or baked goods, there will also be booths for jams, jellies, and other canned goods," said Jane.

"I'll pass that along." Sadie looked around the immaculate kitchen, satisfied that it was in order. "Well … I guess I'd best get to my wagon. I have a lot to do." She moved to a chair where she picked up her shawl. Taking it from her Thompson draped it around her shoulders. She turned with a smile. "Thank you, Captain." She touched his cheek tenderly then pulled her shawl tighter around her.

Squaring her shoulders, Sadie shuffled out the door with Jane and Paul following behind her. Thompson waited until the two women were near the gate before going about his business.

He strolled aimlessly around the fort, trying to collect his jumbled thoughts. As tantalizing aromas came wafting at him from all directions, he knew the women were baking up a storm. His mouth began to salivate in anticipation of what was to come. He watched as the troops went about their various tasks, feeling pleased.

Thompson's attention was drawn to a group intently working a short distance away. His curiosity getting the better of him, he decided to check it out. As he approached, he saw Peters arduously working on something. The men were hooting at something he said. Hearing someone approaching, the men turned as one. Upon seeing Thompson, everyone turned visibly pale.

Peters, intent upon what he was doing, was unaware of Thompson's presence. "Dad-blamed ifn' Ah ain't agoin'a have me sum fun with the captain. Ah want ta see him go under en come up alookin' like a drowned rat!" He began to roar at the picture it presented in his mind. When no one joined in the merriment, he looked up. Seeing Thompson scowling at him sternly, Peters jumped to attention and hastily saluted. "Ain't meanin' ya no disrespect, sir!"

Thompson glowered at him angrily. "It didn't sound like that from where I was standing, Sergeant!" It tickled him to see Peters squirm. He disgustedly pointed to the contraption before him. "I take it, that this is going to be the dunking booth." Thompson was having a difficult time remaining stern. The men visibly squirmed as he looked at Peters to see what he would do.

"Yes, suh," replied Peters, a little hesitantly. "It's nearly ready."

Thompson began to move in for the kill. "Well … I think I'll change my mind … the people can dunk you instead!" Thompson smiled inwardly, when he saw Peters' mouth open in abject disbelief.

"But, suh!" Peters became so flustered and frustrated that he couldn't go on for a moment. Finally he took a deep breath, "Ah've jest been tellin' ever'un thet ya were sich a good sport, en thet ya were agona sit in the dunkin booth!"

It was plain to Thompson, who was enjoying the sergeant's dilemma, that Peters was very discouraged with the turn of events. "Well … this nasty weather has made me change my mind about being dunked!" Peters swallowed as he looked at the men. They were intently watching the interaction between the two men. "No, sir, you aren't going to get me into that dunking apparatus … not even for all the tea in the Boston Harbor!"

Peters didn't know what to do, but it was plain that he didn't want to be the one in the dunking booth. The fact that Thompson refused really looked bad to the men. Finally, he swallowed past the lump in his throat and faced the music. "Very well, suh." Peters spoke so low that everyone had to strain to hear him. "Ah guess sumbidy's got ta do it!" He turned back to continue to work on the dunking booth.

Thompson almost lost his sternness when he saw Peters' look of distress, but he wasn't ready to give him any mercy. "No officer should be expected to have to submit to such a degrading ordeal, Sergeant!" Peters' shoulders drooped even more, but he only worked all the harder.

Seeing Peters in such a dither, Thompson turned and winked at the men, who relaxed. "Peters…"

Peters eyed Thompson suspiciously, "Yes, suh." He stood rigidly at attention with a blank expression on his face.

"As you were, Peters." Peters relaxed. "Sergeant, have you ever known me to break my word … once I agree to do something?"

"No, suh. Thet's whut bothers me the most, suh!"

"Well, now is no exception!" Peters' jaw again dropped. He watched Thompson intently to see if he'd heard correctly. "When I heard your comments a while ago, I decided to have some fun at your expense." The men began to howl, and Peters soon joined them.

"Ah shoulda knowd ya were only a funnin' with me, suh!" Lights began to flash from his eyes, while his demeanor changed drastically. "Ye jest wait til Ah get my chance at ya, then Ah'll play hob with ya' fer funnin' with me!"

They continued to watch eagerly as Thompson moseyed over to critically scrutinize the booth. "Did you fix it so that it wouldn't drop just because someone bumped it?"

"Well now ..." drawled Peters, "Ah don't rightly know, for certain sure, suh." Thompson knew that Peters was toying with him. "Ah guess ya'll have ta wait 'n see, won't ya?"

Thompson shrugged then calmly replied, "I could always refuse to get into it until I had you test it out, Sergeant." The men heckled Peters boisterously when he snorted as he stalked away.

Private Harris couldn't contain himself any longer. "Oh ... I have ... never been so tickled ... in all my life ... as when you got ... the best of ... Peters just now!" The rest of the men could only shake their heads affirmatively.

Smiling broadly, Thompson started away. "Carry on as you were, men." He was impressed at how quickly everything was taking shape. They'd be ready in two days if they progressed the way they had been doing.

A short time later, Corporal Lewis, a young man of twenty, entered the community hall. He scanned the room as if searching for someone. Seeing Hansen and Thompson standing near an unfinished booth, he hurried toward them. When he reached the two men, he saluted.

"As you were, Corporal," commanded Thompson.

Corporal Lewis complied. He slowly began to present his message. "Private Hawks sent me to tell you that there is a covered wagon approaching the fort."

"What direction is it coming from, Lewis?"

"From Salmon, sir."

"Very well. That will be all!"

"Yes, sir." Corporal Lewis, snapping to full attention, saluted before ambling away.

Thompson turned to Hansen. "Carry on, Hansen. I'll come back as soon as I can ... if it's possible."

"Very well, sir." Hansen quickly went back to work.

When Thompson emerged from the community hall, it had stopped raining. He pulled his watch out of his watch fob to scan it intently. He was surprised that it was nearly fifteen hundred hours. Replacing his watch, he hurried over to the stairs leading up to the lookout point, taking them two at a time. "How far away are they, Hawks?"

"Approximately a mile, sir." Lowering the spyglass, he handed it to Thompson.

Thompson looked through the glass a moment and then lowered it. He stood thoughtfully tapping it on his open palm. He lifted it again, focusing it on the wagon. A strange expression came over his face. Again, he lowered the glass, tapping it against his open palm. When the wagon got close enough so that the glass was no longer necessary, Thompson handed it back to Hawks. He took one more look as the wagon approached the gate.

All at once, he yelled, "Praise be!" Thompson called down to the guards at the gate, "Open the gate, Private Townsend." Thompson growing excited descended the stairs two at a time.

Private Townsend complied with Thompson's orders, and Thompson arrived just as the wagon entered the gate. He blinked, struggling to believe what he saw. Slowly, yet deliberately, he strolled over to the wagon as the driver stepped down to help a lady to the ground.

Thompson uttered a glad little cry, as he dove at the woman. Scooping her up, he twirled her around. Finally, he hugged her close, while the driver and the private stared at them.

"You old, scallywag," yelled the woman. "Put me down this instant! You hear?" Thompson complied, but not without first pecking her on the cheek and getting a playful slap for his efforts.

"Now, now," she scolded. "Where are your manners, Captain?" It was plain for all to see that she was pleased with his actions.

The short, plump lady in her late sixties stepped back to critically survey Thompson. Her snow-white hair was styled according to Eastern fashion. A brown hat trimmed with a light-brown ribbon and pink flowers sat askew on her head. Her mischievous blue eyes twinkled from beneath neatly shaped brows.

When she laughed, her face lit up and her eyes, shrouded in wrinkles, danced with merriment. The brown cotton traveling dress she wore was trimmed in white tatted lace around the neck. A white cameo, sitting in the middle of a light-green background and encased in an ornate silver mounting, was clasped at her throat.

Long sleeves, puffed from the shoulder to the elbow, tapered into a 'V' at her wrists. The close-fitting bodice was gathered at the waist with a wide band. The skirt was straight in the front then gathered into a bustle at the back. Black, high-top button shoes completed the effect. White gloves adorned her dainty hands and a brown drawstring bag was clasped at the right wrist.

Thompson kissed her soundly upon the cheek once more. "There! I'll be hanged whether I give a hoot if the whole fort knows that I just kissed my beloved Aunt Eileen Thompson!"

Eileen Thompson smiled in spite of herself. "I do believe this backwoods country has ruined your gentlemanly manners!" She feigned disappointment, but Thompson saw right through her.

"Ah, me thinks, thou dost protest too much, my dear lady," he said, grabbing her hands and bowing low. Lifting her right hand, he kissed the air above it.

Eileen threw her head slightly back laughing joyfully, then playfully cuffed him on the arm. "Enough, you dear, wonderful, foolish man! Enough!"

Thompson excitedly grabbed both of her hands. "Oh, dearest Auntie, won't Kate be beside herself when she sees you!"

"Uh-hum," They turned to face the driver. He was plainly disgusted with the whole situation. All he wanted was to get the trip over with. "Could you tell me where to put her gear?"

"Just put it onto the porch here. We'll take care of it later." The driver didn't need to be told twice, but quickly began unloading Eileen's trunks and luggage from the back of the wagon, muttering to himself about women always being mushy creatures. Thompson whistled at the amount of luggage the driver was stacking on the porch, and hurried over to the wagon to help.

When they were done, the driver got back upon the wagon seat, bellowing at the horses, who strained into their harnesses as the wagon moved toward the gate. "Haw!" He slapped the horses hard on the rump with the reins, causing them to snort. They bolted for a moment. It seemed as if the wagon would flip over, but it corrected itself. All too quickly, the wagon disappeared from view.

Thompson's face clouded over with unspoken anger. Turning to face his aunt he asked, "Did he treat the horses like that while coming here?"

She nodded angrily. "Yes. Several times I told him to go slower, to treat the animals better, but he only became meaner to them. Finally, I figured that if I wanted to help the horses, I'd best remain silent. As we drew near the fort, I gave him a choice piece of my mind ... you can bet it wasn't really the choice part, either!"

Thompson wisely refrained from answering. He put his hand on her elbow, gently guiding her toward home. "Leave your things here for the time being. After you see Kate we'll haul them home." Smiling, Eileen allowed herself to be piloted away.

When they neared Thompson's home, he paused a moment. "When we get to the house, you wait on the porch until I call her out."

Eileen's eyes sparkled with anticipation, "It will be a wonderful surprise to see her expression."

They stepped up on the porch. Thompson winked at his aunt before opening the door. "Kate, honey, would you please come outside a moment?" Closing the door, he stood in front of Eileen. "Don't want her to see you too soon now, do we?"

"No, we don't," she agreed, her blue eyes twinkling merrily.

"Yes," called Kate, as she walked out onto the porch.

"I have a surprise for you."

Blinking in surprise, Kate looked around. Seeing nothing, she turned to look at him wonderingly. "Well ... what is it?"

Paul looked at his spouse intently, all the time appearing daft. "Where's what?"

Kate impatiently stepped forward to punch him lightly on the arm. "Oh you! The surprise ... what else?" She grabbed him impatiently, while trying to look behind him. At the sight of Eileen, Kate took a step backwards, blinking her eyes in absolute dismay. "Oh!" Still not satisfied that she was seeing correctly, she rubbed her eyes. Eileen stepped out from behind Paul just as Kate opened her eyes. "Oh, Auntie, is that really you?"

Eileen chuckled at Kate's expression. "Yes, dear, it's really me!"

"Oh!" Kate lunged forward to throw her arms around Eileen, who met her half way. "I was beginning to think that we would never see you again." She stepped back to look Eileen over critically. "You're still as beautiful as ever."

Eileen gasped and snickered in surprise. "Oh my goodness! I can see that the blarney is still flowing freely!"

They all laughed joyously. Finally Kate excitedly drew her toward the door. "Come on in. We have a surprise for you as well." Eileen allowed herself to be led into the house. When they were inside, Kate gently pushed Eileen into the rocker by the door. "Sit in this rocker, Auntie. We'll be right back!" Kate grabbed Paul's arm pulling him toward the bedroom.

They soon returned, each with a bundle in their arms. Smiling they handed the sleeping infants to Eileen. She gasped, silently taking a child in each arm. Bemused, she intently studied each face, and then looked up at her family misty-eyed. "They're beautiful!" Kate and Paul beamed at the praise bestowed them.

Looking at each other, Paul nodded for Kate to speak. "The boy we named Aaron Joseph … the girl we named Sarah Anna-Heleen. I didn't want to load the wee thing down with too many names, so I decided to combine your name with Aunt Helen's."

Gazing lovingly at each infant, Eileen could only shake her head. Looking up at the proud parents, she smiled. "I guess the biggest surprise is on me!"

Thompson looked dumbfounded. "Didn't you get our letter telling you about the twins?"

"I left New York a month ago. The longing to see the two of you got so overwhelming that I decided to sell my estate so I could come join you."

He watched his beloved aunt hopefully. "Are you going to stay near us permanently?"

"Yes … that is, if you'll have me." She watched each face for negative signs, but found only joy and happiness.

Paul dropped to his knees beside her, tenderly looking into her eyes. "Oh, dearest Auntie, I am beside myself with the joy of it all!"

Kate knelt on her other side. "I have wanted you to join us for so long!"

Eileen blinked back the tears that threatened to spill out of her eyes. "Thank you both so very much! No one could have had a better welcome than this."

Paul and Kate took the infants back to their beds, then returned to join Eileen. "You must be famished," declared Kate. She walked over to stoke the fire in the kitchen stove.

"Not really. I guess I'm just too excited to feel anything else."

"Why don't you try to eat something, while I see to your things?" coaxed Paul.

"Okay. I would appreciate it if you saw to my things."

Paul stooped down and tenderly kissed her cheek. "I won't be long, Auntie. Before I come home, I'll have a cot brought over for you to sleep on." After kissing Kate, he left.

Kate bustled around the kitchen while Eileen removed her hat and hung it on the hook near the door. She then went to the counter to wash off some of the trail dust. "It feels so good to get some of that dust and grime off of me."

"I know. When we finally arrived here at the fort … that was the first thing I wanted to do. Paul heated some water to fill a tub for me that very night." She chuckled at the memory. "I didn't want to come out for a long time, but, the water got so cold, I was forced to. I'll have Paul get some hot water for you to soak your travel weary body in when he gets a chance. Come sit at the table, Auntie, while the food's still hot."

Complying, Eileen took a bite, sighing in pleasure. "This is delicious, my dear. I didn't realize that I was so hungry until I took a bite."

"Thank you, Auntie." Kate, pleased at the compliment, let her take the edge off her hunger before she engaged her in further conversation.

When Eileen was finished, she leaned back and sighed contentedly. "I feel much better now. Thank you, dear."

"Good. Now tell me what really brought you out here! You said you longed to see us," prompted Kate, "but were you excluding part of the story?" She intently watched Eileen's face.

"Truthfully, I was disgusted with the way the young people were acting. There is also the fact that the city is getting so overly-crowded. I began feeling lost in that big old house." She paused thoughtfully before continuing. "I longed for other company besides that of the servants." Tears glistened in her eyes but she hastily brushed them away. "I kept rereading the letters from the two of you, and the yearning to see you both grew more unbearable every day. The long winter months wore tediously upon my nerves, making them more frayed every day. Then one cold crisp snowy day, while I was coming home from a tea with Mrs. Freedman, I looked at the estate … asking myself what was really holding me in New York. You know, my dear, I couldn't for the life of me come up with one good reason for staying!"

"Good! We've wanted you to be with us for this past year and a half, but when you always wrote back that you were too old to travel, it saddened us."

"Well it takes some of us old dogs longer to realize that we really aren't as old as we think we are."

Kate placed her hand gently over Eileen's to squeeze it lightly. "You'll never be old, Auntie!"

Eileen smiled thoughtfully. "I don't know. Sometimes when my lumbago acts up, I'm forced to wonder." Kate squeezed her hand but remained silent. "When I finally made up my mind to sell the estate, I went to Horace Greenly, my lawyer. I asked him to make all of the arrangements. Three weeks later, an English earl from England contacted Mr. Greenly about securing property in New York. Horace sent me a note asking when it would be convenient for him to bring the gentleman by to look at the estate. I sent a note with my butler, Edwardo, telling him that he could bring him around in a week."

Eileen paused so long that Kate grew anxious. "Please go on, Auntie."

"Well, we thoroughly cleaned that house from top to bottom. It's doubtful that it ever got a cleaning like that one for many centuries. You can bet that I made the maids, housekeeper, even the butler clean every nook, every cranny in that old house until it fairly shone." Eileen paused a moment before proceeding. "Even the carriages were polished until they almost blinded the horses."

Kate, amused at Eileen's exaggerations, couldn't resist the temptation to tease. "Perhaps it is a good thing that they wear blinders."

Eileen pursed her lips at the same time drawing her eyebrows together sternly. Seeing Kate's silly expression, she grinned. "Perhaps," she conceded. "Anyway, the house fairly sparkled when Horace brought the gentleman to the estate. She laughed slightly, and then began again. "As we showed that gentleman around, he was so straight laced that he never displayed any emotion whatsoever. Even when we served tea, he was gracious but impassive." Little pinpoints of light shimmered in her eyes. "I began to believe that if the poor old chap smiled, his face would crack into a million pieces!" Kate snickered then willed herself to remain impassive. Eileen went on as though she'd never said anything amiss. "I was never so relieved to see someone leave in all of my life, as I was with that old bore!"

Kate tried to restrain herself but it was no use. She grabbed her sides in a fit of laughter. "Oh … what I wouldn't have given to see you trying to entertain someone so dull, droll, so humorless!"

"You would! Anyway it was decided that if this gentleman bought the estate, then everything went with it … that is … all except some of my pictures, some kitchen items, ornaments, knick-knacks and personal effects. As you know, Kate, I have a very large library of rare books. Those, I informed him, were not for sale. He tried to drop the price on the sale of the estate, but I was emphatic about my decision. When he realized that I wouldn't change my mind, he dropped the subject."

When Eileen smiled, Kate knew that this dear old lady was pleased with herself for denying the gentleman's persistence. This surprised her, because she knew that this grand lady loved people, even delighted in pleasing them. Kate grew impatient when Eileen remained silent. "How long did you have to wait before you got your answer?"

"I waited for nearly a month before Horace came to visit me, and I grew so despondent that I decided to change my mind about the sale of the estate." An impish gleam came into Eileen's eyes. "When Horace finally came to see me, I was writing him a note telling him of my decision. I hadn't quite finished the note when I heard a carriage approach the house. Edwardo came in a few minutes later to inform me that Horace was waiting for me in the drawing room. At that moment, I felt such fear, dread and apprehension that I thought that I would suffocate. Slowly I laid the pen on the desk. Rising, I followed Edwardo from the room."

Kate, who was leaning on her every word, grew impatient. She couldn't wait for her to continue. "What happened next, Auntie?"

"As I didn't want to appear too eager, I paused at the door a moment to gain complete control of my turbulent emotions. When I was sure that I was ready, I entered the parlor. When Horace saw me, his eyes lit up. Smiling broadly he came eagerly forward to clasp my hand. I didn't know what the smile meant, but it surely did put my mind at ease.

"He quickly informed me that he had received a letter from the gentleman stating that he wanted the estate, also that he had enclosed a bank draft with the letter. For a moment, all those feelings of fear, dread and apprehension washed over me. Then the thought of seeing both of you erased it all from my heart … from my mind. It was then that I knew that I was making the right decision.

"Horace told me that he hadn't told me about the letter because he wanted to check out the man's credentials before coming to see me, as he didn't want to get my hopes up prematurely. He found everything in order so came right over. The only stipulation the gentleman made was that he wanted to take the estate over inside of a month.

"At first I wasn't sure that I could be ready to leave in time, but Horace assured me that he would take care of all the legal transactions, travel arrangements and bank business, while I prepared to leave. After thanking him, I asked him to stay for tea, but he politely declined. He left shortly after I had signed the agreement." Eileen started to rise in order to clear the table. "Let me help clean up, dear."

"Those old dishes can just wait. Right now I'm more interested in what happened next."

"Very well, I almost forgot to tell you that when we were first discussing what went or what didn't, the gentleman expressed the desire to retain all of the staff. I told him that he would have to talk with them about that; it was their lives he was talking about.

"When Horace left, I called a staff meeting to inform them that I had sold the estate, also that I would be leaving at the end of one month. I informed them of the gentleman's desire to keep them on, but that it was to be their decision. That was not a happy time, I can tell you.

"Most of the staff, who had been with me for many years, didn't want to see me leave. Edwardo, who took it the hardest, wanted to come with me. The hardest thing I ever had to do was tell that dear, wonderful man that I felt his place was there in New York.

"Dinner that night was very somber, what with everyone struggling to digest the information given them. After dinner I went back to my office, where I tore up the note I'd been writing to Horace, then tossed it into the trashcan. With so much needing to be done, I decided to make some lists. I got out more paper to make the lists, but I quickly got so distraught that I found myself doing more pacing than anything else."

"I can understand that feeling, because I felt that way when we left Ireland."

Eileen patted Kate's hand sympathetically. "I know, dear. I decided that I would walk through the house with my butler, Edwardo, along with my housekeeper, Alisa. Edwardo wrote down what things I was to take while Alisa wrote down what needed to be done in order for me to be ready on time.

"My job was to decide what was going to stay with the estate or go with me. That job took us a few days to complete. The servants flew about in a mad rush to accomplish everything. With everyone feverishly working, it was no surprise that I was ready a day ahead of my departure time.

"Ralph, the gardener, and Edwardo shipped several crates and trunks on ahead, where I picked them up prior to leaving Salmon. Everyone was so great. I would never have made it without them. Horace came over that last evening to give me my tickets along with my travel instructions. While we had tea and crumpets, we chatted about old times. Not long after that, he left."

"The last night at the estate was very difficult for all of us. I went to bed but couldn't sleep. Finally, giving up I went to sit by the window. Snow was falling softly, blanketing everything with a mantle of white. I didn't realize it at first, but tears were also falling down my cheeks. I wasn't sorry that I was going," she hastened to add.

"Somehow I was just saying goodbye to that dear old house, a refuge that had not only sheltered me all of my life, but also my family for many generations back." A lump rose in her throat, making it impossible to go on for a moment. Finally, taking a deep breath she began. "Then, too, it was difficult to let go of all the familiar surroundings I had ever known … everything that was so dear to my heart."

Kate nodded understandingly. "That is always really hard to do."

"I don't know how long I sat by the window before I finally went back to bed. The wind seemed to be scolding me, as it howled, causing tree branches to rattle against the window pane. The creaking house groaned out its nightly refrain. Finally, in the wee hours of the morning, I fell into a light sleep. I was to take the train out of Grand Central Station at two o'clock in the afternoon, so I was able to finish packing my last minute things and eat a hurried meal, and still get there in plenty of time."

Tears filled her eyes, forcing her to take a moment to gain control. Finally, impatiently brushing at the tears she plunged on. "Edwardo surprised me by hugging and kissing me on the cheek. After safely seeing me settled in my Pullman, he said goodbye. Before I could say anything he rushed away."

"It seemed as though I've traveled forever. The worst of the journey was from Salmon to the fort, because that driver drove that team like a mad man! There were times when I feared he would kill the horses or turn the wagon over, thus killing us all. When I tried to get him to go slower, he defiantly drove them all the harder." She shuddered at the memory.

"We had to go up a steep, rutty, twisting trail until we reached the top, then repeated the process going down the other side. He drove so wildly that I had to clutch the wagon seat for fear of falling off, then we had to spend two nights on the trail, which was extremely nerve racking to me."

"Mr. Burns, that was his name, wore a faded, multi-patched yellow plaid shirt with black baggy pants that were held up with black suspenders. He was so fat that his tummy bulged over the waistband of his pants.

"He always had a lighted cigarette dangling between thick lips. Not only was the smoke offensive, but there was also an awful odor coming from his person. I doubt that he'd had a bath in at least six months … maybe even longer." Eileen ran a hand over her face as if that would help her remove the awful memory. "You know, Kate, he reminded me of a hairy old grizzly."

"Sounds downright handsome to me, Auntie," teased Kate.

Eileen eyed her suspiciously, wrinkled her nose disdainfully, then ignored her. "That first night, Mr. Burns pulled off the road near a turbulent river. After unhitching the horses he took them to the water to drink their fill before taking them to a grassy area, where he hobbled them. "

"After Mr. Burns had the team hobbled, he built a roaring fire. Going over to the wagon he rummaged around under the wagon seat. He grunted in satisfaction when he found what he was looking for. I shuddered when he triumphantly displayed a bottle of rotgut whiskey." Kate's nose wrinkled in disdain, but she remained silent.

"He began to imbibe heavily from the bottle's contents while getting dinner ready. At first I didn't want to eat because he was such a dirty, filthy cook, but somehow I got down a few bites of that awful swill!" She shuddered involuntarily.

"After supper he brought two blankets from the back of the wagon, which he threw near the fire. Disgustingly picking up one of the blankets, I wrapped myself up in it. Going over to a tree, I sank to the ground, huddling there all night. I was miserable, bone-weary, but I wasn't about to go to sleep while he was guzzling that garbage!

"Finally, he took the other blanket and wrapped it around himself, then he lay down near the fire. From his loud snoring, I knew he was asleep. Feeling safer, I too went to sleep."

"The wind was so cold at daybreak that I wasn't able to stay warm. I got up to wander around camp in an attempt to get some much needed heat into these stiff old bones. While that old coot was still sleeping soundly, I had a great time with the horses. They nickered softly as I scratched their ears, rubbed their necks, or talked soothingly to them. One of the horses lifted his head and looked toward camp when he nickered. Slowly following his gaze there stood Mr. Burns scowling at me." Kate unconsciously held her breath as she waited expectantly. "I guess he didn't like me fussing over his horses."

Eileen shrugged and chuckled softly. "Ignoring him, I continued to rub the horse's neck until I was good and ready to go back to camp. Mr. Burns had the fire going when I got back, so I went to sit near it, grateful for the warmth it provided.

"He snarled at me in disgust as he rattled off something about my leaving his horse alone. Promptly ignoring me, he rattled the kettles while getting breakfast." Eileen shivered as if cold, then shuddered involuntarily.

"Breakfast was no better than the swill the night before, but I tried to eat some of it, knowing that I needed to keep up my strength. When he took the dishes down to the creek to wash them, I went to the wagon. Climbing inside, I began to rummage through my small satchel for a comb, soap and a towel.

"Finding them, I got out of the wagon and went some distance away from camp to make myself presentable for the day. When I came back, he not only had the wagon loaded, but he also had the horses hitched to the wagon. When I saw how impatiently he was waiting for my return … you can bet your bottom dollar, that I took my own sweet time about putting my things back into my satchel."

Kate smiled in spite of herself. "Finally when I was ready, I climbed down from the back of the wagon, went to the front, where I waited for him to help me up. Grumbling to himself about all weak, feeble-minded women always needing help, he helped me up onto the wagon seat. Still grumbling under his beard, he climbed up. Picking up the reins, he yelled at the poor horses, striking them with the whip."

Anger flashed from Kate's eyes, but she bit her bottom lip in an attempt to control her emotions. "I was grateful when the sun came up as it eased the discomfort in my aching bones. That crazy fool driver drove the horses even harder than the day before." Kate's eyes burned with unspoken anger.

"When we didn't stop for lunch I was grateful, as I didn't want any more of his rotten food. Toward noon the clouds began to gather until they had obscured the sun. The wind ripped through me, once more chilling me to the bone. The bumping, along with the careening of the wagon, began to wear on my nerves.

"I longed for the time when we would make camp. Yet at the same time I dreaded it, for it meant another miserable night. Two hours later, the wind picked up, drawing the impending storm even closer, and lightning flashed with thunder echoing all around us. Static electricity ran along my arms, making my already taut nerves ragged."

"Mr. Burns found a good place to camp. He helped me down before taking care of the horses. I offered to fix supper while he got the fire going. Mr. Burns looked at me as if I was a strange person but grudgingly gave in. I rummaged through his food box, groaning at the scanty contents.

"Realizing there was nothing I could do but make the best of a bad situation, I began to work quickly. Calling him over when it was ready, I covertly watched as he took a bite. When he looked up, he caught me looking at him. Scowling, he quickly looked away. Several times during the meal, I caught him looking at me differently."

The mischievous gleam was back in her eyes. "There were no words of praise, but then I didn't expect any. However, his expressions said a lot."

"After dinner was over, I took the dishes to the creek to clean them up. I returned in time to see him climbing out of the back of the wagon. Removing the cork from his bottle of booze, he swaggered over to the fire.

"You can imagine my surprise when he told me that he'd made a bed in the back of the wagon. He said it wasn't much, but it would keep me out of the storm. Thanking him, I went toward the wagon. I hadn't gone far when the rain began to fall in great torrents, blending with the clapping thunder. Each time lightning flashed it illuminated the ebony night.

"The air was so charged with electricity that my already nerve-racked body grew even more distressed. The bed was as hard as the ground, but as I listened to the rain, I was grateful that I didn't have to sleep out in the open.

"Not long after I got into the crude bed, I heard Mr. Burns crawl under the wagon. I figured he wouldn't get too cold … after all he had that bottle as a bed partner."

"No doubt of that," said Kate.

"In spite of being in out of the rain, I just couldn't stay warm. I huddled there with my arms around my knees in an attempt to get some heat, but it was no use. I could hear Mr. Burns under the wagon, taking deep gulps from his bottle far into the long night. I don't know how soon he fell asleep. I only knew that all at once he was snoring.

"The next morning as the rain was still falling heavily, we didn't try to fix breakfast. After Mr. Burns got the horses hitched to the wagon, he helped me up onto the seat. Surprisingly, he drove the team a little better that morning. Perhaps it was due to the fact that he was too busy watching for deep holes.

"All morning we struggled along, not making very good time. There were times I felt that I'd been right about being too old to travel. The rain finally stopped. As you can see, we were able to make it here to the fort.

"Oh, I just knew every bone was broken, as I was helped down from that wagon. Every muscle … every joint … every little inch of my body … protested. Not only did it do it then, it's still doing it. Oh … when Paul grabbed me … swung me around … I just knew for sure I was going to die!"

Kate hugged Eileen lovingly, "I'm so glad that you're safely here, Auntie."

"Between you, me and the proverbial gate post, I'm very happy to be safe."

Not long after that, Paul returned with several soldiers laden down with trunks, crates or luggage, putting everything on the porch. As they were about to return for another trip, Paul blew a kiss at both ladies. They made several trips, until they had the porch piled high with Eileen's possessions.

Corporal Adams rushed excitedly up to Paul. Saluting, he waited for permission to speak. "At ease, Corporal."

"Sergeant Peters sent me to tell you that a column of soldiers are approaching from Missoula, sir!"

"Very well, Corporal. That will be all." The corporal saluted, then sped away. *Well,* Thompson told himself sternly, *there's definitely no rest for the wicked!* He stepped inside to tell the women that there were soldiers approaching from Missoula. He told them that he had to go see to their needs. Kissing each one in turn, he hastened away. Rushing over to speak to the guard on duty, Thompson saw a column of soldiers approaching the gate. When he readily picked out Colonel Williams among the column, Thompson shuddered involuntarily, knowing that he was about to come face to face with his fate.

CHAPTER 21

The Meeting

Thompson waited for Colonel Williams to enter Thornton's office, hesitating a moment as John, who had escorted Williams to the office, went toward home. Taking a deep breath, Paul entered. Colonel Williams was already seated at Thornton's desk removing papers from his leather bag. He looked up as Thompson remained standing at attention. "As you were, Captain," Thompson lowered his hand. "Take a seat while I scan these papers." The colonel finally looked up from his stack of papers to ask, "Where is Major Thornton right now?"

Thompson answered cautiously. "Major Thornton took three men and rode out toward the Indian village to see if I really did follow orders."

"Do you know this for a fact, Captain?"

"Yes, sir. I sent our scout, Nataka Hansen, out to warn the Indians of Thornton's intentions. He came back yesterday with the report that Thornton had indeed gone to the Indian village. Finding it empty, he apparently followed signs left when the Indians went to their new location. Nataka intercepted them. Then following my orders, he stripped them of their horses, weapons and clothes ... everything that is, but their long-johns."

Williams remained expressionless throughout Thompson's statement. "I see," he replied. "My deepest apologies for taking so long to get back to you, Captain, but there was a lot of excitement at Fort Missoula, as well."

"Oh. I see."

"Let's get started on the situation here, shall we?" Williams picked up a sheet of paper from the pile on the desk, which he quickly scanned. "You state here in this note that Major Thornton gave you orders to annihilate the Indians. Is that correct?"

"Yes, sir."

"Do you still have the orders?"

"Yes, sir." Thompson reached inside his right shirt pocket extracting a piece of paper. After unfolding it, he handed it over to Williams, who scrutinized it thoroughly. Thompson watched the colonel's face, but he could read no expression there.

Williams finally set the paper with his other paper work then raised his head. "You told me in your note that you planned to disobey the orders."

"Thompson nodded affirmatively. "Yes, sir, I did."

"Correct me if I am wrong, but didn't I tell you to carry on because I had problems at Fort Missoula that were more pressing." Thompson nodded but remained silent. Williams looked down at the orders a moment then back to Thompson. "Something must have happened to make Thornton give you such an order."

Thompson leaned forward in his seat to face Williams uneasily. "Sir, may I have permission to speak candidly?"

"Yes, please do, Captain."

"I know what caused him to issue such an order, but I must state that it isn't entirely the Indians' fault."

"Elaborate more fully on that, Captain!"

"There were several Indian tribes who were attacking the settlers around Missoula twenty-one years ago. Because many troops were out on patrols, or engaged in skirmishes, the fort was vulnerable. Chief Swift Eagle's tribe, the tribe we were ordered to eliminate, took advantage of the fort's vulnerability. Riding into the fort with a lot of braves, they raped, murdered or plundered at will. Storm Cloud, Swift Eagle's brother, defiled Thorton's wife Anna, then beat her and left her for dead."

Thompson paused to recollect his thoughts before going on. He finally continued. "When Thornton found out what had happened to Anna he flew into a terrible rage. Then when he learned that she was with child, Thornton slipped over the edge of reasoning. Anna was never allowed to forget what had happened. Thornton took great delight in abusing her every chance he got. Those of us at the fort have endured the brunt of his wrath for many years. Sir, when we came to the fort, his wife Anna befriended my wife Kate. They have become close friends.

"One day Kate stopped Thornton from killing Anna by brandishing a knife at him. Ever since then Major Thornton has hated Kate vehemently. When the major found Anna helping Kate during the birth of our twins, he went on a terrible rampage, nearly killing Anna." Williams' eyes flashed with anger as he listened to Thompson. "Over the years this hatred of the Indians has grown ... festered, until he defied the peace treaty by issuing those orders for their extinction."

When Thompson had finished, Williams sat silently pondering his words. Finally, Williams leaned back in his seat. Taking a deep breath before speaking, "I have only been stationed at Fort Missoula for two years, yet each time I've visited this fort I have been unaware of the turbulent emotions boiling so deeply in him."

"Major Thornton has become very adept at camouflaging his true feelings, sir. When we first came here, I thought he was a great officer. I always tried to obey his orders without question. Then when Anna told my wife what was really happening here I was stunned. At first, I refused to believe it but little by little, his true self began to emerge ... until he has become a very bitter spiteful man."

"I see. Please go on."

"When I first got the orders to annihilate the Indians, I was determined to obey the orders." Thompson paused for a moment, and then continued. "But when we left the fort, my conscience began to plague me. I found myself facing a huge dilemma … one that I didn't know how to handle." Williams waited for him to continue. "Sir, I have never disobeyed an order in all of my years in the service … nor have I ever believed in wantonly taking another human being's life."

Thompson had to stop to collect his jumbled thoughts before he could proceed. "I didn't want innocent blood on my hands, sir. I just didn't know what to do or where to turn. I finally took it to a higher power and then was able to make the decision. I know that disobeying those orders means court martial … even possible death, but I would rather face my maker with my hands clean than to obey an order that was unfounded … unrighteous! Also, since I will be retiring from the service soon, I want to leave with a good service record."

Not giving Williams a chance to speak, Thompson hastened on, "Sir, the Indians have honored the treaty. They do not deserve to be annihilated. I just could not take the life of innocent women or little children! Then when we found them so ill, I knew with a certainty that the orders were very … very … wrong." Thompson grew more passionate about the issue as he spoke. "Do with me as you will, sir, but I am not sorry that I disobeyed those orders!"

Williams began drumming his fingers on his desk as he sat pondering Thompson's comments. Meanwhile Thompson struggled to gain control of his emotions. "I have to agree with you, Captain. The orders were not only unfounded but were completely out of line. Thornton's behavior should have been brought to my attention long before it got to the issuing of these orders."

"I know, sir, but we dared not buck him. The consequences were just too great!"

"We have been having problems at Fort Missoula which have needed my attention for some time as well, so perhaps I wouldn't have been much help then either. I doubt that we would have ever resolved the issue if it hadn't been for John Whipple." As Colonel Williams spoke, Thompson saw a look of awe cross his face. He couldn't help wondering what it meant.

"You see, John saw the family of Jared Martin killed. It was your wife who convinced him to come to Missoula to report their deaths to me. On his way there, he accidentally stumbled into the outlaws' hideout. Just as he was finding a good hiding spot, he heard horses approaching.

"The night of the murders, he saw a horse with strange marking as the thieves sped away. When the outlaws rode into their hideout, John spotted the horse again. He listened to the outlaw leader, Corporal Maines, speak to his lieutenant, Corporal Reno—"

"So, Corporal Reno has been found at last. I never liked the man because of his shifty attitude and laziness. What did you do with him?"

"I'm coming to that in just a moment."

"Excuse me sir … please go on."

Williams eyes twinkled merrily as he continued, "He listened as the two outlaws bragged about their nasty crimes, also what they planned for another family, the Pedersens, later that night. As scared as he was, John waited for the outlaws, who were drinking, gambling or gloating over their evil deeds, to pass out so that he could steal their horses.

Impressed by his young friend, Thompson stared at Williams. "He did?"

"Yes, he did! In my book ... that is one very courageous young man."

"I agree, sir."

Williams sat forward in his seat gazing at Thompson intently. Changing the subject he said, "I commend you, Captain, for standing up to your convictions, for doing what you thought was right. With these facts, I absolve you from disobeying Thornton's orders."

Thompson blinked at him in surprise. "Did I hear you right ... you aren't going to court martial me for disobeying orders?"

Seeing Thompson's look of dismay, Williams smiled, "No, Captain. You did the only thing you could do under the circumstances. Major Thornton went against the treaty when he issued those orders. He could have caused another terrible Indian uprising." Shuddering at the thought, Williams was forced to pause a moment before he could go on. Finally, he continued, "We've had more than enough bloodshed to last us forever! We ... as a people ... no matter the color or race ... have got to learn to live together in peace ... in harmony. If we don't, we'll be forever fighting one another. No, Captain, you can rest assured that you did what was right."

Thompson sighed gratefully, relief flooding his whole being. "Thank you for understanding, sir."

Williams ignored him as he began to rifle through the desk drawers. "Where does Thornton keep his writing paper?"

"In the bottom left-hand drawer, sir."

"Good!" Williams opened the drawer to extract a sheet. "Thompson, I am going to write a letter. I want it sent to Fort Missoula by the most reliable soldier you have." After uncapping the inkbottle, he picked up the pen, dispensed it into the ink and began to write quickly. Thompson rose and crossed over to open the door. Stepping out onto the porch, he looked around. Observing Peters standing several feet from the porch, Thompson suspected that he'd been there in case of trouble. This pleased him. "Peters, come here on the double!"

Peters rushed forward, saluted, then stood rigidly at attention waiting for Thompson to speak. "Yes, suh."

"Sergeant, I want Private Michael Cooper here on the double."

"Yes, suh." Saluting, Peters hurried off toward the barracks. Thompson stepped back into the office to wait.

When Williams was finished, he laid the pen down. Picking up the paper, he blew on it until the ink was dry. Folding the letter, he slipped it into an envelope. After sealing it, he scribbled something onto the front. After wiping the pen, he laid it back onto the desk. Recapping the inkbottle, he rose to walk around the office, surveying the room's contents.

There was a knock at the door, and Private Cooper entered, saluted, then stood rigidly at attention. "As you were, Private," said Williams. Cooper slowly lowered his arm. "You are to carry this envelope to Fort Missoula as fast as possible. Personally deliver it to Major Brown, then wait for his reply. When you have it, hurry back."

"Yes, sir." Taking the envelope that Williams handed him, Cooper stuffed it inside his shirt. Saluting, he hurried out the door, slamming it behind him.

Williams stared at Thompson strangely. "Thompson, did you really have Thornton, along with his men stripped down to their long-johns?"

"Yes, sir."

"What possessed you to do that to them, man? Surely there was another way to detain them."

Thompson sighed and slumped down into a nearby chair. "I discovered he was leaving the fort only a few minutes after his departure. When he wouldn't give me any details of their intended maneuver, I suspected what he was up to. Then a private came to me to tell me that he heard Thornton telling his three hand-picked men discussing their vile plans."

Thompson paused a moment, then went on. "I must admit, sir, that I just flat-out panicked." Thompson looked at Williams to see what he would do, but he remained expressionless. "The only thing that came to me was to detain them anyway I could, in order to give you time to get here. I figured you could decide what to do with the situation."

Williams nodded, but remained silent. "While I waited for Peters to bring the scout to me, the idea of stripping them and taking away their horses popped into my head. Before anything else could be thought of, the scout was in front of me. I gave him those orders then sent him on his way."

"Let the chips fall where they may was the idea, huh?"

Thompson nodded. "Yes, sir."

Williams absently drummed his fingers on the desk. After a few minutes, he folded his hands, "Well … it wasn't the proper thing to do, but I believe if I were in your situation, I might find myself making the same kind of decision."

Williams rose to scrutinize a map on the wall across the room, while Thompson waited with baited breath for the punishment that he was sure was forthcoming. All at once, Williams turned to face Thompson. "I know that I should punish you for what you've done to a superior officer, but, so help me Hannah, when I try to think of a punishment, my mind conjures up the image of Thornton hobbling back to the fort in just his long-johns. It's so dad-blamed funny … that there's no punishment good enough!"

Williams was seized with a fit of sidesplitting laughter. It was awhile before he was able to gain control. Finally, taking a deep breath, Williams went back to his chair, "We won't let the others know that I lost control, will we, Captain? Wouldn't do to see a superior officer so undignified."

Thompson struggled not to laugh, but found it very difficult. "No, sir, it surely wouldn't!"

"Very good, Captain. That will be all."

Thompson rose to salute. "Thank you, sir. Begging your pardon, sir, but would you mind coming with me to see Mrs. Thornton?" Williams looked at him in surprise. "I would like you to see what she has been forced to endure from the major." Williams stuffed his papers into his leather bag before following Thompson out of the office.

When they entered, Anna was sitting up in a chair with a lap robe around her legs. The bruises on her face were starting to change color. She smiled at Thompson sweetly as the two men entered. "Hello, Paul, what brings you here at this time of the day?"

"Colonel Williams is visiting us from Fort Missoula, Anna. I wanted him to come see you."

Anna turned to smile at Williams. "It's so great to see you again, Colonel Williams. How is JaNae?"

Williams reached out to take one of her hands. "She is doing just great! I brought her to the fort to visit with you women while I conducted some business."

"That's wonderful! I would really love to see her."

"I'll see that she knows that." Thompson brought him a chair. Williams placed it in front of Anna then sat down. Gently taking Anna's hands in his, he bowed his head unconsciously rubbing her fingers. It was apparent that he was fighting unspoken anger, while trying to find words to comfort Anna.

Anna was the one to break the silence. "I am getting better now … thanks to the thoughtfulness of Paul and Sergeant Peters. They found me after Carl rushed out of the house." Williams glanced over at Thompson then back to hear Anna say, "Doctor Phelps told me that I could go home tomorrow, if I continue to improve as I have."

"That's just great, Mrs. Thornton."

"Please, sir, just call me 'Anna'." Williams nodded. "I don't want to be reminded of the fact that that animal is my husband!"

Williams tenderly squeezed her hand. "Anna it will be then."

"Thank you." All at once Anna grew excited, "Please stay at our house while you're here, Colonel. Think of it as your home away from home. I doubt that Carl will be back soon. When he goes out on these strange maneuvers, he doesn't usually come back very quickly."

Williams regarded Anna with concern. "I don't want to put you out, ma'am."

She hastened to reassure him. "I'm stuck here for tonight at least, so it's no imposition at all! There are two bedrooms, so when I do come home tomorrow, you won't be in the way at all."

Williams gratefully smiled. "Very well then, we'll gladly take you up on your offer."

"Good!"

Williams rose to go. Gently placing a hand on her shoulder, he looked down into her eyes. "What a pity it is that Major Thornton doesn't know the rare, beautiful jewel he has."

Anna gulped back the tears that threatened to spill from her eyes. "Why ... what a kind thing to say!" Anna watched them leave. She pondered the kind words that Williams had said, promptly storing them away in her mind for the future.

❧❧ ❧❧

Time seemed to fly by for those at Fort Owen, as they worked on preparation for the next day's celebrations. For once, the old fort fairly hummed with laughter and merriment. Williams, who had learned that Thompson would be in the dunking booth, eagerly gave his approval. Watching Thompson struggle with the situation, he puffed out his chest like a strutting rooster. "Yes, sir, I'm going to enjoy dunking you, Captain."

Seeing the amusement on Peters' face, Thompson shrugged nonchalantly then added, "Perhaps, but we'll see!"

The soldiers bantered good-naturedly back and forth, plainly excited about the merriment. Those in charge of the different outdoor contests were busy signing the contestants' numbers. When John Whipple entered Beauty, Peters walked around the horse, looking him over critically. "Ya haf a right beautiful hoss there, Whipple," he announced approvingly. "Howsumever, he 'peers ta be a might bit winded."

John, knowing how Peters delighted in teasing, shrugged his shoulders nonchalantly. "Be that as it may, I know that he'll beat your horse Tulips hands down, Sergeant!"

Peters critically looked the horse over again. "Ah reckon ez how he'll haf him a tough job a doin' that thar deed, Whipple."

Corporal Adams seeing his opportunity quickly seized it. "I'm agona lay my bet on Whipple. A horse that proud, that beautiful, has to be a thoroughbred."

Soon everyone was placing bets on who would win the race. Several entrants would give the two horses a run for their money. While the men haggled over who was going to win the horse race, some of the women were busily arranging their crafts in the different booths, curious to see what the other women had entered. Still others were baking up a storm in their kitchens.

JaNae, who was visiting with the women folk, enjoyed the gaiety. John Whipple walked toward her as she sat visiting with his mother, Hattie. JaNae turned toward him with a smile. "Hello, John." Hattie beamed at the sight of her son, but remained silent as she observed their interactions. It was plain to see that there was a special bond between the two of them.

Hattie remembered JaNae telling how her son had come to the fort and courageously turned in the men who'd been raiding and killing people around the settlements. JaNae had called him a hero. Hattie remembered her telling how he'd made many lifelong friends at the fort, especially to a little dog called Pugger.

JaNae had gone on to explain how John had saved the dog and her pups from drowning. Laughing, she had confessed how she, too, had taken in one of the pups, and how it already thought it was the boss. She had wanted to bring it but thought it best to leave it with Jeffries, the man who runs the stables. Hattie remembered all of this as she watched her son speak to JaNae. She lovingly filed it away in her mother's heart.

"Have you been over to see Mrs. Thompson yet, John?"

"No. I was just thinking of going over there in a minute or two."

"I haven't, either. Would you mind walking over with me?"

"Not at all, JaNae."

Hattie gently scolded John. "You shouldn't call Mrs. Williams 'JaNae'."

JaNae chuckled. "I told him that I preferred to be called JaNae, because calling me Mrs. Williams made me feel old ... unapproachable."

"Oh," replied Hattie in surprise.

"Please, you call me 'JaNae', too, Hattie."

"Very well, then. I will!"

"Won't you come with us, dear? I would love to have your company as well."

"I'd like that very much," said Hattie, pleased to be included.

"Good!" exclaimed JaNae, rising to go.

John fell into step between the two of them. "Say, ain't I the lucky one!" Both women looked at him strangely. "I get to escort two lovely ladies to the Thompson's." Both women punched him lightly in the ribs. "Ah," he cried, feigning great pain, "is that a nice way to treat your escort, ladies?" Both women winked at each other and punched him lightly again. "I guess it is."

They soon reached the Thompson's home. Stepping up onto the porch, they knocked. Kate opened the door. Stepping back, she invited them in. "What a wonderful surprise!" The three entered waiting for Kate to close the door. She pointed toward Eileen, "I'd like you to meet Paul's aunt, Eileen Thompson."

Then turning back to the three visitors, she introduced them. "This is JaNae Williams, wife of Colonel Williams, who is visiting us from Fort Missoula." Eileen rose to shake hands with JaNae. Both women took to each other immediately. "This is Hattie Whipple, who lives here at the fort. The young man is her son, John Whipple." The two shook hands. "John did the chores for me while Paul was away on maneuvers."

JaNae turned to smile sweetly at John. "I'm not surprised about that. He was a great help to the both of us while he was at Fort Missoula."

John was visibly embarrassed at the praise given him. He wanted desperately to change the subject. All at once an idea came to him. "Could I see the new baby, ma'am?"

A mischievous gleam came into Kate and Eileen's eyes. "Sure! Won't you all please be seated?" JaNae and Hattie sat down at the table near Eileen. "John, you sit here," ordered Kate indicating the rocker by the door. John sat down looking at Kate strangely. "I'll be right back."

Eileen rose to follow Kate. "Let me help you, dear." John looked first at Hattie then JaNae. The women's eyes sparkled with delight, but they remained silent.

"Close your eyes, John," cried Kate from the bedroom. Again, John looked at his mother, who only shrugged. Shaking his head slightly, John closed his eyes. The two women emerged from the bedroom, each carrying an infant. Hattie and JaNae giggled. Kate took John's right arm lifting it enough to hold the baby, then placed her son into his arm. "Don't you peek yet," Kate ordered. Lifting the baby from Eileen's arms repeated the process with John's other arm. John's face displayed shock, but he remained silent. When both babies were secure, Kate stepped back. "You can open your eyes now, John."

John's eyes flew open. He stared in wonder as he looked from one infant to the other. "Twins?" The women burst out laughing at John's surprised expression. He looked up at Kate in awe. "Twins!"

"Kate nodded, watching him intently. "That's right, John." He could only stare at each infant in turn. "It was quite a surprise to us, as well."

"I should say!" He paused a moment to get his thoughts together. "What did you name them, ma'am?"

"The boy is Aaron Joseph … the girl is Sarah Anna-Heleen."

"Somehow the names seem to fit them. These tykes are really beautiful!"

"Thank you," said Kate, pleased beyond words. As if on cue, Sarah yawned sleepily. John smiled when her mouth made a sucking motion with her rosebud lips. Aaron on the other hand slept on unconcernedly. John grinned at them both. Kate reached out to take her daughter from him, which she handed to JaNae. Taking her son, she handed him to Hattie. Eileen watched the women as they admired each infant. Kate hovered like a protective hen with her chicks. Finally, the women handed the sleeping infants back to Kate and Eileen, who took them back to their beds.

When they returned, the five of them spent an enjoyable hour together. Finally JaNae rose to go. "I think we've bothered the two of you long enough. I have really enjoyed our visit, Kate." John and Hattie nodded.

Kate spoke for them both. "We have, too, JaNae." She turned to John with an impish grin. "I'll always treasure your shocked expression when you saw the twins."

John laughed good-naturedly at the joke played on him. "I'll not soon forget the trick you pulled, either." That brought peals of laughter from everyone. They hugged each other, bid their goodbyes, then left.

When they were outside, John hugged his mother. "I promised Captain Thompson I'd help him, but I'll be home in time for dinner."

"Very well, Son, see you at dinner." John nodded and walked away as the two women walked toward the community hall.

Anna, who had been released to go home that morning, lay sleeping peacefully in Miles' bed. JaNae quietly entered the house some time later. She tiptoed into the room to check on her. Finding her sleeping peacefully, she tiptoed back out to the kitchen. JaNae searched through the cupboards for the ingredients needed to prepare the evening meal.

She was setting the table when Williams entered, so she stopped long enough to kiss him sweetly upon the lips. He sat at the table chatting with her while she worked. When it was ready, she prepared a good-sized portion on a plate and slipped it onto a cookie sheet. Pouring a cup of coffee, she placed it onto a saucer next to the plate. Adding a napkin under the eating utensils, she took it to Anna's room. She found Anna trying to sit up in bed. Setting the tray onto the dresser, JaNae began to scold Anna. "And what do you think you're doing?"

Anna slumped back down upon the bed. "I thought I would at least come out to the table to eat."

JaNae grew just a little stern with her. "Tonight you are going to stay in bed so that you can conserve your energy for tomorrow." After helping Anna into a better sitting position, she fluffed up the pillows, placing them behind her. That finished, she placed the tray on Anna's lap.

Anna sighed contentedly. "Thank you for being so good to me, Mrs. Williams."

"Please call me 'JaNae'."

"Okay," replied Anna. Picking up her fork, Anna took a bite of her dinner. "Yum!" This is wonderful!"

"Thank you, dear," beamed JaNae. "I'll be back in a little while to take your tray. After the dishes are done, I'll help you get settled for the night."

Anna nodded, "Thank you."

JaNae went back to the kitchen to take her place at the table. They ate in companionable silence. Williams rose, came around to her chair to kiss her tenderly. "Thank you for a superb dinner, honey." JaNae beamed under his praise. "I am going back to help finish up the last minute details for the celebration tomorrow."

"Very well, dear." JaNae went to get Anna's tray so it could be washed with the rest of the dishes. It didn't take her long to clean up the kitchen. Satisfied, she went to help Anna get ready for bed. Removing her apron, she went to sit on the porch swing. As she gently rocked the swing, JaNae listened to the activities in the fort. She felt awed as she watched the sun slip over the horizon.

She thought of Anna Thornton in the bedroom. A great pity engulfed her as she tried to imagine all that Anna had gone through. She couldn't help wondering how a man could be so mean to such a sweetheart like her.

A sweet peace enveloped JaNae, as she thought of the love Jedidiah had for her. So poignant were the feelings that tears filled her eyes, then spilled unnoticed down her cheeks. She wanted Anna to have that same kind of love.

Even as she desired it for her, she knew that she would never have that kind of love with Carl Thornton. Sighing she looked heavenward. "Please, dear God … get Major Thornton out of Anna's life. Let her find someone to love her like my Jedidiah loves me … someone who will fill her life with joy … who will bring a sweet happiness into her life … such as I have in mine. Anna has suffered so much from a man who doesn't have the capacity to see her gentle spirit let alone her kind generosity. There is so much more that I would like to ask of you, but I don't have the ability to express it all. However, Lord, you know what is best, so let thy will be done according to thy sweet will …"

CHAPTER 22

A Time for Fun

Amazingly the morning of the Fourth dawned bright and beautiful, with not a cloud in the sky. It was as though the elements were contributing to the fun that lay ahead. The fort buzzed with activity long before daylight, as the different households prepared for the day's events.

Thompson rose from the breakfast table to help his wife Kate do the breakfast dishes. Paul's Aunt Eileen made the beds and straightened up the house. When the dishes were done, Paul helped Kate with the fussing twins. They were almost ready to go when there was a knock at the door. Thompson walked over, opened it, and then stepped back in surprise. "Why, John, what brings you here?"

As John Whipple stood smiling, Paul noticed a mischievous sparkle in his eyes. "Well … Pa made you a gift, which he asked me to deliver to you." He stepped back to reveal a strange apparatus.

Thompson stared at the contraption a moment, not at all sure what he should do. After mulling it over a moment in his mind, he examined it closely. Finally he looked up at John with a blank expression. "I don't mean to appear ungrateful or dim-witted, but what is this thing anyway?"

John couldn't help but laugh at the expression on Thompson's face. "I asked Pa that very same question the first time I saw it. He said he didn't know a technical name for it, but he called it a twin-baby-buggy."

With brows puckered, his nose wrinkled quizzically. Thompson gawked at John. "A what?"

"Pa called it a twin-baby-buggy."

The buggy was fashioned with heavy, black canvas. It was complete with a pouch to carry the items needed when away from the house, as well as two matching hoods. Brightly colored fringe made from coarse material ran across the front of each hood. Matching quilts adorned each little bed, brightening the dark exterior. All four wheels, the handle and the framework were all made of knotty pine. Everything had been sanded and stained to perfection.

John stepped down from the porch while he began to explain the different parts of the buggy and its uses. "Pa told me that he placed hoods over the beds so that there would be shade on the twins as you walk in the sun. Ma added her touches by making the goose-down mattress, the matching quilts, and the fringe for Pa to place on the front of the hoods. She said it would help dress it up. As you can see, behind each bed is a pouch to put the baby's didies or other paraphernalia in, when you are away from the house.

Listening to John's prattle, Thompson again surveyed the buggy, growing more excited. "Let's bring it inside." Together, they got it inside. "Wow! This is marvelous! Kate will be so thrilled!"

"What's marvelous?" Kate called from the bedroom.

Thompson winked at John in a conspiratorial manner. "Come see, honey."

Kate emerged from the bedroom to gaze around Paul. Her eyes grew large with surprise then sparkled with delight. "Oh, John! How wonderful!" She surprised the young man by giving him a big bear hug. "This is just the ticket!" John turned beet red as he looked at Kate in astonishment. She punched him lightly on the arm. "Don't tell me you've never been hugged before," she teased.

Thompson came to John's rescue, apparently deeply touched by his friend's kind gesture. "Tell Jonathon that we're much obliged for his thoughtfulness."

"I will. Right now I'd better get back to help them get ready to go."

John slipped his hands into his pants pocket. He began to whistle some merry little tune as he ambled toward home. "He is the most thoughtful young man I've ever known." Paul readily concurred. Going to the bedroom, he emerged carrying the sleeping Sarah.

After placing her in the buggy, he went back to get Aaron. Kate was fussing with Sarah's blanket when he returned to place Aaron in the other bed. While Kate adjusted Aaron's quilt, Paul placed the necessary items for the day into the pocket in the back. When they were ready, Paul pushed the buggy out onto the porch where he lifted it onto the ground.

Kate helped Eileen with her shawl then wrapped one around her own shoulders. The women carried their baked goods, leaving Paul to manage the buggy.

When they reached the community hall, Paul stayed with the twins while the women took the baked goods to the designated booths. He wasn't surprised to see so many people gawk at the buggy strangely. Some were impressed, some were envious, still others were flabbergasted. Peters, who was among the latter, studied the buggy's every nook, every cranny. Scratching his head in total amazement, he walked over to Paul. "When Whipple told me he were buildin' this here contraption, Ah shorely thunk he'd gone daft. Ah even poked a lil fun at him jest fer the sport a it. Ah went so far ez to tell him thet ifn' ya liked it, Ah'd eat ma own hat. Well Ah'll be dad-blamed ifn' Ah ain't got ta do that very thin'!"

Thompson couldn't resist the temptation to taunt Peters. "Well, old man, I always did think you had a bad case of hoof-and-mouth disease. What's more, I always feared it'd get you into trouble someday." He couldn't resist adding insult to injury by saying, "Want some salt with that hat, Sergeant?"

Peters grinned in spite of himself. "Might not be sich a bad idea, Cap'n. Might not be a bad idea a'tall."

Everyone was roaring, when Kate and Eileen joined the group. Eileen stood back and watched the merriment, while Kate spoke for both of them. "Can anyone join in this fun or is it a private party?"

Paul reached up to pull her down beside him, wrapping his arm around her shoulder. "Peters just informed us that he told Whipple he'd eat his hat if we liked the gift."

Little points of light shimmered in Kate's eyes. "Since we love the gift, do we get to watch you eat the hat?"

Growing testy, Peters whirled around to storm off, muttering under his breath. "Dad-blamed, persnickety woman nohow. Shoulda knowed ya woulda liked it jest ta spite me." This brought more peals of laughter from the group.

The first part of the morning sped quickly by. The judges completed judging the handiworks, the bake goods and all the menagerie of items on display in all the booths. Kate was pleased to see that Ilse Pedersen won a blue ribbon for her bread, also another ribbon for her three-layered German chocolate cake. Eileen had entered her sugar cookies from a secret recipe handed down through her family. They warranted a blue ribbon. Kate won a blue ribbon for her apple pie. Jane won a blue ribbon for her cherry pie, also for her peach pie.

Sadie Atkinson won several blue ribbons in the women's needlework section. There was one for her wedding ring quilt, one for a crocheted lace tablecloth and several doilies. Several women from the wagon train also won blue ribbons; some won red ribbons, while a couple of others won white ribbons. Kate was impressed with the incredible quality and workmanship of the different items on display.

The twins were really good for once, needing only to be fed or changed a couple of times throughout the morning. Kate pushed the buggy over to a safe spot where they could keep an eye on the twins while still helping with the luncheon. They had just started paring potatoes when Anna, helped by Phelps and another soldier, entered. JaNae followed behind the procession, stopping every so often to greet someone. Kate rushed over to welcome her. "You're looking much better, dear."

Anna, who was pleased to see her friend, smiled as she returned the hug. "Thank you, I am feeling much better."

Kate hugged JaNae, "Hello, JaNae. I trust you're having a good time?"

"I sure am. It's so good to see everyone again." Chatting happily, the women went to help with lunch. Anna, who was allowed to do little simple things, was content to be around her friends.

The first outdoor event of the day was the log splitting contest. Hans Pedersen, his oldest son, Eric, and James Payne, from the wagon train, were the only three contestants. Colonel Williams gave the signal to start. Everyone began to cheer the contestants on.

Those from the wagon train rooted Payne on, while those from the settlement or the fort cheered for one of the Pedersens. Both Pedersens were not only large but were muscle-bound from hard work, whereas Payne was scrawny in appearance. Thompson was impressed at the way Payne's axe bit into the log as he methodically struck it. The Pedersens were just as forceful, however they weren't as methodic.

The yelling grew louder with the flying wood chips. Perspiration broke out on the working men, yet they continued to chip away on their logs. Thompson found himself rooting for all of the contestants, yet he remained silent, watching first one man then another.

The suspense continued to mount as the minutes continued to tick away. With one last mighty swing, Payne drove the axe into the log. With a crackling noise the log fell apart. Just after that, Han's log split apart, then Eric's. Those from the wagon train whooped and hollered as they sprang forward to congratulate Payne.

Even the two Pedersen men joined in. Colonel Williams handed Payne a new pocket-watch, which he proudly held up for all to view. Wiping the perspiration from his face, he smiled triumphantly. "Thank you, sir. I was going to get me another watch when I could, because mine broke on the way here from Wyoming. I don't think I could have gotten a grander one, had I tried."

"Attention everyone," shouted Thompson. "Will the partners of the saw cutting contest come forward to get into place?" Hans Pedersen with his son Eric stood across from each other waiting for the other contestants. Payne and another man from the wagon train took their places. Finally, Nataka and Peters joined the group. The men removed their shirts, laid them on some nearby rocks then stepped back into place. When they were ready, Colonel Williams raised the gun high into the air, paused for effect, then pulled the trigger.

The two Pedersens were well matched, as were Payne and his partner, Clarence Jubal. On the other hand, Peters and Nataka were not well matched. Again, the yelling spectators rooted for their favorite team. Thompson was amazed to see how the Pedersens were in perfect unison, never jamming up the saw. Even though Nataka was frustrated with Peters' sporadic jerking motions, they were doing great. Payne and his partner were almost as good as the Pedersens. *It's going to be interesting,* he thought, *to see who will become the winner.*

Saws continued to whine rhythmically as they sliced through the huge logs. Beads of perspiration broke out on the men's faces. Threads of sweat caused their upper torso to glisten in the sunlight. The shouting mounted in volume as the saw blades sliced through the last part of the logs. Thompson noticed that the log of Peters and Nataka had a long way to go before it would fall off. He couldn't help feeling sorry for them.

Cheers rang out from the crowd when the Pedersens' block fell to the ground. A moment later Payne's team's block also dropped to the ground with a loud thud. Thompson noticed Nataka straighten up to heave a huge sigh of relief. Thompson smiled understandingly at Nataka when he met his glance. Nataka raised his eyes heavenward, shaking his head in dismay. Everyone gathered around the Pedersens, either patting them on the back or pumping their hands vigorously as they congratulated them. Colonel Williams took a small pouch out of his inside pocket. Handing them the previously agreed upon amount of ten dollars to Hans Pedersen he shook his hand. "I have never seen such a well-matched pair of sawyers as I have seen today," praised Williams. "Congratulations!"

"Danke, sir," replied Hans, basking in the glory of the moment.

When the well-wishers surrounded the pair, Thompson was touched. The Pedersens were well liked around the fort and the settlement. They were not only honest in their dealings with everyone, but they were warm, caring, and generous. Thompson was pleased to see that they won the blue ribbon and the pouch.

Colonel Williams began bellowing loudly over the crowd to announce the next event. "The last event before lunch will be the foot race. Will those who are participating please line up at the gate?" The contestants didn't have to be told twice. Nataka, Peters, and John Whipple were among the contestants.

Peters as usual was mouthing off by taunting the runners, namely John. "Ah hopes ya got on yer best runnin' boots, Son. Ah've been a runnin' long a fer ya were ever born."

John calmly took it all in stride. "Only time will tell, sir. I think the one you should watch out for though ... is Nataka."

Peters scowled at Nataka in disgust. "Aw, he's still wet behind the ears compared ta a young feller like me." Everyone laughed at that comment, because they knew that Nataka ran early every morning.

When all of the contestants were ready, Thompson stood in front of them to give them the details of the course. "The race will start from the gate ... follow the road up to the cemetery, over to Walter's spread, around Wilson's farm ... then back the same way. As you know, this will take a mile and a half to complete." The contestants nodded. "Good luck to all of you ... may the best man win." Raising the gun Thompson squeezed the trigger. The runners were off in a flash.

While the runners were completing their course, the men not in the race set up the tables outside for the noon meal. There was a lot of good-natured bantering as they worked. They carried out several large containers of food, while the women told them where to set them. There were two long tables placed close together laden down with desserts.

Two more long tables, also close together, were laden down with large platters of stews, baked beans, a side of beef, a rack of lamb and a big shank of carved ham. Several other tables were prepared for those who would soon be eating. Big bowls of fresh butter and several platters of rolls were placed on these tables. Towels were laid over the food to protect it from flies or other pests.

They were just finishing up when someone shouted that the runners were seen coming toward the fort. Everyone hurried over to the gate to watch the runners come in. Nataka was way out in the lead, with Whipple behind him. Josh Taylor was nip and tuck with a man from the wagon train. Peters was seen coming in way behind them. It was apparent to all watching that Peters was struggling desperately to make it to the fort.

His face was red and his breathing was very labored, yet he remained persistent. Cheers rang out as the men neared the gate. Nataka sprinted in first, making the feat appear easy. Whipple and Taylor came next, in that order, with Peters close behind them. Jeers rang out as they taunted their Sergeant unmercifully.

Staggering like a drunken man, Peters limped through the gate falling upon the ground, struggling for air. "By gum … Ah … must be … gettin' … old, ez Ah … ain't got the … sap Ah use ta haf."

Thompson attempted to comfort him. "I'm so sorry, old man, but the truth is … we're both getting too old to do this kind of thing."

Angrily Peters rose to his feet, growing huffy. Peters reminded Thompson of a barnyard rooster. "Speak fer yerself, suh!" Doing the limp, stagger, shuffle step, he hobbled off muttering to himself. "Dad-blamed body, no how! Ah …"

When someone rang the dinner bell, everyone hurried off to eat. After everyone was seated, Thompson rose to look around. "I have asked Colonel Williams to say grace over the food, which he has graciously accepted."

As Thompson sat down, Williams rose, while all bowed their heads. Williams followed with, "Dear Lord … for what we are about to receive, make us truly grateful. Bless those who are here with us with Thy tender mercies. Please grant them their greatest desires. Keep them in Thy watchful care at all times. Thank Thee, Lord, for everything, Amen."

After Williams sat down the young people began to serve the adults. They, the babies and the younger children had previously been fed. Some of the young people were with the younger children, who had been put down for their naps. Soon everyone was visiting as they ate heartily of the bounty before them. Finally, one by one, they sat back, sighing in great satisfaction.

The young people not only cleared the tables, but they also did the cleanup so that the women could enjoy the rest of the day's events. Kate saw to the twins' needs before turning them over to Sylvia. Kissing each one tenderly, she tucked them in, wrapping their blankets loosely around them. Eileen waited for Kate to join her, then they slipped out into the bright afternoon sunshine.

Thompson walked up to them, kissing each one tenderly. "I just came to tell you that I have to get into my costume for the dunking booth. I'll be back as soon as I'm ready."

When he had gone, Eileen leaned over to whisper to Kate. "I haven't said anything before now, but I'm not going to miss my golden opportunity to dunk that nephew of mine!"

Kate giggled. "That I've got to see! It will be priceless to see Paul's expression when you step up to try your hand at dunking him."

Eileen thought about it a moment, then a smile began to tug at the corners of her lips. "It will at that!" Both laughed harder.

John walked over to join them, watching them suspiciously. "What's so funny, or is this a private joke?"

Kate struggled for control, but it was impossible. Finally gaining control, Kate said, "Paul's aunt ... just told me ... that she was ... going to try to dunk Paul. Won't that be rich?" Again, Kate doubled over with laughter. "Oh ... won't that be rich?"

John considered it a moment, then joined in on the fun. "Oh, it surely will!"

The three of them had just gained their composure when Paul entered the community hall. They gawked in stunned disbelief, unable to resist the opportunity of ribbing him unmercifully. John even whistled at him. Thompson was dressed in a pair of sloppy cut off faded blue jeans. A ragged old checkered shirt, open at the neck, was sleeveless. A frayed straw hat set askew on his head. His army boots drew attention to his knobby, hairy knees, making the ensemble appear even worse.

At first, he looked sternly at each one of them, then joined in the merriment. Finally, he frowned growing defensive. "Well ... I didn't want to get my uniform wet. Besides, I do have permission from Colonel Williams to wear this garb."

"Uh huh," teased Kate, "Well ... all I got to say is that it's a good thing he has given his approval ... because I don't know anyone here who would have."

He sadly stuck out his bottom lip as if to cry. "Ah honey ... is that any way to treat your handsome husband?"

Kate reached up to kiss him on the lips. "I'm so sorry, darling, but honestly speaking ... you aren't handsome in that get up at all."

Thompson pouted, feigning hurt pride. "Ah ..."

He was prevented from adding more when Peters walked up to them. "A right smart git-up ya haf on thar, Cap'n."

"That will be enough said about my costume! You all don't know a good thing when you see it!" The group laughed heartily. Thompson grew testy, "If all you're going to do is make fun of my costume, then I'm getting out of here!" He pivoted around angrily, sticking his nose in the air. Thompson wasn't about to admit it, but he found his attire just as ridiculous as they did.

Soon after leaving the group of tormentors, Thompson got into the dunking booth. When he was situated onto the chair, the curtain was opened. Williams called for a volunteer to dunk him. Peters stepped up to pay the designated dime.

Williams handed him three balls then moved aside for Peters to toss them. "Ah've been waiting fer this here event all mornin', en Ah aim ta dunk ya with each a these balls." Taking one of the balls in his right hand, he pulled his arm back. All at once he brought his arm forward throwing the ball hard at the bull's-eye. Pop! The ball hit dead center, releasing the chair, dropping Thompson into the holding tank of water. Cheers rang out from the crowd.

Thompson rose, gasping for air. He was also shivering from the extreme cold. "Wow! That water must be at least forty below zero!" Two soldiers replaced the chair into its former position, then went back to join the crowd.

Thompson got back up into the chair where he began to taunt Peters. "Just because you got in a lucky shot, doesn't mean you'll get me again, Sergeant!" Peters grinned mischievously as he took the second ball with his right hand and repeated the process. Plop! The ball missed its mark completely.

Thompson couldn't resist chiding him as Peters calmly placed the third ball into his right hand. He toyed with it, like a cat with a mouse. "What did I tell you, Peters?" Finally, he pulled his arm back. Smiling fiendishly, he brought it forcibly forward. Pop! It struck the bull's-eye dead center, releasing the chair, once more plunging Thompson into the holding tank. Cheers rang out amid the laughter.

When Thompson came up gasping for air, Peters walked over to the tank to boast proudly. "Ah've been a practicing ma throwin fer a long spell, Cap'n. Ah been alookin' for'ard ta the chaunce ta dunk ya in this here dunkin' device!"

"You may have gotten me today, Sergeant," admitted Thompson, "but you just wait … your day is coming!" As he climbed back onto the chair, he looked determinedly at Peters. "Even if it takes me the rest of my life."

Peters slapped his thigh as he continued to goad Thompson. "Might be so, Cap'n … but taday's mine!" He turned and walked back over to get into the long line that had been forming. Some of the men missed, at which time Thompson taunted them unmercifully. Then Peters stepped forward to pay for three more balls. Patiently, but deliberately, he tossed the ball, striking the bull's-eye, laughing gleefully each time Thompson went down.

Thompson had just gotten back into the chair and gotten comfortable when his Aunt Eileen stepped up to Colonel Williams. "I want a chance to dunk that nephew of mine, so I want forty cents worth." Thompson stared at her incredulously, while Williams counted out the twelve balls. The rest of the crowd stepped back in anticipation, intently watching Eileen to see how she would fare.

Williams, grinning at the spunky lady, handed her the first three balls, "Good luck, ma'am! For what it's worth, my money's on you!"

"Who would have thought that my own dear auntie would want to take a potshot at me?"

Eileen smiled sweetly. She went so far as to blow him a kiss. "There were all those years of caring for you when you were a little boy, when I kissed your boo-boos or watched over you when you were ill. There are the times when you got into one scrape after another leaving me to bail you out. Finally, I was forced to watch my hair turn prematurely gray from worrying about what you'd do next. I'd say that these facts have more than earned me the right to dunk you as many times as I can, my boy!"

Kate stood in the crowd silently watching the interchange between aunt and nephew, loving them both dearly. Eileen rubbed the ball in anticipation, tickled to see Thompson waiting with bated breath.

Feigning distress, Thompson began to plead for mercy. "But dear Auntie, haven't I repented of those days?"

"You can't soft-soap me like you did when you were a boy, Paul Thompson! I always turned the other cheek when you got into trouble, but now it's payback time!" She drew her arm back, then brought it forward, letting the ball go. Plop! It hit the side of the canvas.

"If you're going to throw like that, Auntie … I don't have anything to worry about.

Eileen took another ball and toyed with it a moment before tossing the ball, effortlessly pulling back then forward releasing the ball. Pop! The ball struck the bull's-eye, releasing the chair and dropping Thompson into the holding tank. When he came up for air, she gave him a piece of her mind. "That will teach you not to taunt your auntie, sir! Now get up in that chair so I can continue."

Thompson obediently complied while looking at his aunt in wonderment. Not quite sure how to take this aunt of his, he just stared at her. "Where did you learn to throw like that, Auntie?"

"You forgot that I grew up with five older brothers. I used to pitch for their ball games all the time." She toyed with the ball in her hand. "I guess it is like riding a horse … once you've learned how, you never forget it." The crowd went wild with joy when she threw the ball at the target. Pop! Down went Thompson with a great splash. The crowd cheered heartily for her to do it again.

Four more times she hit the bull's-eye, dunking her nephew. When he came up the fourth time, she turned to Kate. "I think he has been sufficiently chastised by me. I'm giving you the remaining five balls to try your luck. Kate blinked a moment then looked at Paul in consternation.

"Oh good," cried Thompson, "A reprieve at last!" He made the mistake of play-fully winking at Kate. Her green eyes grew large with surprise, to be replaced with determination. An impish grin played around her lips as she stepped forward to take the first ball. "Remember that I love you, honey," he called. Kate blew him a kiss before tossing the ball. Plop! The ball hit the canvas before dropping into the water. "I knew you'd miss. You couldn't even hit the broad side of the barn if you were inside with both doors shut!"

Williams handed her another ball while smiling encouragingly. Taking the ball, Kate gazed innocently up at him, "Thank you, kind sir." She looked determinedly over at Thompson. "You've asked for it now!" Tossing the ball toward the target, she smiled as the ball hit dead center. Pop! The chair dropped, dumping Thompson into the water. Again the crowd went wild with joy.

Kate took up another ball, which she tossed at the bull's-eye. Plop! The ball had missed its mark. She threw another ball. Again the ball missed the bull's-eye.

"One lucky shot out of four isn't bad for an amateur," teased Thompson.

"We'll see," replied Kate. Picking up the fifth ball, she took careful aim. Pop! Down went Thompson with a great splash.

Cheers rent the air, while some men whistled. "Dunk him again," called Phelps handing her the money for three more balls.

Taking one of the balls, Kate again took careful aim. After drawing back her arm, she brought it swiftly forward. Pop! Down went Thompson amid loud cheers. When Thompson was ready again, Kate picked another ball. She repeated the action as before. Pop! Down went Thompson. By now the crowd was chanting boisterously for her to dunk him again.

Taking the last ball, Kate eyed the bulls-eye thinking of sweet revenge. Thompson looked at her with nervous dread as she studied the target. All at once, she threw the ball. Pop! Again as he went down, the crowd went wild. Grown men whooped and hollered at Kate's tenacity. Brushing her hands emphatically, she tossed her head arrogantly and gazed at him sarcastically. "There ... that will teach you to taunt me, Mr. Thompson!" Amid thunderous applause, Kate walked disdainfully away.

Colonel Williams dropped ten cents into the money pot, picked up three balls and got into position. "I have waited for my turn as patiently as possible, but I will wait no longer." Taking the first ball, he took careful aim, then swiftly threw the ball. Pop! Thompson dropped effortlessly into the tank. Williams waited for him to get back into position then threw another ball. Two more times he was dropped into the water, when Williams accurately slammed the balls into the bull's-eye.

This spurred several of the soldiers on. They again lined up to take their turns. Thompson was one very waterlogged individual as he crawled out of the tank two hours later. Kate met him with a dry towel, kissing him tenderly. "I'm really proud of you, darling." She tweaked him playfully on the ear. "In spite of the awful razzing you received, you still remained cheerful ... even when your wife and your auntie dunked you!"

Thompson grabbed her in a tight, wet, bear hug, kissing her soundly upon the mouth. "You'll pay dearly for that little stunt," he whispered passionately into her hair.

"Ooooo!" replied Kate, raising her eyebrows then rolling her eyes. It was apparent that she was desperately trying to ignore her wet clothes as she replied, "That sounds promising!" Slipping out of his arms, she started away. "I can't wait!" Thompson laughed as they sloshed toward home.

The arm wrestling contest was well under way when he returned. He was just in time to see a large burly man from the wagon train win. Williams presented the man with a blue ribbon and a gold watch, which he waved proudly in the air for his friends to see.

"Gentleman, it's time for the long awaited horse race," called Thompson. "Get your mounts then report in front of the gate."

Men scrambled furiously to get their mounts. John told Josh that he wanted him to ride Blacky in the race, while he rode Beauty. When John emerged with Beauty, Peters snorted. "Ah still thin' thet ole bag a wind ain't got no chance in this here race!"

"The problem with you, Peters," John taunted, "is that you know he's a great horse, even a wonderful horse … so you're afraid of being beaten!"

Again, Peters snorted in disgust, then turned his head and spit. "Ne'er happen! At least not with thet excuse of a hoss!"

John laughed outright. "Just what I surmised … you're afraid of being beaten!"

Peters opened his mouth to reply, but was interrupted by Thompson, who announced, "Let me have your attention, men!" The men fell silent as they turned to face him. "The race will start from just outside of the gate. Go three miles south. You'll come to a huge tree on the left, circle the tree then return to the gate." He paused to look intently at the men. "Are there any questions?"

The men remained silent. "Good! Bring your horses out of the fort. Line up where Adams shows you." Quickly, the men led their horses out to Adams, who showed them where to go. "Mount up!" Thompson ordered. When the men were in their saddles, Thompson raised the gun high into the air then squeezed the trigger. The horses leaped forward, plunging off toward the south.

While they waited for the horsemen to return, the men played horseshoes. The children ran three-legged races or sought out their own games to play. Thompson joined in a game of horseshoes. The older men promptly thrashed him and his partner, Eric Pedersen. "You old fogies, just wait until we're older. By then you will have grown too old to cut the mustard … then we'll see who wins."

"We'll wait," replied one of the winners. "'T'will probably be the onliest way ya'll ever win, too!" That brought peals of laughter from the onlookers.

Thompson laughed good-naturedly and nodded. "You're probably right!" He walked over to Colonel Williams. "Please let me know when the riders are sighted, as I have been assigned cleanup detail."

"You bet."

Since the soldiers were already taking the tables in when Thompson entered the community hall, he helped dismantle the booths. The women had just finished removing their items from the booths. They were trying to get out of the way when Thompson entered. As he helped rip the booths apart, Thompson assigned a few soldiers to carry the mess away. They soon had the room back to its original condition. They placed chairs around the room for the dance later on.

A soldier came up to them as they stepped out into the late afternoon sunshine. "Colonel Williams sent me to tell you that the riders have been spotted, sir."

"Thank you," replied Thompson. All the soldiers, including Thompson, headed through the opened gate where they excitedly lined up along the course.

The first sign of approaching riders was a cloud of dust billowing in the distance. Then tiny specks began to take the form of riders. Shouts rang out as a few men in the crowd cheered their favorite rider on. Soon the excitement became so contagious that everyone was spurring his rider to the finish line. Thompson, standing near Colonel Williams, searched for a glimpse of his friends. All at once he saw them. John and Josh were neck and neck, with Peters close behind.

The shouting of the spectators grew even louder as the horses drew nearer. Josh began to inch forward on Blacky, while Peters' horse Tulips began to lengthen out, closing the gap between Josh and John.

All at once, as if on cue, Beauty began to surge forward. Silence fell over the crowd as they gazed in awe at the thoroughbred. Beauty's nostril's flared, his mane fanned out while his tail flew in the wind. His proud sleek body gleamed in the afternoon sunlight. Beauty's powerful muscles rippled in perfect symmetry, conveying to all there that he was running for the pure love of it. Slowly, yet persistently, Beauty began to eat up the distance to the fort.

Tulips came up beside Blacky then slowly moved out in front of him. Josh leaned down to whisper something to Blacky. The horse's stride lengthened, until he was nearly even with Tulips. Meanwhile, Beauty plunged forward, leaving the two to eat his dust.

The crowd cheered wildly as Beauty crossed the finish line. Meanwhile Blacky began to surge forward in an attempt to outdistance Tulips. Little by little Blacky inched ahead until he easily came in second, with Tulips trailing a full length behind.

As the three came to the winner's circle, Peters feigned anger, but his eyes gave him away. He sprinted over to pummel John proudly on the leg. "Ah takes back all Ah said 'bout yer hoss being an ole bag a wind. That's one purty piece of hossflesh!"

John knew what it cost Peters to make that statement. "Thank you, Sergeant."

Peters casually shrugged. "Aw … Ah could'a beat ya … ya young whippersnapper!"

John couldn't resist boasting, as he proudly stroked the horse, "I tried to tell you that this was some horse, but you would hear none of it. I always knew that Blacky could beat Tulips although you bragged otherwise … Today he proved it."

Again, Peters snorted in disgust. "Ya, Ya, Ya! Jest pour the salt on, now thet ya've gone en opened the wound!"

"I'd feel sorry for you, sir … that is if I could just reach you." John extended his arm as if trying to touch Peters.

"Why ya dirty, little scallywag," scolded Peters. "Be off with ya fer Ah tan yer britches fer ya!" Everyone laughed at Peters' predicament, as John dismounted and laughed merrily.

John dismounted and placed a hand on Peters' shoulder so he could look him in the eyes. "I think you're one of the squarest fellows I've ever known, Sergeant!" Blinking in surprise, Peters could only stare at the young man before him. It was plain to all there that Peters was touched deeply. John slowly walked his horse back to the stable.

Thompson and Colonel Williams were walking toward Thornton's office when Private Harris approached them. Coming to attention, he saluted. "As you were," commanded Thompson.

Harris lowered his arm, visibly relaxing. "Private Hawks wanted me to report to you that some men are approaching the fort."

"Very well." Thompson started to leave.

"Sir, there's more!"

Thompson turned back in surprise. "More? Very well then, go on."

Nervously shifting from one foot to the other, he looked at each one before replying, "They are only wearing ... long-johns, sir!"

Thompson turned to look at Williams expectantly. He wasn't disappointed when Williams became all military as he began to bark orders. "Bring them to Thornton's office on the double, Private!"

"Yes, sir!" Hawks saluted, pivoted, then briskly walked away.

"Follow me," ordered Williams. Thompson followed silently behind. When they had entered Thornton's office Williams closed the door. Turning to face Thompson, he spoke, "We both know that it has to be Thornton's party. I will enter Thornton's living quarters from here where I'll listen behind the door." Thompson nodded once, and then waited for Williams to continue, "Let him come inside and act as though nothing were out of the ordinary."

Thompson saluted, "Yes, sir."

When Williams entered Thornton's living quarters JaNae turned to him in surprise. "I wasn't expecting you for a while, dear."

He quickly kissed her upon the lips. He began gently to lead her toward Anna's room. "It's all right, honey. I want you to go into Anna's room. Please stay there until I come for you! I'll explain later."

Anna who was sleeping peacefully didn't stir when they entered. Williams looked at Anna in concern, then hurried out of the room to position himself behind the door.

He had just gotten settled, when the door flew open. Thornton entered with three other soldiers in the same state as himself. Thompson rose to salute, then stood at attention. The major began bellowing like a mad, angry bull. "What is the meaning of this?"

Thompson struggled to remain calm. "I beg your pardon, sir. What are you referring to?"

"You know full well what I'm talking about!"

"I'm afraid you'll have to fill me in, sir."

"The orders ... you nitwit!"

"What orders are you talking about, sir?"

By now the cords in Thornton's neck were bulging and his face grew red as he began to shake uncontrollably. Without warning, he stuck his face in front of Thompson where he began riling in a fit of blind, demonic rage. "I gave you specific instructions to eliminate the Indians. I distinctly remember telling you that I didn't want you to spare any of them! That meant, Captain ... men, women, and children.

Thompson sighed wearily. "Yes, sir, you did!"

"When I give an order, I expect it to be carried out completely! Then, to make matters worse ... that half-breed, Nataka, ambushed us, took our clothes, boots, horses, even our weapons. If that weren't enough, he forced us to walk back to the fort!" Thornton paused to take a deep breath before going on. He glared at Thompson with such vehemence, such hatred that Thompson shivered in spite of the heat. "I will see that you are stripped of your rank and title, Captain Thompson! Mark ... my ... words!"

Williams silently removed his revolver, stepped out from behind the door to level it right at Thornton's chest. Little pinpoints of light flashed from his angry eyes. His voice was menacing as he began to speak. "I think I've heard all that I need to, or even care to! Raise your arms high then step over to the right of the door."

"Thornton blinked in total astonishment, then his face grew redder as the cords in his neck bulged even more. "What's the meaning of this?" he demanded.

Williams pulled the hammer back on the gun as he took a step closer to Thornton. "You heard me, Major!" barked Williams. "Step over to the right of the door, now!" Thornton and his men did as they'd been told. "Thompson, step outside. Have some soldiers report here on the double ... tell them to come armed!" Moving to the door, Thompson stepped outside. He soon returned with several armed soldiers, one of which was Sergeant Peters. With guns in hand, they waited for further instructions. Thornton scowled, but remained sullenly silent.

The other three men grew morose, even testy. But Miles Thornton spoke for them all, "How dare you point a gun at my father!"

Williams glared at Miles in abhorrence. "Silence, you mangy cur! I think your father should be grateful that I don't just blow him away here and now." Miles, cowed by Colonel Williams' authoritative voice, withdrew into a corner to watch the proceedings. Even though he appeared to be brow beaten, Thompson knew that Miles would strike if given the chance. Williams turned his attention to Peters, "Sergeant, I want Major Thornton taken to the stockade. Place guards around him in four-hour watches!"

Peters saluted then moved toward Thornton. "Come on, Major, suh ... let's go!"

Looking at Thornton disdainfully, Williams hastened to add, "One more thing, Sargeant. See that he is given a bath and a fresh uniform."

"Yes, suh." Peters and several of the armed men escorted Thornton from the office. They walked briskly toward the stockade. Those at the fort watched in wonderment, then began to whisper among themselves.

Shortly afterwards Williams looked first at Miles, then Jennings. Finally, he faced Jones. They presented a disgusting picture, as they stood there in their filthy grimy long-johns. Several days of growth covered their filthy faces. Their eyes were sunken from lack of sleep, giving them a grizzly appearance. Not only was their hair matted or otherwise in terrible disarray, but their bodies also emitted an odor that was not pleasing to the nose.

As they saluted and tried to present a military stance, everything about them reeked of total dishonor to their country. Williams sighed in disgust. "It would please me immensely to throw you in the stockade with Thornton. However, as you were only following orders, count yourselves lucky to get off so easily. If you haven't had a bath and dressed in proper uniform within the hour, I will consider changing my mind. You're dismissed!" Without a backward glance, the three men filed out into the night.

Williams reentered Thornton's living quarters, crossing over to softly knock upon Anna's door. Opening it, JaNae intently scanned her husband face. Anna, who was sitting on the edge of the bed, looked at Williams questioningly. He absently put his arm around his wife's shoulders as he tenderly regarded Anna. He wearily took a deep breath, wiped his brow, then said, "Your husband has returned to the fort, Anna, but he has been arrested."

"He has?" She began to tremble as fear gripped her.

"Yes, ma'am." Williams smiled gently to take the sting out of his next words. "He issued orders that, if they had been carried out, would have caused a terrible bloodbath."

"Oh," she fell silent, trying to digest his statement.

"I will enlighten you as soon as I am able to."

"Thank you, Jedidiah."

"No problem." He and JaNae went into the other room to give Anna some much needed privacy.

CHAPTER 23

May I Have This Dance?

JaNae and Jedidiah Williams emerged from Anna's room walking quietly over to the table. Sighing, JaNae looked sadly up at her husband then placed a hand on the lapel of his jacket. "I feel so sorry for Anna. It seems as though she were fated to be tried or tested at every turn … perhaps even more than most of us are."

Williams nodded absently as he covered her hand with his. "It surely does look that way, doesn't it, honey!"

"I wish that she could have someone to love her the way that you do me, Jedidiah. Nevertheless, that love hasn't come without its own price, has it, darling?"

"No, it really hasn't! But the good Lord saw us through those rough times, even making our love stronger, richer than I ever thought possible." He placed his hands on both sides of her face so that he could look into her brown eyes. His voice grew husky with emotion. "Darling, how do I ever thank you properly for being here as a comforting influence in my life whenever I've needed it the most?"

JaNae shivered in delight. Tears came into her eyes as she looked lovingly up at her husband. "You have thanked me many times over, darling, just by loving me."

Williams bent his head to gently brush his lips across hers. Trembling JaNae snuggled closer as his lips again met hers in a deep passionate kiss. As he crushed her to him, she felt hot fingers of flaming passion envelope her. For a moment time stood still as they hungrily partook of the other's love. Several more times he drank of her sensuous lips then gazed into her love-filled eyes. "I love you, JaNae Williams, with all of my heart and soul."

"And I love you, too, my darling."

Williams was about to kiss her again, when there was a knock at the office door. "Drats!"

Snickering softly, JaNae hid her face in his massive chest. "That's one way to cool things off in a hurry."

Laughing Williams playfully patted her rump then went toward the office to answer the door. "We'll pick up where we left off when I get rid of whoever that is on the other side of that door."

322

"I have a feeling it won't be for a while," teased JaNae. Williams nodded. Stepping into the office, he closed the door behind him. JaNae watched until the door closed, then went back to work.

Williams hurried over to open the outer door, hoping the problem could be solved quickly. Seeing a man from the wagon train, he suspected that he was going to be detained for a while. He motioned for the man to enter, suddenly becoming all business. "Please, won't you come in?"

The man removed his hat before stepping inside. "Thank you, sir. I wonder if I might have a moment of your time to discuss our dilemma with you?"

"Of course." Smiling, Williams politely indicated a chair positioned opposite the desk. "Please, be seated."

"Thank you, sir." The man sank gratefully onto the chair.

Williams sat opposite him and folded his hands on top of the desk. He studied him a moment before speaking. "Now, how may I be of service to you, sir?"

"Well ... first of all ... let me introduce myself. My name is James Edward Payne. I am with the wagon train that's outside the fort." Payne leaned eagerly forward in his chair. "As you know, our wagon master died a few days ago." Williams nodded affirmatively then waited for Payne to continue. "Well, most of those in our group have opted for going on, but we don't have anyone to lead us, because no one is familiar with the territory ahead."

"Where do you want to go?"

"We were thinking of Canada, sir."

"I see."

"I have come to ask if you know of anyone who might be able to help us." He paused a moment, then proceeded. "There are some of us who would like to stay in this area. After hearing some of the settlers say they would like to move on, we were hoping that they might be willing to sell out to us."

Williams sat thoughtfully pondering Payne's words, again listening as Payne went on, "Those wanting to stay have all talked it over. They would sell their wagons to those wanting to go with the train. They would like to apply their Conestogas and their teams as partial payment for the land. Of course we would also pay cash for the remainder."

"That sounds like a fair deal," replied Williams. "Let me think about it for a while then I'll get back to you."

"That would be great, sir. Rising, Payne shook William's hand. "Thank you for giving me time to discuss our situation with you." Turning, he left the office.

Williams leaned back in the chair to contemplate Payne's situation. *What would be the best way for me to handle this?* he wondered. Looking at the leather case he'd brought with him from Fort Missoula, an idea formed. Opening the case, he took out several papers, which he read over for several minutes. Laying the papers back onto the desk, he rose. Placing his hands behind his back, he paced the room. The more he thought about the possibilities, the more his idea appealed to him. Sitting back at the desk, Williams picked up the papers, once more pouring over them.

"That's it!" he exclaimed, slamming his fist hard on the desk. Putting the papers back into the case, he slipped it into a drawer on the right and securely locked it. Satisfied that all was well, he entered the Thornton's living quarters. JaNae turned as he entered, but waited for him to speak. He crossed over to kiss her quickly on the mouth. "I have to go out for a while, but I'll be back in time for dinner."

"Very well, but I won't have it ready for at least an hour, so don't worry about being late."

"Thank you for being so understanding, honey. I need to get this taken care of as soon as possible."

JaNae smiled, "You're easy to please." Williams chuckled as he reentered the office. It wasn't very long until JaNae heard the outer door close softly behind him.

Williams placed his hat firmly upon his head. Stepping off the porch he went in search of Thompson. He found him talking to Peters in the community hall. The two men turned as one when Williams approached. Coming to full attention they saluted. "As you were, men." Both men visibly relaxed. "Come … walk with me for a spell, Captain."

"Yes, sir." Thompson fell into step with him, while Peters walked away. Thompson patiently waited for Williams to speak, curious to know what was on his mind.

As they approached the gates, Williams barked an order to the Sentry. "Open a gate, Private."

"Right away, sir!" Private Harris quickly complied with Williams' command.

After they were outside the gate, they continued in silence until they were a good distance away from the fort. When Williams was satisfied that they wouldn't be interrupted, he turned to face Thompson. "I have a proposition that I would like you to think about, Captain. I don't want you to interrupt me until I have finished speaking."

"Yes, sir."

"Mr. Payne came to see me a few minutes ago to ask for my help in solving their dilemma. They have lost their wagon master and are in great need of another one to lead them to their new homes. It seems they want to go to Canada. While deliberating about what I could do to help them, I came up with your name. You see, while studying your records, I discovered that three years ago you led a group of soldiers up that way."

Thompson intently watched Williams, feeling a little apprehensive. "Yes, sir."

"I also noticed that you have approximately six weeks or so left before you're eligible to retire."

Thompson nodded warily, "That is correct, sir."

"I will give you an early retirement in order to guide these people to their desired destination." Thompson's jaw dropped in amazement. He quickly gained control as he looked at Williams to see if he was serious, but Williams only chuckled. "I'm serious, son. Before you give me an answer, talk it over with your missus. I would like to have an answer before I return to Fort Missoula."

"Thank you, sir, for giving me the opportunity to do such a thing. I will discuss it with Kate then give you an answer as soon as possible."

"Good! Now, for the other part of the dilemma… Payne stated that there were some of those in the train who wanted to settle down around here. He wondered if any of the settlers would be interested in selling out to them."

Thompson grew thoughtful as he listened to Williams. "Payne said that if there were any settlers interested in selling out in order to go with the wagon train, they wondered if these folks would consider taking a Conestoga and the team toward some of the payment. Of course, they would also pay the rest with cash, thus helping those selling out to outfit themselves for the trip ahead."

As Thompson stood thoughtfully considering how to approach the situation, an idea occurred to him. "Most of the settlers will be at the dance tonight, so let's ask them then."

Williams grew excited at the suggestion. "A capital idea, Captain. When you have given me your decision, then we'll talk more."

"Very well, sir." Turning, the men ambled back to the fort, talking amiably about many different subjects. When they were inside the gate, they shook hands then went their separate ways.

Williams went into dinner feeling ravenous. JaNae welcomed him with open arms declaring that it was ready to eat. Anna smiled as she joined them at the table. Williams pulled her chair out and smiled, "How are you feeling this evening, Mrs. Thornton?"

Anna shuddered involuntarily. "Please, call me 'Anna'."

Williams smiled apologetically. "I forgot for a moment."

Anna smiled gratefully. "Thank you. I'm feeling much better now."

"That's great! Do you think you might save a dance for me tonight?"

Anna gulped, immediately drawing within herself. Finally, she was able to put what she was feeling into words. "Carl never allowed me to have fun, let alone go to a dance. If he were to find out that I had fun, there would be the very hob to pay. Besides, I haven't danced for so long that I doubt that I even know how to any more, sir."

Williams patted her hand reassuringly. "As his superior officer, I promise you that he'll never have the opportunity to hurt you again."

JaNae looked at Anna in surprise. "Then it's high time, dear friend, that you had some fun in your life! Besides, Jedidiah is a fantastic dancer … very easy to follow."

Williams winked at her, plainly pleased at her compliment. "Flattery will get you everywhere, madam."

"Why, thank you, kind sir."

Anna watched their good-natured bantering all the while marveling at their love. *Oh,* she thought, *why couldn't I have had someone to love me like that?*

When dinner was over, JaNae went to the bedroom to get the pitcher, which she filled with hot water from the reservoir. She placed the pitcher beside the washbowl. While the women tidied up the kitchen, Williams shaved off the afternoon shadow of stubble, then dressed for the evening festivities.

JaNae wiped the table then paused thoughtfully. "I was wondering if I could fix your hair for the dance, Anna."

Anna smiled as she touched her hair. "Why, I'd really appreciate that! I have a rough time keeping my arm up long enough even to get it combed."

"That's what I thought, so that's why I offered."

As they were putting everything away, Williams emerged from the bedroom dressed in a clean uniform with his boots polished to perfection.

When JaNae saw her husband, her heart skipped a beat, as she remembered their time together earlier. "Umm ... umm ... umm! Oh my goodness! You look really handsome, darling."

"Why, thank you, honey." Williams, his eyes twinkling merrily, bowed elegantly from the waist. "A gentleman always likes to impress the ladies." Laughing at his ridiculous antics, the women shook their heads. "I have some things that must be taken care of before the dance, so I will leave you beautiful ladies to your own devices." He consulted his pocket watch and put it back into his watch fob as he glanced at JaNae. "I'll be back in just a little over an hour. Will that give you enough time to get gussied up?"

JaNae looked at Anna, then turned to Williams. "That's more than enough time."

"Good. I'll see you then." He quickly kissed JaNae before entering the office.

When the door was closed, JaNae turned to Anna and smiled. "We'd better hustle if we want to be ready when he returns." The two women went to Anna's room so that JaNae could fix her friend's hair. When they were done, Anna gazed in awe at the face staring back at her, surprised at what she saw. Tears came into her eyes, rendering her speechless for a moment. Swallowing past the lump in her throat, she turned to look at JaNae. "It's stunning! Thank you so much, my dear, for your kind generosity."

JaNae hugged Anna, impulsively bending to kiss the top of her head. "It is I who am in your debt, my dear, for your letting us stay here." She walked over to Anna's closet in an attempt to change the subject. "Let's see what you have to wear to the dance." After searching through the closet and finding nothing that would flatter Anna, an idea came to her. "I'll be right back." Anna wondered what had made her rush out like that. JaNae soon returned with a lovely peach dress made of taffeta material. She held it up to Anna. "That's just the ticket!"

Anna looked at her strangely. "I ... I ... don't understand."

"I want you to wear this dress tonight." When Anna started to protest, JaNae raised her hand. "I won't accept any argument about it from you, either."

Anna, touched by JaNae's wonderful generosity, began to cry softly. She gently pushed the dress toward JaNae. "But I can't possibly wear your gorgeous dress."

JaNae pretended to be stern, "I said … I wouldn't take any sass." Seeing the looks of indecision on Anna's, she placed her hands gently on Anna's shoulders, "Please allow me this little pleasure."

Anna mutely complied, "Very well." JaNae gently slipped the dress over her head. Poor Anna just stared at her appearance as JaNae buttoned it.

The dress had long puffy sleeves that tapered from the elbow to the wrist with a snug bodice that gathered at the waist. A slightly flared skirt was attached to the bodice. The hem came just to the ankle. When Anna saw her reflection in the mirror, she was totally amazed. Her hair was piled high on her head, with a wisp of hair at each ear. Her blue eyes sparkled with life.

Anna threw her arms around JaNae's neck, hugging her as tight as her broken ribs would allow and kissing her gratefully upon the cheek. "Thank you so much for making this such a wonderful night. I don't think I could have faced being alone ... especially with all that is happening with Carl."

JaNae brushed the tears from her own eyes. "It's my privilege, Anna."

While Anna finished dressing, JaNae went to get ready. She was emerging from the bedroom when Williams entered the living quarters. Catching sight of his beloved wife, dressed in a sky-blue crushed velvet dress, with her raven-colored hair piled atop her head, he whistled softly. JaNae's heart beat faster as she saw the love light in Jedidiah's eyes.

"Wow! You're absolutely beautiful!"

JaNae's eyes moistened with the praise, making her heart swell with love for this wonderful man who was her husband. "Thank you, darling," she whispered tenderly.

"Too bad we are going to a dance, or I'd carry you off … we'd elope!"

JaNae giggled then went over to tenderly kiss him on the lips. "But, kind sir … I'm already married."

Hanging his head dejectedly, he sank onto a chair with a perfect hound-dog expression on his face. "Isn't that the way of it? All the beautiful gals git hitched afer I kin get to em! What rotten, no-good skunk did ja get hitched to anyway?"

JaNae wrinkled her nose at his funny expression and sloppy grammar. Fluttering her lashes beguilingly, she wrapped her arms around his neck, kissed him passionately upon the lips, then snuggled closer. "You, sir!" she whispered in his ear.

Before she could step back, he grabbed her and pulled her onto his lap, enveloping her in a tight embrace. He kissed her passionately. JaNae's heart felt as though it would explode, with the love she felt for him, as she returned kiss for kiss. Finally, he raised his head to gaze at her flushed face. "It's a good thing it's me who gets your kisses," he teased, "or I'd have to get real jealous."

Chuckling, JaNae buried her face in his massive chest. "I keep thinking that I can't love you more and then you do things like this and I find my love growing deeper."

They were interrupted when Anna opened her door to start out. "Oh," she exclaimed in embarrassment, "I didn't mean to interrupt!"

Williams chuckled as he helped JaNae to her feet. "It's all right, Anna. Sometimes I forget myself around this beautiful creature." JaNae punched him lightly in the stomach. "Oh," he cried in mock pain. "Is that any way to treat your beloved husband?"

"I have to agree, Jedidiah. JaNae is very beautiful!"

JaNae blushed prettily then attempted to change the subject. "We'd better go, before they come looking for us."

Catching sight of Anna, Williams whistled appreciatively. "Whew! You're a picture of exquisite beauty yourself, Anna."

Anna beamed at the praise bestowed her, which only caused her to appear more beautiful. "Thank you, Colonel."

Williams' brows wrinkled in displeasure. "If I am to call you 'Anna', then you have to call me 'Jedidiah'."

"Okay. Jedidiah it is, then."

"Good!" Opening the door for the ladies, he waited for them to go outside. Blowing out the lamps, he joined them. They were waiting for him as he stepped off the porch. Extending an arm to each of them, Williams gazed from one to the other. Sighing he said, "What a strange combination. Here I am, a thorn positioned between two lovely roses." The women curtsied at his compliment. Linking their arms through his, they headed toward the community hall.

ꕥ ꕥ

Thompson, walking in a daze after leaving Williams, trudged aimlessly toward home. He paused on the porch to collect his thoughts. Once he'd gained control of his emotions, he opened the door to enter. Kate was standing at the stove fixing dinner while Eileen was setting the table. Both women greeted him cheerfully with a kiss. "Wow! Now that's worth coming home to!" The women smiled then continued to get dinner onto the table.

Thompson went to the counter to get the washbasin, filling it with hot water from the reservoir. Setting the basin back onto the counter, he washed up. Kate watched him covertly, suspecting that something major was troubling him. Turning from the stove, she placed a steaming kettle of stew onto a hot pad. Picking up the pot of coffee, she poured it into the cups at the table. Placing the pot to the back of the stove, she announced that dinner was ready.

When everyone was seated at the table, grace was offered on the food. The only sounds heard were clinking silverware against the plates or bowls being passed. Kate was the first to break the long silence. Watching Paul anxiously toy with his food, she asked, "Is something bothering you, darling?"

Sighing, he continued to toy with his food while he tried to figure out a way to broach the subject. Finally, realizing there was no other way to approach it, he plunged in. "Darling, do you remember the discussion we had just before I went on that last maneuver … you know, the one where I told you that I was going to be eligible to retire in a few months?"

Kate watched him suspiciously before answering. "Yes, I remember."

"Well what would you think if I told you that a possibility has presented itself in a strange way?"

"I'd say, where is it … and what is it?"

"I have been given the opportunity of leading the wagon train to a new destination … Canada."

Kate blinked in surprise. "Really?"

"Yes, really!"

Eileen's eyes darted from one to the other as she listened intently to their conversation. It was obvious that she wanted to ask questions too, but she thought better of it. Before she could say or do anything else, Kate began to ply Paul with question after question, without giving him time to answer. "But wait, you haven't retired … so what about that? You can't just take off without retiring. Besides that, you'll have Thornton down your throat for going against him. So, I guess the question I'm asking is what we have to do first. … How long do we have to prepare ourselves before we leave? What about Aunt Eileen? We just got her here."

Thompson raised his hands in an attempt to try to ward her off. "Whoa, honey! Whoa! Just give me a minute. I'll explain it all to you."

Kate grinned sheepishly. "Guess I did get kind of carried away, didn't I?"

"It's okay, because I have a thousand questions as well. I've had a little longer to think about it than you have. To answer your questions … I really don't know yet. Williams talked with me a few minutes ago. He told me to talk it over with the missus before giving him an answer. Then if we are all for it, he would discuss the deal with me further."

"Oh, I see."

No one spoke for a moment. They were too busy digesting the news. Finally, Thompson looked at the two women lovingly. "I would really like to take this opportunity because I know the way. I think I would like the challenge it would present." Again looking at each of them, he sighed before rushing on. "What really has me concerned is that you have just arrived, Auntie, and it would mean uprooting you again. Also it is very late in the season to be traveling with a slow-moving wagon train, as we may become caught in bad weather with no shelter."

"That's a good point, honey."

Eileen sighed thoughtfully then said, "Well … I have given up a lot to come here to be with the two of you, so what's a little more distance when it means that we can stay close together. I am looking forward to eventually having my own home again, where I can entertain all of you."

Finally, giving food up as a lost cause, Thompson set his spoon on the side of his plate and leaned back in his chair. He looked from one to the other. Taking a deep breath he hastened on, "You both know my feelings concerning the matter, but I must confess that I am concerned for our little family of five. So, since it involves all of us, I want to know how you both feel about it."

A long deadly silence fell over them as each contemplated their decisions. Looking up from her bowl, Eileen took a deep breath and said, "As I stated before, I just want us to be together in the same area, no matter what we have to do to accomplish it. If it means traveling to a new area, then so be it."

"When I married you, Paul Thompson, I promised to go where you went, no matter where that might be ... now is no different." Paul noticed how beautiful Kate was as her eyes sparkled with life and love. "If you want to take on this adventure ... then I say, go for it!"

Paul stared at both of them in wonderment. "Let me get this straight. Are you saying that we should take on this huge undertaking?"

"Yes," they cried as one.

This so overwhelmed Thompson for a moment that he sat speechless, staring into his coffee cup in an attempt to gain control of his emotions. When he was able to face his two favorite women, he looked at each one tenderly. "Thank you for making this so easy for me. I will talk with Colonel Williams at the first opportunity available then let you know what will be happening." Both women nodded, then all fell silent as they finished their dinner, each one pondering what lay ahead.

When dinner was over, Eileen did up the dishes so Kate could get the twins ready for bed. Sylvia had volunteered to take care of the twins so the adults could go to the dance. Paul got ready first so that he could speak with Colonel Williams before the dance. After he had left, the women began to get ready. Eileen wore a light-lavender brocade dress that had puffy sleeves with wide bands that buttoned at the wrists. The close-fitting bodice had a white frilly ruffle.

A white cameo, set on a black background trimmed with a silver mounting, was pinned under the ruffle at her throat. The slightly flared skirt flowed to just above her ankles. Black high-buttoned shoes completed the ensemble. Her hair, combed back from her face, was piled high on her head. Her eyes sparkled with merriment as she brushed an imaginary speck from her dress.

Kate emerged from the bedroom wearing a dark-green dress, which had puffed sleeves that tapered at the elbow and then flowed to a point at her wrists. The simple bodice had a lighter green trim than that of the dress. The same green trim complimented the skirt, which was slightly flared. She had a white cameo, set in a light-green background with a gold mounting, which Kate had pinned at the throat. Matching earrings set off her auburn hair, which was braided then wrapped around her head. Black lace up shoes enhanced the dress.

Thompson entered shortly afterward, whistling appreciatively at the sight of them, "You both are a picture of loveliness all gussied up like that!"

Smiling, Eileen curtsied slightly. "Why, thank you, kind sir."

Kate grinned at the compliment paid them. "My sentiments exactly."

There was a knock at the door preventing Thompson from speaking further. Turning, he opened the door motioning for Peters to enter. "Please, come on in, Sergeant," greeted Paul. When Peters was inside, Thompson closed the door. "What can I do for you?"

"Ah come ta give ya a report en the money we made from the different booths en events we did today," replied Peters.

Kate clapped her hands together excitedly. "Marvelous!" She turned to Paul questioningly. "Do you mind if we sit in on the report?"

"Not at all, honey," he exclaimed. "After all we couldn't have done it without your help."

When they were all seated at the table, Peters presented the report. "We done made over ninety dollars today," he exclaimed proudly.

Thompson blinked in surprise. "We made that much?"

"Yes, sir!" stated Peters. "Most a it were made from the dunkin' booth alone."

"No wonder I felt like a drowned rat when I climbed out of that contraption!"

Peters turned to look at Thompson with the highest form of respect. "What mattered most suh, is that ya was sich a good sport 'bout it all." Thompson shook his head but refrained from speaking. "Ever'one is still talking 'bout it … 'specially the soldiers. The men haf come to respect ya highly, suh." He laughed slightly, then turning to the two women, he winked while smiling broadly. "The soldiers, en all those from the fort en settlement, think ya ladies 'er 'bout the most grandest ladies in these here parts … fer dunkin' the Cap'n!" This brought peals of laughter from the women, followed by a scowl from Thompson.

"I'm not likely to forget what the two of you did to me today! I have vowed to myself that if it takes the rest of my life to accomplish it, I will get even."

"You poor, dear lamb!" soothed Eileen. "I'm here to tell you that it will probably take the rest of your life to get the opportunity … let alone get even."

Thompson, throwing his head back, guffawed with the rest of them. "Auntie, you are a real peach of a woman!"

Eileen's eyes grew misty. "Thank you, Paul. That means more to me than you'll ever know."

Peters rose to leave. "Ah best git goin' or Ah'll be late ta the dance." Turning, he started toward the door, then stopped to address Thompson. "Suh," he began, "Would'ya mind ifn' Ah hed a dance with each a these most beautifulest ladies tonight at the dance?"

Paul was touched that Peters would ask such a request. "I'd be honored if you'd ask them, but I can't answer for them, so you'll have to ask them yourself."

Kate smiled sweetly as she placed her hand lightly on his arm. "I'd be honored to save a dance for you, Sergeant."

"I, too, would be delighted to dance with you, Sergeant."

Peters' chest swelled with joy, making it impossible for him to speak. Finally, in a stuttering manner, Peters spoke, "Tha ... tha ... thank ya both," he stammered. Turning, he hurried out into the night air.

"I doubt that either of you really knows how much you have touched Sergeant Peters."

Kate smiled at her husband. "I think that is one marvelous individual. I meant it when I said I'd be honored to save a dance for him." Eileen remained silent as she pondered the words of Kate and Paul.

When there was another knock at the door Paul went to answer it. Seeing Sylvia standing there expectantly, he reached out to pull her inside. "Thought you might have gotten lost, young lady."

"Sorry I'm late, but I got busy helping Ma and forgot the time."

"Well ... it's better late than never." Turning to the women, he motioned to them to come. "If we are going to the dance, ladies, we'd better get on our way." After helping them on with their wraps, they stepped out into the night.

As the little group slowly trudged toward the community hall, Kate looked up at her husband, "Did you get to speak to Colonel Williams?"

"No. He was busy with other matters."

"I see."

"Let's not think about what may or may not be tonight. This night has been a long time coming, so I plan to enjoy every minute of it with my two favorite girls."

"Lead on, darling. We are right behind you."

As they neared the building, they could hear laughter coming from within, along with the sound of musicians tuning their instruments.

ഏ⊙ല ⊙ൠ

Thornton's cohorts were sleeping in the barracks oblivious to what was going on in the fort. Thornton sat sulking in his cell, angry at the world and everyone in it. As he sat on his cot, he plotted sweet revenge for Nataka and Thompson. As his mind conjured up all the nasty things possible for him to do, the veins in his neck began to bulge. His face grew red with rage and unspent passion.

When he heard laughter floating across the crisp night air and music echoing across the fort, the rage inside grew even more intense. "When I get out of here," he growled, "Thompson is history! First, he disobeyed my orders ... now he permits the men to pull these shenanigans. I'm here in this hole waiting to face the wrath of Williams. It's all Thompson's fault! As for Nataka ... he'll get his, too. When I get out of here, they're ALL going to pay. If they think I worked them hard before … they ain't seen nothing … YET!"

All at once he grabbed his head with both hands, groaning in mortal agony. "Not another headache," he cried aloud. "Won't they ever go away?" Revenge was momentarily forgotten as he writhed around on the bed. The pain in his head grew more intense. The throbbing beat of the music made the headache worse. Thornton longed for a stiff shot of whisky to rid himself of the pain.

A guard coming in to check on him found him thrashing around on the bed. Slipping back outside, he waited for the next change of guard, which was to happen in a few minutes. He heard the two guards' footsteps approaching, then heard one of them go toward the back, where the other guard was positioned.

The other came up to him. After relinquishing his post to the new guard, he hurried over to find Doctor Phelps, who was approaching the community hall with his medical bag in his left hand. After quickly explaining Thornton's condition, the guard went to his barracks to prepare for the dance. Phelps went to check on Thornton.

Thornton was nearly out of his mind with the pain when the new guard admitted Doctor Phelps into the cell. Now incapable of bullying Phelps, he submitted to the examination. Reaching into his black medical bag, Phelps got out his stethoscope to listen to Thornton's heartbeat. He wasn't surprised to hear how irregular it was. Thornton's nose was bleeding … his muscles were twitching.

All at once Thornton began vomiting. He would grab his head then clutch his stomach as he heaved over and over again. There were times when confusion rendered him incapable of normal rationality. Phelps worked over him in an attempt to calm him, so his heart rate and blood pressure would come down. After what seemed like an eternity, the vomiting stopped … his nose stopped bleeding. Thornton slowly grew quieter as the pain lessened. Finally, when he fell into an exhausted sleep, Phelps closed his medical bag. Rising he walked out of the cell.

The guard looked at Phelps in concern. "Is he going to be all right, sir?"

"For the time being."

"Good! I don't like seeing anyone or anything hurt like that."

"Right now what he needs is to be cleaned up … the cell put to rights."

"I'll get on it right away, sir"

"I'll be at the dance if he needs me again." Without another word Phelps hurried over to the community hall.

✧ ✧

After the Thompsons went inside, they found a good place to sit where they could enjoy the action of the dance. Kate noticed the musicians positioned to the left of the door leading into the community hall. They were on a raised platform warming up their instruments. Hank Townsend was sitting on a chair with his broken leg stretched out in front of him. As she watched them, she mentally clicked off their names in her mind.

Hans Pedersen and James Payne were busy tuning their fiddles. Jason Steed was busy tuning his guitar. Hank Townsend would be playing the jew's-harp; Joshua Reed, the accordion; finally Robert Miller, on the harmonica. When they were all ready, each one nodded. As the band began to play "Turkey in the Straw," several people filed out onto the dance floor.

After the song ended, the band played a soft lilting waltz. Thompson turned to Kate bowing gallantly. "May I have this dance?"

Kate took his hand as she rose. "You may."

They glided away, leaving Eileen seated alone. Peters appeared hesitantly before her. "Mite Ah haf this dance, Miss Thompson?"

"Only if you call me 'Eileen'."

"Ah shor'ly will. Eileen, mite Ah please haf this dance?"

"I would be delighted, sir."

Peters scowled slightly. "Beggin' yer pardon … but ifn' Ah'm ta call ya 'Eileen', then ya must call me 'Daniel'."

"Then, 'Daniel' it is." Taking his hand, she moved out onto the dance floor with him.

As they danced, Eileen was very impressed at how smoothly he glided around the room. "You dance very well, Daniel"

Peter's beamed at the compliment. "Why, thank ya, ma'am." All too soon, the dance ended. Peters politely escorted her back to her seat. "Thank ya fer a mite pleasurable dance, Eileen."

"You're very welcome, Daniel," replied Eileen. Peters gallantly doffed his hat as he bowed, then walked calmly away.

Another waltz tantalized the dancers until the floor was filled. Williams watched as John Whipple approached him. "Sir, would you mind if I were to ask your wife for a dance?"

Williams' eyes beamed with pleasure as he watched the nervous young man before him. "Not at all, Whipple," he declared. "Ask away!"

John turned to JaNae, bowing slightly with his hand extended. "May I have the pleasure of this dance, JaNae?"

She turned to wink at Williams, then turned back to smile at John. "I'd love to, sir," she replied. Reaching out to take his hand, she rose, allowing him to guide her to the dance floor. As they danced, JaNae looked at John in surprise. "Wow, you dance divinely, John!"

"Thank you, JaNae." He was greatly pleased by her praise. "My friend Melissa, the one who was killed by Maines' gang, taught me how to dance. She was very precise when it came to doing a dance step just right." He smiled at the memory it evoked.

"She must have been a swell person."

"That she was!" They danced the rest of the dance in silence, each lost in thought.

When John started to take JaNae back to her seat, he saw Colonel Williams walking Anna back to her seat. "Mrs. Thornton looks beautiful tonight, doesn't she, JaNae?"

"Yes, she does."

"I think I'll ask her for the next dance."

"That's a great idea, John."

He saw JaNae back to her seat, then turned to Anna. Bowing politely, he extended his hand. "May I have this dance, Mrs. Thornton?"

"I'd love to." Anna took his proffered hand, letting him help her to her feet. They joined the dancers already on the floor. JaNae and Jedidiah noticed her discomfort but were pleased to see Anna making an effort to mingle with her friends. John also noticed her discomfort, guessing it was because she felt out of place and feared Thornton's repercussions.

Because of her nervousness, her dance steps were erratic, causing her to step on his feet a few times. Though he winced inwardly, he smiled outwardly. "Don't worry about stepping on my feet, ma'am. Who knows, I may be stepping on yours in a minute or two." He was relieved when he felt her relax in his arms.

Throughout the night, JaNae was asked often to dance by the other soldiers, which caused Williams' heart to swell with pride. He turned to where Anna was sitting only to notice that she, too, was dancing. This pleased him because he had worried about her becoming a wallflower.

Looking out at the dance floor he noticed that she was dancing with Nataka Hansen. As he watched them, he remembered what Thompson had disclosed to him. Seeing them together made him feel wonderful, for he'd come to really admire her tenacity. In spite of, or maybe because of her harsh life, these past twenty-five years, Anna had true grit, thought Williams.

After dancing with Anna, John asked Kate for a dance, which she readily accepted. While on the dance floor, she told him that he needed to come visit. She wanted him to tell what had happened in Fort Missoula. He promised to visit within the next few days to tell her all about it.

Those at the fort and those from the settlement had both enjoyed the rare events of the day. They were grateful for the reprieve from Thornton's iron fist. As the night wore speedily on, their hearts became freer as they realized it had truly been an 'Independence Day' in every way. Around eighteen hundred hours, there was a brief intermission for supper.

After everyone had a chance to partake of the repast, Williams rose to walk to the front of the room. "May I have your attention, folks?" Everyone was talking so much, that at first they didn't hear him. Payne struck a sour note on the fiddle that caused the people to face him. He quickly pointed to Colonel Williams, who chuckled. "Thank you, Payne."

When they finally quieted down, he proceeded, "I have something to talk over with all of you. I would appreciate having your undivided attention and your complete silence until I am through."

A hush fell over the crowd. They listened intently when Williams explained Payne's proposal. When he was finished, he reiterated, "Not only are they willing to pay cash for the land, but they would like to know if you'd be interested in taking their teams and their Conestogas as part of the payment on your places. That way you have a way to start over."

Murmurs ran through the crowd. "Wait a moment," cried Williams holding his hands up for silence, "There is more!" Immediately a hush fell over the people as Williams continued. "As to the new leader, that hasn't been decided yet, but when it is, we'll hold a special meeting to make the announcement."

Some nodded, while others sat thoughtfully pondering his words. "I suggest that no one makes a commitment tonight, but that you all wait for a few days to think it over. Discuss it with your spouses before deciding anything." Everyone nodded in agreement then waited for Williams to say more. "That's all that I have to talk about for right now. The night is still young ... let's take advantage of it. Go back to dancing."

When the band began to play again, the floor filled up with dancing couples. It was difficult, but for a time they were able to concentrate on the gaiety of the evening. However, there were little groups that huddled to discuss what this meant for everyone at the fort and the settlement.

The dance broke up a little before daylight. Families from the settlement prepared for the long trip home. Those at the fort or wagon train stayed to clean up the community hall. Williams escorted JaNae and Anna to the Thornton's, while Thompson took Eileen and Kate home. Satisfied that they were all right, the men returned to help. When everything was back in order, the men called goodbye to each other, then went to their homes ... feeling happy.

CHAPTER 24

Enlightenment

Major Carl Thornton woke not only feeling groggy but listless as well. Phelps was examining him closely as Thornton opened his eyes. He tried to protest but didn't have the strength to resist as he lay there waiting for Phelps to finish examining him.

Phelps leaned back to remove the stethoscope from his ears. "Well … how do you feel this morning?"

"Like a ton of lead fell on me!" complained Thornton irritably.

"I'm not at all surprised. Have you been having this pain in your chest, left arm, and these violent headaches for a long time?"

Thornton grew testy. "What's it to you?"

"I need to know so that I can assess the damage to your body. You nearly died of a massive stroke last night."

"Bull!" snarled Thornton. "You're just trying to scare me … but it won't work!"

"I'm very serious, Major Thornton." As Thornton studied Phelps intently, he realized he was telling him the truth. "I want to know if this has been going on for a long duration."

"For about three weeks. They have been getting worse the last two weeks."

"I surmised as much. The reason you are having this pain is the ill temper you have been displaying." Thornton snorted angrily, then again realized that Phelps was telling the truth when his head started throbbing. "If you don't stop getting angry, you'll drop dead of a stroke or blow a major blood vessel."

Phelps placed his stethoscope back into his medical bag. "My advice to you is to stay just as quiet as you possibly can for a while." Thornton groaned but refrained from speaking. "I'll be back to check on you later on today."

Phelps walked toward the cell door. He turned back to see Thornton wearily close his eyes. He watched a moment longer. As he left the stockade, Thornton fell asleep. Strolling to the infirmary, Phelps knew that Thornton could no more control his temper than he could hold his breath for any long period of time. *What a sad waste,* he thought.

Two hours later, the guard awakened Thornton to tell him that Miles was there to see him. Grumbling, Thornton rose to sit on the edge of the bed as he waited for

Miles to be admitted. His head ached so badly that he had a hard time staying alert to all that was going on around him. The clanging of the cell door didn't help any, either.

Miles looked at his parent with grave concern as Thornton sat holding his head in his hands. "Are you having those headaches more often, Pa?"

"Yes. Last night it was so bad that Doctor Phelps was brought in to help me. He told me that I had to find a way to control my temper or I would suffer the consequences." Miles didn't like the sound of that, but wisely refrained from speaking. Thornton tried to raise his head but found it difficult. "But what does he know anyway?"

"Who knows? I'm sure I don't know."

Thornton decided to change the subject. "What's going on out there this morning?"

"Jennings and Jones pulled out before daylight. They said that they wanted to get a place located where we could all meet them when your hearing is over."

"It's good they were able to get away. Their testimonies could have been damaging to my hearing." Miles nodded then waited for his father to continue. "Besides, we will need a place to meet when I'm out of here."

If you get out, thought Miles. "Have they set a time for the hearing?"

"Not that I know of. I think they are waiting for someone from Fort Missoula, or so the rumor goes."

"They have to send for officers that are equal to my rank or higher in order to have the hearing." For a moment he grew angry, but as it caused pain to his head, Thornton tried to calm down.

"Scuttlebutt has it that the wagon train parked outside the fort is looking for a wagon master to lead them to some place in Canada." Miles smirked while shrugging nonchalantly. "As far as I know, there is no one around the fort or the settlement that can take on the job."

"Yes, there is!"

Miles stared at Thornton dumbly. "Who?"

"I sent Thompson up there with a large troop to scout around shortly after he got here to the fort. They were gone nearly five months on that maneuver, so he is very familiar with the area."

"That leaves him out, because as captain of the fort he'll be left in charge until they get a replacement for you."

Thornton grew very angry at Miles' remark. "Sounds like you have me doomed already."

"I didn't mean to sound so pessimistic, Pa. I was just stating what might be a possibility."

Thornton thought about that a moment, then sighed wearily. "Oh it looks really bad ... my going against the treaty ... but it doesn't look good for Thompson, either." Miles nodded but remained silent. "At this point we can't look on the dark side until we have to."

"You're right, Pa. Anything can happen."

Miles walked over to look out of the window, while Thornton pondered the situation he was in. Neither one spoke, as both were lost in deep thoughts. Eventually, Miles turned to look wistfully at Thornton, who was gazing intently at the floor. He wanted to ask him a question, but he feared that it might bring his father's wrath upon him. Thornton raised his head to look over at Miles in time to see his son's expression before he masked his feeling. "What's on your mind, son?"

"I was wondering what had happened to make you hate women so much." When Thornton scowled, Miles flinched in fear.

Sighing, Thornton looked at the floor in an attempt to collect his thoughts. "I guess you have a right to know." He spoke so low that Miles had to strain to hear it. "It came to a head twenty-one years ago, son. I received word that the Lucky Horse Saloon had a new owner."

Miles looked at him in surprise. "Oh I know that seems strange, but the name of the owner was what interested me the most. You see … it was a woman who had purchased it." Miles flopped into the chair near the cot. He listened intently as his father continued. "On a pretense, I organized a detail to do some cleanup around Missoula. After we got there, I gave Peters a list of things to do. I informed him that he was to oversee the work and men. While the men were busy working, I went to visit the Lucky Horse Saloon."

"What I saw was appalling to me. The name of the saloon had been changed to Ruby's Silver Slipper. The atmosphere was drastically different from that of the Lucky Horse." Thornton paused to recollect his thoughts before going on. "The ladies who worked there were also known as ladies of the night." Miles blinked in stunned disbelief as he watched his parent closely.

"At first I thought nothing of it … until the owner of the saloon entered, scantily dressed. She sidled up to me asking me to buy her a drink." Miles noted the anger on his father's face, worried that he would not be able to go on, but Thornton took a deep breath to calm down. "She didn't recognize me at first, which suited me just fine … for a while. Then, as she brazenly kept moving toward me, I could no longer contain the anger that had been welling up inside of me."

"Who in the world was she?"

"She was my mother … Ruby Thornton," grunted Thornton.

"Your mother!"

"Yes," replied Thornton. "My mother."

"Whoa! That must have been a real shocker seeing her there!"

"To say the least. You see, I hadn't seen my mother since I was eleven years old. She left my father for another man." For a moment, the painful memory was more than he could bear, thus making Thornton speechless. Taking a deep breath, he went on, "You should have seen her face when I said, 'Back off, Mother'."

As Thornton scowled, Miles' eyes lit up at the picture conjured forth in his mind. "She jumped back as though she'd been slapped, then stared at me with a mixture of hate and shock." This caused Miles to smile at his father's small victory. "I asked why she walked out on us like she did. Ruby glared at me with such hate that I flinched inwardly. She told me that she never wanted to be married, but her father made her marry my dad, George Thornton ... after he'd found out that the animal had not only molested her ... but had also made her pregnant."

"What a low blow that must have been for her!"

"That was my first thought, until she dropped the surprise that changed all of that."

"What was that?"

"She told me that there was no love for Pa, but when I was born, she hated me with a passion akin to murder. She had plotted for some time to give me away then tell Pa that she'd lost me." Thornton felt the anger well up in him again, but he was determined to stifle it. "I came early, so George had to help deliver me, spoiling Mom's opportunity to get rid of me. It seems that she had to contend with my squalling and the endless diaper changes, and the feedings that I required, because Pa was off drinking, gambling or wreaking havoc on some other unsuspecting woman." Miles felt sorry for what had happened to his father. He wished that he could have spared him somehow.

"Although Mom was glad that Pa wasn't there, she declared that she hated being saddled with a brat even worse." Thornton's face turned ashen as he related the story to Miles. "When I turned ten, a man went to work for Grandpa Higgens, my mother's father. Before long, he and Mom were soon involved in a sordid love affair." Thornton shuddered in an attempt to break free of the feelings of hate and repulsion he felt at the mere mention of his mother's name. "They'd managed to keep it from Pa for nearly a year. Then one night, Pa came home early to find them together." Miles smiled at the thought of what happened next.

"When Pa flew into a terrible rage, they barely escaped with their lives. She dared not return ... even to see her parents. It wouldn't have accomplished anything ... because her father disowned her. To make matters worse, her father forbade her mother, or me, to ever mention Ruby's name around him again."

"The creep!"

"My father, leaving me with my mother's parents, skipped town shortly after that. Ruby said that she had read somewhere that he'd been caught trying to molest another girl. The girl's father had murdered him."

"If he was dead, then why didn't she try to come home?"

"That's what I asked her. She laughed in my face, replying that it was a perfect way out of being my mother. She confessed that she cared even less for whatever did or didn't happen to her own parents!"

Miles whistled softly. He sat processing the information over in his mind. "I'm sorry that you had to go through that, Pa."

For the first time in his life, when Miles saw tears form in his father's eyes, a strange compassion filled him. "Well … I got in the last lick anyway. I told her that she was nothing but a cheap, dirty, slut … that she was fooling herself … if she thought she was every man's delight!" Miles chuckled at the tenacity Thornton had displayed. "When I was finished, I rose, stormed out … never once looking back."

"Good for you, Pa!"

"When I got back to the fort, I found that a band of Indians had attacked the fort, raping, plundering, even killing several people. It was bad enough to learn that your mother had been raped by one of those lousy skunks, but I flew into an awful rage when I found out a while later that she was going to have his child." Miles' jaw went slack with shock.

Thornton didn't notice Miles' expression, but continued. "I demanded that she get rid of the child, but she refused, took you and ran away. It took me several months to track her down, but I finally found her." Miles was listening so intently, that he scooted forward onto the edge of his seat, leaning forward so as not to miss a single word.

"I tried to snatch the child … kill it, like I'd vowed to do … but Hansen stepped in to try calming me down." Thornton smiled fiendishly at the memory. "He pleaded with me to let him and Jane raise the child, which I did only after obtaining a promise from your mother that she would never divulge the fact that she was Nataka's mother."

Jumping to his feet, Miles glared down at his father. "Are you saying that Nataka is my brother?"

"Yes," replied Thornton softly, "Nataka is your half- brother."

"That just can't be true!" Miles clenched then unclenched his fists.

"But it is, son."

"Well, as far as I'm concerned … he is no brother of mine!" Miles sank back onto the chair looking angrily at the floor. "I wished you would have killed him when you had the chance! Since you didn't … I will do it myself!"

Thornton smiled at the intense feeling issuing out of Miles' mouth, feeling pleased with his son's attitude. "I'm glad to hear you say that, son. I may not get the chance for a long time. It gives me peace of mind in knowing that you'll accomplish what I couldn't do."

"You can count on it, sir," vowed Miles vehemently.

Thornton nodded, then forcing himself to stand, he placed a hand on Miles' shoulder. "I know I can count on you to get the job done, son."

"Thanks, Pa." Miles was pleased at the vote of confidence given him. "I'll go now, but I'll return as soon as I can to let you know what is going on."

"Thank you for coming." Thornton looked at his son intently before quickly adding, "I have always loved you, son. I want you to know that!"

Miles swallowed past the lump in his throat as he gazed admiringly at his father. "Thanks for telling me that, Pa. That helps me focus on the job I must do!" Thornton squeezed Miles' shoulder then sank wearily onto the bed. "See you later, Pa." Rising, Miles crossed over to the cell door. He hesitated a moment before going back to sit on the chair. "Pa there is one thing that I would like to ask ... then the subject will be closed forever."

Thornton inhaled wearily then looked over at Miles, "What is it?"

"I've noticed that there are only two saloons in Missoula--one being the Bluebird, the other one is Murphy's. Whatever happened to Ruby's Silver Slipper?"

"It changed hands several times after Ruby was shipped out of town by the Women's Society." An evil grin spread across Thornton's face. "It couldn't have happened to a better person."

"I see," replied Miles thoughtfully.

"About four years ago it changed hands again. A man named Victor Marrow bought it for a song and a prayer. Then a year ago someone knifed him on his way home. His daughter, Eleanor Marrow, is now running it. The man at the feed store told me that he couldn't prove it, but he was sure she was the one who killed him. I wouldn't know about that, because I wouldn't set foot in any saloon run by a woman."

"Guess I better get a move on." Turning, Miles called to the guard, "I'm ready now." As the guard opened the cell door, Miles turned to take one more look at his father. Thornton, who had lain back onto the cot, closed his eyes. Sighing softly, Miles stepped through the doorway. He watched as the guard locked the cell door. Gazing a moment longer at his father, he stepped out into the fresh morning air. A foreboding feeling of impending doom overwhelmed him as he sauntered back to the barracks.

ഔ ഔ

Private Michael Cooper returned to the fort late the afternoon of July Fifth. He met with Colonel Williams and Captain Thompson in Major Thornton's office. Cooper's uniform showed signs of a hard ride. It was not only dusty, but it also smelled of sweat mingled with wood smoke. A full day's growth of whiskers adorned his haggard face. After saluting, he stood rigidly at attention.

"At ease, Private." Williams waited for Cooper to collect his thoughts. "Now let us hear your report!"

"Cooper reached inside of his jacket to extract an envelope, which he handed to Williams. "Major Brown sent this to you while telling me to report that they would start for the fort inside of two hours." Thompson watched as Cooper nervously twisted the hat in his hands. His attention was pulled back to the present when he heard what Cooper had to say. "I left a few minutes after speaking to Major Brown, so they should be close behind me, sir."

"Great! Is there anything else I need to be aware of?"

"No, sir."

"Very well then, keep this trip under your hat. You are to discuss it with no one ... especially Miles Thornton!"

"Yes, sir!"

"That will be all. You're dismissed." Saluting, he pivoted to face the door and walked back outside.

When he was gone, Thompson turned to Williams. "I have come to a decision, sir."

"Good! Tell me about it!"

"I took your advice about talking it over with my family last night before the dance. We are all in agreement that I should lead the wagon train."

"Wonderful! Wonderful!" Jumping to his feet Williams stepped around the desk to shake Thompson's hand vigorously. "I was hoping you'd agree to take on this job."

Thompson grinned at the Colonel's enthusiasm. "I have several requests, though, before we make it official."

"Several?" teased Williams.

Thompson chuckled in spite of himself. "Yes, sir. Because of Miles' hatred for us, I would like to keep it confidential until after the hearing."

Williams nodded understandingly. "That will be no problem at all." He smiled as he looked at Thompson. "You did say several requests, so let's hear the rest."

"Since Sergeant Peters will retire in two days, I plan to ask him to come with us as a scout. Nataka Hansen is still part of the army; however, I would like permission to have him come with us as our lead scout."

"I see no problem there." They were interrupted when someone knocked at the door. "Enter," bellowed Williams. The door opened. Peters stepped inside, came to full attention then saluted. "As you were, Sergeant." Peters relaxed, lowered his arm, then waited for Colonel Williams to speak. "What is it, Sergeant?" It was obvious that Williams was very impatient.

"It's been brought ta ma 'tention thet Corporal Hank Jennings en Private Tom Jones hev done gone en deserted, suh."

"When did they leave?"

"Unknown, suh. The sentry, who were a carin' fer the hosses noticed thet two hosses were a missin' ... Clancy and Herman. The missin' hosses belonged ta them, of course, but it were the missin' hosses that clued us. That's when he comed ta tell me 'bout what he'd found ... so Ah hussled over ta report it, suh."

"I see," replied Williams thoughtfully. "Continue, Sergeant."

"We've searched the fort from top ta bottom en kin't find 'em enywheres." He paused slightly then continued. "When Ah runned inta Miles en saw the smirk on his face en his strange look ... Ah gots ta thinkin', so Ah went ta check their bunks en found their thangs missin'."

"Where does Thornton keep his personnel files?" Angrily Williams pulled out one drawer after another in search of them.

"They are in the last two drawers on the right, sir," directed Thompson.

"Thank you, Captain." Opening the first drawer, Williams began to rifle through the files. Finding those he wanted, he put them onto the desk, slamming the drawer. Thompson and Peters fell silent as Williams studied Jennings' file, then Jones'. "This is interesting, indeed!" Angrily, he handed the files to Thompson.

Thompson looked at each of them, then looked up at Williams in astonishment. "According to these records, Jones and Jennings were through with their hitches two months before they went on their last maneuver."

"That's right. I smell an awfully fat rat here in the works."

Thompson handed the files back to Williams. "I've suspected for some time that Thornton, Miles, and these two scallywags were up to something that was no good! They kept going on maneuvers, no one knowing what they were up to. As I had no reason to look in the files, I never thought to check it out."

"Why would you?" He picked up the pen, dipped it into the inkbottle, then wrote something across the files. When he was finished, he laid them at the left of the desk. "They really aren't deserters, Sergeant ... so let them go where they will, or until they do something to warrant our going after them."

"Ver' well, suh."

"That will be all, Sergeant. You're dismissed."

"Yes, suh." Saluting, Peters shuffled out the door.

Williams leaned forward looking at Thompson thoughtfully. "Now, where were we?"

"We were discussing my several requests, sir."

"That's right, but before we go on, I must admit that this hearing has my mind in a great turmoil. So if it's all right with you, maybe it would be better to wait until the hearing is over, then I can give you my undivided attention."

Thompson rose to go. "That's all right with me, sir. I understand because I'm really worried about that hearing, too."

"Thanks for understanding, Thompson."

Just as Thompson placed his hand on the knob, someone pounded hard on the door. He jumped in surprise, opened it, then moved aside to let Private Harris enter.

After Harris saluted, he hastened to give his message. "Just wanted to tell you that troops from Fort Missoula are approaching, sir."

Williams nodded in acknowledgment. "Thank you, Private. When they get here, bring the officers here right away."

"Yes, sir." Turning, he rushed back out the door.

"You might as well stay, Captain, as this concerns you, too."

"Very well, sir." Thompson reseated himself.

They didn't have long to wait before Major Brown and Major Edwards entered the office. Saluting, they waited for Williams to speak. "At ease, men." The men relaxed. Williams walked over to open the connecting door. Seeing the two women working at the kitchen table, he asked, "JaNae, could we have a pot of coffee and four cups brought to the office?"

"Sure thing dear," she replied. "Just give me a minute."

"Let me get a chair and I'll be out of your way." Stepping inside, he picked up a chair, which he carried back to the office. "Here you go. One of you can sit here." When they were seated, he took the chair behind the desk so he would be facing them.

JaNae entered, carrying a tray with the requested items. Anna followed with a tray, upon which sat four small plates filled with a huge slice of cake. Setting her tray beside JaNae's, which she had already placed on the desk, she quickly retreated. Meantime, JaNae acknowledged the newcomers, when they rose to bow slightly. She smiled as she set the tray on the desk. "Hello, Major Brown, Major Edwards. Fancy seeing you here." Both men smiled politely, but remained silent. "Well, I'll leave you men to your business." Turning, she hurried back to the kitchen making sure to close the door.

Pouring the coffee, Williams set the pot back onto the tray. "Help yourself, men," he added, indicating the plates filled with cake. While they drank their coffee and ate their dessert, they chatted amiably about nothing in particular. The two men secretly wondered why they were there.

Eventually, Williams set his cup onto the tray. Inhaling deeply, he began to address the men. "We have a serious situation here at Fort Owen, which must be resolved at all haste. Major Thornton issued orders for Captain Thompson to annihilate all of the Indians, which included men, women, and children."

The officers remained impassive, but Thompson saw their eyes flash angrily then become veiled as they listened to Williams. "Luckily, Thompson refused to obey those orders, saving this area a lot of bloodshed. Heaven only knows what else! I have called you officers here because you're equal to Major Thornton's rank. You are to sit in on the hearing that will be held at zero nine hundred hours sharp tomorrow morning."

The men nodded as one, then waited for Williams to continue. "Get settled in, eat a good dinner then retire early. I'll see you in the morning." The men again nodded. After saluting, they filed out the door. When Thompson rose to leave, Williams called him back. "Just a minute, Captain!"

Thompson turned back to face Williams. "Yes, sir."

"I want you to send out a detail to alert the settlers, those in the wagon train, as well as those in the fort … that we will meet at sixteen hundred hours tomorrow afternoon to discuss the situation presented by those in the wagon train."

"Right away, sir."

"That will be all," stated Williams smiling. "You're dismissed." After Thompson left, Williams entered Thornton's living quarters to inform Anna of the upcoming hearing.

JaNae was standing by the stove stirring something in a large kettle, while Anna was sitting at the table paring vegetables. "Gosh, what a sweet surprise," said JaNae, laying down the ladle. Coming around the table, she kissed her husband.

"Hi, yourself."

"Hello, Jedidiah," called Anna, smiling sweetly. When she saw the stern expression on Williams' face, the smile faded. She watched him anxiously as he took a seat beside her. She laid the paring knife onto the table, wiped her hands on her apron then placed them onto the table.

Williams took her right hand, placed it into his right, then covered it with his left so that she couldn't pull it away. "I have come to tell you some disturbing news, Anna." JaNae stepped up to him to place a hand on each one's shoulder. "The troops I sent for, to sit in on the hearing have arrived. We have set a time for Carl's hearing for zero nine hundred hours sharp in the morning." Anna grew visibly pale and struggled to remain in control. "I know this won't be easy for you, but be assured that I will not prolong it longer than I absolutely have to."

As Anna's lower lip began to tremble, she fought even harder for self-control. When she felt composed, she smiled weakly at Williams. "Thank you. I know you'll do what you have to just as fast as possible. Please, know that I appreciate your concern for my feelings."

"You are a real jewel, Anna Thornton," declared Williams, touched by her gentle spirit. Releasing Anna's hand, he rose to face his wife. "Don't wait dinner for me, honey, as I have a lot to do before the hearing in the morning."

"Just do what you have to do, darling. We girls will find things to do to keep out of trouble."

A teasing smile tugged at the corners of Williams' mouth while his eyes sparkled. "More like get into trouble, if I know you two."

Both women grinned then JaNae kissed her husband. "You could be right there." Williams kissed JaNae once more before going back into the office.

CHAPTER 25

A Hardened Heart

Kate lay wide-awake, struggling to empty her mind of troubling thoughts, yearning desperately to go back to sleep. Rolling onto her side, she listened to Paul's gentle snoring. Kate couldn't help wondering what the new adventure would be like.

Although it was thrilling to think of exploring new horizons, it was still difficult to leave the known behind, to bravely step out into the unknown. The thought of leaving precious friends behind that she treasured threatened to break her heart.

Turning impatiently onto the other side, she punched her pillow in an attempt to get comfortable, then burrowed deeper under the covers. Still her mind refused to allow her to sleep, so Kate gave into the wanderings of her mind. *How will I ever say my goodbyes to Jane Hansen, Anna Thornton, Ilse Pedersen, Lonna Foster, or Hattie Whipple, just to name a few?* she wondered. Tears came unbidden, soaking her pillow, as she tried to face the future with a brave heart. Somewhere around dawn, Kate fell into a troubled sleep.

Groaning, Kate tried to burrow deeper under the covers as the reveille sounded, but Paul leaned over to kiss her. "It just can't be morning yet," grumbled Kate.

Paul tauntingly caressed her cheek before stealing another kiss. "Oh but it is, my sleepy-headed Irish rose. You better rise and shine, as we have a lot to do before the hearing this morning."

"If I have to," groaned Kate. Stretching, she rose onto her elbow to look over at the sleeping twins. Satisfied that they were fine, she sat up onto the edge of the bed to dress. Paul, already dressed, went to the kitchen to start a fire in the kitchen stove. As Kate hurried to dress, she could hear Paul and Eileen talking about the day's events. A peaceful feeling washed over Kate, causing her to feel right with her world.

Paul had gone out to inspect the troops and do the few chores of the day, as Kate emerged from the bedroom. Eileen, who was already dressed, was making herself presentable for the day. Kate greeted Eileen cheerfully, "Good morning, Auntie. Did you have a good night's sleep?"

"I did. How about yourself?"

"I couldn't shut my mind off until really early this morning. I don't feel like I've even been to bed at all." She walked over to kiss Eileen on the cheek. "Please don't tell Paul. He'll think I don't want him to take on the job of leading the wagon train. I'm just having trouble letting go of the known ... not only that ... I really dread the idea of leaving all of my friends that I've come to love so much."

"Boy, can I relate to that feeling! I think inside of us is the knowledge that we need a change, but breaking out of our comfort zone seems too scary. We have a hard time taking that first step. Somehow, when we do take that first tentative step, we find it really wasn't so bad after all ... at least that's what I keep telling myself."

"This has got to be just as difficult for you, Auntie. Here you are just arriving in a new area, only to have to step out into the unknown again."

"But that's the way life is sometimes, my dear. She fell thoughtfully silent as she filled the coffee pot with water. Placing some grounds into the water, Eileen set the pot in the middle of the stove to heat. Turning to face Kate she added, "My biggest concern is my age." Kate nodded understandingly. "The trip here nearly wore me to a frazzle. I am only just beginning to feel better."

Kate looked at Eileen worriedly. "Maybe we shouldn't take on such a huge undertaking as this."

"That would break Paul's heart. Heaven knows, he never asks for much."

"That's true."

"No, my dear child," stated Eileen shaking her head sadly. "We need to leave anyway. We must follow the course life has set out for us."

"You're right, of course."

Eileen grinned mischievously. "I'm always right! Haven't you figured that out yet?"

Giggling, Kate walked over to hug Eileen lovingly. "You dear old treasure, you!"

"Hey!" cried Eileen in mock pain. "You watch out who you're calling old!" Placing her hands on her hips, Eileen pouted prettily.

Kate laughed at Eileen's funny expression, again kissing her tenderly on the cheek. "I stand corrected, Auntie. However, you are a real treasure ... to me, and I love you so much!"

Eileen turned back to the stove as she brushed at a tear. "Dad-blamed stove must be smoking again, as it's making my eyes water." Turning to take down the lid lifter, she raised the front lid, poking at the wood a few times. After replacing the lid, she hung up the lid lifter.

Kate wisely walked away to let Eileen gain control of her emotions. Filling the washbasin with hot water, she hurriedly made herself presentable while Eileen started preparing breakfast.

Paul returned with a large armload of wood, which he stacked into the wood box. When he was finished, he went back out for more. After putting the kindling near the wood box, Thompson went to haul in the water. As he washed up for breakfast, Thompson sniffed the air appreciatively. "Yum! Breakfast smells heavenly!"

As he reached out to take a piece of bacon, Eileen laughed and slapped at his fingers. "Where are your manners, young man?"

"They went out the door the moment I smelled the bacon frying," Paul patted his stomach appreciatively as he munched on a strip of bacon. "'Sides Auntie, I'm still a growing boy who needs lots of nourishment."

Eileen eyed him critically. "From the looks of you, you're growing from side to side, not upward."

Paul struggled to appear hurt but failed miserably. "Why, Auntie … what a thing to say to your sweet handsome nephew!" This brought peals of laughter from both women. Soon Paul joined in the gaiety of the moment.

"Be seated … we'll see if we can't appease that hearty appetite of yours."

Paul quickly kissed his aunt on the cheek then did as he was told. "Yes, ma'am." After a short prayer, they began to take the edge off of their hunger before engaging in a congenial conversation. When the meal ended, Paul rose to kiss Kate tenderly upon the lips. "I have to be in the hearing for Major Thornton, so I have no idea how long I will be gone."

"Very well. Do you think you could stop on your way to the community hall to ask John to come over and haul some water for me? I need to do the washing."

"I'll ask him right away." Turning, he walked to the door, took his hat from the hook, then left. Eileen rose to clear the table so that she could do the dishes, while Kate went to take care of the twins. She nearly had the kitchen cleaned when there was a knock at the door. Drying her hands on the dishtowel, Eileen went to open the door. "Good morning, John. Please won't you come on in?"

"Good morning, Miss Thompson. How are you today?"

"Just peachy! Thank you for your thoughtfulness and for coming so promptly to help us with these tough tasks."

"No problem ma'am … glad to help in any way I can."

"Good! I'll get the kettles so that you can fill them."

John touched her lightly on the arm as she turned to go. "No … I know where they are … so please let me get them for you."

"That would be helpful." John hurried into the storage room emerging with two large kettles, which he placed on the stove. Taking the two buckets from the counter, he emptied the remaining water into both of the kettles, then went to fill them.

By the time John had the huge kettles and the reservoir filled, Kate had finished feeding the twins. She was about ready to bathe them when John returned with two more buckets of water, which he placed on the counter. Turning to the wood box, he added, "I see that your wood box is nearly full. Since we don't know how long the Captain will be detained in the hearing, plus the fact that you have all of this water to heat, I'll chop some more wood. When the wood has been chopped, I'll stack it just outside the door for easy reach." Whistling, he sauntered out the door.

"I see what you mean about that young man going the extra mile. I really admire him." Between the two women, they had the twins bathed then back into their cribs by the time John had finished with the wood.

"Let me help set up the tubs. When the water is hot enough, I'll fill them."

"I'd appreciate that very much, John. When you have completed that task, come sit here so you can tell us all about your trip to Fort Missoula."

Blushing a little, John pulled out a chair from the table. Plopping onto it, he began, "Well Kate … you were definitely right about my reporting the incident to Colonel Williams."

Kate looked at him in surprise. "I was?"

John nodded, then paused a moment to collect his thoughts, then began to fill them in on what happened. "Kate, do you remember my telling you that I'd seen a horse with strange markings when the men rode away?"

"Yes, I do!"

John told how he had just gotten hidden when he heard approaching horses. "When the outlaws came into view, the leader of the gang was riding it," declared John. He went on to explain what had happened at the campsite. The ladies leaned forward in their seats to ensure that they didn't miss a thing. He told of Maines accusing one of the men of cheating at the card game. He paused a moment to heighten the suspense. The women waited with baited breath as John continued gosspiing, "He shot him." While he talked, he lost his inhibitions, even acting out a lot of the details. Watching him, the women sometimes cried, sometimes laughed or gasped, but continued to listen to every word he said. When he told of stealing the horses, the women looked at him with awe.

Kate clapped her hands together gleefully. "You stole their horses?"

John nodded. "Yes, I did!"

Eileen pondered it a moment, then became very jubilant over his quick thinking, "Oh, how wonderful! That was pure genius!"

"I have to agree with Auntie, that was really smart thinking … but very dangerous. I'm really proud of you, John."

Eileen nodded emphatically. "I should say so."

John blushed at the compliment, but it was plain to see that he enjoyed it, too. "I was very nervous when I was taken in to meet Colonel Williams, but he was not only attentive but considerate. I was surprised when he invited me to stay at his home. Because of their kind generosity, I came to really admire them. They are truly wonderful people."

"JaNae told us that you rescued a mother dog and her pups," prompted Kate. John's eyes lit up at mention of his dog Pugger. He related the story in depth. Again the women clung to his every word. "It was a good thing that you were there when that awful man went to drown them," said Kate.

"Your dog is a real sweetheart, John. Why would anyone want to get rid of her?" It was evident that Eileen was very disturbed by the story.

"I don't know, ma'am."

"Please go on with the story about the outlaws," begged Kate.

"Not long after the outlaws were captured there was a trial. You know, not ever having seen a trial, it was rather interesting. A few times it even got heated. At one point it looked like there would be a terrible ruckus, but Colonel Williams soon had everything back under control. The trial didn't last long as there was some extremely damaging evidence presented. The men were convicted, sentenced to die, then executed at dawn the next morning."

"That must have been a frightening experience, John."

"I agree with Auntie. I doubt that I could have been so calm, cool, or collected like you were," said Kate, plainly awed by his courage and his ability to deal with the situation.

"I am still struggling with anger and a need for revenge, but they are slowly slipping away. What you told me about forgiveness has really helped, Kate. Thank you so much."

"You're more than welcome. I'm glad that it helped."

When the water began to boil, John rose to fill the tubs, careful not to spill the water on the floor. When they were ready, he went to get some cold water to cool the water enough to work with. Refilling the buckets, he placed them on the counter. Promising to return to empty the tubs for her, he went home.

After sorting the clothes into piles, Kate grated a generous portion of lye soap into the hot water. Satisfied that she had enough soap, she placed the scrub board into the water. Putting the clothes in to the soapy water, Kate started the washing. Meanwhile, after cleaning the house, Eileen made a batch of bread.

While the bread was rising, she sorted some beans, washed them adding enough water to keep them from burning, then put them on the stove to cook. She hummed a little Irish ditty as she worked. At one point, Kate stopped the washing to watch her, storing the memory in the deepest recesses of her heart.

She went back to work, while Eileen formed the bread dough into beautifully shaped loaves and put them into greased bread pans. After putting them into the warming oven to rise, she helped Kate hang the clothes on the lines outside.

When the bread was ready to bake, Eileen placed it into the oven. While it baked, she quickly prepared one of her favorite New York desserts for dinner.

Eileen took the bread pans out of the oven, placing them onto racks in the pantry to cool. She had just put the cake into the oven to bake, before there was a knock on the door. "I'll get it," said Eileen going over to open the door. "Good morning, Jane! Won't you please come in?"

"Hello, Eileen." Jane entered. When the door was closed, she walked over to greet Kate. "Hi. I just stopped in to find out how both of you are doing, but as I can see you're up to your armpits in washing, so I won't keep you long."

"Nonsense! I'd welcome a break from this mess!" Drying her hands on her apron, Kate came around the tubs to hug Jane. Remembering her manners, Kate pointed to the rocker near the door. "Please, won't you sit a spell with us?"

"I'd like that," declared Jane sinking into the rocker. "I've been rushing around the house all morning like a chicken with its head chopped off!"

Eileen walked over to pull the coffee pot closer to the front of the stove, "We're suffering from the same syndrome, due to the fact that the twins take up a lot of our time now days."

Kate looked at Jane suspiciously. "How is the family doing, Jane?"

"Fine, although I was a little worried when Henry told me that Miles confronted Nataka near the stables last night."

She frowned in concern, as did Eileen. "Was Nataka hurt?"

"No. Henry said that Miles informed Nataka that his father had told him earlier that day that he was his half- brother, but as far as Miles was concerned, he would never accept that fact." Kate listened intently, concerned for Nataka's safety. "He went on to tell Nataka that he'd kill him the first chance he got for what Nataka did to them at the Indian village."

"What did he do?" questioned Kate.

"We don't know because he won't talk about it. Ever since we took Nataka into our home to raise as our own, I've really tried not to hate Major Thornton, or his son Miles. I really have ... but sometimes it's hard not to hate ... when someone tries to hurt those you love. Being taught that we should love our enemies, I try hard not to hate ... but lately it's getting harder and harder to do."

"I know, but hate only begets hate, which eventually destroys the soul."

"In my heart of hearts I know that what you say is true, but oh ... heaven help me ... it feels wonderful to hate."

"That's just it! It gets to feeling so good that before you know it, it has consumed you," said Kate.

"Well, at least it appears as though Thornton will finally receive his reward."

"We can only hope so," retorted Kate. "As much as I dislike the man, I feel sorry for him." Jane stared at Kate as if she'd lost all her senses. "Hate has consumed Major Thornton so completely, that he has lost all sight of the beauties of this world. What a sad waste of life!"

Deep inside Jane recognized the truth of Kate's words. Rising, she faced them, "Thanks for what you've just said, my dear. I needed to hear that this morning." Kate nodded but refrained from speaking. Jane hugged each of them and turned to go. "I'd best get back to the house to start dinner."

"Thank you for stopping in. I really enjoy your visits a lot, Jane." Kate saw her to the door.

"Me, too," replied Jane. "See you both later." Kate watched until she was out of sight then went back to doing the washing. Eileen poured herself a cup of coffee then moved the coffeepot to the back of the stove. Eileen drank her coffee, then cleaned up the kitchen.

◈ ◈

Anna Thornton awoke feeling a great trepidation about the day's upcoming events. Feelings of anger and hatred toward her husband, Major Carl Thornton, threatened to consume her. She turned on her side, burrowing deeper under the covers. It was no use — sleep eluded her.

Flinging the covers back, she rose to sit on the edge of the bed. *How will I ever get through this day?* she wondered. A desperate need for love and comfort came over her, causing her to tremble. Burying her face into her hands, Anna began to sob. All the years of abuse and rejection came rushing to the surface. It was difficult for her to breathe.

A few minutes later she dried her eyes. After blowing her nose, Anna got into her robe and slippers then tiptoed out to the kitchen. The house was eerily quiet except for the sounds made from the contracting or expanding of the wooden boards. Anna pushed a stray lock of hair from her face as she went to get a drink of water. She drank of the water's cold wet sweetness, grateful for the small reprieve from her troubles.

Replacing the dipper, Anna looked around the room. The thought of going back to the bedroom filled her with dread, but not wanting to wake JaNae and Jedidiah, she slowly made her way back to sit on the edge of the bed. Poignant memories flooded her mind, causing her to fall victim to their agonizing spell.

Fear gripped Anna as she thought of her husband sitting in a cell at the stockade. *What will he do to me when he gets out? Will he get out? If he gets out, will he succeed in killing me this time? Where can I go that he won't find me?* These and other questions ran rampant through her tortured mind.

When she felt she could not bear it any longer, Anna dropped to her knees in prayer, "Oh, dear God," she groaned aloud. "For twenty-four years, I have tried not to complain about my lot with Carl … but it was never easy. Today, Colonel Williams and Carl's superiors will decide his fate. There isn't a thing I can do about it."

Burying her face on the bed, Anna sobbed brokenly, as all of the pent up emotions came flooding out. "Lord, please tell me what to do, so that I may have thy sweet love envelope me." Groaning in agony she continued, "Oh, dear Lord, I really need thy healing balm to sustain me as I face the rigors of this horrible day. Please, Lord…"

◈ ◈

John was so intent upon the thoughts he was thinking that he wasn't paying attention to where he was going. As he rounded the right-hand corner of the stables, he ran smack-dab into someone, nearly knocking him off of his feet. "Whoa there, bully," declared a teasing voice.

John began to stammer in frustration as he reached out to help steady the soldier. "Oh my goodness, I am so sorry, sir!"

The soldier began brushing himself off. "You should be sorry!" The voice seemed familiar to John, but he couldn't quite place to whom it belonged. Then the soldier straightened his uniform while smiling at John.

Excitedly grabbing the soldier's hand, John pumped it vigorously. "Oh, it's you!" It was none other than Sergeant Aimes from Fort Missoula.

Sergeant Aimes chuckled good-naturedly at John's enthusiasm. "Easy there, Tornado Sam!"

John laughed sheepishly as he released Aimes' hand. "I did get a little carried away, didn't I, but danged if I ain't happy to see you!"

Patting John on the shoulder, Aimes smiled broadly. "I'm just as glad to see you. The old fort just hasn't been the same since you left." A mischievous gleam came into his eyes. "There isn't as much excitement now as there was when you were there."

John punched him lightly on the arm. "Ah, go on with you, Aimes! You're just funnin' with me."

"Well … now that I'm forced to think about it … you're right!" Both men laughed heartily, while they pummeled each other on the back, content to be in the other's company.

John anxiously watched his friend. "How have you been, sir?"

"Great! Say, John," declared Aimes poignantly, "don't you think we've become good enough friends for you to call me by my first name?"

"Yes, we are, but the only problem with that is … I don't know what your first name is."

Sergeant Aimes rubbed his chin thoughtfully, "I'd say that was a very good reason not to use my first name. My name is Mitchel, but you can call me 'Mitch' if you'd like."

"'Mitch', it is then," replied John.

"Good! Now, I feel we're officially friends." John smiled happily, knowing that he had a very special friend in Mitchel Aimes. "Say, I met a man in Missoula who says he knows you." John's eyebrows knit together in wonderment. "His name is Doctor McCabe."

"Yes, I know him very well!" John brightened at the mention of McCabe's name. "He was our army doctor for many years, but he retired not too long ago."

"Well, he has set up a thriving practice in Missoula. He told me to tell you and everyone at the fort 'hello' for him."

"I'm glad you told me about him, as I've thought of him often since I got home." The two men visited for a while then parted to do their different jobs, promising to try to see each other before Aimes had to go back to Fort Missoula. John went about his business, happy to have had a chance to visit with his friend Mitchel Aimes.

ഔരെ ഔരെ

Miles Thornton awoke, feeling the same feelings of foreboding doom as he had the day before. Shrugging to rid himself of the feelings, he rose to dress quickly. After he'd made himself presentable, he went to the mess hall to eat a hearty breakfast. Slowly he ambled toward home, not wanting to see his mother, but knowing that he needed to get a clean set of clothing for his father.

When he stepped onto the porch, laughter rang out from inside. Uncontrollable rage consumed him as he swung the door open wide. Anna turned from eating, then gasped as Miles strode angrily into the room. Miles glared at her with such hate that Anna trembled. JaNae laid her fork back onto the plate, preparing to defend Anna from her son should the need arise.

"So ... you're happily contemplating the spectacle Pa has to endure, because of your lousy friend's disobedience," Miles screamed.

Anna looked at him calmly, reminded of how spoiled, selfish and unapproachable he was. "We weren't even talking about your father, Miles. And as far as my being happy about the spectacle he must endure, he brought it upon himself!"

"Why, you are a spiteful old hag!"

He sprang at her as if to strike her, but JaNae stepped between them. "You've come far enough, Mister! You will treat your mother kindly ... or you can leave!" Miles stood looking at her with uncertainty, but seeing the determination in her eyes, he thought better of the attack.

"Whose concern is it how I treat the old hag?"

"I am making it my concern!"

Snorting, Miles hurried into his parents' room, rifled through his father's side of the closet for a clean uniform. Finding what he was after, he went to the chest of drawers for some clean underwear. Grabbing the shoeshine kit and toiletries his father would need, Miles huffily left the room. Without looking at his mother or speaking again, he strode angrily out the door, leaving it wide open.

JaNae calmly went to close the door while Anna began to weep softly. Stopping beside Anna's chair, she attempted to comfort her, "I'm sorry that he treated you that way, Anna."

"I feel so bad that you had to intervene for me, but I doubt that I would have been able to have stopped him otherwise."

"I know."

Miles was still fuming as he walked to the guardhouse. He wished that he'd struck the wench who defended his mother. The guard, seeing his foul mood, immediately opened the door and unlocked the cell to let him enter. Miles never even thought to thank the guard as he entered his father's cell. "Hello, Pa."

Thornton, who was sitting on the edge of his cot when Miles entered, grunted in greeting. He was feeling testy like Miles, or perhaps testier. "I brought you some clean underwear, a clean uniform and other things you'll need, Pa." Miles placed the items on the cot beside Thornton.

"Thanks, son. The guard is seeing to some hot water and a tub so that I can have a bath. These items are a welcome sight. "He absently fingered the items on the cot. "Was your mother there when you got them?"

Miles sneered angrily at the memory of meeting his mother. "Yes, sir, she was cavorting with the Colonel's wife."

This statement caused the anger to mount in Thornton, although he tried not to let Miles see it. "Well it doesn't matter what she thinks or does." Miles nodded, feeling warm inside. "If I'm to be ready on time, you had better go, but know that I love you, son."

"Thank you, Pa. I wish you the best of luck." Turning, Miles yelled for the guard to let him out. As the guard unlocked the cell door, Miles turned to smile at his father once more before leaving.

ↀↁ ↂↃ

Colonel Williams was busy with the setup of the community hall. It wouldn't be long until it was time for Thornton's hearing. This was one part of his job as a colonel that he disliked the most ... that of holding a hearing to determine if a court martial were needed. Yet knowing that it had to be done, he plunged in with great determination.

What bothered him most was the fact that Anna was subjected to Thornton's public disgrace and humiliation. Taking out his pocket watch from the watch fob of his jacket, he scrutinized it carefully then put it back. With only an hour to go before the hearing, he began to bark impatiently at the men to get everything in readiness. When the room was ready, he walked back to the office.

Unlocking the drawer, he placed his notes on top of the desk. After re-locking the drawer, he carefully scanned each paper, organized them, then put them together in a leather folder. Rising, he left the office.

Doctor Phelps caught up to Williams before he reached the community hall. "Sir, I wonder if I might have a moment of your time."

Williams only responded with a grunt. Seeing that Phelps was not going to go away, he turned to face him. "I don't have much time for idle chitchat, Doctor."

"This won't take long, sir, but I think you should be made aware of Thornton's condition."

Williams' eyebrows knit together in concern. "What condition?"

"Last night after the changing of guards, the guard who was relieved of duty came to get me. He told me that Thornton was thrashing around on his cot in terrible agony. When I went to check on him, I found him in a bad way. After examining him, I determined that his blood pressure was dangerously high. He was having extreme pain in his head and he was clutching his left arm. His nose was bleeding profusely, and he was vomiting."

Williams, who had been listening intently, grew very concerned. "What was your diagnosis?"

"Sir, Thornton nearly had a stroke last night, which I suspect was caused by fits of extreme rage."

Williams scratched his head thoughtfully. "I see."

"He told me this morning that he has been having very severe headaches for several weeks but they have gotten worse these past two weeks. I told him that if he didn't learn to calm down, he would have a stroke or blow a blood vessel." Williams nodded but remained thoughtful. "I didn't tell him that he could also have a massive heart attack."

"What do you want me to do about this information?"

"Thornton is so filled with hate, revenge, especially rage, that he can no more control his temper than he can hold his breath for any long period of time. I know this is not a public hearing, but if my suspicions are correct, then at some point in the hearing Major Thornton will lose his temper. It could prove fatal. Time is of the essence, therefore I feel that I should be present at the hearing in case I am needed."

"I tend to agree with you, Doctor. Very well then, come along."

"Thank you," replied Phelps, falling into step with Williams.

When they entered the community hall, the officers, Major Brown and Major Edwards were already seated at the long conference table at the front of the room. Colonel Williams, who had taken his seat, had just spread out his papers when Thompson entered and took a seat near the front of the room. Williams could tell by Captain Thompson's countenance that he was having a difficult time dealing with the situation at hand. The Colonel knew that it was always difficult to see a commanding officer face incriminating charges.

As Thornton was escorted to the community hall, he saw the Hansens standing among the crowd. He began to feel uncontrollable anger mount inside of him. When his eyes fell on Nataka, he glowered at him with such hatred that the young man flinched inwardly, although outwardly he felt calm. As the onlookers gawked at him, Thornton struggled to remain calm, while he plotted revenge against every one of them. Little did he realize the severity of his situation.

Just as they reached the building, Miles stepped out to smile encouragingly at his father. Peters frowned as he felt an overwhelming feeling of repulsion for Miles wash over him, but he smothered it as he watched Miles leaning against the building, his arms folded, sulking like a spoiled brat. *Like father, like son!* mused Peters.

Williams' attention was drawn to the back of the room when Thornton arrived, escorted by Sergeant Peters and Sergeant Aimes. He watched as they walked to the front. They waited for Thornton to take his designated seat. Seeing Thornton's surly expression, Williams couldn't help feeling disgust for the man. *What a shame that he has to be the man Anna married,* he thought. Her beauty, grace, and charm were wasted on this miserable excuse of a man ... a man so consumed with hate that he is blind to the beauties of life around him. Williams was coming to really admire Anna's spunk and tenacity, the more he got to know her.

After consulting his watch, Williams' put it back into his watch fob. Leaning forward, Williams placed his hands on the table. "This preliminary court martial has been convened for and in behalf of Carl Maxwell Thornton. Because of his rank, I have had Major Brown and Major Edwards brought here to act as witnesses, also to decide if a court martial will indeed be deemed necessary."

"Wait a minute," yelled Thornton, growing extremely angry. "Why isn't Captain Thompson being included in these proceedings?"

Williams faced Thornton with great contempt. "That isn't any concern of yours, sir! Besides, we are the ones who will be asking the questions, not you."

The cords in Thornton's neck began to bulge, while his face grew red with unspent rage. "I demand to know why Thompson isn't being charged in these proceedings!" Thornton grew even testier, if that were possible. "I want to know why I was treated like an animal ... forced to walk back to the fort with very little clothing on my person ... then imprisoned for two days like some filthy criminal!"

As Williams leaned back in his seat, disgust for Thornton was displayed on his countenance. "Alright, I'll tell you. Captain Thompson has been absolved from all guilt for disobeying your orders, because they were utterly unjust."

"Aren't I the one in command here ... who has the authority to issue any orders I deem apropos?"

Grabbing a sheet of paper, Williams declared, "We have here in our possession the orders you issued to Captain Thompson. Had he carried them out, it would have meant the lives of many innocent people, both Indians and soldiers alike. Because Captain Thompson had the courage and foresight to go against your orders, he has undoubtedly saved us all from a lot of useless bloodshed."

"With all the Indians dead, how could we have had any, as you call it, 'unnecessary bloodshed'?"

"Williams blinked at him in amazement. "Don't you remember the massacre that happened ten years ago?"

Thornton looked at Williams with a blank expression. "So what has that got to do with my question?"

Williams looked at him in amazement then absolute disgust. "You really don't get it, do you?"

Thornton nodded negatively. "No, sir ... I do not!"

"Someone would have spilled the beans, either wittingly or unwittingly. The news would have reached other Indian tribes. They would have gone on the warpath ... there would have been an imminent uprising."

Thornton shrugged then began to fidget nervously in his seat. The mounting anger continued to escalate inside of him. "I don't believe you."

"That's obvious!" Williams struggled to keep a tight rein on his overwrought emotions. "However, that doesn't matter at this time. What does matter is that I feel that what you did was very cowardly. Not only that, but it was an evil thing for you to attempt to involve Captain Thompson in your fiendish plan. Therefore, it is my recommendation that you are to be tried before a court martial as a coward. I also recommend that you be stripped of your rank as a major, branded as a coward, then booted out of the army with a dishonorable discharge."

As Williams spoke, Thornton grew so irate that it was all that Peters or Aimes could do to restrain him to his chair. "I protest!" Peters, with the aid of Aimes, again struggled to restrain him.

Colonel Williams, ignoring Thornton, turned his attention to the two majors. "What are your feelings toward holding a court martial for Major Thornton?"

Edwards looked over at Thornton with a scowl on his face, "I have seen the orders issued to Captain Thompson." Taking a deep breath, he added, "After hearing Major Thornton's comments just now, I concur with you, sir, that there should be a court martial held for Major Carl Maxwell Thornton!"

Pushing both sergeants from him, Thornton jumped to his feet all the time screaming like a raving maniac, "No! You can't do this to me!"

Ignoring Thornton's outrage, Brown looked down at the table. "I must also concur with Major Edwards' assessment of the situation. It is not only evident that Major Thornton is not only a coward, but he is also mentally incompetent to run this fort. It is my recommendation that he should be given a court martial then removed from his office."

"So be it," declared Williams. "A date for your court martial will be set in the near future."

Thornton grew so violent that he began raving crazily. All at once pushing away from the sergeants, he started toward Colonel Williams. Like a demon from Hell, he began bellowing. "I hate all of you! Ah, my ... " Thornton, grabbing his head, fell backward against his chair, which he knocked over as he crumpled onto the floor. Williams rushed over to where Thornton lay on the floor, anxiously gazing down at him. The others swarmed around him. "Doctor Phelps, get over here immediately!"

Phelps, who had been sitting in the back of the room, grabbed his medical bag and rushed forward. Kneeling beside Thornton, he turned Thornton over so that he could examine him. Feeling for a pulse, he found none. Reaching into his medical bag for his stethoscope, he listened to Thornton's heart in an attempt to find a heartbeat.

Removing the stethoscope from his ears, he looked over at Williams shaking his head negatively. "I'm sorry ... we've lost him, sir! As I feared he would do, Major Thornton became so angry that I assume he has blown an aneurysm." Phelps folded Thornton's arms over his chest then reached up to pull his eyelids closed.

Peters scratched his head, plainly confused by it all. "What does that mean, suh?"

"Isn't that where a person breaks a blood vessel in his brain?" asked Williams.

"Yes, but it can also happen when a vessel ruptures in the abdomen or the heart. I think that is what caused him to die so quickly, but of course I won't know for sure, unless I do an autopsy on him."

Williams ran a hand thoughtfully over his face. Rising, Williams went to his chair and wearily sank into it as he fought to overcome the shock. No one spoke as they waited for him to decide what to do next. He looked up at Phelps questioningly. "Is it possible to leave him here for a while, while I bring the family in to talk to them?"

"Yes," replied Phelps.

"In that case, you're all dismissed, except Captain Thompson, Sergeant Peters and Doctor Phelps. Keep mum about what has transpired here until I have had a chance to inform the family myself." They all nodded, then one by one, the men filed out of the room, leaving the four men alone with Thornton's body. Williams removed the jacket from his uniform covering Thornton's face. "Peters, go get Mrs. Thornton and their son, Miles. Make sure they come in together."

"Right away, suh." Saluting, Peters rushed out of the building.

After Peters had departed, Williams turned to face Thompson. "Is there someone around here who could make a coffin on such short notice?"

"Yes. Carl Jensen makes and sells them in Missoula."

"Do you think he would have one ready, or could he at least build one to use right away?"

"I don't know, sir. When the wagon master died, we purchased a coffin that he was planning to sell in Missoula. I don't know if he has another one started, or if he already has one in storage."

"Check that out as soon as you can. If he doesn't have one, tell him to construct a crude one and we'll pay him for it."

"Yes, sir." Thompson turned and hurried from the room.

As Thompson emerged from the building, Henry Hansen began to bombard him with questions. "What's going on in there? What happened to Thornton? We saw Peters come out, but he wouldn't say anything, so why is everything so secret?"

"I'm not at liberty to say anything as yet, Henry. Everything will be cleared up in a short time. Right now I must go, as I have orders that I must attend to." Hurrying to where Carl Jensen had his shop, he flung the door open to rush in. Carl looked up in surprise, which turned to concern when he saw Thompson struggling to catch his breath. That his face was ashen worried Jensen. "I'm sorry to barge in, Carl, but we have an emergency."

Carl groaned suspiciously then looked down at the roughly constructed coffin he had been working on. "What is the emergency?"

"As you know, we were holding a preliminary court martial for Major Thornton in the community hall."

"I'd heard something about there being a hearing, but really didn't pay too much attention to it."

"Well, when Major Thornton went into one of his famous tirades, he dropped dead."

Carl's mouth dropped in shock as he stared at Thompson. "No!"

"Yes, he did! Colonel Williams sent me to ask if you had a coffin already made. If not, could you quickly build one that we could use?"

Jensen sighed resignedly. "I have one back here that I finished a few weeks ago, but didn't feel satisfied with it enough to sell it in Missoula. Would that be alright?"

"How much do you want for it?"

"Oh … the same price as last time will be fine."

"Thank you. I'll get you the money as quickly as possible. I'll let you know when we'll be ready for it. Meanwhile, please keep this to yourself."

"No problem, sir."

Thompson got back to the community hall just as Miles and Anna were entering it. When Miles saw his father's body on the floor, he rushed forward to kneel on the floor beside him, while Anna sank onto a nearby chair, gasping in horror. Williams held up his hand motioning for silence. "Please hold your comments until I am able to explain what happened." He quickly explained to them all that had transpired, while giving them his condolences. Miles stared angrily at Williams then glared at Thompson. Rising, he rushed blindly from the building to be by himself.

"I really feel sorry for Miles," said Thompson.

Williams looked from Anna to Captain Thompson. "Major Thornton must be buried with full military honors for the rank that he holds, with a twenty-one-gun salute because he was never court-martialed. I will attend to that matter later, but for now I would like to know what we can do for you, Anna?"

Anna twisted her hands in frustration. "Right now, I am so numbed by it all, that I just don't know what to do. I don't even know if I should cry." Losing control, Anna laid her head on Williams' shoulder, sobbing bitterly.

CHAPTER 26

Changing Times

While Thompson walked Anna home, Williams sent Peters to the infirmary to get a stretcher and a blanket. While they were gone, Williams went out to speak to the curious crowd that was milling around. Someone started to speak but Williams held up his hands. "Wait a moment please, and I'll tell you what has been going on in here." A hush immediately fell over the crowd as they stood watching him curiously. "During the preliminary court martial, Major Thornton suddenly died."

Jane gasped. "Carl is dead?"

"Apparently so," said Henry.

Jane looked at her husband with a mixture of sympathy and grief. "I told Doctor Phelps that the day Carl Thornton got his just desserts, I'd laugh, but now that it has happened … all I can feel is extreme pity and sorrow for Anna."

Henry slipped an arm around Jane's shoulders. "I know, honey."

They again turned their attention to Williams. "We will let you know when the funeral will be just as soon as we know. Meanwhile go back to your homes or to your various tasks."

Slowly the crowd began to disperse, leaving Williams standing alone. He turned to re-enter the building when he heard Peters and Private Harris coming toward him with a stretcher. He opened the door, allowing them to enter. Hastening to the front of the room, the two men placed the stretcher next to Major Thornton's body. Working quickly they soon had Thornton on the stretcher.

As they spread a blanket over him, Williams started to speak, "Tell Dr. Phelps that I want an autopsy performed on the major as soon as possible. Have him place the report on my desk as soon as he's finished."

Peters nodded as they lifted the stretcher. "Yes, suh."

After Thornton's body had been taken to the infirmary, Williams sank wearily onto a chair. A while later he began to gather his papers together. All at once he longed to feel JaNae's comforting influence. He quickly stuffed the papers into a leather folder. Rising, he left the community hall.

As he ambled back to the office to prepare his report, he wished that it was nearing his time for retirement but then chided himself for such feelings. *I still have a little over a year before I'm eligible for retirement,* he thought, then sighed audibly.

When Williams entered the office, tantalizing aromas told him that dinner was being prepared. Sitting on the chair at the desk, he took out a key from his pocket. Unlocking the drawer where he'd been keeping his leather case of private papers, he removed the case.

Putting it on the desk, Williams hurriedly stuffed the papers from the hearing inside. Closing the flap, he sat absently stroking the metal clasp. Williams shook himself sternly to rid his mind of the images of Thornton's body lying on the floor. He placed the leather case back into the drawer, locked the drawer then placed the key back into his pocket.

Rising, he went into Anna's living quarters. JaNae was working at the stove while Anna was setting the table. Williams' heart went out to Anna when he saw how drained and tired she appeared.

JaNae, turning from the stove, gently wrapped her arms around his waist. Hungrily he pulled her to him, hugging her tightly against him. Williams was grateful for the calming effect she provided through her love. She kissed him softly. "Get washed up, honey. I just have to dish it up."

"I could really go for something to eat about now." Filling the washbowl with hot water from the reservoir, he set it on the counter. Picking up a bar of soap, he vigorously washed his hands and face. Anna handed him a towel when he was finished, then went to the icebox and set out the butter and some cream for their coffee. She placed these onto the table. Soon they were sitting down to partake of the delicious fare before them.

When they were finished, Williams went back into the office. JaNae rose to clear the table. "JaNae, leave those dishes to me ... go spend some time with Jedidiah." JaNae looked up at Anna in surprise. "You have been so good to me, but I feel that your husband needs you right now. It was really hard for him when Carl died during the hearing."

"You're right, my dear." JaNae kissed Anna tenderly upon the cheek. "You really are a treasure, Anna! I'm so glad that I have gotten to know you better."

For a moment Anna was touched beyond words. She took a deep breath and raised her head to smile. "Thank you. Doing these dishes will help me sort out my feelings about everything, too."

"Very well. I won't be gone too awfully long."

"Take all the time the two of you need. I'll be just fine."

Removing her apron, JaNae flung it across the back of a chair. She went into the office, closing the door behind her. Anna, having finished doing the dishes, was washing the table when Miles walked in. Seeing how upset Miles was, Anna's heart ached for him, although she did not dare show it. "Hello, Miles," Anna greeted him gently. "I know that losing your father has been very difficult for you, but we need to talk. First of all, have you eaten?"

Miles scowled as he roughly approached the table. "No," he snapped, "but I don't want anything right now!" Pulling out a chair from the table, he flopped into it.

"Okay." Anna quickly finished washing the table, then sat across from him, "Son, I know that you don't think much of me, but I am your mother. There are things that we have to decide … now that your father is gone. We don't really have to do it right this minute, Miles … but we ought to do it sometime soon."

"Look, Ma," growled Miles impatiently, "I just want to get out of here after the funeral. I know that Pa had some money stashed away." Anna nodded, waiting for him to continue. "If you will give me a thousand dollars of it, all of his medals and military ribbons, you can do whatever you want with the rest of his things, because it doesn't matter to me."

"I can do that." Rising, she went to her room. Laying Thornton's military medals on the bed, she took out a large leather bag. After placing the medals inside the bag, Anna knelt on the floor to reach under the bed for the cash box. Opening it, she counted out a thousand dollars. Closing the lid, Anna pushed the box back under the bed. Rising, Anna picked up the bag then walked back to the table. "I put your father's military awards in this bag so that they'll be easy to carry around."

Taking the bag from her, Miles placed it onto the floor beside his chair. "Thanks, Ma."

"Here is a thousand dollars of your father's money," said Anna as she laid it onto the table in front of him. "Is there anything else you want?"

Miles thought for a moment then shook his head. "No, this is all I want." He started to count the money, but seemed to lack focus. Rising, he stuffed the money into the right pocket of his pants then bent to pick up the bag. "Would you mind packing my things? You can send them over to the barracks. I can't stand being here any longer."

"I'll do that right away, Miles. Good luck to you, wherever you go," she added with a mother's tender feeling.

"Thanks," replied Miles in surprise. As he looked at her, for a fraction of a moment there was softness in his eyes, which she hadn't seen since he was a little boy. Then just as suddenly as it had appeared … it was gone. "Goodbye, Ma." Turning, he fled from the house. Anna sat thoughtfully wondering what would become of him. Her mother's heart ached, because even though he hated her, he was still flesh of her flesh and she loved him with every fiber of her being. Sighing, she rose to dump the dishwater, then finished putting the kitchen in order. Although she methodically performed the task before her, Anna's mind became a jumble of tortured thoughts.

When the kitchen was in order, Anna went to Miles' room, where she organized his belongings into piles on the bed. Finding two large carpetbags on the floor of his closet, she packed everything neatly into them. Removing his personal items from the shelves and top of the dresser, she stuffed them into the bags as well. After checking to see that she hadn't missed anything, Anna closed the bags making sure they were securely fastened. She knew she wouldn't be able to lift them, so left them until she could find a soldier to help her. When she stepped outside, Anna saw Peters nearing her house on his way to the barracks. She called to him, "Sergeant Peters …"

"Yes, ma'am." Peters rushed over to her. "What kin Ah do fer ya?"

"I wonder if I might impose upon you to carry two bags over to the barracks for Miles?"

"Shore nuff," said Peters, following Anna into the house.

"The bags are in the bedroom." She showed him where the room was, then waited.

Peters lifted the bags from the bed asking, "Good laws-ah-massy, lady! What cha got in here … rocks?" Anna chuckled as he staggered out into the living room. "A good thin' ya didn't try ta heft this yer own sef."

"When I had trouble closing them, I figured that it wouldn't be very wise for me to lift them. My ribs are stronger but not completely healed yet."

"It shorely were good ta see ya dancin' up a storm at the dance."

Anna smiled, pleased at his compliment. "Thank you, Sergeant. That really was fun!"

"Thet it were!" Peters grew thoughtful a moment then roughly pulled himself back to the present. Shifting the bags into a better position, he started toward the door. "Well, Ah'd best be on my way, ez Ah haf a lot to do afer the meeting at sixteen hundred."

"Thank you again, Sergeant. I greatly appreciate your doing this for me."

"Muh pleasure, ma'am!" Starting out the door, he paused to turn back to face her. "Will ya be ta the meetin' later?"

"Yes, I'm interested in what is going to happen around here. Now that Carl's gone, I have to find another place to live."

"See ya there."

After he'd gone, Anna closed the door, then went to sit in one of her stuffed chairs. Her mind whirled with many unanswered questions. *What should I do first? What's going to happen to me? How do I go on?* She still hadn't found any answers to her questions when JaNae entered.

"It's good to see you resting, my dear. I felt really guilty leaving you to clean up the dishes."

"They weren't difficult to do."

"Good. You were right about Jedidiah needing me." Sinking into a chair beside Anna, JaNae sighed contentedly. "Anything interesting happen while I was gone?"

"Miles came over as I was washing the table."

JaNae frowned in concern. "He didn't try to hurt you, did he?"

"No … actually he was very civil."

"Good! After this morning's stunt, I was worried he'd try to hurt you."

"I think he was so numbed by his father's death that he was oblivious to any other thoughts or feelings."

"Perhaps," replied JaNae thoughtfully, "perhaps."

Jedidiah entered the room long enough to tell Anna that he had received the report from Phelps. "The doctor said that Carl's temper was so explosive that he could no more control it than he could stop breathing. When he got so angry at the hearing, it was more than his body could endure. It seems that his heart was really bad, but it was indeed ruptured vessels in his head that took his life."

Frowning, Anna looked at Williams strangely. "I don't understand."

Williams knelt beside her to patiently explain the report. "Doctor Phelps said this happens when the wall of an artery becomes weak; it balloons out. Carl's temper was so bad, that when several weakened arteries in his head burst ... he literally bled to death internally."

"I see. Thank you for explaining it to me so that I could understand it."

"That's no problem, Anna." He rose to quickly kiss JaNae. "I'll be busy the rest of the afternoon, so I won't see you until dinner time." JaNae nodded and both women watched as he walked out of the room.

Williams knocked on Thompson's door, then stepped back to wait. When the door opened, Thompson blinked in surprise. Then quickly coming to attention, he saluted. "Won't you please come in, sir?"

"No, thank you, Captain. I just stopped by to ask you to report to Thornton's office in fifteen minutes. I want to talk to you before we have the meeting with the people from the fort, settlement and the wagon train."

"I'll be right over, sir."

"Thank you, Captain." Turning, he walked off of the porch. Thompson watched as Williams calmly strode toward Thornton's office.

Thompson went back inside, crossing over to the table where Kate was busily folding clothes. "I have to go to Thornton's office to see Williams for a while. I don't know how long I'll be. I should be back long before time for the meeting."

"Don't worry about us. We'll be ready to go fifteen minutes before the meeting. If you aren't here, we'll just walk on over."

"Very well." After kissing Kate tenderly upon the mouth, he strode over to where Eileen was ironing to kiss her on the cheek. "I will see you two beautiful women later." Removing his hat from the hook, he opened the door, turned back for one more glance at his family, blew them another kiss, then reluctantly left.

Williams was already in the office poring over some papers when Thompson entered. After saluting Thompson stood rigidly at attention as he waited for Williams to acknowledge him. "At ease, Captain." Williams, placing the pen near the inkbottle, leaned back in his chair. "Be seated, Thompson." When he was comfortable, Williams began. "I have several things to discuss with you, Captain."

"Yes, sir."

"First of all, I have received orders from my superiors in Washington, decreeing that I permanently terminate all military activities in Fort Owens." Thompson stared at Williams as if he hadn't heard correctly. "That's right … permanently. It seems that those in Washington feel that we no longer need a fort here, because Swift Eagle has honored the peace treaty so faithfully."

"How soon is this going to happen?"

"I have given Major Brown orders to dispense with the fort's contents any way he deems, just as soon as it is possible."

"I see. What will happen to the troops?"

"Some will go to Fort Missoula, some to Fort Benton, while others will be sent to Fort Boise. By giving Major Brown the responsibility to disband the fort, it will free you to concentrate on the needs of the wagon train."

"That's a good idea."

"I am going to issue an early retirement with full honors for these people, which will become effective immediately." He handed the orders to Thompson, who scanned them and then handed them back to Williams. "These men will be notified before the meeting at sixteen hundred hours, so they can make a decision on what they want to do."

"I must confess I'm glad that Corporal Hansen and Corporal Whipple and Sergeant Peters are on the list, sir. After all, they are getting up there in age. They have been here a long time."

"I surmised that when I reviewed their records." Williams smiled kindly at Thompson. "By the way, Anna told me that she and Hansen's wife, Jane, are very close friends. She also told me that Jane helped save your wife's life."

"That's true. Jane has always been a tower of strength whenever anyone was in trouble."

"Between you and me, Captain, Anna Thornton is one spunky lady! Because of all she has been through, I wanted to do something really special for her. When I reviewed Hansen's records, I saw my opportunity." He rose to pace slowly in an effort to collect his thoughts. "It is my understanding that Jane Hansen, your wife Kate, and Anna are not only like sisters, but are inseparable."

Williams stopped and faced Thompson before continuing. "Anna really needs that companionship right now and I don't have the heart to separate that friendship. So I have an idea." Thompson listened with interest as Williams hastened on, "Since the fort is being closed, Anna will be alone. Perhaps she would consider going with your family. I was hoping your wife Kate could lead her in that direction. I have a suspicion, if given the chance they will look out for each other."

Thompson agreed. "I will talk with Kate about it."

Colonel Williams said thoughtfully, "You know, Anna deserves a gold medal for putting up with that maniac's shenanigans. No one would have blamed her if she had cracked him over the head with a double tree! I just can't understand how she survived his barbaric abuse."

"All of us have been asking that very same question, sir."

Leaning back in his chair, he shrugged. "Well enough said about that. You said yesterday that you had some special requests to make."

"Yes, sir, I have."

"Let's hear them then."

"I had wanted to ask that Corporal Henry Hansen, Corporal Jonathon Whipple, and Sergeant Daniel Peters be given an early retirement, but you have already seen to that."

Williams smiled. "Kind of two minds converging as one. Hey?"

"Something like that, I guess. But I had also wanted Nataka released from his contract as scout for the army, so that he and Peters can scout for me."

Williams thought for a moment. "I don't see why that would be a problem, as long as Nataka is in agreement with that. As far as Jonathon Whipple is concerned ... well, his son John did a really brave thing when he helped capture the villains who had been wreaking havoc around the surrounding communities. I feel that he should be rewarded somehow. What better way to accomplish this, than sparing his father from an unnecessary transfer?"

"Thank you for your kind generosity, sir."

"What else did you have on your mind?"

"Would it be all right with you, sir, if I were to talk to them before the meeting?"

"Granted!"

"One last request, sir?" Williams nodded and Thompson went on, "We will need more wagons and teams, sir. With the closing of the fort, I am sure there will be more families that will want to go, so there won't be enough Conestogas to go around."

"A good point," replied Williams thoughtfully.

"We are also going to need more supplies."

"I tell you what. I'll issue orders to Major Brown that you are to have available, at your discretion, anything you might need to outfit those who aren't able to purchase a Conestoga."

"Thank you, sir. We're willing to pay for any services rendered or purchases made."

"Good! Then am I to understand that you are taking on the task?"

Thompson smiled. "You understand correctly, sir."

Williams rose to extend his hand to Thompson. "Good luck, Captain."

Thompson took the proffered hand and shook it heartily. "Thank you, sir."

"Not at all. After studying your records, I knew you were the man for the job." Williams handed Thompson several sheets of papers. "Here are your discharge papers, which are effective tomorrow!"

"Thank you, sir. I must admit, that it seems strange not to be responsible for anything in the military after tomorrow."

"I'll bet it does." Williams leaned forward in his seat to look intently at Thompson. "I want to thank you again for alerting us to the conditions here at the fort ...

also for going against Major Thornton's orders. I really admire your convictions, and your tremendous sense of honor."

Thompson was so touched that he couldn't speak for a moment. Swallowing past the lump in his throat, he tried again. "Thank you for your compliment, sir. I will remember it always." Standing, he looked at Williams with great respect. "John is right, sir. You truly are a giant among men!" Williams blinked in surprise, watching as Thompson saluted and slowly walked out the door.

Thompson not only felt light but was carefree as well. There was a spring to his step and a song on his lips. Excitement gripped him as he thought about the upcoming meeting, yet he wondered if his friends, the Hansens and Whipples, would consent to go with him. He decided to wait for an hour before going over to speak to the two families.

Nataka, absently stepping out of the stable, ran smack into Thompson. They grabbed each other to keep from falling. "I was hoping to run into you, Nataka, but not literally." Thompson couldn't help grinning. Nataka smiled sheepishly, but refrained from returning the sarcastic comment.

"Come walk with me a few minutes, son."

They fell into step while strolling toward the gate. They chatted about their families, and the happenings at the fort. Once they were outside, Thompson guided him away from the fort and beyond the wagon train. Satisfied they wouldn't be interrupted, he plunged in. "What I'm about to tell you must stay between the two of us for now."

"Very well. I understand, sir."

Colonel Williams has asked me to be the new wagon master, and I have requested that you accompany us as the scout. He gave his permission, but only if you are in agreement." Nataka could only stare at him. "It's true, Nataka, I have brought you out here to seek your acceptance to this request."

Nataka stared absently at the scenery before him, then taking a deep breath, he began to speak. "Well, I would like to accept this opportunity, but what about my parents, or my mother, Anna? I just found her ... I don't want to lose her already."

"I can see your dilemma, son, but there is something else I must share with you. Your father has been given an early retirement. I plan to ask him to go with us." Seeing Nataka's indecision, Thompson smiled encouragingly. "While talking to Colonel Williams, he expressed the hope that we could persuade Anna to go with the wagon train. It was suggested that Kate urge her to come along."

"Oh, that sheds a new light on things."

"Why don't we speak to your parents together?"

"That's a great idea! Do you have time to do it now?"

"Yes, as a matter of fact I do. I was on my way to speak to them, but I literally ran into you first," quipped Thompson.

Nataka's eyes twinkled and his mouth twitched naughtily. "I just know how to get your undivided attention, sir ... that's all ... just knock you over."

This was more than Thompson could take, and he burst out laughing heartily. "Come on, before you get too ornery for your own good."

When they entered the Hansen's home, Henry jumped to his feet, coming to full attention while saluting. Thompson smiled. "At ease, Henry. I'm not here on official military business."

Lowering his arm, Henry looked at Thompson anxiously. "Is everything all right, sir? Is something wrong with Kate or the children?"

"No, Henry, everything is just fine. We need to speak with the two of you, if this is a good time." Jane, who was standing at the counter preparing dinner, turned to look at Thompson curiously.

"Anytime is fine for you, Captain," said Henry, as he motioned toward the table. "Let's sit at the table. It's more comfortable."

When they were seated, Henry looked expectantly first at Jane, over to Nataka, then back to Thompson. Jane placed a hand on Paul's shoulder. "Can I get you a cup of coffee or something to eat?"

"A cup of coffee would be really nice, Jane." Bustling about the room, she quickly served all four of them, then sat down next to Henry. After linking her fingers together, she placed them on the table and watched Paul expectantly. "As you both know, the wagon train needs a new wagon master." Both nodded, then waited. "Well ... Colonel Williams has asked me to lead the wagon train to its next destination."

The Hansens stared blankly at Thompson, unable to speak. Finally Henry found his voice. "He has?"

"Yes, he has." I received my discharge orders today, which will become effective tomorrow. He also informed me that he was retiring you, Jonathan Whipple, and Daniel Peters. This will be with full military honors."

Henry and Jane turned visibly pale, sank back in their chairs as they stared at Thompson, unable to take it all in, then he leaned forward to stammer. "I- I- I don't understand! Why would he do that?"

"Well, you see ... I would like you and your family to accompany us. I have requested that Nataka act as scout for the train. Colonel Williams has given his permission. There is more that I would like to tell you, but you must be patient until after the meeting." They all nodded yet mutely watched Thompson rise to go. "Talk it over. Let me know your answer as soon as possible. Right now, I must visit one other family before I can go home to dinner."

Nataka walked Thompson to the door, while his parents remained in their seats ... their mouths gaped open in stunned disbelief.

When Thompson entered his house some time later, Kate pounced on him immediately. "What did Colonel Williams want with you? Well ... perhaps I'm not supposed to know, so you don't need to tell me."

Thompson walked over and kissed her lightly upon the mouth. "You'll know soon enough, my red-haired beauty, so for now, mum's the word."

"I stand chastised," Kate said apologetically. "I guess I was wondering if you told him you'd lead the wagon train." She searched his face for signs to know if he had, but he was so impassive that she turned away.

"Perhaps ..." he replied nonchalantly, "then ... perhaps I didn't." Like a cat toying with a mouse, he strung her along for a few minutes until he couldn't wait to see her expression when he told her that he had indeed spoken to Williams. "We discussed my leading the train." Again he toyed with her like a cat with a mouse.

"Well!" she cried impatiently. "What did you tell him?"

Thompson shrugged his shoulder nonchalantly. "I said I'd do it."

Kate sighed in exasperation and punched him lightly on the arm. She exclaimed, "Oh, you tease! Sometimes I think you need Auntie to whip you back into submission."

"It wouldn't do any good," said Thompson, matter-of-factly. "She tried when I was a strapping young man. It didn't work then. Did it, Auntie?"

Eileen waved him off. "I'm staying out of this conversation."

"See," teased Thompson. "You can't even get help from Auntie!"

Eileen glared at him in mock anger. "You continue to hassle her, and we'll see if it will do any good to whip you into shape!"

Thompson laughed uproariously. "Oh, you're just as much of a big tease as I am, Auntie!"

She looked around to see if there was some unseen person in the room. "Don't tell anyone else. It would spoil my cover as a grouch." Kate and Paul laughed heartily at Eileen's mock severity.

Thompson reached out and hugged her. "Something tells me that it has already gotten out, Auntie."

Sighing resignedly, she walked over to the stove to stoke the fire. After hanging the lid lifter back on the hook, she set a pot of coffee on to heat. "I was afraid the cat was out of the bag. Oh, well, come tell us what you can."

"There isn't any more that I can tell you right now, except that I got my discharge papers, which will be effective tomorrow."

"How long were you planning to keep that from us?" Kate walked over to look at his official documents.

"Until now," laughed Thompson.

"That's what I thought."

Thompson sat at the table with his two favorite women, chatting amiably about nothing in particular but content to be in their presence. While he half listened to their prattle, his mind went back to the interviews with the Whipples. Like the Hansens, they also were stunned beyond words. When he left them, they were staring at each other as if their commander were crazy. The image made Thompson smile.

It wasn't long until dinner was ready. Soon after appeasing their appetites, they chatted about the upcoming meeting, wondering what it would be like. Although they anxiously looked forward to the new adventure, the thought of leaving most of their friends behind left emptiness within. Underlying the excitement of it all was the realization that their lives were about to change … be it for good or bad.

When the meal was over, Thompson helped Eileen with the dishes while Kate took care of the twins. She had just finished, when Paul entered the bedroom. "Are they about ready for night-night?" he asked as he tickled one affectionately under the chin.

Kate grinned as her handsome, he-man husband cooed over his little ones. "Yes, they are."

"Good! Let me help you put them to bed."

"I'd appreciate that very much," sighed Kate. "This afternoon has been a real challenge."

When the twins were settled in for the night, Thompson led the way back into the living room while Kate finished getting ready. Eileen was just putting her hat on when Thompson entered the room. "Are you ready, Auntie?"

"Yes. All except for my shawl, which I'll carry."

Kate hurried out of the bedroom. "I'm ready, too, just as soon as Sylvia gets here."

Just then there was a knock at the door. "Come in," called Thompson.

Sylvia entered. "Sorry I'm late, but I had to help Ma a few minutes."

"You're not late, Sylvia." Kate bustled around, giving her last minute instructions. "I don't know how long the meeting will last, but if you get hungry, there's cake on the counter and milk in the icebox. Just feel free to help yourself."

"Thank you, but I'll be fine."

Thompson opened the door, motioning to the ladies to hurry. "Then we'd best get started. Wouldn't want to get there after the meeting's ended."

Kate giggled as she joined the rest of her family. She quipped, "Keep your shirt on, mister! The last I heard, there wasn't any fire to go to."

"Why you little imp!" Thompson made as if to slap at her, but she just side-stepped him as she slipped out the door.

Eileen shook her head, feigning sternness. "Now you children behave before I spank you both!" This brought peals of laughter from the couple. Eileen smiled in spite of herself, content to be with her family.

They walked companionably along for a while, then Kate broke the silence. "I still can't believe that Carl Thornton is dead. He was such a vile man that I thought he'd be around to torment us for a long time yet."

"I know," replied Thompson absently. "That was an awful shock to see him die in front of us like that."

They were prevented from speaking further about the Major, when the Hansens caught up with them. After their greetings, Thompson turned to Henry. "Well, have you thought over what I asked you earlier?"

"Yes, we have, sir. We think it's a good idea."

"Good! That was what the Whipples thought when I went to see them also." Kate looked at Paul, then back to Jane and Henry, but as they didn't elaborate on what question Paul was referring to, she thought it best not to pry. When they drew closer to the community hall and saw all the people milling around, Thompson was amazed. "Boy, it looks like we'll have a crowd at this meeting!"

Henry blinked in surprise. "It surely does."

Several families were filing into the building as they approached. Thompson waited until Kate and Eileen entered before following them to a row of seats near the front. When they were seated, he noticed that Williams was standing at the front of the room, waiting for all to take their seats so that he could start the meeting. As Thompson looked around the room, he was amazed at how packed it was. He couldn't help but wonder how many of the people would be going on the wagon train with them.

Williams banged on the table in an attempt to be heard above the crowd. "Let me have your attention, ladies and gentlemen." Falling silent, everyone looked toward the front of the room. "Good ... now we can get started." He looked around the room until his eyes met Paul's. "Captain Thompson, would you please come up here a moment?"

Thompson rose to join Williams. Turning to face the people, he started, "I have several things to discuss with all of you. First of all, I would like to inform you that Captain Paul Thompson, discharged from the army effective tomorrow, has consented to be your new wagon master."

A tremendous cheer rang through the people when they heard the news, yet some felt a tremendous loss, losing not only their friend, but their leader. Kate and Eileen beamed at the people's vote of confidence. They even felt a thrill of excitement at the prospects of the new adventure.

There were others in the settlement that felt numbed, because they sensed that changes were about to occur. This frightened them a little. As for Paul, he was experiencing so many emotions that he was having a difficult time dealing with it all.

Williams grinned, pleased that the people were taking it so well. "Captain Thompson was sent to explore the regions around Montana, also part of Canada, shortly after coming to the fort three years ago. That qualifies him for the job."

Again the people cheered and talked excitedly among themselves until it was impossible to get their attention for quite a while. Williams understood their excitement so waited a little bit before trying to get their attentions again.

When Williams failed to get their attention, Peters whistled shrilly. "Listen up, folks," he bellowed.

Williams smiled gratefully. "Thanks, Sergeant Peters." He nodded for Thompson to take his seat. "There is a lot more to tell you, so if you will please settle down, I can get on with it."

The people grew quiet as they turned their attention back to Williams. "I have received orders from my superiors in Washington that Fort Owens is to be terminated as a military post, effective immediately."

The people groaned or gasped in turn, then waited to hear what else he had to say. "Because the Indians have honored the treaty so well, my superiors feel that having a fort here is unnecessary."

The soldiers looked at each other, then back to Williams, alarm written on their faces. "I have assigned Major Brown from Fort Missoula the commission of this fort until it is completely dissolved. The soldiers who are still serving a tour of duty will be sent to other facilities to complete them."

Most of the soldiers managed to remain impassive, though some scowled at the prospect of being separated. Williams continued, "I know that this has been a low blow to most of you, but I know that you'll deal with it like the gentlemen that you are." Most of the soldiers really wanted to finish their tours together, but what could they do but try to face it the best way they could when Williams gave them that kind of praise. "As I stated at the beginning of this meeting, Captain Thompson will be leading the wagon train. He has asked that Sergeant Daniel Peters and Nataka Hansen go along as guides."

A murmur of consent ran through the people, and then all was silent. "Mr. Payne said that there were some from the wagon train who wanted to settle around this area. They wished to buy property of those interested in selling out. However, because of their meager funds, they hoped that those willing to sell out to them would be willing to accept Conestogas with the teams as part of the payment, with cash for the remainder. Some just want to sell their Conestogas and their teams for cash, in order to purchase fares back to their friends or families."

For a moment, Williams stood silently pondering what should be done next, and then he proceeded. "I think that the remainder of this meeting should be devoted to making the lists of those wanting to sell out, those wishing to stay in the area, and those wanting to sell their wagons with teams."

The rest of the meeting consisted of making the lists. When that was finished, the meeting broke up. Some went on their way, while others milled around the little groups of people discussing the news, while others sat in numbed silence. Thompson listened absently as Kate and Eileen discussed what had taken place in the meeting. As one, the three of them turned when they heard their names called. Pedersen hurried to catch up to them. "Hello Hans ... Ilse," greeted Thompson. "What did you think of the meeting?

Linking her arm with Hans, Ilse nodded for him to speak. "Ve vant to speak to ya regarding zee meeting."

"Why don't you come on over to the house, where we can be comfortable? We can all discuss it there. Kate made a cake today, so we can have it and some coffee while we visit."

Hans looked at Ilse, who smiled approvingly, then turned back to Thompson. "Ya, danke. Ve vould like dat." The little group walked along content to be together.

After they entered the house, Thompson walked Sylvia home, while Kate and Eileen prepared refreshments for their guests. Kate motioned to the chairs at the table. "Won't you please be seated? Paul won't be long. We can talk while we eat."

The Petersens pulled out chairs, which they sank gratefully onto. They chatted about everything but the meeting as they waited for Paul to return. All at once the door flew open and Paul stepped inside.

He took a chair next to Hans, watching as refreshments were served. After they had finished, he turned to Hans. "Now my friend, what can I do for you?"

Indicating himself and Ilse, Hans again took over the conversation. "Ve haf talked it over, und ve haf decided to sell our place. Ve vant ta go vith ya."

Kate grew excited by the news. "You do?"

Isle smiled broadly at Kate. "Ya. Ve do not haf so many freunds here, so ve vant to be vith all a ya, no matter vere ya go." All at once, she felt unsure of herself. "Dat's ifn' ya vil haf us."

Paul, becoming elated, clapped his hands together. "If we'll have you? We would be absolutely delighted to have you along!"

"Sehr Gut! Ve know zat ve haf a big family, so it vil take much to make us ready … so ve vould haf understoot yer not vanting us shoudst go vith ya."

"We have been friends ever since Kate and I arrived at the fort three years ago, so we were wondering how we could ever say our goodbyes. We are so glad that you are going to be with us, because now we don't have to be parted from each other!" This brought tears to both couples' eyes.

"Danke, mine freunds," said Ilse. "Danke."

Hans nodded vigorously, as he impatiently blinked the tears from his eyes. "Ya, danke fer being such varm loving freunds to us."

They stayed long enough to have another cup of coffee and get instructions on how to be prepared for the trip. An hour later they went home. They hadn't been gone long when there was a knock on the door. "My but aren't we becoming popular," teased Kate, as she walked over to open the door. "Why hello, Sergeant Peters. What a wonderful surprise!"

"Howdy, ma'am."

"Please, won't you come in?"

"Thank ya, ma'am. Ah would 'preciates ifn' Ah could speak ta the Captain."

Thompson walked over to grasp Peters' hand, which he shook vigorously in greeting. "Hello, Peters. You're just the person I was looking for, so come on in."

"Thank ya, sir." Stepping inside, Peters began twisting his hat nervously.

"Be seated, Sergeant," commanded Thompson.

"Auntie and I are going out to sit on the swing to get a breath of fresh air for a few minutes … giving you men some privacy. Let us know if the twins wake up."

"Thank you, honey. This shouldn't take too long."

"You're a prince of a husband, darling." Kate kissed him quickly upon the mouth, and the women left the men alone.

Thompson waited until they had closed the door before addressing Peters. Reaching into the desk, he took out several sheets of paper, which he handed to Peters. "This document in my hands states that you are officially out of the Army as of this minute."

"Peters took the document, touched it tenderly, then looked up at Thompson. "Ah've looked forward ta this day fer so long, thet now thet it's here, Ah feel sorta strange 'bout it."

"I understand how you feel, Peters, because I felt the same way when I received my walking papers a few hours ago."

"Ah wants ta thank ya, suh, fer recommendin' me ta hep scout fer the wagon train, en Ah promise not ta let ya down, ifn' Ah kin hep it."

"That's why I asked for you to be a scout for us. You have been the best friend a man could ever have, and I wasn't about to let you slip away without first trying to get you to go with us."

Rubbing his eyes, Peters took a deep breath. "Dad-blamed eyes er givin' me a fit taday!" Thompson wisely gave Peters time to gain control of his emotions. Eventually, Peters rose to leave, pausing long enough to add, "Ah thin' yer the squarest man Ah e'er knowed. Ah calls it a real honor, suh, thet ya'd asked me along on this here wagon train. Ah thank ya kindly." Before Thompson could reply, Peters turned and walked out the door.

ॐ ॐ

The Hansens were sitting in their living room alone after the meeting. Sylvia had not returned from babysitting the Thompson twins, and Nataka was still at the meeting. "Henry, do you think it's time for Anna to have a talk with the children?"

Henry sat silently mulling the question over in his mind. "I really don't know, dear. Perhaps we should talk with her first. Let her decide when it's time."

"I know that we need to break the news to them eventually, but I'm really worried how they'll take it."

"It will be rough for a while, but I have enough faith in them to know that they'll come to understand why Anna gave them up. I also believe they will even come to love her for the sacrifices that she has made for their safety."

"I really do hope so, Henry." Both fell silent, lost in their own worlds. "Before we took Nataka, I really didn't have much to do with Anna. I guess I was too busy judging her by Thornton's actions." She sighed at the memory of how she had shunned Anna in the beginning. "Then when she ran away from Thornton to save her son's life, I saw her in a completely new light. I was so ashamed of my previous actions toward her." A look of admiration crossed Jane's face as she continued. "Anna is one grand lady! To love her children enough to let someone else raise them, so that they weren't harmed by that fiend, took a tremendous amount of courage!"

"You're right, honey," agreed Henry emphatically. "She is one really terrific individual. I have not only come to respect her, but I also love her like a sister."

Rising from his chair to kneel beside Jane, Henry enveloped her in his arms and wisely let her cry. "I know you would have done anything to protect Sylvia or Nataka, honey … even if it meant your life."

Throwing her arms around Henry's neck, Jane hugged him tighter to her. "You are so sweet to say that. It makes me feel a lot better for your having said it."

"Henry kissed her cheek tenderly. Placing his hands on both sides of her face, Henry added, "I have been married to you for thirty-seven years, Jane Hansen. I know what you would have done!"

Gasping, June snuggled back into his arms, content to bask in the love she felt for this man. "I love you so much, Henry Hansen!"

"And I love you too, honey. I don't want to be a wet blanket, but now that Carl's dead, Anna is going to need our help more than ever."

"You're right, of course. At least we'll be able to do so without worrying about Carl's rotten intervention." Henry nodded as he drew Jane closer to him.

They were still like this when Nataka entered. "Excuse me," he stammered, turning to go back outside.

"It's all right, son," Henry chuckled, "I was just sparking my sweetheart." His eyes twinkled with merriment as he looked as his wife's red face.

"I could come back," teased Nataka.

"Don't be so silly," scolded Jane. She pushed her hair back from her face in an attempt to gain control of her composure. "This is your home, too!"

"I have something to talk to the two of you about. I would really appreciate it if we could talk before sis gets home."

"Sure, son," Henry anxiously watched Nataka walk toward them. "What's on your mind?"

Nataka sat on the floor next to Jane. Taking her hand in his big one, he began to stroke it absently. "Well, I wanted to tell you that I've known for a long time that Anna Thornton is my real mother."

Jane flinched, turned to look at Henry, then back to Nataka. "You know?"

"Yes, Ma."

Henry watched him suspiciously. "How did you find out?"

"One night when you thought I was asleep, I heard the two of you talking about how Anna was my real mother. Then when I went on the last maneuver with Captain Thompson, I forced him to tell me why she did that." Nataka smiled at the memory. "Oh, he didn't want to at first. But when I told him that I knew that she was my mother, and that I felt that I had the right to know why she gave me away, he told me."

"Oh," answered Jane thoughtfully.

"Ma," cried Nataka with deep feeling, "I will always love you as my mother, but I have come to love Anna just as dearly."

Jane flung her arms around his neck. "Oh, son, I'm so glad, because I was worried that you'd hate her when you found out the truth."

"For a while I did, but when Captain Thompson informed me of what really happened, something inside of me reached out to her." He kissed Jane's hands lovingly, before adding, "When I thought of all that she has been through because of her father, and that skunk, Carl Thornton, I felt sorry for her. Then when I kept visiting her in the infirmary, I realized that I loved her dearly." There was a catch in his voice.

For a moment he couldn't go on. When he was able to continue, he said, "Then as we talked, I felt grateful that she allowed you to raise me so that I could live." Tears glistened in his eyes as he tried to express his thoughts. "How could I hate someone who loved me enough to let me go in order that I might live?"

Jane reached out to tenderly touch Nataka's cheek. "You have always made me proud, son, but never more than you have now!"

That was more than Nataka could bear, so he laid his head on Jane's hand while he shed a few tears. "Thank you, Ma. I'll treasure that comment for the rest of my life!"

A great silence fell over the room, as no one wanted to break the feeling of love that filled their hearts at that moment. Henry crossed over to place a hand on Nataka's shoulder. "There's something else you'd like to say to us, but don't want to hurt our feelings, isn't there, son?"

"Yes there is something I need to say, Pa." Nataka smiled broadly up at his father. "I've always been amazed at how well you could read me."

"Not always, but today something tells me that you're afraid of hurting us." Nataka nodded as he looked at his wonderful parents. "Son, whatever you're afraid of telling us must be mighty important, or you wouldn't be so worried."

"I will always love both of you. We'll always be a family, but right now Anna needs me. She has no one to care for her." When his parents refrained from speaking, Nataka hastened on. "Ma, Pa, you haven't lost me because I'll always be popping in now and again to check in on the three of you."

"You're right, of course." Henry squeezed Nataka's shoulder tenderly. "Son, you have our blessing to do what you feel is right, because we trust you implicitly."

"Thank you, Pa." Nataka watched them both intently. "Would you mind too terribly if I called her Ma?"

"I'd be proud if you did," replied Jane. "She needs to know that you love her, too."

"No wonder I love you both so much!" Nataka gazed proudly from one to the other. "May I still call you Ma and Pa?"

"We'd be hurt if you didn't!"

"I'd be honored if you'd still call me Ma!"

"Good! I must be the luckiest man in the whole world, because I have two mothers!"

All at once, the door flew open. Sylvia bounded inside, rattling the windows as she slammed the door shut. Jane jumped, clutching her chest in fright. "Good grief, girl. Is the devil chasin' ya er somthin'?"

Sylvia grinned sheepishly, "Aw, Ma. I'm just happy."

"Well, ya coulda fooled me. I thought something terrible was happening."

Henry walked over to proudly hug her. Stepping back, he gazed lovingly into her eyes. "You're quite the gal, Sylvia."

Sylvia smiled, as she hugged him back. "Thank you, Pa."

"Come on little family, let's have a family counsel." Henry led the way to the table, taking his place at the head of it. When everyone was seated, he looked around and felt a great love for them all. "Your mother and I have something we'd like to discuss with you."

Sylvia looked at her mother, then back to her father. "There is no easy way to prepare you for what we need to say, so I'm just going to plunge in. As you know, the fort has been shut down." Everyone nodded agreeably. "Well I was retired from the Army effective immediately. After talking with Captain Thompson, your mother and I have decided to go with the wagon train."

Sylvia inhaled sharply and leaned forward in her chair, while looking at her parents as if they had suddenly gone crazy. "Isn't that a little drastic? Why do we have to go out where there are hostile Indians?" As she spoke, she grew more frantic, playing with the ruffle on her sleeve. "I don't want to leave my friends! They mean everything to me. How am I supposed to start over?"

Hansen reached out to take her hand. "But you're failing to see the overall picture, Sylvia. With the fort shutting down, everyone is going in different directions. We are going to lose some of those we love anyway. Since I am no longer in the Army, we have to move someplace else, so why not be with some of our friends? Maybe it will help soften the blow if you know that Mary Pedersen's family is going with us."

"They are? I thought they owned their place, so why are they going with us?"

Henry smiled patiently. "I think you just answered your own question. They're leaving because they want to be with us, too. I know it's hard to start over, but we've done it many times before. We can do it again. Don't think of it as the end of the world but a fresh new beginning."

Sylvia nodded absently. "Very well, Pa. I trust you to make the right choices for our family."

"Thank you, honey. That means a lot to me."

Jane reached over to pat Nataka's hand. Looking at Sylvia, Jane smiled. "Nataka will be scouting for the wagon train, so that's another reason why we want to go."

"Oh, I didn't know that! That makes it easier already."

Everyone laughed heartily, grateful for the release of tension. For the rest of the evening the family spent their time together making plans or discussing what would happen on their new adventure, just happy to be together.

CHAPTER 27

Confessions

The three Thompsons were sitting around the table in the kitchen on the morning of Thornton's funeral. They were dilly-dallying after breakfast, not anxious to start the day. There were so many emotions to deal with and things to do that they felt a little overwhelmed. Sighing, Kate rose to do the dishes, but her heart was definitely not in it. As she started to clear the table, Paul reached out to gently take her hand. "Forget the dishes right now, honey. Let's talk about what we're feeling. ... Okay?"

Smiling, Kate took her seat. "You don't have to twist my arm to get me to forget these blasted dishes. To tell you the truth, I am feeling so many mixed emotions that I don't know what to do."

"I figured as much, honey." Paul turned to look at Eileen. "I assume you are suffering from the same disease ... emotional distress?"

"You could say that," grinned Eileen. "However, I don't know that I would class it as a disease."

"Well maybe you're right, but I have the same problem ... whatever it is. Anyway I've been awake most of the night, just thinking about what lies ahead and what I've learned through the experiences here at the fort."

"So have I," admitted Kate. "As I sat nursing Aaron last night, I remembered the day we arrived at the fort. I was just a new bride ... scared to death of being in an unknown place or meeting strange people. Little did I know then that I would gain so many wonderful friends ... or that I would become a mother of twins. Not only that, but I finally learned to live without the water closet.

"I couldn't help grumbling, at the many times during the day, when I would wade out through the deep snow ... just to get to the outhouse. Then at night, when the fire was out and the house was cold, I had to warm that cold, enamel chamber pot before I could do my duty. Oh, how I longed for the water closet then!" Eileen and Paul laughed at the picture it summoned to their mind.

"There was a lot I had to learn, too," admitted Thompson. "Believe me when I say that I was forced to learn most of it the hard way. When we came to Fort Owens, I had never met a man like Major Thornton. I always thought the superiors I served under back east were bad, but when I met Thornton, he made them look like pussycats. In spite of his crusty attitude, which grew worse every year, I strived to do the best job possible."

Kate nodded understandingly before adding, "Nobody can fault you for that! This past year has proven difficult for everyone here at the fort. However, in spite of the major's nasty disposition, Anna and I were able to cultivate a lasting friendship."

"I guess the turning point for me was when he issued orders for the Indians' annihilation. Going against orders was something I never thought I'd do, but I just couldn't obey those commands. It went against every principle you ever taught me, Auntie. Many times I feared what you would feel or think of my actions."

"I've never been more proud of you than I am now," said Eileen. "It took incredible courage, let alone integrity, to do what you did. You never have to worry about my feelings for you, Paul. I know you are a man of honor."

Thompson had a hard time swallowing past the lump in his throat, and he had to blink several times to clear his vision. Without a word, he reached out to squeeze his aunt's hand. "Oh my beloved Auntie, I'll treasure those words to my dying day."

"Now we don't need to get mushy about it," she scolded. "I'm just stating the facts!"

"Speaking of facts, Auntie, you're just as mushy as the rest of us."

Eileen sighed resignedly with a scowl on her face. "There you go again, trying to ruin my reputation as the world's biggest grouch." This brought peals of laughter from Paul and Kate.

"Oops! I keep forgetting."

"Ya, ya. Any excuse will do when you need one."

Growing serious again, Paul said, "Going back to the Indians, I learned so many valuable lessons. The greatest one of them all is that it matters not the color of a man's skin, or his traditions. It's what's inside a man's heart and mind that matter most. While serving my red brothers, I not only learned to love them, I learned to respect them highly, too. Although I may never again see them in this life, I wonder what will happen to them. I shall carry their images in my mind and heart forever."

"From the stories that you told us, I can almost feel their presence," uttered Kate.

"Montana will always be a special place for me. I've witnessed love, honor, even justice here," the captain concluded.

Eileen sat thoughtfully toying with her apron. She sighed and looked from one to the other. "I have only been here a short time but already I have learned a lot. Perhaps the most important thing I have learned is that people matter, whether they are the richest family on the hill or the poorest beggars in the street.

"For as long as I can remember, I thought the underprivileged never mattered and that they just existed without love or worldly possessions. For that matter, I figured no one wanted them. Coming to the fort I found that I was the green horn.

"Life isn't just for the elite; everyone deserves a better life. These people have lofty goals and hearts bigger than the whole outdoors, with huge desires for a better life for their families. In spite of the crude circumstances, I am learning to adapt. Since my arrival I have felt more love than I ever have in my whole life."

All at once she realized that she was rattling on. Her face turned a bright crisp crimson. "Oh my goodness. Here I am chattering like an old Blue Jay. That's it! I've had my say, so there'll be no more comments from me."

"Oh, Auntie, that is so beautiful! I never knew you felt that way about people. Ever since my parents' death, you have taught me to look inside a person's heart, so I thought you had a different opinion of people. Thank you for telling us about your growth. I love you more at this moment than I ever thought possible."

"Well I have come to realize that there's more to this life than tea parties, operas, or spending money on unnecessary frivolity. I am looking forward to this new adventure because I feel that my horizons will be expanded to greater heights. What greater way to do this than to do it with my family?"

Paul sat rubbing his chin thoughtfully. "It is my opinion that everyone going on this wagon train has the same aspirations. They want something better for their families, a place where they can raise their children to be the best they can be. Yes, it means starting over with just the bare essentials, but underneath lies the hope for something more."

Kate looked from one to the other, smiling sweetly. "You have a great responsibility in leading the people, Paul, but even so we should think of this adventure as turning over a new leaf. I liken it to a brave new tomorrow. The only thing that dampens this is leaving my friends behind."

Paul smiled, knowing he held the biggest secret to their happiness. "What would you say if I told you that you didn't have to leave your friends behind?"

Kate stared at him blankly. "What does that mean?"

"Colonel Williams issued an early retirement for Henry Hansen and Jonathon Whipple. After speaking to each family individually, they have agreed to go with us." By now Kate was growing extremely excited, but Paul wisely ignored her and went on. "Nataka and Peters agreed to scout for the train. Of course, we have already talked to the Pedersens." Paul had to smile at the way Kate clung to his every word. Again he ignored her excitement as he continued. "Lester Foster told me that Williams had spoken to him after the meeting. It seems that Lonna made quite a hit with JaNae, so she talked her husband into assigning them to Fort Missoula."

By now Kate was jubilant, but a little hesitant. "But what about Anna? She can't stay at the fort, so where is she going?"

Again he smiled secretively. "Anna is also coming with us."

Clapping her hands, she rubbed them together gleefully. "Oh wonderful! We won't have to leave our friends behind after all." Then all at once Kate sank back into her chair, looking anxiously at Paul. "Everything would be so complete if Doctor Phelps would consent to go with us. Do you know anything about his plans, Paul?"

Thompson sighed wistfully. "As far as knowing what Doctor Phelps plans to do, nobody knows."

A sly little smile tugged at Eileen's lips. "Now, don't you worry about the good Doctor Phelps. I have an ace or two up my sleeves, which may entice him to go with us. Only time will tell."

Thompson raised his eyebrows teasingly. "I wouldn't touch that statement with a ten foot pole." Eileen scowled but remained silent. Pulling his watch from his watch fob, he scrutinized it intently. "If we're going to be ready in time for the funeral, we had better shake a leg." All began their daily rituals.

✑ ✑

After the funeral, Anna stood near the grave sadly watching as Miles walked over to two waiting horses. He untied the packhorse and tied the reins to the saddle horn. Untying his saddle horse, Miles mounted and rode away, not once looking back.

As Anna watched him ride away, she had a strong feeling that she would never see him again. Anna knew that he had no feelings of love for her, but the mother part of her longed for him to be safe. *What will happen to him?* she wondered.

When he had disappeared, her heart felt heavy with the realization that she was truly alone, and the thought threatened to overwhelm her. All at once she became aware of someone standing beside her, so she slowly turned to discover Nataka intently watching her. Blinking in surprise, Anna looked at him questioningly. *Is that love that I see in his eyes? Could he really know that he is my son? No,* she thought, *Jane and Henry would never have told him.*

"May I walk you home?"

"I would greatly appreciate that, Nataka."

Smiling, Nataka offered her his arm. "Would you take a walk with me before I take you home, so that I can talk to you privately?"

"Sure." Anna looked at him with numbed curiosity. Even though she longed for him to know that he was her son and for him to love her, fear of rejection prevented her from believing that this could be anything but her imagination.

When Nataka guided her away from the cemetery toward a secluded grove of trees, her curiosity became piqued. "What do you have on your mind, Nataka?"

Seeing a large flat rock a short distance away, Nataka guided her to it before answering her questions. When she was comfortably seated, Nataka sat on the grass beside her left knee. Taking one of her hands in his, he began to speak. "I know that you are my mother," he whispered so low that Anna had to strain to hear it.

Anna jumped in fear, then shivered. "What did you say?"

"I know that you are my real mother."

Anna was afraid that she was dreaming again, but just in case she wasn't dreaming, she had to know how he discovered the truth. "How, Nataka? How did you find out the truth?"

"I heard Ma and Pa Hansen talking about it one night several months ago when they thought I was asleep. While on the last maneuver with Captain Thompson, I asked him straight out to tell me the truth, that I felt I had a right to know. He was the one who told me what you went through to protect me from Carl Thornton."

Anna began to weep softly. "Oh I must be dreaming. For so long I have wanted you to know that it wasn't my decision to give you up. I would never have done that … not ever!"

Nataka squeezed her hand gently. "I know that now. That is why I have come to you, to thank you for saving my life. I also want to thank you for allowing the Hansens to raise me." He hesitated, absently stroking her hand. He looked questioningly into her eyes. "Mother, could we start over as mother and son?"

She gently pulled her hand free so she could cup his face in her hands. Gazing intently into his eyes, Anna exclaimed, "Oh, yes! I want that so badly! I want you to know, my son, that I have always loved you with all my heart! I'm very proud to be your mother!"

Nataka trembled. Tears of love and joy sprang into his eyes, falling unheeded down his face. "Thank you for telling me that," declared Nataka brokenly. Anna leaned forward to gently kiss his cheek. Nataka reached out to pull her to him so that he could hug her close. Leaning back, he took both of her hands in his while looking earnestly into her eyes. "Do you mind if I call you 'mother'?"

Fresh tears of joy coursed down Anna's cheeks. "I'd be so proud if you did. So very, very proud."

"I will do all in my power to help you get settled before I have to go with the wagon train."

She smiled sweetly at Nataka. "What if I said I was thinking about going with the wagon train, too?"

Nataka's eyes widened and all at once a big smile swept across his face. "I'd be delighted!" Then Nataka watched her anxiously. "Are you really considering it?"

"Yes, I am. In fact …" Anna paused to add a little suspense before continuing. Seeing the hope in Nataka's eyes, she smiled and said, "I have decided to go, too. I have spoken with Captain Thompson and he has agreed to help me with whatever I need."

"Wonderful!" Nataka said and hugged her excitedly to him. "I know that Ma and Pa Hansen will be as happy about it as I am!"

"Good! Then it's all settled. I will speak to Captain Thompson about helping me get ready to go." Mother and son sat together for a long time in the early morning sunlight, talking and planning for their futures. Eventually, they got up and ambled back to the fort, happy in the knowledge that they could openly express how they felt without fear.

ᢒᥬᥩᢒ ᥩᥬᢒ

As they prepared to return to Fort Missoula, Josh Taylor and Mitchel Aimes, John Whipple's friends, met him at his home to say their last goodbyes. It would be a long time before they would be together. Furthermore, there was always the possibility that they would never be together again.

They chatted amiably for several minutes, then fell silent as the knowledge of their approaching separation overwhelmed them. John gazed from one to the other, filing their images deep within his mind. "I'll never forget either of you, for I will always regard your friendships as some of my most priceless treasures!"

"I know that I'll never forget what you taught me about friendship," stated Aimes. "I have found that when I treat a man squarely, I am the better man for it, even if they don't respond in kind."

"While I was here at the fort, I never had time to miss my family," Josh said. "And I feel as though I have gained two new brothers."

"Thank you both for such high praises," responded John.

A teasing light came into Aimes' eyes. "Just don't let it go to your head, Whipple."

Laughing, John's mother touched Aimes lightly on the shoulder. "Thank you, sir. We, who have to live with him wouldn't want that to happen."

Aimes slapped his leg and burst out laughing heartily. "Oh, you're a lady after my own heart, ma'am." John tried to appear hurt but the twinkle in his eyes gave him away. He soon joined in on the laughter. "John, you have a real peach of a mother!"

"Thank you, Mitch," replied John proudly. "I've always thought so!"

Aimes rose to go. "Well I guess we'd best get back to the barracks to pack. We want to be ready to pull out when the time comes."

John shook each one's hands. "Good luck to both of you!"

Aimes pummeled John heartily on the back. "The same goes for you, too." Josh tried to swallow past the lump in his throat, but he found it difficult to do. Josh surprised Hattie by quickly kissing her on the cheek. "Thank you, Mrs. Whipple, for the wonderful hospitality you extended to me while I stayed with John. I'll always remember you fondly."

"It has been a real pleasure, Josh. You were a joy to have around."

Aimes hugged Hattie much to her delight, then without further ado they departed.

They weren't gone long when an idea came to John. At first he thought it was a little bold of him to think such thoughts. Then as the idea grew on him, he knew he had to find out. Grabbing his hat from the hook by the door, he told his mother that he'd be back soon. Then he bolted out the door like the very devil himself was after him.

Knocking on Anna's door, John stepped back to wait. After Anna opened the door she greeted him cheerfully. "Please come in, John."

"Thank you." John stepped inside, pausing to look around. The Williams', who were sitting at the table, rose to greet him.

JaNae smiled sweetly then hugged him warmly. "Hello, John. We were going to come see you before we left for Fort Missoula, but you've beaten us to it."

"I have an idea that I wanted to speak to the Colonel about. Then, too, I wanted to say my goodbyes before you left."

Williams burst out laughing. "I like how you tried to cover your tracks by stating the latter—you know, that part about wanting to say your goodbyes to us."

JaNae appeared to be very hurt. "I have to agree with Jedidiah. How come it took you so long to get around to us old fogies?"

John blushed to the very roots of his hair. "I didn't mean it that way! I … I just..."

JaNae's heart melted immediately. She surprised John by hugging him quickly, then stepped back. This sweet gesture pleased John immensely.

The fact that John was embarrassed tickled Williams to no end, so he secretly decided to play it to the hilt. "Now you're playing on the sympathies of my dear wife. What nerve!" Immediately Williams turned and walked to the table, where he slumped disgustedly into a chair and scowled.

John first looked at JaNae, then over at Williams. His face turned ashen at the possibility that he'd truly offended his dear friends. It was apparent that he didn't know what to do. JaNae was touched to see John nervously twist his hat in his hand while shuffling his weight from first one foot, then the other. Turning to look critically at her spouse, she saw the twinkle in his eyes. "Jedidiah Williams, you stop your teasing this minute, before you make this poor boy bolt and run."

John began to plead in earnest. "Please, sir. I am so sorry for whatever it was I did. I most humbly beg your pardon!"

Seeing John standing before him, like a whipped puppy, struck at Williams' soft heart. Rising, he walked over to place his hands on John's shoulders. "It is I who must ask for your forgiveness."

John's head jerked up. He stared at Williams in surprise. "Me? Forgive you, sir? But it is I … who have somehow offended you!"

Williams, who shook his head slightly, gently squeezed his shoulders. "You have done nothing but become a victim of my silly teasing." Seeing the look of wonder on John's face, Williams continued, "Seeing your embarrassment, when you thought we were upset with you a moment ago, I couldn't resist the opportunity to tease you … just a little bit." John looked first at JaNae, then over to Anna, who had silently been watching the good-natured bantering.

When he looked at the colonel, whose eyes were flashing impishly, the reality of it all began to sink in. A smile momentarily crossed his face, then faded to nothingness. John paused to think everything over. When it dawned on him what had just happened, he looked up at Williams. Grinning sheepishly, he uttered, "Oh!" Shaking a finger at Williams, he said, "Well, you really got a good one over on me, sir." When Williams burst out laughing, the others joined in.

Growing serious, Williams placed an arm around John's shoulders. After pulling him toward the table, he gently pushed him into a chair. Taking a seat opposite him, Williams prompted, "You said you had an idea that you wanted to discuss with me?"

"Yes, sir." He looked at Williams intently, then seeing only concern mingled with curiosity, he took the plunge. "Is Josh somehow part of the army?"

"No, I hired him as a stable hand to give him something to do."

"Oh."

"Why do you ask?"

"I have come to regard Josh as the brother I never had, sir. I am having a hard time leaving him behind."

"I see," replied Williams. "Go on."

"I wanted to ask him to go with us, but I didn't know if he was a soldier in the army. I must also admit that I wondered why he never wore a uniform if he was."

"Albert Jefferson, the man who took Josh in after his parents' deaths, is enlisted as a corporal." He scratched his head thoughtfully. "I think he has about five or six months left on his hitch. Anyway, I thought it would help the boy adjust to his environment if he had something to do. The idea came to me when I saw how well he treated the horses and other animals around the fort. I knew this was a job for him."

"I don't want to take him away from his family."

"Why don't you ask Josh what he wants? If he wants to go with the wagon train, I'll see what I can do to help ease the burden somehow."

"Thank you, sir."

"I'd do anything I could for you, John. There are times, however, that we have to accept whatever life has to dish out."

"I know, sir. I appreciate all that you have done for me!"

Williams reached out to pat John's shoulder. "I know that, John. That's why I like to help you." Folding his hands in front of him, Williams thought for a moment. He looked at John with a smile on his face. "Why don't you speak to Taylor? Then if he wants to go, I'll intervene with Jefferson on behalf of both of you."

"Thank you, sir." Rising, John grabbed Williams' hand, which he pumped excitedly. "I'll be back in a few minutes to tell you what he has decided." Before Williams could say more, John rushed out of the house.

John found Josh sitting on Aimes' bunk, chattering away a mile a minute. When he saw John, he jumped to his feet, hurrying over to meet him. "Hey, what are you doing here?"

"I came to talk to you for a minute."

Josh pulled John forward. "Come over here … join us."

Aimes looked at John in surprise. "Fancy seeing you here."

"I came to talk to Josh a moment," replied John.

"Ah," teased Aimes, "you don't want to see me, huh?"

"It isn't that at all, Mitch."

"Okay," smiled Aimes.

John started thinking out loud. "I remembered that you still have a long hitch left to serve in the army, Mitch, so I knew that I couldn't ask you to go with us. But Josh doesn't have to worry about that … just about leaving his family, which is probably just as hard."

Josh watched John intently, struggling to figure out what he was getting at. "What are you saying, John?"

"I wish I could take both of you with me, but I can't at this time. So I thought I'd ask you, Josh, if you would go with us on the wagon train."

Aimes plopped excitedly onto the bed. "That's a grand idea! Your family can join you later, Josh, when your father's hitch is up."

John couldn't stand it; he had to know Josh's answer immediately. "Do you want to go with us?"

"You bet your sweet Aunt Petunia, I do! The only problem is my folks. They have been really good to me after my parents died. I don't want to hurt them."

"I understand."

"Then the other problem is that I don't have all of my things with me."

Smiling, Aimes looked over at Josh. "That's not a problem! The wagon train won't be able to leave for a while, so you could send a letter back from your home at Fort Missoula, informing John of your decision."

"Wonderful! That's exactly what I'll do!" The three men talked for a while longer, then John left to walk back to Anna's. With his hands jammed into the pockets of his pants, John whistled contentedly, all the while feeling right with the world.

At Anna's house, John hurriedly told Williams Josh's feelings and his concerns about going. Williams sat thoughtfully pondering a reasonable solution. Coming up with nothing, he promised to think about it. He told John that he would get with Josh and his family when he got back to Fort Missoula. John thanked him profusely. Bidding them both a fond farewell, John went home.

After John left, Williams asked Anna if she had given any thought to what she would like to do now that she was alone. "I have decided to go with the wagon train when it leaves so that I can be with those I care most about. I have talked to Captain Thompson about my going. I told him that I needed help getting outfitted. I also needed to procure a wagon and team. He has assured me that he is working on it."

"Good! I have been concerned about what will happen to you, now that everything's changed in your life."

"Carl has some money set aside, which will help me get a fresh start. There is enough there to live comfortably. Thank you for your great concern for me, but I have wonderful friends to turn to if I need them."

"Wonderful! Then I will leave you in their capable hands."

"Correct me if I'm wrong, Colonel, but didn't you say you have a little over a year left in the army?"

"That's correct." Williams looked at her strangely. "Why do you ask?"

"I have been wondering what will happen to the two of you after your hitch is up."

"We haven't given any thought to that yet. That seems so far in the distant future that we have been taking it one day at a time."

Anna pondered his statement for a moment, looking from one to the other. "It would be so wonderful if you joined us at our new destination."

Williams looked at JaNae, who looked at him hopefully. "I can see by the look on my sweetheart's face that she thinks it's a capital idea! I'll tell you what we'll do. Let us think about it throughout the year and who knows, we may even consider it. Meanwhile you concentrate on traveling to your new destination and getting settled in your new home.

JaNae turned to Anna, "Please write to us when you get settled in your new area because we don't want to lose track of you."

"I will do that! I don't want to lose contact with you, either."

Not long after that, they went out to the waiting troops. After hugging Anna close to her, JaNae kissed her tenderly upon the cheek. "Goodbye, my dear. Good luck to you—always!"

"Thank you for all that you have done for me while you were here," replied Anna. "I will never forget either of you!"

When they stepped back, Williams reached out to hug Anna. "I will always remember the little gem that glowed brightly in spite of her obstacles."

Anna gasped at the beautiful compliment as tears glistened in her eyes. "Thank you, Jedidiah."

"We both would like to thank you for your warm, generous hospitality," added Williams, and JaNae nodded in agreement. "You take good care of yourself. Pray that we may we see each other again. That is our greatest hope."

"Oh I hope so, too," replied Anna. Williams helped JaNae into the surrey, then mounted. As they started toward the head of the column, Anna called out, "Good luck to both of you!" JaNae waved. Williams paused long enough to salute her smartly, then he continued to ride to the head of the column.

"Forward-ho!" bellowed Williams. Slowly, the company moved out of the gate and disappeared from view. Sighing, Anna went back into the house.

She hadn't been inside long when there was a knock at the door. Opening the door, she smiled when she saw the Hansen family standing on the porch. "Please, won't you come on in?"

When they were inside Anna offered them a seat. "This is a wonderful surprise."

Henry looked at Jane then back to Anna. "We are here because we feel that it is time to get a lot of things out in the open."

Anna flinched inwardly, then felt hope well up inside. "I see," she calmly replied.

Sensing her discomfort, Henry leaned forward in his seat to look at her compassionately. "Let me be the one to start it. May I?"

"Of course," Anna sighed in relief.

Henry took a deep breath before plunging in. "Sylvia, there is a secret that the three of us have withheld from you all of your life. We feel that it's time it was brought out in the open." Sylvia scowled at her father in bewilderment but wisely refrained from speaking. "Something happened prior to your birth that required our remaining quiet." He turned to Anna, who took up the story.

"A little over seventeen years ago, I discovered that I was going to have a child. I feared for the baby's life because of how Carl had treated me around Miles." Anna watched Sylvia's face anxiously. Sylvia sat in her chair so expressionlessly. "There were so many questions that needed to be answered, but I didn't know where to get those answers. Seeing no reaction from Sylvia, Anna continued, "so I went to the two people I knew I could trust ... your parents."

I wanted this child with all of my heart, but what would happen if it were a boy? Would he turn out to be as rotten as Miles? There was no doubt in my mind, whatsoever, that Carl would do all in his power to make it so. Then I was forced to wonder what would happen if it were a girl. With Miles so jealous of his father's attention, he would think nothing of hurting her. As much as Carl hated women, and he was always abusing me, how would he feel if it were a girl? Deep inside, I knew that he would also abuse her. I just couldn't let that happen."

"What does all of this have to do with me?"

"I am coming to that," replied Anna. Shrugging her shoulders, Sylvia continued to listen. "When Nataka was born, Carl wanted me to kill him." Gasping, Sylvia leaned forward to cling to Anna's every word. "That's right, Nataka is my son." Sylvia looked at her parents, then back to Anna in amazement.

Anna hesitated as the painful memories came flooding back. She swallowed several times to stifle the urge to scream. Indian war whoops, women screaming in terror, gunshots reverberating throughout the fort, played over and over in her mind. She shuddered in an attempt to break free of the mental demons. Rising, she walked over to the counter to get a drink of water. This helped to calm her down some, then she went back to her seat.

She absently smoothed out a fold in her apron before wringing her hands. Seeing no other way around her feelings, she began to speak. "While Carl was away on one of his mysterious maneuvers, a band of warriors attacked the fort. They violated the women and murdered several people." Again, she was forced to pause as painful memories threatened to choke her. She brushed impatiently at the tears running down her cheeks as she struggled for control, drawing inner strength from deep within.

Eventually, she was able to go on. "Storm Cloud, Chief Swift Eagle's brother, broke in here and took advantage of me. When he was through, he beat me mercilessly, leaving me to die! Carl was furious when he learned what had happened. Later when he found out I was going to have Storm Cloud's child, he went into a blind rage. He demanded that I get rid of the unborn child.

"When I refused, he swore that he would kill it, so I took Miles and ran away to protect the unborn child. Nataka wasn't very old when Carl found me and attempted to carry out his threat. Henry intervened, pleading with Carl to let them ... your mom and dad... raise Nataka as their own. Carl, knowing that this would hurt me even more, consented but only if I promised to never tell Nataka that I was his mother."

"What a creep!" Sylvia squirmed uncomfortably in her seat, anxious to know more. "What did you do?"

"I had no choice but to comply if I were to spare Nataka's life ... so I consented."

"Oh," replied Sylvia thoughtfully.

"So, there I was expecting another child. I didn't know what to do. I didn't want to give it up, but I didn't want it to suffer like I did, either. After explaining my dilemma to your folks, we decided that they would claim the child as theirs."

Sylvia jumped as though she'd been slapped, then stared dumbly at each of the adults. "What are you saying?"

Anna looked at her calmly. "I am your mother, Sylvia."

Sylvia jumped to her feet, glaring defiantly at Anna. "I don't believe you! You're a rotten liar!"

Henry rose to place his hands on Sylvia's shoulders. "Now wait a minute, honey. It's the truth!"

Sylvia screamed passionately. "No! I can't ... I won't believe it!"

Henry looked at her tenderly as he said, "I know it's hard to believe something like this could be true, but believe me, Sylvia, honey. It is true!"

"Then all of my life has been nothing but a lie?"

"We have always loved you as our own, but we knew that someday we would have to tell you the truth."

Sylvia turned to glare at Anna venomously as she clenched her fists. She opened and closed her fists repeatedly, screaming at the top of her lungs. "I hate you! I hate you! I hate you!" Before Henry or Jane could say anything to her, Sylvia ran from the house.

Tears ran unheeded down Anna's cheeks, as she stared at the closed door, feeling as if a knife had been driven through her heart. Carl is dead, thought Anna, but he is still striking out from beyond the grave. All at once becoming aware of someone touching her shoulder, she looked up to see Henry gazing at her with heartfelt compassion. "Oh, Henry, I always feared she'd be angry," quietly declared Anna, "but never did I think she would hate me so passionately."

Jane came to stand beside her. "This is an awful shock to her right now, as it has turned her world upside down. We must give her enough space to mull it over in her heart and mind."

"Time is what she needs most of all," replied Henry. "Lots and lots of time."

"You're right, of course." Sighing, Anna added hopefully, "I just hope she will find it in her heart to forgive me ... someday!"

❧❧❧

After rushing from Anna's home, Sylvia stood on the porch, struggling to gain control of her overwrought emotions. *It just can't be true,* she thought. *It just can't be!* When she tried to take in a deep breath of the fresh air, the pain inside seemed to stifle her efforts. She blinked several times to stem the flow of tears, but that only made her eyes smart. Seeing the stable, an uncontrollable urge to get away enveloped her.

Raising her head high in an effort to maintain her dignity, Sylvia strolled briskly toward the stable. Jared Waterman, stepping out from one of the stalls, approached her. It was apparent that something was bothering her, but he wisely refrained from asking her how she was. "Kin I hep ya, Miss Sylvia?"

"I want a horse saddled for me immediately."

"Yes, ma'am!" Turning, he walked to a nearby stall.

While she waited, Sylvia paced impatiently back and forth around the stable entrance. She had to swallow several times to keep the tears in check and her anger under control. A few minutes later, Jared led a buckskin mare named 'Buttercup' over to her. Lifting her chin defiantly, she took the reins from him. "Thank you, Jared."

"You're very welcome, Miss Sylvia. Glad to be of service." She nodded curtly before turning her attention to the buckskin. "Let me help you mount, Miss."

"Thank you. I'd appreciate the help." When she was seated comfortably in the saddle, Sylvia turned the horse sharply to the right. Leaving the stable, she rode toward the gate. Arriving at the gate, the guard opened it for her then wished her happy riding. Nodding an acknowledgment, she silently rode away.

Sylvia's slightly protruding chin quivered as anger, mingled with pain, began to surge through her. She angrily jabbed her heels into the sides of Buttercup to speed her on. Snorting, the mare began to run as if her very life depended on it. The wind tore at the pins in Sylvia's hair, sending them flying. Her hair blew helter-skelter about her face.

As they raced on, the wind threatened to take her very breath away. Tears, long held in check, began to stream unheeded down her face. Because of her inner turmoil, Sylvia was unaware of a rider gaining on her. Her only thought was to get as far away from the fort as possible. Confusion, frustration, disgust, and blinding rage all vied for dominance in her already tortured mind.

Pinpoints of light flashed in her eyes, her teeth were clenched tightly, and there was a pout to her lips. *Surely, this is only an awful nightmare and I'll awaken soon.* Even as these thoughts formed in her mind, Sylvia knew that she was deluding herself.

As she raced along, she yelled out loud, "Why! ... Why did I have to find out now ... that ... I'm really Sylvia Thornton ... not Sylvia Hansen?" The horror of the statement caused her to shudder as if gripped in the throes of the ague. "No! It just can't be true!" Again, she shuddered in an attempt to clear away the fog from her mind. Again, she yelled, "Of all the people in the world to have as a father, I had to be saddled with that skunk!" Without concern for her horse, Sylvia kicked Buttercup hard in the ribs. The horse snorted, jumped in surprise, then attempted to run harder.

Again, Sylvia screamed aloud, "I hate you, I hate all of you!" Sobbing hysterically, she raised her fist heavenward, yelling even louder, "Do you hear me? I hate all of you for deceiving me and for making my life nothing but an ugly, shameless lie. Oh, how you must have laughed ... even gloated ... behind my back ... all the while knowing that I felt so safe and secure!" All at once, with shoulders sagging, she slumped over the saddle. "Oh, how I wish I were dead!" Great soul-racking sobs shook her frame as she gave vent to all of her pent up emotions.

When the worst of the anger and pain had subsided, she became aware of the buckskin's labored breathing. Knowing that Buttercup wasn't to blame for what was happening ... that she was being unfair to her pet, Sylvia decided to consider Buttercup's needs.

Reaching down to stroke the mare's neck, she was surprised to feel so much lather. In that moment, Sylvia felt ashamed of herself for her treatment of Buttercup. Pulling gently on the reins, she slowed Buttercup to a brisk walk, then to a canter. Eventually, she brought her to a gentle gait to cool her down.

Pounding hooves behind her alerted Sylvia to the presence of another rider. She whirled around in her saddle to defiantly face the rider. Seeing that it was Nataka looking at her with great concern, she snarled impatiently, "What do you want?"

"I saw you leave the fort. When I saw you spur your horse on, I decided to see what was up." Sylvia remained sullenly silent. "Sis, what's wrong?"

Fresh tears began to flow down Sylvia's cheeks. "It's awful," she sobbed, "Truly awful!"

Nataka reached out for one of Sylvia's trembling hands. Securing it, he squeezed it gently. "There is a spot close by where we can talk in private. Let's get down ... see if we can talk it out. Okay?" Sylvia could only nod. He was so afraid that she would bolt, that Nataka continued holding on to her hand as they walked the horses to a secluded spot nearby. Turning loose of her hand, he dismounted and came around to her side to help her down. She absently allowed him to lead her to a large log, where they could sit together. When they were comfortable, Nataka gently squeezed her hand. "Now, Sis," he began, "tell me all about it."

Sylvia buried her face in her hands, sobbing brokenly. "I just found out that Anna Thornton is our real mother!"

"I know," stated Nataka matter-of-factly.

Raising her head, Sylvia stared at Nataka in shock. "You know?"

"Yes!"

"How? ... When?"

"I have suspected it for several months now, but I knew for sure when I was out on the last maneuver with Captain Thompson." Sylvia looked at him critically while waiting for him to continue. "I told him that I had heard Ma and Pa talking about it one night when they thought I was asleep. I felt that since we were going to go against Thornton's orders, I deserved to know. So he told me all about us."

Sylvia stared at him incredulously. "You aren't angry?"

"When I first heard about it, I was. After hearing the facts, I've had time to sort it out. I have come to appreciate what she did to save my life." Sylvia shuddered but remained silent. "Thornton bought our mother for a lousy bottle of whisky, which he gave to her father." Flinching, Sylvia watched Nataka for signs that he was lying. Seeing only the truth, she wondered at the statement. Nataka went on to tell of how Anna had run away to save his life when Thornton threatened to kill him. "If it wasn't for the fact that the Hansens volunteered to take me, Thornton would have carried out his promise."

"That's awful!"

"When she found that she was going to have another baby, she didn't know what to do. She didn't want the child to be ruined like Miles, so again Ma and Pa Hansen volunteered to take you. It nearly broke Anna's heart to give you up, but she knew that it was the only way to protect you from the abuse that Carl and Miles would have heaped upon you, Sis."

"I don't believe you!" Sylvia jumped to her feet to stare defiantly down at him. With her hands on her hips, she looked like a naughty child throwing a tantrum, yet there was so much pain in her countenance that Nataka's heart ached for her. "If Anna cared so much, then why didn't she find a way to keep us?" Sylvia didn't give Nataka a chance to answer, but moved a short distance away. "I'll tell you why!" She spun back to approach Nataka. "Because she was spineless, gutless and just plain didn't care! That's why! If she had really wanted to keep us so badly, then she should have tried harder to hide all of us from that animal!"

"That animal, as you so aptly called him, would have hunted until he had found her. Then there would have been the hob to pay for sure. Think about it for a minute. You'll realize that it wouldn't have borne well for you, either. He would have, with Miles' help, made you so miserable that your life wouldn't have been worth living! If Anna had broken her word to Major Thornton and taken me with her, he never would have listened to reason. I would be dead!"

Sylvia knew that he was right, but wasn't about to admit it. "You're just being melodramatic! After all, he isn't God! He's just an evil, vile old man!"

"He is evil — vile to the core — but he's always had a way of getting what he wanted. No, Sis. Anna would never have been able to pull it off."

Sylvia's mind raced to find more reasons to support her anger, not really wanting to let go. Strangely, the hurting felt almost good to her soul because it helped release the excruciating agony within; but finally, reluctantly she accepted the truth. Dropping wearily onto the log, Sylvia's shoulders began to shake violently. Fresh tears, glistening in her eyes, threatened to spill out. Burying her face in Nataka's shoulder to hide the pain, she began to sob as though her life were about to end.

Nataka wisely held her, allowing her to cry it out. When she grew calmer, he continued to hold her close, feeling concern for his precious sister. He reached in to his pocket and extracted his handkerchief. Handing it to her, he waited while Sylvia mopped at the tears on her face. Blowing her nose, she declared, "I really don't want to go out there in that awful wilderness … with … those filthy savages." She paused to blow her nose once more before adding, "But most of all, I wish I were dead!"

Nataka jumped as though he had just been dealt an awful blow, but wisely waited until he could gain control of his emotions. Sighing sadly, he looked at his sister. "Do you remember when we were kids … how we wondered at our different skin coloring … how we heard things about me being different?"

Sylvia nodded thoughtfully. "Yes, I do."

"Now we know why. It was because of the way I was born. Sis … because I'm a half-breed … am I one of those filthy savages? Please don't hate me for who I am." The pained expression on Nataka's face caused Sylvia to flinch in shame. "It hasn't always been easy for me growing up with you, Ma and Pa. You had a fair complexion with light colored eyes, while my skin and eyes were so dark. Growing up, I used to wonder why I tanned so easily, while you burned. You were content to be with people, while I preferred the animals or being outdoors."

Nataka reached down to pluck a blade of grass. For a few minutes, he toyed with it while he again collected his thoughts. It seemed that both needed a moment to assimilate all the new information about relationships and to find relief from their pain and heartache. Sylvia was silent as well. Breaking the joined silence, Nataka began to speak, "As to your wishing that you were dead, Sis…. well, I can't even imagine my life without you as my sister. While struggling to sort out my life … many times thinking I was a strange misfit … I drew on your love and strength.

"Because Ma and Pa Hansen raised you, you are the sweet loveable young lady you are. You've brought so much joy into my otherwise humdrum existence, that I would have been miserable indeed without you. Sylvie, I'm so proud that you're my sweet sister." Even though Nataka was still stinging from Sylvia's uncharacteristic words from a few moments ago, he desired to alleviate her pain as much as possible.

Sylvia, also sensing Nataka's hurt from her insensitive words, hastened to repair the inflicted damage, "That was awfully rotten of me to say what I did. Please forgive me!"

"It's forgiven." Nataka grinned, bending his head to thoughtfully continue stroking the blade of grass in his hand. He threw the blade of grass onto the ground. Looking into Sylvia's troubled eyes, he said, "It took me a lot of time to come to grips with the truth, Sis. It will take some time for you to sort it out, too. However, let me repeat the fact that if you had been raised with Anna, who knows what you would have been like, let alone if you would have survived Carl's, or Miles' abuse. I know that right now you can't see past the deceit, or the pain, but I think Anna did the only brave thing she could do … love you enough to let you go!

"Once I understood why Anna did what she did, I began to feel better about myself. As far as I'm concerned, I'm proud of having another mother … like Anna." Sylvia started to speak, but Nataka held up a hand to lightly touch her lips to silence her. "I still feel a great love for Ma and Pa Hansen that will never change. In fact, we both owe our lives to the two of them. I love them more at this moment than I ever did before."

Sylvia stiffened for a moment, again starting to speak, but Nataka hastened on, "No matter how you feel about not being told sooner, Anna would have risked your safety by telling you before now."

Sylvia looked unconvinced as she wavered between acceptance and denial. "I don't know about that!"

"Sis, life can be so cruel, but I firmly believe that the roughest trial has a way of working out for our good. … if we let time take its course." Seeing the scowl on Sylvia's face and knowing how it always made her furious, Nataka reached out and playfully tweaked her nose.

Jumping in surprise, Sylvia covered up the tender member before Nataka could tweak it again. "Oh … you dirty rat!"

She reached out to punch him on the arm but he jumped out of her way. As he started for the horses, he called back, "Do what you want, Sis, but I'm hungry. I'm going home to see if I can persuade Ma to feed me."

Watching Nataka stride toward the horses, Sylvia snorted in disgust. As she watched him, she gave in to the imp on her shoulder, "Which one?"

Nataka paused, then grinned back at her and said, "Whichever one can get it fixed the quickest!" It seemed that Nataka, too, had an imp on his shoulder, for he couldn't resist the impulse to strike back. "You know, Sis, I'm going to like having two mothers. When one doesn't meet my demands, I'll be able to wheedle my way around the other."

Sylvia shook her head, loathing the idea of calling Anna 'Mother'. "You can do what you want, but I'm going home."

Sylvia watched as Nataka mounted Hurricane, doffed his hat, then galloped toward home. Something inside her triggered the impulse to strike back at him for tweaking her nose. "If that rat thinks he's going to pull a fast one on me, then he's got another think coming!" Sylvia rushed over to the buckskin mare, who nickered softly in response to her touch. "Buttercup, ole girl … are we going to stand still for this?"

Buttercup, now fully rested, tossed her head up and down while flicking her tail. Sylvia, who was stroking the horse as she talked to her, felt Buttercup quiver in antici-pation. Mounting, Sylvia turned the mare toward home. Leaning over her neck she gave the command, "Come on girl, let's show him what we're made of!" Giving vent to her competitive spirit, Sylvia nudged the horse into a full run, quickly gaining on Nataka. As they passed him, his mouth gaped open in stunned disbelief. She giggled impetuously. "If you think you're going to get away with tweaking my nose, mister, well ... you've got another think coming. I'm going to beat you home!"

"We'll just see about that, miss smarty pants!" He hunkered over the saddle, giving Hurricane his head. "Go boy! GO!"

Off they raced. For a time, their troubles were forgotten, left behind in the billowing dust. For years Montana had been home to them, their family and their friends. Now new adventures were waiting for them ... just around the corner.

About the Author

Having visited Montana for years from her nearby home in Idaho, Mabel G. Ebner has developed a love, even a reverence, for the state's scenic beauty and wildlife. She has expressed these feelings through her multiple talents and creativity. One can appreciate this in her acrylic paintings of mountains, waterfalls, moose, elk and other related subjects.

She is self-educated in creative writing, and she has demonstrated a love of playing with words — painting pictures with them. When reading her descriptions in this book, one is able to visualize the swirling, boiling rapids, hear the rushing waters, smell the nearby pines, feel the cool breezes, and taste the delicious food cooked over campfires.

This is Mabel's first novel, but not her first published writing. She published a book of poetry titled *Reflections of the Soul*. Her poem "Grandeur" from that work was included in *Of Diamonds and Rust*, an international poetry publication. Her poem, "Silent Killer" (about cancer), was published first on the Internet at poetry.com. She then received an Editor's Choice certificate from the International Poetry contest. It was later published in *Poet's Elite 2000*.

She has also written stories for adults and children, songs, plays and other as yet unpublished poems.

Drawing upon real life experiences has helped Mabel portray the characters, the drama and the emotions accompanying each story in this novel. She says her talent and inspiration come from her Heavenly Father. She and her husband, Maurice, have one daughter, Jennifer. They have also recently become grandparents. Mabel has sometimes paused during health challenges, but "quit" is not in her vocabulary.

Mabel already has additional sequel novels in mind. Be sure to look for the following titles from this series:

Montana: A Brave New Tomorrow

Montana: Autumn's Lengthening Shadows

Montana: In the Hands of Time

Montana: United Again

Montana: Whispers from the Future

www.ingramcontent.com/pod-product-compliance
Lightning Source LLC
Chambersburg PA
CBHW020248120726
47904CB00001B/129